STAR WARS
ROLEPLAYING GAME

Saga Edition
Revised Core Rulebook

CHRISTOPHER PERKINS, OWEN K.C. STEPHENS, RODNEY THOMPSON

CREDITS

ORIGINAL STAR WARS® ROLEPLAYING GAME DESIGNERS
Bill Slavicsek, Andy Collins, JD Wiker

SAGA EDITION DESIGNERS
Christopher Perkins, Owen K.C. Stephens, Rodney Thompson

DEVELOPER AND EDITOR
Gary M. Sarli

LUCAS LICENSING EDITORS
Sue Rostoni, Jonathan Rinzler

DESIGN MANAGER AND MANAGING EDITOR
Christopher Perkins

DIRECTOR OF RPG R&D
Bill Slavicsek

PRODUCTION MANAGERS
Josh Fischer, Randall Crews

IMAGING TECHNICIANS
Travis Adams, Bob Jordan

SAGA EDITION ART DIRECTOR
Paul Hebron

COVER DESIGNER
Scott Okumura

GRAPHIC DESIGNERS
Keven Smith, Leon Cortez, Michael Martin

DIAGRAM PHOTOGRAPHY
Jay Sakamoto

ARCHIVIST
Bryn Jennings

GRAPHIC PRODUCTION SPECIALIST
Angelika Lokotz

INTERIOR ARTISTS
Daniel Falconer, Langdon Foss, 4G Squared, Daniel Gelon, D. Alexander Gregory, Matt Hatton, Raven Mimura, Vinod Rams, Ramon Perez, Andrew Robinson, Marc Sasso, Greg Staples, Mark Tedin, Chris Trevas, Lucasfilm Ltd.

PLAYTESTERS
Joseph Al-Khazraji, Ian Allen, Michael Beeler, Newell Curlee, James Hamilton, Doug Hyatt, Lj Stephens, Brett Thompson, Clay Venable, Shay Wells

SPECIAL THANKS
Leland Chee, Andy Collins, Jonathan Gibbons, Rob Heinsoo, Scott Sarli, Mark Valetutto, Jeff Waddill, Rob Watkins, James Wyatt

---

Some rules mechanics are based on the *Star Wars Roleplaying Game* Revised Core Rulebook by Bill Slavicsek, Andy Collins, and JD Wiker, the original DUNGEONS & DRAGONS® rules created by E. Gary Gygax and Dave Arneson, and the new DUNGEONS & DRAGONS game designed by Jonathan Tweet, Monte Cook, Skip Williams, Richard Baker, and Peter Adkison.

This Wizards of the Coast game product contains no Open Game Content. No portion of this work may be reproduced in any form without written permission. To learn more about the Open Gaming License and the d20 System License, please visit www.wizards.com/d20

U.S., CANADA, ASIA, PACIFIC, & LATIN AMERICA
WIZARDS OF THE COAST, INC.
P.O. BOX 707
RENTON, WA 98057-0707
QUESTIONS? 1-800-324-6496

GREAT BRITAIN
HASBRO UK LTD
CASWELL WAY
NEWPORT, GWENT NP9 0YH
GREAT BRITAIN
PLEASE KEEP THIS ADDRESS FOR YOUR RECORDS

EUROPE
WIZARDS OF THE COAST, BELGIUM
'T HOFVELD 6D
1702 GROOT-BIJGAARDEN
BELGIUM
+32 2 467 3360

WWW.WIZARDS.COM

WWW.STARWARS.COM

ISBN: 978-0-7869-4356-2
620-10796720-001-EN
9 8 7 6 5 4 3 2 1
FIRST PRINTING: MAY 2007

©2007 LUCASFILM LTD. & ® OR ™ WHERE INDICATED. ALL RIGHTS RESERVED.
USED UNDER AUTHORIZATION.

DUNGEONS & DRAGONS, D20 SYSTEM, Wizards of the Coast, and their respective logos are trademarks of Wizards of the Coast in the U.S.A. and other countries. This material is protected under the copyright laws of the United States of America. Any reproduction or unauthorized use of the material or artwork contained herein is prohibited without the express written permission of Wizards of the Coast, Inc. This product is a work of fiction. Any similarity to actual people, organizations, places, or events is purely coincidental. Printed in the U.S.A.

Contents

- Foreword 5
- **Introduction** 6
  - This Is *Star Wars* 7
  - This Is a Roleplaying Game 7
  - This Is the *Star Wars* Roleplaying Game 7
  - Characters 8
  - What You Need to Play 8
  - Dice 8
  - The Three Eras of Play 8
  - The Basics 9
  - Game Play 9
  - What's Next? 10
  - Character Creation 13

- **Chapter 1: Abilities** ... 16
  - Your Ability Scores 17
  - The Abilities 18
  - Changing Ability Scores 19

- **Chapter 2: Species** 20
  - Choosing a Species 21
  - Species Characteristics 22
  - Humans 23
  - Bothans 23
  - Cereans 24
  - Duros 25
  - Ewoks 25
  - Gamorreans 26
  - Gungans 26
  - Ithorians 27
  - Kel Dor 28
  - Mon Calamari 28
  - Quarren 29
  - Rodians 29
  - Sullustans 30
  - Trandoshans 31
  - Twi'leks 31
  - Wookiees 32
  - Zabrak 32

- **Chapter 3: Heroic Classes** 34
  - Choosing a Heroic Class 35
  - Class and Level Bonuses 36
  - Level-Dependent Benefits 36
  - Class Descriptions 37
  - Jedi 38
  - Noble 42
  - Scoundrel 45
  - Scout 48
  - Soldier 50
  - Multiclass Characters 54

- **Chapter 4: Skills** 56
  - Skills Summary 57
  - How Do Skills Work? 58
  - Types of Skill Checks 58
  - Trying Again 58
  - Favorable and Unfavorable Circumstances 59
  - Time and Skill Checks 60
  - Checks without Rolls 60
  - Combining Skill Attempts 61
  - Ability Checks 61
  - Skill Descriptions 61

- **Chapter 5: Feats** 78
  - Acquiring Feats 79
  - Prerequisites 79
  - Feat Descriptions 79

- **Chapter 6: The Force** .. 90
  - The Force through the Ages ... 91
  - Using the Force 92
  - Force Points 92
  - The Dark Side 93
  - Force Powers 95
  - Force Power Descriptions 96
  - Force Talents 100
  - Force Techniques 101
  - Force Secrets 103
  - Force-Using Traditions 103

- **Chapter 7: Heroic Traits** 108
  - Details 109
  - Destiny 112

- **Chapter 8: Equipment** . 116
  - Money 117
  - Restricted Items 118
  - Weapons 119
  - Melee Weapons 120
  - Ranged Weapons 124
  - Explosives 130
  - Armor 131
  - Equipment 133
  - Services and Expenses 140
  - Encumbrance 140

- **Chapter 9: Combat** 142
  - Combat Sequence 143
  - Combat Statistics 144
  - Initiative 149
  - Surprise 149
  - Types of Actions 150
  - Special Combat Rules 155

- **Chapter 10: Vehicles** .. 164
  - Scale 165
  - Vehicle Types 166
  - Vehicle Combat Statistics ... 167
  - Characters in Vehicles 169
  - Starting the Battle 169
  - Vehicle Combat Actions 170
  - Special Vehicle Combat Rules 173
  - Vehicle Descriptions 174

- **Chapter 11: Droids** 184
  - A Droid's Life 185
  - Creating a Droid Hero 185
  - Droid Traits 187
  - Droid Systems 188
  - Modifying Droids 197
  - Sample Droids 197

- **Chapter 12: Prestige Classes** 204
  - Prestige Classes 205
  - Ace Pilot 206
  - Bounty Hunter 207
  - Crime Lord 209
  - Elite Trooper 211
  - Force Adept 212
  - Force Disciple 214
  - Gunslinger 216
  - Jedi Knight 217
  - Jedi Master 219
  - Officer 220
  - Sith Apprentice 222
  - Sith Lord 224

- **Chapter 13: Galactic Gazetteer** 226
  - Life in the Galaxy 227
  - Planets of the Galaxy 228
  - Travel in the Galaxy 237

- **Chapter 14: Gamemastering** 238
  - The Role of the Gamemaster .. 239
  - Running a Game Session 242
  - Building an Encounter 247
  - Awarding Experience Points 248
  - Other Rewards 248
  - Building an Adventure 249
  - Building a Campaign 251
  - Hazards 252
  - Gravity 256
  - Visibility 257

- **Chapter 15: Eras of Play** 258
  - The Rise of the Empire Era .. 259
  - The Rebellion Era 260
  - The New Jedi Order Era 261
  - Main Characters 261
  - Supporting Characters 266

- **Chapter 16: Allies and Opponents** 272
  - Beasts 273
  - Beast Descriptions 275
  - Nonheroic Characters 277
  - Character Archetypes 278
  - Other Species 284

- **Index** 286

- **Character Sheet** 287

Welcome to the latest edition of the *Star Wars Roleplaying Game*. Whether you're an experienced player or new to the game, you're in for a real treat.

Why the new edition? First and foremost, we wanted the "definitive" core rulebook to encompass all six feature films—something that wasn't possible until after the release of Episode III: *Revenge of the Sith* in 2005. Secondly, Wizards of the Coast had stepped away from the roleplaying game for a few years to focus on the *Star Wars Miniatures Game*. After the successful launch of the miniatures line, we knew that we wanted a roleplaying game rulebook that embraced our pre-painted plastic miniatures—over 500 of them and counting. And what a great opportunity to give *Star Wars Miniatures Game* players another way in which to use their miniatures! Lastly, we wanted to make good on a promise to treat this game as a living document shaped by fan feedback and the latest breakthroughs in game design. Like the *Star Wars* saga itself, the game evolves.

So, here it is: the first roleplaying game rulebook to span the complete *Star Wars* film saga. What else could we call it but the Saga Edition?

This rulebook doesn't change how roleplaying games are played: You still need those wacky dice, your imagination, a love for all things *Star Wars*, and a few good friends. However, it boldly reinvents the game by allowing players to customize their characters in ways never before possible. Characters gain access to more feats as well as new suites of talents. Every level gained promises something new and exciting. We've even taken a few pointers from the miniatures game and streamlined the combat rules. We've also simplified the skill system and devised Force rules that feel more elegant and true to the *Star Wars* milieu.

The book incorporates Episode III content (of course!) as well as a few surprises. Like its predecessors, the Saga Edition rulebook promises new adventures in the *Star Wars* galaxy and delivers a rules system that doesn't apologize for breaking new ground.

Believe it or not, it's been thirty years since George Lucas gave us his first film in the *Star Wars* saga. I was 9 years old when the movie premiered on May 25, 1977. Truth be told, I was the boy on my block with the *Star Wars* posters tacked to his bedroom walls, shelves lined with *Star Wars* action figures, and yes, *Star Wars* bed sheets. Many of the "dry years" between Episode VI and Episode I were spent playing electronic games such as X-Wing, TIE Fighter, and Dark Forces. Somewhere along the way, I became an adult, and shortly before the release of *The Phantom Menace*, I rekindled my passion for *Star Wars* and unleashed my inner child by becoming the editor-in-chief of *Star Wars Gamer* magazine. In this role, I was able to meet the people behind the *Star Wars* legacy, even work with them. I visited Skywalker Ranch, read film scripts stamped "confidential," attended conventions, followed Peter Mayhew around like a happy little dog, and enjoyed frequent behind-the-scenes glimpses of filmmaking magic. It stuns me to think of how much *Star Wars* has remained a part of my life in spite of all of the things that can occupy one's time.

Thirty years—what a cause for celebration! Perhaps for this reason alone, the time seemed right to revisit this great game, make it better, and give it a facelift. I'm as proud of this book as anything I've worked on, and I've been doing game design since I was seventeen. As a follow-up, Wizards of the Coast plans to unveil more products in its new line of roleplaying game supplements and accessories. I hope you're as excited by them as I am. More importantly, I hope this book fills many of your evenings and weekends with adventure, laughter, and fond memories of a galaxy far, far away.

Christopher Perkins
Christopher Perkins
January 7, 2007

INTRODUCTION

The *Star Wars* films depict an amazing galaxy of strange aliens, wondrous machinery, mystical powers, epic struggles, great heroes, and terrible villains. From the moment the first Star Destroyer blazed across the screen, the story of *Star Wars* captivated the world. With this game, you can re-create the story of the films or craft your own adventures in the *Star Wars* universe. All you need is some dice, a few friends, and your imagination.

This Is Star Wars

Blasters; X-wing starfighters; lightsabers; clone troopers; the Force. . . .

Star Wars is space fantasy at its best, full of action, adventure, and a sense of wonder. The heroes are larger than life. The villains are utterly evil. The universe has a lived-in, well-used look and feel to it. It's a familiar story, but it's never been told quite this way before. It has mythic elements that speak to the heart of the audience. It's epic in scope; everything appears on a grand scale. And it's fun. Vehicles move very fast. Things blow up. We want to cheer for the good guys and boo the bad guys. And, sometimes, we want to be a part of that faraway galaxy.

This Is a Roleplaying Game

It's a game of your imagination, where you get to tell stories by taking on roles of the main characters—characters you create. It's a game that offers a multitude of choices to those characters—more choices than even the most sophisticated computer game, because the only limit to what you can do is what you can imagine. The story is like a movie, except all of the action takes place in your imagination. There's no script to the movie (other than a rough outline used by the Gamemaster); you decide what your character says and does. The Gamemaster is the director and special effects designer, deciding what the story is about and taking on the roles of all the other characters—the villains, the extras, the special guest stars. The Gamemaster also keeps track of the rules, interprets the outcome of actions, and describes what happens. Together, players and Gamemaster create a story, and everybody has a great time.

This Is the Star Wars Roleplaying Game

Combine the fabulous elements of the *Star Wars* universe with the imagination-powered engine of a roleplaying game, and the faraway galaxy draws nearer. Everything you need is in this book except the dice. Check out The Basics, starting on page 9, to get an idea of the fundamentals of the game.

When you're ready, flip through the rest of this book. It offers a wealth of options, allowing you to play in any *Star Wars* era. It lets you play the good guys, the bad guys, or the guys in between if you want to add a little ambiguity to an otherwise black-and-white universe.

When you play the *Star Wars Roleplaying Game*, you create a unique fictional character that lives in the imaginations of you and your friends. One person in the game, the Gamemaster (GM), controls the villains and other people who live in the *Star Wars* universe. Through your characters, you and your friends face the dangers and explore the mysteries that your Gamemaster sets before you.

Anything is possible in the *Star Wars Roleplaying Game*. You can have your character try anything you can think of. If it sounds good and the dice fall in your favor, the action succeeds. The Basics section has more details.

Now, get ready. It's a long time ago in a galaxy far, far away. And the Force is with you. Enjoy!

CHARACTERS

Your characters are the stars of the movie, the main characters in the game. We sometimes refer to them as "heroes," not in the "good guy" sense per se, but in the sense of the main protagonists of the story. Each character's imaginary life is different. Your character might be . . .

- A tough blaster-for-hire.
- A Padawan learner seeking to gain power in the Force.
- A brash starfighter pilot.
- A gambler looking to make the next big score.
- A grizzled spacer making a living on the space lanes.
- A smuggler with a heart of gold.
- A young senator from a prosperous world.
- A Rebel spy.
- A Jedi Knight wielding a lightsaber in defense of the Republic.
- A galactic scout exploring the hyperspace lanes.
- A soldier trained for war in the Outer Rim.
- Or any other kind of character you can imagine.

WHAT YOU NEED TO PLAY

Here's what you need to start playing the *Star Wars Roleplaying Game*:

- This book, which tells you how to create and play your character.
- A copy of the character sheet (on page 287)
- A pencil and scratch paper.
- One or two four-sided dice (d4), four or more six-sided dice (d6), an eight-sided die (d8), two ten-sided dice (d10), a twelve-sided die (d12), and a twenty-sided die (d20).
- A miniature from the *Star Wars Miniatures Game* line to represent your character.
- A battle map with 1-inch squares to put your miniature on.

Players should read the front sections of this book, the parts dealing with character creation, skills, feats, and equipment. The rest of the book is for the Gamemaster, providing advice for running the game, opponents to throw at the players' characters, and a few starting points for adventures.

DICE

The rules abbreviate dice rolls with phrases such as "4d6+2," which means "four six-sided dice plus 2" (generating a number between 6 and 26). The first number tells you how many dice to roll (all of which are added together), the number after the "d" tells you what type of dice to use, and any number after that indicates a quantity that is added to or subtracted from the result.

Some examples:

3d6: Three six-sided dice, generating a number from 3 to 18. This is the amount of damage that a blaster pistol deals.

2d8: Two eight-sided dice, generating a number from 2 to 16. This is the amount of damage that a lightsaber deals in the hands of a 1st-level Jedi.

THE THREE ERAS OF PLAY

The *Star Wars Roleplaying Game* supports adventures and campaigns set in many different eras, three of which are described in detail in this book. You can set your campaign in the time of the prequel movies (Episodes I–III). Known as the Rise of the Empire era, this is a period when the Republic's power is waning, war grips the galaxy, and the Jedi Council still holds sway over ten thousand Jedi Knights. This time period pre-dates the Empire but includes the tumultuous Clone Wars.

Or, you can go forward in time to the classic period of galactic civil war and play in the Rebellion era, when the power of the Empire is supreme and those capable of using the Force are few and far between. This is the time described in the original *Star Wars* films (Episodes IV–VI).

Or, jump to a time twenty years after the Battle of Endor and participate in the events surrounding the invasion of the galaxy. Aliens from beyond the edge of known space have begun an incursion into the New Republic as forces conspire to threaten the hard-won peace in the era of The New Jedi Order (as described in the Del Rey Books novel series).

In addition, the rules in this book can be used to support campaigns set in other eras. For example, in the distant past the Jedi and Sith warred for the fate of the galaxy, as described in Dark Horse Comics' *Tales of the Jedi* and *Knights of the Old Republic* series, as well as the *Knights of the Old Republic* video game series. Alternately, you may choose to set your game in the Legacy era, as popularized in Dark Horse Comics' *Legacy* series: Forty years after

The New Jedi Order era, the Empire has once again risen to power and the Sith have regained control of the galaxy. Although these time periods are not explicitly covered in this book, the rules herein can be used as a basis for play in these eras.

The Basics

A long time ago in a galaxy far, far away...

With this compelling phrase, every *Star Wars* film thunders onto the screen. These epic movies enthrall us with a mix of space fantasy, high adventure, and mythology. We thrill to the adventures of Luke Skywalker and Han Solo, Qui-Gon Jinn and Obi-Wan Kenobi, Anakin Skywalker and Padmé Amidala. We imagine ourselves piloting X-wing starfighters down the Death Star trench or engaging in fight-to-the-death lightsaber duels with Darth Maul, Count Dooku, or General Grievous.

With the *Star Wars Roleplaying Game*, you can experience this epic saga in a whole new way. Imagine yourself as a Jedi in training or a Republic Senator, a brave starfighter pilot or a powerful Wookiee. Whether you want to be a player or the Gamemaster, this book is your portal to the action-packed *Star Wars* galaxy.

The Core Mechanic

The *Star Wars Roleplaying Game* uses a core mechanic to resolve all actions. This central game rule keeps play fast and intuitive. Whenever you want to attempt an action that has some chance of failure, you roll a twenty-sided die (or "d20"). To determine whether your character succeeds at a task (such as an attack or the use of a skill), you do this:

- Roll a d20.
- Add any relevant modifiers.
- Compare the result to a target number.

If the result equals or exceeds the target number (set by the GM or given in the rules), your character succeeds at the task at hand. If the result is lower than the target number, you fail.

The Gamemaster

When you play the *Star Wars Roleplaying Game*, you're participating in an interactive story. Players take on the roles of unique characters, called heroes. One player serves as the Gamemaster, a combination director, narrator, and referee. The GM describes situations, asks the players what their characters want to do, and resolves these actions according to the rules of the game. The GM sets each scene, keeps the story moving, and takes on the roles of the opponents and other characters that the players' heroes encounter in each adventure. If you're the GM, you should read through all sections of this book; you don't need to memorize it, but you do need to have an idea of where to find things once play begins.

Heroes

If you're a player, you take the role of a hero—one of the "stars" of the *Star Wars* saga that you, the other players, and the GM all help to develop. You create your character with the help of the game rules that follow, according to your own vision for the type of hero you want to play. As your character participates in adventures, he or she gains experience points (XP) that help him or her improve and become more powerful.

For more information on character creation, see page 13.

Game Play

This overview gives you enough of the basics to get a feel for how this roleplaying game works. The chapters that follow take these basic concepts and expand upon them.

Important! You don't have to memorize the contents of this book to play the game. It's a game, not homework. Once you understand the basics, start playing! Use this book as a reference during play. The table of contents and index should help you find a specific topic easily. When in doubt, stick to the basics, keep playing, and have fun. You can always look up an obscure rule after your game session ends, but remember that you don't have to sweat the details in the middle of play.

Rolling Dice

We've already explained the basic rule that forms the foundation of the game—roll a d20, add a modifier, and try to get a result that's equal to or greater than the target number. Whenever your character tries to accomplish something significant, the GM asks you to roll a d20.

Important! Not every action requires a die roll. Roll dice in combat and other dramatic situations when the success of an action is in doubt.

The d20 is used to determine results in combat and when making skill checks and ability checks. In other words, the d20 determines whether or not you succeed at an action.

The other dice (d4, d6, d8, d10, and d12) are used to determine what happens after you succeed. Usually, the other dice come into play after making a successful attack roll to determine how much damage the attack deals to the target.

A Game Session

In the *Star Wars Roleplaying Game*, the Gamemaster and players get together to tell a story through the play of the game. We call these group-created stories "adventures." A *Star Wars* adventure features plenty of action, lots of opportunities for combat, cool villains, epic plots, and a sense of wonder and grandeur.

Typically, the game consists of adventures that resemble episodes in the movie saga. One adventure might play out in a single game session; another might stretch across several evenings of play. A session can last as long as you're comfortable playing, from as short as one hour to as long as a 12-hour marathon. Most groups get together and play for two to four hours at a time. The game can be stopped at any time and restarted when the players get back together.

Each adventure consists of interrelated scenes. A scene might feature some kind of challenge or roleplaying encounter, or it could revolve around combat. When there's no combat going on, play is much more casual. The GM describes the scene and asks the players what their characters do. When combat breaks out, game play becomes more structured, and the action takes place in rounds.

What Characters Can Do

A character can try to do anything you can imagine, just so long as it fits the scene the GM describes. Depending on the situation, your character might want to:

- Listen at a door
- Use a computer terminal
- Explore a location
- Converse with an alien
- Bargain with a merchant
- Intimidate a thug
- Talk to an ally
- Pilot a vehicle
- Search for a clue
- Bluff an official
- Repair an item
- Swing across a repulsorlift shaft
- Move
- Duck behind a bulkhead
- Attack an opponent

Characters accomplish these things by making skill checks, ability checks, or attack rolls, all of which entail a modified d20 roll.

What's Next?

If you're new to roleplaying games, you might be wondering how to proceed. After you've read over these basics to get an understanding of the game, check out The First Game Session (see below). This example of play provides some insight into how a roleplaying game session plays out. Then review the first few chapters of the book. When you're ready, use the Character Creation overview (page 13) and a copy of the character sheet from the back of the book to create a character. (You can also download a copy of the character sheet from our website at **www.wizards.com/starwars**.) When you, your Gamemaster, and the other players are ready, start playing!

Setup

After you've created a hero, get together with the rest of your gaming group for your first adventure. Prior to this, the GM has developed a storyline for the adventure. She might buy a complete, ready-to-play adventure or grab one off of the Internet. Alternately, the GM might develop one using the guidelines in Chapter 14: Gamemastering.

Pick an evening or a weekend afternoon or some other convenient time when you and your friends can spend a few hours playing the *Star Wars Roleplaying Game*. Decide on how much time you want to spend playing. (Two to four hours is a good length for a game session.)

Where should you play the game? Anywhere that's comfortable. The place should have a flat surface to roll dice on, such as a kitchen table. The GM sits so that the other players can't look over her shoulder or peek at her adventure notes. She needs enough room to spread out the rulebook and any other materials she might have for the game session, including other *Star Wars* books, a battle map, miniatures, a pencil or pen, dice, and her adventure notes.

General Advice

The first couple of game sessions you play might be a little uneven as everyone learns how the game works and gets comfortable with the idea of roleplaying. Remember that these rules are guidelines, a framework and structure for playing *Star Wars* adventures in a roleplaying game environment. A roleplaying game is a living game; it evolves and develops as you play it. If something isn't working for your group, and the entire group agrees, make a change. But wait until you've played a few times with the official rules before you decide to tinker.

The First Game Session

You and your friends have reviewed the basic rules and created 1st-level characters. Your Gamemaster has reviewed the rules and is ready to run her first adventure. You've agreed upon a time and place to play. Then the time arrives and the game begins!

Sitting around the table, with dice and snacks scattered in all directions, the players gather. Michele is the GM. She takes her place at the head of the table. Chris sits in the next seat; he's running Sia-Lan, a female Jedi. Next to Chris is Mike, practicing his Wookiee sounds to inject a little authenticity into his character, Rorworr the scout. Across the table, Penny makes some last-minute notes on her character sheet, adding a little more detail to Vor'en the soldier. Next to Penny, Brian anxiously waits to get started. He's running Deel Surool, the crafty scoundrel.

Michele has selected a number of *Star Wars* miniatures from her collection to use in tonight's game. The figures will help the players visualize the action in certain situations and will speed along play. She's got a miniature to represent each of the players' characters, and she places them in the middle of the table. She leaves a few others hidden on the floor beside her. She'll use these later to represent opponents that will challenge and compete with the heroes.

Michele doesn't have a specific character for herself. While the players each run a single hero, the Gamemaster narrates the story, adjudicates the rules, and plays all of the GM characters—the supporting cast that serves as allies and opponents for the heroes.

Anyway, it looks like everyone's ready to get started. Michele answers a few last-minute rules questions, then begins the game.

Michele (GM): *A long time ago, in a galaxy far, far away . . . it is the time of the Republic, about twenty-two years before the days of the Empire and the first Death Star battle station. Supreme Chancellor Palpatine leads the Republic, Mace Windu and Yoda lead the Jedi Council, and the start of the Clone Wars is still a few weeks away.*

You're in a spaceport cantina on Corellia, a prominent world in the galactic core. The place is pretty busy for a weekday afternoon, though it's not packed to capacity. You see humans and a variety of other species drinking, laughing, and talking quietly near the bar, in shadowy booths, and at a scattering of freestanding tables. Among those you see are the other players' characters. Why don't you each take a moment to describe yourselves?

Chris (Sia-Lan): *You see a young woman with brown hair sitting alone in one of the booths. She's sipping a clear liquid and watching the crowd. Her hairstyle and outfit mark her as a Jedi. She's a Padawan learner, if any of you know anything about the specifics of the Jedi order. She has a lightsaber hanging at her side, but it's probably hidden beneath the table.*

Mike (Rorworr): *There's a young male Wookiee standing at the bar. He's exchanging words with the bartender. He's tall, but perhaps a bit thin when compared to other Wookiees you may have seen. He's got a bowcaster slung across his back, and he's nursing a huge mug of some foamy liquid.*

Penny (Vor'en): *My character sits in a corner booth, his back to the wall as he nonchalantly studies the crowd. He's got dark eyes and an intense gaze, and he looks strong and capable. He's wearing bits and pieces of light body armor. If he has any weapons—and you're sure he does—they're either hidden under the table or in the booth's darker shadows.*

Brian (Deel): *You also see a young male Twi'lek—you know, the guys with the head-tails, like Bib Fortuna—sitting at one of the tables in the middle of the room. He's playing sabacc with a few of the spacers, and it looks like he's begun to amass more than his share of credits.*

Michele (GM): *Okay. You've all noticed each other, but you don't know each other yet. Before anything else happens, why don't each of you make a Perception check for me?*

The players each roll a d20 and add their Perception skill modifier to get a result. If a character doesn't have the Perception skill as a trained skill, the player still gets to apply his Wisdom modifier (if any) to the roll. After all the players have made the skill check, they let the GM know the results.

Chris (Sia-Lan): *Sia-Lan got a 15.*
Mike (Rorworr): *17 for Rorworr!*
Penny (Vor'en): *I rolled an 8.*
Brian (Deel): *The amazingly perceptive Deel Surool got a 22.*

Michele consults her notes, checking to see what the DC for the Perception check is. She nods and makes a note or two, just to keep the players guessing.

Michele (GM): *Vor'en the soldier, even though he's watching the room, fails to notice something that the rest of you successfully spot. The rest of you see a Human male who looks a lot like Senator Alastar Treen of Corulag. He's dressed like most of the other spacers in the cantina, and he's deep in conversation with a Rodian female.*

Just then, you all see the cantina doors slide open as a group of tough-looking thugs enters the room. The bartender yells, "Hey, no blasters in here!" He ducks behind the bar, just in time, as one of the thugs casually fires a blaster bolt in his direction. There are four thugs—two Humans, a Rodian, and a Gamorrean. The Gamorrean wields a vibroblade, and the other three are armed with blaster pistols. The Gamorrean grunts something foul and gestures toward the table where the senator is sitting.

"For the Separatists!" shouts one of the Humans with a sneer as he prepares to target Senator Treen.

Everyone make an Initiative check!

The players each roll a d20 and add their Initiative skill modifier to get a result. If a character doesn't have the Initiative skill as a trained skill, the player still gets to apply his Dexterity modifier (if any) to the roll. Michele rolls a single Initiative check for the group of thugs, and one for the disguised senator and his companion.

Chris (Sia-Lan): *Sia-Lan got an 18.*
Mike (Rorworr): *10 for Rorworr!*
Penny (Vor'en): *Vor'en got a 12.*
Brian (Deel): *The fast-acting Deel Surool got a 15.*

Michele writes down the initiative order, from highest result to lowest. She jots down:

Sia-Lan 18
Deel 15
Thugs 13 (her roll)
Vor'en 12
Rorworr 10
Senator 7 (her roll)

Michele (GM): *The thugs look like they're gunning for the senator. Sia-Lan, what are you going to do?*

Chris (Sia-Lan): *I leap out of the booth and position myself between the senator and the thugs as my first move action. As my second move action I draw my lightsaber. As a free action, I activate the lightsaber and shout, "This man is under the protection of the Jedi Knights!"*

Michele (GM): *Your lightsaber hums to life. Deel, you're next. What are you going to do?*

Brian (Deel): *Helping a senator and a Jedi could be profitable. Deel tips his table over and crouches behind it to get some cover. I guess that's a move action. Then he pulls out his blaster for his second move action.*

Michele (GM): *When the table crashes onto its side, sabacc card-chips and credits scatter across the floor. The spacers you were playing with dive for cover.*

Brian (Deel): *Oops, I forgot about the sabacc game in all the excitement. No matter, I guess. Most of the credits belonged to Deel, anyway.*

Michele (GM): *The thugs act next. The two humans each take a shot at the Jedi who's standing between them and the senator. The Rodian thug takes a shot at Deel, and the Gamorrean rushes forward to slice at the Jedi with his vibroblade.*

Chris (Sia-Lan): *I'm going to use the table next to me to protect myself from the blaster shots.*

Michele (GM): *Sure. That gives you cover against all the thugs, but increases your Reflex Defense by +4.*

Michele makes the attack rolls for the two thugs. The first one gets an 11. The second one gets a 19.

Sia-Lan's Reflex Defense when she uses cover to protect herself is 19. That means she blocks the first bolt, but the second bolt gets through.

Michele rolls 3d6 damage for the successful blaster pistol attack. The total is 11. Sia-Lan has 22 hit points, so the attack reduces her hit points to 11.

The rest of the round continues, with Michele finishing up the thug's actions, then Vor'en, Rorworr, and Senator Treen acting in turn. Each round plays out in this order until one side or the other is defeated or flees. Then the heroes would get a chance to meet each other and find out why the senator is in disguise and under attack. And so begins this *Star Wars* adventure!

Character Creation

Make sure you review Chapters 1 through 9 before using this overview when creating a *Star Wars* character. Make a copy of the character sheet from the back of this book to use as a record of your character.

Characters generally begin play at 1st level and attain additional levels as they complete adventures.

1. Generate Ability Scores

Every character has six abilities that represent the character's basic strengths and weaknesses. These abilities—Strength, Dexterity, Constitution, Intelligence, Wisdom, and Charisma—affect everything a hero does, from fighting to using skills.

A score of 10 or 11 in an ability is average. Higher scores grant bonuses, and lower scores give penalties. When you create your character, you'll want to put your higher scores into the abilities most closely associated with your character's class.

Use one of the methods described in Chapter 1: Abilities to generate your six ability scores. Record the scores on a piece of scrap paper and put them aside for the moment.

2. Select Your Species

As a *Star Wars* character, you aren't limited to simply being Human. There are a variety of species available, from Mon Calamari to Wookiee. Select the species you want to play from those presented in Chapter 2: Species.

Each species has its own set of special abilities and modifiers. Record these traits on your character sheet.

3. Choose Your Class

A class provides you with a starting point for your character, a frame upon which you can hang skills, feats, and various story elements. Choose a class from those presented in Chapter 3: Heroic Classes and write it on your character sheet.

4. Assign Ability Scores

Now that you know what species and class you want your character to be, take the scores you generated earlier and assign each to one of the six abilities: Strength, Dexterity, Constitution, Intelligence, Wisdom, and Charisma. Then make any adjustments to these scores according to the species you selected.

For guidance, each class description indicates which abilities are most important for that class. You might want to put your highest scores in the abilities that accentuate the natural benefits of the class.

Record your ability scores on your character sheet. Record your ability modifiers as well.

5. Determine Combat Statistics

In combat, you need to know your character's hit points, defenses, damage threshold, attack bonuses, and speed, as well as how many Force Points he has to spend.

Hit Points

Each character can withstand a certain amount of damage before falling unconscious or dying. This ability to take damage and keep on functioning is represented by the character's hit points.

Your class determines how many hit points you have at 1st level, as shown below:

CLASS	STARTING HIT POINTS
Noble, scoundrel	18 + Constitution modifier
Scout	24 + Constitution modifier
Jedi, soldier	30 + Constitution modifier

For example, if your character belongs to the scoundrel class and you have a 12 Constitution, you start with 19 hit points (18 plus 1 for your Constitution bonus).

Your hit points increase as you gain levels, as described on page 37.

Defenses

Determine your character's defenses as follows:

Reflex Defense: 10 + your heroic level or armor bonus + Dexterity modifier + class bonus + natural armor bonus + size modifier

Fortitude Defense: 10 + your heroic level + Constitution modifier + class bonus + equipment bonus

Will Defense: 10 + your heroic level + Wisdom modifier + class bonus

When you take your first level in a heroic class, you gain class bonuses on two or more defenses, as shown on page 36.

If you wear armor, you must substitute your armor bonus for your heroic level when calculating your Reflex Defense. For example, a 1st-level soldier with a Dexterity of 12 wearing a blast helmet and vest (+2 armor bonus) has a Reflex Defense of 13 (10 + 2 armor + 1 Dex + 1 class). Some types of armor also provide an equipment bonus to your Fortitude Defense in addition to an armor bonus to your Reflex Defense (as noted in Table 8–7: Armor, page 132).

Damage Threshold
Attacks that deal massive amounts of damage can impair or incapacitate you regardless of how many hit points you have remaining. Your damage threshold determines how much damage a single attack must deal to reduce your combat effectiveness or, in some cases, kill you.

A Small or Medium character's damage threshold is equal to his or her Fortitude Defense. Record this number on your character sheet.

Base Attack Bonus

Your character's class determines your base attack bonus. Record this number on the character sheet.

Jedi and soldiers have a base attack bonus of +1 at 1st level; nobles, scoundrels, and scouts have a base attack bonus of +0 at 1st level.

Melee Attack Bonus

To determine your melee attack bonus, add your Strength modifier to your base attack bonus. Certain feats and talents might provide additional modifiers, so make adjustments as necessary.

Ranged Attack Bonus

To determine your ranged attack bonus, add your Dexterity modifier to your base attack bonus. Certain feats and talents might provide additional modifiers, so make adjustments as necessary.

Speed

Your character's species determines her speed. Most species have a speed of 6 squares. Ewoks have a speed of 4 squares because they are Small.

Force Points

Your character begins play with 5 Force Points. Indicate this in the space provided on the character sheet.

If you end up taking the Force Boon feat (page 85), you gain an additional 3 Force Points.

Destiny Point

If your GM uses the optional destiny rules described in Chapter 7: Heroic Traits, your character begins play with 1 Destiny Point. Indicate this in the space provided on the character sheet.

6. SELECT SKILLS

Skills represent how well a character accomplishes dramatic tasks other than combat, such as disabling a tractor beam generator or climbing a sheer surface.

Each class comes with a list of class skills. From this list, you get to pick a number of skills in which your character is considered trained. The number of trained skills your character gets depends on the class you've selected and your character's Intelligence modifier. Once you've selected your character's trained skills, determine the skill check modifier for each skill.

The skill check modifier for trained skills is one-half your character level (rounded down) + the relevant ability modifier + 5. If you are untrained in a skill, the skill check modifier is one-half your character level (rounded down) + the relevant ability modifier. (In other words, you get a +5 bonus on skill checks made using trained skills.)

Some skills cannot be used untrained. See Chapter 4: Skills for more information.

7. SELECT FEATS

Feats are special features that provide a character with new capabilities or improvements.

Your character begins play with at least one feat. If you are playing a Human, you get a bonus feat. In addition, your class also gives you several starting feats that you get for free.

Select your feats from Chapter 5: Feats and record them on the character sheet. Some feats may affect the information you've already recorded, so make adjustments as necessary.

8. SELECT A TALENT

At 1st level, your character gets a talent (a special class feature). Choose a talent from any of the talent trees presented in your character's class description. Some talents have prerequisites that must be met before they can be selected.

9. DETERMINE STARTING CREDITS AND BUY GEAR

Your character's class determines how many credits you start play with. Use your credits to purchase equipment for your character. Chapter 8: Equipment describes weapons, armor, and gear you can select from.

10. FINISH YOUR CHARACTER

The last details you need to add to your character sheet help you visualize and roleplay your character. You need a name, of course—something that fits your class, species, and the *Star Wars* galaxy. You should also determine your character's age, gender, height, weight, eye and hair color, skin color, and any relevant background information you want to provide. (Make sure to run your ideas past your Gamemaster so that he or she can fit them into the campaign.)

Chapter 7: Heroic Traits provides guidelines that can help you with these details and characteristics.

Chapter 1
Abilities

Just about every dice roll you make is going to get a bonus or penalty based on your character's abilities. A tough character has a better chance of surviving a freezing night on Hoth. A perceptive character is more likely to notice stormtroopers sneaking up from behind. A stupid character is less likely to find a concealed panel that leads to a secret cargo compartment. Your ability scores tell you what your modifiers are for rolls such as these.

Your character has six abilities: Strength (abbreviated Str), Dexterity (Dex), Constitution (Con), Intelligence (Int), Wisdom (Wis), and Charisma (Cha). Each of your character's above-average abilities gives you a benefit on certain die rolls, and each below-average ability gives you a disadvantage on other die rolls. You roll your scores randomly, assign them to the abilities you like, raise and lower them according to your character's species, and then raise them as your character advances in experience.

Your Ability Scores

To create an ability score for your character, roll four six-sided dice (4d6). Disregard the lowest die and total the three highest dice.

This roll gives you a number between 3 (horrible) and 18 (tremendous). The average ability score for the typical galactic citizen is 10 or 11, but your character is not typical. The most common ability scores for player characters (heroes) are 12 and 13. (The average hero is above average.)

Make this roll six times, recording the result each time on a piece of paper. Once you have all six scores, assign each score to one of your six abilities. At this step, you need to know what kind of person your character is going to be, including his species and class, in order to know where best to place your character's ability scores. Remember that choosing a species other than Human causes some of these ability scores to change (see Table 2–1: Species Ability Adjustments).

Ability Modifiers

Each ability, after changes made because of species, has a –5 to +5 modifier. Table 1–1: Ability Modifiers shows the modifier for each ability, based on its score.

The modifier is the number you add to or subtract from the die roll when your character tries to do something related to that ability. For instance, you add or subtract your Strength modifier to your roll when you try to hit someone with a vibroblade. You also apply the modifier to some numbers that aren't die rolls, such as when you add or subtract your Dexterity modifier to your Reflex Defense. A positive modifier is called a bonus and a negative modifier is called a penalty.

Rerolling

If your scores are too low, you may scrap them and reroll all six scores. Your scores are considered too low if your total modifiers (before changes according to species) are 0 or less, or if your highest score is 13 or lower.

Table 1-1: Ability Modifiers

SCORE	MODIFIER	SCORE	MODIFIER	SCORE	MODIFIER
1	−5	12–13	+1	24–25	+7
2–3	−4	14–15	+2	26–27	+8
4–5	−3	16–17	+3	28–29	+9
6–7	−2	18–19	+4	30–31	+10
8–9	−1	20–21	+5	etc....	etc....
10–11	0	22–23	+6		

Planned Generation

Instead of rolling dice, you may select the scores you want by using the planned character generation method. This requires a bit more thought and effort on your part, since you need to know what kind of character you want to play so you can select your scores appropriately. Determine your species and class beforehand, then select your scores as outlined below.

Your character's ability scores all start at 8. You have 25 points to spend to increase these scores, using the costs shown below. After you select your scores, apply any species modifiers.

SCORE	COST	SCORE	COST	SCORE	COST
8	0	12	4	16	10
9	1	13	5	17	13
10	2	14	6	18	16
11	3	15	8		

Standard Score Package

The third method of determining ability scores is the standard score package, a balanced mix of scores designed to quickly create hero characters. Assign the scores to the abilities as you like. After you assign your scores, apply species modifiers.

The standard score package is:
15, 14, 13, 12, 10, and 8.

The Abilities

Each ability partially describes your character and affects some of your character's actions. The description of each ability includes a list of notable characters along with their scores in that ability.

Strength (Str)

Strength measures your character's muscle and physical power. This ability is especially important for soldiers because it helps them prevail in physical combat.

You apply your character's Strength modifier to:
—Melee attack rolls.
—Damage rolls for melee and thrown weapons. (Exceptions: Grenades don't have their damage modified by Strength.)
—Climb, Jump, and Swim checks (the skills with Strength as the key ability).
—Strength checks (for breaking down doors and the like).

Dexterity (Dex)

Dexterity measures hand-eye coordination, agility, reflexes, and balance. This ability is the most important ability for scoundrels, but it's also high on the list for characters who want to be good shots with ranged weapons (such as blaster pistols) or who want to handle the controls of a starship or speeder fairly well.

You apply your character's Dexterity modifier to:
—Ranged attack rolls, such as with blasters.
—Reflex Defense, provided the character can react to the attack.
—Acrobatics, Pilot, Ride, and Stealth checks (the skills where Dexterity is the key ability).

Constitution (Con)

Constitution represents your character's health and stamina. Constitution adds to a hero's hit points, so it's important for everyone, but most important for soldiers and Jedi.

You apply your Constitution modifier to:
—Each die roll for gaining additional hit points (though a penalty can never drop a hit point roll below 1; a character always gains at least 1 hit point each time he or she goes up a level).
—Fortitude Defense, for resisting poison, radiation, and similar threats.
—The Endurance skill.

If a character's Constitution changes, his or her hit points should also increase or decrease accordingly.

Intelligence (Int)

Intelligence determines how well your character learns and reasons. Intelligence is important for scouts, nobles, and any character who wants to have a wide assortment of skills.

You apply your character's Intelligence modifier to:
—The number of languages your character knows at the start of the game.
—The number of trained skills you have.

—Knowledge, Mechanics, and Use Computer checks (the skills with Intelligence as the key ability).

Beasts have Intelligence scores of 1 or 2. Sentient creatures have scores of at least 3.

When a character's Intelligence score permanently increases or decreases, its number of trained skills and known languages also changes. For example, if Paul's Wookiee scout increases his Intelligence from 13 to 14, his Int modifier goes from +1 to +2. Paul's Wookiee gains one new trained skill (chosen from his class skills) and one new language. The Wookiee's greater Intelligence allows him to utilize things he had learned but never before applied properly.

Wisdom (Wis)

Every creature has a Wisdom score. Wisdom describes a character's willpower, common sense, perception, and intuition. Compared to Intelligence, Wisdom is more related to being in tune with and aware of one's surroundings, while Intelligence represents one's ability to analyze information. An "absent-minded professor" has a low Wisdom score and a high Intelligence score. A simpleton with low Intelligence might nevertheless have great insight (high Wisdom). Wisdom is the most important ability for scouts, but it's also important to characters wishing to be in-tune with their environment or characters who like to gamble. If you want your character to have keen senses, put a high score in Wisdom.

You apply your character's Wisdom modifier to:

—Will Defense, generally for resisting certain Force attacks.

—Perception, Survival, and Treat Injury checks (the skills with Wisdom as the key ability).

—The number of Force powers you learn when you take the Force Training feat.

When a Force-using character's Wisdom score permanently increases or decreases, his number of known Force powers also changes. For every instance of the Force Training feat that you have, you gain one Force power (or an additional use of an already-known Force power) for every point by which your Wisdom modifier increases. If you instead suffer a permanent reduction in your Wisdom modifier, you lose access to the same number of Force powers; you must choose which Force powers (or extra uses of the same Force power) you lose.

Charisma (Cha)

Every creature has a Charisma score. Charisma measures a character's force of personality, persuasiveness, personal magnetism, ability to lead, and physical attractiveness. It represents actual strength of personality and force of presence, not merely how others perceive you in a social setting. Charisma is most important for nobles and Jedi.

You apply your Charisma modifier to:

Intelligence, Wisdom, and Charisma

A character with a high Intelligence score is curious, knowledgeable, and prone to using big words. A character with a high Intelligence but low Wisdom may be smart but absent-minded, or knowledgeable but lacking in common sense. A character with a high Intelligence but a low Charisma may be a know-it-all or a reclusive scholar. The smart character lacking in both Wisdom and Charisma usually puts her foot in her mouth.

A character with a low Intelligence mispronounces and misuses words, has trouble following directions, or fails to get the joke.

A character with a high Wisdom score may be sensible, serene, "in tune," alert, or centered. A character with a high Wisdom but a low Intelligence may be aware, but simple. A character with a high Wisdom but a low Charisma knows enough to speak carefully and may become an adviser or "power behind the throne" rather than a leader.

A character with a low Wisdom score may be rash, imprudent, irresponsible, or "out of it."

A character with a high Charisma may be beautiful, handsome, striking, personable, and confident. A character with a high Charisma but a low Intelligence can usually pass herself off as knowledgeable, until she meets a true expert. A charismatic character with a low Wisdom may be popular, but he doesn't know who his real friends are.

A character with a low Charisma may be reserved, gruff, rude, fawning, or simply nondescript.

—Deception, Gather Information, Persuasion, and Use the Force checks (skills with Charisma as the key ability).

Changing Ability Scores

Over time, your character's ability scores can change. Ability scores can increase without limit.

- At 4th, 8th, 12th, 16th, and 20th level, a heroic character increases two ability scores by 1 point each.
- As a character ages, some ability scores go up and others go down. See Table 7-2: Aging Effects (page 110) for details.

When an ability score changes, all attributes associated with that score change accordingly. For example, when Sia-Lan becomes a 4th-level Jedi, she increases her Dexterity from 15 to 16 and increases her Charisma from 13 to 14. Now she's harder to hit, better at using ranged weapons, and all of her Dexterity-based and Charisma-based skills improve as well.

Chapter II
Species

The *Star Wars* galaxy contains a bewildering variety of species, each with its own unique outlook and civilization. Although Humans dominate the known galaxy, there are many intelligent alien species that can be encountered wherever you travel.

Humans live among the Core Worlds, throughout the Mid Rim, and even on the worlds of the Outer Rim Territories. Most of the alien species have their own homeworlds and colonies, but individuals can be found anywhere, thanks to the prevalence of hyperspace travel. The promise of profit and power often lure members of all species to the same areas, including spaceports and metropolitan cities.

Sometimes it's easy to believe that all Rodians are outlaws or all Wookiees are short-tempered, but the truth is that every member of every species is unique. Depending on the era in which your campaign is set, nonhuman species have different social advantages or disadvantages, as explained in the Era Notes: Species sidebar (page 23).

Choosing a Species

After you roll your ability scores and before you write them on your character sheet, choose your character's species. At the same time, you'll want to select your character's class, since species affects how well the character can do in each class. Once you've decided your character's species and class, assign ability scores to particular abilities. Alter the scores according to the species (see Table 2-1: Species Ability Modifiers) and continue detailing your character.

You can play a character of any species presented in this chapter, but certain species do better pursuing certain classes.

Your character's species provides plenty of clues as to the sort of person he or she is, how he or she feels about characters of other species, and what motivates him or her. Remember, however, that the species descriptions only apply to the majority of people. In each species, some individuals diverge from the norm, and your character can be one of these. Don't let a description hinder you from detailing your character as you like.

Species Characteristics

Your character's species determines some of his or her qualities.

Ability Adjustments

Find your character's species on Table 2-1: Species Ability Adjustments and apply the adjustments that you see there to your character's ability scores. If the changes raise a score above 18 or lower it below 3, that's okay.

For example, a Rodian gets a +2 species bonus on his Dexterity score and a –2 penalty on his Wisdom and Charisma scores. Knowing this, the player puts her best score rolled (15) in Dexterity and sees it increase to 17. She doesn't want a Wisdom or Charisma penalty for her character, so she puts above-average scores (13 and 12) in Wisdom and Charisma. These drop to 11 and 10, for neither a bonus nor a penalty.

Table 2-1: Species Ability Adjustments

SPECIES	ABILITY ADJUSTMENTS
Human	None
Bothan	+2 Dex, –2 Con
Cerean	+2 Int, +2 Wis, –2 Dex
Duros	+2 Dex, +2 Int, –2 Con
Ewok	+2 Dex, –2 Str
Gamorrean	+2 Str, –2 Dex, –2 Int
Gungan	+2 Dex, –2 Int, –2 Cha
Ithorian	+2 Wis, +2 Cha, –2 Dex
Kel Dor	+2 Dex, +2 Wis, –2 Con
Mon Calamari	+2 Int, +2 Wis, –2 Con
Quarren	+2 Con, –2 Wis, –2 Cha
Rodian	+2 Dex, –2 Wis, –2 Cha
Sullustan	+2 Dex, –2 Con
Trandoshan	+2 Str, –2 Dex
Twi'lek	+2 Cha, –2 Wis
Wookiee	+4 Str, +2 Con, –2 Dex, –2 Wis, –2 Cha
Zabrak	None

Common Languages

The *Star Wars* galaxy is home to millions of languages, but picking languages for your character doesn't need to be daunting. A few of the more common languages are listed below. Among these, Basic is the most widely spoken. Other prevalent languages include Huttese (particularly common in the Outer Rim), Binary (used by droids and programmers), and Bocce (a trade language that can be spoken by almost any species).

- Basic
- Binary
- Bocce
- Bothese
- Cerean
- Dosh
- Durese
- Ewokese*
- Gamorrean
- Gunganese*
- High Galactic
- Huttese
- Ithorese
- Jawa Trade Language*
- Kel Dor
- Mon Calamarian
- Quarrenese
- Rodese
- Ryl
- Shyriiwook
- Sullustese
- Zabrak

* Local language not widely spoken except on its planet of origin.

> "The ability to speak does not make you intelligent."
> — Qui-Gon Jinn

Known Languages

The primary language used throughout known space is called Basic. Most characters can speak Basic, and all characters understand it even if they can't speak it. Nonhuman characters can also speak, read, and write the language associated with their species; for example, Bothans speak, read, and write Bothese as well as Basic.

Characters with an Intelligence bonus know how to speak, read, and write other languages as well. For each point of Intelligence bonus, a character can speak, read, and write one additional language of his choice.

Some species (Gamorreans and Wookiees, for example) are incapable of speaking any language other than their native tongue, but they can learn to read and write other languages just fine.

HUMAN

Humans

Humans dominate the Core Worlds and can be found in virtually every corner of the galaxy. They are the ancestors of early spacefaring pioneers, conquerors, traders, travelers, and refugees. Humans have always been people on the move. As a result, they can be found on almost every inhabited planet. As a species, Humans are physically, culturally, and politically diverse. Hardy or fine, light-skinned or dark, Humans remain one of the most dominant species throughout all eras of play.

Personality: Human personality runs the gamut of possibilities, though members of this species tend to be highly adaptable, tenacious, and willing to keep striving no matter the odds. They are flexible and ambitious, diverse in their tastes, morals, customs, and habits.

Physical Description: Humans average about 1.8 meters tall. Skin shades run from nearly black to very pale, hair from black to blond. Men are usually taller and heavier than women. Humans achieve maturity about the age of 15 and rarely live beyond 100.

Homeworlds: Various, including Coruscant (page 229), Corellia, Naboo (page 233), Tatooine (page 236), and Alderaan.

Languages: Humans speak, read, and write Basic. They often learn other languages as well, including obscure ones.

Example Names: Anakin, Arani, Bail, Ben, Beru, Biggs, Boba, Corran, Dack, Dané, Galak, Garm, Han, Jango, Jodo, Lando, Leia, Luke, Mace, Mara, Obi-Wan, Owen, Padmé, Qui-Gon, Sia-Lan, Rann, Talon, Vor'en, Wedge, Winter.

Adventurers: Humans aren't afraid to try anything, and Human adventurers are the most audacious, daring, and ambitious members of an audacious, daring, and ambitious species. A Human can earn glory by amassing power, wealth, and fame. More than any other species, Humans champion causes rather than territories or groups.

Human Species Traits

Humans share the following species traits:

Medium Size: As Medium creatures, Humans have no special bonuses or penalties due to their size.

Speed: Human base speed is 6 squares.

Bonus Trained Skill: Humans are versatile and accomplished at many tasks. A Human character chooses one additional trained skill at 1st level. The skill must be chosen from the character's list of class skills (see Chapter 3: Heroic Classes).

Bonus Feat: Humans gain one bonus feat at 1st level (see Chapter 5: Feats).

Automatic Language: Basic.

Bothans

Native to Bothawui, these short, fur-covered humanoids have had hyperspace travel for thousands of years. Bothans use information as a measure of wealth and power, even wielding it as a weapon when necessary. The

Era Notes: Species

Nonhuman characters have some restrictions placed upon them, depending on the era in which your campaign is set. These restrictions are described below.

The Rise of the Empire (50 to 0 years before Episode IV)
During the time that saw the erosion of the Old Republic and the rise of the Empire, including the period around Episodes I–III, all species participated in a more or less cosmopolitan galaxy. The only restrictions on your choice of an alien species in this time frame refer to species that have not yet "been discovered" by the galaxy at large. Ewoks, therefore, are not available if your campaign is set in this era.

The Rebellion (0 to 5 years after Episode IV)
The Empire was particularly entrenched with anti-alien sentiments. During this period of galactic history, most alien species were either enslaved or subjugated by the Empire. In the Outer Rim, nonhuman species continued to carry on their lives as normally as they were able, but in the more civilized regions, nonhumans were relegated to the status of second-class citizens—or worse. Many aliens joined the Rebellion, fighting alongside humans in an effort to throw off the shackles of oppression and tyranny. Ewoks show up late in this era, during the Battle of Endor, and free Wookiees rarely appear due to their status as slaves of the Empire.

Late in this era, with the decline of the Empire and the birth of the New Republic, nonhumans once again take a prominent and equal role in the affairs of the galaxy.

The New Jedi Order (25+ years after Episode IV)
All alien species are available without restriction in this time frame. The era is marked by the New Republic's battle against the Yuuzhan Vong invaders and tainted by growing distrust of the Jedi Knights.

BOTHAN

Bothan SpyNet, one of the largest intelligence agencies during most eras, plays an important role in the Galactic Civil War.

Culturally, Bothans don't believe in direct conflict because it destroys people, material, and even information. They prefer behind-the-scenes manipulation, watching and waiting for information that they can use to gain status and influence. This attitude makes espionage a natural part of their culture. While others often find Bothans to be manipulative and irritating, no one wants to lose access to their SpyNet. As a result, nearly all groups have at least some contact with the Bothans.

Personality: Bothans are curious, manipulative, crafty, suspicious, and even a bit paranoid. They can be irritating, but they are also loyal and brave.

Physical Description: Bothans are covered with fur that ripples in response to their emotional state. They have tapered ears, and both male and female Bothans sport beards. They average about 1.6 meters tall and have a maturity rate and life span slightly greater than Humans.

Homeworld: The industrial world of Bothawui (page 228), with various colony worlds throughout the Mid Rim Territories.

Languages: Bothans speak, read, and write Bothese and Basic.

Example Names: Borsk Fey'lya, Karka Kre'fey, Koth Melan, Tav Breil'lya, Tereb Ab'lon.

Adventurers: Bothan adventurers, often SpyNet operatives, engage in daring missions at great personal risk. In addition, many Bothan heroes serve as soldiers, pilots, and diplomats. Their curiosity leads some to be explorers and scouts.

Bothan Species Traits

Bothans share the following species traits:

Ability Modifiers: +2 Dexterity, –2 Constitution. Bothans are agile but not particularly resilient.

Medium Size: As Medium creatures, Bothans have no special bonuses or penalties due to their size.

Speed: Bothan base speed is 6 squares.

Iron Will: Bothans have above-average willpower and gain a +2 species bonus to their Will Defense.

Conditional Bonus Feat: Bothans are natural spies and investigators. A Bothan with Gather Information as a trained skill gains Skill Focus (Gather Information) as a bonus feat.

Automatic Languages: Basic and Bothese.

Cereans

Cereans are a sophisticated and cultured humanoid species native to Cerea, a world on the fringes of known space. Their elongated heads distinguish them from most other humanoid species.

Cereans established contact with the rest of the galaxy shortly before the Galactic Republic was transformed into the Empire, swiftly gaining fame as expert astrogators, cryptographers, and economists. Few patterns or trends escape the notice of a Cerean.

Cerean society is matriarchal, and the Cerean culture's traditional values emphasize living in harmony with nature and minimizing any impact on the environment from technology. The peaceful philosophies of the Jedi appeal to Cereans, and many join the Order.

Personality: Cereans tend to be calm, rational, and extremely logical.

Physical Description: Cereans average about 2 meters tall, with elongated craniums housing binary brains. They have a maturity rate and life span similar to those of Humans.

Homeworld: The blissful planet Cerea (page 228).

Languages: Cereans speak, read, and write Cerean and Basic.

Example Names: Ki-Adi, So Leet, Sylvn, Ti-Dal, Maj-Odo.

Adventurers: Cereans who become adventurers do so in spite of their peaceful traditions. Still, when a cause or situation leads down this path, a Cerean tries to keep these traditions intact, avoiding aggression when possible. The binary brain allows a Cerean to constantly weigh both sides in any disagreement and give two points of view equal consideration. This ability extends even to issues surrounding the Force, and a Cerean Force-user often contemplates the light side and the dark side simultaneously.

Cerean Species Traits

Cereans share the following species traits:

Ability Modifiers: +2 Intelligence, +2 Wisdom, –2 Dexterity. Cereans are bright and intuitive but less coordinated than most other species.

CEREAN

Medium Size: As Medium creatures, Cereans have no special bonuses or penalties due to their size.

Speed: Cerean base speed is 6 squares.

Intuitive Initiative: A Cerean may choose to reroll any Initiative check, but the result of the reroll must be accepted even if it is worse. Despite their general lack of coordination, Cereans' reaction speed is superior to that of most other species.

Conditional Bonus Feat: A Cerean with Initiative as a trained skill gains Skill Focus (Initiative) as a bonus feat.

Automatic Languages: Basic and Cerean.

Duros

Tall, hairless humanoids from the Duro system, Duros were one of the first species to become a major influence in the Galactic Republic, and many respected scholars credited the Duros with creating the first hyperdrive. The Duros have a natural affinity for space travel, possessing an innate grasp of the mathematical underpinnings of astrogational computations. Many tales are swapped in cantinas about Duros astrogators calculating the coordinates for supposedly impossible jumps in their heads. Although not as numerous as Humans, the Duros are almost as omnipresent; all but the smallest settlements in known space feature Duros populations.

The Duros species has existed on other worlds in isolation from the rest of their kind, evolving in slight different directions from the baseline species. The most populous and well-known near-Duros species are the Neimoidians, a people rarely encountered during the Rebellion era.

Personality: A Duros tends to be intense and adventurous, always seeking to learn what's at the end of the next hyperspace jump. They are a proud, self-sufficient, fun-loving people who also have a tendency toward gregariousness.

Physical Description: Duros average about 1.8 meters tall. They are hairless, with large eyes and wide, lipless mouths. Skin color ranges from blue-gray to deep azure.

Homeworld: The orbiting cities of the Duro system (page 230).

Languages: Duros speak and are literate in Durese and Basic.

Example Names: Baniss Keeg, Ellor, Kadlo, Kir Vantai, Lai Nootka, Monnda Tebbo.

Adventurers: Duros adventurers include hyperspace explorers, star charters, and spacers of all descriptions. They also tend to gravitate toward the sciences, including engineering and astrogation. Some Duros shun exploration in favor of smuggling and trading, and a small number go into diplomatic professions.

Duros Species Traits

Duros share the following species traits:

Ability Modifiers: +2 Dexterity, +2 Intelligence, –2 Constitution. Duros are agile in mind and body, but they aren't a physically hardy people.

Medium Size: As Medium creatures, Duros have no special bonuses or penalties due to their size.

Speed: Duros base speed is 6 squares.

Expert Pilot: As natural spacers, a Duros may choose to reroll any Pilot check, but the result of the reroll must be accepted even if it is worse.

Automatic Languages: Basic and Durese.

Ewoks

Intelligent omnivores native to one of the moons orbiting Endor, Ewoks are almost unknown prior to the Battle of Endor. Ewoks live in tree-dwelling tribes with gender-based division of labor; males hunt, forage, and make weapons, while females raise young and handle other domestic tasks. Ewok culture revolves around complex animistic beliefs involving the giant trees of the forest moon.

Although technologically primitive, Ewoks are clever, inquisitive, and inventive. Skittish and wary when first introduced to machines, their curiosity soon overcomes fear.

Personality: Ewoks tend to be curious, superstitious, and courageous, though they can be fearful around things that are strange and new.

Physical Description: Ewoks average about 1 meter tall. Their fur color and pattern varies widely.

Homeworld: The forest moon of Endor (page 230).

Languages: Ewoks speak Ewokese. They have no written form of their language. They can learn to speak Basic.

Example Names: Asha, Chirpa, Deej, Kneesaa, Latara, Logray, Malani, Nippet, Paploo, Shodu, Teebo, Wicket, Wiley.

Adventurers: An Ewok adventurer may be motivated by a love of excitement, a natural inquisitiveness, or a warrior's quest. Collecting powerful "magic" items from fallen opponents is sure way to earn the respect of the tribe.

Duros

Ewok

Ewok Species Traits

Ewoks share the following species traits:

Ability Modifiers: +2 Dexterity, –2 Strength. Ewoks are very agile but somewhat weak.

Small Size: As Small creatures, Ewoks gain a +1 size bonus to their Reflex Defense and a +5 size bonus on Stealth checks. However, their lifting and carrying limits are three-quarters of those of Medium characters.

Speed: Ewok base speed is 4 squares.

Primitive: Ewoks do not gain Weapon Proficiency (pistols, rifles, or heavy weapons) as starting feats at 1st level, even if their class normally grants them.

Scent: Ewoks have a keen sense of smell. At close range (within 10 squares), Ewoks ignore concealment and cover for purposes of Perception checks, and they take no penalty from poor visibility when tracking (see Survival skill, page 73).

Sneaky: An Ewok may choose to reroll any Stealth check, but the result of the reroll must be accepted even if it is worse.

Conditional Bonus Feat: Ewoks are skilled foragers. An Ewok with Survival as a trained skill gains Skill Focus (Survival) as a bonus feat.

Automatic Languages: Ewokese (speak only).

Gamorreans

Gamorreans are green-skinned, porcine creatures from native to Gamorr. Their tendency toward violence makes them valued as criminal enforcers; though viewed as mindless brutes, they don't care so long as they are paid to fight.

Gamorrean civilization revolves around the never-ending wars between their clans. Preferring large melee weapons in combat, many see ranged weapons as cowardly. Males live to fight; females farm, hunt, and manufacture weapons. Inter-clan hatred rarely fades, and anyone hiring Gamorreans should be aware of their clans to avoid infighting.

Personality: Gamorreans are brutish, violent, and proud. They respect physical prowess and have no problem facing death against a foe they feel they are on at least equal footing with.

Physical Description: Gamorreans average about 1.8 meters tall, with thick green skin covering powerful muscles. Close-set eyes, a thick snout, tusks, and small horns give them a distinct look.

GAMORREAN

Homeworld: The preindustrial world of Gamorr (pae 231).

Languages: Gamorreans speak Gamorrean. They have no written version of the language. They can learn to understand but not speak other languages.

Example Names: Gartogg, Jubnuk, Ortugg, Ugmush, Venorra, Warlug.

Adventurers: Some Gamorreans leave their homeworld as slaves but later escape or buy out their contracts. Others sell their contracts, finding employment as bodyguards or enforcers. A Gamorrean is constantly at war; it's only a matter of figuring out who the enemy is. Gamorrean heroes tend to select the soldier class.

Gamorrean Species Traits

Gamorreans share the following species traits:

Ability Modifiers: +2 Strength, –2 Dexterity, –2 Intelligence. Gamorreans possess greater physical power, but have limited agility and intelligence.

Medium Size: As Medium creatures, Gamorreans have no special bonuses or penalties due to their size.

Speed: Gamorrean base speed is 6 squares.

Primitive: Gamorreans do not gain Weapon Proficiency (pistols, rifles, or heavy weapons) as starting feats at 1st level, even if their class normally grants them.

Great Fortitude: Gamorreans gain a +2 species bonus to their Fortitude Defense, accounting for their great physical resistance.

Bonus Feat: Gamorreans gain Improved Damage Threshold as a bonus feat.

Automatic Languages: Basic (cannot speak) and Gamorrean (speak only).

Gungans

GUNGAN

The Gungans are omnivorous humanoids native to the swamps of Naboo. Technologically advanced, they rely mostly on biotech, growing instead of building their homes and production facilities.

While their culture is peaceful, it evolved from a series of long, bloody clan wars, and Gungans still admire strength and cunning. Most communities are devoted to farming or manufacturing goods that are then traded to other Gungan settlements, but they will reluctantly trade with the Humans of Naboo.

Personality: Gungans tend to be inquisitive, cautious, and suspicious.

Physical Description: Gungans range from 1.6 to 2 meters tall, with two eyestalks, floppy ears, and long tongues.

Homeworld: Naboo (page 233).

Languages: Gungans speak, read, and write Gunganese and Basic.

Example Names: Fassa, Jar Jar, Rugor, Tarpals, Toba, Tobler Ceel, Yoss.

Adventurers: Many Gungans leave their underwater cities to explore. Since the treaty with the Humans of Naboo, some Gungans—perhaps driven by an impulse to regain the warrior spirit of old—have taken a larger step into galactic society.

Gungan Species Traits

Gungans share the following species traits:

Ability Modifiers: +2 Dexterity, –2 Intelligence, –2 Charisma. Gungans are agile but aren't particularly witty or astute.

Medium Size: As Medium creatures, Gungans have no special bonuses or penalties due to their size.

Speed: Gungan base speed is 6 squares. They have a swim speed of 4 squares.

Expert Swimmer: A Gungan may choose to reroll any Swim check, but the result of the reroll must be accepted even if it is worse. In addition, a Gungan may choose to take 10 on Swim checks even when distracted or threatened.

Hold Breath: Gungans are at home either in air or water. A Gungan can hold his breath for a number of rounds equal to 25 times his Constitution score before he needs to make Endurance checks to hold his breath (see the Endurance skill, page 66).

Lightning Reflexes: Gungans gain a +2 species bonus to their Reflex Defense, accounting for their uncanny ability to avoid danger.

Low-Light Vision: Gungans ignore concealment (but not total concealment) from darkness.

Weapon Familiarity: Gungans with the Weapon Proficiency (simple weapons) feat are proficient with the atlatl and the cesta (see page 121).

Automatic Languages: Basic and Gunganese.

Ithorians

Ithorians are tall humanoids whose appearance leads many to refer to them colloquially as "Hammerheads." Peaceful and gentle, Ithorians are widely recognized as talented artists, brilliant agricultural engineers, and skilled diplomats.

Ithorians are perhaps the greatest ecologists in the galaxy, devoting their technology to preserving the natural beauty of their homeworld's jungles. They live in "herds," dwelling in cities that hover above the surface of their planet and striving to maintain the ecological balance in the "Mother Jungle."

Ithorians also travel the galaxy in massive "herd ships," masterpieces of environmental engineering that carry a perfect replica of their native jungle. Many look forward to trading for the exotic wares the Ithorians bring from distant planets.

Personality: Ithorians tend to be calm, peaceful, tranquil, and gentle.

Physical Description: Ithorians are humanoid, ranging in height from 1.8 to 2.3 meters tall, with long necks that curl forward and end in dome-shaped heads. They have two mouths, one on each side of their neck, producing a stereo effect when they talk.

Homeworld: Ithor (page 231), or a specific herd ship.

Language: Ithorians speak stereophonic Ithorese and Basic.

Example Names: Fandomar, Momaw, Oraltor, Tomla, Trangle, Umwaw.

Adventurers: Ithorians tend to concentrate on peaceful professions. They love to meet new beings and see new places. Often, wanderlust leads them to explore the greater galaxy for a time before they eventually return home.

> "WHY DO I SENSE WE'VE PICKED UP ANOTHER PATHETIC LIFE FORM."
> – OBI-WAN KENOBI

Ithorian Species Traits

Ithorians share the following species traits:

Ability Modifiers: +2 Wisdom, +2 Charisma, –2 Dexterity. Ithorians are wise and deliberate thinkers whose personable nature allows them to get along well with others, but they are not agile.

Medium Size: As Medium creatures, Ithorians have no special bonuses or penalties due to their size.

Speed: Ithorian base speed is 6 squares.

Iron Will: Ithorians have above-average willpower and gain a +2 species bonus to their Will Defense.

Bellow: As a standard action, an Ithorian can open all four of its throats and emit a terrible subsonic

ITHORIAN

bellow. The Ithorian makes a special attack roll (1d20 + its character level) and compares the result to the Fortitude Defense of all creatures and unattended objects in a 6-square cone. A successful hit deals 3d6 points of sonic damage; if the attack misses, the target takes half damage instead.

Each use of this ability moves the Ithorian –1 step along the condition track (see Conditions, page 148).

An Ithorian can choose to add more dice (d6s) to the damage it deals with its bellow, but each additional 1d6 of damage moves the Ithorian another –1 step along the condition track.

Survival Instinct: An Ithorian may choose to reroll any Survival check, but the result of the reroll must be accepted even if it is worse.

Conditional Bonus Feat: Ithorians like to maintain close ties with nature. An Ithorian with Knowledge (life sciences) as a trained skill gains Skill Focus (Knowledge [life sciences]) as a bonus feat.

Automatic Languages: Basic and Ithorese.

Kel Dor

The Kel Dor evolved on Dorin, a world with an atmosphere consisting mostly of helium and a gas that is unique to that world. As such, Kel Dor cannot breathe on planets with common nitrogen/oxygen atmospheres. Conversely, Dorin's atmosphere is toxic to most nonnative life (see page 253).

On other planets, Kel Dor dwellings provide their native atmosphere (stored in large tanks). When outside, Kel Dor must wear breath masks and goggles. They can neither see nor breathe without these devices. Most Kel Dor breath masks include vocoders that amplify the wearer's speech; while their vocal cords function normally in their native atmosphere, Kel Dor must shout to produce sound in other environments. Their eyesight, however, is enhanced when they are away from Dorin.

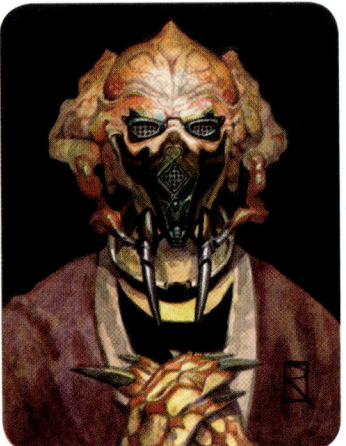

KEL DOR

Personality: Calm and kind, the Kel Dor never turn away a being in need. Still, most believe in quick, simple justice (even engaging in vigilantism).

Physical Description: The average Kel Dor stands between 1.6 and 2 meters tall. Their skin ranges from peach to deep red, and most have black eyes.

Homeworld: The technological planet of Dorin (page 229).

Languages: The Kel Dor speak, read, and write Kel Dor and Basic.

Example Names: Dorn Tlo, Plo Koon, Torin Dol.

Adventurers: Kel Dor commonly become diplomats, bounty hunters, and Jedi. Given their altruism and sense of justice, many enter law enforcement.

Kel Dor Species Traits

Kel Dor share the following species traits:

Ability Modifiers: +2 Dexterity, +2 Wisdom, –2 Constitution. Kel Dor are quick and wise, but they suffer from weaker constitutions than other species.

Medium Size: As Medium creatures, Kel Dor have no special bonuses or penalties due to their size.

Speed: Kel Dor base speed is 6 squares.

Keen Force Sense: Kel Dor may choose to reroll any Use the Force check made to search their feelings or sense the Force, keeping the better of the two results.

Low-Light Vision: Kel Dor ignore concealment (but not total concealment) from darkness.

Special Equipment: Kel Dor suffer limitations outside their native atmosphere. Without protective goggles, a Kel Dor is considered blind (see page 254). Without an antiox breath mask, a Kel Dor begins to suffocate (see Endurance, page 66). A replacement mask costs 2,000 credits (500 on Dorin), and a year's supply of filters costs 200 credits (50 on Dorin). Kel Dor characters begin play with these items at no cost.

An antiox breath mask is poisonous to other species (see page 255).

Automatic Languages: Basic and Kel Dor.

Mon Calamari

Amphibious land-dwellers, the Mon Calamari share their Outer Rim homeworld with the aquatic Quarren. They tend to be soft-spoken but vigorously defend causes that inspire them. Mon Calamari suffered under great oppression under the Galactic Empire; thus, it was one of the first worlds to declare support for the Rebel Alliance.

Mon Calamari are widely recognized for their keen analytical and organizational abilities, and they have developed a reputation as being among the foremost ship designers in the galaxy. They see everything they create as a work of art, not just as a tool or weapon.

MON CALAMARI

Personality: Creative, quiet, and inquisitive, the Mon Calamari are dreamers who cherish peace but aren't afraid to fight for the causes they believe in.

Physical Description: The average Mon Calamari stands 1.8 meters tall. They have high-domed heads, large eyes, and smooth, mottled skin.

Homeworld: The watery world of Mon Calamari (page 232).

Languages: The Mon Calamari speak, read, and write Mon Calamarian and Basic. They tend to learn Quarrenese as well.

Example Names: Ackbar, Bant, Cilghal, Ibtisam, Jesmin, Oro, Perit, Rekara.

Adventurers: Mon Calamari seek their dreams among the stars. They are idealistic and daring, often attaching themselves to causes that seem hopeless or lost right from the start. They strive to prove that even thinkers and dreamers can be brave and daring when the need arises.

Mon Calamari Species Traits

Mon Calamari share the following species traits:

Ability Modifiers: +2 Intelligence, +2 Wisdom, –2 Constitution. Mon Calamari are bright and prudent, but they have relatively frail physiques.

Medium Size: As Medium creatures, Mon Calamari have no special bonuses or penalties due to their size.

Speed: Mon Calamari base speed is 6 squares. They have a swim speed of 4 squares.

Breathe Underwater: As amphibious creatures, Mon Calamari can't drown in water.

Expert Swimmer: A Mon Calamari may choose to reroll any Swim check, but the result of the reroll must be accepted even if it is worse. In addition, a Mon Calamari may choose to take 10 on Swim checks even when distracted or threatened.

Low-Light Vision: Mon Calamari ignore concealment (but not total concealment) from darkness.

Conditional Bonus Feat: Keenly perceptive, a Mon Calamari with Perception as a trained skill gains Skill Focus (Perception) as a bonus feat.

Languages: Basic and Mon Calamarian.

Quarren

The Quarren hail from the distant Outer Rim world of Mon Calamari, sharing the world with the sentient humanoid species of the same name. The Mon Calamari live on the surface of the world, while the more isolationist Quarren dwell in oxygen-filled cities in the deep recesses of the oceans.

Offworld, Quarren generally stay clear galactic politics. Instead, they often become involved with shadowy occupations such as pirates, smugglers, and spy networks. Many Quarren blame both the Empire and the Rebels (even more than the Mon Calamari) for their homeworld's devastation during the Galactic Civil War.

Personality: Practical and conservative, Quarren tend to hate change and distrust anyone who displays overt optimism and idealism.

Physical Description: The average Quarren stands 1.8 meters tall. They have leathery skin and heads that resemble four-tentacled squids, hence the name "squid head" sometimes used by others.

Homeworld: The watery planet Mon Calamari (page 232).

Languages: Quarren speak, read, and write Quarrenese and Basic. They tend to learn Mon Calamarian as well.

Example Names: Kelmut, Seggor, Tessek, Tsillin, Vekker, Vuhlg.

Adventurers: Quarren leave their homeworld to escape their dependency on the Mon Calamari. They tend to seek out the fringes of society, operating as scoundrels or nobles in criminal organizations.

Quarren Species Traits

Quarren share the following species traits:

Ability Modifiers: +2 Constitution, –2 Wisdom, –2 Charisma. Quarren are extremely resilient and physically tough, though they tend toward deficiencies in wisdom and social graces.

Medium Size: As Medium creatures, Quarren have no special bonuses or penalties due to their size.

Speed: Quarren base speed is 6 squares. They have a swim speed of 4 squares.

Breathe Underwater: As amphibious creatures, Quarren can't drown in water.

Expert Swimmer: A Quarren may choose to reroll any Swim check, but the result of the reroll must be accepted even if it is worse. In addition, a Quarren may choose to take 10 on Swim checks even when distracted or threatened.

Low-Light Vision: Quarren ignore concealment (but not total concealment) from darkness.

Conditional Bonus Feat: Adept traders and negotiators, Quarren with Persuasion as a trained skill gains Skill Focus (Persuasion) as a bonus feat.

Automatic Languages: Basic and Quarrenese.

Rodians

Rodians hail from the Tyrius star system in the Mid Rim, their homeworld humid and choked with heavy rain forests teeming with dangerous life forms. In this hostile environment, the Rodians evolved into brutal hunters and killers to survive. As a result, Rodian culture centers around the concept of "the hunt." Their art glorifies violence and the act of stalking prey. The more intel-

QUARREN

ligent and dangerous a hunter's prey, the more honorable the hunt. Rodians have numerous annual festivals that exist solely to honor such activities.

Since joining the rest of the galaxy's spacefaring species, the Rodians have come to view bounty hunting as the most honorable profession in existence, and many have found great success in this field.

Personality: Rodians tend to be violent, tenacious, and dedicated.

Physical Description: Humanoid, with multifaceted eyes, a tapered snout, and deep green skin, the average Rodian stands 1.6 meters tall.

Homeworld: The industrial world of Rodia (page 234).

Languages: Rodians speak, read, and write Rodese and Basic, but many learn to speak Huttese as well.

Example Names: Andoorni, Beedo, Chido, Doda, Greedo, Greeata, Kelko, Navik, Neela, Neesh, Wald.

Adventurers: Rodian adventurers leave their homeworld to improve their skills, hoping to one day return and claim the title of Hunt Master. To this end, they take on roles that allow them to flex their hunting skills and increase their battle prowess, most commonly working as bounty hunters or mercenaries.

Rodian Species Traits

Rodians share the following species traits:

Ability Modifiers: +2 Dexterity, –2 Wisdom, –2 Charisma. Rodians are quick and well coordinated but often act before thinking things through and are often rude and try to bully others.

Medium Size: As Medium creatures, Rodians have no special bonuses or penalties due to their size.

Speed: Rodian base speed is 6 squares.

Heightened Awareness: A Rodian may choose to reroll any Perception check, but the result of the reroll must be accepted even if it is worse.

Low-Light Vision: Rodians ignore concealment (but not total concealment) from darkness.

Conditional Bonus Feat: Rodians are taught how to track and survive in the wilderness of Rodia from a very young age. A Rodian with Survival as a trained skill gains Skill Focus (Survival) as a bonus feat.

Automatic Languages: Basic and Rodese.

Sullustans

To survive the natural perils of their harsh, volcanic homeworld, the Sullustans evolved in the planet's numerous caves. They prefer to dwell underground, constructing highly advanced cities of such great beauty that wealthy sightseers come from all over the galaxy to visit them. Living underground helped the Sullustans to develop acute senses, and they are renowned for their navigational and piloting skills.

This friendly, gregarious species enjoys interacting with unique, unusual, and interesting beings. When Old Republic scouts first visited their homeworld, the Sullustans quickly embraced galactic civilization. The Sullustan manufacturing company SoroSuub is one of the largest non-Human-owned interstellar corporations in the galaxy. In fact, the company is so powerful that it has become the official government of Sullust, and more than half of the planet's population is on its payroll.

Personality: Sullustans tend to be pragmatic, pleasant, and fond of practical jokes.

Physical Description: Humanoid with large round eyes, big ears, and jowls, the average Sullustan stands 1.5 meters tall.

Homeworld: The volcanic, technological world Sullust (page 235).

Languages: Sullustans speak, read, and write Sullustese and Basic.

Example Names: Aril Nunb, Dllr Nep, Nien Nunb, Sian Tevv, Syub Snunb.

Adventurers: Sullustan adventurers enjoy exploring the galaxy, conducting business, and pulling pranks to see how others react. They are inquisitive and love to discover things through personal experience, sometimes being a bit reckless.

Sullustan Species Traits

Sullustans share the following species traits:

Ability Modifiers: +2 Dexterity, –2 Constitution. Sullustans are quick, agile, and good with ranged weapons, but they are not as hardy as other species.

Medium Size: As Medium creatures, Sullustans have no special bonuses or penalties due to their size.

Speed: Sullustan base speed is 6 squares.

Darkvision: Sullustans ignore concealment (including total concealment) from darkness. However, they cannot perceive colors in total darkness.

RODIAN

SULLUSTAN

Expert Climber: Sullustans are adept at climbing in their underground homes. A Sullustan may choose to take 10 on Climb checks even when distracted or threatened.

Heightened Awareness: A Sullustan may choose to reroll any Perception check, but the result of the reroll must be accepted even if it is worse.

Automatic Languages: Basic and Sullustese.

TRANDOSHANS

The reptilian Trandoshans are known for their great strength and warlike natures. Many of these beings dedicate themselves to martial training, and some follow the path of the hunter on their native world. A few have even become renowned (or infamous) bounty hunters in galactic society. Trandoshans have a long-standing enmity with Wookiees, and the two species have fought often over the centuries.

Trandoshans (who refer to themselves as "T'doshok") have supersensitive eyes that can see into the infrared range. They shed their skin several times in the span of their lives and can even regenerate lost limbs, but their clawed hands have difficulty with fine manipulation of objects.

Personality: Violent, brutal, and driven, Trandoshans love to compete but can show compassion and mercy as the situation warrants.

Physical Description: Trandoshans range from 1.8 to 2.1 meters tall. Their scaly hides offer additional defense against attacks.

Homeworld: Trandosha (page 237).

Language: Trandoshans speak, read, and write Dosh and Basic.

Example Names: Bossk, Fusset, Krussk, Ssuurg, Tusserk.

Adventurers: A Trandoshan adventurer craves the thrill of battle. Some leave Dosha to become bodyguards or mercenaries. Others set out to find new places to hunt and explore. A few use their warrior traditions to become soldiers, some even developing into bounty hunters as time goes by.

TRANDOSHAN SPECIES TRAITS

Trandoshans share the following species traits:

Ability Modifiers: +2 Strength, –2 Dexterity. Trandoshans are powerful but lack agility.

Medium Size: As Medium creatures, Trandoshans have no special bonuses or penalties due to their size.

Speed: Trandoshan base speed is 6 squares.

Darkvision: Trandoshans ignore concealment (including total concealment) from darkness. However, they cannot perceive colors in total darkness.

Limb Regeneration: A Trandoshan regrows a lost limb in 1d10 days. At the end of that time, all persistent penalties associated with the loss of the limb are removed.

Natural Armor: Trandoshans have thick scales that provide a +1 natural armor bonus to their Reflex Defense. A natural armor bonus stacks with an armor bonus.

Bonus Feat: Rugged and resilient, Trandoshans gain Toughness as a bonus feat.

Automatic Languages: Basic and Dosh.

TWI'LEKS

From the dry, rocky world of Ryloth, Twi'leks have made a place for themselves along the galactic rim. These tall, thin humanoids include a variety of distinct subraces, but are all instantly recognizable by the tentacular "head-tails" (called *lekku*) that protrude from the backs of their heads.

Sly, calculating beings, Twi'leks prefer to avoid trouble and stick to the shadows until an opportunity to act without undue danger to themselves presents itself. Their entrepreneurial spirit frequently leads them to positions of influence, and Twi'lek corporate executives and ambassadors are no less common than unscrupulous Twi'lek freighter captains and crime lords.

Personality: Twi'leks are calculating, pragmatic, and charismatic people. Generally, they try to avoid being swept up in open conflict, preferring instead to duck into the shadows where they can observe, plan, and prepare to profit from the outcome.

Physical Description: Humanoids with long head-tails, the average Twi'lek stands between 1.6 and 2 meters tall. Skin tones include white, green, blue, red, and orange, among others.

Homeworld: Twi'leks come from the planet Ryloth (page 234).

Languages: Twi'leks speak, read, and write Ryl and Basic. They can also communicate with one another using their lekku (a form of sign language). Some also learn Huttese.

Example Names: Bib Fortuna, Deel Surool, Firith Olan, Koyi Komad, Lyn Me, Oola, Tott Doneeta.

TRANDOSHAN

TWI'LEK

Adventurers: Twi'lek adventurers generally prefer to work behind the scenes, letting others stand in the full light of day. Many wind up in business (whether legal or illegal), performing as entertainers, or even serving as diplomats.

Twi'lek Species Traits

Twi'leks share the following species traits:

Ability Modifiers: +2 Charisma, –2 Wisdom. Twi'leks make convincing diplomats but are relatively weak-willed.

Medium Size: As Medium creatures, Twi'leks have no special bonuses or penalties due to their size.

Speed: Twi'lek base speed is 6 squares.

Deceptive: Naturally gifted at manipulation, a Twi'lek may choose to reroll any Deception check, but the result of the reroll must be accepted even if it is worse.

Great Fortitude: Twi'leks gain a +2 species bonus to their Fortitude Defense. Twi'leks have great health with a natural resistance to toxins and illness.

Low-Light Vision: Twi'leks ignore concealment (but not total concealment) from darkness.

Automatic Languages: Basic and Ryl.

Wookiees

Wookiees are widely recognized as one of the strongest and fiercest intelligent species in the galaxy. Wookiees have many customs and traditions that revolve around honor and loyalty, including the special bond called the honor family and the sacred pledge called the life debt. A Wookiee never uses his or her climbing claws in combat; doing this is considered dishonorable and a sign of madness.

Personality: Wookiees tend to be honorable, rash, loyal, and short-tempered.

Physical Description: Wookiees are large furry bipeds ranging in height from 2 to 2.3 meters.

Homeworld: The forest world of Kashyyyk (page 232).

Language: Wookiees speak Shyriiwook, consisting of complex grunts and growls. They understand Basic but lack the ability to speak it.

Example Names: Chewbacca, Gorwooken, Groznik, Low-bacca, Ralrra, Rorworr, Salporin.

Adventurers: Wookiee adventurers usually start out as wanderers or explorers, but some find this path by forming an honor family with (or owing a life debt to) other adventures.

Wookiee Species Traits

Wookiees share the following species traits:

Ability Modifiers: +4 Strength, +2 Constitution, –2 Dexterity, –2 Wisdom, –2 Charisma. Wookiees are powerful and hardy, but they aren't

WOOKIEE

agile, tend to be impulsive, and have little patience for diplomacy.

Medium Size: As Medium creatures, Wookiees have no special bonuses or penalties due to their size.

Speed: Wookiee base speed is 6 squares.

Extraordinary Recuperation: A Wookiee regains hit points at double the normal rate (see Natural Healing, page 148).

Rage: Once per day, a Wookiee can fly into a rage as a swift action. While raging, the Wookiee temporarily gains a +2 rage bonus on melee attack rolls and melee damage rolls but cannot use skills that require patience and concentration, such as Mechanics, Stealth, or Use the Force.

A fit of rage lasts for a number of rounds equal to 5 + the Wookiee's Constitution modifier. At the end of its rage, a Wookiee moves –1 persistent step along the condition track (see Conditions, page 148). The penalties imposed by this condition persist until the Wookiee takes at least 10 minutes to recuperate, during which time the Wookiee can't engage in any strenuous activity.

Weapon Familiarity: Wookiees with the Weapon Proficiency (rifles) feat are proficient with the bowcaster.

Skills: Wookiees are great climbers and may choose to take 10 on Climb checks even when distracted or threatened. Known to pull the ears off gundarks, they may choose to reroll any Persuasion check made to intimidate others, but the result of the reroll must be accepted even if it is worse.

Automatic Languages: Basic (cannot speak) and Shyriiwook.

Zabrak

The Zabrak are an early spacefaring race distinguished by patterns of vestigial horns on their heads. Zabrak hail from many worlds and have been spacefarers for so long that they define themselves and each other according to their colony of origin.

ZABRAK

The harshness of Iridonia, their homeworld, forged in the Zabrak an iron will to survive. Driven to escape their world, they sought to obtain the knowledge of space flight. When Duros scouts began exploring the Mid Rim Territories, they encountered Zabrak in eight sovereign colonies in five different systems. Though subjugated under the harsh rule of the Empire, the Zabrak colonies eventually regained their independence.

Zabrak possess a great amount of confidence, and they believe that there is nothing they can't accomplish. While this innate attitude could lead to feelings of superiority, most Zabrak don't look down on others. They believe in themselves and are proud and strong, but they rarely project any negativity toward those of other species.

Personality: Zabrak tend to be dedicated, intense, and focused, sometimes appearing obsessive and single-minded to other species.

Physical Description: Humanoid, distinguished by patterns of vestigial horns atop their heads. The average Zabrak stands 1.8 meters tall.

Homeworld: Iridonia (page 231) or one of eight colonies in the Mid Rim region of space.

Language: Zabrak speak, read, and write Zabrak and Basic.

Example Names: Aagh Odok, Eeth Koth, Kooth Aan.

Adventurers: Zabrak adventurers love to explore the galaxy. No challenge is too big to deter a Zabrak. They range from scoundrels on distant colony worlds, to noble diplomats and merchants, to scouts, soldiers, and even Jedi.

Zabrak Species Traits

Zabrak share the following species traits:

Ability Modifiers: Zabrak have no ability score adjustments.

Medium Size: As Medium creatures, Zabrak have no special bonuses or penalties due to their size.

Speed: Zabrak base speed is 6 squares.

Heightened Awareness: Having strong survival instincts and quick reactions, a Zabrak may choose to reroll any Perception check, but the result of the reroll must be accepted even if it is worse.

Superior Defenses: Adapted to a very tough and trying environment, Zabrak gain a +1 species bonus to all of their defenses.

Automatic Languages: Basic and Zabrak.

Star Wars heroes seek credits, glory, justice, fame, influence, and knowledge, among other goals. Some of these goals are honorable, some base. Each character chooses a different way to achieve these goals, from brutal combat power to subtle skills to mastery of the Force. Some adventurers prevail and grow in experience, wealth, and power. Others die.

A character class is the frame upon which you build your hero. It isn't meant to be rigid or confining. Instead, a class provides a starting point from which you can develop in any direction you see fit. Don't think of a class as restrictive; instead, a class is defining. When you choose a class for your character, you're laying the foundation of a concept that will grow and expand as you play. A class provides structure. How you develop your character is entirely up to you. You get to choose talents and feats as you advance—and you can take levels in other classes as you go along if that better serves the concept at the core of your hero.

Choosing a Heroic Class

Five basic classes, known as heroic classes, are available in the Star Wars Roleplaying Game. Characters with levels in heroic classes are called heroic characters, or heroes. Unlike nonheroic supporting characters, heroic characters have many special abilities that make them extraordinary.

At 1st level, you must choose a heroic class for your character. The five heroic classes are:

Jedi: The Jedi are the guardians of peace and justice in the galaxy. They learn to master the Force, and their trademark weapon is the lightsaber.

Noble: The noble is a shrewd bargainer and negotiator who inspires confidence and makes a great leader.

Scoundrel: The scoundrel is a tricky, skillful rogue who succeeds by stealth instead of brute force.

Scout: The scout is a cunning, skilled explorer trained to operate in the vast wilderness of space and backwater worlds.

Soldier: A warrior with exceptional combat capability and unequaled skill with weapons.

The Multiclass Character

As your character advances in level, he or she may add new classes. Adding a new class gives the character a broader range of abilities, but all advancement in the new class is at the expense of advancement in the character's other class or classes. A noble, for example, might become a noble/soldier. Adding the soldier class would give her proficiency in more weapons, a better Fortitude Defense, and so on, but it would also mean that she doesn't gain new noble talents and thus is not as powerful a noble as she otherwise would have become. Rules for creating and advancing multiclass characters can be found at the end of this chapter.

> **Class Level vs. Character Level**
>
> The *Star Wars Roleplaying Game* uses the terms *class level* and *character level* to mean different things. Class level pertains to a character's level in a particular class. Character level pertains to a character's total experience. So, a character who has only one class has a character level and a class level that are the same. (A 7th-level Jedi has a character level of 7th and a class level of 7th.) But for a character with more than one class, class level and character level are different. A 4th-level scout/3rd-level scoundrel has a character level of 7th, with a scout class level of 4th and a scoundrel class level of 3rd.

Class and Level Bonuses

An attack roll is a combination of three numbers, each representing a different factor: a random factor (the number you roll on the d20), a number representing the character's innate abilities (the ability modifier), and a bonus representing the character's experience and training. This third factor depends on the character's class and level. Each class table summarizes the figures for this third factor.

Base Attack Bonus

Check the table for your character's class. Your character's base attack bonus applies to all attack rolls. Use the bonus that corresponds to the character's class level.

If a character has more than one class, add the base attack bonuses for each class together to determine the character's base attack bonus.

Damage Bonus

Your character deals extra damage on melee and ranged attacks equal to one-half her character level, rounded down. A 1st-level character, therefore, has a damage bonus of +0.

For example, a 4th-level soldier armed with a heavy blaster deals 3d8+2 points of damage with the weapon. A 12th-level soldier armed with the exact same weapon deals 3d8+6 points of damage.

Defenses

Your character has three defense scores. Defenses are discussed fully on page 145.

Reflex Defense: 10 + your heroic level or armor bonus + Dexterity modifier + class bonus + natural armor bonus (if any) + size modifier

Fortitude Defense: 10 + your heroic level + Constitution modifier + class bonus + equipment bonus

Will Defense: 10 + your heroic level + Wisdom modifier + class bonus

Heroic Level

Your heroic level is the sum of all levels you have in heroic classes (Jedi, noble, scoundrel, scout, soldier) and prestige classes (see Chapter 12). It does not include levels in the nonheroic character class (see page 277) or beast class (see page 273). For example, if you were a scout 6/soldier 2, you would have a heroic level of 8, adding that number to all of your defense scores.

Class Bonuses to Defenses

When you take your first level in a heroic class, you gain class bonuses on two or more defenses, as shown below:

CLASS	CLASS BONUSES TO DEFENSES
Jedi	+1 Reflex Defense, +1 Fortitude Defense, +1 Will Defense
Noble	+1 Reflex Defense, +2 Will Defense
Scoundrel	+2 Reflex Defense, +1 Will Defense
Scout	+2 Reflex Defense, +1 Fortitude Defense
Soldier	+1 Reflex Defense, +2 Fortitude Defense

Class bonuses do not stack; you only apply the best bonus from all your classes to each defense score. Continuing the previous example, if you were a scout 6/soldier 2, you would have a +2 class bonus to your Fortitude Defense (this is the better bonus, granted by being a soldier) and a +2 class bonus to your Reflex Defense (also the better bonus, granted by being a scout). If you later added a level of noble, you would also gain a +2 class bonus to your Will Defense.

Level-Dependent Benefits

In addition to attack bonuses and saving throw bonuses, all characters gain other benefits from advancing in level. Table 3-1: Experience and Level-Dependent Benefits summarizes these additional benefits.

XP: This column shows the experience point total needed to achieve a given character level. For multiclass characters, XP determines overall character level, not individual class levels.

Feats: This column indicates the levels at which a character gains feats. These feats are in addition to any bonus feats granted in the class descriptions and the bonus feat granted to Humans at 1st level.

Ability Increases: This column indicates the levels at which a character gains ability score increases. Upon gaining 4th, 8th, 12th, 16th, and 20th level, a character increases two of his or her ability scores by 1 point each. The player chooses which two ability scores to improve. A player cannot apply both ability increases to a single ability score, and the ability improvements are permanent.

Table 3-1: Experience and Level-Dependent Benefits

CHARACTER LEVEL	XP	FEATS	ABILITY INCREASES
1st	0	1st	—
2nd	1,000	—	—
3rd	3,000	2nd	—
4th	6,000	—	1st, 2nd
5th	10,000	—	—
6th	15,000	3rd	—
7th	21,000	—	—
8th	28,000	—	3rd, 4th
9th	36,000	4th	—
10th	45,000	—	—
11th	55,000	—	—
12th	66,000	5th	5th, 6th
13th	78,000	—	—
14th	91,000	—	—
15th	105,000	6th	—
16th	120,000	—	7th, 8th
17th	136,000	—	—
18th	153,000	7th	—
19th	171,000	—	—
20th	190,000	—	9th, 10th

For example, a noble with a starting Dexterity of 13 and a starting Charisma of 15 might improve to Dex 14 and Cha 16 at 4th level. At 8th level, the same character might improve Charisma again (from 16 to 17) and increase any one of the other five abilities by 1 as well.

Ability score increases are retroactive. For example, if you increase your Intelligence score from 13 to 14, you immediately gain an additional trained skill chosen from your class skills and an additional language. Similarly, if a Jedi with two instances of the Force Training feat increased his Wisdom from 13 to 14, he would gain two Force powers (for a total of six).

Multiclass Characters: For multiclass characters, ability increases are gained according to overall character level, not class level. Thus, a 3rd-level noble/1st-level soldier is a 4th-level character overall and eligible for her first two ability score boosts.

Class Descriptions

The rest of this chapter, up to the section on multiclass characters, describes each class. These descriptions are general. Individual members of a class may differ in their attitudes, outlooks, and other aspects.

Game Rule Information

Game rule information follows the general class description. Not all of the following categories apply to every class.

Abilities

This entry tells you which abilities are most important for a character of that class. Players can "play against type," but a typical character of a class puts his or her highest ability scores where they'll do the most good. (Or, in game-world terms, the character is attracted to the class that most suits his or her talents, or for which he or she is best qualified.)

Hit Points

A 1st-level heroic character begins play with a certain number of hit points determined by his or her class:

CLASS	STARTING HIT POINTS
Noble, scoundrel	18 + Constitution modifier
Scout	24 + Constitution modifier
Jedi, soldier	30 + Constitution modifier

A character's hit points increase each time he or she gains a level. The type of die rolled depends on the class in which the level is gained, as shown below:

CLASS	HIT POINTS/LEVEL
Noble, scoundrel	1d6 + Constitution modifier
Scout	1d8 + Constitution modifier
Jedi, soldier	1d10 + Constitution modifier

The character always gets at least 1 hit point with each new level, regardless of the player's die roll and the character's Constitution modifier.

Class Table

This table details how a character improves as he or she gains levels. Class tables include the following information:
Level: The character's level in the class.

Base Attack Bonus: The character's base attack bonus. Apply this bonus to the character's attack rolls and damage rolls.

Class Features: Level-dependent class abilities, alternating between talents and bonus feats.

Class Skills

Every class has a list of class skills. Once a player selects a class for his character, he chooses a number of trained skills from the character's list of class skills. The exact number of trained skills a player can choose at 1st level depends on the character's class:

CLASS	NUMBER OF TRAINED SKILLS
Jedi	2 + Intelligence modifier
Noble	6 + Intelligence modifier
Scoundrel	4 + Intelligence modifier
Scout	5 + Intelligence modifier
Soldier	3 + Intelligence modifier

Put another way, a character's trained skills represent a subset of that character's class skills. Every time a character picks up a new class, his list of class skills grows to include those of the new class, but the only way to gain new trained skills after 1st level is to take the Skill Training feat (page 88).

For example, a noble gets 6 trained skills at 1st level. If she has a +1 Intelligence modifier, her total becomes 7 trained skills. The noble then selects 7 skills from her list of class skills, which then become trained skills for her.

For more information on trained skills, see Chapter 4: Skills.

CLASS FEATURES

This entry details special characteristics of the class, including starting feats that the character gets for free at 1st level, special talents uniquely flavored to the class, and bonus feats.

JEDI

Jedi combine physical training with mastery of the Force. Jedi concentrate on battle prowess, defense, and lightsaber training. Additionally, they are ambassadors of the Jedi order, protecting the Republic from all dangers. Few are strong enough in the Force and have the devotion to walk the Jedi's path, but those few are awarded with a powerful ally. They walk in a larger world than those who neither feel nor heed the Force.

EXPLOITS

All Jedi journey into the galaxy at large to further their own knowledge and to help those in need. They take their responsibility seriously, considering even mundane missions to be personal tests. Most Jedi follow the light side, but some become darksiders and use the Force for evil or selfish intent. Those imbued with the light side refrain from using the Force for every task, preferring to find other solutions and save the Force for when it is truly needed. Those who succumb to the dark side use every advantage at their disposal, wielding the Force to solve problems as a soldier would use a blaster to destroy a stingfly.

TABLE 3-2: THE JEDI

LEVEL	BASE ATTACK BONUS	CLASS FEATURES
1st	+1	Defense bonuses, lightsaber, starting feats, talent
2nd	+2	Bonus feat
3rd	+3	Talent
4th	+4	Bonus feat
5th	+5	Talent
6th	+6	Bonus feat
7th	+7	Build lightsaber, talent
8th	+8	Bonus feat
9th	+9	Talent
10th	+10	Bonus feat
11th	+11	Talent
12th	+12	Bonus feat
13th	+13	Talent
14th	+14	Bonus feat
15th	+15	Talent
16th	+16	Bonus feat
17th	+17	Talent
18th	+18	Bonus feat
19th	+19	Talent
20th	+20	Bonus feat

Class Skills (trained in 2 + Int modifier): Acrobatics, Endurance, Initiative, Knowledge (all skills, taken individually), Perception, Pilot, Use the Force

Characteristics

The Jedi's strength flows from the Force, granting her special powers. This character often masters the ability to feel the living Force in the world within her. Charisma and Wisdom are the most important abilities for a Jedi, although any of the other abilities are nearly as important.

Background

A Jedi typically starts out as a Padawan learner attached to a Jedi Master. (Prior to 1st level, the character trained as a student with the Jedi Council. She begins her heroic career at 1st level when she is selected as a Padawan learner.) The Jedi has a genuine desire to use the Force to help the people of the galaxy. A Jedi has a deep connection to her mentor and the Jedi order but often operates with only tangential contact with either master or order.

Still, not all who study the Jedi arts are actually members of the Jedi order. During the Old Sith Wars (thousands of years before the Battle of Yavin), many Sith acolytes and initiates are often members of this class before becoming a Sith apprentice under a particular Sith Lord (see page 224). This class is also common among other Force traditions with strong ties to the Jedi arts, such as the Jensaarai (see page 106).

Examples of Jedi in Star Wars

Luke Skywalker (after training under Obi-Wan Kenobi and Yoda), Obi-Wan Kenobi, Anakin Skywalker, Mace Windu, Bastila Shan, Quinlan Vos.

Game Rule Information

Jedi have the following game statistics.

Abilities

A Jedi should be gifted in all abilities, but Wisdom and Charisma are most important. Strength and Dexterity are also useful.

Hit Points

Jedi begin play at 1st level with a number of hit points equal to 30 + their Constitution modifier. At each level after 1st, Jedi gain 1d10 hit points + their Constitution modifier.

Sia-Lan Wezz, Female Human Jedi

Force Points

Jedi gain a number of Force Points equal to 5 + one-half their character level (rounded down) at 1st level and every time they gain a new level in this class. Any Force Points left over from previous levels are lost.

Class Features

All of the following are features of the Jedi class.

Defense Bonuses

At 1st level, you gain a +1 class bonus to your Fortitude Defense, Reflex Defense, and Will Defense.

Lightsaber

You start play with a lightsaber provided by your Master. Later, you can build your own lightsaber (see Build Lightsaber, below).

Starting Feats

At 1st level, you gain the following bonus feats:
  Force Sensitivity
  Weapon Proficiency (lightsabers)
  Weapon Proficiency (simple weapons)

Talents

At 1st level and every odd-numbered level thereafter (3rd, 5th, 7th, etc.), you select a talent from any of the following talent trees. You may choose a talent from any tree you wish, but you must meet the prerequisites (if any) of the chosen talent. No talent can be selected more than once unless expressly indicated.

JEDI CONSULAR TALENT TREE

Jedi that follow the path of the consular are skilled negotiators and talented ambassadors. You prefer to use the strength of your words and the wisdom that the Force provides to solve conflicts.

Adept Negotiator: As a standard action, you can weaken the resolve of one enemy with your words. The target must have an Intelligence of 3 or higher, and it must be able to see,

> ### BUILDING A LIGHTSABER
> You can build a lightsaber if you have at least seven heroic levels as well as the Force Sensitivity and Weapon Proficiency (lightsabers) feats. You must spend 1,500 credits to obtain the basic components and 24 uninterrupted hours constructing the weapon. At the end of this time, make a DC 20 Use the Force check; you can't take 20 on this check. If the check succeeds, you complete the lightsaber's construction. If the check fails, you must spend another 24 hours dismantling and rebuilding the flawed weapon.
>
> Once the lightsaber is constructed, you must spend a Force Point to attune it (a full-round action). From that point on, you gain a +1 bonus on attack rolls made with your scratch-built lightsaber. No one else who wields the weapon gains this bonus.
>
> You can build a double-bladed lightsaber instead of a normal lightsaber, but the cost for components increases to 3,000 credits.

hear, and understand you. Make a Persuasion check; if the result equals or exceeds the target's Will Defense, it moves –1 step along the condition track (see Conditions, page 148). The target gets a +5 bonus to its Will Defense if it is highter level than you. If the target reaches the end of the track, it does not fall unconscious; instead, it cannot attack you or your allies for the remainder of the encounter unless you or one of your allies attacks it or one of its allies first. This is a mind-affecting action.

Force Persuasion: You can use your Use the Force check modifier instead of your Persuasion check modifier when making Persuasion checks. You are considered trained in the Persuasion skill for purposes of using this talent. If you are entitled to a Persuasion check reroll, you may reroll your Use the Force check instead (subject to the same circumstances and limitations).

Prerequisite: Adept Negotiator.

Master Negotiator: If you successfully use the Adept Negotiator talent (see above), your target moves an additional –1 step along the condition track (–2 steps total). This is a mind-affecting effect.

Prerequisite: Adept Negotiator.

Skilled Advisor: You can spend a full-round action advising an ally, thereby granting her a +5 bonus on her next skill check. If you spend a Force Point, the bonus increases to +10. The target must be able (and willing) to hear and understand your advice. You cannot advise yourself. This is a mind-affecting effect.

JEDI GUARDIAN TALENT TREE
Jedi that follow the path of the guardian are more combat-oriented than other Jedi, honing their skills to become deadly combatants.

Acrobatic Recovery: If an effect causes you to fall prone, you can make a DC 20 Acrobatics check to remain on your feet.

Battle Meditation: The Jedi technique known as Battle Meditation allows you and your allies to work together seamlessly and with a level of precision that can only come from the Force. As a full-round action, you can spend a Force Point to give you and all allies within 6 squares of you a +1 insight bonus on attack rolls that lasts until the end of the encounter. This bonus does not extend to allies outside the range of the effect, even if they move within 6 squares of you later on. Allies who benefit from the Battle Meditation must remain within 6 squares of you to retain the insight bonus, and they lose it if you are knocked unconscious or killed. This is a mind-affecting effect.

Elusive Target: When fighting an opponent or multiple opponents in melee, other opponents attempting to target you with ranged attacks take a –5 penalty. This penalty is in addition to the normal –5 penalty for firing into melee (see Shooting or Throwing into a Melee, page 161), making the penalty to target you –10.

Force Intuition: You can use your Use the Force check modifier instead of your Initiative modifier when making Initiative checks. You are considered trained in the Initiative skill for purposes of using this talent. If you are entitled to an Initiative check reroll, you may reroll your Use the Force check instead (subject to the same circumstances and limitations).

Resilience: You can spend a Force Point as a swift action to move +2 steps along the condition track (see Conditions, page 148).

JEDI SENTINEL TALENT TREE
The Jedi that follow the path of the sentinel are the true enemies of the dark side, hunting down evil and stopping the spread of darkness wherever they go. You are a master of subtlety and difficult to tempt with the dark side, even when constantly confronted with its power.

Clear Mind: You may reroll any opposed Use the Force check made to avoid being detected by other Force-users. You must take the result of the reroll, even if it is worse.

Dark Side Sense: Jedi following the path of the sentinel become exceptionally talented at rooting out evil. You may reroll any Use the Force check made to sense the presence and relative location of characters with a Dark Side Score of 1 or higher. You must take the result of the reroll, even if it is worse.

Dark Side Scourge: Against creatures with a Dark Side Score of 1 or higher, you deal extra damage on melee attacks equal to your Charisma bonus (minimum +1).

Prerequisite: Dark Side Sense.

Force Haze: You can spend a Force Point as a standard action to create a "haze" that hides you and your allies from the perceptions of others. You can hide a number of creatures in line of sight equal to your class level. Make a Use the Force check and compare the result to the Will Defense of any opponent that moves into line of sight of any creature hidden by your Force haze. If

> "MY ALLY IS THE FORCE, AND A POWERFUL ALLY IT IS."
> – JEDI MASTER YODA

your check result beats the opponent's Will Defense, all hidden creatures are treated as if they had total concealment against that opponent.

The Force haze lasts up to 1 minute but is dismissed instantly if anyone hidden by the Force haze makes an attack.

Prerequisite: Clear Mind.

Resist the Dark Side: You gain a +5 Force bonus to all Defense scores against Force powers with the *[dark side]* descriptor and Force powers originating from any dark Force-user (that is, any Force-user whose Dark Side Score equals his Wisdom score).

Prerequisite: Dark Side Sense.

LIGHTSABER COMBAT TALENT TREE

The lightsaber is the chosen weapon of the Jedi. Not as clumsy or random as a blaster, the lightsaber is an elegant weapon for a more civilized combatant. The following talents allow you to improve your prowess with a lightsaber.

Block: As a reaction, you may negate a melee attack by making a successful Use the Force check. The DC of the skill check is equal to the result of the attack roll you wish to negate, and you take a cumulative –5 penalty on your Use the Force check for every time you have used Block or Deflect since the beginning of your last turn. You must have a lightsaber drawn and ignited to use this talent, and you must be aware of the attack and not flat-footed.

Deflect: As a reaction, you may negate a ranged attack by making a successful Use the Force check. The DC of the skill check is equal to the result of the attack roll you wish to negate, and you take a cumulative –5 penalty on your Use the Force check for every time you have used Block or Deflect since the beginning of your last turn. You must have a lightsaber drawn and ignited to use this talent, and you must be aware of the attack and not flat-footed.

You can use this talent to deflect some of the barrage of shots fired from a ranged weapon set on autofire. If you succeed on the Use the Force check, you take half damage if the autofire attack hits and no damage if the autofire attack misses. This talent has no effect on other area attacks (such as grenades, missiles, and flamethrowers).

This talent cannot be used to negate attacks made by Colossal (frigate) or larger-size vehicles unless the attack is made with a point-defense weapon.

Lightsaber Defense: As a swift action, you can use your lightsaber to parry your opponents' attacks, gaining a +1 deflection bonus to your Reflex Defense until the start of your next turn. You must have a lightsaber drawn and ignited to use this talent, and you don't gain the deflection bonus if you are flat-footed or otherwise unaware of the incoming attack.

You can take this talent multiple times; each time you take this talent, the deflection bonus increases by +1 (maximum +3).

Weapon Specialization (lightsabers): You gain a +2 bonus on melee damage rolls with lightsabers.

Prerequisite: Weapon Focus (lightsabers) feat (see page 89).

Lightsaber Throw: You can hurl a lightsaber as a standard action, treating it as a thrown weapon. You are considered proficient with the thrown lightsaber, and you apply the normal range penalties to the attack roll (see Table 8-5: Range Penalties). The thrown lightsaber deals normal weapon damage if it hits.

If your target is no more than 6 squares away, you can pull your lightsaber back to your hand as a swift action by making a DC 20 Use the Force check.

Redirect Shot: This talent allows you to redirect a deflected blaster bolt along a specific trajectory so that it damages another creature or object in its path. Once per round when you successfully deflect a blaster bolt, you can make an immediate ranged attack against another target with which you have line of sight. Apply the normal range penalties to the attack roll (see Table 8-5: Range Penalties), not counting the distance the bolt traveled to reach you. If the attack succeeds, it deals normal weapon damage to the target.

Only single blaster bolts can be redirected in this manner. Barrages from autofire weapons and other types of projectiles can't be redirected.

Prerequisites: Deflect, base attack bonus +5.

Build Lightsaber

At 7th level and beyond, you can build your own lightsaber (see the Building a Lightsaber sidebar).

Bonus Feats

At each even-numbered level (2nd, 4th, 6th, etc.), you gain a bonus feat. This feat must be selected from the following list, and you must meet any prerequisites for that feat.

Acrobatic Strike, Cleave, Combat Reflexes, Dodge, Double Attack, Dual Weapon Mastery I, Dual Weapon Mastery II, Dual Weapon Mastery III, Great Cleave, Improved Charge, Improved Disarm, Martial Arts I, Martial Arts II, Martial Arts III, Melee Defense, Mobility, Quick Draw, Power Attack, Powerful Charge, Rapid Strike, Running Attack, Skill Focus, Skill Training, Strong in the Force, Triple Attack, Triple Crit, Weapon Finesse, Weapon Focus (lightsabers).

CREDITS

A 1st-level Jedi starts play with 3d4 × 100 credits.

Noble

Members of the noble class use their intelligence and natural charisma to make their way in the galaxy. From true royalty to elected officials, military commanders to crime lords, traders, merchants, ambassadors, holovid stars, and influential corporate magnates, character types who appear in the noble class are varied and numerous. Some bring honor to the name. Others are sly, treacherous, and dishonorable to the core. With a winning smile, a golden tongue, a powerful message, or a knack for making compromises, the noble commands respect, makes friends, and inevitably influences people.

Exploits

Most nobles wind up in dangerous situations because of something they believe in or because their job calls for it. Others hope to use their negotiating talents to navigate a course through the troubles around them, or seek to find profit in the troubles of others. Whatever their initial motivations, nobles usually wind up taking to a cause and a goal that sustains them through the roughest missions. An adventuring noble might be a senator's aide, a free trader, a diplomat, a true prince or princess, or an outlaw's lieutenant. Nobles often feel responsible for others, though some consider themselves to be better than those around them.

Characteristics

The noble fosters feelings of good will and honesty, or at least the illusion of such, to succeed. Where other classes shoot first, the noble starts out asking questions and hopes to finish by negotiating a deal. The noble believes she can be more effective with words and deeds than with violence, though some draw a blaster when push comes to shove. The noble is more comfortable in civilized regions of space, where law and order have some meaning. Of all the classes, nobles have the best diplomatic and bargaining skills. They're good talkers, negotiators, and bluffers. They have a knack for inspiring others, and they make good leaders.

Background

Nobles come to their profession in a variety of ways. Altruistic nobles believe it is their duty and responsibility to serve and lead. More selfish nobles seek the fame, wealth, and power often associated with the positions they aspire to. Power-hungry nobles take advantage of the system and wind up helping others only to help themselves. The halls of power are calling. How the noble answers can make all the difference.

Examples of Nobles in Star Wars

Leia Organa, Padmé Amidala, Bail Organa, Talon Karrde, Jabba the Hutt, Chancellor Valorum, Supreme Chancellor Palpatine.

Game Rule Information

Nobles have the following game statistics.

Abilities

Charisma is undoubtedly a noble's most important ability score, as the noble's skill at interacting with others and projecting a sense of confidence are crucial for his or her success. Wisdom and Intelligence form the basis of other important skills, so these ability scores are also significant.

Hit Points

Nobles begin play at 1st level with a number of hit points equal to 18 + their Constitution modifier. At each level after 1st, nobles gain 1d6 hit points + their Constitution modifier.

Force Points

Nobles gain a number of Force Points equal to 5 + one-half their character level (rounded down) at 1st level and every time they gain a new level in this class. Any Force Points left over from previous levels are lost.

Class Features

All of the following are features of the noble class.

Defense Bonuses

At 1st level, you gain a +1 class bonus to your Reflex Defense and a +2 class bonus to your Will Defense.

Starting Feats

You begin play with the following feats:
Linguist*
Weapon Proficiency (pistols)
Weapon Proficiency (simple weapons)
* *You must meet the prerequisite of this feat (minimum Intelligence 13) to gain it.*

ARANI KORDEN, FEMALE HUMAN NOBLE

Talents

At 1st level and every odd-numbered level thereafter (3rd, 5th, 7th, etc.), you select a talent from any of the following talent trees. You may choose a talent from any tree you wish, but you must meet the prerequisites (if any) of the chosen talent. No talent can be selected more than once unless expressly indicated.

INFLUENCE TALENT TREE

One of your greatest strengths is your ability to exert influence over your opponents.

Presence: You can make a Persuasion check to intimidate a creature as a standard action (instead of a full-round action).

Demand Surrender: Once per encounter, you can make a Persuasion check as a standard action to demand surrender from an opponent who has been reduced to one-half or less of its hit points. If your check result equals or exceeds the target's Will Defense, it surrenders to you and your allies, drops any weapons it is holding, and takes no hostile actions. If the target is higher level than you, it gains a +5 bonus to its Will Defense. If you or any of your allies attack it, it no longer submits to your will and can act normally. You can only use this talent against a particular target once per encounter. This is a mind-affecting effect.

Prerequisite: Presence.

Improved Weaken Resolve: As Weaken Resolve (see below), except that the target doesn't stop fleeing from you if it is wounded.

Prerequisites: Presence, Weaken Resolve.

Weaken Resolve: Once per round, when you deal damage equal to or greater than the target's damage threshold, make a Persuasion check as a free action; if the result equals or exceeds the target's Will Defense, you fill the target with terror, causing it to flee from you at top speed for 1 minute. The target can't take standard actions, swift actions, or full-round actions while fleeing, and the target stops fleeing and can act normally if it is wounded. As a free action or reaction, the target can spend a Force Point (if it has not already spent one earlier in the round) to negate the effect. The effect is automatically negated if the target's level is equal to or higher than your character level. This is a mind-affecting fear effect.

Prerequisite: Presence.

INSPIRATION TALENT TREE

Nobles are renowned for their ability to inspire their followers and urge them to greatness. You can often get results out of their friends, allies, and followers that other leaders cannot.

All of the talents in this tree are mind-affecting effects. Moreover, you can't use any of these talents on yourself.

Bolster Ally: As a standard action, you can bolster an ally within line of sight, moving him +1 step along the condition track (see Conditions, page 148) and giving him a number of bonus hit points equal to his character level if he's at one-half his maximum hit points or less. Damage is subtracted from the bonus hit points first, and any bonus hit points remaining at the end of the encounter go away. You can't bolster the same ally more than once in a single encounter, and you can't bolster yourself.

Ignite Fervor: Whenever you hit an opponent with a melee or ranged attack, you can (as a free action) choose to give one ally within your line of

TABLE 3-3: THE NOBLE

LEVEL	BASE ATTACK BONUS	CLASS FEATURES
1st	+0	Defense bonuses, starting feats, talent
2nd	+1	Bonus feat
3rd	+2	Talent
4th	+3	Bonus feat
5th	+3	Talent
6th	+4	Bonus feat
7th	+5	Talent
8th	+6	Bonus feat
9th	+6	Talent
10th	+7	Bonus feat
11th	+8	Talent
12th	+9	Bonus feat
13th	+9	Talent
14th	+10	Bonus feat
15th	+11	Talent
16th	+12	Bonus feat
17th	+12	Talent
18th	+13	Bonus feat
19th	+14	Talent
20th	+15	Bonus feat

Class Skills (trained in 6 + Int modifier): Deception, Gather Information, Initiative, Knowledge (all skills, taken individually), Perception, Persuasion, Pilot, Ride, Treat Injury, Use Computer

sight a bonus to damage on his next attack equal to his character level. Once his fervor has been ignited, the affected ally doesn't need to remain within line of sight of you; if his next attack misses, he loses the bonus to damage granted by this talent. You can't ignite fervor in yourself.

Prerequisites: Bolster Ally, Inspire Confidence.

Inspire Confidence: As a standard action, you can inspire confidence in all allies in your line of sight, granting them a +1 morale bonus on attack rolls and a +1 morale bonus on skill checks for the rest of the encounter or until you're unconscious or dead. Once inspired, your allies don't need to remain within line of sight of you. You can't inspire confidence in yourself.

Inspire Haste: As a swift action, you can encourage one of your allies within line of sight to make haste with a skill check. On that ally's next turn, that ally can make a skill check that requires a standard action as a move action instead.

Inspire Zeal: Whenever an ally within line of sight of you makes an attack that moves an opponent down the condition track (such as by dealing damage that equals or exceeds the target's damage threshold), that ally moves the target an additional –1 step down the condition track.

Prerequisites: Bolster Ally, Inspire Confidence, Ignite Fervor.

LEADERSHIP TALENT TREE

A born leader, you know how to take charge and lead your companions and followers to success.

All of the talents in this tree are mind-affecting effects. Moreover, you can't use any of these talents on yourself.

Born Leader: Once per encounter, as a swift action, you grant all allies within your line of sight a +1 insight bonus on attack rolls. This effect lasts for as long as they remain within line of sight of you. An ally loses this bonus immediately if line of sight is broken or if you are unconscious or dead.

Coordinate: A noble with this talent has a knack for getting people to work together. When you use this talent as a standard action, all allies within your line of sight grant an additional +1 bonus when they use the aid another action until the start of your next turn (see Aid Another, page 151).

You may select this talent multiple times; each time you do, the bonus granted by the coordinate ability increases by +1 (to a maximum of +5).

Distant Command: Any ally who gains the benefit of your Born Leader talent (see above) does not lose the benefit if their line of sight to you is broken.

Prerequisite: Born Leader.

Fearless Leader: As a swift action, you can provide a courageous example for your allies. For the remainder of the encounter, your allies receive a +5 morale bonus to their Will Defense against any fear effect. Your allies lose this benefit if they lose line of sight to you, or if you are killed or knocked unconscious.

Prerequisite: Born Leader.

Rally: Once per encounter, you can rally your allies and bring them back from the edge of defeat. As a swift action, any allies within your line of sight who have less than half their total hit points remaining gain a +2 morale bonus to their Reflex Defense and Will Defense and a +2 bonus to all damage rolls for the remainder of the encounter.

Prerequisites: Born Leader, Distant Command.

Trust: You can give up your standard action to give one ally within your line of sight an extra standard action or move action on his next turn, to do with as he pleases. The ally does not lose the action if line of sight is later broken.

Prerequisites: Born Leader, Coordinate.

LINEAGE TALENT TREE

You lead a privileged life and reap the benefit of an upbringing beyond most citizens of the galaxy.

Connections: You are able to obtain licensed, restricted, military, or illegal equipment without having to pay a licensing fee or endure a background check, provided the total cost of the desired equipment is equal to or less than your character level × 1,000 credits. In addition, when obtaining equipment or services through the black market, you reduce the black market cost multiplier by 1. See Restricted Items (page 118) for details.

Educated: Thanks to your well-rounded education, you may make any Knowledge check untrained.

Spontaneous Skill: Sometimes you surprise others with your skill. Once per day, you may make an untrained skill check as though you were trained in the skill. Exception: You cannot use this talent to make an untrained Use the Force check as though you were trained in the skill unless you have the Force Sensitivity feat (page 85).

You can select this talent multiple times; each time you do, you can use it one additional time per day.

Prerequisite: Educated.

Wealth: Each time you gain a level (including the level at which you select this talent), you receive an amount of credits equal to 5,000 × your noble level. You can spend these credits as you see fit. The credits appear in a civilized, accessible location of your choice or in your private bank account.

Bonus Feats

At every even-numbered level (2nd, 4th, 6th, etc.), you gain a bonus feat. This feat must be selected from the following list, and you must meet any prerequisites for that feat.

Armor Proficiency (light), Cybernetic Surgery, Exotic Weapon Proficiency, Linguist, Melee Defense, Skill Focus, Skill Training, Surgical Expertise, Weapon Finesse, Weapon Proficiency (advanced melee weapons), Weapon Proficiency (rifles).

CREDITS

A 1st-level noble starts play with 3d4 × 400 credits.

Scoundrel

Scoundrels are rogues—good, bad, and neutral—who either live outside the law or fight against it in order to get the upper hand. They can come from any world or region of the galaxy. Most use their intelligence and dexterity to accomplish tasks, and many rely on charisma as a fallback when all else fails. The scoundrel gets by with bravado, cunning, duplicity, and trickery. They live by their wits, lying, cheating, stealing, and even fighting when the need arises.

Exploits

Many scoundrels live a life of adventure for the excitement it provides. Others go adventuring to advance their illicit careers. Some are good-hearted rogues in it for the thrill or to right a wrong done to them or those they love. Others are despicable knaves who serve only one master—the greed that swells inside them. More often, a adventurous scoundrel falls somewhere in the middle, changing allegiance and attitudes as the political climate changes, until something larger than himself sets him on a particular course through the galaxy. Adventurous scoundrels call themselves smugglers, pirates, outlaws, gamblers, slicers, con artists, thieves, rogues, and spies.

Characteristics

Scoundrels have a knack for getting into and out of trouble. They have an instinct for self-preservation that keeps them alive, but it's usually tempered with a need to experience the thrills that their profession has to offer, and many adventurous scoundrels are also saddled with a sense of honor that sometimes makes them go against their natural inclinations.

Background

Scoundrels don't often start out seeking to defy authority and break the law. Some are thrust into the profession as a means of rebellion. Others wind up on the wrong side of the law due to bad luck, poor decisions, or circumstances beyond their control. The skills they pick up along the way make them great members of any mission team.

Examples of Scoundrels in Star Wars

Han Solo, Lando Calrissian, Dash Rendar, Dexter Jettster, Ghent, Watto.

Game Rule Information

Scoundrels have the following game statistics.

Abilities

Dexterity and Intelligence are a scoundrel's most important ability scores, because he must have quick reflexes and a sharp wit to survive. Charisma is important for talking one's way out of trouble, and Wisdom is useful for spotting trouble before it finds the scoundrel.

Hit Points

Scoundrels begin play at 1st level with a number of hit points equal to 18 + their Constitution modifier. At each level after 1st, scoundrels gain 1d6 hit points + their Constitution modifier.

Table 3-4: The Scoundrel

Level	Base Attack Bonus	Class Features
1st	+0	Defense bonuses, starting feats, talent
2nd	+1	Bonus Feat
3rd	+2	Talent
4th	+3	Bonus Feat
5th	+3	Talent
6th	+4	Bonus Feat
7th	+5	Talent
8th	+6	Bonus Feat
9th	+6	Talent
10th	+7	Bonus Feat
11th	+8	Talent
12th	+9	Bonus Feat
13th	+9	Talent
14th	+10	Bonus Feat
15th	+11	Talent
16th	+12	Bonus Feat
17th	+12	Talent
18th	+13	Bonus Feat
19th	+14	Talent
20th	+15	Bonus Feat

Class Skills (trained in 4 + Int modifier): Acrobatics, Deception, Gather Information, Initiative, Knowledge (all skills, taken individually), Mechanics, Perception, Persuasion, Pilot, Stealth, Use Computer

Force Points
Scoundrels gain a number of Force Points equal to 5 + one-half their character level (rounded down) at 1st level and every time they gain a new level in this class. Any Force Points left over from previous levels are lost.

CLASS FEATURES
All of the following are features of the scoundrel class.

Defense Bonuses
At 1st level, you gain a +2 class bonus to your Reflex Defense and a +1 class bonus to your Will Defense.

Starting Feats
You begin play with the following feats:
   Point Blank Shot
   Weapon Proficiency (pistols)
   Weapon Proficiency (simple weapons)

Talents
At 1st level and every odd-numbered level thereafter (3rd, 5th, 7th, etc.), you select a talent from any of the following talent trees. You may choose a talent from any tree you wish, but you must meet the prerequisites (if any) of the chosen talent. No talent can be selected more than once unless expressly indicated.

FORTUNE TALENT TREE
Many scoundrels like to gamble with destiny, putting everything on the line and trusting fate (or the Force) to bring them fortune, fame, and success.

Fool's Luck: As a standard action, you can spend a Force Point to gain one of the following benefits for the rest of the encounter: a +1 luck bonus on attack rolls, a +5 luck bonus on skill checks, or a +1 luck bonus to all your defenses.

Fortune's Favor: Whenever you score a critical hit with a melee or ranged attack, you gain a free standard action. You must take the extra standard action before the end of your turn, or else it is lost.

Gambler: You gain a +2 competence bonus on Wisdom checks when you gamble (see the Gambling sidebar on the next page).

You can select this talent multiple times; each time you take this talent, the competence bonus increases by +2.

Knack: Once per day, you can reroll a skill check and take the better result.

You can select this talent multiple times; each time you select this talent, you can use it one additional time per day.

Lucky Shot: Once per day, you can reroll an attack roll and take the better result.

You can select this talent multiple times; each time you select this talent, you can use it one additional time per day.

Prerequisite: Knack.

MISFORTUNE TALENT TREE
Your mother always said you were trouble. Now, your enemies know it, too.

Dastardly Strike: Whenever you make a successful attack against an opponent that is denied its Dexterity bonus to Reflex Defense, the target moves −1 step along the condition track (see Conditions, page 148).

Disruptive: By spending two swift actions, you can use your knack for causing trouble and instigating chaos to disrupt your enemies. Until the start of your next turn, you suppress all morale and insight bonuses applied to enemies in your line of sight.

Skirmisher: If you move at least 2 squares before you attack and end your move in a different square from where you started, you gain a +1 bonus on attack rolls until the start of your next turn.

Sneak Attack: Any time your opponent is flat-footed or otherwise denied its Dexterity bonus to Reflex Defense, you deal an extra 1d6 points of damage with a successful melee or ranged attack. You must be within 6 squares of the target to make a sneak attack with a ranged weapon.

You may select this talent multiple times. Each time you select it, your sneak attack damage increases by +1d6 (maximum +10d6).

Walk the Line: As a standard action, you can do or say something that catches your enemies off guard. All opponents within 6 squares of you and in your line of sight take a −2 penalty to their defenses until the start of your next turn. The penalty is negated if line of sight is broken.

Prerequisite: Disruptive.

DEEL SUROOL, MALE TWI'LEK SCOUNDREL

SLICER TALENT TREE

You move like a ghost through the HoloNet and can hack into enemy mainframes and computer systems with astonishing grace.

Gimmick: You can issue a routine command to a computer (see page 76) as a swift action.

Master Slicer: You may choose to reroll any Use Computer check made to improve access on a computer, keeping the better of the two results.

Prerequisite: Gimmick.

Trace: You can substitute your Use Computer skill for any Gather Information check as long as you have access to a computer network.

SPACER TALENT TREE

You prowl the space lanes seeking wealth, fame, adventure, or something more. You're also pretty good with vehicles in general.

Hyperdriven: Once per day while aboard a starship, you can add your scoundrel class level as a bonus on a single attack roll, skill check, or ability check. The decision to add this bonus can be made after the result of the roll or check is known.

Spacehound: You take no penalty on attack rolls in low-gravity or zero-gravity environments, and you ignore the debilitating effects of space sickness (see Zero-Gravity Environments, page 257). In addition, you are considered proficient with any starship weapon.

Starship Raider: You gain a +1 bonus on attack rolls while aboard a starship. This bonus applies to attacks made with starship weapons as well as personal weapons used aboard a starship.

Prerequisite: Spacehound.

Stellar Warrior: Whenever you roll a natural 20 on an attack roll made aboard a starship, you gain one temporary Force Point. If the Force Point is not used before the end of the encounter, it is lost.

Prerequisite: Spacehound.

Bonus Feats

At every even-numbered level (2nd, 4th, 6th, etc.), you gain a bonus feat. This feat must be selected from the following list, and you must meet any prerequisites for that feat.

Deadeye, Dodge, Melee Defense, Mobility, Precise Shot, Quick Draw, Rapid Shot, Running Attack, Skill Focus, Skill Training, Vehicular Combat, Weapon Proficiency (advanced melee weapons).

CREDITS

A 1st-level scoundrel starts play with 3d4 × 250 credits.

GAMBLING

Characters can win or lose credits by betting on swoop races or playing games of chance, such as sabacc and jubilee. Use these rules whenever a character plays against the house, gambles against other characters, or takes his chances on games of pure chance.

Gambling against the House: When gambling against the house, such as when playing the jubilee wheel or betting on the outcome of a race, you must declare how many credits you want to wager as your stake. A Wisdom check determines whether you win or lose, and by how much:

WISDOM CHECK RESULT	WINS OR LOSSES
Less than 5	Lose entire stake
5–9	Lose half of stake
10–14	Break even; keep entire stake
15–19	Win stake ×2
20–24	Win stake ×5
25 or higher	Win stake ×10

Gambling against Other Characters: When gambling against other opponents, including GM characters and other heroes, each participant declares an amount to wager and makes a Wisdom check. The character with the highest result wins; if two participants are tied for the highest result, they split the winnings. Each participant other than the winner compares his check result against the winner's result, using the difference in scores to determine how much money is deducted from his stake and added to the winner's take.

DIFFERENCE	CHANGE IN WINNINGS
1–4	Break even; keep your entire stake
5–9	Give 1/2 of stake to winner
10 or more	Lose it all; give entire stake to winner

Games of Pure Chance: When you play a game of pure chance, Wisdom checks never come into play. Simply roll 1d20 and consult the chart below:

D20 RESULT	OUTCOME
1–15	Lose entire stake
16	Lose half of stake
17	Break even; keep entire stake
18	Win stake ×2
19	Win stake ×5
20	Win stake ×10

Scout

Scouts are natural explorers and adventurers, full of curiosity and trained to handle the out-of-the-way locations where they often operate. Scouts tend to be independent, signing on when the credits are good and their skills are best utilized and tested. Scouts understand the lay of the land and the orbit of the stars. They know how to recognize danger and locate the basic necessities for survival. The scout seeks knowledge, tries to solve mysteries, and wants to be the first to see something new and different. The scout learns to find a path through the wild regions, often becoming a decent pilot along the way, and usually learns how to protect himself from whatever hides over the next hill or beyond the most distant nebula.

Table 3-5: The Scout

Level	Base Attack Bonus	Class Features
1st	+0	Defense bonuses, starting feats, talent
2nd	+1	Bonus Feat
3rd	+2	Talent
4th	+3	Bonus Feat
5th	+3	Talent
6th	+4	Bonus Feat
7th	+5	Talent
8th	+6	Bonus Feat
9th	+6	Talent
10th	+7	Bonus Feat
11th	+8	Talent
12th	+9	Bonus Feat
13th	+9	Talent
14th	+10	Bonus Feat
15th	+11	Talent
16th	+12	Bonus Feat
17th	+12	Talent
18th	+13	Bonus Feat
19th	+14	Talent
20th	+15	Bonus Feat

Class Skills (trained in 5 + Int modifier): Climb, Endurance, Initiative, Jump, Knowledge (all skills, taken individually), Mechanics, Perception, Pilot, Ride, Stealth, Survival, Swim

Exploits

Many scouts become adventurers to see what's in the next star system. They pick up skills that make them excellent members of any team. They are usually the best trackers, trailblazers, and survivalists the galaxy has to offer. Some scouts are scientists and researchers who learn the skills of the profession so they don't have to rely on others. Some sell their services to the highest bidder. More often, the adventurous scout has a good heart, a sense of honor, and a burning desire to embrace the wild regions of the galaxy and learn to conquer them—either figuratively or literally. Adventurous scouts call themselves rangers, outriders, hunters, explorers, guides, adventurous scholars, and vanguards.

Characteristics

Scouts temper insatiable curiosity with excellent survival instincts. They make use of dexterity and intelligence, as well as wisdom, to spot and avoid dangers. The scout has an undying faith in himself and his abilities that sometimes allows the scout to call upon reserves and an inner strength to get out of tough situations. Scouts like to be the first to reach any location, although they also want to reach it in one piece. They can be gruff or silent, jovial or talkative. They are confident and brave, and they often appreciate the wonders that the galaxy has to offer.

Background

Scouts come to their profession in search of something, usually knowledge or secrets or the answers to the mysteries of the ages. Scholars, while possibly associated with an institute of learning or a particular government, often forsake the halls of academe for the pure research of working in the field. Pathfinders and explorers may work for a government or a military institution, or they may take on freelance contracts from anyone willing to pay for their services. Many scouts develop into bounty hunters, especially those who combine military skills with their tracking and searching abilities. Every group of adventurers benefits from having a scout in the party.

Examples of Scouts in Star Wars

Chewbacca, Wicket the Ewok, Captain Tarpals.

Game Rule Information

Scouts have the following game statistics.

Abilities

Most of the scout's key skills rely on Dexterity, Intelligence, and Wisdom. Strength is also useful for the scout trained in athletic skills.

Hit Points

Scouts begin play at 1st level with a number of hit points equal to 24 + their Constitution modifier. At each level after 1st, scoundrels gain 1d8 hit points + their Constitution modifier.

Force Points

Scouts gain a number of Force Points equal to 5 + one-half their character level (rounded down) at 1st level and every time they gain a new level in this class. Any Force Points left over from previous levels are lost.

Class Features

All of the following are features of the scout class.

Defense Bonuses

At 1st level, you gain a +1 class bonus to your Fortitude Defense and a +2 class bonus to your Reflex Defense. (See page 145 for more information on defenses.)

Starting Feats

You begin play with the following feats:
  Shake It Off*
  Weapon Proficiency (pistols)
  Weapon Proficiency (rifles)
  Weapon Proficiency (simple weapons)
  * You must meet the prerequisite of this feat (minimum Constitution 13 and trained in the Endurance skill) to gain it.

Talents

At 1st level and every odd-numbered level thereafter (3rd, 5th, 7th, etc.), you select a talent from any of the following talent trees. You may choose a talent from any tree you wish, but you must meet the prerequisites (if any) of the chosen talent. No talent can be selected more than once unless expressly indicated.

KELKO, MALE RODIAN SCOUT

AWARENESS TALENT TREE

You are exceptionally good at noticing things and avoiding perilous situations.

Acute Senses: You may choose to reroll any Perception check, but the result of the reroll must be accepted even if it is worse.

Expert Tracker: You take no penalty on Survival checks made to follow tracks while moving your normal speed. (Without this talent, you take a –5 penalty on Survival checks made to follow tracks while moving your normal speed.)
Prerequisite: Acute Senses.

Improved Initiative: You may choose to reroll any Initiative check, but the result of the reroll must be accepted even if it is worse.
Prerequisite: Acute Senses.

Keen Shot: You take no penalty on your attack roll when attacking a target with concealment (but not total concealment).
Prerequisite: Acute Senses.

Uncanny Dodge I: You retain your Dexterity bonus to your Reflex Defense regardless of being caught flat-footed or struck by a hidden attacker. You still lose your Dexterity bonus to your Reflex Defense if you are immobilized.
Prerequisites: Acute Senses, Improved Initiative.

Uncanny Dodge II: You cannot be flanked. You can react to opponents on opposite sides of you as easily as you can react to a single attacker.
Prerequisites: Acute Senses, Improved Initiative, Uncanny Dodge I.

CAMOUFLAGE TALENT TREE

You learn quickly how to blend in with your environment.

Hidden Movement: You're very good at hiding when mobile. You take no penalty on your Stealth check when moving your normal speed.
Prerequisite: Improved Stealth.

Improved Stealth: You may choose to reroll any Stealth check, but the result of the reroll must be accepted even if it is worse.

Total Concealment: Any situation that would give you concealment (see page 156) grants you total concealment instead.
Prerequisites: Hidden Movement, Improved Stealth.

FRINGER TALENT TREE

You're especially skilled at "getting by" on backwater worlds.

Barter: You may reroll any Persuasion check made to haggle (see the Persuasion skill, page 71). You must, however, accept the result of the reroll.

Fringe Savant: Whenever you roll a natural 20 on a skill check during an encounter, you gain one temporary Force Point. If the Force Point is not used before the end of the encounter, it is lost.

Long Stride: Your speed increases by 2 squares if you are wearing light armor or no armor. If you have a natural fly, climb, or swim speed, it increases by 2 squares as well. You cannot use this talent if you are wearing medium or heavy armor.

Jury-Rigger: You may reroll any Mechanics check made to accomplish a jury-rigged repair (see the Mechanics skill, page 68). You must, however, accept the result of the reroll.

SURVIVOR TALENT TREE

As an explorer of dangerous places, you are trained to react to danger swiftly and adroitly, as well as navigate difficult terrain and reduce damage.

Evasion: If you are hit by an area attack (see Area Attacks, page 155), you take half damage if the attack hit you. If the area attack misses you, you take no damage.

Extreme Effort: You can spend two swift actions to gain a +5 bonus on a single Strength check or Strength-based skill check made during the same round.

Sprint: When you use the run action, you can move up to five times your speed (instead of the normal four times your speed).

Surefooted: Your speed is not reduced by difficult terrain (see Difficult Terrain, page 159).

Bonus Feats

At every even-numbered level (2nd, 4th, 6th, etc.), you gain a bonus feat. This feat must be selected from the following list, and you must meet any prerequisites for that feat.

Armor Proficiency (light, medium, or heavy), Careful Shot, Deadeye, Dodge, Far Shot, Linguist, Mobility, Point Blank Shot, Precise Shot, Rapid Shot, Running Attack, Skill Focus, Skill Training, Sniper, Vehicular Combat, Weapon Proficiency (advanced melee weapons).

CREDITS

A 1st-level scout starts play with 3d4 × 250 credits.

SOLDIER

Soldiers combine discipline with martial skills to become the best pure warriors in the galaxy. Soldiers can be stalwart defenders of those in need, cruel marauders, or brave adventurers. They can be hired guns, noble champions, or cold-hearted killers. They fight for glory, for honor, to right wrongs, to gain power, to acquire wealth, or simply for the thrill of battle.

EXPLOITS

Many soldiers see adventures, raids on enemy strongholds, and dangerous missions as their jobs. Some want to defend those who can't defend themselves; others seek to use their muscle to carve their own place of importance in the galaxy. Whatever their initial motivation, most soldiers wind up living for the thrill of combat and the excitement of adventure. Adventuring soldiers call themselves guards, bodyguards, champions, enforcers, mercenaries, warriors, soldiers of fortune, or simply adventurers.

CHARACTERISTICS

Soldiers have the best all-around fighting abilities, and an individual soldier develops styles and techniques that set him apart from his peers. A given soldier might be especially capable with certain weapons, another trained to execute specific combat maneuvers. As soldiers gain experience, they get more opportunities to develop their fighting skills.

BACKGROUND

Most soldiers come to the profession after receiving at least some amount of formal training from a military organization, local militia, or private army. Some attend formal academies; others are self-taught and well tested. A soldier may have taken up his weapon to escape a mundane life. Another may be following a proud family tradition. Soldiers in a particular unit share a certain camaraderie, but most have nothing in common except battle prowess and the desire to apply it to a given situation.

EXAMPLES OF SOLDIERS IN STAR WARS

Admiral Ackbar, Corran Horn, Captain Panaka, Captain Typho, General Crix Madine, Kyle Katarn, Wedge Antilles, Zam Wesell.

Vor'en Kurn, Male Human Soldier

Game Rule Information

Soldiers have the following game statistics.

Abilities

Since most combat in the Star Wars universe uses blasters and other ranged weapons, Dexterity is the soldier's most important ability score, followed closely by Constitution and Strength. Don't underestimate the importance of Intelligence and Wisdom, however, since many of a soldier's useful skills are based on these abilities.

Hit Points

Soldiers begin play at 1st level with a number of hit points equal to 30 + their Constitution modifier. At each level after 1st, soldiers gain 1d10 hit points + their Constitution modifier.

Force Points

Soldiers gain a number of Force Points equal to 5 + one-half their character level (rounded down) at 1st level and every time they gain a new level in this class. Any Force Points left over from previous levels are lost.

Class Features

All of the following are features of the soldier class.

Defense Bonuses

At 1st level, you gain a +1 bonus to your Reflex Defense and a +2 bonus to your Fortitude Defense.

Starting Feats

You begin play with the following feats:
  Armor Proficiency (light)
  Armor Proficiency (medium)
  Weapon Proficiency (pistols)
  Weapon Proficiency (rifles)
  Weapon Proficiency (simple weapons)

Talents

At 1st level and every odd-numbered level thereafter (3rd, 5th, 7th, etc.), you select a talent from any of the following talent trees. You may choose a talent from any tree you wish, but you must meet the prerequisites (if any) of the chosen talent. No talent can be selected more than once unless expressly indicated.

ARMOR SPECIALIST TALENT TREE

You can maximize the benefits of wearing armor while reducing or eliminating some of its drawbacks.

Armor Mastery: The maximum Dexterity bonus of your armor improves by +1. You must be proficient with the armor you are wearing to gain this benefit.
  Prerequisite: Armored Defense.

Table 3-6: The Soldier

Base Level	Attack Bonus	Class Features
1st	+1	Defense bonuses, starting feats, talent
2nd	+2	Bonus Feat
3rd	+3	Talent
4th	+4	Bonus Feat
5th	+5	Talent
6th	+6	Bonus Feat
7th	+7	Talent
8th	+8	Bonus Feat
9th	+9	Talent
10th	+10	Bonus Feat
11th	+11	Talent
12th	+12	Bonus Feat
13th	+13	Talent
14th	+14	Bonus Feat
15th	+15	Talent
16th	+16	Bonus Feat
17th	+17	Talent
18th	+18	Bonus Feat
19th	+19	Talent
20th	+20	Bonus Feat

Class Skills (trained in 3 + Int modifier): Climb, Endurance, Initiative, Jump, Knowledge (tactics), Mechanics, Perception, Pilot, Swim, Treat Injury, Use Computer

Armored Defense: When calculating your Reflex Defense, you may add either your heroic level or your armor bonus, whichever is higher. You must be proficient with the armor you are wearing to gain this benefit.

Improved Armored Defense: When calculating your Reflex Defense, you may add your heroic level plus one-half your armor bonus (rounded down) or your armor bonus, whichever is higher. You must be proficient with the armor you are wearing to gain this benefit.

Prerequisite: Armored Defense.

Juggernaut: Your armor does not reduce your speed or the distance you can move while running. You must be proficient with the armor you are wearing to gain this benefit.

Prerequisite: Armored Defense.

Second Skin: When wearing armor with which you are proficient, your armor bonus to your Reflex Defense and equipment bonus to your Fortitude Defense increase by +1.

Prerequisite: Armored Defense.

BRAWLER TALENT TREE

You like to get "up close and personal" with your enemies and engage them in melee combat.

Expert Grappler: You gain a +2 competence bonus on grapple attacks (see page 153).

Gun Club: You can use a ranged weapon as a melee weapon without taking a penalty on your attack roll. (Normally you take a −5 penalty on attack rolls made with an improvised weapon.) The weapon is otherwise treated as a club in all respects.

If you are using a rifle with a mounted bayonet (see page 121) or vibro-bayonet (see page 124), you may wield that weapon as a double weapon. The bayonet or vibrobayonet end is treated normally, and the other end is treated as a club.

Melee Smash: You deal +1 point of damage with melee attacks.

Stunning Strike: When you damage an opponent with a melee attack, your opponent moves an additional −1 step along the condition track (see page 149) if your attack roll result equals or exceeds the target's damage threshold.

Prerequisite: Melee Smash.

Unbalance Opponent: You are skilled at keeping your opponents off balance in melee combat. During your action, you designate an opponent no more than one size category larger or smaller than you. That opponent doesn't get to add his Strength bonus on attack rolls when targeting you. (If the opponent has a Strength penalty, he still suffers that penalty.) The opponent's Strength modifier applies to damage, as usual. You can select a new opponent on your next turn.

Prerequisite: Expert Grappler.

COMMANDO TALENT TREE

You use advanced combat tactics to take down enemies quickly, shield your comrades, and endure whatever challenges are thrown your way.

Battle Analysis: As a swift action, you can make a DC 15 Knowledge (tactics) check. If the check succeeds, you know which allies and opponents in your line of sight are reduced to at least half of their maximum total hit points.

Cover Fire: When you make a ranged attack with a pistol or rifle, all allies within 6 squares of you when the attack is made gain a +1 bonus to Reflex Defense until the start of your next turn. Allies within range don't need to be within your line of sight to gain the bonus.

Prerequisite: Battle Analysis.

Demolitionist: When you use the Mechanics skill to place an explosive device, the explosion deals +2 dice of damage. You may take this talent multiple times; its effects stack.

Draw Fire: You can distract opponents and convince them that you are the most tempting (or most dangerous) target in an area. As a swift action, make a Persuasion check and compare the result to the Will Defense of all opponents within line of sight. If the check result exceeds an opponent's Will Defense, that opponent cannot attack any character within 6 squares of you until the start of your next turn as long as you do not have cover against that opponent. (The affected opponent may still attack you, however.)

Harm's Way: Once per round, you may spend a swift action to shield a single adjacent ally from attacks, taking the damage and suffering the ill effects in your ally's stead. Until the start of your next turn, any attack made against the protected ally affects you instead. You may elect not to shield your protected ally against a given attack, provided the decision is made before the attack roll is made.

Prerequisite: Trained in the Initiative skill.

Indomitable: Once per day as a swift action, you can move +5 steps on the condition track (see Conditions, page 148). This does not remove any persistent conditions that may be affecting you (see page 149).

You can select this talent multiple times. Each time you select this talent, you can use it one additional time per day.

> "YOUR FRIEND IS QUITE A MERCENARY. I WONDER IF HE REALLY CARES ABOUT ANYTHING . . . OR ANYBODY."
>
> — LEIA ORGANA

Tough as Nails: You can catch a second wind one extra time per day (see Second Wind, page 146). If you have this talent and the Extra Second Wind feat (see page 85), you can catch your second wind a total of three times per day.

WEAPON SPECIALIST TALENT TREE
You are highly trained at using specific weapons.

Devastating Attack: Choose a single exotic weapon or weapon group with which you are proficient. Whenever you make a successful attack against a target using such a weapon, you treat your target's damage threshold as if it were 5 points lower when determining the result of your attack.

You may select this talent multiple times. Each time you select this talent, it applies to a different exotic weapon or weapon group.

Penetrating Attack: Choose a single exotic weapon or weapon group with which you are proficient. Whenever you make a successful attack against a target using such a weapon, you treat your target's damage reduction as if it were 5 points lower when determining the result of your attack.

You may select this talent multiple times. Each time you select this talent, it applies to a different exotic weapon or weapon group.

Prerequisite: Weapon Focus with chosen exotic weapon or weapon group.

Weapon Specialization: Choose a single exotic weapon or weapon group with which you are proficient. You gain a +2 bonus on damage rolls with such weapons.

You may select this talent multiple times. Each time you select this talent, it applies to a different exotic weapon or weapon group.

Prerequisite: Weapon Focus with chosen exotic weapon or weapon group.

Bonus Feats
At every even-numbered level (2nd, 4th, 6th, etc.), you gain a bonus feat. This feat must be selected from the following list, and you must meet any prerequisites for that feat.

Armor Proficiency (heavy), Bantha Rush, Careful Shot, Charging Fire, Cleave, Combat Reflexes, Coordinated Attack, Crush, Deadeye, Double Attack, Dual Weapon Mastery I, Dual Weapon Mastery II, Dual Weapon Mastery III, Exotic Weapon Proficiency, Far Shot, Great Cleave, Improved Charge, Improved Disarm, Martial Arts I, Martial Arts II, Martial Arts III, Melee Defense, Mighty Swing, Pin, Point Blank Shot, Power Attack, Precise Shot, Quick Draw, Rapid Shot, Rapid Strike, Running Attack, Shake It Off, Skill Focus, Skill Training, Sniper, Throw, Toughness, Trip, Triple Attack, Triple Crit, Vehicular Combat, Weapon Focus, Weapon Proficiency (advanced melee weapons), Weapon Proficiency (heavy weapons).

CREDITS
A 1st-level soldier starts play with 3d4 × 250 credits.

Multiclass Characters

A character may add new classes as he or she progresses in levels. Multiclassing improves a character's versatility at the expense of focus.

Class and Level Features

As a general rule, the abilities of a multiclass character are the sum of the abilities of each of the character's classes.

Level

"Character level" is a character's total number of levels. It derives from overall XP earned and is used to determine when feats and ability score boosts are gained, as per Table 3-1: Experience and Level-Dependent Benefits. "Class level" is the character's level in a particular class, as per the individual class tables. For the single-class hero, character level and class level are the same.

Hit Points

Each time you gain a new level, roll a hit point die (the size of the die depends on the class in which the level is gained) and add the result to your character's hit point total. Your character's Constitution modifier applies to each hit point die roll.

For example, a 1st-level scout who becomes a 1st-level scout/1st-level soldier gains a number of additional hit points equal to 1d10 + the character's Constitution modifier. A few game sessions later, the character gains a second level in the scout class, becoming a 2nd-level scout/1st-level soldier, whereupon her hit points increase by 1d8 + the character's Constitution modifier.

Base Attack Bonus

Add the base attack bonus of each class to get the character's base attack bonus. For instance, a 6th-level noble/2nd-level soldier has a base attack bonus of +6 (+4 for noble, +2 for soldier).

Defenses

Each time a character gains a new level, his Reflex Defense, Fortitude Defense, and Will Defense need to be adjusted to account for the increase in character level.

A character who takes his first level of a new class also gains a class bonus to one or more of his defenses; however, this class bonus does not stack with other class bonuses.

Skills

When you select a new class, you do not gain any new trained skills. However, your list of class skills expands to include those of the new class. If you take the Skill Training feat (page 88), you may choose your new trained skill from the class skill list of any class in which you have levels.

For example, Arani is a multiclass noble/soldier who takes the Skill Training feat. Her new trained skill may be chosen from the noble's list of class skills or the soldier's list of class skills.

Starting Feats

When you select a new class, you do not gain all of its starting feats. Select one feat from the list of starting feats. For example, a 1st-level noble decides to take a level of soldier and gains one feat of his choice from the soldier's list of starting feats; he selects Weapon Proficiency (rifles).

Talents

If a character gains a talent as a consequence of gaining a level, he must select a talent associated with the class in which he gained the level. For example, Arani is a 2nd-level noble who decides to take a level in the soldier class, which grants her a talent. She must select her new talent from the soldier talent trees (or from Force talent trees, if she has the Force Sensitivity feat), since it was a soldier level that granted her the talent.

Feats

For multiclass characters, feats are received at 3rd level and every three character levels thereafter, regardless of individual class level (see Table 3-1: Experience and Level-Dependent Benefits).

A multiclass character that gains a class bonus feat must select it from the bonus feats available to that particular class. For example, Arani is a 2nd-level noble/1st-level soldier who decides to take a second level in the soldier class. Doing so grants her a bonus feat, which she must select from the soldier's list of bonus feats (page 53).

Ability Increases

For multiclass characters, abilities are increased every four character levels, regardless of individual class level (see Table 3-1: Experience and Level-Dependent Benefits).

Adding a Second Class

When a single-class character gains a level, he or she may choose to increase the level of his or her current class or pick up a new class at 1st level. The GM may restrict the choices available according to how he or she handles classes, skills, experience, and training. For instance, the character may need to find a teacher to instruct him in the ways of the new class. Additionally, the GM may require the player to declare what class his or her hero is "working on" before he or she makes the jump to the next level, so the character has time to practice new skills. In this way, gaining the new class is the result of previous effort rather than a sudden development.

The character gains the base attack bonus, class bonuses to defense, and class skills, as well as hit points of the appropriate die type and a talent associated with the new class.

Picking up a new class is not exactly the same as starting a character in that class. Some of the benefits for a 1st-level hero represent the advantage of training while young and fresh, with lots of time to practice. When picking up a new class, a hero does not receive the following starting benefits given to characters that begin their careers in that class.

- Starting feats (select only one of the starting feats)
- Maximum, tripled hit points from the first die
- Starting credits

Advancing a Level

Each time a multiclass character achieves a new level, he either increases one of his current class levels by one or picks up a new class at 1st level.

When a multiclass character increases one of his classes by one level, he gets all the standard benefits that characters get for achieving that level in that class: more hit points, possible bonuses on attack rolls, better defense scores, and one or more new class features (such as a talent or bonus feat). In addition, a multiclass character has the option to take any starting feat for that class as a bonus feat.

How Multiclassing Works

Arani, a 4th-level noble, decides she wants to expand her repertoire by learning some soldiering. When Arani reaches 10,000 XP, she becomes a 5th-level character. Instead of becoming a 5th-level noble, however, she becomes a 4th-level noble/1st-level soldier. How exactly she picked up this new area of focus isn't critical to the campaign, though the player and GM are encouraged to create an in-game reason and opportunity for the hero to do so.

Now, instead of gaining the benefits of a new level of noble, she gains the benefits of becoming a 1st-level soldier. She gains a 1st-level soldier's hit points (1d10 + her Constitution modifier), a 1st-level soldier's +1 base attack bonus, a soldier's +2 class bonus to Fortitude Defense, and a soldier talent. Because she gained a level, all of her defenses (Reflex, Fortitude, and Will) increase by 1.

The benefits described above are added to the scores Arani already had as a noble. She doesn't gain any of the benefits a 5th-level noble gains.

On achieving 15,000 XP, Arani becomes a 6th-level hero. She decides she'd like to continue along the soldier path, so she increases her soldier level instead of her noble level. Again she gains the soldier's benefits for attaining a new level rather than the noble's. At this point, Arani is a 4th-level noble/2nd-level soldier. Her combat skill is a little better than a 4th-level noble's would be because she has learned something about fighting during her time as a soldier. Her base attack bonus is +5 (+3 from her noble class and +2 from her soldier class). Her Reflex, Fortitude, and Will Defenses each increase by 1.

At each new level, Arani decides whether to increase her noble level or her soldier level. Of course, if she wants to have even more diverse abilities, she could acquire a third class, such as scoundrel. At some point, she may also qualify for a prestige class (see Chapter 12: Prestige Classes). In general, a character can multiclass as many times as there are classes available.

Chapter IV
Skills

Deel Surool, a scoundrel, can walk quietly behind an Imperial shuttle, crouch in a shadow, and carefully listen for a stormtrooper commander giving orders to its troops. If Vor'en Kurn, a soldier, were to try the same thing, he'd be more likely to make so much noise the stormtroopers would hear him. He, however, could dash into the shuttle and take its controls, flying it away while the stormtroopers fire at it impotently. These actions and many more are determined by the skills that characters have (in this case, Perception, Pilot, and Stealth).

Skills Summary

Your character's skills represent a variety of abilities, and you get better at them as you go up in level. A skill check takes into account your training (trained skill bonus), natural talent (ability modifier), and luck (the die roll). It may also take into account your species' knack for certain skills or the armor you're wearing (armor check penalty), among other things.

Trained Skills vs. Untrained Skills

When you make a character, you are allowed to select a number of skills as trained skills. Your character receives a number of trained skills based on his or her character class and Intelligence modifier (minimum of 1 trained skill). Trained skills are selected from the character's list of class skills at 1st level, and a character may acquire new trained skills by taking the Skill Training feat (page 88). The major difference between a trained skill and an untrained skill is that you gain a +5 bonus on skill checks if you're trained in the skill. However, some skills (such as Use the Force) can't be used untrained.

Using Skills

To make a skill check, roll:

1d20 + one-half your character level + key ability modifier + miscellaneous modifiers

If you are trained in the skill, add +5 to the skill check result.

A skill check is made just like an attack roll or a saving throw. The higher the roll, the better. You're either trying to get a result that equals or exceeds a certain Difficulty Class (DC), or you're trying to beat another character's check result. For instance, to sneak quietly past a guard, Deel needs to beat the guard's Perception check with a Stealth check.

When adding "one-half your character level," always round down (a 1st-level character adds +0).

The "key ability modifier" is the character's bonus or penalty for the skill's associated ability (Strength, Dexterity, Constitution, Intelligence, Wisdom, or Charisma). The key ability of a skill is noted in its description and on Table 4–2: Skills.

"Miscellaneous modifiers" include armor check penalties and bonuses provided by talents, feats, or equipment.

Some skills can't be used untrained. These skills are noted on Table 4-4: Skills. If your character is not trained in these particular skills, you are not allowed to make any kind of check with them.

How Do Skills Work?

A character begins play with a number of trained skills based on his or her starting heroic class (Jedi, noble, scoundrel, scout, or soldier) and Intelligence modifier. A character must choose his or her trained skills from a larger list of class skills, as shown in Table 4-1: Trained Skills by Class.

For example, Rorworr (a 1st-level Wookiee scout) gets 5 trained skills for being a scout. Since his Intelligence score is 12, he gets 1 additional trained skill, for a total of 6 trained skills. These skills must be selected from the scout's list of class skills. Rorworr selects Climb, Initiative, Mechanics, Perception, Pilot, and Stealth as his trained skills.

Making Skill Checks

When your character makes a skill check, roll 1d20 and add one-half your character level + your key ability modifier + any miscellaneous modifiers + 5 (if the character is trained in the skill). Success depends on the difficulty of the task at hand.

Example: Rorworr, a 1st-level Wookiee scout with an Intelligence of 12, tries to open the lock on an Imperial detention cell to free an imprisoned Rebel operative. First he attempts a Mechanics check. Rorworr is trained in the skill, so he can attempt the check (Mechanics skill checks cannot be made untrained). He rolls 1d20 and adds one-half his level (+0), his Intelligence modifier (+1), and his trained skill bonus (+5). He gets a 13. Unfortunately, the GM knows that the lock on the cell door as a DC of 15. Having failed his check and pressed for time, Rorworr shoots the lock with his blaster.

Advancing Skills

Since a character's skill modifiers are based on character level, they automatically increase as the character gains levels. When a character reaches 2nd level, all of his skill modifiers—in both trained and untrained skills—increase by 1. A character's skill modifiers can also be increased by other means.

Types of Skill Checks

When you use a skill, you make a skill check to see how well you do. The higher the result on your skill check, the better you do. Based on the circumstances, your result must equal or exceed a particular number (a DC or the result of an opposed skill check) for you to use the skill successfully. The harder the task, the higher the number you need to roll.

Circumstances can affect your check. If you're free to work without distractions, you can make a careful attempt and avoid simple mistakes. If you have lots of time, you can try over and over again, assuring that you eventually succeed. If others help you, you may succeed where otherwise you would fail.

Opposed Check

Some skill checks are opposed checks. They are made against a randomized number, usually another character's skill check result. For example, to sneak up on a guard, you need to beat the guard's Perception check result with your Stealth check result. You make a Stealth check, and the GM makes a Perception check for the guard. Whoever scores the higher result wins the contest.

For ties on opposed checks, the character with the higher skill modifier wins. For instance, if a Stealth check opposed by a Perception check results in a tie, the sneaker's Stealth check modifier would be compared to the noticer's Perception check modifier. If those scores are the same, roll again.

Check Against a Difficulty Class (DC)

Some checks are made against a Difficulty Class (DC). The DC is a number set by the GM (using the skill rules as a guideline) that you must score as a result on your skill check to succeed. For example, climbing the outer wall of a ruined warehouse may have a DC of 15. To climb the wall, you must get a result of 15 or better on a Climb check.

Untrained Checks

Some skills can be used only if you are trained in the skill. If you don't have Use the Force, for example, regardless of your class, ability scores, and experience level, you just don't know enough about using the Force to attempt to manipulate it consciously. Skills that can't be used untrained are marked with a "No" in the "Untrained" column on Table 4-2: Skills.

Trying Again

In general, you can try a skill check again if you fail, and you can keep trying indefinitely. Many skills, however, have natural consequences for failing that must be accounted for. Some skills can't be tried again once a check has failed for a particular task. For most skills, when a character has succeeded at a given task, additional successes are meaningless.

For example, if Deel Surool misses a Mechanics check to open a mechanical lock, he can try again and keep trying. If, however, an alarm sounds when the Mechanics check is missed by 5 or more, then failing has its own penalty.

Similarly, if Rorworr misses a Climb check, he can keep trying, but if he misses by 5 or more, he falls (after which he can get up and try again if the fall wasn't too far or too painful).

Table 4-1: Trained Skills by Class

CLASS	NUMBER OF TRAINED SKILLS	CLASS SKILLS
Jedi	2 + Int modifier	Acrobatics, Endurance, Initiative, Knowledge (all skills, taken individually), Perception, Pilot, Use the Force
Noble	6 + Int modifier	Deception, Gather Information, Initiative, Knowledge (all skills, taken individually), Perception, Persuasion, Pilot, Ride, Treat Injury, Use Computer
Scoundrel	4 + Int modifier	Acrobatics, Deception, Gather Information, Initiative, Knowledge (all skills, taken individually), Mechanics, Perception, Persuasion, Pilot, Stealth, Use Computer
Scout	5 + Int modifier	Climb, Endurance, Initiative, Jump, Knowledge (all skills, taken individually), Mechanics, Perception, Pilot, Ride, Stealth, Survival, Swim
Soldier	3 + Int modifier	Climb, Endurance, Initiative, Jump, Knowledge (tactics), Mechanics, Perception, Pilot, Swim, Treat Injury, Use Computer

If a skill carries no penalty for failure, you can take 20 and assume that you keep trying until you eventually succeed (see Checks without Rolls, page 60).

Rerolling

Some species traits, talents, and other special abilities allow you to reroll a skill check. You must declare that you are using this option immediately after making the check but before any effects are resolved. Furthermore, you must accept the result of the reroll, even if it is worse. For all purposes, the result of the reroll is treated as the real result of your skill check.

Keeping the Better Result: Some species traits, talents, and other special abilities are more flexible, allowing you to reroll but keep the better of the two results. In most cases, this is more restricted and only available a limited number of times per day (such as the Knack talent, page 46) or requires you to spend a Force Point (such as the Force Power Adept talent, page 214). As always, you must declare that you are using this option immediately after making the check but before any effects are resolved.

Multiple Rerolls: Sometimes you have more than one species trait, talent, or other special ability that allows you to reroll the same skill check. In this case, you may choose to take each reroll one at a time in whatever order you wish, resolving each one before deciding whether to use another.

For example, a Cerean scoundrel makes an Initiative check. Dissatisfied with the result, he decides to use the Cerean species trait that allows him to reroll his Initiative check, keeping the new result. Unfortunately, the second roll is even worse, so he decides to use the Knack talent (page 46) to reroll one more time, this time keeping the better of the second and third rolls. Alternatively, he could have opted to use Knack first, keeping the better of the first and second rolls, and then (if necessary) use his Cerean species trait to roll a third time, keeping the third result instead of the better of the first two.

Favorable and Unfavorable Circumstances

Some situations may make a skill easier or harder to use, resulting in a bonus or penalty to the skill modifier for the skill check, or a change to the skill check's DC. It's one thing for Kelko, a Rodian scout, to hunt down enough food to eat while he's camping for the day on the forest moon of Endor, using a Survival check. Foraging for food while crossing 100 kilometers of Tatooine's Jundland Wastes is an entirely different matter.

The GM can alter the odds of success in four ways to take into account exceptional circumstances:

- Give the skill user a +2 circumstance bonus to represent circumstances that improve performance, such as having the perfect tool for the job, getting help from another character (see Combining Skill Attempts, page 61), or possessing unusually accurate information.
- Give the skill user a –2 circumstance penalty to represent circumstances that hamper performance, such as being forced to use improvised tools or possessing misleading information.
- Reduce the DC by 2 (or assign penalties to an opposed check) to represent circumstances that make the task easier, such as having a friendly audience or performing work that doesn't have to be perfect.
- Increase the DC by 2 (or add bonuses to an opposed check) to represent circumstances that make the task harder, such as having a hostile audience or performing work that must be flawless.

Circumstances that affect your ability to perform the skill change your skill modifier. Circumstances that modify how well you have to perform the skill to succeed change the DC. A bonus on your skill modifier and a reduction in the check's DC have the same result—they create a better chance that you will succeed. But they represent different circumstances, and sometimes that difference is important.

For example, Deel Surool the Twi'lek scoundrel wants to befriend a group of Trandoshan thugs drinking in a cantina. Before beginning his performance, Deel listens to the Trandoshans so that he can judge their mood. Doing so improves his chances of taking the right approach when introducing himself, giving him a +2 bonus to the skill modifier for his Persuasion check. The Trandoshans are in a good mood because they recently received a sizable payoff, so the GM reduces the bonus they receive for an indifferent attitude to +0. (Deel's attempt at diplomacy isn't better just because the Trandoshans are in a good mood, so he does not get a bonus to add into his skill modifier.)

However, the leader of the gang, a Human bounty hunter, has been unable to locate the Wookiee he's tracking, and he's suspicious of Deel. (Didn't the datafile suggest the Wookiee was often seen in the company of a Twi'lek?) He gains a +2 bonus to his Will Defense to resist being persuaded (in addition to the normal +2 for being indifferent).

Deel rolls a 6 and adds +8 for his skill modifier (including +2 for his impromptu research). His result is 14. The Trandoshans have a Will Defense of 13, so Deel's skill check result is high enough to shift their attitudes to friendly, but not their leader (Will Defense 16). The Trandoshans applaud Deel Surool and offer to buy him drinks, but their leader eyes him suspiciously.

Time and Skill Checks

A skill's description tells you whether using a skill is a standard action, a move action, a swift action, a full-round action, or a free action. Some skills can take minutes or hours to use.

In general, using a skill that requires concentration (and thus distracts you from being fully aware of what's going on around you) provokes an attack of opportunity from an opponent if you are within that opponent's threatened area when you attempt the skill check. See Attacks of Opportunity, page 155, for more information.

Checks without Rolls

A skill check represents an attempt to accomplish some goal, usually in the face of some sort of time pressure or distraction. Sometimes, though, you can use a skill under more favorable circumstances and eliminate the luck factor.

Taking 10

When you're not in a rush and not being threatened or distracted, you may choose to take 10. Instead of rolling 1d20 for the skill check, calculate your result as if you had rolled a 10 (an average roll on a d20). For many relatively routine tasks, taking 10 results in a success.

Distractions, threats, and danger make it impossible for a character to take 10. You also can't take 10 when using a skill untrained, though the GM may allow exceptions for truly routine activities.

Example: Rorworr the Wookiee has a Climb skill modifier of +10. The steep, rocky slope he's climbing has a DC of 15. With a little care, he can take 10 and succeed automatically. But partway up the slope, a bounty hunter begins taking blaster shots at him from up above. Rorworr needs to make a Climb check to reach the bounty hunter, and this time he can't take 10. He must make the skill check normally while under attack.

Taking 20

When you have plenty of time (generally 2 minutes for a skill that can normally be checked in 1 round), and when the skill being attempted carries no penalty for failure, you can take 20. Taking 20 represents making multiple rolls, assuming that eventually you will roll a 20. Instead of rolling 1d20 for the skill check, calculate the result as if you had rolled a 20. Taking 20 means you keep trying until you get it right. Taking 20 takes twenty times as long as making a single check.

Example: Rorworr comes to a cliff face. He takes 10 to make the climb, for a result of 20 (10 plus his +10 skill modifier). However, the DC is 23, and the GM tells him that he fails to make progress up the cliff. (His check result is at least high enough that he doesn't fall.) Rorworr can't take 20 because there is a penalty associated with failure (falling, in this case).

Later, Rorworr finds a small bunker in the cliffside and searches it. The GM notes in the Perception skill description that each 1-square area takes a full-round action to search (and she secretly assigns a DC of 15 to the attempt). She estimates that the floors, walls, and ceiling of the bunker make up about twenty squares (about 45 square meters), so she tells Rorworr's player that it takes 2 minutes to search the whole bunker. Rorworr rolls 1d20 and adds his +5 skill modifier. The result of 11 fails. Now Rorworr declares that he is going to search the bunker high and low, for as long as it takes. The GM takes the original time of 2 minutes and multiplies it by 20, for 40 minutes. That's how long it takes Rorworr to search the whole bunker in exacting detail. Now Rorworr's player treats his roll as if it were 20, for a result of 25. That's more than enough to beat the DC of 15, and Rorworr finds a datapad discarded in a waste disposal unit.

Combining Skill Attempts

When more than one character tries the same skill at the same time and for the same purpose, their efforts may overlap.

Individual Events

Often, several characters attempt some action, and each succeeds or fails on his or her own.

For example, Rorworr and each of his companions need to climb a slope to get to the top. Regardless of Rorworr's result, the other characters need successful checks, too. Every character makes a skill check.

Cooperation

Sometimes the individual heroes react to the same circumstance, and they can work together to help each other out. In this case, one hero is considered the leader of the effort and makes a skill check while each helper makes a skill check against DC 10. (You can't take 10 on this check.) For each helper who succeeds, the leader gets a +2 circumstance bonus (as per the rule for favorable circumstances). In many cases, a character's help won't be beneficial, or only a limited number of characters can help at the same time. The GM limits cooperation as she sees fit for the circumstances.

For instance, if Kelko has been badly wounded, Vor'en Kurn can try a Treat Injury check to keep him from dying. One other character can help Vor'en. If the other hero makes a Treat Injury check against DC 10, then Vor'en gets a +2 bonus on the Treat Injury check he makes to help Kelko. The GM rules that two characters can't help Vor'en at the same time because a third person would just get in the way.

Cooperation may not require all the characters to make the same skill check. If Kelko and Deel Surool try to find information about an illegal business on a Hutt's datapad, only one can make a Use Computer check. While Kelko is actually checking the datapad, Deel Surool realizes his Knowledge (business) may be able to give hints on what to look for. Surool can make a DC 10 Knowledge (business) check to give Kelko a +2 bonus to his Use Computer check.

Ability Checks

Sometimes you try to do something to which no specific skill applies. In these cases, you make an ability check: Roll 1d20 and apply the appropriate ability modifier. The GM assigns a DC, or sets up an opposed check when two characters are engaged in a contest using one ability against another. The character who rolls highest acts first.

In some cases, a test of one's ability doesn't involve luck. Just as you wouldn't make a height check to see who is taller, you don't make a Strength check to see who is stronger. When two characters arm wrestle, for example, the stronger character simply wins. In the case of identical scores, then make opposed Strength checks.

EXAMPLE ABILITY CHECK	KEY ABILITY
Forcing open a jammed or locked door	Strength
Tying a rope	Dexterity
Holding one's breath	Constitution
Navigating a maze	Intelligence
Remembering to lock a door	Wisdom
Getting yourself noticed in a crowd	Charisma

Skill Descriptions

This section describes each skill, including common uses and typical modifiers. Characters can sometimes use skills for other purposes than those listed here. For example, you might be able to impress the members of a starfighter squadron by making a Pilot check.

Here is the format for skill descriptions. Headings that do not apply to a particular skill are omitted in that skill's description.

Skill Name (Key Ability)

Trained Only; Armor Check Penalty

The skill name line and the line beneath it include the following information.

Key Ability: The abbreviation for the ability whose modifier applies to the skill check.

Trained Only: If "Trained Only" appears on the line beneath the skill name, you must be trained in that skill to use it. If "Trained Only" is omitted, the skill can be used untrained except for some uses. If any special notes apply to trained or untrained use, they are covered in the Special section.

Armor Check Penalty: If "Armor Check Penalty" appears on the line beneath the skill name, a character takes a penalty on skill checks made with this skill if he's wearing armor with which he is not proficient. The size of the armor check penalty depends on the type of armor: light, –2; medium, –5; or heavy, –10. For example, Rorworr the Wookiee scout is proficient with light armor only. If he attempts to swim in medium armor, he takes a –5 armor check penalty on his Swim check.

Retry: Any circumstances that apply to successive attempts to use the skill successfully. If this paragraph is omitted, the skill check can be tried again without any inherent penalty other than consuming additional time.

Special: Any special notes that apply, such as rules regarding untrained use and whether or not you can take 10 or take 20 when using the skill.

Time: How much time it takes to make a check with this skill, if that information hasn't already been covered elsewhere.

Table 4-2: Skills

SKILL (KEY ABILITY)	USE UNTRAINED?	ARMOR CHECK PENALTY?	JEDI	NOBLE	SCOUNDREL	SCOUT	SOLDIER
Acrobatics (Dex)	Yes[1]	Yes	C	—	C	—	—
Climb (Str)	Yes	Yes	—	—	—	C	C
Deception (Cha)	Yes	No	—	C	C	—	—
Endurance (Con)	Yes	Yes	C	—	—	C	C
Gather Information (Cha)	Yes	No	—	C	C	—	—
Initiative (Dex)	Yes	Yes	C	C	C	C	C
Jump (Str)	Yes	Yes	—	—	—	C	C
Knowledge (Int)	Yes[1]	No	C	C	C	C	C[2]
Mechanics (Int)	No	No	—	—	C	C	C
Perception (Wis)	Yes[1]	No	C	C	C	C	C
Persuasion (Cha)	Yes	No	—	C	C	—	—
Pilot (Dex)	Yes[1]	No	C	C	C	C	C
Ride (Dex)	Yes	Yes	—	C	—	C	—
Stealth (Dex)	Yes	Yes	—	—	C	C	—
Survival (Wis)	Yes[1]	No	—	—	—	C	—
Swim (Str)	Yes	Yes	—	—	—	C	C
Treat Injury (Wis)	Yes[1]	No	—	C	—	—	C
Use Computer (Int)	Yes[1]	No	—	C	C	—	C
Use the Force (Cha)[3]	Yes[1]	No	C	—	—	—	—

C *Class skill*

1 *Some uses of the skill require that you be trained in the skill.*

2 *Knowledge (tactics) only.*

3 *Any character with the Force Sensitivity feat treats Use the Force as a class skill.*

Acrobatics (Dex)
Armor Check Penalty

You can move at normal speed across difficult terrain, keep your balance while walking on a narrow surface, take less damage from a fall, slip free of restraints or a grappling foe, and get up from prone safely. In addition to the specific options listed below, you can use Acrobatics to perform typical tumbling, flipping, or gymnastic maneuvers.

Balance: A successful Acrobatics check allows you to move at half speed along a narrow surface such as a ledge or wire. The DC of the Acrobatics check varies with the width of the surface (see below). If the surface is slippery or unstable, increase the DC by 5. A failed check means you fall prone and must make a DC 15 Reflex save to catch the ledge or wire.

NARROW SURFACE	ACROBATICS DC
8–15 cm wide	10
4–7 cm wide	15
Less than 4 cm wide	20

You are considered flat-footed while balancing, and thus you lose your Dexterity bonus to your Reflex Defense (if any). If you are trained in Acrobatics, you aren't considered flat-footed while balancing.

If you take damage while balancing, you must immediately make another Acrobatics check against the same DC to keep from falling.

Cross Difficult Terrain (Trained Only): With a successful DC 15 Acrobatics check, you can move through difficult terrain at your normal speed.

Escape Bonds: With a successful Acrobatics check, you can slip free of restraints (DC varies; see table below), wriggle through a tight space (DC 20), or escape from a grapple (DC = the grappler's grapple check). The DC to slip free of a restraint depends on the type of restraint (see table).

It takes an attack action to escape a grapple. It takes a full-round action to escape a net or to move 1 square through a tight space. It takes 1 minute to escape from ropes, binder cuffs, or manacles.

RESTRAINT	ACROBATICS DC
Ropes	Opponent's Dex check + 10
Net	15
Binder cuffs	25

Fall Prone (Trained Only): If you are trained in Acrobatics and succeed at a DC 15 check, you can drop to a prone position as a free action (instead of a swift action).

Reduce Falling Damage (Trained Only): With a successful DC 15 Acrobatics check, you can treat a fall as if it was 3 meters (2 squares) shorter when determining damage. For every 10 points by which you beat this DC, you can subtract an additional 3 meters from the fall for determining damage. If you make this check and take no damage from the fall, you land on your feet.

If you are struck by a falling object, you can reduce the damage you take by half with a successful DC 15 Acrobatics check (see Falling Objects, page 254).

Stand Up from Prone (Trained Only): If you are trained in Acrobatics and succeed at a DC 15 check, you can stand up from a prone position as a swift action (instead of a move action).

Tumble (Trained Only): If you succeed at a DC 15 Acrobatics check, you can tumble through the threatened area or fighting space of an enemy as part of your move action without provoking an attack of opportunity. Each threatened square or occupied square that you tumble through counts as 2 squares of movement.

Special: You can't take 10 or take 20 on an Acrobatics check.

If you are trained in Acrobatics, you gain a +2 dodge bonus to your Reflex Defense when fighting defensively (see Fighting Defensively, page 152).

Climb (Str)
Armor Check Penalty

Use this skill to scale a cliff, to get to a window on the second story of a building, or to climb up an antenna array after falling out of an airway at the bottom of a floating city.

Climb Surface: With each successful Climb check, you can advance up, down, or across a slope or a wall or other steep incline (or even a ceiling with handholds). A slope is considered to be any incline of less than 60 degrees; a wall is any incline of 60 degrees or steeper. You can climb at one-half of your speed as a full-round action. You can move half that far—one-fourth of your speed—as a move action.

A failed Climb check indicates that you make no progress, and a check that fails by 5 or more means that you fall from whatever height you have already attained.

The DC of the check depends on the circumstances of the climb:

DC	EXAMPLE WALL OR SURFACE
0	Slope too steep to walk up; knotted rope with a wall to brace against.
5	Rope with a wall to brace against or a knotted rope, but not both.
10	Surface with ledges to hold on to and stand on, such as a very rough wall.
15	Surface with adequate handholds and footholds (natural or artificial), such as a very rough natural rock surface or a tree; an unknotted rope.
20	Uneven surface with some narrow handholds and footholds.
25	Rough surface, such as a natural rock wall or a brick wall.
25	Overhang or ceiling with handholds but no footholds.
—	Perfectly smooth, flat, vertical surface cannot be climbed.
-10*	Climbing inside an air duct or other location where one can brace against two opposite walls (reduces normal DC by 10).
-5*	Climbing a corner where you can brace against perpendicular walls (reduces normal DC by 5).
+5*	Surface is slippery (increases normal DC by 5).

These modifiers are cumulative; use any that apply.

Since you can't move to avoid an attack while climbing, opponents get a +2 bonus on attack rolls against you, and you lose any Dexterity bonus to your Reflex Defense.

Any time you take damage while climbing, make a Climb check against the DC of the slope or wall. Failure means you fall from your current height and sustain the appropriate falling damage (see Falling Damage, page 255).

Accelerated Climbing: You try to climb more quickly than normal, but you take a -5 penalty on Climb checks. Accelerated climbing allows you to climb at your full speed as a full-round action. You can move half that far—one-half of your speed—as a move action.

Catching Yourself When Falling: It's practically impossible to catch yourself on a wall while falling. Make a Climb check (DC = the wall's DC + 20) to do so. A slope is relatively easier to catch yourself on (DC = the slope's DC + 10).

Making Handholds and Footholds: You can make your own handholds and footholds by pounding pitons into a wall. Doing so takes 1 minute per piton, and one piton is needed per meter. As with any surface with handholds and footholds, a wall with pitons in it has a DC of 15. In the same way, a climber with an ice axe or similar implement can cut handholds or footholds in an ice wall.

Special: Someone using a rope can haul a character upward (or lower the character) by means of sheer strength. Use the encumbrance rules (see page 140) to determine how much weight a character can lift.

You can take 10 while climbing, but you can't take 20.

DECEPTION (CHA)

You can make the untrue seem true, the outrageous seem plausible, and the nefarious seem ordinary. The skill encompasses conning, fast-talking, misdirection, forgery, disguise, and outright lying. Use a Deception check to sow temporary confusion, pass as someone you're not, get someone to turn his head in the direction you point, or pass faked documents off as genuine.

Deceive: When you want to make another character believe something that is untrue, you can attempt to deceive them. You can deceive a target in one of two ways: by producing a deceptive appearance or by communicating deceptive information.

Deceptive Appearance: When you produce a deceptive appearance, such as disguising your appearance or producing forged documents, make a Deception check opposed by the Perception check of any target that sees the deception. If you succeed, that character believes that the appearance is authentic. If you fail, the target detects the deception. Creating a deceptive appearance requires at least 1 minute (10 rounds) for simple deceptions, 10 minutes for moderate deceptions, 1 hour for difficult deceptions, 1 day for incredible deceptions, or 2 weeks (10 days) for outrageous deceptions. You can rush and create the deception in less time (treating it as if it were one step easier, to a minimum of simple), but you take a -10 penalty on your Deception check. In all cases, make a single Deception check at the time you create the deceptive appearance and compare your check result to the Perception check of any character who encounters it.

Deceptive Information: When you communicate deceptive information, such as telling a lie or distorting facts to lead the target to a false conclusion, make a Deception check against the Will Defense of any target that can understand you. If you succeed, the target believes that what you're telling them is true. While most cases of deceptive information are either verbal or written (requiring the target to be able to understand you), you can deceive with gestures, body language, facial expressions, and so forth. Communicating deceptive information requires at least a standard action for simple deceptions, a full-round action for moderate deceptions, and 1 minute (10 rounds) or even more for difficult, incredible, or outrageous deceptions. You can rush and communicate your deception in less time (treating

Table 4-3: Deceptions

DECEPTION	CHECK MODIFIER	DESCRIPTION
Simple	+5	A simple deception works in the target's favor or matches the target's expectations, and it requires nothing you don't have on hand. Simple deceptions include convincing a junk dealer to buy some stolen droids; disguising yourself as someone nonspecific of similar size, species, and gender; and creating a false ID that will pass casual inspection but not careful scrutiny.
Moderate	+0	A moderate deception is believable and doesn't affect the target much one way or the other, and you have most of the props you need. Moderate deceptions include convincing a suspicious guard that you're not a thief; disguising yourself as a member of another species or gender; and creating a false ID good enough to pass visual scrutiny but not electronic screening.
Difficult	–5	A difficult deception is a little hard to believe, puts the target at some kind of risk, or undergoes scrutiny. Examples include convincing a group of thugs that you're willing and able to beat them in a cantina fight, forging starship transponder codes, impersonating an officer well enough to give troops orders, and creating false official documents good enough to pass electronic screening.
Incredible	–10	An incredible deception is hard to believe, presents a sizable risk to the target, or requires passing intense scrutiny. Incredible deceptions include convincing a reputable starship dealer to buy a stolen Imperial shuttle, impersonating someone well enough to convince an old friend, and forging false credits.
Outrageous	–20	An unlikely deception is almost too unlikely to consider or requires material you just don't have. Outrageous deceptions include impersonating a Jedi (without any Force sensitivity) well enough to fool another Jedi, claiming to be the Emperor in disguise and giving orders to stormtroopers, and forging important documents with no proper tools or examples to work with.

> "UH, HAD A SLIGHT WEAPONS MALFUNCTION BUT, UH . . . EVERYTHING'S PERFECTLY ALL RIGHT NOW. WE'RE FINE. WE'RE ALL FINE HERE NOW. THANK YOU. HOW ARE YOU?"
>
> – HAN SOLO

as if it were one step easier, to a minimum of simple), but you take a –10 penalty on your Deception check. If your deceptive information is written, recorded, or otherwise preserved for later viewing, your original Deception check result is compared to the Will Defense of all targets who later read or observe your deception.

In some cases, you convey both a deceptive appearance and deceptive information. For example, if you create a falsified document (such as an official report, a letter from a senator, or orders from a military commander), you have to produce something that looks authentic (deceptive appearance) while also creating believable content (deceptive information). In this case, make a single Deception check and compare it to both the target's Perception check and Will Defense. Similarly, you might disguise yourself as an Imperial general (deceptive appearance) and then give fake orders to a stormtrooper (deceptive information). In this example, you make one Deception check ahead of time to create the disguise and another Deception check at the time you give the stormtrooper his new orders.

Favorable and unfavorable circumstances weigh heavily on the outcome of a deception. Two circumstances can weigh against you: The deception is hard to believe, or the action that the deception requires the target to take goes against the target's self-interest, nature, personality, or orders.

If it's important, the GM can distinguish between a deception that fails because the target doesn't believe it and one that fails because it just asks too much of the target. For instance, if the deception demands something risky of the target, and your Deception check fails by 10 or less, then the target didn't so much see through the deception as prove reluctant to go along with it even if he believes it's true. If your Deception check fails by 11 or more, he has seen through the deception (and would have done so even if it had not placed any demand on him).

A successful Deception check indicates that the target reacts as you wish, at least for a short time, or the target believes something that you want him to believe. For example, you could use a deception to put someone off guard by telling him someone was behind him. At best, such a deception would make the target glance over his shoulder. It would not cause the target to ignore you and completely turn around. Alternatively, you could use a deception to make a starship captain believe that he has orders to take his vessel to Tatooine. If successful, the captain would carry out his new "orders" even though that would take quite some time, but as soon as he encounters contradictory information (such receiving contradictory orders from his real commander, or arriving at Tatooine and discovering that no one sent for him) he will realize that he has been fooled.

Creating a Diversion to Hide: You can use Deception to help you hide. A successful Deception check that equals or exceeds the target's Will Defense gives you the momentary diversion you need to attempt a Stealth check while the target is aware of you (see the Stealth skill, page 72).

Feint: Make a Deception check as a standard action to set the DC of your opponent's Initiative check. If you beat your opponent's roll, that target is treated as flat-footed against the first attack you make against him in the next round. You take a –5 penalty against non-humanoid creatures or against creatures with an Intelligence lower than 3.

Retry: Generally, a failed Deception check makes the target too suspicious for you to try another deception in the same circumstances. For feinting in combat, you may retry freely.

Special: You can take 10 when making a deception (except for feinting in combat), but you can't take 20.

Time: A deception takes at least a standard action, but can take much longer if you try something elaborate. Disguises that require major changes to your physical outline, or forged documents with many safeguards, can take hours or even days.

Endurance (Con)
Armor Check Penalty
You can push yourself beyond your normal physical limits.

Force March: Each hour of walking after 8 hours requires you to attempt a DC 10 Endurance check (+2 per hour after the first). If you fail, you move –1 persistent step along the condition track (see Conditions, page 148). You can only remove this persistent condition by resting for 8 hours.

Hold Breath: You can hold your breath for a number of rounds equal to your Constitution score. After this period of time, you must succeed on a DC 10 Endurance check in order to continue holding your breath. The DC increases by +2 per additional round. If you fail, you must breathe or you move –1 step on the condition track (see page 149). If you reach the bottom of the condition track, you fall unconscious. If you are still unable to breathe on your next turn after falling unconscious, you die.

Ignore Hunger: You can go without food for a number of days equal to your Constitution modifier (minimum 1 day). After this time, you must succeed on an Endurance check each day or move –1 persistent step along the condition track (see page 149). You can only remove this persistent condition by eating a nutritious meal. The DC is 10 on the first day and increases by +2 each day thereafter.

Ignore Thirst: You can go without water for a number of hours equal to three times your Constitution score. After this time, you must succeed on an Endurance check each hour or move –1 persistent step along the condition track (see page 149). You may only remove this persistent condition by drinking at least 1 liter of water; for creatures that are not Medium size, multiply the water required by 10 for every size category above Medium or divide it by 10 for every size category below Medium. The DC is 10 on the first day and increases by +2 each day thereafter.

Run: You can run as a full-round action. When you run, you can move up to four times your speed in a straight line (or three times your speed in a straight line if you are wearing heavy armor or carrying a heavy load). You lose any Dexterity bonus to your Reflex Defense while you're running, since you can't actively avoid attacks.

You can run for a number of rounds equal to your Constitution score without any trouble. If you want to continue running after that, you must succeed on a DC 10 Endurance check. You must check again each round in which you continue to run, and the DC of the Endurance check increases by 1 for each previous check you made. When you fail a check, you move –1 persistent step on the condition track (see Conditions, page 148). You can only remove this persistent condition by resting for the same length of time that you were running. During this rest period, you can only move your speed.

Sleep in Armor: You can sleep while wearing armor by succeeding at an Endurance check (DC 10 for light armor, DC 15 for medium armor, and DC 20 for heavy armor). If you fail, you don't sleep and move –1 persistent step along the condition track (see page 149). You can only remove this persistent condition by sleeping for 8 hours.

Swim/Tread Water: Each hour that you swim, you must succeed on a DC 15 Endurance check or move –1 persistent step along the condition track (see page 149). You can only remove this persistent condition by resting (not swimming or treading water) for the same length of time that you were swimming. Each consecutive hour of swimming increases the DC by +2. If you are only treading water, reduce the DC by 5.

Gather Information (Cha)

Use this skill to make contacts, learn local new stories and gossip, and acquire secrets.

Learn News and Rumors: Major news stories and popular local rumors can be unearthed with a DC 10 Gather Information check. Learning the detailed, unclassified facts of a news story or determining the veracity of a rumor requires a DC 20 check and 50 credits in bribes.

Learn Secret Information: "Secret information" includes anything unavailable to the general public. Examples include a classified police report, a hidden location, military blueprints, installation security procedures, and computer access codes. Learning a piece of secret information typically requires a DC 25 check and 5,000 credits in bribes; however, information that's especially difficult to obtain (such as the technical blueprints of the Death Star) might require a DC 30 or higher skill check and cost 50,000 credits or more, at the GM's discretion. If the check fails by 5 or more, someone notices that you're asking questions and comes to investigate, arrest, or silence you.

Locate Individual: Make a Gather Information check to locate a specific individual—either someone you know by name or someone with the skill, item, or information you need. The DC of the check is 15 if the target is relatively easy to locate; if the target isn't well known or has taken strides to conceal

his or her presence and/or activities, the DC is 25 and the information costs 500 credits in bribes.

Special: You can take 10 on a Gather Information check, but you can't take 20. A successful Persuasion check can reduce the monetary cost of a Gather Information check (see the Persuasion skill, page 71).

Some information is beyond the reach of a Gather Information skill check. For example, characters searching for Darth Vader won't find him by speaking with tribes of Ewoks on the Forest Moon of Endor, no matter how many Ewoks they question.

Time: Each Gather Information check represents 1d6 hours of time spent talking to informants, scanning HoloNet news broadcasts, or perusing information kiosks.

INITIATIVE (DEX)
Armor Check Penalty

Use this skill to gain the advantage in combat.

Start Battle: An Initiative check sets the order of combat when a fight starts. Each character aware of the fight makes an Initiative check and goes in order from highest to lowest.

When piloting a vehicle in combat, you must apply the vehicle's size modifier to your Initiative check (see Table 10–1: Vehicle Sizes, page 166).

Avoid Feint: When an opponent attempts to feint in combat, you oppose his Deception check with an Initiative check. If you meet or beat his check result, his feint attempt fails.

Special: You can take 10 on an Initiative check, but you can't take 20.

JUMP (STR)
Armor Check Penalty

Use this skill to leap over pits, vault low fences, or jump down from a tree's lowest branches.

Long Jump: The DC of a running long jump is equal to the distance cleared (in meters) multiplied by 3. For example, clearing a 3-meter-wide (2-square-wide) pit requires a successful DC 9 Jump check. If you do not get at least a 4-square running start, the DC is doubled.

High Jump: The DC of a running high jump is equal to the distance cleared (in meters) multiplied by 12. For example, landing atop a 1.5-meter-high (1-square-high) ledge requires a successful DC 18 Jump check. If you use a pole of sufficient height to help you vault the distance, the DC is halved. If you do not get at least a 4-square running start, the DC is doubled.

Jump Down: If you intentionally jump down from a height, you can attempt a DC 15 Jump check to take falling damage as if you had dropped 3 meters (2 squares) fewer than you actually did. If you succeed on this check and take no damage, you land on your feet.

Special: You can take 10 when making a Jump check. If there is no danger associated with failing, you can take 20. Distance covered by a long jump or high jump counts against your maximum movement in a round; distance covered by jumping down does not.

KNOWLEDGE (INT)

Knowledge encompasses a number of unrelated skills. Knowledge represents a study of some body of lore, possibly an academic or even scientific discipline.

Each time you select Knowledge as a trained skill, you must choose a field of study from the list below:

Bureaucracy: Business procedures, legal systems and regulations, and organizational structures

Galactic lore: Planets, homeworlds, sectors of space, galactic history, and the Force

Life sciences: Biology, botany, genetics, archaeology, xenobiology, medicine, and forensics

Physical sciences: Astronomy, astrogation, chemistry, mathematics, physics, and engineering

Social sciences: Sociology, psychology, philosophy, theology, and criminology

Tactics: Techniques and strategies for disposing and maneuvering forces in combat

Technology: Function and principle of technological devices, as well as knowledge of cutting edge theories and advancements.

Common Knowledge: You can answer a basic question about a subject related to your field of study with a DC 10 check. For example, a DC 10 Knowledge (life sciences) check is enough to know that Rodians are skilled hunters.

Expert Knowledge (Trained Only): You can make a Knowledge check as a swift action to answer a question within your field of study that requires some level of expertise. The DC of the check ranges from 15 (for simple questions) to 25 (for tough questions). The GM may adjust the DC depending on the character's personal experience. For example, a DC 20 Knowledge (galactic lore) check might reveal specific information about the inhabitants of the planet Dathomir, but the DC may be lower if the character making the check has actually been there.

Retry: No, you can't reroll a failed Knowledge check. The roll represents what you know, and thinking about a topic a second time doesn't let you know something you never learned in the first place.

Special: You can take 10 when making a Knowledge check, but you can't take 20.

MECHANICS (INT)
Trained Only

You can bypass locks and traps, set and disarm explosives, fix malfunctioning devices, and modify and repair damaged droids.

Disable Device (requires security kit): You can use this skill to disarm a security device, defeat a lock or trap, or rig a device to fail when it is used.

The effort takes a full-round action, and the DC depends on the intricacy or complexity of the item being disabled or sabotaged, as shown below:

DEVICE	DC*	EXAMPLES
Simple	15	Sabotage a mechanical device, jam a blaster, bypass a basic mechanical lock
Tricky	20	Sabotage an electronic device, bypass a basic electronic lock
Complex	25	Disarm an electronic security system, bypass a complex mechanical or electronic lock

* If you attempt to leave behind no trace of the tampering, increase the DC by 5.

If the Mechanics check fails by 5 or more, something goes wrong. If it's a trap, you spring it. If it's some sort of sabotage, you think the device is disabled, but it still works normally.

> "FOR A MECHANIC, YOU SEEM TO DO AN EXCESSIVE AMOUNT OF THINKING."
> – C-3PO

Handle Explosives: Setting a simple explosive to blow up at a certain spot doesn't require a check, but connecting and setting a detonator does. Also, placing an explosive for maximum effect against a structure calls for a check, as does disarming an explosive device.

Setting a detonator, placing an explosive device, or disarming an explosive device is a full-round action.

Set Detonator: Most explosives require a detonator to go off. Connecting a detonator to an explosive requires a DC 10 check. Failure means that the explosive fails to go off as planned. Failure by 10 or more means the explosive goes off as the detonator is being installed.

You can make an explosive difficult to disarm. To do so, you choose the disarm DC before making your check to set the detonator (it must be higher than 10). Your DC to set the detonator is equal to the disarm DC – 5. For example, you might decide to make the disarm DC 20. The DC to set the detonator and disarm the explosive becomes 15 (instead of the normal 10).

Place Explosive Device: Carefully placing an explosive against a fixed structure or vehicle (a stationary, unattended inanimate object) increases the damage dealt by exploiting weaknesses in its construction. The GM makes the check (so that you don't know exactly how well you've done). One a result of 15 or higher, you ignore the damage reduction of any object to which the explosives are attached. On a result of 25 or higher, the explosive deals double damage to the structure or vehicle against which it's placed. On a result of 35 or higher, it deals triple damage. In all cases, it deals normal damage to all other targets within its burst radius.

Disarm Explosive Device (requires a security kit): Disarming an explosive that has been set to go off requires a check. The DC is usually 15, unless the one who set the detonator chose a higher disarm DC (see Set Detonator above). If you fail the check, you do not disarm the explosive. If you fail it by 5 or more, the explosive detonates while you are adjacent to it.

Jury-Rig: You can make temporary repairs to any disabled mechanical or electronic device, from a simple tool to a complex starship component. Jury-rigging is a full-round action and requires a successful DC 25 check. If you use a tool kit, you gain a +5 equipment bonus on the check. A jury-rigged device gains +2 steps on the condition track. At the end of the scene or encounter, the jury-rigged device moves –5 steps along the track and becomes disabled again. (See Conditions, page 148.)

Modify Droid (requires tool kit): You can make a Mechanics check to modify a droid (see Modifying Droids, page 197).

Recharge Shields: When acting as the shield operator on a vehicle or operating a device with a shield rating, you can spend three swift actions on the same turn or on consecutive turns to make a DC 20 Mechanics check to recharge the vehicle's shields. If successful, you restore 5 points to its shield rating, up to its normal maximum.

Regulate Power: When acting as the engineer on a vehicle or operating a device, you can spend three swift actions to make a DC 20 Mechanics check to regulate its power. If you are successful, the vehicle moves +1 step on the condition track (see Conditions, page 148).

Repair (requires tool kit): You can repair a damaged or disabled droid or object (including devices and vehicles). This requires at least 1 hour of work, at the end of which time you must make a Mechanics check. Only one character may repair a given droid or object at a time, but other characters may use the aid another action to assist (see page 151).

Repair Droid (requires a tool kit): You can spend 1 hour and make a DC 20 Mechanics check to repair a damaged or disabled droid, restoring hit points equal to the droid's character level and removing any persistent conditions currently affecting the droid. A droid can attempt to repair itself, but it takes a –5 penalty on its skill check.

Repair Object: You can spend 1 hour and make a DC 20 Mechanics check to repair a damaged or disabled object, restoring 1d8 hit points and removing any persistent conditions currently affecting the device or vehicle. If you are on board a damaged vehicle while you attempt to repair it, apply any penalties from the vehicle's position on the condition track on your Mechanics check. (Major vehicle repairs are best attempted in a garage, hangar, dry dock, or other specialized facility.)

Retry: You can usually retry a Mechanics check. In some specific cases, however, a failed Mechanics check has negative ramifications that prevent repeated checks (see Disable Device, above, for example).

Special: You can take 10 or take 20 on a Mechanics check. When making a Mechanics check to accomplish a jury-rig repair, you can't take 20.

PERCEPTION (WIS)

Use this skill to perceive threats as well as your surroundings.

The distance between you and whatever you're trying to perceive affects your Perception check, as do solid barriers and concealment.

Avoid Surprise: A Perception check made at the start of a battle determines whether or not you are surprised (see Surprise, page 149). A Perception check made to avoid surprise is a reaction.

Eavesdrop: A DC 10 Perception check allows you to eavesdrop on a conversation. You must be able to understand the language being spoken. The DC increases to 15 in relatively noisy areas (such as a cantina) or 25 in particularly loud areas (such as a droid factory). Eavesdropping on a conversation is a standard action.

Hear Distant or Ambient Noises: A DC 10 Perception check allows you to detect and identify distant or ambient noises. Actively listening for distant or ambient noises is a standard action.

Notice Targets: A Perception check lets you hear or spot other targets or detect someone or something sneaking up on you from behind. If the target is actively attempting to remain undetected, your Perception check is opposed by the target's Stealth check. If the target is not making any special effort to avoid detection, the Perception check DC is determined by the target's size: Colossal, DC –15; Gargantuan, DC –10; Huge, DC –5; Large, DC 0; Medium, DC 5; Small, DC 10; Tiny, DC 15; Diminutive, DC 20; Fine, DC 25.

For every 10 squares of distance between you and the target, you take a –5 penalty on your Perception check. You also take a –5 penalty if the target has concealment or cover, or a –10 penalty if it has total concealment or total cover.

Detecting a target that enters your line of sight is a reaction. Actively looking or listening for hidden enemies (including those to whom you do not have a line of sight) is a standard action.

You can also notice if a character has a concealed weapons or objects. Make a Perception check opposed by the target's Stealth check result. If you win the opposed check, you notice the concealed object. If you win the opposed check by 5 or more, you can tell what kind of object is concealed (for example, distinguishing a blaster from a datapad).

Search: You can carefully examine a 1-square area or a 1-cubic-meter volume of goods as a full-round action. A DC 15 Perception check allows you to find clues, hidden compartments, secret doors, traps, irregularities, and other details not readily apparent within that area. The GM may increase the DC for especially obscure well-hidden features.

You can also search a character for concealed weapons or objects. Make a Perception check opposed by the target's Stealth check result. If you win the opposed check, you find the concealed object. You receive a +10 circumstance bonus on your Perception check if you physically touch the target to search for concealed items; this requires a full-round action and can only be used on a willing, pinned, or helpless target.

Sense Deception: You can use Perception to see through deceptive appearances made using the Deception skill. If your Perception check meets or exceeds the result of the Deception check, you realize that you're being deceived. Your Perception check to sense the deception is a reaction.

Table 4-4: Attitude Steps

ATTITUDE	THE CREATURE...
Hostile	Takes risks to harm you, usually attacking on sight
Unfriendly	Wishes you ill but won't go out of its way to harm you
Indifferent	Regard you as neither a threat nor an ally and probably doesn't attack you
Friendly	Wishes you well but won't take life-threatening risks on your behalf
Helpful	Take risks to help you

Sense Influence: Make a Perception check to determine whether someone is under the influence of a mind-affecting Force power or other method of coercion (assuming the effect isn't obvious). This requires a full-round action and a successful DC 20 check.

Retry: You can make a Perception check every time you have the opportunity to notice something as a reaction. As a swift action, you may attempt to see or hear something that you failed (or believe you failed) to notice previously.

Special: You can take 10 or take 20 when making a Perception check. Taking 20 means you spend 2 minutes attempting to notice something that may or may not be there.

Persuasion (Cha)

You can influence others with your tact, subtlety, and social grace, or you can threaten them into being more cooperative.

Change Attitude: As a full-round action, you can make a Persuasion check to adjust the attitude of a creature with an Intelligence of 2 or higher using words, body language, or a combination of the two. The target must be able to see you. Apply a modifier to the check based on the target's current attitude toward you: hostile –10, unfriendly –5, indifferent –2, friendly +0 (see Table 4-4: Attitude Steps). If the check equals or exceeds the target's Will Defense, the target's attitude shifts one step in your favor. If the target creature cannot understand your speech, apply a –5 penalty on your Persuasion check. You may attempt to change the attitude of a given creature only once per encounter.

Haggle: Whenever you use the Gather Information skill, you can make a Persuasion check as a swift action to reduce by half the amount you must pay to acquire the information you desire. Conversely, you can use this skill as a full-round action to increase or reduce the sell price of a desired item by 50%. The DC depends on the attitude of the individual (or individuals) with whom you're dealing: unfriendly DC 30, indifferent DC 25, friendly DC 20, helpful DC 15. You can't haggle with creatures that are hostile toward you or creatures that have an Intelligence of 2 or lower. No matter how adept you are at haggling, a creature won't pay more for an item that can easily be obtained elsewhere for the standard listed price.

Intimidate: As a full-round action, you can make a Persuasion check to force a single creature with an Intelligence of 1 or higher to back down from a confrontation, surrender one of its possessions, reveal a piece of secret information, or flee from you for a short time. The creature must be able to see you. Your check result must equal or exceed the target's Will Defense for the intimidation attempt to succeed. Apply a modifier to the check based on the threat the target perceives from you:

SITUATION	MODIFIER
Target is helpless or completely at your mercy	+5
Target is clearly outnumbered or disadvantaged	+0
Target is evenly matched with you	–5
You are clearly outnumbered or disadvantaged	–10
You are helpless or completely at the target's mercy	–15

You can't force the target to obey your every command or do something that endangers its life or the lives of its allies. A creature you successfully intimidate becomes one step more hostile toward you as soon as you are no longer an imminent threat (see Table 4-4: Attitude Steps).

Retry: If you fail a Persuasion check, you cannot make any further Persuasion checks against the targeted creature for 24 hours.

Special: You can take 10 on a Persuasion check, but you can't take 20.

Pilot (Dex)

Use this skill to operate a vehicle. Basic operation of a vehicle does not require a skill check or special training, but performing evasive maneuvers and difficult stunts does.

Whenever you make a Pilot check, you must apply the vehicle's size modifier to your check (see Table 10-1: Vehicle Sizes, page 166).

Avoid Collision: You can make a DC 15 Pilot check as a reaction to reduce or negate the damage from a collision (see Avoid Collision, page 173).

Dogfight: When operating a flying vehicle, you can make a Pilot check as a standard action to engage in a dogfight (see Dogfight, page 171).

Engage the Enemy (Trained Only): When piloting a vehicle in combat, you can choose to make a Pilot check instead of an Initiative check to determine your place in the initiative order.

Increase Vehicle Speed (Trained Only): You may make a DC 20 Pilot check as a swift action to make your vehicle perform beyond its normal limits. (You can't take 10 on this check.) If the check fails, your vehicle's speed does not increase, and your vehicle moves −1 step on the condition track (see Conditions, page 148). If you succeed, your vehicle's speed increases by 1 square until the start of your next turn. For every 5 points by which you exceed the DC, your vehicle's speed increases by an additional 1 square.

Ram: You can make a Pilot check as part of a full-round action to collide intentionally with a target (see Ram, page 172).

Special: You can take 10 when making a Pilot check except when attempting to increase a vehicle's speed. You can't take 20 on a Pilot check.

RIDE (DEX)
Armor Check Penalty
Use this skill to ride any kind of mount, such as a tauntaun, dewback, or bantha.

Ride Mount: Typical riding actions don't require checks. You can saddle, mount, ride, and dismount without a problem. Mounting or dismounting an animal is a move action. Some tasks, such as those undertaken in combat or other extreme circumstances, require checks. In addition, attempting trick riding or convincing the animal to do something unusual also requires a check.

RIDING TASK	DC
Guide with knees	10
Stay in saddle	10
Cover	15
Soft fall	15
Leap	15
Control mount in battle	20
Fast mount or dismount	20*

* Armor check penalty applies.

Control Mount in Battle: As a move action, you can attempt to control a mount while in combat. If you fail, you can do nothing else that round. You do not need to roll for riding animals specifically trained for battle.

Fast Mount or Dismount: You can mount or dismount as a swift action. If you fail the check, mounting or dismounting is a move action. (You can't attempt a fast mount or dismount unless you can perform the mount or dismount as a move action this round, should the check fail.)

Guide with Knees: You can react instantly to guide your mount with your knees so that you can use both hands in combat or to perform some other action. Make the check at the start of your round. If you fail, you can only use one hand this round because you need to use the other to control your mount.

Leap: You can get your mount to leap obstacles as part of its movement. Use your Ride skill modifier or the mount's Jump skill modifier, whichever is lower, to see how far the mount can jump (see the Jump skill, page 68). A DC 15 Ride check is required to stay on the mount when it leaps.

Soft Fall: You react instantly when you fall off a mount, such as when it is killed or when it falls, to try to avoid taking damage. If you fail, you take 1d6 points of falling damage (see Falling Damage, page 255).

Stay in Saddle: You can react instantly to try to avoid falling when your mount rears or bolts unexpectedly or when you take damage.

Use Mount as Cover: You can react instantly to drop down and hang alongside your mount, using it as one-half cover. You can't attack while using your mount as cover. If you fail, you don't get the cover benefit.

Special: You can take 10 when making a Ride check, but you can't take 20.

Time: Ride is a move action, except when otherwise noted for the special tasks listed above.

STEALTH (DEX)
Armor Check Penalty
Use this skill to slink past a sentry without being heard, catch your enemy off-guard, snipe from a concealed location, or perform sleight of hand.

Sneak: Your Stealth check sets the DC for Perception checks made to notice you. If an opponent's Perception check equals or exceeds your Stealth check, your opponent notices you.

Any circumstance that hampers your ability to sneak imposes a −2 penalty on your check, while favorable circumstances grant a +2 bonus. For example, sneaking across a surface littered with debris imposes a −2 penalty on your Stealth check, while a room filled with abundant hiding places grants a +2 bonus on your check.

If you move more than your speed in any given round, you take a −5 penalty on your Stealth check. If you move more than twice your speed in any given round, you take a −10 penalty on your Stealth check.

Your size provides a modifier to your Stealth checks: Fine, +20; Diminutive, +15; Tiny, +10; Small, +5; Medium, +0; Large, −5; Huge, −10; Gargantuan, −15; Colossal, −20.

Conceal Item: As a standard action, you can attempt to conceal an item (such as a weapon) on your person. The concealed object must be at least one size smaller than you, and you get a modifier on your skill check based on the object's relative size: One size smaller, −5; two sizes smaller, +0; three sizes smaller, +5; four or more sizes smaller, +10.

Other characters may notice a concealed object with a successful Perception check (opposed by your Stealth check result), but only if you do not have total concealment. A character gains a +10 circumstance bonus on his Perception check if he physically touches you to search for concealed items; this requires a full-round action that can only be performed if you're a willing, pinned, or helpless target.

Drawing a concealed item is a move action.

Create a Diversion to Hide: You can use the Deception skill (page 64) to help you be stealthy. A successful Deception gives you the momentary diversion you need to attempt a Stealth check even though people are aware of you. While the others turn their attention from you, you can make a Stealth check (as normal, and at no penalty) if you can reach a hiding place of some kind as a move action.

Pick Pocket: With a successful Stealth check, you can pilfer a small, hand-sized object from a target within reach. Your Stealth check is opposed by the target's Perception check, and the target gains a +5 bonus. If you fail by 4 or less, you are unable to take the item, but the target does not notice the effort. If you fail by 5 or more, you are unable to take the item and the target catches you in the act.

> "I'D PREFER A STRAIGHT FIGHT TO ALL THIS SNEAKING AROUND."
> – Han Solo

Sleight of Hand: You can palm hand-sized objects, perform minor feats of legerdemain, or attempt to perform a minor action without being noticed (such as flipping a switch, pulling out a thermal detonator, or drawing a pistol under the cover of a table). All such efforts are opposed by observer's Perception check. Any observer that beats your Stealth check notices the action you attempted, and knows how you did it.

Snipe: After making a ranged attack from hiding, you can try to hide again. You must be at least 2 squares from the target, and you must already have successfully used Stealth to hide from the target. Make a new Stealth check (as normal, but with a –10 penalty) as a move action. If you succeed, you remain hidden; otherwise, your location is revealed.

Special: You can take 10 when making a Stealth check, but you can't take 20.

Survival (Wis)

Use this skill to hunt and forage, guide a party safely through arid wastelands, identify signs that gundarks live nearby, or avoid quicksand and other natural hazards.

Basic Survival: Once per day, you can make a DC 15 Survival check to avoid natural hazards and keep yourself safe and fed in the wild for the next 24 hours. You can provide food and water for one additional person for every 2 points by which your check result exceeds 10.

Endure Extreme Temperatures (requires field kit): Once per day, you can make a DC 20 Survival check to ignore the effects of extreme cold or extreme heat for the next 24 hours (see Extreme Temperatures, page 254).

Know Direction: As a full-round action, you can ascertain which direction is north by succeeding on a DC 10 Survival check (assuming you're somewhere where cardinal directions matter).

Track (Trained Only): To find tracks or to follow them requires a full-round action and a successful Survival check. The DC of the check depends on the surface and the prevailing circumstances, as given below. You must

make another Survival check every time the tracks become difficult to follow, such as when other tracks cross them or when the terrain or prevailing circumstances change.

You move at half normal speed while tracking. You can choose to move your normal speed instead, but you take a –5 penalty on Survival checks made to follow tracks.

SURFACE	DC
Soft ground	10
Firm ground	20
Hard ground	30

Soft Ground: Any surface (fresh snow, thick ash, wet mud) that holds clear impressions of footprints.

Firm Ground: Any outdoor surface (lawns, fields, woods) or exceptionally soft or dirty indoor surface (dusty floors, thick carpets) that can capture footprints of a creature's passage.

Hard Ground: Any surface that doesn't hold footprints at all (bare rock, concrete, metal deck plates).

CIRCUMSTANCE	DC MODIFIER
Every 3 creatures in the group being tracked	–1
Every day since the trail was made	+1
Every hour of rain since the trail was made	+1
Fresh snow cover since the trail was made	+5
Poor visibility	+5
Tracked target hides trail (and moves at half speed)	+5
Largest creature being tracked	
Huge or bigger	–10
Large	–5
Medium	+0
Small	+5
Tiny or smaller	+10

Special: You can take 10 when making a Survival check. You can take 20 if there is no danger or penalty for failure, but it takes twenty times as long as normal to do so.

Swim (Str)
Armor Check Penalty

Using this skill, a land-based creature can swim, dive, navigate underwater obstacles, and so on.

Swim: A successful Swim check allows you to swim one-quarter your speed as a move action or one-half your speed as a full-round action. Roll once per round. If you fail, you make no progress through the water. If you fail by 5 or more, you go underwater and must hold your breath (see the Endurance skill, page 66) until you reach the surface by succeeding on a Swim check.

The DC for the Swim check depends on the situation:

SITUATION	DC
Calm water	10
Rough water	15
Stormy water	20

Retry: A new check is allowed the round after a check is failed.

Special: You can take 10 when making a Swim check, but you can't take 20.

Treat Injury (Wis)

Use this skill to keep a badly wounded friend from dying, to heal the injured, or to treat a diseased or poisoned character.

First Aid (requires a medpac): As a full-round action, you can administer first aid to an unconscious or wounded creature. If you succeed on a DC 15 Treat Injury check, the creature regains a number of hit points equal to its character level, +1 for every point by which your check result exceeds the DC. Using a medical kit grants a +2 equipment bonus on your skill check. If the skill check succeeds, the tended creature cannot benefit from additional first aid for 24 hours.

You can administer first aid on yourself, but you take a –5 penalty on your Treat Injury check.

Long-Term Care: If you tend to a creature for 8 consecutive hours, that creature regains hit points equal to its character level in addition to those recovered from natural healing (see Natural Healing, page 148). A creature can only benefit from long-term care once in a 24-hour period. You can tend one creature at a time if untrained, or up to six simultaneously if trained. You can't give long-term care to yourself.

Perform Surgery (Trained Only; requires a surgery kit): You can perform surgery to heal damage to a wounded creature, remove a persistent condition, or install a cybernetic prosthesis (see page 137). Any of these operations requires 1 hour of uninterrupted work, at the end of which time you must make a Treat Injury check. If you fail your check, the surgery does not yield any benefit (but any resources used are still lost). In addition, if you fail your check by 5 or more, the creature takes damage equal to its damage threshold. If this damage reduces the creature to 0 hit points, it dies (see 0 Hit Points, page 146).

Heal Damage: You can make a DC 20 Treat Injury check to perform surgery on a wounded creature, healing an amount of damage equal to the creature's Constitution bonus (minimum 1) × the creature's level. If you fail the check, the creature instead takes damage equal to its damage threshold. If the creature was already at 0 hit points, it dies unless it can spend a Force Point to save itself (see page 93). You can perform surgery on yourself to heal damage, but you take a –5 penalty on your skill check. Performing surgery to heal damage also removes any persistent conditions afflicting the target.

Install a Cybernetic Prosthesis: You must have the Cybernetic Surgery feat (see page 83) to install a cybernetic prosthesis on a living being. At the end of the procedure, make a DC 20 Treat Injury check. If the check succeeds, the prosthesis is installed properly. If the check fails, the prosthesis is not properly installed; however, you can try again after another uninterrupted hour of surgery. You can install a cybernetic prosthesis on yourself, but you take a –5 penalty on your skill check.

Revivify (Trained Only; requires a medical kit): As a full-round action, you can revive a creature that has just died. You must reach the dead creature within 1 round of its death to revive it, and you must succeed on a DC 25 Treat Injury check. Using a medpac grants a +2 equipment bonus on the skill check. If the check succeeds, the creature is unconscious instead of dead. If the check fails, you are unable to revive the creature.

Treat Disease (Trained Only; requires a medical kit): Treating a diseased character requires 8 hours. At the end of that time, make a Treat Injury check against the disease's DC (see Disease, page 254). If the check succeeds, the patient is cured and no longer suffers any ill effects (including persistent conditions caused by the disease). You can treat one creature at a time if untrained, or up to six simultaneously if trained.

Treat Poison (Trained Only; requires a medical kit): As a full-round action, you can treat a poisoned character. Make a Treat Injury check; if the result equals or exceeds the poison's DC (see Poison, page 255), you successfully detoxify the poison in the character's system and the patient no longer suffers any ill effects (including persistent conditions caused by the poison).

Treat Radiation (Trained Only; requires a medical kit): Treating an irradiated character requires 8 hours. At the end of that time, make a Treat Injury check against the radiation's DC (see Radiation, page 255). If the check succeeds, the patient is cured and no longer suffers any ill effects (including persistent conditions caused by the radiation). You can treat one creature at a time if untrained, or up to six simultaneously if trained.

Special: You can take 10 when making a Treat Injury check, but you can't take 20.

Use Computer (Int)

Use this skill to access secured files and defeat security systems.

Access Information (requires computer attitude of indifferent or better): Getting information through a computer requires you to connect to the appropriate network (such as the HoloNet, or its equivalent in other eras) and locate the files you seek. Connecting to a network (a full-round action) doesn't require a skill check if you use a computer that's already linked to it. However, establishing a connection to a network using a remote computer requires a DC 10 Use Computer check. You can also get information without connecting to a network if you use a computer whose memory contains that information; the GM decides what information a computer's memory actually holds.

Finding information on a single topic requires a set amount of time (see below); at the end of this time, you must make a Use Computer check. The time required and the check DC are determined by the type of information sought. For example, locating general information about a senator is easier than locating specific information (such as the senator's date of birth), which is easier than finding private information (such as the senator's private comm

Table 4-5: Computer Attitude Steps

Attitude	The Computer...
Hostile	Treats you as a hostile intruder and attempts to trace your location and isolate your connection.
Unfriendly	Treats you as an unauthorized user and blocks your access to its programs and information.
Indifferent	Treats you as a guest or visitor and grants you access to non-secret programs and information (as long as this does not conflict with previous commands).
Friendly	Treats you as an authorized user and grants you access to any programs and non-secret information (as long as this does not conflict with previous commands). You may add any equipment bonus provided by the computer to your Use Computer checks.
Helpful	Treats you as if you are its owner or administrator, granting access to all of its programs and information (even if doing so overrides previous commands). You may add any equipment bonus provided by the computer to your Use Computer checks.

channel code), which is easier than uncovering secret information (such as the senator's cred stick code).

Information	DC	Time Required
General	15	1 minute (10 rounds)
Specific	20	10 minutes
Private	25	1 hour
Secret*	30	1 day (8 hours)

* Secret information can only be accessed on a computer that is helpful toward you.

Astrogate (Trained Only): You can plot a safe course through hyperspace. Doing so usually requires 1 minute, at the end of which time you must succeed on a Use Computer check. Various factors influence the DC of the check (see Astrogation, page 237).

Disable or Erase Program (Trained Only; requires computer attitude of helpful): You can disable or erase a program on a computer that is helpful toward you (See Table 4-5: Computer Attitude Steps). Disabling or erasing a program takes 10 minutes and requires a DC 15 Use Computer check.

Improve Access (Trained Only): As a full-round action, you can make a Use Computer check to adjust the attitude of a computer in order to gain access to its programs and information. You must be able to communicate with the computer either through a direct interface (such as a keypad) or by connecting to it through an appropriate network (such as the HoloNet). Apply a modifier on the check based on the computer's current attitude toward you: hostile -10, unfriendly -5, indifferent -2, friendly +0 (see Table 4-5: Computer Attitude Steps). If the check equals or exceeds the computer's Will Defense, the computer's attitude shifts one step in your favor. If you fail, the computer's attitude does not change. If you fail by 5 or more, the computer's becomes one step worse (for example, indifferent to unfriendly) and the computer notifies the computer's administrator of the access attempt.

A hostile computer can be dangerous. If a computer becomes hostile or if you fail any Use Computer check made to improve access to a hostile computer, it traces your exact location and notifies the nearest security personnel. In addition, if you fail by 5 or more when attempting to improve access to a hostile computer, it isolates your connection and rejects any further attempts you make to access it for 24 hours.

Issue Routine Command (requires computer attitude of friendly or better): As a standard action, you can issue a routine command to a computer. Examples include turning a computer on or off, viewing and editing documents or recordings in its memory, printing a hard copy of a document or image on a flimsiplast sheet, opening or closing doors that the computer controls, and the like.

Issuing routine commands doesn't normally require a Use Computer check. However, if another character issues a contradictory command, the computer follows the command of the character toward whom it has a better attitude (for example, it follows a command from someone toward whom it is helpful over someone toward whom it is friendly). If the computer has the same attitude toward both characters, make an opposed Use Computer check against the competing character. If you succeed, your command takes effect. If you fail, the opposing character's command takes effect.

Reprogram Droid (Trained Only; requires tool kit): You can make a check to reprogram a droid to obey a new master, copy data stored in its memory banks, change its trained skills, erase memories selectively, or erase its memory entirely (resetting the droid to its factory preset status). The DC for any of these actions is equal to the droid's Will Defense. Reprogramming a droid takes 10 minutes.

Special: You can take 10 on Use Computer checks. You can take 20 on a Use Computer check except when attempting to improve access.

When a computer is friendly or helpful toward you, you gain an equipment bonus on all Use Computer checks made with that computer equal to its Intelligence bonus.

Use the Force (Cha)
Requires the Force Sensitivity feat

You draw upon the Force to help you recover from injuries, gain special insights, or perform other remarkable acts. You must have the Force Sensitivity feat (page 85) to be trained in this skill.

Activate Force Power (Trained Only): You make a Use the Force check to use a Force power (see Force Powers, page 95). This use of the skill requires no action.

Force Trance (Trained Only): As a full-round action, you can enter a Force trance with a DC 10 Use the Force check. In this state, you remain fully aware of your surroundings. Each hour you remain in the trance, you regain a number of hit points equal to your character level. You can emerge from the trance as a swift action. If you remain in a Force trance for 4 consecutive hours, you emerge from the trance fully rested (as though you'd rested for 8 hours).

While you're in a Force trance, you can go ten times as long as normal without food or water (see the Endurance skill, page 66).

Move Light Object (Trained Only): As a move action, you can use the Force to telekinetically lift and move a relatively light object within your line of sight. A successful DC 10 Use the Force check allows you to move an object weighing up to 5 kg a distance of 6 squares in any direction. As a standard action, you can use the object as a projectile weapon, but the DC increases to 15. If your Use the Force check beats the target's Reflex Defense, the object hits and deals 1d6 points of bludgeoning damage.

Search Your Feelings: As a full-round action, you can make a DC 15 Use the Force check to determine whether a particular action will yield favorable or unfavorable results to you in the immediate future (10 minutes or less). For example, you can make the check to determine whether destroying a dark side artifact will have immediate unforeseen repercussions. The answer does not take into account the long-term consequences of a contemplated action. Using the above example, a successful check would not portend a future encounter with vengeful darksiders angered by the destruction of the dark side artifact. (The GM must assess the immediate consequences of the action, based on what he knows about the circumstances.)

Sense Force (Trained Only): You automatically sense disturbances in the Force. A location that is strong in the dark side of the Force can be sensed out to a range of 1 kilometer. A relative, companion, or close friend in mortal danger or great pain can be sensed out to a range of 10,000 light years. A great disturbance, such as the destruction of an entire populated planet or the distress of a whole order of allies, can be sensed anywhere in the same galaxy. As a full-round action, you can make a DC 15 Use the Force check to determine the distance and general direction to the location of the disturbance.

As a full-round action, you can use this ability to actively sense other Force-users out to a range of 100 kilometers. If you succeed on a DC 15 Use the Force check, you know how many Force-users are within range, their approximate distance and direction from you, and whether you've met them before or not. Another Force-user within range can try to conceal her presence from you by making an opposed Use the Force check. If she equals or exceeds your Use the Force check, you don't sense her presence at all.

Sense Surroundings: As a swift action, you can make a DC 15 Use the Force check to ignore the effects of cover and concealment when making Perception checks to detect or observe targets. Increase the DC by 5 if this ability is used against targets with total cover.

Telepathy: As a standard action, you can establish a telepathic link with a distant creature. Through the link, you can exchange emotions or a single thought, such as "Go!", "Help!", or "Danger!" The target must have an Intelligence of 2 or higher, and the distance between you and the target determines the DC (see below). Against an unwilling target, you must make a Use the Force check against the target's Will Defense; if the check fails, you cannot establish a telepathic link or attempt to telepathically contact the target for 24 hours unless the target becomes a willing one.

TELEPATHY DISTANCE	DC
Same planet	15
Same system	20
Same region/quadrant of the galaxy	25
Different region/quadrant of the galaxy	30

Special: You can't make Use the Force checks unless you have the Force Sensitivity feat (see page 85). Use the Force is a class skill for any character with the Force Sensitivity feat.

You can take 10 on a Use the Force check, but you can't take 20.

> "THE ABILITY TO DESTROY A PLANET IS INSIGNIFICANT NEXT TO THE POWER OF THE FORCE."
> —DARTH VADER

A feat is a special feature that either gives your character a new capability or improves one he or she already has. Unlike skills and talents, your choice of feats is not restricted by your class. Any character can take any feat as long as the prerequisites are met.

Acquiring Feats

Choose the feats you feel best represent your character's interests and capabilities. Each character gets one feat when the character is created (at 1st level). At 3rd, 6th, 9th, 12th, 15th, and 18th level, characters gain another feat (see Table 3-1: Experience and Level-Dependent Benefits, page 37). For multiclass characters, feats are gained according to total character level, not by individual class levels.

Additionally, classes get bonus feats chosen from special lists (see the class descriptions in Chapter 3: Heroic Classes). Humans also get a bonus feat at 1st level, chosen from any feat the character qualifies for.

Prerequisites

Some feats have prerequisites. A character must have the listed ability score, feat, trained skill, or base attack bonus in order to select or use that feat. A character can gain a feat at the same level at which he or she gains the prerequisite(s).

A prerequisite that contains a numerical value is a minimum; any value higher than the one given also meets the prerequisite. For instance, the prerequisites for the Cleave feat are "Strength 13, Power Attack." Any character with a Strength score of 13 or higher and the Power Attack feat meets the prerequisites. You can't use a feat if you've lost a prerequisite. For example, if your Strength drops below 13 for any reason, you can't use the Power Attack feat until your Strength returns to 13 or higher.

Feat Descriptions

Here is the format for feat descriptions.

Feat Name

A description of what the feat does or represents in plain language, with no game mechanics.

Prerequisite(s): A minimum ability score, another feat or feats, a minimum base attack bonus, a special skill requirement, and/or a minimum level in a class that a character must have to acquire this feat. This entry is absent if a feat has no prerequisite.

Benefit: What the feat enables you (the character) to do.

Normal: What a character who does not have this feat is limited to or restricted from doing. If not having the feat causes no particular drawback, this entry is absent.

Table 5-1: Feats

FEAT	PREREQUISITES	BENEFIT
Acrobatic Strike	Trained in Acrobatics	Gain +5 bonus on next attack against opponent you tumble past.
Armor Proficiency (heavy)	Armor Proficiency (light), Armor Proficiency (medium)	No penalty on attacks and no armor check penalty while wearing light, medium, or heavy armor.
Armor Proficiency (light)	—	No penalty on attacks and no armor check penalty while wearing light armor.
Armor Proficiency (medium)	Armor Proficiency (light)	No penalty on attacks and no armor check penalty while wearing light or medium armor.
Bantha Rush	Str 13, base attack bonus +1	Push opponent 1 square after making a successful melee attack.
Burst Fire	Str 13, Weapon Proficiency (heavy weapons), proficient with weapon	Take a −5 penalty on an autofire attack to gain +2 dice damage.
Careful Shot	Point Blank Shot, base attack bonus +2	If you aim, gain +1 bonus on the attack roll.
Charging Fire	Base attack bonus +4	Make ranged attack at the end of a charge, at a −2 penalty.
Cleave	Str 13, Power Attack	Extra melee attack after dropping target.
Combat Reflexes	—	Gain additional attacks of opportunity.
Coordinated Attack	Base attack bonus +2	Automatic success with aid another action at point blank range.
Crush	Pin, base attack bonus +1	Deal unarmed or claw damage to a pinned opponent.
Cybernetic Surgery	Trained in Treat Injury	Install a cybernetic prosthesis onto a living being.
Deadeye	Point Blank Shot, Precise Shot, base attack bonus +4	If you aim, deal extra damage.
Dodge	Dex 13	Gain a +1 dodge bonus to Reflex Defense against a selected target.
Double Attack	Base attack bonus +6, proficient with weapon	Make extra attack during full attack, −5 penalty to all attacks
Dreadful Rage	Rage species trait, base attack bonus +1	Rage bonus to attacks and damage increases to +4.
Dual Weapon Mastery I	Dex 13, base attack bonus +1	Take a −5 penalty on attacks when attacking with two weapons or both ends of a double weapon.
Dual Weapon Mastery II	Dex 15, base attack bonus +6, Dual Weapon Mastery I	Take a −2 penalty on attacks when attacking with two weapons or both ends of a double weapon.
Dual Weapon Mastery III	Dex 17, base attack bonus +11, Dual Weapon Mastery I, Dual Weapon Mastery II	Take no penalty on attacks when attacking with two weapons or both ends of a double weapon.
Exotic Weapon Proficiency	Base attack bonus +1	Wield an exotic weapon without penalty.
Extra Rage	Rage species trait	Rage one additional time per day.
Extra Second Wind	Trained in Endurance	Gain an additional second wind per day.
Far Shot	Point Blank Shot	Range penalties for short-, medium-, and long-ranged attacks are reduced.
Force Boon	Force Sensitivity	Gain three additional Force Points at each level.
Force Sensitivity	Non-droid	You can make Use the Force checks and gain access to Force talents.
Force Training	Force Sensitivity	Learn a number of Force powers equal to 1 + your Wis modifier (minimum 1).
Great Cleave	Str 13, Power Attack, Cleave, base attack bonus +4	No limit to cleave attacks each round.
Improved Charge	Dex 13, Dodge, Mobility	You can charge without moving in a straight line.
Improved Defenses	—	Gain +1 bonus to all defenses.
Improved Disarm	Int 13, Melee Defense	Gain +5 bonus on melee attacks to disarm an opponent.
Improved Damage Threshold	—	Damage threshold increases by 5.

Feat	Prerequisite	Benefit
Linguist	Int 13	Gain bonus languages equal to 1 + your Int modifier (minimum 1).
Martial Arts I	—	Increase damage from unarmed attacks by one die step; gain +1 dodge bonus to Reflex Defense.
Martial Arts II	Martial Arts I, base attack bonus +3	Increase damage from unarmed attacks by one die step; gain +1 dodge bonus to Reflex Defense.
Martial Arts III	Martial Arts I, Martial Arts II, base attack bonus +6	Increase damage from unarmed attacks by one die step; gain +1 dodge bonus to Reflex Defense.
Melee Defense	Int 13	Trade attack bonus on melee attacks for a dodge bonus to Reflex Defense.
Mighty Swing	Strength 13	Spend two swift actions to deal extra damage in melee.
Mobility	Dex 13, Dodge	Gain +5 dodge bonus to Reflex Defense against some attacks of opportunity.
Pin	Base attack bonus +1	Grappled opponent is pinned for 1 round, can't move, and loses its Dexterity bonus to Reflex Defense.
Point Blank Shot	—	+1 bonus on ranged attacks and damage against point blank foes.
Power Attack	Str 13	Trade attack bonus for damage on melee attacks (up to your base attack bonus).
Powerful Charge	Medium or larger size, base attack bonus +1	Gain +2 bonus on your attack roll while charging and deal extra damage.
Precise Shot	Point Blank Shot	No –5 penalty for shooting into melee.
Quick Draw	Base attack bonus +1	Draw weapon as a swift action.
Rapid Shot	Str 13, base attack bonus +1, proficient with weapon	Take a –2 penalty on a ranged attack roll to deal +1 die of damage.
Rapid Strike	Dex 13, base attack bonus +1, proficient with weapon	Take a –2 penalty on a melee attack roll to deal +1 die of damage.
Running Attack	Dex 13	Move before and after making an attack.
Shake It Off	Con 13, trained in Endurance	Spend two swift actions to move +1 step along the condition track.
Skill Focus	—	Gain +5 competence bonus on skill checks with one trained skill.
Skill Training	—	You become trained in one class skill.
Sniper	Point Blank Shot, Precise Shot, base attack bonus +4	You ignore soft cover when making a ranged attack.
Strong in the Force	—	Roll d8s instead of d6s when you spend a Force Point.
Surgical Expertise	Trained in Treat Injury	You can perform surgery in 10 minutes instead of 1 hour.
Throw	Trip, base attack bonus +1	Throw a grappled opponent up to 1 square beyond your reach and deal damage.
Toughness	—	Gain +1 hit point per character level.
Trip	Base attack bonus +1	Trip an opponent that you've grappled, knocking it prone.
Triple Attack	Base attack bonus +9, Double Attack (chosen weapon), proficient with chosen weapon	Make second extra attack during full attack, additional –5 penalty to all attacks
Triple Crit	Proficient with weapon, base attack bonus +8	Deal triple damage on a critical hit.
Vehicular Combat	Trained in Pilot	Negate one attack per round against the vehicle you're piloting.
Weapon Finesse	Base attack bonus +1	Use Dex modifier instead of Str modifier on attack rolls with light melee weapons and lightsabers.
Weapon Focus	Proficiency with weapon	+1 bonus on attack rolls with selected weapon
Weapon Proficiency	—	Ignore –5 penalty on attack rolls with weapons of a particular type.
Whirlwind Attack	Dex 13, Int 13, Melee Defense, base attack bonus +4	Make one melee attack against each opponent within reach.

Special: Additional facts about the feat that may be helpful when you decide whether to acquire the feat.

ACROBATIC STRIKE

Your dexterous maneuvers and skilled acrobatics allow you to slip past a foe's defenses and deliver an accurate strike against him.

Prerequisite: Trained in the Acrobatics skill.

Benefit: If you succeed in tumbling to avoid an attack of opportunity (see the Acrobatics skill, page 62), you gain a +5 bonus on the next attack that you make against that foe as long as the attack occurs before the end of your current turn.

ARMOR PROFICIENCY (HEAVY)

You are proficient with heavy armor (see Table 8-7: Armor) and can wear it without impediment.

Prerequisites: Armor Proficiency (light), Armor Proficiency (medium).

Benefit: When you wear heavy armor, you take no armor check penalty on attack rolls or skill checks. Additionally, you benefit from all of the armor's special equipment bonuses (if any).

Normal: A character who wears heavy armor with which she is not proficient takes a –10 armor check penalty on attack rolls as well as skill checks made using the following skills: Acrobatics, Climb, Endurance, Initiative, Jump, Stealth, and Swim. Additionally, the character gains none of the armor's special equipment bonuses.

ARMOR PROFICIENCY (LIGHT)

You are proficient with light armor (see Table 8-7: Armor) and can wear it without impediment.

Benefit: When you wear light armor, you take no armor check penalty on attack rolls or skill checks. Additionally, you benefit from all of the armor's special equipment bonuses (if any).

Normal: A character who wears heavy armor with which she is not proficient takes a –2 armor check penalty on attack rolls as well as skill checks made using the following skills: Acrobatics, Climb, Endurance, Initiative, Jump, Stealth, and Swim. Additionally, the character gains none of the armor's special equipment bonuses.

ARMOR PROFICIENCY (MEDIUM)

You are proficient with medium armor (see Table 8-7: Armor) and can wear it without impediment.

Prerequisite: Armor Proficiency (light).

Benefit: When you wear medium armor, you take no armor check penalty on attack rolls or skill checks. Additionally, you benefit from all of the armor's special equipment bonuses (if any).

Normal: A character who wears medium armor with which she is not proficient takes a –5 armor check penalty on attack rolls as well as skill checks made using the following skills: Acrobatics, Climb, Endurance, Initiative, Jump, Stealth, and Swim. Additionally, the character gains none of the armor's special equipment bonuses.

BANTHA RUSH

You can shove your opponents around the battlefield to gain a tactical advantage.

Prerequisite: Strength 13, base attack bonus +1.

Benefit: After making a successful melee attack against an opponent up to one size category larger than you, you can choose to move that opponent 1 square in any direction as a free action. You can't bantha rush an opponent that's being grabbed or grappled, and you can't bantha rush your opponent into a solid object or another creature's fighting space.

BURST FIRE

When using a ranged weapon in autofire mode, you can fire a short burst at a single foe.

Prerequisites: Strength 13, Weapon Proficiency (heavy weapons), proficient with weapon.

Benefit: When using a ranged weapon with autofire capability in autofire mode, you may fire a short burst as a single attack against a single target. You take a –5 penalty on the attack roll but deal +2 dice of damage. For example, a weapon that deals 3d10 points of damage deals 5d10 points of damage instead.

The effects of this feat do not stack with the extra damage provided by the Deadeye or Rapid Shot feat.

Special: Firing a burst expends five shots and can only be done if the weapon has at least five shots remaining.

Normal: Autofire uses ten shots, targets a 2-square-by-2-square area, and can't be aimed at a specific target. Without this feat, if you attempt an autofire attack at a specific target, it simply counts as a normal attack and all the extra shots are wasted.

CAREFUL SHOT

You are particularly skilled at aiming your attacks.

Prerequisites: Point Blank Shot, base attack bonus +2.

Benefit: If you aim before making a ranged attack (see Aim on page 154), you gain a +1 bonus on your attack roll.

CHARGING FIRE

You are able to make ranged attacks while charging.

Prerequisite: Base attack bonus +4.

Benefit: When you charge, you may make a ranged attack instead of a melee attack at the end of your movement. Unlike a normal charge, your momentum does not help overcome your target, so you gain no bonus on attack roll. As with a normal charge, you still take a −2 penalty to your Reflex Defense.

Normal: You can make a single melee attack with a +2 bonus on your attack roll at the end of a charge.

Cleave

You can follow through with a powerful melee attack.

Prerequisites: Strength 13, Power Attack.

Benefit: If you deal an opponent enough damage to reduce its hit points to 0, you get an immediate extra melee attack against another opponent within your reach. You cannot adjust 1 square before making this extra attack. The extra attack is with the same weapon and at the same bonus as the attack that dropped the previous opponent. You can use this ability once per round.

Combat Reflexes

You can respond quickly and repeatedly to opponents who let their guard down.

Benefit: When opponents leave themselves open, you may make a number of additional attacks of opportunity equal to your Dexterity modifier.

For example, a character with a Dexterity of 15 can make a total of three attacks of opportunity in a round: the one attack of opportunity every character is entitled to, plus two more attacks because of his +2 Dexterity bonus. If four stormtroopers move through the character's threatened area, he can make attacks of opportunity against three of the four. You still only make one attack of opportunity on a single opponent.

With this feat, you may also make attacks of opportunity while flat-footed.

Normal: A character without the Combat Reflexes feat can make only one attack of opportunity per round and can't make attacks of opportunity while flat-footed. (See Attacks of Opportunity, page 155, for more information.)

Coordinated Attack

You are skilled at coordinating your attacks with your allies.

Prerequisite: Base attack bonus +2.

Benefit: You are automatically successful when using the aid another action to aid an ally's attack or suppress an enemy as long as the target is adjacent to you or within point blank range.

Normal: You must make an attack roll against a Reflex Defense of 10 to gain the benefits of the aid another action.

Crush

You can deal damage to a creature that you've grappled.

Prerequisites: Pin, base attack bonus +1.

Benefit: If you successfully pin an opponent with a grapple attack (see the Pin feat, page 87), you can immediately deal bludgeoning damage to it equal to your unarmed damage or claw damage, whichever is greater.

Cybernetic Surgery

You can perform the surgical procedures necessary to graft cybernetic components onto living flesh.

Prerequisite: Trained in the Treat Injury skill.

Benefit: You can install a cybernetic prosthesis (see page 137) on a living being. The surgical procedure takes 1 hour of uninterrupted work, after which you must make on a DC 20 Treat Injury check. If the check succeeds, the prosthesis is installed correctly. If the check fails, the prosthesis is not properly installed; however, you can try again after another uninterrupted hour of surgery.

Special: You can install a cybernetic prosthesis on yourself, but you take a –5 penalty on the Treat Injury skill check. If you have the Surgical Expertise feat (see page 88), you can install a cybernetic prosthesis in 10 minutes instead of 1 hour.

Deadeye

You are skilled at picking off enemies with well-aimed ranged attacks.

Prerequisites: Point Blank Shot, Precise Shot, base attack bonus +4.

Benefit: If you aim before making a ranged attack (see Aim, page 154) and the attack hits, increase the damage you deal by an additional weapon die. For example, if you score a hit with a blaster pistol using the Deadeye feat, the blaster shot deals 4d6 points of damage (instead of the normal 3d6 points).

The effects of this feat do not stack with the extra damage provided by the Burst Fire or Rapid Shot feat.

Dodge

You are adept at dodging blows.

Prerequisite: Dexterity 13.

Benefit: During your turn, you designate an opponent and receive a +1 dodge bonus to your Reflex Defense against attacks from that opponent. You can select a new opponent on any action.

A situation that makes you lose your Dexterity bonus to Reflex Defense (if any) also makes you lose dodge bonuses. Also, dodge bonuses stack with each other, unlike most other types of bonuses.

Double Attack

You can make an additional attack during a round of combat.

Prerequisites: Base attack bonus +6, proficient with chosen weapon.

Benefit: Choose a single exotic weapon or one of the following weapon groups: advanced melee weapons, heavy weapons, lightsabers, pistols, rifles, simple weapons. When you use the full attack action, you may make one additional attack when wielding such a weapon. However, you take a –5 penalty on all attack rolls until your next turn because you're trading precision for speed.

Normal: Making a single attack is a standard action.

Special: You may select this feat multiple times. Each time you select this feat, it applies to a different exotic weapon or weapon group.

Dreadful Rage

You deal horrendous damage while raging.

Prerequisites: Rage species trait, base attack bonus +1.

Benefit: While raging, your rage bonus on melee attack rolls and melee damage rolls increases to +5.

Normal: A character with the rage species trait gains a +2 rage bonus on melee attack rolls and melee damage rolls while raging.

Dual Weapon Mastery I

You are adept at fighting with two weapons and double weapons.

Prerequisites: Dexterity 13, base attack bonus +1.

Benefit: When you attack with two weapons or with both ends of a double weapon as a part of a full attack action, you take a –5 penalty (instead of a –10 penalty) on all attack rolls until the start of your next turn. You only gain this reduced penalty if you are wielding a weapon with which you are proficient.

Normal: If you use a full attack action to make more than one attack on your turn (see Full Attack, page 154), you take a –10 penalty on all attack rolls for the round.

Dual Weapon Mastery II

You are a master at fighting with two weapons and double weapons.

Prerequisites: Dexterity 15, base attack bonus +6, Dual Weapon Mastery I.

Benefit: When you attack with two weapons or both ends of a double weapon as a part of a full attack action, you take a –2 penalty (instead of a –10 penalty) on all attack rolls until the start of your next turn. You only gain this reduced penalty if you are wielding a weapon with which you are proficient.

Normal: If you use a full attack action to make more than one attack on your turn (see Full Attack, page 154), you take a –10 penalty on all attack rolls for the round.

Dual Weapon Mastery III

You can wield two weapons or a double weapon without penalty.

Prerequisites: Dexterity 17, base attack bonus +11, Dual Weapon Mastery I, Dual Weapon Mastery II.

Benefit: When you wield two weapons or attack with both ends of a double weapon as a part of a full attack action, you take no penalty on your attack rolls. You only gain this benefit if you are wielding a weapon with which you are proficient.

Normal: If you use a full attack action to make more than one attack on your turn (see Full Attack, page 154), you take a –10 penalty on all attack rolls for the round.

Exotic Weapon Proficiency

Choose an exotic weapon, such as bowcaster or atlatl (see Exotic Weapons, page 119). You understand how to use that type of exotic weapon in combat.

Prerequisite: Base attack bonus +1.

Benefit: You make attack rolls with the weapon normally.

Normal: A character who uses a weapon without being proficient with it takes a –5 penalty on attack rolls.

Special: You can gain this feat multiple times. Each time you take the feat, it applies to a different weapon.

Extra Rage

You can fly into a rage more often.

Prerequisite: Rage species trait.

Benefit: You can rage one additional time per day.

Special: You can take this feat multiple times; each time you take the feat, you can rage one additional time per day.

Extra Second Wind

You tend to come back from the edge of oblivion more often.

Prerequisite: Trained in the Endurance skill.

Benefit: You can catch your second wind one additional time per day, but you can still only catch a second wind once per encounter (see Second Wind, page 146).

Normal: A hero can catch his or her second wind once per day.

Special: A nonheroic character that takes this feat for the first time can catch a second wind once per day.

You can take this feat multiple times; each time you take this feat, you can catch a second wind one additional time per day.

Far Shot

You are better at shooting distant foes.

Prerequisite: Point Blank Shot.

Benefit: When you use a ranged weapon against targets at short, medium, or long range, the range category is considered one less. In other words, you take no penalty on ranged attack rolls against targets at short range, a –2 penalty on ranged attack rolls made against targets at medium range, and a –5 penalty on a ranged attack rolls made against targets at long range.

Normal: When making a ranged attack roll, a character takes a –2 penalty against targets at short range, a –5 penalty against targets at medium range, and a –10 penalty against targets at long range.

Force Boon

You are able to draw upon the Force more often than less skilled users.

Prerequisite: Force Sensitivity.

Benefit: You gain three additional Force Points at each level.

Force Sensitivity

You are Force-sensitive, allowing you to call on the Force and learn to draw on its power.

Prerequisite: Cannot be a droid.

Benefit: You can make Use the Force checks, and Use the Force is considered a class skill for you. In addition, whenever you gain a new talent, you have the option of selecting a Force talent instead. You must meet the prerequisites of the Force talent to select it (see Force Talents, page 100).

Normal: You can't make Use the Force checks (page 77) or select Force talents unless you have the Force Sensitivity feat.

Force Training

You learn one or more Force powers (see Force Powers, page 95).

Prerequisites: Force Sensitivity, trained in the Use the Force skill.

Benefit: You add to your Force power suite a number of Force powers equal to 1 + your Wisdom modifier (minimum 1). You can add the same power more than once.

Special: You can take this feat more than once. Each time you take this feat, you add to your Force suite a number of new Force powers equal to your Wisdom modifier.

If your Wisdom modifier permanently increases, you immediately gain a number of Force powers equal to the number of Force Training feats you have taken.

Great Cleave

You can wield a melee weapon with such power that you can strike multiple times when you drop your opponents.

Prerequisites: Strength 13, Power Attack, Cleave, base attack bonus +4.

Benefit: As the Cleave feat (page 83), except that you have no limit to the number of times you can use it per round.

Improved Charge

You can charge around obstacles.

Prerequisites: Dexterity 13, Dodge, Mobility.

Benefit: You can make a charge (see page 152) without having to move in a straight line, and you can alter your direction when making a charge to avoid obstacles. All other charge rules apply.

Normal: A character must charge in an unobstructed straight line.

Improved Defenses

You are skilled at fending off attacks of many forms.

Benefit: You gain a +1 bonus to your Reflex Defense, Fortitude Defense, and Will Defense.

Improved Disarm

You are skilled at disarming opponents in melee combat.

Prerequisites: Intelligence 13, Melee Defense.

Benefit: You gain a +5 bonus on any melee attack roll made to disarm an opponent. In addition, if you fail to disarm your opponent, he doesn't get to make a free attack against you.

Normal: See the normal disarm rules on page 152.

Improved Damage Threshold

You are harder to take down in a fight.

Benefit: You increase your damage threshold by 5 (see Damage Threshold, page 146).

Normal: A creature without this feat has a damage threshold equal to its Fortitude Defense plus its size modifier (+5 for Large, +10 for Huge, +20 for Gargantuan, or +50 for Colossal).

Special: You can take this feat more than once. Its effects stack. Each time you take this feat, increase your damage threshold by 5.

Linguist

You pick up languages quickly and easily.

Prerequisite: Intelligence 13.

Benefit: You gain a number of bonus languages equal to 1 plus your Intelligence bonus (minimum of 1). See the sidebar on page 22 for a list of common languages.

Special: You can take this feat more than once. Each time you take this feat, you gain a number of additional languages equal to 1 plus your Intelligence bonus (minimum of 1).

Martial Arts I

You are adept at fighting unarmed.

Benefit: Damage dealt by your unarmed attacks increases by one die step: 1d3 becomes 1d4, 1d4 becomes 1d6, and 1d6 becomes 1d8. In addition, you gain a +1 dodge bonus to your Reflex Defense.

Normal: The amount of damage you deal with a successful unarmed attack is based on your size: Small, 1d3; Medium, 1d4; Large, 1d6.

Special: A situation that makes you lose your Dexterity bonus to Reflex Defense (if any) also makes you lose dodge bonuses. Also, dodge bonuses stack with each other, unlike most other types of bonuses.

Martial Arts II

You are a master at fighting unarmed.

Prerequisites: Martial Arts I, base attack bonus +3.

Benefit: Damage dealt by your unarmed attacks increases by one die step: 1d4 becomes 1d6, 1d6 becomes 1d8, and 1d8 becomes 1d10. In addition, you gain a +1 dodge bonus to your Reflex Defense (which stacks with the dodge bonus granted by the Martial Arts I feat).

Normal: The amount of damage you deal with a successful unarmed attack is based on your size: Small, 1d3; Medium, 1d4; Large, 1d6.

Special: A situation that makes you lose your Dexterity bonus to Reflex Defense (if any) also makes you lose dodge bonuses. Also, dodge bonuses stack with each other, unlike most other types of bonuses.

Martial Arts III

Your martial arts prowess is second to none.

Prerequisites: Martial Arts I, Martial Arts II, base attack bonus +6.

Benefit: Damage dealt by your unarmed attacks increases by one die step: 1d6 becomes 1d8, 1d8 becomes 1d10, and 1d10 becomes 1d12. In addition, you gain a +1 dodge bonus to your Reflex Defense (which stacks with the dodge bonus granted by the Martial Arts I and Martial Arts II feats).

Normal: The amount of damage you deal with a successful unarmed attack is based on your size: Small, 1d3; Medium, 1d4; Large, 1d6.

Special: A situation that makes you lose your Dexterity bonus to Reflex Defense (if any) also makes you lose dodge bonuses. Also, dodge bonuses stack with each other, unlike most other types of bonuses.

Melee Defense

You are trained at using your combat ability for defense as well as offense.

Prerequisite: Intelligence 13.

Benefit: When you use a standard action to make a melee attack, you can take a penalty of up to −5 on your attack roll and add the same number (up to +5) as a dodge bonus to your Reflex Defense. This number may not exceed your base attack bonus. The changes to attack rolls and Reflex Defense last until the start of your next turn.

Normal: A character without the Melee Defense feat can fight defensively while using the attack action to take a −5 penalty on his attack roll and gain a +2 dodge bonus to his Reflex Defense.

Mighty Swing

You are capable of delivering jarring melee attacks.

Prerequisite: Strength 13.

Benefit: You can spend two swift actions in the same round to deal +1 die of damage on your next melee attack in the same round.

The effects of this feat do not stack with the extra damage provided by the Rapid Strike feat.

Mobility

You are skilled at moving past opponents and avoiding opportunistic attacks.

Prerequisites: Dexterity 13, Dodge.

Benefit: You get a +5 dodge bonus to Reflex Defense against attacks of opportunity caused when you move out of or into a threatened area (see Attacks of Opportunity, page 155).

A situation that makes you lose your Dexterity bonus to Reflex Defense (if any) also makes you lose dodge bonuses. Dodge bonuses stack with each other, unlike most types of bonuses.

Pin
You are skilled at immobilizing grappled foes.
Prerequisite: Base attack bonus +1.
Benefit: If you succeed on a grappling attack and your opponent fails the opposed grapple check, your opponent is automatically pinned until the start of your next turn. A pinned creature can't move or take any actions while pinned, and it loses its Dexterity bonus (if any) to Reflex Defense.
Special: You cannot use the Pin and Trip feats during the same round. You can use the Pin and Crush feat in the same round, however.

Point Blank Shot
You are skilled at making well-placed shots with ranged weapons at point blank range.
Benefit: You get a +1 bonus on attack and damage rolls with ranged weapons against opponents within point blank range (see Table 8–5: Weapon Ranges, page 129).

Power Attack
You can make exceptionally powerful melee attacks.
Prerequisite: Strength 13.
Benefit: On your action, before making an attack roll, you may choose to subtract a number from all melee attack rolls and add the same number to all melee damage rolls. This number may not exceed your base attack bonus. The penalty on attacks and bonus on damage applies until the start of your next turn.
Special: If you attack with a two-handed weapon, or with a one-handed weapon wielded in two hands, instead add twice the number subtracted from your attack rolls. You can't add the bonus from Power Attack to the damage dealt against an object or vehicle.

Powerful Charge
You can charge with extra force.
Prerequisites: Medium or larger size, base attack bonus +1.
Benefit: When you charge, you gain an additional +2 bonus to your melee attack roll. If your melee attack hits, you deal additional damage equal to one-half your level.

Precise Shot
You are skilled at timing your ranged attacks so that you don't hit your allies by mistake.
Prerequisite: Point Blank Shot.
Benefit: You can shoot or throw a ranged weapon at an opponent engaged in melee combat with one or more of your allies without taking the standard –5 penalty (see Shooting or Throwing into a Melee, page 161).

Quick Draw
You can draw and holster weapons with startling quickness.
Prerequisite: Base attack bonus +1.
Benefit: You can draw or holster a weapon as a swift action instead of as a move action.

Rapid Shot
You can make two quick shots with a ranged weapon as a single attack.

Prerequisites: Strength 13, base attack bonus +1, proficient with weapon.

Benefit: When using a ranged weapon, you may fire two shots as a single attack against a single target. You take a –2 penalty on your attack roll, but you deal +1 die of damage with a successful attack.

Special: Using this feat fires two shots and can only be done if the weapon has sufficient ammunition remaining. The effects of this feat do not stack with the extra damage provided by the Burst Fire feat (page 82) or Deadeye feat (page 84).

Rapid Strike
You can make two quick strikes with a melee weapon as a single attack.

Prerequisites: Dexterity 13, base attack bonus +1, proficient with weapon.

Benefit: When using a melee weapon, you may make two strikes as a single attack against a single target. You take a –2 penalty on your attack roll, but you deal +1 die of damage with a successful attack.

The effects of this feat do not stack with the extra damage provided by the Mighty Swing feat.

Running Attack
You can move as you attack.

Prerequisite: Dexterity 13.

Benefit: When making an attack with a melee or ranged weapon, you can move both before and after the attack, provided that your total distance moved is not greater than your speed.

Shake It Off
You have learned to shake off debilitating conditions.

Prerequisites: Constitution 13, trained in the Endurance skill.

Benefit: You can spend two swift actions instead of three swift actions to move +1 step along the condition track (see Conditions, page 148).

Normal: It takes three swift actions to move +1 step along the condition track.

Skill Focus
One of your skills is particularly well honed.

Benefit: You gain a +5 competence bonus on skill checks made with one trained skill of your choice.

Special: This feat may be selected multiple times. Its effects do not stack. Each time you take this feat, it applies to a different trained skill.

Skill Training
You are considered trained in a new skill.

Benefit: Choose one untrained skill from your list of class skills. You become trained in that skill.

Special: This feat may be selected multiple times. Each time you take this feat, it applies to a different class skill.

Sniper
You are particularly adept at hitting the right target in a crowd.

Prerequisites: Point Blank Shot, Precise Shot, base attack bonus +4.

Benefit: You always ignore soft cover (that is, cover provided by a character, creature, or droid) when you make a ranged attack.

Normal: You can only ignore cover if you aim (see page 154) before making a ranged attack.

Strong in the Force
You have a particularly strong connection to the Force.

Benefit: When you spend a Force Point to adjust the result of an attack roll, skill check, or ability check, you roll d8s rather than d6s.

Surgical Expertise
You can perform skillful surgical procedures quickly.

Prerequisite: Trained in the Treat Injury skill.

Benefit: You can perform surgery in 10 minutes.

Normal: Performing surgery typically takes 1 hour (see the Treat Injury skill, page 74).

Throw
You can throw a creature that you've grappled.

Prerequisites: Trip, base attack bonus +1.

Benefit: If you successfully trip an opponent with a grapple attack, the opponent falls prone in any unoccupied space you desire up to 1 square beyond your reach and takes bludgeoning damage equal to your unarmed attack damage. A thrown opponent is no longer considered grappled.

Toughness
You are tougher than normal.

Benefit: You gain +1 hit point per character level.

Trip
You are skilled at tripping grappled foes.

Prerequisite: Base attack bonus +1.

Benefit: If you succeed on a grappling attack (see page 153) and your opponent fails the opposed grapple check, it falls prone in its space and is no longer considered grappled.

A prone opponent takes a –5 penalty on melee attack rolls. Melee attacks made against a prone target gain a +5 bonus, while ranged attacks made against a prone target take a –5 penalty.

Special: You cannot use the Pin and Trip feats during the same round.

Triple Attack
You can make an additional attack during a round of combat.

Prerequisites: Base attack bonus +11, Double Attack (chosen weapon), proficient with chosen weapon.

Benefit: Choose a single exotic weapon or one of the following weapon groups: advanced melee weapons, heavy weapons, lightsabers, pistols, rifles, simple weapons. When you use the full attack action, you may make one additional attack when wielding such a weapon. However, you take a –5 penalty on all attack rolls until your next turn because you're trading precision for speed. The extra attack and penalty stack with those of Double Attack.

Normal: Making a single attack is a standard action.

Special: You may select this feat multiple times. Each time you select this feat, it applies to a different exotic weapon or weapon group.

Triple Crit
Choose one type of weapon, such as a blaster pistol, vibrodagger, or lightsaber. You deal more damage on a critical hit with that weapon.

Prerequisites: Proficient with weapon, base attack bonus +8.

Benefit: When you score a critical hit with the selected weapon, you deal triple damage. You may select "unarmed attack" as a weapon for purposes of this feat.

Normal: A critical hit normally deals double damage to the target.

Special: You can gain this feat multiple times. The effects do not stack. Each time you take this feat, it applies to a different weapon.

Vehicular Combat
You can avoid attacks made against your vehicle.

Prerequisite: Trained in the Pilot skill.

Benefit: Once per round (as a reaction), when you are piloting a vehicle or starship, you may negate a weapon hit by making a successful Pilot check. The DC of the skill check is equal to the result of the attack roll you wish to negate.

In addition, while you are piloting a vehicle, you are considered proficient with pilot-operated vehicle weapons. (The vehicle descriptions in Chapter 10 indicate which weapons are operated by the pilot.)

Weapon Finesse
You are especially skilled at using weapons one that can benefit as much from Dexterity as from Strength.

Prerequisite: Base attack bonus +1.

Benefit: When using a light melee weapon or a lightsaber, you may use your Dexterity modifier instead of your Strength modifier on attack rolls.

Weapon Focus
Choose a single exotic weapon or weapon group. You are especially good at using these weapons. You can choose unarmed strike or grapple for your weapon for purposes of this feat.

Prerequisite: Proficient with selected exotic weapon or weapon group.

Benefit: You gain a +1 bonus on all attack rolls you make using the selected exotic weapon or weapon group.

Special: You can gain this feat multiple times. Its effects do not stack. Each time you take the feat, it applies to a new exotic weapon or weapon group.

Weapon Proficiency
You are proficient with a particular kind of weaponry.

Benefit: Choose one of the following weapon groups: advanced melee weapons, heavy weapons (which includes vehicular weapons and starship weapons), lightsabers, pistols, rifles, and simple weapons. You are proficient with all weapons of the selected group. For more information on weapon groups, see page 119.

Normal: If you wield a weapon with which you are not proficient, you take a –5 penalty to your attack rolls.

Special: You can gain this feat multiple times. Each time you take the feat, it applies to a different weapon group. You cannot take exotic weapons as a weapon group; instead, you must select the Exotic Weapon Proficiency feat (see page 84) to gain proficiency with a specific exotic weapon (such as the bowcaster or flamethrower).

Whirlwind Attack
You can strike nearby opponents in an amazing, spinning melee attack.

Prerequisites: Dexterity 13, Intelligence 13, Melee Defense, base attack bonus +4.

Benefit: As a full-round action, you can make an area attack with your melee weapon, striking every opponent within your reach. This whirlwind attack uses the area attack rules (see Area Attacks, page 155); you make one attack roll and apply the result to every target in range.

Chapter VI
The Force

The Force is an energy field generated by all living things. It surrounds and penetrates everything, binding the galaxy together. There are two sides to the Force. Peace, serenity, and knowledge form the light side, while the dark side consists of aggression, anger, and fear. The universe is a place of balance: life and death, creation and destruction, love and hate. As such, both sides of the Force are part of the natural order.

Some beings are more attuned to the Force than others. Whether they understand it or not, they can feel the Force flowing through them. Of those that are sensitive to the Force, beings that study its ways can learn to manipulate its energy. The Jedi fall into this category, using their knowledge of the Force to give them their powers. But theirs is not the only Force-using tradition. The Sith, the Nightsisters of Dathomir, and others embrace the dark side of the Force, while a variety of alien cultures, such as Ewok shamans and Ithorian eco-priests, call the light side of the Force by different names. Understanding of the Force manifests in many ways.

The Force through the Ages

For most of the history of the Republic, the Jedi were looked upon as defenders and protectors of justice. By their example, belief in the Force was accepted if not always understood. Most beings could not perceive the Force directly; they could only see it manifest in those attuned to it, such as the Jedi. At times over the years, the dark side came to the forefront, such as during the ancient Sith Wars, but in general the champions of the light side helped keep the galactic peace.

During the Rise of the Empire era, the Force is a powerful component of everyday life. The Jedi are visible, active proponents of the Force. Regardless of what an individual may believe about the Force, it's hard to deny the power demonstrated by the Jedi. As the Clone Wars rage across the galaxy, Jedi are seen at the forefront of battles, and the Force impacts the lives of soldiers and citizens alike.

Later, in the wake of the destruction of the Jedi order and the rise of the Empire, the Force comes to be looked upon as an arcane religion practiced by misguided fools. The Empire outlaws the Jedi and attempts to stamp out anyone who demonstrates an affinity for the Force. Propaganda and politics keep the local systems in line and succeed in driving Force-users underground, where they live in fear and obscurity.

If your campaign is set in the Rebellion era (around the time of Episodes IV–VI), the Force has faded from common knowledge. Those who can manipulate the Force keep their skills hidden to avoid the notice of the Empire. Even members of the Imperial hierarchy, despite the presence of Darth Vader, consider the Force to be outdated and insignificant compared to the military might of the Empire. In many ways, that's just how the Emperor wants it. Even the Emperor, one of the most powerful Force-users in the galaxy, keeps his Force abilities secret from the general public and most of his subordinates. The few Force-users that exist during this period are either hiding from the Empire, working for the Empire, or trying to ignore the presence of the Force. The Rebel Alliance has begun to use the Force as a rallying cry, adopting the Jedi salutation, "May the Force be with you," as its own. Because of this, the few Force-sensitive beings that can actually use the Force begin to reach out to the Alliance. And, of course, Luke Skywalker begins his training during this time.

If your campaign is set in The New Jedi Order era, the Force has regained a place in everyday society and a new fellowship of Jedi has come to prominence under the tutelage of Luke Skywalker. Many beings in the New Republic, however, harbor varying degrees of mistrust and fear toward Force-users. These negative feelings are due, in part, to the actions of a few rogue Jedi who have taken the law into their own hands and have begun to rebel against Luke Skywalker's leadership. The memories of a host of darksiders that plagued the galaxy since the time of Darth Vader and the Emperor add fuel to the fire of fear, and the political machinations of members of the Republic Council have begun to fan these flames. Force-users of this period, then, are finding that acceptance of the Force among the general population may turn into a bad thing—at least as far as they are concerned. Tensions are already high, as this era is marked by the invasion of the Yuuzhan Vong.

Using the Force

The Force is a mystical energy field that surrounds and binds all living things in the galaxy. More than just a source of power for those sensitive to its presence, the Force can affect the fates of even ordinary citizens who have no aptitude for its use. In the *Star Wars Roleplaying Game*, there are two ways that players may call upon the Force for assistance. The first way, usable by all characters, comes in the form of Force Points. The second way, usable only by characters with the Force Sensitivity feat, is through the Use of Force skill and associated Force powers.

Force Points

Force Points represent a character's knack for using the Force to aid her actions. A character need not be Force-sensitive to use Force Points; they represent the presence of the Force in all forms of life, and though some call it luck, others believe that it is the will of the Force that grants a person aid. For a Force-sensitive character, it represents a conscious decision to call upon the Force for assistance. Characters without the Force Sensitivity feat don't realize that the Force is aiding their actions, only that they are trying hard to succeed.

Gaining Force Points

You get 5 Force Points at 1st level. When you gain a new level, you lose any unspent Force Points from the previous level but gain a number of Force

Points equal to 5 + one-half your new character level (rounded down). Some prestige classes grant a higher number of Force Points at each level (see Chapter 12).

Example: Deel Surool, a 1st-level scoundrel, gains 5 Force Points at 1st level and spends only four of them before achieving 2nd level. When he hits 2nd level, he loses the unspent Force Point from the previous level, but he gains 6 Force Points (5 + one-half his new character level).

Using Force Points

On your turn, you may spend a Force Point as a free action to roll 1d6 and add the result to a single attack roll, skill check, or ability check. You can do this once per round. At 8th level, when you spend a Force Point, you instead roll 2d6 and take the best die result as your bonus; at 15th level, you roll 3d6 and take the best die result as your bonus. This is summarized below:

CHARACTER LEVEL	NUMBER OF DICE ROLLED
1st–7th	1d6
8th–14th	2d6*
15th or higher	3d6*

* Only count the highest die result.

Some talents, Force techniques, Force secrets, and Force powers require you to spend a Force Point to activate. In addition, if you are a Force-user, you may spend 1 Force Point as a swift action to return a single spent Force power to your active suite of Force powers (see Force Powers, page 95, for more information).

If you are reduced to 0 hit points and would be killed, you can spend a Force Point as a reaction to avoid death and instead fall unconscious (see 0 Hit Points and Falling Unconscious, pages 146–147).

Finally, you can spend 1 Force Point as a swift action to lower your Dark Side Score by 1 (see The Dark Side, below).

Unless noted otherwise, you can spend only one Force Point per round.

The Dark Side

The Force has two aspects, one light and one dark. The dark side lurks in the shadows, whispering to Force-users, tempting them with quick and easy access to power. While seemingly stronger, the dark side is only easier. It consists of the destructive impulses of all living beings. Anger, fear, hatred, and aggression are expressions of the dark side, and such emotions can quickly lead a Force-user down the dark side's corrupting path. Early on in her training, a Force-user finds that the dark side greatly enhances her abilities. After a time, the dark side demands more and more of those in its embrace.

Beware the Dark Side
Most players don't want their Jedi characters to slip over to the dark side of the Force. If you want a campaign where all the heroes must constantly strive against the lure of the dark side, then the GM should increase a character's Dark Side Score for even the most minor transgressions. If you want a campaign where the heroes have more room to explore options, or if you don't want slipping to the dark side to be a major theme of the campaign, then the GM should consider increasing a character's Dark Side Score only for major or moderate transgressions.

Dark Side Score

Your Dark Side Score measures the extent to which you've been corrupted by the dark side of the Force. A 1st-level character begins play with a Dark Side Score of 0. The only way to increase one's Dark Side Score is to commit evil acts.

A character who commits an evil act increases his Dark Side Score by 1. What constitutes an evil act is discussed under Dark Side Transgressions, below. Regardless of how many evil acts a character commits, the maximum Dark Side Score a character can possess is equal to his Wisdom score. Thus, a character with a Wisdom of 15 can have a maximum Dark Side Score of 15.

A character whose Dark Side Score equals his Wisdom score has fully embraced the dark side and is wholly evil. A hero who falls to the dark side becomes a GM character (unless the GM wants to allow the player to continue playing the dark side character as a sort of campaign anti-hero).

Dark Side Transgressions

The GM should use the considerations detailed below as guidelines for whether or not to increase a character's Dark Side Score. The guidelines are separated by degree: Major transgressions are acts that definitely deserve

> "The dark side of the Force is a pathway to many abilities some consider to be unnatural."
> – Supreme Chancellor Palpatine

an increase, moderate transgressions are acts that probably deserve an increase, and minor transgressions are acts that could be considered dark but probably don't deserve an increase.

Major Transgressions
Any of the following transgressions should increase a character's Dark Side Score by 1:

Performing a blatantly evil act: This includes deliberately killing or injuring another character who hasn't done anything wrong or who honestly seeks redemption for evil acts he performed in the past.

Using a Force power with the [dark side] descriptor: A few Force powers are, by their very nature, evil. Examples of Force powers with the [dark side] descriptor include *Force lightning*, which channels dark energy, and *dark rage*, which feeds on negative emotions.

Using the Force in anger: Using the Force in anger or hatred is bad, but this can be hard to enforce. It's difficult to determine the emotion a character is experiencing. The GM should increase a character's Dark Side Score by 1 in these situations only when the player specifically states that his character is feeling fear, anger, hatred, pride, jealousy, greed, vengeance, and so forth.

Moderate Transgressions
Any of the following transgressions might increase a character's Dark Side Score by 1, at the GM's discretion:

Using the Force to cause undue harm: Many uses of the Force are not overtly of the dark side, but they can be harmful or even fatal in their applications. When a Force power that isn't specifically tied to the dark side is used to harm living beings, the GM should consider increasing the character's Dark Side Score by 1.

Performing a questionably evil act: Some acts, while seemingly cruel, aren't necessarily evil. The GM should consider the intent behind the action before deciding to increase a character's Dark Side Score. For example, it may be a transgression to deliberately kill or injure (or allow someone else to kill or injure) a character known to have committed evil acts without remorse, but who is otherwise helpless.

Minor Transgressions
The following transgressions should probably not increase a character's Dark Side Score, unless the GM feels there's good cause to make an exception:

Performing a dubiously evil act: Increase a character's Dark Side Score only when the act is out of proportion to the situation. In most cases, the GM shouldn't increase a character's Dark Side Score for a single incident, but multiple incidents may indicate that the character has an unconscious cruel streak. For example, a hero who kills an opponent in combat while ignoring opportunities to end the situation without the loss of life might deserve a increased Dark Side Score, though a specific situation might not appear quite so clear-cut.

> ### Heroes and the Dark Side
> A GM may decide to run a completely heroic campaign. In this case, the GM can rule that once a Force-using character becomes dark, that character becomes a GM character and is no longer under the control of the player. If you're the GM, consider this option carefully before implementing it, because it takes away player freedom. If you put this rule in place at the start of your campaign, then it just becomes part of the rules and everyone is aware of the consequences of walking down the dark path.

Dark Side Score Tracker
The Dark Side Score tracker is a useful tool for tracking a hero's devotion to the dark side. The Dark Side Score tracker is represented as a row of 24 numbered boxes at the bottom of your *Star Wars* character sheet (page 287).

A character's Dark Side Score tracker should have a number of empty boxes equal to the character's Wisdom score. Any extra boxes should be shaded in or blacked out. For example, Set Harth has a Wisdom of 11, so his Dark Side Score tracker looks like this:

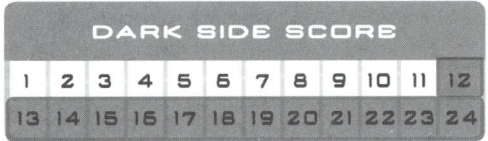

Whenever a hero's Dark Side Score increases by 1, the player fills in one of the empty boxes on the character's Dark Side Score tracker. When a character has no more empty boxes on his Dark Side Score tracker, he is considered to be dark. He is now effectively lost to the dark side and has little hope of finding redemption.

Whenever a character's Wisdom score increases by 1, he gets an additional empty box on his Dark Side Score tracker. This box remains empty until his Dark Side Score increases by 1.

A hero who still has empty boxes on his Dark Side Score tracker may be tainted by the dark side, but not beyond redemption. A tainted character can rid himself of the dark side's taint by atoning.

Atoning
A hero tainted by the dark side can work his way back to the light through heroic deeds, the use of Force Points, and by atoning for past misdeeds. A dark character's only path back to the light is to accomplish a truly epic act of heroism against the dark and in the service of the light.

Effectively, the tainted character accomplishes this by reducing his Dark Side Score. A character can sacrifice 1 Force Point to reduce his Dark Side Score by 1 and clear one box on his Dark Side Score tracker. This form of atonement represents a period of meditation, reflection, and absolution on the part of the character. If desired by the player and GM, this can be worked into the campaign as part of an adventure, but it isn't necessary. It can occur between adventures.

In addition, an act of dramatic heroism by the character—if performed without calling upon the dark side—reduces the character's Dark Side Score by 1 and clears one box on his Dark Side Score tracker.

A dark character can't reduce his Dark Side Score by atoning. Such a character's only option is an act of dramatic heroism (see below).

Dramatic Heroism

A dark character may attempt to turn away from the dark side by performing an act of dramatic heroism without calling upon the dark side of the Force. Such an act should require extreme personal cost, be made in a selfless manner, and provide a significant benefit to the galactic balance.

Darth Vader performed such an act of dramatic heroism at the end of *Return of the Jedi* when he sacrificed his own life to save his son and destroy the Emperor. Kyp Durron (in the expanded *Star Wars* universe) performed a similar act of dramatic heroism by destroying the Sun Crusher, a super weapon prototype. Additionally, Jedi history tells of a Jedi named Bastila Shan (from *Knights of the Old Republic*) falling to the dark side, but in an act of dramatic heroism she turned the Republic fleet against Darth Malak using a powerful form of Battle Meditation.

If the GM accepts the act as being appropriately heroic, dramatic, and selfless, the character's Dark Side Score drops to 1, and he clears all but one of the boxes on his Dark Side Score tracker (so that he has a number of empty boxes equal to one less than his Wisdom score). In addition, the dark side exacts a final toll by drawing away all of the character's current Force Points. Henceforth, the character must strive to walk the path of the light side.

FORCE POWERS

Force powers are special abilities available to anyone who takes the Force Training feat (page 85). They allow characters to do astonishing things such as play tricks with the minds of others, move heavy objects, see into the future, and even blast foes with terrible arcs of lightning.

LEARNING FORCE POWERS

A character who takes the Force Training feat (see page 85) automatically learns a number of Force powers of her choice equal to 1 + her Wisdom modifier (minimum 1). A character can learn additional Force powers by taking the Force Training feat again or by increasing her Wisdom modifier.

SELECTING FORCE POWERS

Choosing your Force powers can be something of an art. If you choose poorly, you might be stuck with a Force power that you can't use very well. When selecting Force powers, remember the following:

Like feats, Force powers cannot be changed once selected (not without your GM's approval, anyway). Also, some Force powers are inherently more difficult to trigger than others. For example, *Force stun* requires a DC 20 (or higher) Use the Force check to activate, which means that a low-level character attempting to use the power will fail more often than he succeeds.

Don't forget that you can select the same Force power more than once if you want to be able to have multiple uses of that power in your suite. At low levels, it is sometimes more useful to have extra uses of an easy-to-trigger power than a new power that is more difficult to activate.

For example, Sen Udo-Mal is a 1st-level Jedi with a Wisdom score of 11 (+0 modifier). He takes the Force Training feat at 1st level and immediately gains a Force power. He chooses *battle strike*. At 3rd level, he takes the Force Training feat again, which allows him to learn a new Force power; he chooses *mind trick*. At 4th level, Sen Udo-Mal raises his Wisdom score from 11 to 12, thereby increasing his ability modifier from +0 to +1; at that time, he gains two additional Force powers (one for each instance of the Force Training feat), so he chooses *move object* and *surge*.

USING FORCE POWERS

When your character uses a Force power, make a Use the Force check (see page 77). The check result determines the power's effect.

Some Force powers have all-or-nothing effects. Other Force powers have multi-tiered effects, and your Use the Force check result determines the maximum effect you can achieve, although you can always choose a lesser effect. If your Use the Force check is too low to activate the Force power's baseline effect, nothing happens and the action is wasted.

Using a Force power removes it from your character's active "suite" of Force powers, regardless of whether the Use the Force skill check succeeds or fails.

Your Force Power Suite: Your character's Force powers collectively form a suite. When your character uses a Force power, it's like playing a card and putting it in a discard pile. The power takes effect, and it's no longer available to the character . . . at least for a while.

Regaining Force Powers: You have different ways to regain spent Force powers so that you can use them again:

—When combat is over and you have a chance to rest for 1 minute, you regain all of your Force powers.

—If you roll a natural 20 on a Use the Force check, you regain all spent Force powers at the end of your turn.

—You can spend a Force Point as a reaction and immediately regain one spent Force power.

—Some unique abilities (such as the Force Focus talent) allow you to regain spent Force powers in other ways.

Force Power Descriptors

Some Force powers are more strongly tied to one side of the Force than the other. These Force powers carry either the [light side] descriptor or the [dark side] descriptor. Powers that target creatures' minds carry the [mind-affecting] descriptor.

Dark Side: Using a Force power with the [dark side] descriptor increases your Dark Side Score by 1. You cannot use a Force Point to modify your Use the Force check when activating a Force power with the [dark side] descriptor. Dark side powers stem from powerful negative emotions and include *dark rage* and *Force lightning*.

Light Side: If you have a Dark Side Score of 1 or higher, you cannot use a Force Point to modify your Use the Force check when activating a Force power with the [light side] descriptor. Light side powers are generally beneficial and include *sever Force* and *vital transfer*.

Mind-Affecting: A Force power with the [mind-affecting] descriptor has no effect on creatures that are mindless (that is, creatures with no Intelligence score) or creatures that are immune to mind-affecting effects.

Force Power Descriptions

The following Force powers are available to any character with the Force Sensitivity feat (see page 85). Each Force power includes the following information:

Force Power Name [Descriptor]

If a Force power has a descriptor, it appears in square brackets after the Force power's name. The name of the power is followed by a brief description of the Force power's effect. **Time:** The type of action needed to use or activate the Force power. **Target:** The targets affected by the Force power.

Make a Use the Force check. The results of the Use the Force check are described here.

Special: Some Force powers have special rules, which are covered here.

Battle Strike

You use the Force to enhance your battle prowess. **Time:** Swift action. **Target:** You.

Make a Use the Force check. The result of the check determines the effect, if any:

DC 15: Gain a +1 Force bonus on your next attack roll and deal an additional 1d6 points of damage if the attack hits.

DC 20: As DC 15, except you deal an additional 2d6 points of damage.

DC 25: As DC 15, except you deal an additional 3d6 points of damage.

Special: You can spend a Force Point to deal an additional 2d6 points of damage on your next attack.

Dark Rage [Dark Side]

You become enraged as the dark side flows through you. **Time:** Swift action. **Target:** You.

Make a Use the Force check. The result of the check determines the effect, if any:

DC 15: You gain a +2 rage bonus on melee attack rolls and melee damage rolls until the end of your turn.

DC 20: As DC 15, except the rage bonuses increase to +4.

DC 25: As DC 15, except the rage bonuses increase to +6.

Special: While consumed by rage, you cannot use skills or perform tasks that require patience or concentration.

You can spend a Force Point to extend the duration of your *dark rage* until the end of the encounter.

Farseeing

You gain a vague, momentary impression of events happening around a particular being in some distant place. **Time:** Full-round action. **Target:** One creature you know or have met before.

Make a Use the Force check. If your check result is less than the target's Will Defense, you gain no information (including whether the target is alive or dead) and cannot use this Force power against the same target for 24 hours. If your check result equals or exceeds the target's Will Defense, you can sense whether the target is alive or dead and gain a vague sense of its immediate surroundings, what it's currently doing, and any strong emotions it is presently feeling. A dead target has a Will Defense of 30 for purposes of this Force power.

Special: If you successfully use this Force power, you can spend a Force Point to gain a clear mental image of the target's surroundings, as well as other creatures and objects within 6 squares of it.

Force Disarm

You disarm an opponent by using the Force to pull the weapon from his grasp. **Time:** Standard action. **Target:** One creature within 6 squares and within line of sight.

Make a Use the Force check. Use this check in place of your attack roll when attempting to disarm the target (see Disarm, page 152). If your disarm attack succeeds, you may choose to let the item drop to the ground in the target's fighting space or have the item fly into your hand (in which case you must have a free hand to catch it).

Special: Feats that improve disarm attacks (such as Improved Disarm) do not apply to *Force disarm*.

You can spend a Force Point to damage or destroy the target weapon instead. If your disarm attack succeeds, the weapon takes damage equal to your Use the Force check result. You must declare that you are using this option before making your disarm attack.

Force Grip

You use the Force to choke or crush your enemy. **Time:** Standard action. **Target:** One target within 6 squares or within line of sight.

Make a Use the Force check. The result of the check determines the effect, if any:

DC 15: The target takes 2d6 points of damage. If your Use the Force check equals or exceeds the target's Fortitude Defense, the target can take only a single swift action on his next turn.

DC 20: As DC 15, except the target takes 4d6 points of damage.

DC 25: As DC 15, except target takes 6d6 points of damage.

Special: You may maintain your concentration on the targeted creature to continue damaging it from round to round. Maintaining the *Force grip* is a standard action, and you must make a new Use the Force check each round.

You can spend a Force Point to deal an additional 2d6 points of damage with your *Force grip*.

Force Lightning [Dark Side]

You blast an enemy with deadly arcs of Force energy. **Time:** Standard action. **Targets:** One target in line of sight and within 6 squares of you.

Make a Use the Force check. Make one roll and compare the result to the target's Reflex Defense. If the attack hits, the target takes 8d6 points of Force damage and moves –1 step along the condition track (see Conditions, page 148). If the attack misses, the target takes half damage and does not move along the condition track.

Special: You can spend a Force Point to move a target an additional –1 step along the condition track when you successfully hit it with *Force lightning*.

Force Slam

You pound one or more creatures with the Force. **Time:** Standard action. **Targets:** All targets within a 6-square cone and within line of sight.

Make a Use the Force check. Make one roll and compare the result to each target's Fortitude Defense. If the result equals or exceeds a target's Fortitude Defense, it takes 4d6 points of Force damage and is knocked prone. If the result is less than a target's Fortitude Defense, it takes half damage and is not knocked prone. This is an area effect.

Special: When you use this power, you can spend a Force Point to deal an additional 2d6 points of damage to targets in the area.

Force Stun

You call upon the Force to overload an enemy's senses, potentially stunning it. **Time:** Standard action. Targets: One creature within 6 squares or within your line of sight.

Make a Use the Force check. Compare the result to the target's Will Defense. If the check result equals or exceeds the target's Will Defense, the target moves −1 step along the condition track (see Conditions, page 148). For every 5 points by which you exceed the target's Will Defense, the target moves an additional −1 step along the condition track.

Special: When you use this power, you can spend a Force Point to move the target an additional −1 step along the condition track.

Force Thrust

You use the Force to push a target away from you. **Time:** Standard action. Targets: One object or character within 12 squares and within line of sight.

Make a Use the Force check. The target makes a Strength check. If you beat the target's Strength check, you push it back 1 square plus an additional square for every 5 points by which you exceed the target's check result. If you push the target into a larger object, the target takes 1d6 points of damage.

The target adds its size modifier to its Strength check: Colossal, +20; Gargantuan, +15; Huge, +10; Large, +5; Medium, +0; Small, −5; Tiny, −10; Diminutive, −15; Fine, −20. In addition, it gets a +5 stability bonus if it has more than two legs or is otherwise exceptionally stable.

Special: You can spend a Force Point to apply a −5 penalty to the target's Strength check to resist your *Force thrust*. Additionally, if you successfully push the target into a larger object, you deal an additional 2d6 points of damage from the extreme force of the thrust.

Mind Trick [mind-affecting]

You use the Force to alter a target's perceptions or plant a suggestion in its mind. **Time:** Standard action. **Target:** One Intelligence 3 or higher creature in line of sight and within 12 squares of you.

Make a Use the Force check. If you equal or exceed the target's Will Defense, you may choose one of the following effects:

—You create a fleeting hallucination that distracts the target and enables you to use the Stealth skill even if the target is aware of you.

—You perform a feint so that the next attack you make against the target ignores its Dexterity bonus to Reflex Defense (if any).

—You make an otherwise unpalatable suggestion seem completely reasonable to the target. You must be able to communicate with the target, and the suggestion can't obviously threaten the target's life. The target won't realize later that what he did is unacceptable.

—You fill the target with terror, causing it to flee from you at top speed for 1 minute. The affected creature stops fleeing if it is wounded. The effect is negated if the target's level is equal to or higher than your character level. This is a fear effect.

Special: If you are making a suggestion, you may spend a Force Point to improve the target's attitude by one step, plus one additional step for every 5 points by which your Use the Force check exceeds the target's Will Defense.

Move Object

You telekinetically move a target up to 6 squares in any direction using the Force. **Time:** Standard action. **Target:** One character or object within 6 squares or within your line of sight.

Make a Use the Force check. The result of the check determines the maximum size of the target you can lift (see below). If the target is a creature that resists your attempt, your Use the Force check must also exceed the target's Will Defense. You can hurl the target at (or drop it on) another target in range if your Use the Force check exceeds the second target's Reflex Defense. Both targets take damage determined by your Use the Force check result.

DC 15: Move object up to Medium size (deals 2d6 points of damage)
DC 20: Move object up to Large size (deals 4d6 points of damage)
DC 25: Move object up to Huge size (deals 6d6 points of damage)
DC 30: Move object up to Gargantuan size (deals 8d6 points of damage)
DC 35: Move object up to Colossal size (deals 10d6 points of damage)

Special: You may maintain your concentration on the targeted object to continue to move it from round to round. Maintaining the *move object* power is a standard action.

If you use *move object* against a hovering or flying target (such as a speeder or starship), the target can oppose your Use the Force check with a grapple check as a reaction. If the target wins the opposed check, you are unable to move the target.

You may spend a Force Point to increase the maximum size of the object by one category and deal an additional 2d6 points of damage (maximum size Colossal [frigate], 12d6 damage). Alternatively, you may spend a Destiny Point (see page 112) to increase the maximum size of the object by three

> "THE FORCE CAN HAVE A STRONG INFLUENCE ON A WEAK MIND."
> — OBI-WAN KENOBI

categories and deal an additional 6d6 points of damage (maximum size Colossal [station], 16d6 damage).

Negate Energy

You spontaneously negate a single attack that deals energy weapon damage, such as a lightsaber or blaster. **Time:** Reaction. **Target:** One attack made against you that deals energy weapon damage.

Make a Use the Force check. If the result of the check equals or exceeds the damage dealt by the energy weapon, the attack is negated and you take no damage. If your check result is less than the amount of damage dealt, you fail to negate the attack and take damage as normal.

Special: You must be aware of the attack (and not flat-footed) to negate it. If you are successful, you can spend a Force Point to regain hit points equal to the damage of the negated attack, up to a maximum of your full normal hit points.

Rebuke

You harmlessly absorb or deflect one Force power or used against you, perhaps even turning it against its creator. **Time:** Reaction. **Target:** One Force power directed at you.

Make a Use the Force check. If your result equals or exceeds the check result of the power directed at you, you harmlessly redirect it and suffer no ill effects. If you result exceeds the check result of the power directed at you by 5 or more, you may choose to turn the Force power against its creator, who suffers the effect.

Special: If you successfully reflect a Force power back at its originator, the originator may attempt to rebuke the power as well. If he reflects it back again, both you and the originator are affected by the Force power. You can spend a Force Point as a reaction to suffer no ill effects from a Force power that has been rebuked twice—once by you and once by the power's originator.

Sever Force [Light Side]

You can block another Force-user's access to the Force, preventing him from spending Force Points and making it difficult for him to use Force powers. **Time:** Standard action. **Target:** One Force-using creature with a Dark Side Score of 1 or higher that is within 12 squares and within line of sight.

Make a Use the Force check. If your Use the Force check equals or exceeds the target's Will Defense, the effect (if any) is determined by your check result:

DC 25: The target cannot spend Force Points for a number of hours equal to its Dark Side Score.

DC 30: As DC 25, plus the target moves –1 step along the condition track (see page 149) each time it uses a Force power in the same timeframe.

DC 35: As DC 35, except the target moves –2 steps along the condition track each time it uses a Force power in the same timeframe.

Special: This Force power has no effect on targets with a Dark Side Score of 0.

You can spend a Force Point to double the duration of the effect. Alternatively, you can spend a Destiny Point (see page 112) to increase the duration to a number of days equal to the target's Dark Side Score.

Surge

The Force enables you to jump great heights and distances as well as move quickly. **Time:** Swift action. **Target:** You.

Make a Use the Force check. The result of the check determines the effect, if any:

DC 10: You gain a +10 Force bonus on Jump checks and your speed increases by 2 squares until the start of your next turn. The Force bonus on Jump checks includes the adjustment for increased speed.

DC 15: As DC 10 except: +20 Force bonus on Jump checks, speed increases by 4 squares.

DC 20: As DC 10 except: +30 Force bonus on Jump checks, speed increases by 6 squares.

Special: You can spend a Force Point to increase the power's Force bonus on Jump checks by 10 and increase your speed by an additional 2 squares.

Vital Transfer [Light Side]

You use your own life force to heal another living creature, using the Force as a conduit. **Time:** Standard action. **Target:** One creature touched.

Make a Use the Force check. The result of the check determines the effect, if any:

DC 15: The target heals hit points equal to 2 × its character level.
DC 20: The target heals hit points equal to 3 × its character level.
DC 25: The target heals hit points equal to 4 × its character level.

Each time you use *vital transfer*, you take half as much damage as you heal (rounded down).

Special: You may spend a Force Point to avoid taking any damage when you use this Force power. You may spend a Destiny Point (see page 112) to move the target +5 steps on the condition track in addition to healing it normally.

Force Talents

Force talents work exactly like the talents presented in Chapter 3: Heroic Classes; however, they are available only to characters with the Force Sensitivity feat (see page 85). Any time a character with the Force Sensitivity feat would normally gain a talent (such as from gaining an odd-numbered level in a heroic class), he or she may instead select a Force talent from one of the four Force talent trees presented below. If a character with the Force Sensitivity feat is a member of a Force tradition (see page 106), he or she may instead select a Force talent from that tradition's individual Force talent tree.

Alter Talent Tree

The Force grants you considerable power over your environment as well as others around you.

Disciplined Strike: Whenever you use a Force power that has a cone effect (such as *Force slam*), you may exclude a certain number of targets from the effects of that power. The number of targets that you may exclude in this manner is equal to your Wisdom modifier (minimum of 1).

Telekinetic Power: Whenever you roll a natural 20 on your Use the Force check to activate the *Force disarm, Force grip, Force slam, Force thrust,* or *move object* Force powers, you may choose to use that Force power again immediately as a free action. You may direct the second use of the Force power against any eligible target.

Telekinetic Savant: Once per encounter as a swift action, you may return one of these Force powers to your suite without spending a Force Point: *Force disarm, Force grip, Force slam, Force thrust,* or *move object*.

You may select this talent multiple times. Each time you select it, you may use this talent one additional time per encounter.

CONTROL TALENT TREE

You have learned how to regulate your own body systems, control your emotions, and channel the Force.

Damage Reduction 10: You can spend a Force Point as a standard action to gain damage reduction 10 for 1 minute (see Damage Reduction, page 158).

Equilibrium: As a swift action, you can spend a Force Point to remove all debilitating conditions affecting you and return to a normal state (see Conditions, page 148).

Force Focus: As a full-round action, you may make a DC 15 Use the Force check. If the check succeeds, you regain one spent Force power of your choice.

Force Recovery: Whenever you use your second wind (see Second Wind, page 146), you regain a number of additional hit points equal to 1d6 per Force Point you possess (maximum 10d6).

Prerequisite: Equilibrium.

DARK SIDE TALENT TREE

The path to the dark side of the Force is the quick and easy path, granting amazing power but forever dominating the destinies of those in its grasp.

You must have a Dark Side Score of 1 or higher to select talents from this tree; if your Dark Side Score is ever reduced to 0, you lose access to all talents in this talent tree until your Dark Side Score increases.

Power of the Dark Side: You allow your hatred to fuel your attacks. Whenever you spend a Force Point to modify an attack roll, you may choose to roll an additional bonus die and take the best result. However, doing so increases your Dark Side Score by 1.

For example, a 1st-level character with this talent could increase his Dark Side Score by 1 to roll 2d6 instead of 1d6, taking the best die result and applying it as a bonus on his attack roll.

Dark Presence: As a standard action, you grant yourself and all allies within 6 squares of you a +1 Force bonus to all defenses until the end of the encounter. These bonuses are lost if you fall unconscious or die. Affected allies that move out of range lose the benefits for as long as they remain out of range.

Prerequisites: Charisma 13, Power of the Dark Side.

Revenge: Whenever an ally of equal or higher level than you is killed or reduced to 0 hit points within your line of sight, you gain a +2 Force bonus on attack rolls and damage rolls until the end of the encounter. (Since Force bonuses do not stack, you don't get a higher bonus if more than one ally falls in the same encounter.)

Prerequisites: Dark Presence, Power of the Dark Side.

Swift Power: Once per day, you can use a Force power that normally takes a standard action or move action as a swift action.

Prerequisite: Power of the Dark Side.

SENSE TALENT TREE

Your attunement to the Force grants you uncanny powers of perception.

Force Perception: You can make a Use the Force check instead of a Perception check to avoid surprise, notice enemies, sense deception, or sense influence (see the Perception skill, page 70). You are considered trained in the Perception skill for purposes of using this talent. If you are entitled to a Perception check reroll, you may reroll your Use the Force check instead (subject to the same circumstances and limitations).

Force Pilot: You can use your Use the Force check modifier instead of your Pilot check modifier when making Pilot checks. You are considered trained in the Pilot skill for purposes of using this talent. If you are entitled to a Pilot check reroll, you may reroll your Use the Force check instead (subject to the same circumstances and limitations).

Foresight: You may spend a Force Point to reroll an Initiative check, keeping the better of the two rolls. Additionally, if you roll a natural 20 on the Initiative check reroll, you immediately regain the Force Point spent to activate this talent.

Prerequisite: Force Perception.

Gauge Force Potential: By focusing on a specific creature in your line of sight, you can gauge how strong in the Force it is. This takes a standard action and requires a Use the Force check. If your check result meets or beats the target's Will Defense, you know whether or not it has the Force Sensitivity feat, you know how many Force powers it knows (but not which ones, specifically), and you know how many Force Points it has currently.

Prerequisite: Force Perception.

Visions: Whenever you use the *farseeing* Force power, you can spend a Force Point as a swift action to see into the target's past or future instead of the glimpsing the target in the present. You declare how far into the target's past or future you wish to look, up to a maximum of 1 year per your character level. Any information gained about a target's future is subject to change, depending on whether steps are taken to alter that future.

Prerequisites: Force Perception, *farseeing*.

FORCE TECHNIQUES

Force techniques represent a deeper understanding of the Force and, like martial skills, usually come with years of practice. A few gifted or devoted Force-users learn to master them more quickly. In general, Force techniques are only available to characters with levels in certain Force-using prestige classes (such as the Force adept, Jedi Knight, and Sith apprentice).

Whenever you gain access to a new Force technique, select it from the following list. Once selected, a Force technique cannot be changed.

Force Point Recovery

At the end of an encounter, you automatically recover 1 Force Point spent during the encounter.

You may select this Force technique multiple times; each time you take it, you recover an additional Force Point spent during an encounter.

Force Power Mastery

Choose a single Force power. You may take 10 on Use the Force checks to activate this Force power even when distracted or threatened.

You may select this Force technique multiple times; each time you select this Force technique, it applies to a different Force power.

Improved Force Trance

Each hour you remain in a Force trance (see the Use the Force skill, page 77), you regain a number of hit points equal to 2 × your character level.

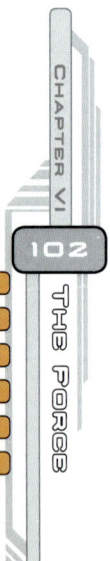

> ### Disturbances in the Force
> All life shines in the Force, very much the way gravity wells in realspace are reflected in hyperspace. A single person not particularly attuned to the Force flickers like a candle in the night, making but the slightest impression in the Force. A Force-user shines more brightly, especially when manipulating the Force. Each time a Force-user calls upon the Force, a slight tremor ripples through it that can be perceived by other Force-users. Used sparingly and in harmony with the natural balance, such ripples can barely be detected. When a user constantly calls upon the Force to alter the world around him, the ripples become quakes that can be felt at great distances. Such quakes attract attention, making those who have less refined control over the Force or who rely on the Force too frequently the target of more powerful Force-users. It is believed that through such methods the Empire was able to hunt down stray Force-users in the years leading up to the Galactic Civil War.

Improved Move Light Object
You may make a Use the Force check to move a light object as a swift action instead of a move action. Using the light object as a projectile weapon requires a move action (instead of a standard action).

Improved Sense Force
You may use the sense Force ability of the Use the Force skill (see page 77) as a move action rather than a full-round action.

Improved Sense Surroundings
You may use the sense surroundings ability of the Use the Force skill (see page 77) as a free action rather than a swift action.

Improved Telepathy
Whenever you use the telepathy ability of the Use the Force skill (see page 77), you can reroll your Use the Force check and keep the better result.

Force Secrets
Skilled Force-users can learn to manipulate their Force powers in intriguing ways. Force secrets represent a sublime connection of the Force and are usually available only to powerful Force-users such as Force disciples, Jedi Masters, and Sith Lords (see Chapter 12: Prestige Classes).

Activating a Force secret costs either a Force Point or a Destiny Point (as noted in its description), and the normal limits on spending Force Points and Destiny Points during a round apply. (See Chapter 7: Heroic Traits for more information on Destiny Points.)

Whenever you learn a new Force secret, select it from the following list. Once selected, a Force secret cannot be changed.

Devastating Power
When using a Force power that deals damage, you can spend a Force Point to increase the power's damage dice by 50%. Alternatively, you can spend a Destiny Point to double the number of damage dice.

Distant Power
When using a Force power that has a range expressed numerically, you can spend a Force Point to multiply the range by 10. Alternatively, you can spend a Destiny Point to increase the range to anywhere in the same star system.

This Force secret does not remove line of sight requirements.

Multitarget Power
When using a Force power that affects a single target, you can spend a Force Point to affect one additional target. Alternatively, you can spend a Destiny Point to affect one target per four character levels.

Quicken Power
When using a Force power that requires a standard action or move action to activate, you can spend a Force Point to activate the power as a swift action instead. Alternatively, you can spend a Destiny Point to activate the power as a reaction instead.

Shaped Power
When using a Force power with a cone area effect (such as *Force slam*), you can spend a Force Point to instead affect a line 1 square wide and (5 × cone's length) squares long. Alternatively, when using a Force power with a cone area effect, you can spend a Destiny Point to instead affect one or more targets of your choice within a number of squares of you equal to the cone's length.

Force-Using Traditions
Even those who don't believe in the Force and aren't particularly attuned to its flow can call upon the Force without understanding exactly what they are doing. When a stroke of amazing luck occurs, or fate seems to be on your side and helps you accomplish a difficult objective, it could be the Force coming to your aid. In game terms, the expenditure of Force Points by non-Force-using characters represents this unconscious, tenuous connection to the Force that all living beings share. When a Force-using character calls on the Force in this way, he or she knows exactly what's happening.

The most prominent and well-known Force-users in the galaxy are the Jedi. However, the Jedi are not the only ones who have learned to manipulate the Force. Other Force-users sometimes attribute their abilities to sources other than the Force, such as magic or gods, but they are all using the energy to manipulate the world around them. In game terms, anyone with the Force Sensitivity feat has the ability to master the Use the Force skill and learn Force powers, though many of these beings will never go down this particular path.

Other Force-using traditions include dark side cults (such as the Sith), and obscure, isolated sects such as the Witches of Dathomir and the Sorcerers of Tund. Some know the Force for what it is but approach its use in a different way from the Jedi. Others know the Force by a different name. Either way, it remains the mystic energy that binds the galaxy together and gives Force-users their powers.

Membership: The conditions for being considered a member of a given Force tradition are outlined in the description. A character may be a member of more than one Force tradition, but this is uncommon.

THE JEDI

There is no emotion; there is peace.
There is no ignorance; there is knowledge.
There is no passion; there is serenity.
There is no death; there is the Force.
—from The Jedi Code

For centuries, the group of philosophers that would eventually become the Jedi contemplated the mysteries of the energy field known as the Force. Eventually, some of the group's members mastered the Force. After that, they dedicated themselves to using their newfound skills and powers for good, helping those in need. In the thousands of years that followed, the Jedi served as protectors of the Galactic Republic. Answering to their own Jedi council and operating in concordance with the Judicial Department of the office of the Supreme Chancellor, the Jedi became the guardians of peace and justice in the galaxy.

The Jedi, in addition to battling interstellar criminals and settling galactic disputes, served as mediators, defenders, and teachers. Because of their sense of honor and the epic challenges they undertook, the Jedi became legends, serving as symbols of the best the Republic had to offer. With lightsabers at their sides and the power of the Force flowing through them, the Jedi accomplished the tasks set before them with dedication and seeming invincibility. But invincibility was only an illusion. Jedi often died in the defense of freedom and justice.

During the Rise of the Empire era (circa Episodes I–III), ten thousand Jedi served the Republic and defended its vast territory. They identified potential recruits early in life, usually within the first six months of a child's existence. As infants, those attuned to the Force and accepted by the Jedi Council were taken to begin their training. Older children, if identified later in life as being Force-sensitive, were refused training in most cases; the Jedi believed that the fear and anger in older children made them too susceptible to the dark side, and so it was unwise to train them. All characters playing in this era that are Jedi Padawan learners (Jedi class level 1st through 6th) have a master (Jedi class level 7th or higher). While there may be times when the master and the Padawan travel together, most of their interaction happens between adventures, while all characters are training and improving. The master is a GM character, offering training, advice, and aid when the GM feels such aid is appropriate and necessary. Unfortunately, by the end of this time period, Anakin Skywalker has turned to the dark side and the Emperor has slaughtered nearly all the Jedi.

During the Rebellion era, the Jedi purge has been completed. All but a handful of Force-users, let alone fully trained Jedi, were exterminated or corrupted to the dark side and placed in the service of the Emperor. Force-sensitive individuals, such as Luke Skywalker and Leia Organa, were hidden from the Empire and cut off from their heritage. More powerful Force-users, such as Obi-Wan Kenobi and Yoda, purposely disappeared and worked to stay unnoticed. Jedi characters in this era eventually attract a teacher, though the training these Force-users provide is haphazard at best. A would-be Jedi learns by experience, through occasional meetings with other Force-users, and even by studying with beings who follow other Force traditions. It's not easy, which is why Jedi in this period are few and far between, and few reach the level of power exhibited in earlier or later periods. A Gamemaster wishing to simulate this experience might require the potential character to

> "THE FORCE IS WHAT GIVES THE JEDI HIS POWER. IT'S AN ENERGY FIELD CREATED BY ALL LIVING THINGS. IT SURROUNDS US AND PENETRATES US. IT BINDS THE GALAXY TOGETHER."
> – OBI-WAN KENOBI

THE JEDI CODE

Jedi are the guardians of peace in the galaxy.
Jedi use their powers to defend and protect, never to attack others.
Jedi respect all life, in any form.
Jedi serve others rather than ruling over them, for the good of the galaxy.
Jedi seek to improve themselves through knowledge and training.
—from The Jedi Code

The philosophy known as the Jedi Code was created to keep young Jedi students from being drawn to the dark side. It was taught by the Jedi council to hundreds of thousands of Jedi throughout the ages, Obi-Wan Kenobi and Master Yoda taught parts of it to Luke Skywalker, and Luke Skywalker passed on what he had learned to his students at the Jedi academy.

At its heart, the Jedi Code provides simple instructions for living in touch with the Force. A Jedi never uses the Force to gain wealth or personal power. Instead, a Jedi uses the Force to find knowledge and enlightenment. Anger, fear, aggression, and other negative emotions lead to the dark side, so Jedi are taught to act only when they are at peace with the Force.

Jedi are encouraged to find nonviolent solutions whenever possible. They should act from wisdom, using persuasion and counsel instead of Force powers and violence. When all else fails, or to save a life, a Jedi must sometimes resort to battle in order to resolve a particularly dangerous situation. Though combat may sometimes be the best answer, it should never be the first option a Jedi explores.

Because of their connection to the Force, the Jedi sense its flow and draw upon its energy. While doing so, a Jedi sometimes perceives disturbances in the Force. These disturbances can be explained by the presence of powerful Force-users in the area, or intense emotions that cry out in the Force, such as when the life of the planet Alderaan was extinguished by the Death Star. There are even times when such disturbances result in feelings of urgency or premonitions that spur a Jedi to a place or situation where she is needed. This aspect and manifestation of the Force is covered by the Use the Force skill.

have at least one non-Force-using class level before allowing them to take levels in the Jedi class.

In The New Jedi Order era, Luke Skywalker has trained about one hundred Jedi and identified perhaps a dozen others in need of training. Prominent Force-users such as Mara Jade Skywalker and Corran Horn help Skywalker train and coordinate the efforts of these Jedi, while promising students such as the Solo children and Ganner Rhysode show great promise for the future. Jedi characters again receive a higher-level mentor who provides training and advice between adventures or when the Gamemaster deems such interaction to be warranted and important to a mission.

Membership: Any character with the Force Sensitivity feat can become a member of the Jedi tradition by being accepted as an apprentice by a Jedi Knight or Jedi Master.

THE SITH

Peace is a lie, there is only passion.
Through passion, I gain strength.
Through strength, I gain power.
Through power, I gain victory.
Through victory, my chains are broken.
The Force shall free me.
—from The Sith Code

An ancient order of Force-users devoted to the dark side and determined to destroy the Jedi, the Sith have existed in many forms throughout the history of the Galaxy. The original Sith were a near-Human population on Korriban, subjugated and ruled by outcast Dark Jedi several thousand years before the Battle of Yavin. The name "Sith" eventually came to refer to the dark side cult that ruled the Sith people (that is, the "Lords of the Sith"). When the Old Republic discovered the Sith Empire thousands of years later, it led to the Great Hyperspace War, the first of a long series of conflicts that ravaged the galaxy over the next few millennia. Eventually, the Sith Empire (now known as the "Old Sith") was destroyed, and all it left behind were ancient holocrons and the ruined tombs and temples on Korriban, Yavin 4, and a handful of other planets throughout the galaxy.

The current incarnation of the Sith (the "New Sith") is the result of another Dark Jedi who broke away from the order. Two thousand years before the Battle of Yavin, this Dark Jedi had come to the understanding that the true power of the Force lay not through contemplation and passivity but by tapping into one's emotions and the dark side. Renaming himself Darth Ruin, he stole a Sith Holocron from the archives of the Jedi order and began gathering followers to his banner. Awakening beliefs from the dark past, the new Sith cult continued to grow, driven by the promise of new powers attainable by tapping into the hateful energies of the dark side. It was only a matter of time before the order self-destructed. Internecine struggles by power-hungry Sith practitioners dwindled their numbers. Weakened by infighting, the Sith were easily wiped out by the Jedi at the Battle of Ruusan, one thousand years after Darth Ruin founded the order.

However, one Sith had the cunning to survive. Darth Bane restructured the cult so that there could only be two—no more, no less: a master and an apprentice. Bane adopted cunning, subterfuge, and stealth as the fundamental tenets of the new Sith order. Bane took an apprentice. When that apprentice succeeded him, that new Sith Lord would take an apprentice. Thus, the Sith quietly continued for centuries, until the time of Darth Sidious. With great cunning and treachery, Sidious fomented a galactic civil war within the Republic, seized control of the Galactic Senate, wiped out the Jedi order, and replaced the Old Republic with the Galactic Empire. With Sidious as the Emperor and Darth Vader as his loyal apprentice, the Sith ruled the galaxy and plunged it into darkness. It remained so for decades until a new hope arose to bring Darth Vader back from the dark side and extinguish the menace of the Sith.

The Sith order rises once again in the Legacy era, some 140 years after the Battle of Yavin. The new Sith are led by the enigmatic Darth Krayt and serve as dark side enforcers to the reincarnated Empire. Though the Sith are not as common as the Jedi were during the days of the Old Republic, it is not uncommon to have a Sith apprentice or Sith Lord attached to an important mission or garrison.

Membership: Any character with the Force Sensitivity feat can become a member of the Sith tradition by being accepted as an apprentice by a Sith Lord. During the Rise of the Empire era, there can be only one Sith Lord and one Sith apprentice. Thus, the only way to join the Sith tradition during this era is to wait (or arrange) for one of the two Sith to die.

Other Force-Using Traditions

The Jedi and the Sith are not the only Force-users in the galaxy. Several other traditions have sprung up over the course of history, some lasting for many years and some extinguished during Darth Vader's purge of the Jedi. Most such Force-users receive only rudimentary training, while others develop their own skills and abilities by simple trial and error. A few of the more organized Force-using sects have learned a great deal about the Force and can become powerful even without the benefit of thousands of years of tradition and philosophy. On the whole, the Jedi order typically attempts to root out these Force-users and assimilate them, or at least keep tabs on them.

The following two Force-using sects are suitable for use in the *Star Wars Roleplaying Game*, though certainly there are others that would work as well. Each tradition has a Force talent tree associated with it; like the Force talents presented earlier in the chapter, these talents are available only to characters with the Force Sensitivity feat (page 85), and even then only if the character is a member of that tradition.

The Jensaarai

The Jensaarai sect of Force-users came into existence near the end of the Clone Wars and is relatively young compared to other Force traditions. Founded by an Anzati Dark Jedi, Nikkos Tyris, the Jensaarai blend teachings of Jedi and Sith philosophy to form something altogether different. Unfortunately, a short time after Tyris and a band of rogue Jedi split off to form their movement, the Jedi Council dispatched several Jedi Knights to put an end to their rebellion. The Jedi accomplished their mission, killing Tyris and his comrades, but unknowingly leaving behind the families and students of the new Jensaarai tradition. The surviving Jensaarai laid in wait as Darth Vader's purge of the Jedi swept through the galaxy, coming close to extinction themselves on occasion but surviving nonetheless. After the fall of the Empire, Luke Skywalker and Corran Horn discovered the Jensaarai and made them fast allies, even bringing some of them into the New Jedi Order.

The Jensaarai walk a dangerous line between light and darkness. Though their dark Jedi Masters died early at the hands of the Council's agents, the Jensaarai followers retained much of the philosophy (if not the Sith secrets) that Tyris had used to found the order. The Jensaarai resemble both the Jedi and the Sith in many ways; they construct and wield lightsabers, they defend their planet from hostile forces, and they have a strong grasp of the Force and its ways. Still, they remain quite different in other respects. Jensaarai Defenders construct suits of armor, fashioning them after creatures they feel fit their personalities, and they can be violent and ruthless when necessary. Though many Jensaarai Defenders run the risk of falling to the dark side, very few actually do, as discipline and awareness of the repercussions of their actions are two of the most important tenets of Jensaarai training.

Membership: Any character with the Force Sensitivity feat can become a member of the Jensaarai tradition by being accepted as an apprentice by a Force adept or Force disciple who is a member of the Jensaarai. In addition, any character with the Force Sensitivity who is native to the Suarbi system (during the Rise of the Empire era and onward) is likely a member of the Jensaarai tradition.

JENSAARAI DEFENDER TALENT TREE

The Jensaarai walk a thin line between light and darkness, using the teachings of both the Jedi and the Sith to create their own unique traditions. Only Force-users that are part of the Jensaarai tradition may select talents from this tree.

Attune Armor: As a full-round action, you may spend a Force Point to attune a suit of armor to the Force, permanently increasing its armor bonus by +2. In addition, the maximum Dexterity bonus of the attuned armor permanently improves by +1. Only you can benefit from wearing the attuned armor; the benefits do not apply if someone else dons the armor.

Force Cloak: As a swift action, you can surround yourself with an invisible bubble of Force power that shields you and anything you're carrying from electronic surveillance. The bubble also blocks all electronic sensors and communications. The Force cloak lasts for as long as you concentrate (a standard action) or until the start of your next turn.

Force Cloak Mastery: As the Force Cloak talent, except that you can expand the bubble to envelop a number of creatures (including yourself) equal to your character level.

Prerequisite: Force Cloak.

Linked Defense: As a swift action, you can take a penalty of up to –5 on your attack roll and add the same number (up to +5) as a Force bonus to an ally's Reflex Defense, provided the ally is within your line of sight when you activate this talent. The bonus you confer cannot exceed your base attack bonus. The changes to your attack rolls and your ally's Reflex Defense last until the start of your next turn.

The Witches of Dathomir

Native to the planet Dathomir, the witches were some of the first non-Jedi Force-users encountered by Luke Skywalker during his quest to rebuild the Jedi Order. Some 600 years before the Clone Wars, the Jedi Order banished a Jedi named Allya to the primitive planet of Dathomir. In exile, she founded her own sect of Force adepts, selectively breeding with a group of exiled arms dealers, and within decades had created a Force-using society to rule. Though ruthless, Allya maintained a strict rule of law (even authoring a tome called the Book of Law for her followers to use as an example). After Allya's death, the society fragmented into six clans, and despite Allya's command to never concede to evil, some of the witches she trained fell to the dark side, becoming the Nightsisters.

The Witches of Dathomir are part of a primitive culture with a strong yet rudimentary grasp of the Force. Though much of their own knowledge is derived from the Jedi arts, over the centuries their lifestyle and philosophies have shaped their knowledge of the Force to fit their own needs. The Witches of Dathomir train and ride fearsome rancors, using the Force to communicate with them. Though their tribal organization makes them seem primitive, they are sophisticated and knowledgeable Force-users who, despite their rustic lifestyle, have evolved Force powers seemingly unheard of to other sects.

Membership: Only female natives of Dathomir (from the Rise of the Empire era onward) with the Force Sensitivity feat can be members of the Witches of Dathomir tradition.

DATHOMIRI WITCH TALENT TREE

The Force-using witches of the planet Dathomir are primitive yet powerful beings. They use ancient training handed down for generations as the basis of their powers.

Adept Spellcaster: You may use any Force power that normally requires a swift action, move action, or standard action as a full-round action instead. If you choose to do so, you may reroll your Use the Force check to activate that power, but you must accept the result of the reroll, even if it is worse.

Charm Beast: You may make a Use the Force check in place of a Persuasion check when attempting to change the attitude of an undomesticated creature with an Intelligence of 2 or less. Additionally, you do not take the normal –5 penalty on the check if the creature can't speak or understand your language.

Command Beast: Whenever you manage to shift the attitude of a beast to indifferent or friendly, you may treat that creature as a domesticated animal—but for you only (it remains undomesticated in its response to other creatures). Additionally, you may use this beast as a mount, as per the Ride skill (see page 72), provided that it is at least one size category larger than you and has a comfortable place for you to sit. For more information on beasts, see page 273.

Prerequisite: Charm Beast.

Flight: As a swift action, you can spend a Force Point to fly. You gain a fly speed equal to your land speed, and you can ascend at half speed or descend at double speed. The flight lasts until the start of your next turn; if you're still airborne at that time, you fall.

Prerequisite: Adept Spellcaster.

Chapter VII
Heroic Traits

What does your character look like? How old is he (or she)? What sort of first impression does he make? What led him to become a hero?

This chapter covers a miscellany of topics that apply to your character. It helps you establish your character's identity and place in the *Star Wars* universe and make him or her more lifelike—like a main character in a *Star Wars* movie or novel. For many players, this is the true expression of roleplaying: defining the character that you are going to play.

When you first play a character, it's fine to leave some of the details sketchy. Over time, as adventures play out, you'll get a better sense of who you want your character to be. You'll develop your character's details much the way an author develops a character over several chapters in a novel or over several novels in a series.

Details

This section offers advice as you determine details about your character, including his or her name, age, appearance, and personality. Start with some idea about your character's background and personality, and use that idea to develop the details that bring your character to life.

Name

Invent or choose a name that fits your character's species and class. Chapter 2: Species contains some examples of alien names. A name is a great way for you to start thinking about your character's background. For instance, a Rodian scout might be named after a great Rodian hunter of the past, and the Rodian may be striving to live up to that heritage. Alternatively, the name could be that of an infamous traitor, and the hero could be bent on proving that she's not like her namesake.

A name can also tell a lot about a character and help establish an image in your mind and the minds of the other players. It doesn't have to be descriptive, but you want it to fit the type of character you're going to play. Use the sample names to help you make up a name that has the appropriate *Star Wars* feel.

Age

Your character's age is pretty much up to you (subject to the Gamemaster's approval). A character reaches 1st level in a heroic class at the point when he or she steps out of mundane life and into the drama of the story, either by choice or through circumstances beyond the character's control. That could be as a young adult for a Padawan learner, as a 20-year-old adult (such as in the case of Luke Skywalker in *A New Hope*), or as an even older character, depending on your character concept.

Table 7-1: Age by Species

SPECIES	CHILD	YOUNG ADULT	ADULT	MIDDLE AGE	OLD	VENERABLE
Human	1–11 years	12–15 years	16–40 years	41–59 years	60–79 years	80+ years
Bothan	1–11 years	12–16 years	17–45 years	46–65 years	66–84 years	85+ years
Cerean	1–10 years	11–15 years	16–35 years	36–53 years	54–64 years	65+ years
Duros	1–9 years	10–14 years	15–35 years	36–49 years	50–69 years	70+ years
Ewok	1–9 years	10–13 years	14–29 years	30–44 years	45–59 years	60+ years
Gamorrean	1–6 years	7–12 years	13–29 years	30–39 years	40–44 years	45+ years
Gungan	1–12 years	13–15 years	16–35 years	36–54 years	55–64 years	65+ years
Ithorian	1–13 years	14–17 years	18–44 years	45–69 years	70–84 years	85+ years
Kel Dor	1–11 years	12–15 years	16–44 years	45–59 years	60–69 years	70+ years
Mon Calamari	1–11 years	12–16 years	17–40 years	41–57 years	58–79 years	80+ years
Quarren	1–11 years	12–16 years	17–40 years	41–57 years	58–79 years	80+ years
Rodian	1–12 years	13–15 years	16–35 years	36–49 years	50–59 years	60+ years
Sullustan	1–9 years	10–14 years	15–39 years	40–55 years	56–69 years	70+ years
Trandoshan	1–11 years	12–14 years	15–34 years	35–49 years	50–59 years	60+ years
Twi'lek	1–12 years	13–15 years	16–44 years	45–59 years	60–79 years	80+ years
Wookiee	1–12 years	13–17 years	18–300 years	301–350 years	351–399 years	400+ years
Zabrak	1–8 years	9–14 years	15–44 years	45–55 years	56–69 years	70+ years

Table 7-1: Age by Species gives age ranges for the various species presented in Chapter 2: Species. As your hero ages, his or her physical ability scores (Strength, Dexterity, and Constitution) decrease and his or her mental ability scores (Intelligence, Wisdom, and Charisma) increase, as shown in Table 7-2: Aging Effects). The effects of each aging step are cumulative. However, none of a character's ability scores can be reduced below 1 in this way.

First, generate your ability scores as defined in Chapter 1. Then, once your starting age is determined, apply the modifiers shown on Table 7-2: Aging Effects. Note that the methods described for determining ability scores yield the scores of an adult character. For example, when a character reaches middle age, her Strength, Dexterity, and Constitution scores each drop 1 point, while her Intelligence, Wisdom, and Charisma scores each increase by 1 point. When she becomes old, her physical ability scores all drop an additional 2 points, while her mental ability scores increase by 1 again. So far she has lost a total of 3 points from her Strength, Constitution, and Dexterity scores and gained a total of 2 points to her Wisdom, Intelligence, and Charisma scores due to aging.

On the other hand, a child would start with a total penalty of –4 to Strength and Constitution and a –2 penalty to all other abilities (adjustments are cumulative for both the child and young adult categories). As he advances to young adulthood, these penalties would be reduced to –1 for each ability score. He would thus "gain" 3 points to both his Strength and Constitution and 1 point to each of his other ability scores. When he later becomes an adult, he would gain 1 point to each of his ability scores.

Jedi live longer than the average member of their species. While a typical Human lives well into his or her 80s, a Human Jedi might live well into his or her 100s. The upper limit for a character powerful in the Force can be twice as much or more than a typical member of a species.

Table 7-2: Aging Effects

Child	–3 to Str and Con; –1 to Dex, Int, Wis, and Cha
Young adult	–1 to Str, Dex, Con, Int, Wis, and Cha
Adult	No modifier
Middle age	–1 to Str, Dex, and Con; +1 to Int, Wis, and Cha
Old	–2 to Str, Dex, and Con; +1 to Int, Wis, and Cha
Venerable	–3 to Str, Dex, and Con; +1 to Int, Wis, and Cha

APPEARANCE

Decide what your character looks like using the descriptions of the various species in Chapter 2: Species as a starting point. Characters with high Charisma scores tend to be better looking than those with low Charisma scores, though a character with high Charisma could have strange looks, giving him or her a sort of exotic beauty.

You can use your hero's looks to tell something about his personality and background. For example:

—Deel Surool, the Twi'lek scoundrel, always has a smirk on his lips, no matter what situation he finds himself in. He treats life as a joke where only he knows the punch line. He wears the latest fashions and comes off as being mildly superior to everyone around him.

—Vor'en Kurn, the Human soldier, has a rough, dark look that speaks of the life he has led. His mercenary nature shows through in the way he moves, the way he wears his armor, and the way his twin blasters hang at his sides. His eyes are cold, dead, uncaring. You know he means business and that he's dangerous just by looking at him.

—Sia-Lan Wezz, the Human Jedi, appears confident and in control. She wears her Jedi robes and lightsaber proudly, and her fresh, young face glows with enthusiasm and hope. You know you can trust her, and you know she takes her role very seriously. Perhaps even a bit too seriously.

HEIGHT AND WEIGHT

Table 7-3: Height and Weight presents average heights and weights for the different species presented in Chapter 2: Species. Your character may be of average height and weight, or you can make your character lighter, heavier, shorter, or taller. Think about what your character's abilities might say about her height and weight. If she is weak but agile, she may be thin. If she is strong and tough, she may be tall or just heavy.

PERSONALITY

Decide how your character acts, what she likes, what she wants out of life, what scares her, and what makes her angry. Your character's species is a good place to start when thinking about personality, but it's a bad place to stop. Make your Wookiee (or whatever) different from every other Wookiee.

Personality is a summary of how your character usually acts. Make sure it's interesting and fun for you to play. Give your character good points and bad points. Think about his code of ethics. Will your character do anything for the right price, or is there a line he just won't cross? Is your character cheerful or dour, optimistic or pessimistic, honorable or dishonorable? These are just some of the factors that could go into your character's personality.

A handy trick for making an interesting personality for your character is including some sort of conflict in his nature. For example, Deel the scoundrel is generally self-centered, but he looks out for his close friends. He may be tempted to help them, even if it goes against his best interests, so long as he can justify doing so.

Your character's personality can change over time. Just because you've written some personality notes on your character sheet doesn't mean you can't let your character grow and develop the way real people do.

TABLE 7-3: AVERAGE HEIGHT AND WEIGHT

SPECIES	AVERAGE HEIGHT	AVERAGE WEIGHT
Human, male	1.8 m	75 kg
Human, female	1.6 m	55 kg
Bothan	1.6 m	55 kg
Cerean, male	2.0 m	78 kg
Cerean, female	1.8 m	58 kg
Duros	1.8 m	70 kg
Ewok	1.0 m	30 kg
Gamorrean	1.8 m	140 kg
Gungan	1.8 m	70 kg
Ithorian	2.0 m	90 kg
Kel Dor	1.8 m	70 kg
Mon Calamari	1.8 m	72 kg
Quarren	1.8 m	72 kg
Rodian	1.6 m	60 kg
Sullustan	1.5 m	55 kg
Trandoshan	2.0 m	80 kg
Twi'lek, male	1.8 m	55 kg
Twi'lek, female	1.6 m	55 kg
Wookiee, male	2.2 m	125 kg
Wookiee, female	2.0 m	100 kg
Zabrak	1.8 m	75 kg

BACKGROUND
Decide what your character's life has been like up until now. Here are a few questions to get you thinking:

How did she decide to become a hero?

How did she acquire her class? A soldier, for example, might have been in a planetary militia, she may come from a family of soldiers, she may have trained in a martial school, or she may be a self-taught mercenary.

Where did she get her starting equipment? Did she assemble it piece by piece over time? Was it a parting gift from a parent or mentor? Do any items have special significance to her?

What's the worst thing that's ever happened to her?

What's the best thing that's ever happened to her?

Does she stay in contact with her family? What do they think of her?

Only your GM needs to know all the details of your background. You can tell the other players as much or as little as you see fit. You can get as complex as you like, or keep your character's background simple. Has she traveled around the galaxy a lot? What's her home planet like? What does she think of the Republic (or Rebellion, or Empire, or whatever)? Does she know any of the other players' characters from before the campaign started? If not, what's her connection to the rest of the team?

GOALS
Your character might have a number of objectives that he or she hopes to accomplish. These are the things that motivate your character. Does he seek wealth or love? Revenge or power? That's up to you and your GM.

Goals can be immediate or long-term. They can also change during play, and new goals can be added all the time. Think of goals as what's motivating your character right now, though some long-term goals might fade to the background until circumstances warrant.

DESTINY
Destiny plays a large role in the *Star Wars* universe. As a young boy, Anakin Skywalker is told that his destiny is to bring balance to the Force. Padmé's destiny is to give birth to the twins, Luke and Leia, so that they can fulfill their own destinies. Luke Skywalker learns that his destiny is to redeem his father, Darth Vader, so that balance to the Force is restored. Leia's destiny is to save the Rebellion from annihilation at the hands of the Empire and help forge the New Republic. The destiny mechanic helps players and Gamemasters recognize that all heroes—and even major villains—have significant roles to play in the fate of the galaxy. Destiny rewards players for good roleplaying and gives Gamemasters new plot hooks to use when designing adventures.

The rules presented below are optional. A Gamemaster may decide to use Destiny Points or not; however, the decision to use them should be made before the campaign gets underway, so that each player can decide whether or not to embrace a destiny for her character from the outset.

Although conceivably any character—heroic or nonheroic—has a destiny to fulfill, only heroic characters receive Destiny Points and receive in-game benefits for pursuing their destinies. Nonheroic characters don't receive Destiny Points; their destinies, whatever they may be, exist purely on a story level.

CHOOSING A DESTINY
Players don't need to choose destinies for their heroes at the start of the campaign—or ever, for that matter. Not every hero has a destiny that must be fulfilled before the end of the campaign, and even players who want their characters to have destinies need to give their characters—and the campaign—a chance to develop first. It may take several adventures before players understand where the campaign is going and what goals their heroes are likely to pursue.

Choosing a destiny can be handled in one of two ways: Either the player can select an appropriate destiny for her hero (based on what's happening in the campaign), or the Gamemaster can select a secret destiny for the hero. If the player chooses a destiny for her character, the GM should challenge the player to fulfill her destiny by presenting conflicting situations where the smartest and most beneficial decision might force the character to choose between doing what is best for her fellow heroes and taking steps toward her destiny. If the GM secretly chooses the hero's destiny, he must present challenges that let the character move closer to achieving her destiny, imparting benefits when the character is moving in the right direction and imposing penalties when the character does something that takes her far from the destined path. The GM-selected "secret destiny" forces the player to take her character through a period of self-discovery, as she learns which actions lead her closer to—or farther from—her destiny. In essence, this mirrors Luke Skywalker's struggle at the end of *The Empire Strikes Back*, when he must choose between redeeming his father and falling prey to the corruption of the dark side.

A character with a destiny gains short-term benefits whenever he makes significant progress toward fulfilling it, while a character who pursues goals that move him farther away from his destiny suffers short-term negative effects. Conversely, a character without a destiny has nothing to gain and nothing to lose.

DESTINY POINTS
Destiny Points are resources that a player can use to help fulfill whatever destiny has been set before her character. A 1st-level character begins play with 1 Destiny Point and gains another Destiny Point at each level. A Destiny Point allows a hero to perform a nearly impossible task or survive against all odds.

Only a character with a destiny can gain or spend Destiny Points.

Spending Destiny Points

Spending a Destiny Point does not take an action and grants one of the following benefits:

- Automatically score a critical hit (no attack roll required).
- Automatically cause an attack made against you to miss (even once the attack is resolved).
- Act out of turn (thus changing your position in the initiative order).
- Take damage that would otherwise harm another character within your reach.
- Increase the effect of some Force powers (as noted in their descriptions).
- Use some applications of Force secrets (as noted in their descriptions).
- Immediately gain 3 Force Points (see Force Points, page 92).

A character may accumulate as many Destiny Points as she has levels. Thus, a 5th-level character may have as many as 5 Destiny Points if she doesn't spend any of them.

When a character fulfills his destiny, he can choose to keep the Destiny Points he has remaining or transfer some or all of them to allied characters. A character who retains his unspent Destiny Points can't spend them until he chooses a new destiny. A character who chooses to give away some or all of his Destiny Points can't give more than 1 Destiny Point to any single ally. Under no other circumstances may a character transfer his Destiny Points to another character.

For example, Sia-Lan fulfills her destiny by redeeming a powerful darksider, after which she still has 2 unspent Destiny Points. Sia-Lan decides to give Vor'en and Rorworr—two of her compatriots—1 Destiny Point each, leaving her with 0 Destiny Points.

Sample Destinies

The following sample destinies should provide a starting point for any character wishing to take advantage of the destiny rules. Each destiny includes a brief description, with examples.

Destiny Bonus: When a character accomplishes a goal or performs a task that clearly moves him closer to fulfilling his destiny (GM's determination), he gains this short-term benefit.

Destiny Penalty: When a character does something that clearly moves him away from his destiny (GM's determination), he suffers this short-term negative effect.

Destiny Fulfilled: When a character fulfills his destiny, he gains these permanent benefits. Sometimes fulfilling a destiny has other effects as well; these are also covered here.

Corruption

Your destiny is to corrupt an individual, organization, or location. You may seek to turn a person to the dark side or indoctrinate a group of people in the ways of evil. Your destiny may also be to become corrupted yourself, either by another character, an organization, or a series of life-changing events that unfold over time. The corruption should be a long-term goal requiring a great deal of time and effort.

Examples of this destiny include the Emperor's corruption of Anakin Skywalker, a dark Force-user transforming a Jedi shrine into a temple of evil, or an Imperial officer convincing an Alliance cell to betray the Rebellion.

Additionally, a character's destiny may be to allow herself to be corrupted by the dark side; her fall into darkness becomes the path to achieving this destiny.

Destiny Bonus: For 24 hours, you and any allies within 10 squares of you gain a +1 destiny bonus on skill checks and ability checks.

Destiny Penalty: You take a –2 penalty on all skill checks and ability checks for 24 hours.

Destiny Fulfilled: Increase two ability scores of your choice by +1 each. In addition, if your Dark Side Score (see page 94) is less than your Wisdom score, your Dark Side Score increases until it's equal to your Wisdom score, signifying that you've turned to the dark side (see The Dark Side, page 93).

Destruction

Your destiny is to destroy a person or object, for good or evil. A Rebel agent's destiny might be to destroy a tyrannical Imperial Moff presiding over his home planet, while a darksider may be destined to destroy a powerful Jedi training site used to bolster the ranks of the Jedi order. The target of this destiny should be something very difficult to reach, either because it's heavily guarded or well hidden. Examples of this destiny include Darth Vader's destruction of the Emperor, Lando Calrissian's destruction of the Death Star II, or A-wing pilot Arvel Crynyd's destruction of the *Executor*.

Destiny Bonus: For 24 hours, you and any allies within 10 squares of you gain a +2 destiny bonus on all damage rolls.

Destiny Penalty: You take a –2 penalty on all damage rolls for 24 hours.

Destiny Fulfilled: Increase one ability score of your choice by +2.

Discovery

Your destiny is to discover a person, species, object, or location that was either previously lost or unknown to the civilized galaxy. This could be as simple as seeking out the remains of a long-dead hero, or as rare as finding a vergence in the Force. A scout's destiny might be to find a thus-far-uncharted world that helps solve a galactic crisis, while a scoundrel's destiny might be to chart a new route through the Deep Core, allowing the Rebel Alliance to sneak past the Empire's security web. The thing being discovered should be something that can only be found as the result of a long-term search or serendipitous events that only occur because the character long ago set down the path that would lead to that discovery.

Examples of this destiny include Qui-Gon Jinn's discovery of Anakin Skywalker on Tatooine or Kyle Katarn's discovery of the Valley of the Jedi.

Destiny Bonus: For 24 hours, you and any allies within 10 squares of you gain a +1 destiny bonus to all defenses (Reflex, Fortitude, and Will).

Destiny Penalty: You take a –1 penalty to your defenses (Reflex, Fortitude, and Will) for 24 hours.

Destiny Fulfilled: You gain a permanent +1 destiny bonus to your defenses (Reflex, Fortitude, and Will).

Education

Your destiny is to train or educate another being or group of beings in some way. In some cases, this could mean taking a young Padawan learner and molding her into an eventual Jedi Master, or it could mean training fresh-faced Rebel Alliance recruits and molding them into a crack team of SpecForce operatives. Characters with this destiny are not merely teachers providing mundane training. The education that this destiny demands must be of great importance to the galaxy, and should lay the groundwork for the beneficiaries of your tutelage to go on to fulfill destinies of their own. Only when the training is complete can this destiny be fulfilled, and the process should take many months or years to complete.

Examples of this destiny include Obi-Wan Kenobi's training of Anakin Skywalker, Yoda's training of Luke Skywalker, or Grand Admiral Thrawn's training of Captain Pellaeon.

Destiny Bonus: For 24 hours, you and any allies within 10 squares of you gain a +1 destiny bonus on skill checks and ability checks.

Destiny Penalty: You take a –2 penalty on all skill checks and ability checks for 24 hours.

Destiny Fulfilled: You gain a permanent +5 destiny bonus on checks made with one class skill of your choice.

Redemption

Your destiny is to redeem a character that has been corrupted or otherwise turned to evil. Many Jedi seek to turn their fallen brethren away from the dark side. A Rebel agent might seek to turn his brother, an Imperial officer, away from the evil Empire, redeeming him back to the side of justice and freedom. The target of this destiny should be someone that has fallen from the light in some way, whether that means turning to the dark side of the Force or simply siding with evil over good. Turning someone away from their wicked ways is usually very difficult and requires far more than simple persuasion. Often a character that fulfills this destiny does not survive it, and sometimes neither does their redeemed target. Additionally, you may be your own target for this destiny, making your own redemption the means of fulfilling it.

Examples of this destiny include Luke Skywalker turning Darth Vader away from the dark side and Revan's redemption of Bastila Shan on the Star Forge.

Destiny Bonus: You gain a Force Point.

Destiny Penalty: You lose one Force Point. If you have no Force Point to lose, you take a –1 penalty on attack rolls until you gain a level.

Destiny Fulfilled: The Dark Side Score of the redeemed character is reduced to 1, and he loses any remaining Force Points. You gain a number of Force Points equal to 3 + the number of Force Points the redeemed character lost.

Rescue

Your destiny requires you to save a person from death or an object from destruction. Often characters with this destiny will not know which person or object they're meant to save, let alone when or how to do so. They simply must be in the right place at the right time. A hero might spend months traveling with his allies before fulfilling his destiny by saving one of their lives. Conversely, a Rebel agent might engage in years' worth of espionage on his home planet, only to find that his destiny is to save a local Imperial magistrate who betrays the Empire after having her life saved.

Examples of this destiny include Han Solo saving Luke Skywalker's life at the Battle of Yavin and Wicket the Ewok rescuing Leia from the scout troopers on Endor.

Destiny Bonus: For 24 hours, you and any allies within 10 squares of you gain a +2 destiny bonus on all damage rolls.

Destiny Penalty: You take a –2 penalty on all attack rolls for 24 hours.

Destiny Fulfilled: Increase two ability scores of your choice by +1 each.

Death and Destiny

Achieving one's destiny may yield great benefits, but the path of destiny can be perilous. Many characters in the *Star Wars* saga perish attempting to fulfill their destinies. If a Force-sensitive character dies while fulfilling (or attempting to fulfill) his destiny, the Gamemaster may allow the dead character to manifest as a Force spirit. If a non-Force-user perishes while pursuing or achieving his destiny, the GM may decide that the character's sacrifice or untimely death imparts some benefit upon his surviving allies.

Force Spirit: A Force-user who dies in the process of fulfilling his destiny may manifest as a Force spirit. For a Jedi or other good Force-user, this means transforming into a translucent blue spirit that can appear before his former allies. For a darksider, this means becoming an evil dark side spirit that can linger on, continuing to spread the influence of the dark side.

If a character with the Force Sensitivity feat dies while fulfilling her destiny, that character may become a Force spirit, retaining her consciousness (and her Intelligence, Wisdom, and Charisma scores) but becoming completely incorporeal. The Force spirit can manifest at will and can vanish just as easily. It can also walk through walls and exist in the vacuum of space. Additionally, Force spirits can travel anywhere in the galaxy instantly with a mere thought. However, Force spirits have no substance and cannot interact physically with creatures or objects in the universe.

When a hero dies and becomes a Force spirit, that Force spirit becomes a GM-controlled character. Under the GM's control, a Force spirit might serve as a guide, advising heroes in times of dire need and sharing valuable information or wisdom it held in life.

Noble Sacrifice: Whenever a character willingly sacrifices himself for a noble cause, particularly while fulfilling his destiny, he can bolster the resolve of his surviving comrades and allies. For example, when Arvel Crynyd crashed his A-wing into the bridge of the *Executor*, it was a turning point in the Battle of Endor. When a character dies fulfilling his destiny in such a way, all allies within the same star system gain a +1 destiny bonus on attack rolls and a +1 destiny bonus to defenses (Reflex, Fortitude, and Will) for 24 hours.

Vengeance: When a valued ally falls in the pursuit of his destiny, it can have powerful effects on those present at the time of his death. When a character dies fulfilling his destiny, any ally who witness his death may choose to become filled with a desire to avenge her fallen comrade, gaining a +2 destiny bonus on attack rolls and damage rolls for 24 hours. Since revenge leads to the dark side, any Force-user who chooses to gain these bonuses must immediately increase his Dark Side Score by 1 (see page 93).

Chapter VIII
Equipment

In a galaxy of high-tech wonders, the only limits to what types of equipment are commercially available depend on the inventors, merchants, and corporations that manufacture and supply them. Most of the items described in this chapter are available through legitimate arms and equipment traders.

Money

The galactic economy turns on the wealth and products of billions of worlds. Throughout the history of known space, money has gone by many names, but the basic unit always came back to the "credit." As the Republic waned and the Rise of the Empire approached (circa Episodes I–III), Republic credits (also called "dataries") no longer had much value beyond the Core Worlds and the Inner Rim. Instead, local currencies became popular. More often, people living and working in the distant regions wanted to trade in hard currency, not electronic credit chips.

This changed when the Empire came to power. By the time of the Rebellion era (circa Episodes IV–VI), Imperial credits were accepted everywhere. Even the Alliance used this currency, as it was the standard throughout known space until the Empire finally fell.

The New Republic, of course, minted its own credits after the victory at Endor and the establishment of the new galactic government. However, individual planets, regions, and sectors also adopted their own currencies, and the Imperial remnants issued their own scrip. Exchange rates fluctuated wildly throughout this period. The New Republic credit was established ten years after the Battle of Endor and eventually emerged as the leading currency by the time of The New Jedi Order era.

Carrying Credits

The most common methods for keeping track of your credits are the credit chip or cred stick. These contains memory algorithms that can securely monitor the amount of credits available to the owner and accurately add to and subtract from that amount as transactions occur.

Wealth Beyond Credits

Some characters with access to a ship deal in commodities. Han Solo, for example, smuggled goods from place to place before hooking up with the Rebel Alliance. Other characters might be legitimate traders, buying and selling commodities to pay their way across the galaxy (and subsidize the adventures in which they wind up participating). Guilds and governments regulate trade. Charters and licenses are granted, cargo is regularly inspected, trade routes are established, and port fees are posted. In general, small freighters might come to the attention of local ports and the occasional inspection vessel, but independent traders are otherwise given a lot of freedom when they conduct their business.

Table 8-1: Trade Goods gives baseline prices for fairly broad categories of goods. The Gamemaster can get more specific, add or remove items depending on supply and demand in the campaign, and adjust prices to reflect such fluctuations in the market. Also, prices can vary greatly in different regions of space, different star systems, and even between different planets within the same star system.

Table 8-1: Trade Goods

COMMODITY	COST
Animal, common	100
Animal, exotic	2,000
Animal, livestock	500
Art, common	100
Art, quality	1,000
Art, precious	10,000
Bacta, 1 liter (1 kg)	100
Food, common (1 kg)	10
Food, quality (1 kg)	20
Food, exotic (1 kg)	50
Fuel, 1 liter (1 kg)	50
Gems, semiprecious (1 gram)	100
Gems, precious (1 gram)	1,000
Gems, exotic (1 gram)	10,000
Holovid	10
Metal, common (1 metric ton)	2,500
Metal, semi-precious (1 kg)	200
Metal, precious (1 kg)	10,000
Ore, common (1 metric ton)	1,500
Spice, common (1 kg)	1,000
Spice, exotic (1 gram)	20
Textiles, common (1 meter)	5
Textiles, quality (1 meter)	20
Textiles, exotic (1 meter)	100
Water, 1 liter (1 kg)	1

Selling Items

Sometimes you'll come into possession of an item that you don't want. We're not talking about commodities here. Commodities are valuable goods that can easily be exchanged almost like cash. We're talking about individual items from the lists presented later in this chapter. In general, a merchant will buy used equipment at half its listed price. If you have a blaster and want to upgrade to a heavy blaster pistol, you can sell the smaller blaster for half price.

Restricted Items

Some objects require licenses to own or operate, or are restricted to qualifying organizations or individuals. In such cases, a character must pay a license fee to own the object legally. A license fee is a separate expense, purchased in addition to the object to which it applies.

The four restriction ratings are as follows:

Licensed: The owner must obtain a license to own or operate the object legally. Generally, the license is not expensive, and obtaining it has few if any additional legal requirements.

Restricted: Only specifically qualified individuals or organizations are technically allowed to own the object. However, the real obstacles to ownership are time and money; anyone with sufficient patience and cash can eventually acquire the necessary license.

Military: The object is sold primarily to legitimate police and military organizations. A military rating is essentially the same as restricted (see above), except that manufacturers and dealers are generally under tight government scrutiny and are therefore especially wary of selling to private individuals.

Illegal: The object is illegal in all but specific, highly regulated circumstances.

Getting a License

To get a license, you must pay the fee required to file the application. The amount of the fee is a percentage of the object's normal cost, as listed in Table 8-2: Restricted Objects. Once you've paid the fee, make a Knowledge (bureaucracy) check against the DC listed in the Skill DC column. You can't take 10 or take 20 on this check. On a success, your license is approved and will be available to you in a number of days as listed in the Time Required column. On a failure, you spend a number of days as listed in the Time Required column, but you are not granted the license and your application fee is lost. You may try again as often as you like if you have the time and credits to do so.

Whether you succeed or fail on your Knowledge (bureaucracy) check, your request is recorded in public records. The more restricted the license, the more in-depth the background check required, and this leaves an increasingly detailed electronic trail for others to follow.

Table 8-2: Restricted Objects

RESTRICTION RATING	LICENSE FEE[1]	BLACK MARKET COST	SKILL DC	TIME REQUIRED
Licensed	5%	×2	10	1 day
Restricted	10%	×3	15	2 days
Military	20%	×4	20	5 days
Illegal	50%	×5	25	10 days

1 *The license fee is given as a percentage of the licensed object's base cost.*

You can choose to secure a license through illicit means. If you want to bribe an official, make a Persuasion check instead of a Knowledge (bureaucracy) check. If you want to fabricate a false identity or steal another person's identity, make a Deception check instead of a Knowledge (bureaucracy) check. If either of these checks fails by 5 or more, the local authorities are alerted to your activities.

The Black Market

Almost anything is available on the black market. However, you must make a Gather Information check to locate a black market merchant who has the object you seek. The DC of the check is listed in the Skill DC column of Table 8-2: Restricted Objects, and the GM may apply a bonus or penalty to the check depending on the circumstances. (For example, finding a black market dealer on the smuggler's moon of Nar Shaddaa is relatively easy and may warrant a +5 bonus on the check.) If you succeed on the Gather Information check, you find a black market merchant who has access to the item you seek. If you fail, you can try again later. If you fail by 5 or more, someone notices you've been asking questions and comes to capture, interrogate, or silence you.

Once you find someone who can get the item for you, you'll have to pay two, three, four, or five times the item's normal price (as listed in the Black Market Cost column of Table 8-2: Restricted Items) and wait some time for the item to become available (as listed in the Time Required column).

Weapons

The galaxy is a dangerous place. Most people have access to some kind of weapon, and those who travel the space lanes often carry a blaster or some other weapon as a means of defense. A weapon's legality depends on where you are. No one would look twice at a character wearing a blaster at his side in Mos Espa or Nar Shaddaa. The same character would do well to conceal it while visiting the gleaming metropolis of Coruscant.

Weapon Groups

Discriminating combatants choose their weapons very carefully. However, a character who knows how to load and fire a slugthrower pistol can handle a blaster pistol just as expertly. Thus, weapons are categorized based on their form and function, and a character who takes the appropriate Weapon Proficiency feat (see page 89) is considered skilled with all of the weapons in that group. Exotic weapons such as bowcasters and flamethrowers are exceptions: An exotic weapon is unique in form and function, and requires special training (that is, the Exotic Weapon Proficiency feat) to wield proficiently.

Advanced Melee Weapons

The most common advanced melee weapons are bladed vibro weapons with ultrasonic generators built into their hilts or handles. A vibro weapon's ultrasonic blade gives the weapon more cutting power with less effort. Advanced melee weapons include the electrostaff, force pike, vibrodagger, vibroblade, vibrobayonet, and vibro-ax.

Exotic Weapons

Unlike other weapon groups, you must select the Exotic Weapon Proficiency feat each time you want to learn how to use a different exotic weapon. Exotic weapons include the amphistaff, atlatl, bowcaster, cesta, and flamethrower.

Heavy Weapons

Large, powerful weapons that usually require a brace or tripod to operate fall under the category of heavy weapons, as do even larger weapons mounted to vehicles and starships. Heavy weapons include the blaster cannon, grenade launcher, heavy repeating blaster, missile launcher, and E-Web repeating blaster.

Lightsabers

This group includes the standard lightsaber (a handgrip hilt that projects a single blade of energy) and all lightsaber variants, including the double-bladed lightsaber (as wielded by Darth Maul in Episode I: *The Phantom Menace*). Lightsabers ignore damage reduction unless noted otherwise. However, a target's shield rating reduces a lightsaber's damage normally.

Pistols

Pistols are ranged weapons that can be fired with one hand. Types of pistols include the blaster pistol (the most common firearm in the *Star Wars* universe), the heavy blaster pistol, the hold-out blaster, the sporting blaster, the ion pistol, and the slugthrower pistol.

Rifles

Rifles deal more damage and have a greater range than pistols, but you take a –5 penalty on attack rolls if you wield a rifle with one hand (regardless of the weapon's size relative to you). Weapons in this group include the blaster carbine, blaster rifle, heavy blaster rifle, sporting blaster rifle, light repeating blaster, ion rifle, and slugthrower rifle.

Simple Weapons

Simple weapons include weapons that require no special training to use, such as the club, combat gloves, knife, mace, quarterstaff, stun baton, grenades, and thermal detonator. Also included are primitive weapons such as the spear, net, sling, and bow.

WEAPON SIZES

The size of a weapon compared to your size determines whether the weapon is light, one-handed, two-handed, or too large for you to use.

Light: If the weapon's size is smaller than your size (a Human using a Small weapon, such as a blaster pistol), then the weapon is light. Light weapons can be used while grappling, and light melee weapons can be used with the Weapon Finesse feat (page 89).

One-Handed: If the weapon's size category is the same as your size (a Human using a Medium weapon, such as a heavy blaster pistol), then the weapon is one-handed.

Two-Handed: If the weapon's size category is one step larger than your size (a Human using a Large weapon, such as a light repeating blaster), then the weapon requires two hands to use (and sometimes a special mount such as a tripod).

Too Large to Use: If the weapon's size category is two or more steps larger than your size (an Ewok using a Large weapon, such as a blaster cannon), the weapon is too large to use. The exceptions to this are vehicle- or starship-mounted mounted weapons, which are housed in a unit that aids in their use.

WEAPON QUALITIES

When you choose a weapon for your character, refer to Table 8-3: Melee Weapons and Table 8-4: Ranged Weapons for details about the various weapon types. The weapon qualities on these tables are explained below:

Weapon Group: A weapon's group tells you which Weapon Proficiency feat you need to be considered proficient with the weapon. If you don't have the appropriate feat, you take a –5 penalty on attacks made with the weapon.

Size: The weapon's size (see Weapon Sizes, above).

Cost: The weapon's cost in credits.

Damage: The damage the weapon deals with each hit. Melee weapons also add the wielder's Strength bonus to damage, or twice the wielder's Strength bonus when wielded in two hands.

Double weapons have two damage entries separated by a slash; these represent the damage dealt by each end of the double weapon.

Stun Damage: If the weapon has a stun setting, its stun damage is listed here (see Stunning, page 162, for more information). Ranged weapons set to stun have a maximum range of 6 squares unless noted otherwise.

Rate of Fire: Ranged weapons have either a single-shot setting (S) or an autofire setting (A). A few weapons have both settings and can be set to either single-shot mode or autofire mode as a swift action. Only ranged weapons that hold multiple shots of ammunition can have an autofire setting.

Weight: The weapon's weight in kilograms.

Damage Type: The type of damage a weapon deals. Some creatures and objects take more or less damage from weapons that deal a certain type of damage (see Damage Reduction, page 158). Some weapons deal more than one type of damage, depending on how the weapon is used:

And: The weapon deals both types of damage simultaneously.

Or: The weapon deals one type of damage or the other, chosen immediately before making the attack roll.

Double weapons sometimes deal a different damage type depending on which end of the weapon is used; in this case, the two damage types are separated by a slash.

(Ion): See Ion Damage, page 159, for special rules governing ion weapons.

Availability: Some weapons have limited availability, as noted below.

Licensed, Restricted, Military, or Illegal: Ownership of the weapon is limited to certain individuals (see Restricted Items, page 118).

Rare: A rare weapon is generally available only on its planet of origin (for example, Naboo for the atlatl and cesta, or Kashyyyk for the bowcaster) or by acquiring it directly from the manufacturer. When available on the open market elsewhere, rare items usually cost double the listed price.

MELEE WEAPONS

Used in close combat, melee weapons usually deal bludgeoning, slashing, or piercing damage, depending on the weapon's design. Some combine powered components to augment the user's own strength. Many types of melee weapons are widely available and have few governmental or legal restrictions. Civilians, law enforcement agents, and military personnel alike carry these items.

A character's Strength modifier is always applied to a melee weapon's attack roll and damage roll.

MELEE WEAPON DESCRIPTIONS

The various types of melee weapons presented in Table 8-3: Melee Weapons are described below.

Amphistaff
Exotic Weapon

An amphistaff is a serpentine creature genetically engineered by the Yuuzhan Vong to serve as a weapon. The amphistaff can become as rigid as stone or as flexible as rope, and it can contract the muscles around its head and tail to form razor-sharp edges.

The amphistaff has three distinct weapon forms: quarterstaff, spear, or whip. Switching from one weapon form to another takes a swift action.

Quarterstaff Form: A rigid amphistaff has all the qualities of a quarterstaff (see below).

Spear Form: A rigid amphistaff can be wielded or thrown as a spear (see below). The spear's head is poisonous: If the target takes damage and the attack roll equals or exceeds its Fortitude Defense, the target moves –1 persistent step on the condition track (see Conditions, page 148).

Whip Form: A flexible amphistaff has a reach of 2 squares (see Reach, page 161). The whip's tail deals 1d4 points of piercing damage (plus the wielder's Strength modifier) and is poisonous: If the target takes damage and the attack roll equals or exceeds its Fortitude Defense, the target moves –1 persistent step on the condition track. Instead of dealing damage with the whip, the wielder may use it to pin or trip the target (see Grapple, page 153) as though he was using the Pin or Trip feat (see Chapter 5: Feats); the wielder must be proficient with the amphistaff but doesn't need to have the Pin or Trip feat to use this feature of the weapon.

In any of its weapon forms, an amphistaff may be coaxed by its wielder to spit venom up to 10 squares away (a standard action). If this ranged attack hits both the target's Reflex Defense and Fortitude Defense, the target moves –1 persistent step on the condition track. An amphistaff can only spit venom once every 24 standard hours.

Atlatl
Exotic Weapon

A Gungan weapon, the atlatl adds speed and power as an extension of a throwing arm, allowing the user to hurl energy balls farther than with just an unaided toss. If forced into close combat, the wielder can use the atlatl as a clublike melee weapon. Although the atlatl is considered an exotic weapon, Gungans are treated as proficient if they have the Weapon Proficiency (simple weapons) feat.

Bayonet
Simple Weapon

When mounted on a rifle, a bayonet allows you to use the rifle as a melee weapon much like a spear. When wielding a rifle with a mounted bayonet, you threaten squares within your reach (even if you used the rifle to make a ranged attack on your last turn), and you can use it to make attacks of opportunity. A bayonet requires two hands to use when mounted on a rifle.

A bayonet cannot be used on a rifle with a folded stock. A bayonet detached from a rifle is treated as a knife; a mounted bayonet deals more damage than the knife because of the added leverage and bulk.

Cesta
Exotic Weapon

Another Gungan weapon, the cesta is a flexible pole used to hurl small energy balls. It can also be used as a stafflike melee weapon. Although the cesta is considered an exotic weapon, Gungans are treated as proficient if they have the Weapon Proficiency (simple weapons) feat.

Club/Baton
Simple Weapon

Powered by the wielder's brute strength, clubs break an opponent's bones, or worse. They are the favored weapons of thugs. Batons (a variety of the club) are used by police forces on relatively peaceful worlds in crowd-control situations.

Combat Gloves
Simple Weapon

A pair of padded gloves provides extra hitting power thanks to their weight and the materials used to construct them. Anyone who expects to get into a fistfight or a brawl probably wants to wear combat gloves. They provide a +1 bonus to damage on a successful unarmed attack.

Combat gloves are two sizes smaller than their wearer (for example, a pair of combat gloves designed for a Human are Tiny). Because of how they are worn, combat gloves can't be disarmed or dropped.

Electrostaff
Advanced Melee Weapon

An electrostaff is a double weapon: Each end has an electromagnetic pulse generator that discharges upon impact, allowing it to deal blunt-force wounds. If desired, either electromagnetic pulse can be set to stun its target instead. The staff is made of a resilient phrik alloy that gives it DR 20; this damage reduction applies even against lightsaber attacks.

Electrostaffs are not common except during the Clone Wars. The IG-100 Series MagnaGuard droid (see page 201) typically carries an electrostaff.

An electrostaff requires two energy cells to operate.

Force Pike
Advanced Melee Weapon

Force pikes are 1-meter-long poles topped with power tips. A two-setting power dial located near the bottom of the pike allows the user to set the weapon to "lethal" or "stun." Although primarily a vibro weapon, the force pike also delivers an electrical shock through its tip, dealing both piercing and energy damage.

A force pike requires two energy cells to operate.

Table 8-3: Melee Weapons

ADVANCED MELEE WEAPONS	COST	DAMAGE	STUN DAMAGE	WEIGHT	TYPE	AVAILABILITY
Tiny						
Vibrodagger[1]	200	2d4	—	1 kg	Slashing or piercing	—
Small						
Vibroblade	250	2d6	—	1.8 kg	Slashing or piercing	Licensed
Medium						
Vibrobayonet	350	2d6	—	1 kg	Piercing	Licensed
Force pike	500	2d8	2d8	2 kg	Piercing and energy	Restricted
Large						
Electrostaff	3,000	2d6/2d6	2d6/2d6	2 kg	Bludgeoning and energy	Restricted
Vibro-ax	500	2d10	—	6 kg	Slashing	Restricted
EXOTIC WEAPONS	**COST**	**DAMAGE**	**STUN DAMAGE**	**WEIGHT**	**TYPE**	**AVAILABILITY**
Medium						
Atlatl[2]	50	2d4	—	1.5 kg	Bludgeoning	Rare
Large						
Amphistaff[1,3]	—	Special	—	2 kg	See description	Rare
Cesta[2,3]	100	2d4	—	1.8 kg	Bludgeoning	Rare
LIGHTSABERS	**COST**	**DAMAGE**	**STUN DAMAGE**	**WEIGHT**	**TYPE**	**AVAILABILITY**
Small						
Lightsaber, short[1]	2,500	2d6	—	0.5 kg	Energy and slashing	Rare
Medium						
Lightsaber[1]	3,000	2d8	—	1 kg	Energy and slashing	Rare
Large						
Lightsaber, double	7,000	2d8/2d8	—	2 kg	Energy and slashing	Rare

Knife
Simple Weapon
While many weapons rely on highly advanced technology, knives still see wide use. A knife is completely silent and serves well in close-combat skirmishes.

Lightsaber
Lightsaber
The lightsaber, simple in design yet difficult to wield and master, features a handgrip hilt that projects a blade of pure energy. The traditional weapon of the Jedi, the lightsaber stands as a symbol of their skill, dedication, and authority.

The blade of a lightsaber is generated by an energy cell and focused through crystals within the hilt. The saber can cut through most materials (except another lightsaber blade, an energy shield, or a few exotic materials), given enough time. Because only the handgrip has any weight, unskilled users have difficulty judging the position of the blade. The lightsaber's true potential becomes apparent in the hands of a fully trained Jedi, who can defend and attack with the weapon, deflecting shots or striking opponents with the glowing blade.

A lightsaber requires a special energy cell to operate (the cost is ten times the price of an ordinary energy cell, but it lasts almost indefinitely).

Table 8-3: Melee Weapons Cont.

SIMPLE WEAPONS	COST	DAMAGE	STUN DAMAGE	WEIGHT	TYPE	AVAILABILITY
Tiny						
Knife[1]	25	1d4	—	1 kg	Slashing or piercing	—
Small						
Club/baton	15	1d6	—	0.5 kg	Bludgeoning	—
Stun baton	15	1d6	2d6	0.5 kg	Bludgeoning	—
Medium						
Mace	50	1d8	—	2.5 kg	Bludgeoning	—
Spear[1]	60	1d8	—	1.5 kg	Piercing	—
Bayonet	50	1d8	—	1 kg	Piercing	Licensed
Large						
Quarterstaff	65	1d6/1d6	—	1.8 kg	Bludgeoning	—
UNARMED	**COST**	**DAMAGE**	**STUN DAMAGE**	**WEIGHT**	**TYPE**	**AVAILABILITY**
Unarmed, Small character	—	1d3	—	—	Bludgeoning	—
Combat gloves	150	+1	—	0.4 kg	Bludgeoning	—
Unarmed, Medium character	—	1d4	—	—	Bludgeoning	—
Combat gloves	250	+1	—	0.5 kg	Bludgeoning	—

1 *Can be thrown.*
2 *Can be used to hurl energy balls (see Table 8-4: Ranged Weapons).*
3 *Reach weapon.*

Lightsaber, Double-Bladed
Lightsaber
The double-bladed lightsaber consists of two sabers fused at their hilts. These weapons are rare and require even greater skill to wield than single-bladed lightsabers. One or both blades can be ignited at once.

With both blades ignited, a double-bladed lightsaber is a double weapon. You can attack with both ends of the weapon as a full-round action, but both attack rolls take a −10 penalty (although certain feats and talents can reduce these penalties).

A double-bladed lightsaber requires two special energy cells to operate (the cost of each is ten times the price of an ordinary energy cell, but it lasts almost indefinitely).

Lightsaber, Short
Lightsaber
Small Jedi characters such as Master Yoda favor the short lightsaber, sometimes called a *shoto*. Jedi skilled at two-weapon fighting often use the shoto as their off-hand weapon of choice.

A short lightsaber requires a special energy cell to operate (the cost is ten times the price of an ordinary energy cell, but it lasts almost indefinitely.)

Mace
Simple Weapon
The mace is a weapon made of metal, consisting of a heavy ball atop a handle.

Quarterstaff
Simple Weapon

A quarterstaff is made of wood, plasteel, or a metal alloy. A user can strike with either end of the quarterstaff, taking full advantage of any openings in an opponent's defenses.

A quarterstaff is a double weapon. You can attack with both ends of the weapon as a full-round action, but both attack rolls take a -10 penalty; certain feats and talents can reduce these penalties.

Spear
Simple Weapon

A common weapon used by hunters and warriors in primitive cultures, the spear is a long wooden pole with a sharp end fashioned from stone or metal. Members of more advanced cultures enjoy using spears for sport, though these weapons are usually constructed out of a durable metal alloy. Spears can be used as thrown weapons.

Stun Baton
Simple Weapon

A short club with a power pack in the handle, the stun baton can be activated to produce a stunning charge when it strikes a target (see Stunning, page 162).

A stun baton requires an energy cell to operate.

Vibro-Ax
Advanced Melee Weapon

This powerful vibro weapon features an energy cell that causes the blade to vibrate rapidly when activated. This gives the weapon far greater power than a standard axe, with minimal effort from the wielder.

A vibro-ax requires two energy cells to operate.

Vibrobayonet
Advanced Melee Weapon

When mounted on a rifle, a vibrobayonet allows you to use a rifle as a potent melee weapon. Even if you used the rifle to make a ranged attack on your last turn, you still threaten squares within your reach as long as your rifle has a mounted vibrobayonet, and you can use it to make attacks of opportunity. A vibrobayonet requires two hands to use when mounted on a rifle.

A vibrobayonet cannot be used when mounted on a rifle with a folded stock. A vibrobayonet detached from a rifle functions as a vibrodagger; a mounted vibrobayonet deals more damage than the vibrodagger because of the added leverage and bulk.

A vibrobayonet requires an energy cell to operate. (Its power does not drain energy from the rifle's power pack.)

Vibroblade
Advanced Melee Weapon

The vibroblade is a close-combat weapon favored by soldiers and mercenaries throughout the galaxy. It resembles a short sword with a high-tech look and feel. Vibroblades are illegal in most urban areas.

A vibroblade requires an energy cell to operate.

Vibrodagger
Advanced Melee Weapon

Assassins and petty thugs favor the smallest of the vibro weapons, the vibrodagger. A number of civilians carry it for defense. It alone among vibro weapons is subject to very little regulation, since it is viewed as a common tool for crafters and explorers.

A vibrodagger requires an energy cell to operate.

RANGED WEAPONS

At any given time, hundreds of manufacturers are creating and marketing a wide array of ranged weapons. These weapons run the gamut from small, concealable handheld weapons to tripod-mounted cannons that require a small crew to operate.

WEAPON RANGES

All ranged weapons apply the wielder's Dexterity modifier to the attack roll. Ranged attacks made at point blank range suffer no penalty. However, ranged attacks made at short, medium, or long range take a penalty on the attack roll, as shown in Table 8-5: Weapon Ranges.

Improvised Thrown Weapons: While some weapons are meant to be thrown, it is physically possible to throw almost any weapon of your size or less. You take a -5 penalty on an attack roll made with an improvised thrown weapon. In addition, unless the weapon is light, the improvised thrown weapon is treated as inaccurate (see above).

RANGED WEAPON DESCRIPTIONS

The various types of ranged weapons presented in Table 8-4: Ranged Weapons are described below.

Blaster Cannon
Heavy Weapon

Portable, shoulder-fired blaster cannons fire powerful bolts of energy. Often used as an antivehicle weapon, the blaster cannon has the range and power to inflict devastation on troops and structures alike.

A blaster cannon is an area effect weapon. It deals full damage to the target if the attack hits its Reflex Defense (half damage if it has the Evasion talent) and half damage if it misses (no damage if it has the Evasion talent).

> "HOKEY RELIGIONS AND ANCIENT WEAPONS ARE NO MATCH FOR A GOOD BLASTER AT YOUR SIDE, KID."
>
> – HAN SOLO

Any creature or object adjacent to the target takes half damage if the attack hits (none if it has the Evasion talent) and no damage if it misses.

A blaster cannon requires a power pack to operate. After 10 shots, the power pack must be replaced.

Blaster Carbine
Blaster Rifle (see text)

This small blaster rifle has a short barrel and compact two-handed grip, making it look more like a long pistol than a rifle. Some blaster carbines, such as the E-5 used by B1 battle droids, have a retractable stock. A blaster carbine without a retractable stock costs 850 credits (instead of 900 credits).

Because of its compact design, a blaster carbine can always be used to make an attack of opportunity even if its stock is not folded.

A blaster carbine requires a power pack to operate. After 50 shots, the power pack must be replaced.

Blaster, E-Web Repeating
Heavy Weapon

The E-Web repeating blaster can normally only be fired when mounted on a tripod. When mounted on a tripod, it is treated as one size smaller for purposes of being wielded (allowing a Medium character to operate it with two hands).

The E-Web repeating blaster only operates in autofire mode (see Autofire, page 156) and requires a power generator to operate (see page 139).

Normally, the E-Web repeating blaster requires a second crewman to regulate the weapon's power generator; this second crewman must spend a standard action while adjacent to the weapon to regulate its power. After you regulate the E-Web repeating blaster's power, it will function normally until the beginning of your next turn. If the weapon's power is not regulated (that is, if a second crewman has not done so since the same initiative count on the previous round), apply a –2 penalty on all attack rolls made with the weapon.

Blaster, Heavy Repeating
Heavy Weapon

The heavy repeating blaster is a fearsome weapon typically operated from a bunker emplacement or mounted on a combat vehicle. The heavy repeating blaster operates only in autofire mode (see Autofire, page 156). If you use a heavy repeating blaster without a tripod or other mount, you cannot brace the weapon before making an autofire attack.

A heavy repeating blaster requires a power pack to operate. After 20 shots, the power pack must be replaced. This weapon can also be attached to a power generator for longer use.

Blaster Pistol
Pistol

The word "blaster" is a blanket term for literally thousands of different designs from hundreds of manufacturers, such as the popular BlasTech DL-18. Blasters are popular with urban police forces, traders, and anyone who needs to pack respectable firepower in an easily carried package.

A blaster pistol requires a power pack to operate. After 100 shots, the power pack must be replaced.

Retractable stocks

Some weapons, such as the E-11 blaster rifle used by stormtroopers and the E-5 blaster carbine used by battle droids, have a retractable stock. Only rifles and pistols (and rifle- or pistol-like exotic weapons) can have a retractable stock. Extending or folding a retractable stock is a move action.

When the stock is folded, the following rules apply:
- Treat the weapon as a pistol for purposes of proficiency and range.
- You cannot brace the weapon while using it in autofire mode (see page 156), even if it is an autofire-only weapon.

When the stock is extended, the following rules apply:
- Treat the weapon as a rifle for purposes of proficiency and range.
- You take a –5 penalty on attack rolls with the weapon if you use it in one hand (regardless of its size relative to you).

Blaster Pistol, Heavy
Pistol

Heavy blaster pistols were invented to provide the sort of firepower one expects from a blaster rifle, but in a compact and easily carried sidearm. The weapon produces additional "punch" by drawing heavily on its power pack, reducing the number of shots the power pack can provide (compared to a regular blaster pistol). Han Solo uses a heavy blaster pistol, the BlasTech DL-44.

A heavy blaster pistol requires a power pack to operate. After 50 shots, the power pack must be replaced.

Blaster Pistol, Hold-Out
Pistol

Small, palm-sized blasters see widespread use in weapon-restricted areas. Hold-out blasters are commonly found in the possession of undercover agents, gamblers, scoundrels, or nobles seeking to protect themselves. They are sometimes carried as a backup weapon for more lethal characters.

Because of its compact design, a hold-out blaster pistol grants a +5 equipment bonus on Stealth checks made to conceal the weapon.

A hold-out blaster requires an energy cell to operate. After 6 shots, the energy cell must be replaced.

Table 8-4: Ranged Weapons

EXOTIC WEAPONS	COST	DAMAGE	STUN DMG	RATE OF FIRE	WEIGHT	TYPE	AVAILABILITY
Medium							
Flamethrower[1]	1,000	3d6	—	S	7 kg	Fire	Military
Large							
Bowcaster	1,500	3d10	—	S	8 kg	Energy and piercing	Licensed, Rare
HEAVY WEAPONS	**COST**	**DAMAGE**	**STUN DMG**	**RATE OF FIRE**	**WEIGHT**	**TYPE**	**AVAILABILITY**
Medium							
Grenade launcher	500	Special	Special	S	5 kg	Varies	Military
Large							
Blaster, heavy repeating	4,000	3d10	—	A	12 kg	Energy	Military
Blaster cannon[1]	3,000	3d12	—	S	18 kg	Energy	Military
Missile launcher[1]	1,500	6d6	—	S	10 kg	Slashing	Military
Huge							
Blaster, E-Web repeating[2]	8,000	3d12	—	A	38 kg	Energy	Military
PISTOLS	**COST**	**DAMAGE**	**STUN DMG**	**RATE OF FIRE**	**WEIGHT**	**TYPE**	**AVAILABILITY**
Tiny							
Blaster pistol, hold-out	300	3d4	—	S	0.5 kg	Energy	Illegal
Small							
Blaster pistol	500	3d6	2d6	S	1 kg	Energy	Restricted
Blaster pistol, sporting	300	3d4	2d4	S	1 kg	Energy	Licensed
Ion pistol	250	3d6 ion	—	S	1 kg	Energy (ion)	Licensed
Slugthrower pistol	250	2d6	—	S	1.4 kg	Piercing	Licensed
Medium							
Blaster pistol, heavy	750	3d8	2d8	S	1.3 kg	Energy	Military

Blaster Pistol, Sporting
Pistol

This short, compact blaster is used for small-game hunting or personal defense. Princess Leia Organa used a DDC Defender sporting blaster when she first appeared in Episode IV: *A New Hope*.

A sporting blaster requires an energy cell to operate. After 6 shots, the energy cell must be replaced. A sporting blaster can also be attached to a power pack, but after 100 shots the power pack must be replaced.

Blaster Rifle
Rifle (see text)

The basic blaster rifle is standard issue to soldiers across the galaxy. Some blaster rifles, such as the BlasTech E-11 (or its "clone," the SoroSuub Stormtrooper One), have a retractable stock. A blaster rifle without a retractable stock costs 900 credits (instead of 1,000 credits).

A blaster rifle requires a power pack to operate. After 50 shots, the power pack must be replaced.

Table 8-4: Ranged Weapons

RIFLES	COST	DAMAGE	STUN DMG	RATE OF FIRE	WEIGHT	TYPE	AVAILABILITY
Medium							
Blaster carbine	900	3d8	2d8	S, A	2.2 kg	Energy	Restricted
Blaster rifle	1,000	3d8	2d8	S, A	4.5 kg	Energy	Restricted
Blaster rifle, sporting	800	3d6	2d6	S	4 kg	Energy	Licensed
Ion rifle	800	3d8 ion	—	S	3.1 kg	Energy (ion)	Restricted
Slugthrower rifle	300	2d8	—	S, A	4 kg	Piercing	Restricted
Large							
Blaster, light repeating	1,200	3d8	—	A	6 kg	Energy	Military
Blaster rifle, heavy	2,000	3d10	2d10	S, A	6 kg	Energy	Military
SIMPLE WEAPONS	**COST**	**DAMAGE**	**STUN DMG**	**RATE OF FIRE**	**WEIGHT**	**TYPE**	**AVAILABILITY**
Tiny							
Energy ball[3]	20	2d8	—	S	0.25 kg	Energy	Licensed, Rare
Grenade, frag[1]	200	4d6	—	S	0.5 kg	Slashing	Military
Grenade, ion[1]	250	4d6 ion	—	S	0.5 kg	Energy (ion)	Restricted
Grenade, stun[1]	250	—	4d6	S	0.5 kg	Energy	Restricted
Thermal detonator[1]	2,000	8d6	—	S	1 kg	Energy	Illegal
Small							
Sling	35	1d4	—	S	0.3 kg	Bludgeoning	—
Medium							
Bow	300	1d6	—	S	1.4 kg	Piercing	—
Large							
Net	25	—	—	S	4.5 kg	—	—

1 *Area attack weapon (see Area Attacks, page 155).*
2 *An E-Web repeating blaster mounted on a tripod is treated as a Large weapon.*
3 *For purposes of range, treat as a thrown weapon if thrown by hand, a simple weapon if hurled by an atlatl, or an accurate simple weapon if hurled by a cesta.*

Blaster Rifle, Heavy
Rifle

The heavy blaster rifle is a larger, more powerful version of the blaster rifle (see above) often used by clone troopers, stormtroopers, and other troops during battles on open terrain. Because of its size, it is not well suited to close-quarters fighting.

A heavy blaster rifle requires a power pack to operate. After 30 shots, the power pack must be replaced.

Blaster Rifle, Light Repeating
Rifle

The light repeating blaster is the largest rifle-style weapon carried by military personnel. It is an autofire-only weapon (see Autofire, page 156).

A light repeating blaster requires a power pack to operate. After 30 shots, the power pack must be replaced. This weapon can also be attached to a power generator for longer use.

Blaster Rifle, Sporting
Rifle

Sporting blaster rifles are popular with the galactic elite as well as among "fringers" living in isolated colonies. Sporting blaster rifles are legal in most systems, and special permits must be obtained to carry them on many Core worlds. Luke Skywalker kept a sporting blaster rifle in his landspeeder on Tatooine.

Sporting blaster rifles often have a targeting scope mounted on them (see page 140), but the scope is not included in cost listed on Table 8-4: Ranged Weapons.

A sporting blaster rifle requires a power pack to operate. After 50 shots, the power pack must be replaced.

Bow
Simple Weapon

The bow is a typical hunter's weapon on low-tech worlds, but it is also used for sport on high-tech planets. A primitive bow and its arrows are made of wood and augmented with metal or stone, while more advanced versions tend to be made from durable, lightweight composite materials.

The wielder's Strength modifier applies to damage dealt with a bow. A bow only holds a single arrow at a time, but it can be reloaded as a free action. A quiver of 10 arrows costs 20 credits and weighs 0.8 kg.

Bowcaster
Exotic Weapon

The bowcaster is crafted exclusively by the Wookiees of Kashyyyk. A fusion of modern and ancient technologies, the weapon hurls an explosive energy quarrel at incredible speed, much like an archaic rail gun. Although the bowcaster is an exotic weapon, Wookiees are treated as proficient if they have the Weapon Proficiency (rifles) feat.

A quiver of 10 quarrels costs 50 credits and weighs 1 kg.

Flamethrower
Exotic Weapon

The flamethrower is a ranged weapon that shoots a cone of burning chemicals 6 squares long and 6 squares wide at the terminus. Make a single attack roll and compare it to the Reflex Defense of every target within this area. A successful attack deals 3d6 points of fire damage to the target; if the attack misses, the target takes half damage instead. A target with the Evasion talent (see page 50) takes half damage from a successful attack and no damage if the attack misses.

Reloading the flamethrower is a full-round action. The weapon can be used five times before its chemical supply is depleted. Replacement chemical cartridges for the flame-thrower cost 200 credits and weigh 4 kg each.

Grenade, Frag
Simple Weapon

The standard fragmentation grenade unleashes metal shrapnel with explosive force, slicing up anyone within the 2-square burst radius. It is designed to explode on contact after it is thrown, dealing damage in the same turn it is hurled.

Table 8-5: Weapon Ranges

TYPE OF RANGED WEAPON	POINT BLANK (NO PENALTY)	SHORT (–2 ATTACK)	MEDIUM (–5 ATTACK)	LONG (–10 ATTACK)
Heavy weapons	0–50 squares	51–100 squares	101–250 squares	251–500 squares
Pistols	0–20 squares	21–40 squares	41–60 squares	61–80 squares
Rifles	0–30 squares	31–60 squares	61–150 squares	151–300 squares
Simple weapons[1]	0–20 squares	21–40 squares	41–60 squares	61–80 squares
Thrown weapons[2]	0–6 squares	7–8 squares	9–10 squares	11–12 squares

2 Includes bows, slings, and energy balls hurled from atlatls and cestas.
3 Includes grenades and thrown melee weapons such as spears and lightsabers.

When you make an area attack with a frag grenade, you make a single attack roll and compare the result to the Reflex Defense of every target in the grenade's burst radius. Creatures you hit take full damage, and creatures you miss take half damage. A target with the Evasion talent (see page 50) takes half damage from a successful attack and no damage if the attack misses.

Grenade, Ion
Simple Weapon

When the object of a mission is to capture droids or vehicles, mercenary units, military personnel, and local law enforcement agencies use ion grenades. The standard ion grenade unleashes a brief electrostatic pulse that disables droids, electronic devices, and vehicles within its 2-square burst radius. It is designed to explode on contact after it is thrown, effectively dealing damage in the same round it is hurled.

When you make an area attack with an ion grenade, you make a single attack roll and compare the result to the Reflex Defense of every target in the grenade's burst radius. Droids, vehicles, electronic devices, and cybernetically enhanced creatures you hit take full damage, and those you miss take half damage. In addition, the ion damage has a chance of pushing such targets down the condition track (see Ion Damage, page 159). Creatures without cybernetics take half of the ion damage on a hit or no ion damage on a miss, and they suffer no other ill effects. A target with the Evasion talent (see page 50) takes half damage from a successful attack and no damage if the attack misses.

Grenade, Stun
Simple Weapon

When the object of a mission is to detain or subdue rather than kill, mercenary units, military personnel, and local law enforcement agencies use stun grenades. The standard stun grenade unleashes concussive energy that knocks out creatures within its 2-square burst radius. It is designed to explode on contact after it is thrown, dealing damage in the same round it is hurled.

When you make an area attack with a stun grenade, you make a single attack roll and compare the result to the Reflex Defense of every target in the grenade's burst radius. Creatures you hit take full stun damage, and creatures you miss take half stun damage. In addition, the stun damage has a chance of pushing targeted creatures down the condition track (see Stunning, page 162). A target with the Evasion talent (see page 50) takes half stun damage from a successful attack and no stun damage if the attack misses its Reflex Defense.

Droids, vehicles, and objects are immune to stun damage.

Grenade Launcher
Heavy Weapon

Grenade launchers are military weapons that greatly improve the range of grenades. Grenades fired by grenade launchers always explode on impact, regardless of timers or other considerations. The type of grenade used determines the damage, type, and burst radius. Grenade launchers cannot be used to hurl thermal detonators because these devices are simply too big and heavy (although some larger grenade mortars can hurl thermal detonators as well).

A grenade launcher holds four grenades and has to be reloaded as a full-round action. A grenade launcher can be mounted on a rifle (this takes 1 minute and requires a DC 15 Mechanics check) or used as a separate weapon.

Ion Pistol
Pistol

An ion pistol fires a stream of energy that wreaks havoc on electrical systems, making it effective against droids, vehicles, electronic devices, and cybernetically enhanced creatures. It deals full damage against such targets and has a chance of pushing its target down the condition track (see Ion Damage, page 159). Creatures without cybernetics take half damage from a successful attack and suffer no other ill effects.

An ion pistol requires a power pack to operate. After 30 shots, the power pack must be replaced.

Ion Rifle
Rifle

An ion rifle is simply a larger version of the ion pistol (see above). An ion rifle requires a power pack to operate. After 20 shots, the power pack must be replaced.

Missile Launcher
Heavy Weapon

A missile launcher fires a high-speed projectile with an explosive warhead. The standard missile unleashes metal shrapnel with explosive force, shredding targets within a 2-square radius.

A missile launcher is an area effect weapon. Make a single attack roll and compare it to the Reflex Defense of every target within the blast radius. A successful attack deals full damage to the target; if the attack misses, the target takes half damage instead. A target with the Evasion talent (see page 50) takes half damage from a successful attack and no damage if the attack misses.

A missile launcher holds four missiles and can be reloaded as a full-round action. Replacement missiles are bought in pre-loaded magazines that hold four missiles. Magazines cost 200 credits and weigh 5 kg.

Net
Simple Weapon

Nets are used for hunting and fishing in primitive cultures and for nonlethal crowd control in more advanced ones.

A net allows you to initiate a grab (see page 152) or grapple (see page 153) against a character at range. A character that is grabbed or grappled can attempt to escape the net (requiring a DC 15 Acrobatics check) or break out of it (requiring a DC 20 Strength check). You can use the Pin and Trip feats with a net, but you cannot use the Crush or Throw feats.

Sling
Simple Weapon

A primitive weapon, the sling hurls metal bullets or stones. The wielder's Strength modifier applies to damage dealt with a sling.

Slugthrower Pistol
Pistol

A slugthrower pistol fires metal bullets—called "slugs"—instead of energy bolts.

Slugthrowers are mostly found on backwater fringe worlds where blasters aren't readily available. They don't need power packs; instead, they employ clips that hold 10 slugs apiece. Clips cost 20 credits and weigh 0.1 kg.

Slugthrower Rifle
Rifle

A slugthrower rifle is the larger cousin of the slugthrower pistol. It doesn't need a power pack; instead, it takes clips, and each clip holds 20 slugs. Clips cost 40 credits and weigh 0.2 kg.

Thermal Detonator
Simple Weapon

The thermal detonator is a fist-sized sphere containing baradium, a powerful explosive. Outlawed throughout known space except for highly regulated demolitions professionals, the thermal detonator produces a fusion reaction that generates a rapidly expanding field of searing heat and blast energy. Disguised as a bounty hunter, Princess Leia threatened Jabba with a thermal detonator at the beginning of Episode VI: *Return of the Jedi*.

A thermal detonator's timer can be set for 6 seconds (1 round) to as high as an 18-second delay (3 rounds), counting down until it explodes or is reset to its safe position.

When you make an area attack with a thermal detonator, you make a single attack roll and compare the result to the Reflex Defense of every target in the grenade's 4-square burst radius. Creatures hit take full damage, and creatures missed take half damage. A target with the Evasion talent (see page 50) takes half damage from a successful attack and no damage if the attack misses its Reflex Defense.

EXPLOSIVES

Sometimes a mission calls for the use of more powerful explosives than either grenades or thermal detonators. Set explosives aren't ranged weapons and can't be used like grenades. Placing an explosive requires a Mechanics check (see page 68).

When set and activated, the charge's timer begins counting down. Standard timers can be set with as much as an hour delay. Longer delays require specialized timers.

With a successful Mechanics check, explosives ignore the damage reduction of objects to which they're attached. Particularly good Mechanics check results can increase the damage even more (see the Handle Explosives use of the Mechanics skill, page 68). Multiple explosives rigged to explode at the same time deal extra damage: Every time you double the number of explosives used, you add +2 dice of damage. For example, two blocks of detonite deal 7d6 points of damage, while four blocks deal 9d6 points of damage.

Table 8-6: Explosives

WEAPON	COST	DAMAGE	DAMAGE TYPE	WEIGHT	SIZE	AVAILABILITY
Explosive charge	1,500	10d6*	Energy	0.5 kg	Diminutive	Restricted
Detonite	500	5d6*	Energy	0.1 kg	Fine	Restricted
Timer	250	–	–	0.1 kg	Fine	Licensed

The explosion damages everything in a 1-square burst radius.

Explosive Charge

Explosive charges are highly restricted, usually only available to military or law enforcement specialists or specialized construction units. Han Solo and his strike team used explosive charges to take out the shield generator on Endor in Episode VI: *Return of the Jedi*.

An explosive charge delivers a lot of destructive energy to a specific point, making it perfect for demolishing structures or clearing rubble. It causes negligible damage beyond its 1-square burst radius. Of course, collateral damage and subsequent explosions usually accompany the use of an explosive charge.

Detonite

Detonite is a contact explosive that comes in tiny claylike blocks. It can be shaped or molded around a target and crammed into small cracks. Detonite is very stable in its normal forms and requires a timer to be set off.

Armor

Protective armor exists in the *Star Wars* universe, but only the lightest types see widespread use. Heavier armor is considered to be too expensive, too restrictive, and just not worth the trouble unless it serves an additional function (such as providing environmental protection, as in the case of Imperial snowtrooper armor). See Table 8-7: Armor for the list of armor types.

Many forms of armor are restricted or even illegal outside of approved military uses. In locations where armor isn't prohibited, the wearer of armor identifies himself as someone who either expects to cause trouble or expects trouble to come his way.

Armor Qualities

If you choose armor for your character, refer to Table 8-7: Armor (page 132) for details about the various armor types. The armor qualities on the table are explained below:

Cost: The cost of the armor. Armor sized for Small characters costs half as much, while armor for Large characters costs double the listed price. Some armor has limited availability:

Armor Bonus to Reflex Defense: When you are wearing the armor, you add this value as an armor bonus to your Reflex Defense (instead of adding your heroic level to your Reflex Defense).

Equipment Bonus to Fortitude Defense: When you are wearing the armor, you add this value as an equipment bonus to your Fortitude Defense. Some types of armor do not provide an equipment bonus to your Fortitude Defense.

Maximum Dex Bonus: This is the maximum bonus you can apply to your Reflex Defense from Dexterity when wearing this type of armor. Heavier armor limits your mobility, reducing your ability to avoid attacks. For example, an armored flight suit has a maximum Dexterity bonus of +3. A character with a Dexterity of 18 normally gains a +4 bonus to his Reflex Defense from Dexterity, but if he's wearing an armored flight suit, he only applies a +3 bonus to his Reflex Defense.

Speed: Medium and heavy armor reduces your speed to three-quarters normal (rounded down). Table 8-7 shows this reduction if you have a speed of 6 squares or 4 squares. In addition, when wearing heavy armor, you can only move up to three times your speed when running (instead of four times your speed).

Weight: The weight of the armor. Armor fitted for Small characters weighs half as much. Armor fitted for Large characters weighs twice as much.

Availability: Some armor has limited availability, as indicated below.

Rare: This armor is generally only available by going to its planet of origin or by acquiring it directly from its wearer (for example, getting vonduun crabshell armor from a Yuuzhan Vong warrior). When available on the open market elsewhere, these items usually cost double the listed price, sometimes much more.

Licensed, Restricted, Military, or Illegal: Ownership of the armor is limited to certain people, as described in Restricted Items (see page 118).

Table 8-7: Armor

ARMOR (CHECK PENALTY)	COST	ARMOR BONUS TO REF DEFENSE	EQUIP BONUS TO FORT DEFENSE	MAX DEX BONUS	SPEED (6 SQ.)	SPEED (4 SQ.)	WEIGHT	AVAILABILITY
Light Armor (−2)								
Blast helmet and vest	500	+2	–	+5	–	–	3 kg	–
Flight suit, padded	2,000	+3	+1	+4	–	–	5 kg	–
Combat jumpsuit	1,500	+4	–	+4	–	–	8 kg	Licensed
Flight suit, armored	4,000	+5	+2	+3	–	–	10 kg	Licensed
Vonduun crabshell	–	+5	+5	+4	–	–	5 kg	Rare
Stormtrooper armor	8,000	+6	+2	+3	–	–	10 kg	Military, Rare
Medium Armor (−5)								
Ceremonial armor	5,000	+7	–	+2	4 sq.	3 sq.	13 kg	Restricted
Corellian powersuit	10,000	+7	–	+3	4 sq.	3 sq.	20 kg	Restricted
Battle armor	7,000	+8	+2	+2	4 sq.	3 sq.	16 kg	Military
Heavy Armor (−10)								
Armored spacesuit	12,000	+9	+3	+1	4 sq.[1]	3 sq.[1]	35 kg	Restricted
Battle armor, heavy	15,000	+10	+4	+1	4 sq.[1]	3 sq.[1]	30 kg	Military

1 *When running in heavy armor, you can only move up to three times your speed (instead of four times).*

Armor Check Penalty

While wearing armor with which you are not proficient, you take an armor check penalty on attack rolls as well as skill checks made using the following skills: Acrobatics, Climb, Endurance, Initiative, Jump, Stealth, and Swim. The type of armor worn determines the size of the penalty: light, −2; medium, −5; heavy, −10. Additionally, you do not gain the armor's equipment bonuses. For example, a character not proficient with light armor who dons a suit of stormtrooper armor takes a −2 penalty on attack rolls and certain skill checks (see above). In addition, he does not gain the armor's equipment bonus on Perception checks and cannot apply the armor's equipment bonus to his Fortitude Defense.

Armor Descriptions

The types of armor given on Table 8-7: Armor are described below.

Armored Spacesuit
Heavy Armor
This bulky coverall contains a sealed life support system that provides everything the wearer needs to survive for 24 hours in the vacuum of space or any other hostile environment.

Battle Armor
Medium Armor
Battle armor combines protective metal or composite plates with a padded jumpsuit to form a layer of protection. While off-the-rack battle armor is available, most users cobble together their gear from various sources.

Battle Armor, Heavy
Heavy Armor
Similar to regular battle armor, heavy battle armor features more plating than padding, including various pieces molded to fit the user, such as breastplates and armor covering the arms and legs.

Blast Helmet and Vest
Light Armor
This armor consists of a lightweight helmet and a composite vest that, when worn together, offer limited protection against incoming attacks.

Ceremonial Armor
Medium Armor
Ceremonial armor blends practicality with ornate design. Republic Guards and Imperial Royal Guards wear different styles of ceremonial armor. A typical

suit of ceremonial armor consists of a helmet, durable breast guard, shoulder guards, and articulated greaves for the arms and legs.

Combat Jumpsuit
Light Armor

This heavily padded jumpsuit is designed to provide limited protection against physical and energy trauma without overly restricting the wearer's movement.

Corellian Powersuit
Medium Armor

This suit of body armor contains an energized exoskeleton and a series of servomotors that boosts the wearer's physical strength. Used by professional soldiers, mercenaries, and bounty hunters, the powersuit requires skill and training to use effectively.

The Corellian powersuit grants its wearer a +2 equipment bonus to Strength, but only if the wearer has the Armor Proficiency (medium) feat.

Flight Suit, Armored
Light Armor

A combat-ready flight suit that provides additional protection against vacuum for limited periods, this armor comes in various models, including the Corellian TX-3 (favored by various pirate gangs) and the Imperial TIE flight suit (worn by TIE fighter pilots throughout the Empire). An armored flight suit provides up to 10 hours of life support, allowing its wearer to survive in the vacuum of space or any other hostile environment.

Flight Suit, Padded
Light Armor

Favored by starfighter pilots all over the galaxy, the one-piece padded flight suit protects against decompression, g-forces, and harmful environments. It provides limited protection against attacks as well. A padded flight suit comes with a matching helmet and gloves that seal around the wearer and provide up to 10 hours of life support, allowing him to survive in the vacuum of space or any other hostile environment.

Stormtrooper Armor
Light Armor

Worn by the elite soldiers of the Galactic Empire, stormtrooper armor comes in a variety of models based around a standard white-and-black shell. Filled with electronics that assist and augment the stormtrooper in his duties, it includes rudimentary environmental protection, three-phase sonic filtering, and visual amplification.

Variants of this armor also exist, including snowtrooper armor, sandtrooper armor, and clone trooper armor. Each has slightly different details, but all include the basic characteristics common to all stormtrooper armor. Though

> ### TO WEAR ARMOR OR NOT
> A character's Reflex Defense can be improved with armor; however, a character who wears armor chooses to apply the armor's bonus to Reflex Defense instead of his heroic level. He also chooses to take a penalty on certain skill checks (see Armor Check Penalty, page 132).
>
> As a character gains levels, armor becomes less enticing. For example, a 5th-level heroic character has little reason to wear armor that grants an armor bonus of +5 or less, unless the armor confers some other useful benefit or the character has the Armored Defense or Improved Armored Defense talents (see page 52). Still, some characters enjoy the benefit of having a higher Fortitude Defense and damage threshold; against very dangerous opponents, armor can literally be the difference between life and death.

unavailable on the open market, these suits can occasionally be found on the black market (or sometimes much higher).

Stormtrooper armor (including all variants) grants a wearer who has the Armor Proficiency (light) feat a +2 equipment bonus on Perception checks as well as low-light vision. Stormtrooper armor also includes an integrated comlink in the helmet, allowing hands-free communication.

Wearing snowtrooper armor (18,000 credits) makes you immune to the effects of extreme cold (see Extreme Temperatures, page 254).

Wearing sandtrooper armor (18,000 credits) makes you immune to the effects of extreme heat (see Extreme Temperatures, page 254).

Vonduun Crabshell Armor
Light Armor

Yuuzhan Vong warriors wear this bioengineered "living armor" into battle. The armor clings to its wearer's body like a parasite until its wearer dies or decides to remove it. It is not found anywhere except in the hands of the Yuuzhan Vong (see page 285).

EQUIPMENT

A sample of common equipment available during the time periods covered in this book is given on Table 8-8: Equipment. Refer to the descriptions below for other pertinent information.

COMMUNICATIONS DEVICES

Communications devices in the *Star Wars Roleplaying Game* are assumed to use the same basic set of frequencies. The primary differences between them lie in range, size, and what kind of data (audio, visual, or holo) they can carry. If two or more communication devices are within range of one another and share a data type, they can communicate.

Comlink

A personal communications transceiver, the comlink consists of a receiver, a transmitter, and a power source. Comlinks come in a variety of shapes and styles.

Short-range comlinks have a range of 50 kilometers or low orbit, and they can be built into helmets and armor; for example, stormtrooper armor includes a helmet equipped with a short-range comlink.

A long-range comlink has a range of 200 kilometers or high orbit, and it requires with a backpack-sized comset. For double the cost, a long-range comlink can be miniaturized to a wrist-sized unit.

Encryption: A comlink can have hardwired encryption routines (adding +10 to the DC of all Use Computer checks made to intercept your transmission) for ten times the base cost.

Video Capability: A comlink can have video capability (two-dimensional images in addition to audio) for twice the base cost.

Holo Capability: A comlink can have holo capability (three-dimensional images in addition to audio) for five times the base cost.

Pocket Scrambler

This is a simple add-on device that can be attached to any normal communications device, such as a comlink and more advanced transceiver. The pocket scrambler automatically encodes any outgoing message so that it can be read only by a communications device equipped with a linked pocket scrambler. Anyone who intercepts the scrambled message must make a DC 30 Use Computer check to decrypt it.

Vox-Box

A vox-box is a simple audio playback unit with 12 preprogrammed phrases in Basic ("Yes." "No." "Maybe." "Greetings." "Go away." "How much?" "Please take me to someone with authority." "I understand." "I need assistance." "I can help you." "I mean no harm." "I am hungry."), each with its own button. These devices are useful to races that understand Basic but can't speak it (such as Gamorreans and Wookiees). Devices that speak these phrases in other languages also exist.

Altering one or more of a vox-box's preprogrammed phrases requires a DC 10 Use Computer check.

COMPUTERS AND STORAGE DEVICES

A computer includes any electronic device that stores and processes data. Its Intelligence score represents its processing capability and is relevant when making Use Computer checks (see page 75).

- If a computer's attitude toward you is friendly or helpful, it grants an equipment bonus equal to its Intelligence bonus (if any) on any Use Computer check you make using that computer.

- A computer's Will Defense is equal to 15 + its Intelligence modifier. When attempting to improve your access to a computer (see page 76), your Use Computer check result must equal or exceed the computer's Will Defense.

Storage Devices: Some computers are very simple and used only for recording, storing, or viewing data. Some storage devices include a basic operating system and display that allows for the manual viewing, entry, and editing of data, but these are more expensive.

Code Cylinder

A compact encoded security device issued to many military, political, or corporate officials, a code cylinder accesses computer data via a droid's scomp link or provides entry into restricted facilities. Each cylinder features the user's personal security clearance data. High-ranking personnel may carry more than one cylinder, each with different access codes encrypted within them. Republic citizens, Imperial officers, and New Republic personnel use them to facilitate security measures.

Code cylinders are storage devices with Intelligence 10 and Will Defense 15. Improving your access to a code cylinder is difficult because the cylinder has a starting attitude of hostile (see page 75). If your Use Computer check fails by 5 or more, the code cylinder's self-destruct programming activates and ruins the cylinder.

Credit Chip

The credit chip is a small, flat card that features a security codeout and credit algorithm memory stripes. The chip can hold a specified number of credits appropriate to the government that issued it, or it can draw from a specific account held by the user. Credit chips not only allow quick and easy transfers of funds but also protect users from theft.

Credit chips are storage devices with Intelligence 10 and Will Defense 15. Improving your access to a credit chip is very difficult because the chip has a starting attitude of hostile (see page 75). Once it is friendly, you can draw from the account to which it is linked. If you fail by 5 or more on your Use Computer check to improve access, the credit chip's security program detects the intrusion attempt and self-destructs.

Modifying a credit chip so that government and bank computers think that it draws on a different account or that it has a different value stored is almost impossible: The central bank's computers have Will Defense 30 and a starting attitude of hostile (see page 75); even worse, you won't know if your check succeeded until after you attempt to use the modified credit chip. If you fail, the government or bank computer orders the chip's self-destruct programming to activate, ruining the chip. If you fail by 5 or more, the chip's self-destruct programming activates and the government or bank computer has traced your location, dispatching security personnel to apprehend you.

Table 8-8: Equipment

COMMUNICATION DEVICES	COST	WEIGHT
Comlink, short-range	25	0.1 kg
Comlink, long-range	250	1 kg
Pocket scrambler	400	0.5 kg
Vox-box	200	0.1 kg
COMPUTERS AND STORAGE DEVICES	**COST**	**WEIGHT**
Code cylinder	500	0.1 kg
Credit chip	100	0.1 kg
Datacards, blank (10)	10	0.1 kg
Datapad	1,000	0.5 kg
Datapad, basic	100	0.3 kg
Holoprojector, personal	1,000	0.5 kg
Portable computer	5,000	2 kg
DETECTION AND SURVEILLANCE DEVICES	**COST**	**WEIGHT**
Electrobinoculars	1,000	1 kg
Glow rod	10	1 kg
Fusion lantern	25	2 kg
Recording unit		
Audiorecorder	25	0.1 kg
Holorecorder	100	0.1 kg
Videorecorder	50	0.1 kg
Sensor pack	1,500	9 kg
LIFE SUPPORT	**COST**	**WEIGHT**
Aquata breather	350	0.2 kg
Breath mask	200	2 kg
Atmosphere canister/filter	25	1 kg
Flight suit	1,000	3 kg
Space suit	2,000	15 kg
MEDICAL GEAR	**COST**	**WEIGHT**
Bacta tank (empty)	100,000	500 kg
Bacta, 1 liter[1]	100	2 kg
Cybernetic prosthesis	1,500[2]	Varies
Medical kit	600	20 kg
Medpac	100	1 kg
Surgery kit	1,000	10 kg

SURVIVAL GEAR	COST	WEIGHT
All-temperature cloak	100	1.5 kg
Chain (3 meters)	25	2.5 kg
Field kit	1,000	10 kg
Jet pack	300	30 kg
Liquid cable dispenser (15 meters)	10	0.2 kg
Ration pack	5	0.1 kg
Syntherope (45 meters)	20	2.5 kg
TOOLS	**COST**	**WEIGHT**
Binder cuffs	50	0.5 kg
Energy cell	10	—
Fire extinguisher	50	3 kg
Mesh tape	5	0.5 kg
Power generator	750	15 kg
Power pack	25	0.1 kg
Power recharger	100	1 kg
Security kit	750	1 kg
Tool kit	250	1 kg
Utility belt	500	4 kg
WEAPON AND ARMOR ACCESSORIES	**COST**	**WEIGHT**
Bandolier	100	2 kg
Helmet package	4,000	1 kg
Holster		
Concealed	50	0.2 kg
Hip	25	0.5 kg
Targeting scope		
Standard	100	0.2 kg
Enhanced low-light	1,000	1.2 kg

1 It takes 300 liters of bacta to fill a bacta tank.

2 The cost of a cybernetic prosthesis does not include the surgical cost to install it (500 credits).

Data Card
A data card is a simple storage device with Intelligence 2. Intended solely as external storage for a computer, it has no interface for direct display, editing, or entry of data.

Datapad
These handheld personal computers serve as notebooks, day planners, calculators, and sketchpads. In addition to performing basic computer functions, datapads can interface with larger computer networks directly or via comlink.

A datapad is a computer with Intelligence 12. Simpler datapads also exist (Intelligence 10, 100 credits), but they are actually just storage devices with display, input, and editing capability; they have no ability to run programs.

Holoprojector, Personal
A handheld, personal hologram transmitter can be used to view real-time or recorded three-dimensional images or to pass the information through a comlink connection. This storage device has Intelligence 2 and enough memory to store about 1 hour of a holo recording or 1,000 holo images.

Portable Computer
Compact and light enough to be carried in an attaché case or backpack but powerful enough to run fairly complex programs, portable computers are the information technology of choice for anyone who needs access to a lot of data while on the go. As such, they are particularly popular with traveling business executives, military commanders in the field, and slicers.

A portable computer has Intelligence 14.

DETECTION AND SURVEILLANCE DEVICES
Some detection devices augment a character's natural ability to perceive its environment (for example, macrobinoculars), providing a bonus or reducing penalties on Perception checks. Others use sensors to scan their surroundings beyond the normal visual and audible range.

Electrobinoculars
This device magnifies distant objects in most lighting conditions. An internal display provides data on range, relative and true azimuths, and elevation. Viewing options include zoom and wide-vision observation. Electrobinoculars also feature radiation sensors and a nightvision mode that grants darkvision (see Darkvision, page 257) out to the user's normal range of sight.

Electrobinoculars reduce the range penalty on Perception checks to –1 for every 10 squares of distance (instead of –5 for every 10 squares of distance).

Glow Rod
A glow rod is a portable illumination device that projects a beam of light up to 6 squares.

Fusion Lantern
A hand-held light source larger than a glow rod, the fusion lantern produces light and heat. The light spreads out from the lantern, producing illumination in a 6-square radius.

Recording Unit
This storage device is an audio, video, or holo recorder with a playback feature. It has Intelligence 1 and 1 memory unit. You can modify a recording (edit, erase, or rearrange the order of events) with a DC 15 Use Computer check. However, anyone can make an opposed Perception check (if observing the recording) or opposed Use Computer check (if inspecting the data from the recording) to detect any modifications you have made. Editing or modifying a recording without first uploading it to a computer can be difficult: Add the recording unit's Intelligence modifier (–5) to any Use Computer checks you make to change the recording.

Audio Recorder: An audio recorder stores 100 hours of high-quality sound.

Video Recorder: A video recorder stores 10 hours of high-quality video.

Holo Recorder: A holo recorder stores 1 hour of high-quality holos.

Sensor Pack
A portable scanning device, the sensor pack is a bulky rectangle featuring a variety of dials and switches, a readout display, and a scanning dish. It provides general details on comm signals, life forms, and hazards within 1 kilometer. Operating a sensor pack requires a standard action and grants a +5 circumstance bonus on your Perception checks until the end of your next turn.

LIFE SUPPORT
The Star Wars Roleplaying Game includes many hostile environments, ranging from deep oceans to poisonous atmospheres to the vacuum of space. These devices enable creatures to function in such environments.

Aquata Breather
While underwater, an Aquata Breather can provide up to 2 hours of breathable air through its mouthpiece. Qui-Gon Jinn and Obi-Wan Kenobi used Aquata Breathers while swimming to Otoh Gunga in Episode I: The Phantom Menace, and Obi-Wan Kenobi used his again when evading clone troopers on Utapau in Episode III: Revenge of the Sith.

Breath Mask
This personal atmosphere-filtering system consists of a mask that fits over the nose and mouth and a hose connecting the mask to a portable life-

support system. A breath mask provides 1 hour of breathable atmosphere before the filter and atmosphere canister must be replaced. A functional breath mask grants immunity to inhaled poisons, including poisonous atmospheres. A breath mask offers no protection from extreme temperatures or hard vacuum.

A breath mask system can be built into a suit of armor; Darth Vader's armor contains such a system.

Replacing the filter and atmosphere canister requires a DC 10 Mechanics check.

Flight Suit
The flight suit is a one-piece coverall (plus a helmet) that provides life support, protects the wearer from hostile environments, and prevents the wearer from succumbing to the adverse effects of high-velocity flying. A flight suit includes a matching helmet and gloves that seal around the wearer and provide up to 10 hours of life support.

As long as you have life support remaining, you are immune to any hostile atmosphere or inhaled poison hazard. The suit also grants a +1 equipment bonus to your Fortitude Defense.

Space Suit
This bulky coverall contains a sealed life support system that provides everything the wearer needs to survive for 24 hours in the vacuum of space or any other hostile environment.

As long as you have life support remaining, you are immune to any atmosphere or inhaled poison hazard. The suit also grants a +2 equipment bonus to your Fortitude Defense.

MEDICAL GEAR
Medical equipment by itself does not restore lost hit points—it can only help when used with the Treat Injury skill (see page 74). Several common types of medical equipment are described below.

Bacta Tank
This large, specialized tank is filled with the powerful healing agent, bacta, which promotes rapid healing.

A bacta tank can be used in conjunction with surgery (see Treat Injury skill, page 74). If the Treat Injury check is successful, the patient heals a number of hit points equal to its character level in addition to that provided by Surgery.

A bacta tank can also be used when treating disease, poison, or radiation in a creature. In this case, the bacta tank grants a +5 equipment bonus on your Treat Injury check.

A bacta tank and a supply of bacta is expensive, so such medical equipment is usually found only in hospitals, aboard capital ships, and within major military bases. Each hour of treatment consumes one liter of bacta, which costs 100 credits. A typical tank holds up to 300 liters of bacta, and the tank must hold at least 150 liters at all times to provide any benefit. Only one creature can be immersed in the tank at any given time.

Cybernetic Prosthesis
Prosthetic replacements in the *Star Wars* universe frequently take the form of mechanical simulations powered by tiny high-capacity battery packs and motivated by the recipient's bioelectrical impulses. In effect, someone who loses a limb or an extremity can have an electronic replacement that acts (and in some cases looks) just like the original.

Cybernetic prosthetic devices are unusual, but hardly rare. Luke Skywalker gains a cybernetic replacement for his right hand, lost in battle against Darth Vader—who, in turn, had much of his own body replaced with cybernetics years before.

Attaching a cybernetic prosthesis requires the Cybernetic Surgery feat (see page 83). Once attached, the cybernetic replacement performs as well as the original limb or extremity. Common cybernetic prosthetics include arms, hands, legs, feet, and various internal organs. In addition to the cost of the prosthesis, the recipient must also cover the cost of the surgery (see Table 8–9: Services and Expenses, page 144).

Unlike other creatures, a creature with cybernetic prosthetics takes full damage from weapons and attacks that deal ion damage.

Because the Force is present in all living things, but not machines, creatures with cybernetic prosthetics take a –1 penalty on Use the Force checks for each prosthetic replacement (to a maximum penalty of –5).

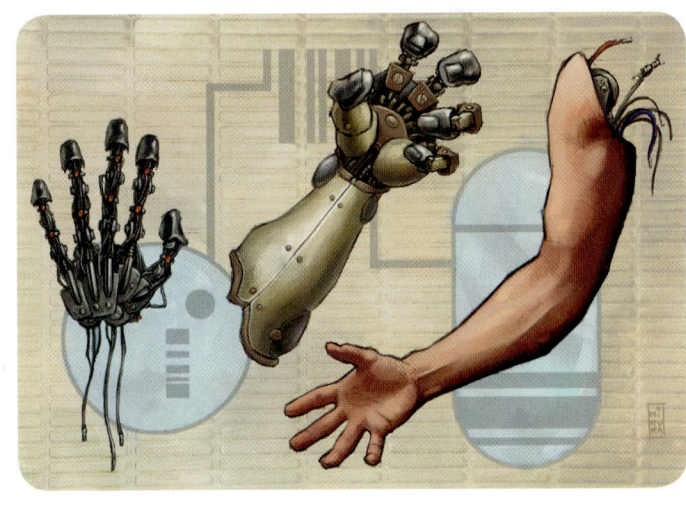

Medical Kit

This backpack-sized medical kit includes almost everything a first responder needs to save a life: diagnostic scanners, anti-venom, medicine to counteract the effects of contaminated water and radiation poisoning, burn treatments, defibrillators, respirator, shock blankets, pressure cuffs, a collapsible repulsorlift stretcher for patient transport (capable of hovering with 160 kg load), and even limited surgical tools. In addition, a medical kit has six external pouches for carrying expendable medical supplies, such as medpacs.

You need a medical kit to revive a dying character, treat disease, treat poison, or treat radiation (see the Treat Injury skill, page 74).

Medpac

Medpacs are compact packages designed to both equip a trained medic for work in the field and to allow untrained individuals to apply first aid in emergencies. A medpac contains bandages, bacta, synthetic flesh, coagulants, stimulants, and other medicines designed to help an injured patient recover quickly.

Once you use a medpac, its contents are expended even if your Treat Injury check is not successful. Any given creature can only benefit from the use of a medpac once in a 24-hour period. (See the Treat Injury skill, page 74, for more information.)

Surgery Kit

This small kit contains the instruments a character needs to perform surgery on a wounded character using the Treat Injury skill (see page 74). You must be trained in the Treat Injury skill to perform surgery using a surgery kit.

Survival Gear

Whether you're exploring the Dune Sea of Tatooine or scaling the volcanic mountains of Mustafar, you need the right equipment to survive. The most important considerations are food, water, shelter, and a way to signal for help. On many worlds, a lack of survival gear leads to a quick death.

All-Temperature Cloak

This wrap-around cloak protects its wearer from the elements, providing a +5 equipment bonus to its wearer's Fortitude Defense against extreme heat or cold (see Extreme Temperatures, page 254).

Chain

This 3-meter (2-square) length of chain has damage reduction 10 and 5 hit points. It has Strength 44 and can safely support over 5 metric tons of weight, and it can be broken with a DC 32 Strength check.

Field Kit

Essentially a backpack full of survival gear, the typical field kit contains two condensing canteens with built-in water purification systems, a sunshield roll, a week's worth of food rations, two glow rods, two breath masks, 24 filters, 12 atmosphere canisters, and an all-temperature cloak.

You need a field kit to make a Survival check to endure extreme temperatures (see the Survival skill, page 73).

Jet Pack

A jet pack is a propulsion system that a character can strap on, allowing flight over short distances. Arm and wrist controls are employed for maneuvering. Activating a jet pack is a swift action, and you gain a fly speed of 6 squares until the end of your turn. A jet pack has 10 charges and can be run continuously; no swift action is required to activate the jet pack on subsequent rounds of use.

Routine maneuvers do not require a Pilot check, but you must make a DC 20 Pilot check if you land after moving more than 12 squares during the same turn; on a failure, you fall prone.

A jet pack can lift up to 180 kg while flying. Replacement fuel cells cost 100 credits.

Liquid Cable Dispenser

Cable dispensers contain a special liquid that instantly solidifies upon contact with either atmosphere or vacuum to form a tough, lightweight, flexible cable. The dispenser contains enough liquid for 15 meters (10 squares) of cable and is refillable at authorized outlets. The cable has Strength 28 and can safely support up to 560 kg, and it can be broken with a DC 24 Strength check.

Ration Pack

Ration packs are compact meals that take up little room (you can fit six in a pouch designed to carry a datapad) but have all the requirements to nourish a person for one day. Each ration pack is geared for a range of species. The food isn't appetizing, and it doesn't include water, but it does prevent malnutrition.

Syntherope

Although not as compact and convenient as a liquid cable dispenser, syntherope is stronger and more durable. A coil contains 45 meters (30 squares) of syntherope, and unlike liquid cable it is meant to be reused. Syntherope has Strength 30 and can safely support up to 720 kg, and it can be broken with a DC 25 Strength check.

Tools

Any object designed to make a task easier—or take care of it entirely—is essentially a tool. Most technical jobs can be performed with a security kit or tool kit, but some devices not included in those packages don't fit under any other category, and are presented here.

Binder Cuffs

Binder cuffs are durasteel restraints designed to lock two limbs of a prisoner together, normally the wrists of ankles, but it is possible to lock one arm to one leg or use the binder cuffs to hook a prisoner to a tree. The cuffs have damage reduction 10, 20 hit points, and Strength 40. Breaking them requires a DC 30 Strength check, and removing them without the seven-digit release code requires a DC 25 Mechanics check. The binder cuffs can be attached to the limbs of any creature of Large, Medium, or Small size.

Energy Cell

This small battery provides power for devices, including certain types of weapons. An energy cell appears as a small, flat disk. An energy cell can be recharged with a power recharger.

Fire Extinguisher

A full-round blast from this tool produces a chemical cloud that provides total concealment (see page 156). Those inside the cloud can't see targets outside the cloud, and those outside the cloud can't see targets inside the cloud. The cloud spreads 1 square in all directions for every round it is activated. It dissipates after 3 rounds (no matter how large the cloud). Each full-round blast depletes one-tenth of the fire extinguisher's chemical supply.

If used for its intended purpose, the extinguisher can put out a fire of up to 10 squares in size at a rate of 1 square per round before it is depleted.

Reloading the fire extinguisher is a full-round action. Replacement chemical cartridges for the extinguisher cost 25 credits each.

Mesh Tape

The usefulness of mesh tape is limited only by a character's imagination. Mesh tape adhesive has Strength 15 and can support up to 90 kg indefinitely (and up to 180 kg for up to 5 rounds). Mesh tape itself has Strength 20 when used to bind another character and requires a DC 20 Strength check to break.

A roll provides 30 meters (20 squares) of tape, 5 centimeters wide.

Power Generator

A power generator is a small fusion reactor that provides continuous power for heavy weapons, vehicles, structures, and machinery. It can power anything up to a Gargantuan vehicle or structure indefinitely, a Colossal vehicle or structure for 1 day, and a vehicle or structure of Colossal (frigate) size for 1 hour. After that, it is disabled and must be repaired.

If a power generator is destroyed while in use, its fusion reactor overloads and explodes, venting plasma into the surrounding area. When a fusion reactor explodes, make an attack roll (1d20+10) against the Reflex Defense of every target within 4 squares. If the attack succeeds, the target takes 8d6 points of energy damage. If the attack misses, the target takes half damage. A target with the Evasion talent (see page 50) takes half damage if the attack succeeds or no damage if the attack misses. This is an area attack

Power Pack

A power pack is a compact rectangular battery that fits into the grip or barrel of an energy weapon, such as a blaster, to provide the power needed to fire it. A power pack can be recharged with a power recharger.

Power Recharger

A power recharger is used to recharge a power pack or energy cell. The recharge process takes 4 hours, and only one power pack or energy cell may be recharged at a time. A power recharger holds enough power to recharge 100 packs or cells, but is normally connected to a ship's or building's power supply, allowing it effectively unlimited recharge capacity.

Security Kit

A security kit is a set of special tools for bypassing electronic and mechanical locks. It usually includes electronic components and dedicated sensor devices. On most worlds, possession of a security kit is illegal for anyone who doesn't have the proper permits, such as members of law enforcement agencies and professional security experts.

A security kit is required to bypass traps or security systems using the Mechanics skill (see page 68). A security kit contains a comlink that monitors frequencies typically used by silent alarms, so the user can know if such an alarm has been triggered at any point during the operation.

Tool Kit

You need a tool kit to reprogram a droid or to repair a damaged droid or vehicle. A tool kit also makes repairing devices much simpler.

The standard tool kit represents a broad collection of tools designed to take apart, analyze, modify, and rebuild almost any technological device. Most technicians personalize their tool kits over the course of years, but almost all contain at least an electroshock probe (for shorting out electronic components or soldering wires), fusion cutter (for cutting apart durasteel and similar materials), hydrospanner (to tighten and loosen all forms of screws and fasteners), laser welder (for connecting things), power calibrator (both for analyzing circuitry and to act as an emergency power cell), power prybar (for forcing things open), probe sensors, sonic welder (for connecting things when you can't afford a fire), various circuits and connector wires, vibrocutters (for things that don't call for a fusion cutter), and welding goggles (so you don't burn out your eyes).

Many of these tools can be used as makeshift weapons. They all qualify as simple weapons, but since they aren't designed for combat, they impose a –5 penalty on attack rolls. (Droids with such tools on tool mounts don't suffer these penalties, since they don't have to deal with an oddly shaped handle.) Different tools deal different damage: electroshock probe, 1d8 ion; fusion cutter, 2d6 energy; laser welder, 1d8 energy; power prybar, 1d8 bludgeoning; sonic welder, 1d8 energy.

Utility Belt
A utility belt has several pouches containing a three-day supply of food capsules, a medpac, a tool kit, a spare power pack, a spare energy cell, a glow rod, a comlink, a liquid cable dispenser with a small grappling hook, and a couple of empty pouches for whatever else the wearer wants to add (up to 0.5 kg per pouch).

WEAPON AND ARMOR ACCESSORIES
A number of off-the-shelf accessories can enhance one's performance on the battlefield.

Bandolier
Since there are so many types of weapons, there are an equally large number of ammunition types. Depending upon the weapons the wearer carries, a bandolier may contain energy cells or power packs (for blasters), clips (for slugthrowers), explosive bolts (for bowcasters), magazines (for missile launchers), grenades, knives, or any number of other forms of ammunition.

A bandolier has 12 slots that can each hold a single Tiny weapon (such as a grenade or a knife) or a single piece of equipment weighing up to 0.5 kg. Any item on the bandolier can be retrieved as a move action.

Helmet Package
When installed in the helmet of a suit of armor, this electronic package allows the armor to grant the wearer a +2 equipment bonus on Perception checks as well as low-light vision. In addition, it includes an integrated hands-free comlink. Stormtrooper armor and its variants include such a system (MFTAS, or Multi-Frequency Target Acquisition System), already included in its statistics. Installing a helmet package takes 1 hour and a DC 20 Mechanics check.

Holster
Holsters are generally available for all Medium or smaller weapons. (Larger weapons are usually carried on shoulder straps, hangers, or baldrics that cost as much as a hip holster.) A holster for a melee weapon is usually called a sheath.

Hip Holster: This holster holds the weapon in an easily accessed—and easily seen—location.

Concealed Holster: A concealed holster is designed to help keep a weapon out of sight (see the Stealth skill, page 72). In most cases, this is a shoulder holster (the weapon fits under the wearer's armpit, presumably beneath a jacket, vest, or cloak). Small or Tiny weapons and single-bladed lightsabers can be carried in concealed waistband holsters (often placed inside the wearer's waistband in the small of the back). Tiny weapons and single-bladed lightsabers can also be carried in ankle, boot, or wrist holsters.

A concealed holster allows you to draw a concealed weapon as a move action instead of a standard action, but you take a –5 penalty on your Stealth check to conceal the weapon.

Targeting Scope
A targeting scope is a sighting device that makes it easier to hit distant targets. However, it affords a very limited field of view, making it difficult to use. Installing a targeting scope on a rifle or pistol requires 10 minutes and a DC 10 Mechanics check.

Standard: A standard targeting scope reduces the range by one category (for example, from medium to short range). However, you must aim at your target to gain this benefit, and you lose the benefit if you change targets or lose line of sight to your target (see Aim, page 154).

Enhanced Low-Light: A low-light targeting scope functions the same as a standard targeting scope in normal light. However, after aiming at a target, it allows the wielder to ignore concealment (but not total concealment) from darkness when attacking that target.

SERVICES AND EXPENSES
A brief listing of common services and expenses is given on Table 8–9: Services and Expenses. The cost figures on the table are guidelines only; the cost of certain services and expenses may be higher in isolated or primitive areas.

ENCUMBRANCE
Encumbrance rules determine how much your equipment slows you down. Encumbrance comes in two parts: encumbrance by armor and encumbrance by total weight.

ENCUMBRANCE BY ARMOR
Your armor defines your maximum Dexterity bonus to Reflex Defense, your armor check penalty, your speed, and how fast you move when you run (see Armor, page 131). Unless your character is weak or carrying a lot of gear, that's all you need to know. The extra gear your character carries, such as weapons and medpacs, won't slow your character down any more than his or her armor already does.

If your character is carrying a really heavy load, however, then you'll need to calculate encumbrance by weight.

ENCUMBRANCE BY WEIGHT
If you want to determine whether your character's gear is heavy enough to slow him or her down (more than any armor already does), add up the weight of all the armor, weapons, and gear the character is carrying. If the total equals or exceeds the square of one-half your character's Strength score,

he or she is carrying a heavy load. For example, a character with Strength 12 is carrying a heavy load if the total weight of his or her armor and gear is 36 kg (0.5 × 12, squared) or more.

When carrying a heavy load, a character takes a −10 penalty on checks made using the following skills: Acrobatics, Climb, Endurance, Initiative, Jump, Stealth, and Swim. A heavy load also reduces the character's speed to three-quarters normal (rounded down). A character can move up to three times his or her speed when running with a heavy load (instead of four times).

Carrying Capacity

The amount of weight that you can lift (in kilograms) is based on your Strength score and determined by the following formula: (Strength score)^2 × 0.5. For example, a character with Strength 15 can lift 112.5 kg (15 × 15 × 0.5).

A character can strain to lift an amount of weight (in kilograms) equal to his Strength score squared, but he or she can only stagger around with it. While overloaded in this way, the character loses any Dexterity bonus to Reflex Defense and can only move 1 square per round (as a full-round action).

A dragged object has less effective weight depending on the resistance of the surface: normal ground, 1/2; smooth surface or wheels, 1/5; completely frictionless (such as pulling an object in zero-g or on a repulsorlift), 1/10. Dragging an object over rough ground is no easier than lifting it.

Bigger and Smaller Creatures: Larger creatures can carry more weight depending on size category: Large (×2), Huge (×5), Gargantuan (×10), and Colossal (×20). Smaller creatures can carry less weight depending on size category: Small (×0.75), Tiny (×0.5), Diminutive (×0.25), Fine (×0.01).

Table 8-9: Services and Expenses

SERVICE	COST
DINING (PER MEAL)	
Luxurious	150
Upscale	50
Average	10
Budget	2
LODGING (PER DAY)	
Luxurious	200
Upscale	100
Average	50
Budget	20
MEDICAL CARE	
Bacta tank treatment (per hour)	300
Long-term care (per day)	300
Medpac treatment	300
Surgery (per hour)	500
Treat disease (per day)	500
Treat poison (per hour)	100
Treat radiation (per day)	1,000

TRANSPORTATION	COST
Taxi, local	10
Passage, steerage (up to 5 days)	500
Passage, average (up to 5 days)	1,000
Passage, upscale (up to 5 days)	2,000
Passage, luxurious (up to 5 days)	5,000
Chartered space transport (up to 5 days)	10,000
UPKEEP (PER MONTH)	
Luxurious	10,000
Wealthy	5,000
Comfortable	2,000
Average	1,000
Struggling	500
Impoverished	200
Self-sufficient	100
VEHICLE RENTAL (PER DAY)	
Speeder bike	20
Landspeeder, average	50
Landspeeder, luxury	100
Airspeeder	500
Shuttle, interplanetary	1,000
Shuttle, interstellar	2,000

The galaxy is a dangerous place, and sometimes you have to fight to survive. Whether the enemy takes the form of battle droids or stormtroopers, a dark Force-user or a rampaging rancor, you need to be able to defend yourself. Using blasters, vibroblades, and lightsabers, heroes regularly get caught up in blazing firefights, wild cantina brawls, and mesmerizing lightsaber duels. You can try to bluff your way out of a tough situation, attempt to sneak away when your opponent is distracted, or even dazzle an enemy with your charming personality. But when all else fails, nothing beats having a good blaster at your side.

This chapter details the combat rules, covering the basics first. The back end of the chapter looks at some of the more unusual strategies that heroes can employ, including using vehicles in combat. Many special abilities and forms of damage that affect combat are covered in Chapter 14: Gamemastering.

Combat Sequence

Combat takes place in a series of rounds, with each character taking one turn each round. Generally, combat runs in the following way:

Step 1. The GM determines which characters are aware of their opponents at the start of the battle. If at least some combatants are unaware of their opponents, a surprise round happens before regular rounds begin. If there is a surprise round, each combatant starts the battle flat-footed. A flat-footed character doesn't add a Dexterity bonus to his Reflex Defense. Once combatants act, they are no longer flat-footed.

Step 2. The combatants who are aware of the opponents can act in the surprise round, so they make an Initiative check. In initiative order (highest to lowest), combatants who started the battle aware of their opponents each take a single action (a standard action, a move action, or a swift action; no full-round actions allowed) during the surprise round. Combatants who were unaware do not get to act in the surprise round.

Step 3. Combatants who have not yet made an Initiative check do so. All combatants are now ready to begin their first regular round. If all combatants were aware of their opponents when the battle began, there is no surprise round and this is the first step in the combat sequence. If there is no surprise round, no one starts flat-footed (everyone was alert enough to be ready for a fight).

Step 4. Combatants act in initiative order.

Step 5. When everyone has had a turn, the combatant with the highest initiative acts again, and steps 4 and 5 repeat until combat ends.

The Combat Round

Each round represents 6 seconds in the game world. In the real world, a round is an opportunity for each character involved in a combat to take one or more actions. Anything a person could reasonably do in 6 seconds, your character can do in 1 round.

Each round begins with the character with the highest Initiative check result and then proceeds, in descending order, from there. Each round uses the same initiative order. When a character's turn comes up in the initiative sequence, that character performs his entire round's worth of actions.

For almost all purposes, there is no relevance to the end of a round or the beginning of a round. The term "round" works like the word "month." A month can mean either a calendar month, or a span of time from a day in one month to the same day the next month. In the same way, a round can be a segment of game time starting with the first character to act and ending with the last, but it usually means a span of time from one round to the same initiative number in the next round. Effects that last a certain number of rounds end just before the same initiative number that they began on.

Actions in Combat

Every round, on your character's turn, you may take a standard action, a move action, and a swift action (in any order). You may take a move action or a swift action in place of a standard action, but not the other way around. You may also take a swift action in place of a move action, but not the other way around. Finally, you may sacrifice all three of these actions to perform a single full-round action on your turn.

STANDARD ACTION
|
MOVE ACTION
|
SWIFT ACTION

Standard Action: A standard action is usually the most important action you'll take in a round, and it often consists of some sort of attack—swinging a lightsaber, firing a blaster, throwing a punch, hurling a grenade, and so on. You can perform one standard action on your turn.

Move Action: A move action represents physical movement. The most common move action is moving your speed. Standing up from a prone position, opening a door, and drawing a weapon are also move actions. You can perform one move action on your turn, or two if you give up your standard action.

Swift Action: Most swift actions enable you to perform your standard action. Examples include switching a weapon's mode and dropping a held item. You can perform one swift action on your turn, or two if you give up either your standard action or your move action, or three if you give up both your standard action and your move action.

Full-Round Action: A full-round action consumes all of your effort during a given round, effectively replacing all other actions on your turn. Some uses of skills require a full-round action to complete. Examples include bypassing a lock (using the Mechanics skill), searching an area for clues (using the Perception skill), and entering a Force trance (using the Use the Force skill). A full-round action can't span multiple rounds; for example, you cannot perform a full-round action that replaces your move action and swift action in the first round and your standard action in the following round.

Free Actions and Reactions

Some actions take such a negligible amount of time that they can be performed in addition to other actions or they can happen out of turn:

Free Action: Free actions consume almost no time or effort, and you may take one or more free actions even when it isn't your turn. Examples include calling out to your friends for help and taunting a foe. The GM puts reasonable limits on what counts as a free action. Reciting the epic history of the Rodian hunter clans takes several minutes (or more) and therefore isn't a free action. You can't take free actions when you're flat-footed.

Reaction: A reaction is an instantaneous response to someone else's action, and you can use a reaction even if it is not your turn. Examples of reactions include making a Perception check to notice a bounty hunter sneaking up behind you and instantly activating a Force power to absorb damage from an incoming blaster bolt.

Combat Statistics

Several fundamental statistics determine how well you do in combat. This section summarizes these statistics.

Attack Roll

Attacking is a standard action. When you make an attack roll, roll 1d20 and add the appropriate modifiers. If your result is equal to or higher than the target's Reflex Defense, you hit and deal damage (see Damage below).

Your attack roll with a melee weapon or unarmed attack is:

1d20 + base attack bonus + Strength modifier

Your attack roll with a ranged weapon is:

1d20 + base attack bonus + Dexterity modifier + range penalty (if any)

Base Attack Bonus: Your class and level determine your base attack bonus.

Strength Modifier: Strength helps you swing a weapon harder and faster, so your Strength modifier applies to melee attack rolls.

Dexterity Modifier: Since Dexterity measures coordination and steadiness, your Dexterity modifier applies to attacks with ranged weapons.

Range Penalty: A ranged weapon can attack a target at point blank, short, medium, or long range. If you make a ranged attack against a target within the weapon's point blank range, you take no penalty on the attack roll; your penalty on attack rolls increases to –2 at short range, –5 at medium range, and –10 at long range (see Table 8–5: Weapon Ranges, page 129).

Critical Hits

When you roll a natural 20 on your attack roll (the d20 comes up "20"), the attack automatically hits, no matter how high the defender's Reflex Defense. In addition, you score a critical hit and deal double damage. All targets are subject to critical hits, even inanimate objects.

Automatic Misses

When you roll a natural 1 on your attack roll (the d20 comes up "1"), the attack automatically misses, no matter how high the bonus on the attack roll is.

DAMAGE

When you hit with an attack, you deal damage that reduces the enemy's hit points (see Hit Points, below).

Damage with a melee weapon or thrown melee weapon is calculated as follows:

Weapon damage + one-half heroic level (rounded down) + Strength modifier

Damage with a ranged weapon is calculated as follows:

Weapon damage + one-half heroic level (rounded down)

Weapon Damage: A hit always deals at least 1 point of damage, even if penalties to damage bring the damage result below 1.

One-Half Heroic Level: Weapons are simply more dangerous in the hands of powerful heroes (and villains).

Strength Modifier: When you hit with a melee weapon or thrown melee weapon, you add your Strength modifier to damage. When you hit with a melee weapon that you are wielding two-handed, you add double your Strength bonus (if any) to the damage. This higher Strength modifier does not apply to two-handed melee attacks with light weapons.

DEFENSES

Your defenses represent your ability to avoid taking damage and overcome attacks against the body and mind. You have three defense scores:

Reflex Defense: 10 + your heroic level or armor bonus + Dexterity modifier + class bonus + natural armor bonus + size modifier

Fortitude Defense: 10 + your heroic level + Constitution modifier + class bonus + equipment bonus

Will Defense: 10 + your heroic level + Wisdom modifier + class bonus

Your species, talents, feats, and actions may grant additional bonuses to one or more of these defenses. For example, Gamorreans gain a +2 species bonus to Fortitude Defense, while a character with the Improved Defenses feat (page 85) gains a +1 bonus to all three defenses.

Reflex Defense

Your Reflex Defense (Ref) represents how hard you are to hit in combat, and most attacks target a creature's Reflex Defense. If an opponent's attack roll equals or exceeds your Reflex Defense, the attack hits.

Heroic Level: Your heroic level is the sum of all levels you have in heroic classes (Jedi, noble, scoundrel, scout, soldier) and prestige classes (see Chapter 12). It does not include levels in the nonheroic class (see page 277) or beast class (see page 273).

Armor Bonus: Your armor bonus is determined by the armor you wear (see Table 8–7: Armor, page 132). If you are wearing armor, add your armor bonus to your Reflex Defense instead of your heroic level. This represents the difference between using your innate skill to avoid injury and counting on your armor to absorb the damage from incoming attacks.

Dexterity Modifier: Nimble targets are more difficult to hit than slow ones. Add your Dexterity modifier to your Reflex Defense. If you are flat-footed or unaware of an attack, you lose your Dexterity bonus (but not a penalty) to your Reflex Defense. If you are helpless (for example, knocked unconscious), calculate your Reflex Defense as if you had a Dexterity score of 0 (–5 modifier).

Size Modifier: Smaller creatures are harder to hit than bigger ones. Apply the appropriate size modifier to your Reflex Defense (and only your Reflex Defense). Size modifiers are as follows: Colossal, –10; Gargantuan, –5; Huge, –2; Large, –1; Medium, +0; Small, +1; Tiny, +2; Diminutive, +5; Fine, +10.

Fortitude Defense

Your Fortitude Defense (Fort) represents your ability to resist the effects of poison, disease, and radiation, as well as your ability to ignore effects that would incapacitate a normal being.

Heroic Level: Your heroic level is the sum of all levels you have in heroic classes (Jedi, noble, scoundrel, scout, soldier) and prestige classes (see Chapter 12). It does not include levels in the nonheroic class (see page 277) or beast class (see page 273).

Constitution Modifier: Tougher, healthier targets are more difficult to hurt than weaker ones, so you add your Constitution modifier to your Fortitude Defense. A nonliving target (that is, any target without a Constitution score, such as a droid) instead adds its Strength modifier to its Fortitude Defense.

Equipment Bonus: Some kinds of armor provide an equipment bonus to your Fortitude Defense (see Table 8-7: Armor, page 132).

Will Defense

Your Will Defense (Will) represents your willpower and your ability to resist certain Force powers and other effects that attack your mind.

Heroic Level: Your heroic level is the sum of all levels you have in heroic classes (Jedi, noble, scoundrel, scout, soldier) and prestige classes (see Chapter 12). It does not include levels in the nonheroic class (see page 277) or beast class (see page 273).

Wisdom Modifier: Strong-willed characters are harder to influence than weak-willed ones. You add your Wisdom modifier to your Will Defense. When you are unconscious, you have an effective Wisdom score of 0 (-5 modifier).

Speed

Your speed tells you how far you can move with a single move action. Your speed depends mostly on your species, although certain kinds of armor can reduce your speed (see Armor, page 131). Some creatures, droids, and vehicles have a natural climb, burrow, fly, and/or swim speed in addition to their normal land speed. Any effect that reduces speed affects all of a creature's movement modes unless noted otherwise.

Speed is measured in squares. Each square represents 1.5 meters (about 5 feet).

Fly: A creature with a fly speed is capable of flight, but not if it is carrying a heavy load (see Encumbrance, page 140).

Hit Points

Hit points (sometimes abbreviated "hp") represent two things in the game world: the ability to take physical punishment and keep going, and the ability to turn a serious blow into a graze or near miss. As you become more experienced, you become more adept at parrying strikes, dodging attacks, and rolling with blows such that you minimize or avoid significant physical trauma, but all this effort slowly wears you down. Rather than trying to keep track of the difference between attacks and how much physical injury you take, hit points are an abstract measure of your total ability to survive damage.

As long as you have at least 1 hit point, you can act normally on your turn.

Second Wind

If you are reduced to one-half your maximum hit points or less, you can catch a second wind as a swift action. This action heals one-quarter of your full hit point total (rounded down) or a number of hit points equal to your Constitution score, whichever is greater. You can catch a second wind only once per day. Certain feats or talents may allow you to catch a second wind more often, but never more than once in a single encounter.

Only heroic characters can catch a second wind; nonheroic characters, creatures, objects, devices, and vehicles cannot. Exception: A nonheroic character that takes the Extra Second Wind feat (page 85) can catch a second wind once per day.

0 Hit Points

A creature reduced to 0 hit points moves -5 steps on the condition track and falls unconscious (see Falling Unconscious, below). However, if the damage that reduced the creature to 0 hit points equals or exceeds its damage threshold, the creature is killed instead (see Damage Threshold, below).

A droid, object, or vehicle reduced to 0 hit points moves -5 steps on the condition track and is disabled (but repairable). However, if the damage that reduced it to 0 hit points equals or exceeds its damage threshold, the droid, object, or vehicle is destroyed instead. A destroyed droid, object, or vehicle cannot be repaired.

Damage Threshold

Attacks that deal massive amounts of damage can impair or incapacitate you regardless of how many hit points you have remaining. Your damage threshold determines how much damage a single attack must deal to reduce your combat effectiveness or, in some cases, kill you. Your damage threshold is calculated as follows:

Damage threshold = Fortitude Defense + size modifier

Size Modifier: Creatures, droids, and vehicles larger than Medium size gain a size bonus to their damage threshold. This size bonus is +5 for Large, +10 for Huge, +20 for Gargantuan, and +50 for Colossal.

When a single attack made against you deals damage that equals or exceeds your damage threshold, but not enough damage to drop you to 0 hit points, you move -1 step along the condition track (see Conditions, page 148). If the damage reduces you to 0 hit points, you are dead.

Droids, Objects, and Vehicles: A droid, object, or vehicle reduced to 0 hit points by an attack that deals damage equal to or greater than its damage threshold is destroyed.

Spending a Force Point: If you are reduced to 0 hit points by an attack that deals damage equal to or greater than your damage threshold, you can avoid death by immediately spending a Force Point, even if you spent a Force Point earlier in the round. A character who spends a Force Point in this fashion remains at 0 hit points, moves −5 steps along the condition track (see Conditions, page 148), and falls unconscious.

If a droid is reduced to 0 hit points by an attack that deals damage equal to or greater than its damage threshold, it may spend a Force Point in this manner to be disabled instead of destroyed.

Improved Damage Threshold: You can increase your damage threshold by taking the Improved Damage Threshold feat (page 86).

Falling Unconscious

A creature pushed to the bottom of the condition track (see Conditions, page 148) or reduced to 0 hit points falls unconscious. When you fall unconscious, you fall prone and are unable to take any actions. After 1 minute (10 rounds), you make a DC 10 Constitution check. On a success, you move +1 step on the condition track, regain consciousness, recover hit points equal to your level, and can act normally on your next turn (although you start prone). If the check fails, you remain unconscious for 1 hour, after which you can attempt another Constitution check. You make a new Constitution check every hour until you regain consciousness. If you fail by 5 or more points, or if you roll a natural 1 on your Constitution check, you are dead. You can't take 10 on the Constitution check.

If you fail a Constitution check to regain consciousness, your condition becomes persistent (see page 149), which means that you can't heal damage

naturally and you can't use the recover action (see page 154) until you've had surgery performed on you or until you get eight consecutive, uninterrupted hours of rest.

An unconscious character or creature subjected to a coup de grace attack (see page 154) or an attack that deals damage equal to or greater than its damage threshold dies immediately.

A character or creature that receives any kind of healing while unconscious immediately revives and can get up to fight again (but starts prone); the healed character or creature has a number of hit points equal to the amount of healing it received, and it moves +1 step on the condition track.

Droids: When a droid is disabled (the equivalent of being unconscious), it moves –5 steps on the condition track, falls prone, and is unable to take any actions. It remains inert and inoperative until repaired (see the Mechanics skill, page 68). A droid that is repaired immediately reactivates and can get up to fight again (but starts prone). The repaired droid gains a number of hit points equal to the amount repaired, and it moves +1 step on the condition track.

Objects, Devices, and Vehicles: When an object, device, or vehicle is disabled, it moves –5 steps on the condition track and no longer functions. It remains inert and inoperative until repaired (see the Mechanics skill, page 68). A repaired object, device, or vehicle gains a number of hit points equal to the amount repaired, and it moves +1 step on the condition track.

Death

A character or creature that dies cannot be brought back to life except under special circumstances (see the revivify ability of the Treat Injury skill, page 74). Similarly, a destroyed droid, object, or vehicle cannot be repaired.

The *Star Wars* galaxy is a vast and perilous wilderness, and heroes who fight against evil and tyranny sometimes make the ultimate sacrifice. When a hero dies, the only thing a player can do is bid her character a fond farewell and roll up a new one.

Natural Healing

A living creature that gets eight consecutive, uninterrupted hours of rest regains hit points equal to its level. A living creature cannot heal naturally if it has any persistent conditions (see next page), and a creature can only benefit from natural healing once in a 24-hour period.

In addition to the hit points gained from natural healing, a creature can regain additional hit points from first aid or long-term care (see Treat Injury skill, page 74).

CONDITIONS

Certain debilitating attacks reduce one's combat effectiveness instead of one's hit points. Examples include a stun grenade blast, a force march, a paralyzing venom, or long-term exposure to extreme temperatures. Multiple conditions have cumulative effects and can quickly drive a creature from its normal state to unconsciousness or disable an otherwise functional droid, device, or vehicle.

Physically debilitating attacks are usually made against the target's Fortitude Defense, while mentally debilitating attacks target one's Will Defense. Either type of attack pushes the target along the same track.

The Condition Track

A creature, droid, object, or vehicle not affected by any debilitating conditions is assumed to be in a "normal state," which represents one end of the condition track. Each debilitating effect to which it succumbs moves it one or more steps along the condition track. A creature pushed to the last step on the condition track falls unconscious (see Falling Unconscious, above). A droid, object, or vehicle pushed to the last step on the condition track is disabled until repaired using the Mechanics skill (see page 68).

When a device is pushed down the condition track, apply the indicated penalty on skill checks to any skill check made using the device.

When a vehicle is pushed down the condition track, all of the vehicle's occupants suffer the same penalties as the vehicle itself until the vehicle is disabled. Penalties imposed by multiple condition tracks are cumulative; in other words, a vehicle's occupants suffer the effects of their own personal condition tracks in addition to the effects of the vehicle's condition track.

Removing Conditions

You can improve your condition by spending three swift actions to use the recover action, moving +1 step along the condition track. You can spend all three swift actions in a single round or spread them out across consecutive rounds. For example, you could spend a swift action at the end of one turn and two swift actions at the start of your next turn to move +1 step along the condition track. Certain situations may prevent you from spending swift actions to move toward a normal state on the condition track (see Persistent Conditions, below).

Resting for eight consecutive, uninterrupted hours usually removes all debilitating conditions afflicting a creature and returns it to its normal state. Some causes of debilitation, such as poison and hunger, may prevent a creature from improving its condition or returning to its normal state until the cause of the debilitation is treated (see Persistent Conditions, below).

Normal state (no penalties)
−1 step ↕ +1 step
−1 penalty to all defenses; −1 penalty on attack rolls, ability checks, and skill checks
−1 step ↕ +1 step
−2 penalty to all defenses; −2 penalty on attack rolls, ability checks, and skill checks
−1 step ↕ +1 step
−5 penalty to all defenses; −5 penalty on attack rolls, ability checks, and skill checks
−1 step ↕ +1 step
Move at half speed; −10 penalty to all defenses; −10 penalty on attack rolls, ability checks, and skill checks
−1 step ↕ +1 step
Helpless (unconscious or disabled)

Persistent Conditions

Some hazards and attacks (such as poison and disease) result in a persistent condition that cannot be removed except in certain circumstances. Any time a condition is persistent, you cannot use the recover action (see page 154) to move steps up the condition track, and you do not regain any hit points from natural healing. However, once a persistent condition is removed by satisfying the requirements stated in its description, you can move up the condition track and heal normally.

Persistent conditions do not prevent you from moving up the condition track by means other than the recover action or resting for 8 hours. For example, an unconscious creature that fails its first Constitution check has a persistent condition from its injuries, but it still moves +1 step on the condition track when it makes a successful Constitution check to regain consciousness.

Multiple Persistent Conditions: Sometimes you are affected by more than one persistent condition. For example, you might be poisoned after already suffering the effects of a disease. In this case, you must satisfy the requirements for removing all of these persistent conditions before you can move up the condition track.

INITIATIVE

In every round during combat, each combatant gets to do something. The combatants' Initiative checks determine the order in which they act, from highest to lowest.

INITIATIVE CHECKS

At the start of a battle, each player makes an Initiative skill check for his character. (A character can make an Initiative check untrained.) The GM rolls Initiative checks for the opponents. All combatants act in order, from the highest Initiative check result to the lowest. A character's initiative count remains the same for all rounds of the combat unless a character takes an action that causes her place in the initiative order to change (see Special Initiative Actions, page 161).

The GM should write the names of the characters on a piece of scrap paper in initiative order. That way, in subsequent rounds the GM can move quickly from one character to the next. If two combatants have the same Initiative check result, the character with the highest Initiative check modifier acts first. If there is still a tie, roll a die.

To save time, the GM can make a single Initiative check for all of the bad guys, rolling 1d20 and adding the lowest Initiative check modifier in the group. That way, each player gets a turn each round and the GM also gets one turn. At the GM's option, however, he can make separate Initiative checks for different groups of opponents or even for individual foes. For instance, the GM may make one Initiative check for an Imperial officer and another check for his squad of stormtroopers.

JOINING A BATTLE

If characters enter a battle after it has begun, they make their Initiative check at that time and act whenever their turn comes up in the existing order.

FLAT-FOOTED

In any battle that begins with a surprise round (see Surprise, below), you start the battle flat-footed. You remain flat-footed until your first regular turn in the initiative order. You can't apply your Dexterity bonus (if any) to your Reflex Defense while flat-footed.

SURPRISE

When combat starts, if you are not aware of your enemies but they are aware of you, you're surprised. If you know about your opponents but they don't know about you, you surprise them.

AWARENESS AND SURPRISE

Sometimes all the combatants on a side are aware of their opponents; sometimes none are; sometimes only some of them are. Sometimes a few combatants on each side are aware and the other combatants on each side are unaware.

Determining Awareness

The GM determines who is aware of whom at the start of a battle. She may call for Perception checks to see how aware the characters are of their opponents. Some example situations:

- The mission team enters a cantina and immediately spots a gang of Rodians. Alert and watchful, the Rodians also notice the heroes. Both sides are aware; neither is surprised. The heroes and the Rodians make Initiative checks, and the battle begins.
- While exploring an abandoned armory, the heroes are being watched by a pack of Jawas. The Jawas lurk in hiding places, waiting for the right time to strike and defend their new lair from the intruders. Sia-Lan spots one of the Jawas as it tries to sneak behind a partially destroyed battle droid. The Jawas shriek and leap from their hiding places, surrounding the heroes. The Jawas and Sia-Lan each get to act during the surprise round. The other heroes, caught unaware, can't act. After the surprise round, the first regular round of combat begins.
- The mission team advances down a dark corridor in the space-station fortress of Grumbog, an alien warlord, using glow rods to light the way. At the end of the corridor, three of Grumbog's soldiers have set up an E-Web repeating blaster. They fire the weapon, sending a powerful blast down the corridor. That's the end of the surprise round. After determining whether any of the heroes were hit and calculating damage, the GM announces that the first regular round of combat begins. The mission team is in a tough spot, since they are facing a powerful weapon and still can't see who is attacking them.

The Surprise Round

If some but not all of the combatants are aware of their opponents, a surprise round happens before regular rounds begin. The combatants who are aware of their opponents can act in the surprise round, so they make Initiative checks. In initiative order (highest to lowest), combatants who started the battle aware of their opponents each take a single action—a standard action, a move action, or a swift action—during the surprise round. If no one is surprised, a surprise round doesn't occur.

Unaware Combatants: Combatants who are unaware at the start of battle do not get to act in the surprise round. Unaware combatants are flat-footed because they have not acted yet, so they do not apply their Dexterity bonus (if any) to their Reflex Defense.

TYPES OF ACTIONS

The fundamental combat actions of moving and attacking cover most of what you want to do in a battle. They're all described here and summarized in Table 9-1: Actions in Combat.

STANDARD ACTIONS

A standard action is usually the most important action you'll take in a round, and it often consists of some sort of attack—swinging a lightsaber, firing a blaster, throwing a punch, hurling a grenade, and so on. You can perform one standard action in a given round of combat.

A standard action could be any one of the following:

Attack with a Melee Weapon

With a melee weapon, you can strike any enemy in a square you can threaten. Small and Medium characters threaten the squares adjacent to them. Bigger creatures may threaten a larger number of squares, as defined by their reach (see Reach, page 161).

Two-Handed Melee Weapons: When you wield a melee weapon two-handed, add double your Strength bonus (if any) to the damage. This higher Strength modifier does not apply to light weapons (weapons smaller than your size).

Improvised Weapons: Sometimes objects not crafted to be weapons get used: chairs, bottles, crates, and so on. Because these objects are not designed for such use, characters who use improvised weapons are treated as not proficient with them and take a –5 penalty on their attack rolls. The GM determines the size and damage dealt by an improvised weapon.

Attack with a Ranged Weapon

With a ranged weapon, you can throw or shoot at any target within your line of sight. A target is in line of sight if there are no obstructions (including other characters) between you and the target. The maximum range of a ranged attack depends on the weapon used (see Table 8-5: Weapon Ranges, page 129).

A ranged weapon can attack a target at point blank, short, medium, or long range. If you make a ranged attack against a target within the weapon's point blank range, you take no penalty on the attack roll; your penalty on attack rolls increases to –2 at short range, –5 at medium range, and –10 at long range.

Improvised Thrown Weapons: Sometimes objects not crafted to be weapons get thrown: small rocks, vases, pitchers, lightsabers, and so forth. Because these objects are not designed for such use, characters who use improvised thrown weapons are treated as not proficient with them and take a –5 penalty on their attack rolls. The GM determines the size and damage dealt by an improvised thrown weapon.

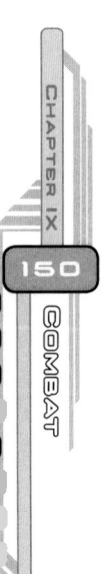

Table 9-1: Statistics for Objects

OBJECT	DR[1]	HIT POINTS	DAMAGE THRESHOLD	STRENGTH (BREAK DC[2])	OBJECT	DR[1]	HIT POINTS	DAMAGE THRESHOLD	STRENGTH (BREAK DC[2])
Manufactured Objects					**Bindings**				
Fine (comlink)	–	1	5	1 (10)	Mesh tape	–	1	15	20 (20)
Diminutive (datapad)	–	1	5	1 (10)	Liquid cable	–	2	19	28 (24)
Tiny (computer)	–	2	5	1 (10)	Syntherope	–	4	20	30 (25)
Small (storage bin)	2	3	6	4 (12)	Chain	10	5	26	32 (26)
Medium (desk)	5	5	10	10 (15)	Binder cuffs	10	20	25	40 (30)
Large (bed)	5	10	20	10 (15)	**Locks**				
Huge (conference table)	10	10	35	20 (20)	Cheap	–	1	5	1 (10)
Gargantuan (small bridge)	10	20	55	40 (30)	Average	2	5	10	10 (15)
Colossal (house)	10	30	85	80 (50)	Good	5	10	15	20 (20)
Tools and Weapons					High security	10	120	30	50 (35)
Computer console	–	5	10	10 (15)	Ultrahigh security	20	150	35	60 (40)
Weapon, Tiny (hold-out blaster)	5	2	10	10 (15)	**Barriers**				
Weapon, Small (blaster pistol)	5	5	12	15 (17)	Metal bars (2 cm thick)	10	30	25	40 (30)
Weapon, Medium (blaster rifle)	5	10	15	20 (20)	Permacrete wall (30 cm thick)	10	150	30	50 (35)
Weapon, Large (heavy blaster rifle)	10	10	17	25 (25)	Metal wall or hull (15 cm thick)	10	150	35	60 (40)
Weapon, Huge (E-Web)	10	20	30	30 (30)	Wooden door (5 cm thick)	5	25	10	10 (15)
					Metal door or airlock (5 cm thick)	10	50	30	50 (35)
					Blast door (50 cm thick)	10	750	40	70 (45)

1 *Lightsabers ignore an object's damage reduction.*
2 *The DC of the Strength check to disable the object.*

Aid Another

As a standard action, you can aid an ally's next skill check or attack roll, or you can interfere with an enemy's attacks.

Aiding a Skill Check or Ability Check: You can help another character achieve success on her skill check or ability check by making the same kind of skill check or ability check in a cooperative effort. If you roll a 10 or higher on your check, the character you are helping gains a +2 bonus on her check. You can't take 10 on a skill check or ability check to aid another.

Aiding an Attack Roll: In combat, you can aid another character's attack by forcing an opponent to avoid your own attacks, making it more difficult for him to avoid your ally. Select an opponent and make an attack against a Reflex Defense of 10. If you succeed, you grant a +2 bonus on a single ally's next attack roll against that opponent.

Suppressing an Enemy: In combat, you can distract or interfere with an opponent, making his attacks more difficult. Select an opponent and make an attack against a Reflex Defense of 10. If you succeed, that opponent takes a –2 penalty on its next attack roll.

Attack an Object

Sometimes you need to attack an object such as a door, a control console, or a held weapon, either to destroy it or to bypass it. An unattended, immobile object has a Reflex Defense of 5 + its size modifier; an unattended, moving object has a Reflex Defense of 10 + its size modifier. If you hit it, you deal damage as normal. However, an object usually has damage reduction (DR), which means that any attack that hits it has its damage reduced by the indicated amount. (Lightsabers ignore an object's damage reduction.) An object reduced to 0 hit points is disabled. If the damage that reduces the object to 0 hit points also equals or exceeds the object's damage threshold, the object is destroyed instead.

Like characters, objects become increasingly debilitated if they take a lot of damage at once. If an object takes damage from a single attack that equals or exceeds its damage threshold, it moves –1 step on the condition track. An object that moves –5 steps on the condition track is disabled.

Held, Carried, or Worn Objects: A held, carried, or worn object is much harder to hit than an unattended object and has a Reflex Defense equal to 10 + the object's size modifier + the Reflex Defense of the holder (not counting armor bonus or natural armor bonus, if any).

Table 9-2: Statistics for Substances

SUBSTANCE	DR	HIT POINTS
Paper (flimsiplast, durasheet)	—	1
Rope (syntherope, liquid cable)	—	1 per cm of thickness
Soft plastic (synthmesh, synthleather)	—	1 per cm of thickness
Glass (duraplex, plastex)	—	1 per cm of thickness
Ice or delicate crystal	—	1 per cm of thickness
Ceramic (ceramisteel)	—	1 per cm of thickness
Hard plastic (duraplast, plasteel)	2	2 per cm of thickness
Wood (synthwood or any natural variety)	5	5 per cm of thickness
Light metal (transparisteel)	5	5 per cm of thickness
Stone (permacrete, ferrocrete)	10	5 per cm of thickness
Metal (durasteel, quadanium steel)	10	10 per cm of thickness
Heavy metal (duranium, lanthanide)	10	15 per cm of thickness
Exotic metal (neutronium, Mandalorian steel)	20	20 per cm of thickness

Multipart Objects: Very large objects can have separate hit point totals for different sections. For example, you can break the window of an airspeeder without destroying the whole speeder.

The Right Weapon for the Job: The GM may determine that certain weapons just can't deal damage effectively to certain objects. For example, you will have a hard time breaking open a blast door with a cesta or cutting a cable with a club. The GM may also rule that certain attacks are especially successful against some objects. For example, it's easy to sheer or ignite a curtain with a lightsaber.

Strength: All objects have a Strength score that represents their innate ability to bear weight (see Encumbrance, page 140). An object supporting weight in excess of its heavy load moves -1 step along the condition track immediately and another -1 step each round on the same initiative count. If an object is supporting weight in excess of twice its heavy load, it is immediately disabled.

Breaking an Object: When you try to break something with sudden force rather than by dealing regular damage, use a Strength check to determine whether you succeed. The DC depends more on the construction of the item than on the material (see Table 9-1: Statistics for Objects), but it is usually equal to 15 + the object's Strength modifier. Attempting to break an object is a standard action. If the object has moved steps down the condition track, apply the condition penalty to the object's break DC.

Object Statistics: Use Table 9-1: Statistics for Objects and Table 9-2: Statistics for Substances to determine or extrapolate the statistics for any given object.

Charge

As a standard action, you can move your speed (minimum 2 squares) in a straight line through unobstructed terrain, and then make a melee attack at the end of your movement. You gain a +2 bonus on your attack roll and take a -2 penalty to your Reflex Defense until the start of your next turn. You cannot charge through low objects, difficult terrain, or squares occupied by enemies, but allies do not hinder your charge.

Disarm

As a standard action, you may attempt to disarm an opponent, forcing him to drop one weapon (or other object) that he is holding.

Making a Disarm Attack: Make a normal melee attack roll against your opponent, who gets a +10 bonus to his Reflex Defense. If your opponent is holding the weapon with more than one hand, you take a -5 penalty on your attack roll to disarm him.

If the attack succeeds, your opponent is disarmed. If you successfully disarm your opponent with an unarmed attack, you can take the disarmed weapon. Otherwise, it's on the ground at your opponent's feet (in his fighting space).

If your disarm attack fails, your opponent can make an immediate free attack against you.

Improved Disarm: If you have the Improved Disarm feat (see page 85), you get a +5 bonus on your melee attack roll to disarm an opponent, and your opponent doesn't get to make an immediate free attack against you if your disarm attack fails.

Ranged Disarm: If you have the Ranged Disarm talent (see page 217), you can attempt to disarm your opponent with a ranged attack. If the attack fails, your opponent doesn't get an immediate free attack against you.

Fight Defensively

As a standard action, you can concentrate more on protecting yourself than hurting your enemies. You can take a -5 penalty on your attack rolls and gain a +2 dodge bonus to your Reflex Defense until the start of your next turn. If you choose to make no attacks until your next turn (not even attacks of opportunity), you gain a +5 dodge bonus to your Reflex Defense until the start of your next turn.

Acrobatics: If you are trained in the Acrobatics skill, you instead get a +5 dodge bonus to your Reflex Defense when you fight defensively, or a +10 dodge bonus if you choose to make no attacks.

Grab

As a standard action, you can make a grab attack. A grab attack is treated as an unarmed attack except that it doesn't deal damage and you take a -5 penalty on the attack roll. You can only grab an opponent up to one size category larger than yourself, and only one opponent at a time.

Until it breaks the grab, a grabbed creature takes a –2 penalty on attack rolls unless it uses a natural weapon or a light weapon. Additionally, it cannot move until it breaks the grab. Breaking the grab is a standard action and automatically clears one grabber per character level. (The grabbed creature chooses which grabbers it clears if there are any left over.)

Grapple

A grapple attack is an improved version of the grab attack (see above). You can only make a grapple attack (a standard action) if you have the Pin feat, the Trip feat, or both. You can only grapple an opponent up to one size category larger than you, and only one opponent at a time.

A grappling attack is treated as an unarmed attack except that it deals no damage. If the grappling attack hits, you and the target immediately make opposed grapple checks. A grapple check is 1d20 + base attack bonus + Strength or Dexterity modifier (whichever is higher) + size modifier (see below). If your check result equals or exceeds the target's check result, the target is grappled.

The effects of a grapple depend on the specific feat or combination of feats you are using (see the feat descriptions in Chapter 5: Feats): Pin, Pin and Crush, Trip, or Trip and Throw.

Alternatively, if you are armed with a light weapon, you may deal damage with that weapon if you win the opposed grapple check; no attack roll is necessary.

Size modifiers for the grapple check are as follows: Fine, –20; Diminutive, –15; Tiny, –10; Small, –5; Medium, +0; Large, +5; Huge, +10; Gargantuan, +15; Colossal, +20.

MOVE ACTIONS

A move action represents physical movement. The most common move action is moving your speed. You can perform one move action on your turn, or two if you give up your standard action. With the exception of specific movement-related skills, most move actions don't require skill checks. In some cases (such as shouldering open a stuck door), ability checks might be required.

Move actions include the following:

Move

You can move up to your speed as a move action. Even moving 1 square is considered a move action.

Nonstandard modes of movement are also covered by this type of action, including climbing and riding an animal.

Draw or Holster a Weapon

Drawing or holstering a weapon is a move action.

Quick Draw: If you have the Quick Draw feat (page 87), you can draw or holster a weapon as a swift action instead of a move action.

Manipulate an Item

Manipulating an item includes drawing or holstering a weapon, picking up an item, loading a weapon, opening a door, or moving a heavy object.

Retrieve a Stored Item: Retrieving an item out of a backpack, carrying case, or other closed container requires two move actions, one to open the container and one to get the item. Holsters, utility belts, and bandoliers are not considered to be closed containers for this purpose.

Stand Up

Standing up from a prone position requires a move action.

Acrobatics: If you are trained in the Acrobatics skill (see page 62), you can stand up from a prone position as a swift action with a successful DC 15 Acrobatics check.

Withdraw

You can withdraw from combat as a move action. To withdraw, the first 1 square of your movement must take you out of your opponent's threatened area by the shortest possible route. If you must move more than 1 square to escape the threatened area, you can't withdraw. You can move normally (take a move action) in order to escape an opponent, but you provoke an attack of opportunity when doing so.

Once you clear the threatened area, you may continue to move, up to a total of half your speed.

You can disengage from more than one opponent in the same action, but only if you can clear all threatened areas in your first 1 square of movement.

Disengaging protects you from attacks of opportunity during your first square of movement, but you may provoke attacks of opportunity later in your turn (for example, you may move through another character's threatened area).

SWIFT ACTIONS

Things that require very little time or effort can be accomplished with a swift action. Some actions, feats, and talents require one or more swift actions to perform. You normally get one swift action per round, but you can take a second swift action instead of a standard action or move action, and you can take three swift actions in a round if you give up both your standard action and move action. Multiple swift actions usually have to occur on the same round or consecutive rounds, and some actions require that the multiple swift actions be consecutive (that is, no other action interrupts them). This is noted in the action's description.

Swift actions include the following:

Activate an Item

A swift action allows you to activate an item. Starting a vehicle, turning on a computer, and lighting a fusion lantern are all examples of activating an item.

Aim
2 Swift Actions

You can take two consecutive swift actions in the same round to more carefully line up a ranged attack. When you do so, you ignore all cover bonuses to your target's Reflex Defense on your next attack. You still must have line of sight to the target, however.

You lose the benefits of aiming if you lose line of sight to your target or if you take any other action before making your attack.

Careful Shot: If you have the Careful Shot feat (page 82), you gain a +1 bonus on your ranged attack roll when you take the time to aim first.

Deadeye: If you have the Deadeye feat (page 84), you deal extra damage when you take the time to aim first.

Catch a Second Wind

As a swift action, you can catch a second wind (see Second Wind, page 146). You can only catch a second wind once per day. Only heroic characters can catch a second wind; nonheroic characters, objects, devices, and vehicles cannot.

Extra Second Wind: This feat (described on page 85) allows a heroic character to catch a second wind one extra time per day (but never more than once in a single encounter). A nonheroic character that takes the Extra Second Wind feat can catch a second wind once per day.

Drop an Item

Dropping an item is a swift action (but picking one up is a move action). You can drop an item so that it falls on the ground in your fighting space or lands in an adjacent square.

Fall Prone

Falling into a prone position requires a swift action.

Acrobatics: If you are trained in the Acrobatics skill (see page 62), you can fall prone as a free action with a successful DC 15 Acrobatics check.

Recover
3 Swift Actions

You can spend three swift actions in the same round or across consecutive rounds to move +1 step on the condition track (see Conditions, page 148). You cannot use the recover action while affected by a persistent condition (see Persistent Conditions, page 149).

Switch Weapon Mode

Some weapons have multiple weapon modes. Examples include blaster pistols, which have both a lethal setting and a stun setting, and blaster carbines, which have both a single-shot mode and an autofire mode. Switching to another weapon mode takes a swift action.

FULL-ROUND ACTIONS

A full-round action consumes all of your effort during a given round, effectively replacing all other actions on your turn. A full-round action can't span multiple rounds; for example, you cannot perform a full-round action that replaces your move action and swift action in the first round and your standard action in the following round.

Full-round actions include the following:

Coup de Grace

As a full-round action, you can use a melee weapon to deliver a coup de grace to a helpless creature or droid. You can also use a ranged weapon, provided you are adjacent to the target. You automatically score a critical hit, dealing double damage. A defender reduced to 0 hit points by the coup de grace dies instantly, or, in the case of a droid, is destroyed. An unconscious or disabled defender hit by a coup de grace also dies or is destroyed instantly.

You can't deliver a coup de grace against a vehicle or object.

Full Attack

As a full-round action, you can make more than one attack. To gain extra attacks, you must be wielding two weapons, wielding a double weapon, or using a special ability that grants extra attacks. When making multiple attacks, you may resolve your attacks in any order desired, declaring the target of each attack immediately before making the attack roll. Extra attacks granted from different sources are cumulative. Any penalties associated with gaining an extra attack apply to all attacks that character makes until the start of his next turn.

Attacking with Two Weapons: As a full-round action, a character armed with two weapons can attack once with each weapon, but the character takes a –10 penalty on all attacks for the round. This penalty assumes that the character is proficient with the weapon in hand; apply an additional –5 penalty on the attack roll if the character is not proficient with the weapon.

A character armed with three or more weapons still only gains one extra attack, but that character may choose which weapon it wishes to use for this extra attack each round.

Attacking with a Double Weapon: As a full-round action, a character armed with a double weapon (such as a double-bladed lightsaber) can attack once with each end of the weapon, but the character takes a –10 penalty on all attacks for the round. This penalty assumes that the character is proficient with the weapon; apply an additional –5 penalty on the attack roll if the character is not proficient with the weapon. (A character who chooses to attack with only one end of a double weapon can do so as a standard action.)

Dual Weapon Mastery: The Dual Weapon Mastery feats (see page 84) reduce the –10 penalty on attack rolls when fighting with two weapons or both ends of a double weapon. A character with all three Dual Weapon Mastery feats negates the –10 penalty entirely.

Double Attack and Triple Attack: The Double Attack feat (see page 84) allows a character to make one extra attack during a full attack, but the character takes a –5 penalty on all attacks until the start of his next turn. The Triple Attack feat (see page 89) allows a character to make one extra attack in addition to that granted by Double Attack, giving the character an additional –5 penalty (total –10 penalty) on all attacks until the start of his next turn. If the character is armed with more than one weapon, he may choose which weapon (or weapons) he will use to make each extra attack.

Run
You can run as a full-round action, moving up to four times your speed in a straight line (or three times your speed in a straight line if wearing heavy armor or carrying a heavy load). See the Endurance skill (page 66) for running rules.

Special Combat Rules
This section describes various special rules that arise during combat. The rules are presented alphabetically by topic.

Area Attacks
Certain weapons and effects, such as grenades, autofire weapons, or the *Force slam* power, target all creatures in a given area instead of a single target.

When you make an area attack, you make a single attack roll and compare the result to the Reflex Defense of every target in the area. Creatures you hit take full damage, and creatures you miss take half damage.

Autofire Weapons: A weapon set on autofire targets a 2-square-by-2-square area (see Autofire, below, for more information).

Burst Radius: Grenades and explosives usually have a burst radius. When you make an area attack with such a weapon, you must decide where to center the burst before you make the attack roll. The center of a burst is always on the corner of a square (at the "crosshairs").

Splash Weapons: Some weapons have a splash radius. When you make an attack against a target, that target takes full damage if your attack roll equals or exceeds the its Reflex Defense, and half damage if the attack misses. Also compare your attack roll against the Reflex Defense of every target adjacent to the primary target; these adjacent targets take half damage if the attack hits or no damage if the attack misses.

Evasion: A character with the Evasion talent (see page 50) takes half damage from a successful area attack and no damage from an area effect that misses his Reflex Defense.

Attacks of Opportunity
If an enemy moves out of a square adjacent to you or performs an action that forces him to let down his guard, you can make a single, immediate attack against that enemy (even if you've already acted during the round). This is called an attack of opportunity.

You can only make attacks of opportunity with melee weapons, natural weapons, pistols, carbines, and any weapon with a folded stock. You may also make attacks of opportunity while unarmed if you have the Martial Arts I feat.

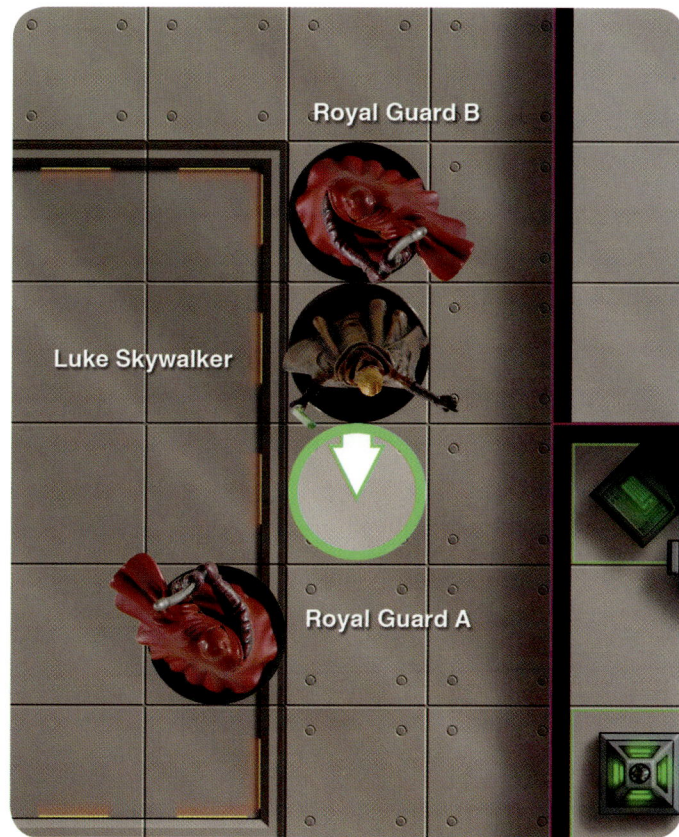

Diagram 9-1: Attack of Opportunity I
Luke Skywalker moves 1 square and attacks Royal Guard A. He provokes an attack of opportunity from Royal Guard B.

Provoking an Attack of Opportunity

Two actions can provoke attacks of opportunity:

- Moving out of a threatened square.
- Performing an action that distracts you from defending yourself and lets your guard down while within a threatened square.

Most characters threaten the squares adjacent to them; larger characters threaten all squares within their reach (see Reach, page 161). A creature only threatens an area if it is armed with a natural weapon, a melee weapon, a pistol, a carbine, or any weapon with a folded stock.

Moving Out of a Threatened Square: When you move out of a threatened square, you generally provoke an attack of opportunity. You do not provoke an attack of opportunity if you use the withdraw action (see page 153) or if you successfully tumble (see Acrobatics skill, page 62).

Performing an Action that Distracts You: Some actions, when performed in a threatened area, provoke attacks of opportunity because they make you divert your attention from the fight at hand. The following actions provoke attacks of opportunity:

- Making an unarmed attack without the Martial Arts I feat
- Aiming
- Loading a weapon
- Picking up an item
- Retrieving a stored item
- Moving into an enemy's square
- Using any skill that distracts you or forces you to drop your guard (GM's determination)

Making an Attack of Opportunity

An attack of opportunity is a single free attack, and you can only make one attack of opportunity per round. You don't have to make an attack of opportunity if you don't want to. An attack of opportunity is always made at your full attack bonus, minus any situational penalties you suffer.

You can't make an attack of opportunity if you're flat-footed.

Combat Reflexes: If you have the Combat Reflexes feat (page 83), you can make more than one attack of opportunity during a round, and you may make an attack of opportunity while flat-footed. However, you may only make one attack of opportunity per provoking action. (Moving any number of squares is treated as a single provoking action.)

AUTOFIRE

Any ranged weapon that has an autofire setting can be set on autofire as a swift action. Table 8-4: Ranged Weapons (page 126) indicates whether or not a specific weapon has an autofire setting. Some weapons, such as E-Web repeating blasters, operate only in autofire mode.

Autofire is treated as an area attack (see Area Attack, page 155). You target a 2-square-by-2-square area, make a single attack roll at a –5 penalty, and compare the result to the Reflex Defense of every creature in the area. Creatures you hit take full damage, and creatures you miss take half damage. Autofire consumes ten shots or slugs, and it can only be used if the weapon has ten shots or slugs in it.

Autofire-Only Weapons: If you are using an autofire-only weapon, you may brace your weapon by taking two swift actions in the same round immediately before making your attack. When you brace an autofire-only weapon, you take only a –2 penalty on your attack roll when making an autofire attack or using the Burst Fire feat (see below).

Only heavy weapons, rifles, and pistols with an extended stock (see page 125) can be braced.

Burst Fire: The Burst Fire feat (see page 82) allows you to use a weapon set on autofire against a specific creature instead of an area. You take a –5 penalty on your attack roll but deal +2 dice of damage. Using burst fire expends half as many shots or slugs (five instead of ten). This is not considered an area attack, so the damage cannot be reduced using the Evasion talent (see below).

Evasion: A character with the Evasion talent (see page 50) takes half damage from a successful autofire attack and no damage from an autofire attack that misses his Reflex Defense (also see Burst Fire, above).

CONCEALMENT

Concealment encompasses all circumstances where nothing physically blocks a blow or shot but where something interferes with an attacker's accuracy. An attack that would normally hit might actually miss because the target has concealment. A target might gain concealment from fog, smoke, poor lighting, tall grass, foliage, or other effects that make it difficult to pinpoint the target's location.

To determine whether your target has concealment from your ranged attack, choose a corner of your square. If any line from this corner to any corner of the target's square passes through a square or border that provides concealment, the target has concealment. When making a melee attack against an adjacent target, your target has concealment if his space is entirely within an effect that grants concealment (such as a cloud of smoke).

If you attack a target with concealment, you take a –2 penalty on your attack roll. Multiple sources of concealment (such as a defender in a fog at night, with no illumination) do not apply additional penalties.

If you attempt to notice a target with concealment, you take a –5 penalty on your Perception check.

Ignoring Concealment: Concealment isn't always effective. For instance, a character with low-light vision ignores concealment from darkness (but not total concealment; see below). Likewise, a character with darkvision ignores all concealment from darkness (even total concealment).

Fog, smoke, foliage, and other visual obstructions work normally against characters with darkvision or low-light vision.

Total Concealment

If you have line of effect to a target but not line of sight (for instance, if he is in total darkness or if you're blinded), he is considered to have total concealment from you. You can't attack an opponent that has total concealment, though you can attack into a square that you think he occupies. If you attack a target with total concealment, you take a –5 penalty on your attack roll. You can't make an attack of opportunity against an opponent with total concealment, even if you know what square or squares the opponent occupies.

If you attempt to notice a target with total concealment, you take a –10 penalty on your Perception check.

Cover

Creatures and terrain features can provide cover against attacks. A creature with cover gains a +5 cover bonus to its Reflex Defense, no matter how many creatures and terrain features are between it and the attacker. Terrain features that provide cover include trees, walls, vehicles, and cargo crates.

To determine whether an enemy has cover, choose a corner of the attacker's square. If any line from this corner to any corner of the target's square passes through a barrier or any square occupied by a creature, the target has cover. The target does not have cover if the line runs along or touches the edge of a wall or other square that would otherwise provide cover.

An adjacent enemy never has cover.

Big Creatures and Cover: Any creature with a fighting space larger than 1 square determines cover against melee attacks slightly differently than smaller creatures. Such a creature can choose any square that it occupies to determine whether an opponent has cover against its melee attacks. Similarly,

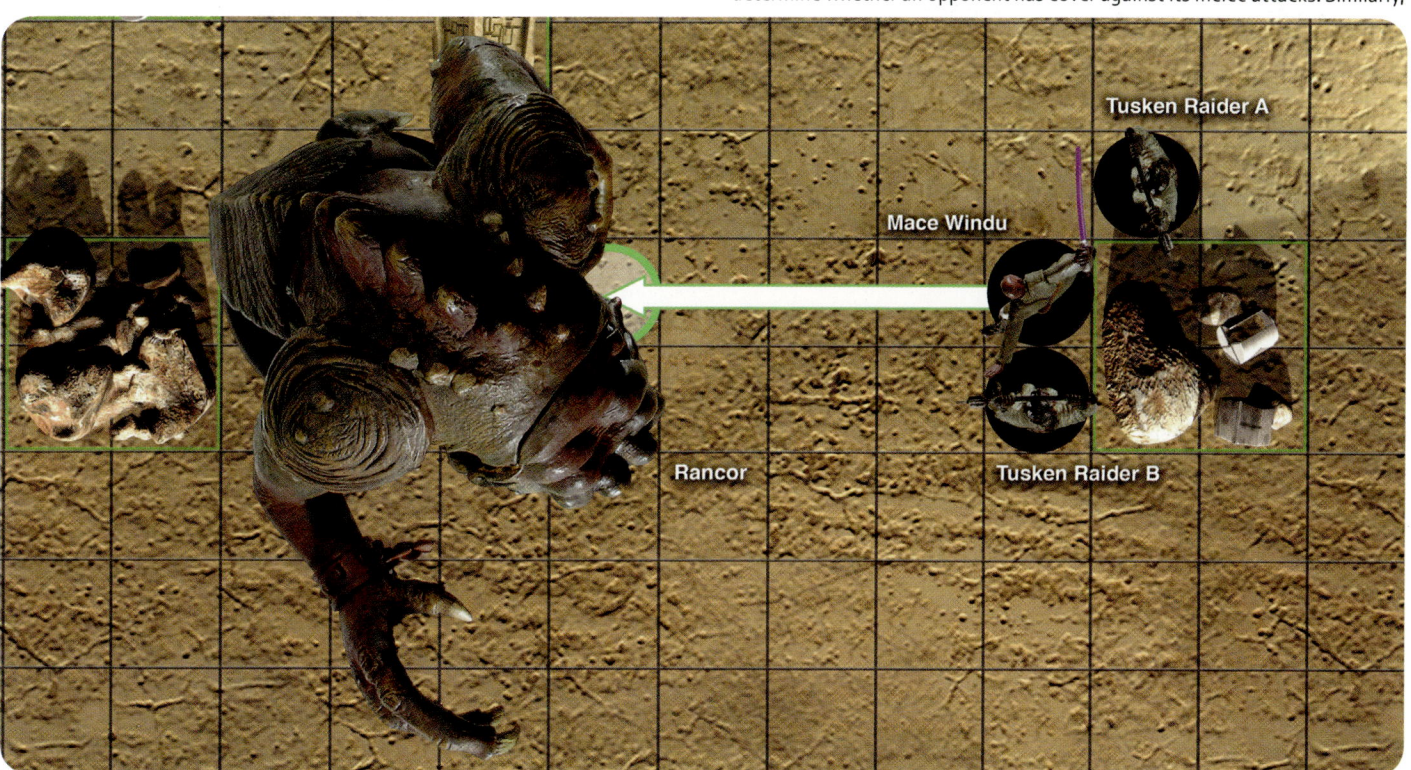

Diagram 9-2: Attack of Opportunity II
Mace Windu moves more than 1 square and attacks the Rancor with his lightsaber. Mace provokes attacks of opportunity from both Tusken Raiders (who are armed with gaffi sticks) as he moves out of their threatened squares. He also provokes an attack of opportunity from the Rancor as he moves through its threatened area (the Rancor has reach).

when making a melee attack against such a creature, you can pick any of the squares it occupies to determine whether it has cover against you.

Cover and Attacks of Opportunity: You can't make an attack of opportunity against an opponent with cover relative to you.

Cover and Stealth Checks: You can use cover to make a Stealth check. Without cover, you usually need concealment (see above) to make a Stealth check.

Low Objects and Cover: Low objects provide cover to creatures in those squares. However, the attacker ignores low objects in its own fighting space and adjacent squares. Low objects in the attacker's space and in adjacent squares don't provide cover to enemies; essentially, the attacker shoots over them.

Improved Cover
In some cases, cover may provide a greater bonus to Reflex Defense. For instance, a character peering around a corner or through a narrow aperture has even better cover than a character standing behind a low wall or a landspeeder. In such situations, double the normal cover bonus to Reflex Defense (+10 instead of +5). A creature with improved cover takes no damage from area attacks that fail to hit its Reflex Defense. Furthermore, improved cover provides a +5 bonus on Stealth checks.

The GM may impose other penalties or restrictions to attacks depending on the details of the cover. For example, to strike effectively through a gun port, you need to use a long thrusting weapon, such as a lightsaber. A vibro-ax just isn't going to get through a narrow slit.

Total Cover
If you don't have line of effect to your target (for instance, if he is completely behind a high wall), he is considered to have total cover from you. You can't make an attack against a target that has total cover.

Damage Reduction (DR)
A creature or object with damage reduction (DR) ignores a certain amount of damage from every attack. The amount of damage it ignores is always indicated; for example, an object with DR 10 ignores the first 10 points of damage from each attack.

Damage reduction is sometimes bypassed by one or more specific damage types (noted after the DR value). For example, a creature with DR 5/energy ignores 5 points of damage from any source except one that deals energy damage (such as from a blaster). Similarly, a creature with DR 10/piercing or slashing ignores 10 points of damage from any source except one that deals piercing or slashing damage.

Certain talents grant damage reduction. When a character with multiple types of damage reduction takes damage, use whichever damage reduction value most benefits the character, based on the type of damage. For example, if a character with DR 1 and DR 10/energy is struck by a blaster, it's better for the character to apply his DR 1 against the attack (since DR 10/energy is bypassed by blaster).

Lightsabers: Lightsaber ignore damage reduction unless specifically noted otherwise.

Diagonal Movement
Moving diagonally costs double. When moving or counting along a diagonal path, each diagonal counts as 2 squares, as shown in Diagram 9–3. If a character moves diagonally through low objects or difficult terrain, the cost of movement doubles twice (that is, each square counts as 4 squares).

A character can't move diagonally past the corner or end of a wall that extends to a grid corner.

Difficult Terrain

Broken ground, buckled deck plating, and similar obstacles are collectively referred to as difficult terrain. It costs twice as much to move into a square containing difficult terrain. Creatures of Large size and bigger must pay the extra cost for moving across difficult terrain if any part of their fighting space moves into such a square.

Difficult terrain does not block line of sight or provide cover.

Encumbrance and Speed

Wearing medium or heavy armor or carrying a heavy load reduces your character's speed to three-quarters normal (4 squares if your base speed is 6 squares, or 3 squares if your base speed is 4 squares). While wearing heavy armor or carrying a heavy load, you can run at triple your speed.

A character with a fly speed cannot fly while carrying a heavy load.

Fighting Space

The squares that a creature occupies on the battle map are collectively referred to as its fighting space. Small and Medium creatures (including most characters) have a fighting space of 1 square. Large creatures have a fighting space of 4 squares (2 squares on a side). Huge creatures have a fighting space of 9 squares (3 squares on a side). Gargantuan and Colossal creatures have much larger fighting spaces.

Flanking

If you are making a melee attack against an opponent and you have an ally on the other side of the opponent so that the opponent is directly between the two of you, you are flanking that opponent. You gain a +2 flanking bonus on your melee attack roll. See Diagrams 9-4 and 9-5 for examples of flanking.

You don't gain a flanking bonus when making a ranged attack.

Helpless Opponents

A helpless opponent—one who is bound, sleeping, unconscious, or otherwise at your mercy—is an easy target. You can sometimes approach a target that is unaware of your presence, get adjacent to it, and treat it as helpless. If the target is in combat or some other tense situation, and therefore in a state of acute awareness and readiness, or if the target can use its Dexterity bonus to improve its Reflex Defense, then that target can't be considered unaware. Further, any reasonable precautions taken by a target—including stationing bodyguards, placing its back to a wall, or being able to make Perception checks—also precludes catching that target unaware and helpless.

Attacking a Helpless Opponent: A melee attack against a helpless opponent gains a +5 bonus on the attack roll (equivalent to attacking a prone target). A ranged attack gets no special bonus. In addition, a helpless opponent can't add its Dexterity bonus (if any) to its Reflex Defense. In fact, its Dexterity score is treated as if it were 0, so its Dexterity modifier to Reflex Defense is –5.

Ion Damage

Ion pistols and ion rifles emit powerful bursts of electrostatic energy that can disable droids, vehicles, and electrical devices in much the same way that stun weapons can incapacitate living creatures.

When you make a successful attack with a weapon that deals ion damage, first subtract half of the ion damage from the target's hit points. Creatures that do not have cybernetic prosthetics are singed by the ion energy but suffer no other ill effects. Droids, vehicles, electronic devices,

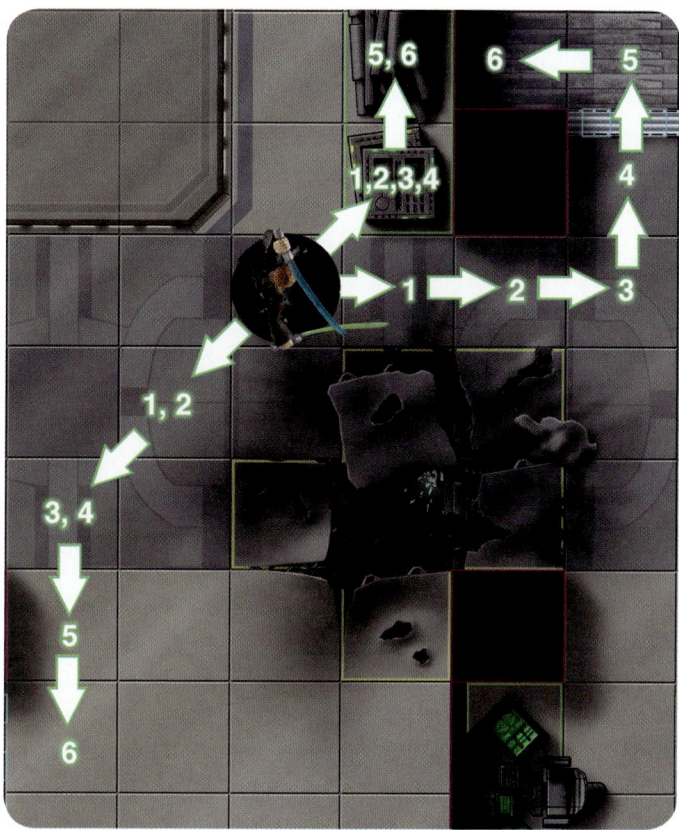

Diagram 9-3: Movement
Moving diagonally costs double. A character can't move diagonally past a corner or end of a wall. Moving through low objects also cost double. If a character moves diagonally through low objects, the cost of movement doubles twice.

and cybernetically enhanced creatures may suffer additional effects, as noted below:

- If the ion damage reduces the target's current hit points to 0, the target moves –5 steps on the condition track and is either knocked unconscious or disabled (see Falling Unconscious, page 147).
- If the ion damage (before being halved) equals or exceeds the target's damage threshold, the target moves –2 steps on the condition track.

LINE OF SIGHT

A character can target an enemy that he can see, which is to say, any enemy within his line of sight. Draw an imaginary line from any point in the attacker's fighting space to any point in the target's fighting space. If the player who controls the attacking character can draw that line without touching a square that provides total cover (a wall, closed door, or similar barrier) or total concealment (thick smoke, total darkness, or anything else that prevents visibility), that character has line of sight to the target.

A line that nicks a corner or runs along a wall does not provide line of sight. Other characters and creatures, low objects, difficult terrain, and pits do not block line of sight.

Line of Effect: Line of effect works just like line of sight, but it ignores squares that provide total concealment. For example, a character who is blind or in total darkness doesn't have line of sight to any target, but that character has line of effect to any target that doesn't have total cover.

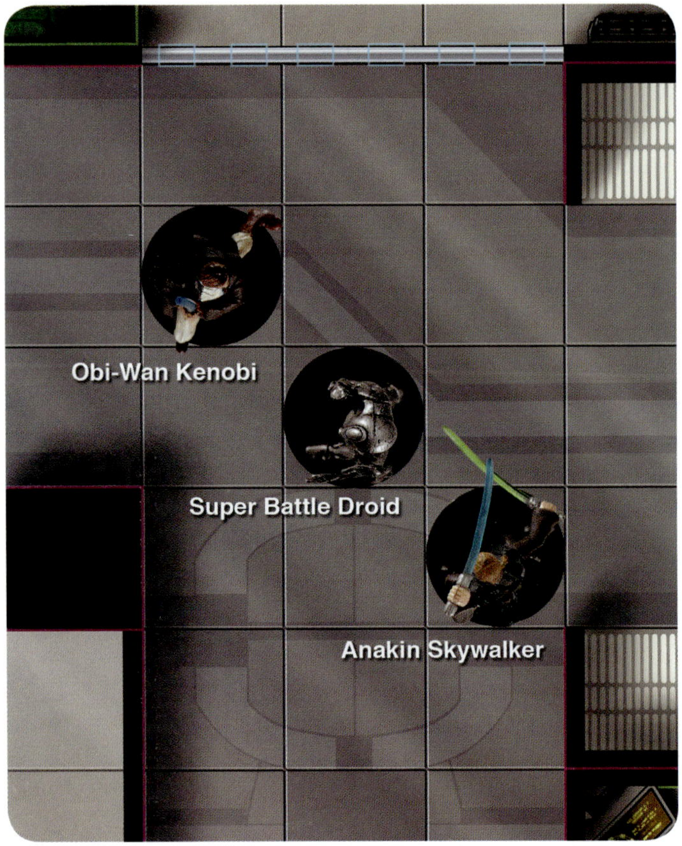

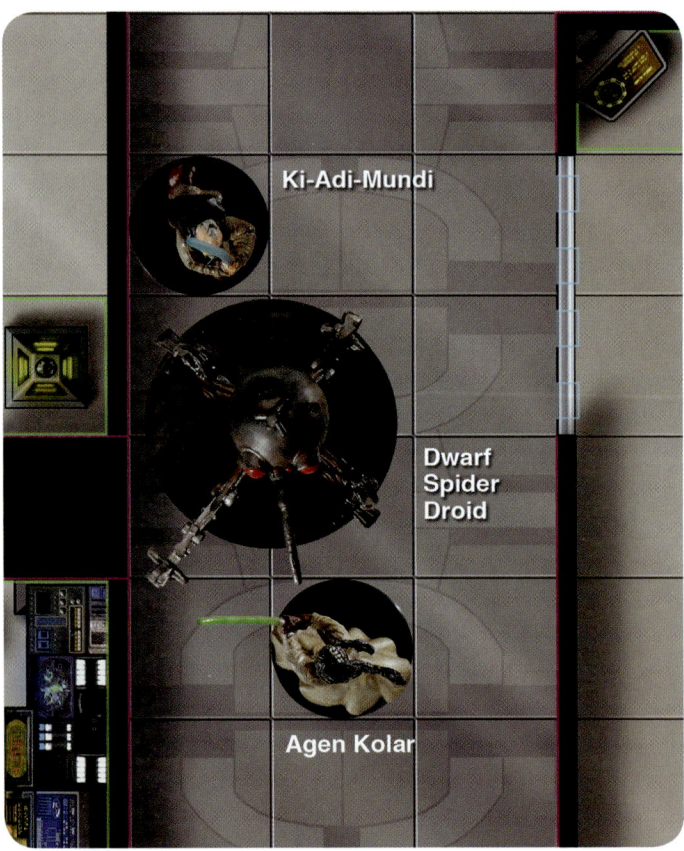

DIAGRAM 9-4: FLANKING I
ANAKIN SKYWALKER AND OBI-WAN KENOBI ARE FLANKING THE SUPER BATTLE DROID. THEY EACH GAIN A +2 FLANKING BONUS ON MELEE ATTACKS AGAINST THE DROID.

DIAGRAM 9-5: FLANKING II
KI-ADI-MUNDI AND AGEN KOLAR ARE FLANKING THE DWARF SPIDER DROID. THEY EACH GAIN A +2 FLANKING BONUS ON MELEE ATTACKS AGAINST THE DROID.

Moving Through Occupied Squares

Sometimes you can pass through an occupied square.

Ally: You can move through a square occupied by any character, creature, or droid that doesn't consider you an enemy.

Dead or Unconscious Enemy: You can move through a square occupied by an enemy that doesn't present an obstacle, such as one who is dead, unconscious, or disabled.

Much Larger or Smaller Enemy: Any character can move through a space occupied by an enemy three or more size categories larger or smaller than the moving character.

Tumbling: A character trained in Acrobatics can attempt to tumble through an enemy's fighting space (see the Acrobatics skill, page 62).

Prone Targets

Various attacks, talents, feats, and Force powers can knock a character prone. A prone character takes a –5 penalty on melee attack rolls. Melee attacks made against a prone character gain a +5 bonus, while ranged attacks made against a prone character take a –5 penalty. Being prone may also give a character total cover instead of normal cover (for example, being prone behind a low wall), subject to the GM's discretion.

Reach

A creature's reach determines the distance it can reach when making a melee attack. A creature threatens all squares within its reach. Small and Medium characters have a reach of 1 square, which means they can make melee attacks only against targets in adjacent squares. Larger creatures tend to have a greater reach and, consequently, a bigger threatened area.

Bigger Creatures: A creature with greater-than-normal reach (more than 1 square) can still attack opponents directly next to it. A creature with greater than normal reach usually gets an attack of opportunity against an opponent when the opponent approaches it, because the opponent must enter and move within its threatened area before making a melee attack.

Smaller Creatures: A Fine, Diminutive, or Tiny creature must be in your space to attack you; moving into your square provokes an attack of opportunity. You can attack into your own space if you need to with a melee attack (but not a ranged attack), so you can attack very small opponents normally.

Shield Rating (SR)

Some droids, devices, and vehicles have a shield rating (SR). Whenever a target with SR takes damage from an attack, reduce the damage by the shield rating. The remaining damage (if any) is dealt to the target's hit points, subtracting damage reduction normally.

Shield Damage: If the damage dealt by an attack exceeds the target's SR, reduce the shield rating by 5. This reduction is cumulative, so a target's shield rating can eventually be reduced to zero. A character may recharge the shields of a device or vehicle by spending three swift actions on the same or consecutive rounds to make a DC 20 Mechanics check; if the check succeeds, the target's SR improves by 5 points (up to its normal maximum). A droid may recharge its own shields by spending three swift actions on the same or consecutive rounds to make a DC 20 Endurance check; if the check succeeds, its current shield rating improves by 5 points (up to its normal maximum).

Shooting or Throwing into a Melee

If you shoot a ranged weapon or throw a weapon at an opponent that is adjacent to one or more of your allies, you take a –5 penalty on your attack roll. This penalty accounts for the fact that you're trying not to hit your allies.

Precise Shot: If you have the Precise Shot feat (page 87), you don't take this penalty.

Special Initiative Actions

Usually you act as soon as you can in combat, but sometimes you want to act later, at a better time, or in response to the actions of someone else.

Delay

By choosing to delay, you take no action when your turn in the initiative order arrives. Instead, you act normally at whatever later initiative point you decide to act. When you delay, you voluntarily reduce your own initiative count for the rest of the encounter. When your new, lower initiative count comes up later in the same round, you can act normally. You can specify this new initiative result or just wait until some time later in the round and act at that time, thus fixing your new initiative result at that point.

Delaying is useful if you need to see what your friends or enemies are going to do before deciding what to do yourself. The price you pay is lost initiative. You never get back the time you spend waiting to see what's going to happen.

Example: Deel and Vor'en approach a locked hatch, behind which they expect to encounter a crime boss and his thugs. Vor'en's initiative count is 22, but he delays. He wants to open fire on the crime boss with his heavy blaster rifle, so he delays. On initiative count 14, Deel uses his Mechanics skill to unlock and open the door. Now Vor'en can move through the doorway and fire a shot at the crime boss, but his initiative is reduced to 13 (just after Deel's initiative of 14). For the rest of the battle, Vor'en acts on initiative count 13.

Multiple Characters Delaying: If multiple characters delay their actions, the one with the highest Initiative check modifier has the advantage. If two or more delaying characters both want to act on the same initiative count, the one with the highest Initiative check modifier gets to go first.

Ready

Readying lets you prepare to take an action later, after your turn is over but before your next turn has begun. You can ready a single standard action or move action. To do so, specify the standard action or move you will take and the circumstances under which you will take it. Then, any time before your next turn, you may take the readied action in response to those circumstances (assuming they occur).

Initiative Consequences of Readying: The count on which you took your readied action becomes your new initiative result. If you come to your next action and have not yet performed your readied action, you don't get to take the readied action (though you can ready the same action again). If you take your readied action in the next round, before your regular action, your initiative rises to that new point in the order of battle, and you do not get your regular action in that round.

Example: Kelko and his friend Sia-Lan have just encountered a trio of Tusken Raiders in the wilds of Tatooine. On initiative count 14, Kelko specifies that he is going to fire his blaster at the first Raider that tries making an attack. On count 10, Sia-Lan moves next to Kelko and readies an attack with her lightsaber so that she can strike any foe that comes within 1 square of her position. On count 7, the Tusken Raiders charge, brandishing their gaffi sticks. As soon as the lead Raider raises his weapon, Kelko fires his blaster, but misses. Next, Sia-Lan swings at the first Raider to reach her and drops him. Other Raiders, however, reach Sia-Lan and attack her. From this point on, both Kelko and Sia-Lan act on initiative count 7 (and before the Raiders).

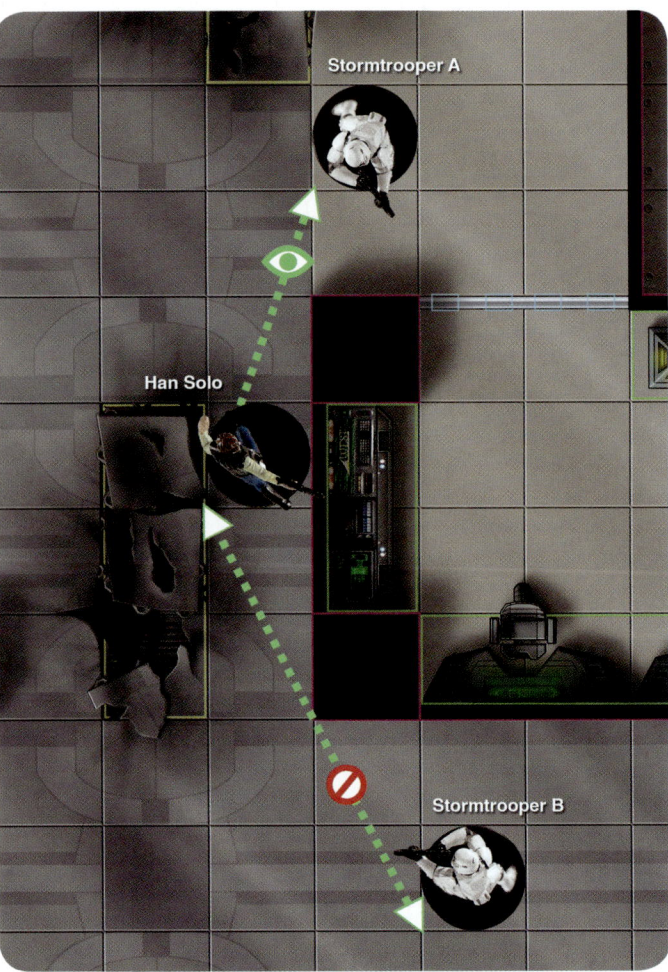

DIAGRAM 9-6: LINE OF SIGHT
TWO CHARACTERS HAVE LINE OF SIGHT TO EACH OTHER IF THERE'S AT LEAST ONE CLEAR LINE BETWEEN THEIR SPACES. A LINE THAT NICKS A CORNER OR RUNS ALONG A WALL DOES NOT PROVIDE LINE OF SIGHT. A CHARACTER NEEDS LINE OF SIGHT TO AN ENEMY TO ATTACK THAT ENEMY. HAN SOLO HAS LINE OF SIGHT TO STORMTROOPER A, BUT NOT TO STORMTROOPER B.

SQUEEZING

Creatures of Large size and bigger can squeeze through small openings and down narrow hallways that are at least half as wide as their fighting space, provided they end their movement in an area that they can normally occupy. Big droids and vehicles can't squeeze at all, unless they can compress their frames to accommodate the tighter space.

Creatures of Large size or bigger cannot squeeze past enemies.

STUNNING

Sometimes you'd rather knock an enemy unconscious than kill him. That's why many weapons have stun settings and why stun batons and stun grenades are popular with law enforcement agencies throughout the galaxy.

Various melee weapons and blasters have a stun setting, and switching a weapon to its stun setting (or resetting it to normal damage) is a swift action. Some stun weapons, such as stun grenades, only have a stun setting. Unless otherwise noted, the stun setting on a blaster weapon has a maximum range of 6 squares (no range penalties).

Only creatures can be stunned. Droids, vehicles, and objects are immune to stunning effects.

When you make a successful attack with a weapon that deals stun damage, subtract half of the stun damage from the target's hit points. Additional effects may occur as well, depending on the amount of damage dealt:

- If the stun damage reduces the target's current hit points to 0, the target moves −5 steps on the condition track and is knocked unconscious (see Falling Unconscious, page 147).

- If the stun damage (before being halved) equals or exceeds the target's damage threshold, the target moves −2 steps on the condition track.

A creature knocked unconscious by a stunning effect does not die if it rolls a natural 1 on its Constitution check to regain consciousness or if it fails the check by 5 or more points. It simply remains unconscious.

Unarmed Attacks

Striking for damage with punches, kicks, and head butts is essentially like attacking with a melee weapon. Unarmed attacks deal normal bludgeoning damage.

A Medium character normally deals 1d4 points of bludgeoning damage (plus Strength modifier) with a successful unarmed attack; a Small character deals 1d3 points of bludgeoning damage (plus Strength modifier). Certain talents, feats, or special abilities may increase the damage a character deals with his unarmed attacks.

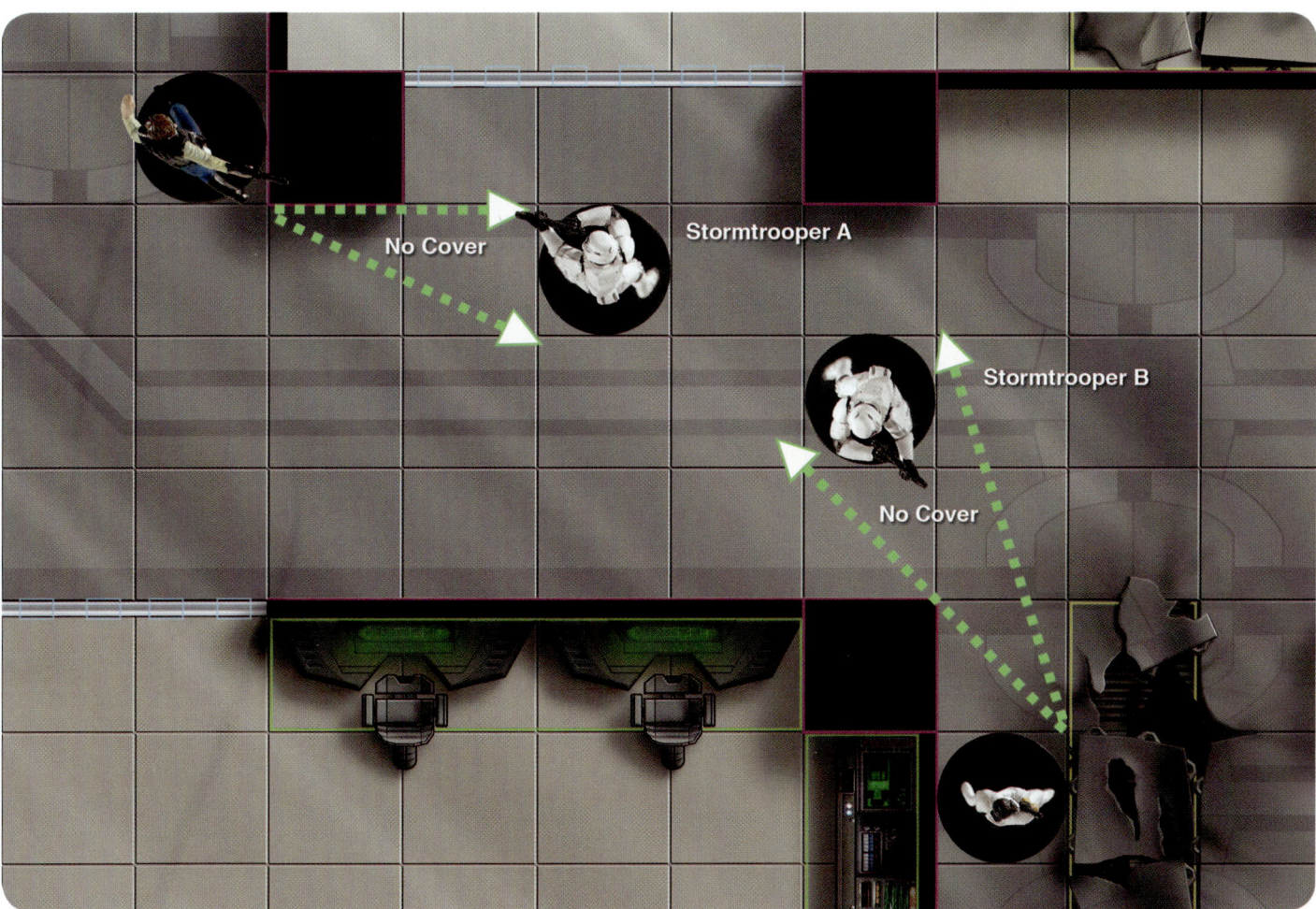

Diagram 9-7: Cover and Line of Sight
A line that runs along a wall or that nicks a corner of a wall does not provide cover. Stormtrooper A does not have cover from Han Solo. Stormtrooper B does not have cover from Princess Leia. Han and Leia do not have line of sight to one another.

Chapter X
Vehicles

Vehicles in the *Star Wars* universe run the gamut from ponderous armored walkers and capital ships to agile airspeeders and starfighters. Despite this variety, the basic purpose of all vehicles remains similar: moving passengers from one place to another. Of course, the places involved in this journey can greatly affect the form and function of the vehicle.

These rules come into play whenever vehicles figure prominently on the battlefield—whether that battlefield happens to be on a planet's surface or in the dark void of space. The movement and combat rules presented here cover all types of vehicles, from planetary vehicles to starships.

In most respects, vehicles follow the same rules as characters, insofar as they have movement, actions, and the capacity to take damage.

Scale

These rules use two scales: character scale and starship scale. If the encounter involves both vehicles and characters on foot, use character scale. If the scene involves vehicles only, use starship scale.

Character Scale

Character scale is identical to the standard movement scale. Combat is carried out on a grid in which each square equals 1.5 meters (about 5 feet).

In character scale, most vehicles are large enough to occupy multiple squares on the battle grid. How many squares a vehicle occupies is determined by the vehicle's size (and the same holds true for characters and creatures). Vehicles of Colossal (frigate) size or greater are not placed on the battle map; they are either off the map (perhaps providing fire support), or the battle takes place inside them.

In character scale, more than one surface vehicle cannot occupy the same space on the battle grid, and a collision occurs whenever a vehicle enters a square occupied by a creature, obstacle, or other vehicle (see Collisions, page 173).

Starship Scale

In starship scale, each square of the grid is abstract, representing a variable amount of space depending on the vehicles involved. In most cases, one square is hundreds or even thousands of meters wide. In starship scale, the grid itself represents relative movement, not absolute movement, so several starships in orbit might be drifting together at many kilometers per second even as they move around one another.

At starship scale, a vehicle can pass through squares occupied by allies, but not squares occupied by enemies.

> ### Starship Battles
> You can play out starship battles using the *Star Wars Miniatures: Starships Battles* starter set, which comes with a battle mat, a rulebook, and several pre-painted plastic starship miniatures. In addition, you can purchase *Starship Battles* booster packs and add more ships to your fleets.
>
> The *Starship Battles* rules are easy to learn, and if you want to play out a starship battle as the backdrop for your roleplaying game campaign, you can do so. However, the *Starship Battles* rules don't let you modify ship statistics to account for the presence of heroes from the roleplaying game, nor do they allow you to run battles that involve anything but starships. If you want to stage a starship battle that hinges on the participation of the heroes or other characters, use the rules in this chapter.

Vehicle Types

The term "vehicle" encompasses both planetary vehicles (such as airspeeders, landspeeders, and walkers) and starships (such as starfighters, space transports, and capital ships). The major difference between planetary vehicles and starships is that planetary vehicles generally do not travel in the vacuum of space. Rules that pertain only to planetary vehicles or starships are called out specifically.

Planetary Vehicles

Planetary vehicles are further subdivided into ground vehicles and air vehicles.

Ground Vehicle: The most basic vehicles in the *Star Wars* universe, ground vehicles only operate on (or very near) a planetary surface.

Speeder: Speeders are common sights on the technologically advanced worlds. Equipped with repulsorlift drive technology, they hover above the ground at a height of anywhere from a few centimeters to several meters and can achieve remarkable speeds. Speeders ignore penalties for difficult terrain.

Tracked: Tracked vehicles have treads or tracks looped around a large number of wheels, providing great traction but making them less maneuverable at higher speeds—and extremely loud at any speed. Tracked vehicles ignore penalties for difficult terrain and take half damage from collisions with obstacles at least one size category smaller than them.

Walker: Walkers move about on two or more legs, literally walking over the terrain. Walkers retain their balance by means of finely tuned gyroscopes and offer a fairly smooth ride. They rely on even footing, however, and when they topple, the results can be disastrous. Walkers ignore obstacles that are three or more sizes smaller than them.

Wheeled: Wheeled vehicles move on one or more wheels (most commonly two to four). Faster and more maneuverable than tracked or walker vehicles, wheels are a cheap alternative to repulsorlift technology for light and fast vehicles.

Air Vehicle: Air vehicles generally operate above a planetary surface, but within the planet's atmosphere.

Airspeeders: Airspeeders are repulsorlift vehicles that can travel anywhere up to about 300 kilometers above ground level, but they are incapable of true space flight. Because they fly so high above the ground, they ignore penalties for terrain or obstructions. Of all planetary vehicles, airspeeders are the most maneuverable.

Starships

Starships are vehicles capable of interplanetary and interstellar travel. They are further subdivided into starfighters, space transports, capital ships, and space stations.

Starfighter: Starfighters are small, agile starships of Gargantuan size or smaller. Though they can travel in atmosphere, they excel at space combat. Starfighters can function with as few as one crewmember (the pilot).

Space Transport: Space transports are mid-size starships of Colossal or Colossal (frigate) size with fewer than 200 hit points. Most space transports are designed for moving passengers or cargo, but some are used as gunships, drop ships, or assault shuttles.

Table 10-1: Vehicle Sizes

VEHICLE SIZE	SIZE MODIFIER[1]	EXAMPLES
Colossal (station)	–10	*Executor*-class Star Dreadnought, Death Star
Colossal (cruiser)	–10	*Imperial*-class Star Destroyer, MC80 Mon Calamari cruiser
Colossal (frigate)	–10	Corellian corvette *(Tantive IV)*, Nebulon-B frigate
Colossal	–10	AT-AT, YT-1300 light freighter *(Millennium Falcon)*
Gargantuan	–5	AAT-1 repulsor tank, X-wing starfighter
Huge	–2	AT-ST walker, TIE fighter
Large	–1	Speeder bike, X-34 landspeeder

1 *Apply this size modifier to the vehicle's Reflex Defense, as well as to Initiative and Pilot checks made by the vehicle's occupants.*

Capital Ship: Capital ships include all starships of Colossal (frigate) size or larger. Capital ships usually carry hundreds if not thousands of crewmembers and passengers, and some are large enough to house other capital ships within their hangar bays. Some very large transports and colony ships fall into this category despite not being designed for combat.

Space Station: Though not technically modes of transportation, space stations have statistics like other starships. A space station can have a population in the thousands or millions, depending on its size. Most space stations are immobile, the Death Star being a notable exception.

Vehicle Combat Statistics

All vehicle statistics that are relevant to combat are described below.

Vehicle Size

Vehicles use similar size categories as creatures, as shown on Table 10–1: Vehicle Sizes. The Colossal size category is further subdivided to differentiate particularly massive starships and space stations.

A vehicle's size modifier applies to the vehicle's Reflex Defense, as well as to Initiative and Pilot checks made by the vehicle's occupants.

Attacks

Any vehicle equipped with weapons can make attacks against enemies within range. An attack roll with a vehicle weapon is calculated as follows:

1d20 + base attack bonus + vehicle's Intelligence modifier + range modifier

Base Attack Bonus: Use the base attack bonus of the gunner (which, in some cases, may be the pilot).

Intelligence Modifier: A vehicle's computer improves the accuracy of the vehicle's weapon systems, and the vehicle's Intelligence score measures the quality of the computer.

Range Modifier: A vehicle weapon can attack a target at point blank, short, medium, or long range. If you make a ranged attack against a target within the weapon's point blank range, you take no penalty on the attack roll. Your penalty on attack rolls increases to –2 at short range, –5 at medium range, and –10 at long range (see Table 10–2: Vehicle Weapon Ranges).

Critical Hits

As in character combat, when you roll a natural 20 on your attack, you automatically hit and deal double damage.

Automatic Misses

If you roll a natural 1 on your attack, you automatically miss.

Table 10-2: Vehicle Weapon Ranges

WEAPON TYPE	CHARACTER SCALE (IN SQUARES)				STARSHIP SCALE (IN SQUARES)			
	PT. BLANK	SHORT	MEDIUM	LONG	PT. BLANK	SHORT	MEDIUM	LONG
Blaster cannon	0–120	121–240	241–600	601–1,200	0–1	2	3–4	5–8
Ion cannon	0–300	301–600	601–1,500	1,501–3,000	0–2	3–4	5–10	11–20
Laser cannon	0–150	151–300	301–750	751–1,500	0–1	2	3–5	6–10
Missile or torpedo	0–450	451–900	901–2,250	2,251–4,500	0–3	4–6	7–15	16–30
Point-defense[1]	0–150	151–300	301–750	751–1,500	0–1	2	3–5	6–10
Tractor beam[1]	0–150	151–300	301–750	751–1,500	0–1	2	3–5	6–10
Turbolaser[1]	0–600	601–1,200	1,201–3,000	3,001–6,000	0–4	5–8	9–20	21–40

1 *This weapon can only be mounted on a vehicle of Colossal (frigate) size or larger.*

Damage

When you hit with a vehicle weapon, you deal damage according to the type of weapon (listed in each vehicle's statistics). Damage dealt by a vehicle weapon is calculated as follows:

Weapon damage × damage multiplier

Damage Multiplier: After rolling the weapon damage dice, multiply the result by the listed damage multiplier. For example, when you fire a vehicle weapon that deals 6d10×2 damage, roll 6d10 and multiply the result by 2.

Defenses

A vehicle's defenses represent how difficult it is to hit or overload its systems. Unlike characters, vehicles do not have a Will Defense. However, vehicles have a Reflex Defense and a Fortitude Defense which are calculated as follows:

Reflex Defense = 10 + vehicle's Dexterity modifier + size modifier + armor bonus or pilot's heroic level
Fortitude Defense = 10 + vehicle's Strength modifier

Reflex Defense (Ref)

Whenever you make an attack against a vehicle, compare your attack roll to the target's Reflex Defense (abbreviated "Ref"). If you equal or exceed the vehicle's Reflex Defense, you hit it and deal damage.

Size Modifier: Use the vehicle's size modifier instead of your own when calculating the vehicle's Reflex Defense (see Table 10-1: Vehicle Sizes).

Armor Bonus: Use the vehicle's armor bonus instead of your own when calculating the vehicle's Reflex Defense. You may add your heroic level instead of this armor bonus.

Dexterity Modifier: A vehicle's Dexterity modifier represents how well it can move out of harm's way. If the pilot is flat-footed, or if the vehicle is out of control or attacked by an undetected opponent, the vehicle loses its Dexterity bonus to its Reflex Defense. If the vehicle is at a full stop, powered down, or disabled, it is treated as if it has a Dexterity score of 0 (–5 penalty to Reflex Defense).

Fortitude Defense (Fort)

Vehicles use their Fortitude Defense (abbreviated "Fort") to determine their damage threshold (see below).

Strength Bonus: A vehicle's Strength bonus represents its overall toughness and durability.

Hit Points

Vehicles have hit points, just like characters. Hit points are abstract, meant to represent not only the vehicle's physical mass but also the robustness or fragility of its systems.

Damage Threshold

Like creatures, vehicles have a damage threshold, calculated as follows:

Damage threshold = Fortitude Defense + size modifier

Facing and Firing Arcs

Just as in character combat, vehicle facing and fire arcs are not used. It's assumed that the pilot is orienting the ship in the most advantageous way possible during combat, and most vehicles in the *Star Wars* universe are quite maneuverable in any event.

Size Modifier: Apply the following size modifiers to a vehicle's damage threshold: Large, +5; Huge, +10; Gargantuan, +20; Colossal, +50; Colossal (frigate), +100; Colossal (cruiser), +200; Colossal (station), +500.

If a vehicle takes damage from a single attack that equals or exceeds its damage threshold, the vehicle moves −1 step on the condition track (see Conditions, page 148). A vehicle pushed to the bottom of the condition track is disabled and comes to a complete stop immediately. If the vehicle was flying in a gravity well at the time it became disabled, it immediately falls 150 meters (100 squares) plus another 300 meters (200 squares) every round until it either hits the surface or is reactivated. Resolve falling damage normally (see Falling Damage, page 255).

If a vehicle is reduced to 0 hit points by an attack that deals damage equal to or greater than its damage threshold, it is destroyed. In addition, all of the vehicle's occupants take half damage from the attack.

Crew Cover

Most vehicles provide at least some cover to their passengers. Passengers gain a cover bonus to their Reflex Defense against any attacks that target them instead of the vehicle. A vehicle can provide no cover, normal cover (+5 cover bonus), improved cover (+10 cover bonus), or full cover. You cannot attack a target that has full cover.

The cover a vehicle provides to its passengers is included in its statistics (see Vehicle Descriptions, page 174).

Speed

Every vehicle has a speed, given in squares. The pilot may move a vehicle up to its listed speed as a move action, and up to four times its speed with the all-out movement action (see page 172).

Starships and airspeeders have a separate listing for their speed in starship scale.

Maximum Velocity: This is the maximum speed a vehicle may move in character scale. It is seldom relevant in combat because such speeds quickly move the vehicle off the battle map and out of range.

Characters in Vehicles

A character in a vehicle fills one of several possible roles, which determines what the character can do. A character can fill several roles at once, but most roles may only be filled by one character at a time. For example, an X-wing pilot also acts as the vehicle's commander and gunner, while her astromech droid usually acts as a copilot, shield operator, and engineer. On the other hand, an Imperial-class Star Destroyer with thousands of crewmembers still has only one pilot, one commander, and so forth. You can change roles from round to round, but you can only start filling a particular role if no other crewmember has filled that role since your last turn.

Pilot: The pilot of the vehicle controls its movement. Most vehicles have only one position from where the vehicle can be piloted. Piloting a vehicle is, at a minimum, a move action, which means that the pilot can do something else with his standard action and swift action. A vehicle can have only one pilot at one time. The pilot adds the vehicle's size modifier and Dexterity modifier on all Initiative and Pilot checks.

Copilot: A copilot can help the pilot by using the aid another action (see Aid Another, page 170). The copilot must be seated in a location where he can see in front of the vehicle and advise the pilot (in most cases, this location is the cockpit). Aiding the pilot is a standard action, leaving the copilot with a move action and swift action each round to do something else. A vehicle can have only one copilot at a time.

Gunner: Most military vehicles and some civilian vehicles have built-in weapons. Any weapon not controlled by the pilot or co-pilot requires a gunner to operate. A vehicle can have as many gunners as it has gunner positions.

Commander: The commander coordinates the various crewmembers and stations aboard the vehicle, analyzes the battle as it unfolds, and looks for weaknesses in the enemy's vehicles and tactics. A vehicle can only have one commander at a time.

System Operator: The system operator manages the vehicle's shields, sensors, and communications. A vehicle can only have one system operator at a time.

Engineer: The chief engineer keeps the ship running even as it takes debilitating damage to its systems, diverting power from overloaded circuits to keep the ship functional. The engineer also leads efforts to repair damage to the hull between battles. A vehicle can only have one chief engineer at a time.

Other Crew: Other crewmembers can fill many supporting roles, coordinating troops or starfighters, administering medical care, guarding sensitive areas, and providing general maintenance. These crewmembers can assist others on some skill checks; for example, the members of a repair team may assist the chief engineer in his duties on capital ships.

Passenger: All other personnel aboard the vehicle are considered passengers. Passengers have no specific role in the vehicle's operation but may take actions aboard the vehicle or replace crewmembers as needed.

Starting the Battle

Unless noted otherwise, climbing aboard a vehicle is a move action, and powering up a vehicle requires a second move action.

Initiative

There are two options for determining initiative in vehicle combat. First, each character can make a separate Initiative check. This is probably the best method if most or all characters are aboard the same vehicle, but it can result in a lot of delayed or readied actions as passengers wait for pilots to

Weapon Batteries

A weapon battery is a cluster of up to six identical weapons. If a starship has weapon batteries, special rules apply when a gunner aids another gunner in the same battery. First, the aiding gunner automatically grants a +2 bonus on the attack roll; no attack roll is required to determine whether the aid another attempt is successful. Second, for every three points by which the attack roll exceeds the target's Reflex Defense, the target is hit by another weapon in the battery, adding +1 die to the weapon's damage. (Apply this extra damage before applying the weapon's damage multiplier, if any.) If a starship has weapon batteries, its statistics include the modified attack bonus because these weapons are usually fired as a group. However, the weapons may still fire independently without this bonus, if you wish.

In addition, a weapon battery can also aid another weapon battery. In this case, only one gunner in the aiding battery needs to make an attack roll against Reflex Defense 10. If successful, add a +2 bonus on the attack roll for every weapon in the aiding battery. Unlike weapons in the same battery, there is no chance that these extra weapons hit the target, regardless of how much the attack roll exceeds the target's Reflex Defense.

perform maneuvers. An alternative is to make an Initiative check for each vehicle, using the pilot's Initiative check modifier. This is particularly appropriate when characters are in separate vehicles, since it allows everyone aboard the same vehicle to act more or less simultaneously.

Special: If you are trained in the Pilot skill (see page 71), you can choose to make a Pilot check instead of an Initiative check to determine your place in the initiative order. In any event, you must apply the vehicle's size modifier to your check (see Table 10-1: Vehicle Sizes, page 166).

Vehicle Combat Actions

The types of actions you can take during a single turn don't change when you're aboard a vehicle.

Some of the actions described below can only be performed by particular crewmembers. In this case, the eligible crewmembers are listed in parentheses following the action's name.

Standard Actions

A standard action could be any one of the following:

Aid Another

As a standard action, you can aid an ally's next skill check, ability check, or attack roll.

Aiding a Skill Check or Ability Check: You can help another character achieve success on her skill check or ability check by making the same kind of skill check or ability check in a cooperative effort. If you roll a 10 or higher on your check, the character you are helping gains a +2 bonus on her check. You can't take 10 on a skill check or ability check to aid another. Only the copilot can assist on Pilot checks, and only the commander can assist on Use Computer checks. Any crewmember can aid any other skill check.

Aiding an Attack Roll: In combat, you can aid another character's attack by providing improved targeting data or by coordinating that attack with other vehicle actions. A gunner can grant a +2 bonus on another character's attack roll by making an attack against a Reflex Defense of 10.

A sensor operator can grant a +2 bonus on another character's attack roll by making a DC 10 Use Computer check.

A vehicle's commander can grant a +2 bonus on another character's attack roll by making a DC 10 Knowledge (tactics) check.

Attack with Melee Weapon

With a melee weapon, you can strike any enemy in a square you can threaten. You can only threaten squares within your reach from the vehicle's space, and you don't threaten spaces around the vehicle at all if it grants total cover. For example, a Jedi on a speeder bike could attack targets adjacent to the bike with his lightsaber, but the same Jedi couldn't do so while inside an AT-AT.

You can't make a melee attack in starship scale, except within the confines of the vehicle you occupy.

Attack with Ranged Weapon

With a ranged weapon, you can throw or shoot at any target within your line of sight, as long as your vehicle does not grant you total cover. For example, clone troopers can fire their blasters at targets outside a LAAT/i gunship as long as the ship's doors are open. Range modifiers apply normally for your weapon.

You cannot make a personal ranged attack in starship scale, except within the confines of the vehicle you occupy.

Attack with Vehicle Weapon
Gunner Only

Any gunners (including the pilot, if there are pilot-operated weapons on the vehicle) can make an attack with their vehicle weapon as a standard action. The maximum range and the range modifiers of a vehicle weapon attack depend on the weapon used (see Table 10-2: Vehicle Weapon Ranges).

Capital Ships: Capital ship weapons are designed for long-range bombardment against large or immobile targets, and they have difficulty tracking very small enemies. When attacking a target of less than Colossal size, a vehicle that is Colossal (frigate) size or larger takes a –20 penalty on its attack rolls. Point-defense weapons are specifically designed to attack smaller targets and do not take these penalties.

Trained Pilot: If you are trained in the Pilot skill, you gain a +2 bonus on all attacks made with any vehicle weapon identified as being crewed by the pilot.

Attack Run
Pilot Only

As a standard action, you can move up to your vehicle's speed (minimum 2 squares) in a straight line through unobstructed terrain directly toward your target, and then make an attack with a vehicle weapon at that target at the end of your movement. You gain a +2 bonus on your attack roll and take a –2 penalty to your vehicle's Reflex Defense until the start of your next turn. In starship scale, you cannot make an attack run through squares occupied by enemies, but allies do not hinder your attack run.

Dogfight
Pilot Only

As a standard action, the pilot of an airspeeder or starfighter can initiate a dogfight against an enemy airspeeder or starfighter in an adjacent square (starship scale). Make a Pilot check at a –5 penalty, opposed by the enemy's Pilot check. If you succeed, you and the target vehicle are engaged in a dogfight.

Consequences of Dogfighting: A vehicle engaged in a dogfight must select the dogfight action on every turn, and it cannot move out of its current square until it disengages (see below). While engaged in a dogfight, you cannot attack any target outside the dogfight.

Firing into a Dogfight: If another vehicle fires into a dogfight, it takes a –5 penalty on its attack roll unless the gunner has the Precise Shot feat.

Attacking in a Dogfight: Make an opposed Pilot check as a standard action. If you win the opposed check, you may make a single attack with a vehicle weapon as a swift action. If you fail, you cannot attack the target, and any gunners on your vehicle take a –5 penalty on any attack rolls they make until your next turn.

Disengaging from a Dogfight: Make an opposed Pilot check as a move action. If you win the opposed check, you successfully disengage from the dogfight and may move a number of squares equal to your speed. If you fail, you remain in the dogfight, and any gunners on your vehicle take a –5 penalty on any attack rolls they make until your next turn.

Attack of Opportunity: If an enemy starfighter tries to move through your square or an adjacent square, you may attempt to initiate a dogfight as an attack of opportunity. If successful, the enemy starfighter must stop moving.

Fight Defensively
Pilot Only

As a standard action, you can concentrate more on protecting your vehicle than hurting your enemies. You and all gunners on your vehicle take a –5 penalty on your attack rolls and your vehicle gains a +2 dodge bonus to its Reflex Defense until the start of your next turn. If you choose to make no attacks, your vehicle gains a +5 dodge bonus to its Reflex Defense and all gunners on your vehicle take a –10 penalty on their attack rolls until the start of your next turn.

Trained Pilot: If you are trained in the Pilot skill, your vehicle instead gains a +5 dodge bonus to its Reflex Defense when you and your gunners take a –5 penalty on attack rolls, or a +10 dodge bonus if you choose to make no attacks on your turn.

MOVE ACTIONS
Move actions include the following:

Move
Pilot Only

You can move up to your vehicle's speed. The only restriction for vehicle movement is that you cannot reenter a square you just left.

SWIFT ACTIONS
Swift actions include the following:

Aim
Gunner Only

Just as in character combat, you can aim before making a ranged attack (see Aim, page 154).

> "THAT SHIP SAVED MY LIFE QUITE A FEW TIMES. SHE'S THE FASTEST HUNK OF JUNK IN THE GALAXY."
> — LANDO CALRISSIAN

Full Stop
Pilot Only

If you haven't already used a move action or full-round action to move your vehicle this turn, you can spend a swift action to bring your vehicle to a full stop. After that, the vehicle is considered stationary.

You cannot bring a vehicle to a full stop if you used all-out movement (see below) on your last turn.

Increase Vehicle Speed
Pilot Only

If you are trained in the Pilot skill, you may make a DC 20 Pilot check as a swift action to push your vehicle beyond its normal limits. (You can't take 10 on this check.) If the check fails, your vehicle's speed does not increase, and your vehicle moves −1 step on the condition track (see Conditions, page 148). If you succeed, your vehicle's speed increases by 1 square until the start of your next turn. For every 5 points by which you exceed the DC, your vehicle's speed increases by an additional 1 square.

Raise or Lower Shields
System Operator Only

By spending a swift action, you can activate or deactivate the shields on your vehicle. Shields are generally kept inactive in noncombat situations to reduce strain on the vehicle's systems, and raising shields is often perceived as evidence of hostile intent, so many commanders prefer to keep their shields down unless they are expecting trouble.

Recharge Shields
System Operator Only; 3 swift actions

By spending three swift actions during the same turn or on consecutive turns, you can make a DC 20 Mechanics check to increase your current shield rating by 5, up to the vehicle's normal maximum.

Reroute Power
Engineer Only; 3 swift actions

By spending three swift actions during the same turn or on consecutive turns, you can make a DC 20 Mechanics check to move your vehicle +1 step on the condition track (see Conditions, page 148).

FULL-ROUND ACTIONS

Full-round actions include the following:

All-Out Movement
Pilot Only

As a full-round action, you can move up to four times your vehicle's speed. All of this movement must be in a straight line, and you can't avoid collisions while doing so (see Avoid Collision, page 173). Your vehicle loses its Dexterity bonus to Reflex Defense until the beginning of your next turn.

You can't use all-out movement unless you moved on your last turn.

Because most power is diverted to the engines when using all-out movement, gunners on board your vehicle cannot attack until the start of your next turn.

Maximum Velocity (character scale only): If you use all-out movement on your turn, you may move up to your vehicle's maximum velocity with all-out movement on your next turn. If you move your vehicle's maximum velocity, you must either continue moving at the vehicle's maximum velocity or use all-out movement as your action on the following turn.

Full Attack
Gunner Only

If you are capable of making more than one attack (because you have the Double Attack feat or a similar ability), you must make a full attack to get those extra attacks. A pilot who spends at least a move action every round moving his vehicle cannot make a full attack action unless the vehicle has already been brought to a full stop.

Ram
Pilot Only

As a full-round action, you can attempt to ram a target by moving your vehicle into the target's fighting space. You must have sufficient movement to reach the target's fighting space, and the ram is treated as an area effect. You can use your vehicle to ram just about anything, including another vehicle, a creature, or a structure.

Make a Pilot check at a −10 penalty against the target's Reflex Defense. If the check succeeds, your vehicle, the target, and all passengers aboard vehicles involved in the collision (including you) take the amount of damage listed in Table 10-3: Collision Damage. Assuming you're alive and conscious, you can continue moving through the target's fighting space if your vehicle has any movement left. Otherwise, your vehicle is pushed out of the target's fighting space and into the nearest available squares, and your turn ends.

If your Pilot check fails, your vehicle, the target, and all passengers aboard vehicles involved in the collision (including you) take half damage. In addition, your vehicle is pushed out of the target's fighting space and into the nearest available squares, at which point your turn ends.

All-Out Movement: If the colliding vehicle is moving all-out or moving at maximum velocity (see All-Out Movement, above), double the damage caused by the collision.

Vehicular Evasion: If you have the Vehicular Evasion talent (page 207), you can reduce or negate the damage your vehicle and its passengers take when rammed by another vehicle.

REACTIONS

As always, a character may make any number of reactions during a round. Reactions include the following:

Avoid Collision
Pilot Only

Any time your vehicle is subject to a collision, you can make a DC 15 Pilot check as a reaction. If you succeed on the check, all targets involved in the collision take half damage (see Collisions, below, for more information).

You can't attempt to avoid a collision when you intentionally ram a target (see Ram, above).

Starship Scale: Collisions are easier to avoid at starship scale. If you succeed on the Pilot check to avoid a collision in starship scale, no collision occurs.

SPECIAL VEHICLE COMBAT RULES

Vehicles have a few additional rules during combat that are different from those used with characters.

AREA ATTACKS

Except as noted here, area attacks work the same for vehicles as they do for characters.

Starship Scale: Because of the size of each square compared to the size of starships, area attacks (including autofire, burst radius weapons, and splash weapons) are resolved as attacks on a single target in starship scale unless the weapon is specifically listed as having a starship-scale area attack.

AUTOFIRE

If your vehicle weapon is capable of autofire, you can use it to make an area attack in character scale, just as in character combat.

Strafe Attacks: Instead of attacking a 2-square-by-2-square area, airspeeders and starfighters may attack a number of squares in a straight line as they fly over them. Doing this requires the attack run action (see page 171), and the area attack applies to a straight line 1 square wide and 5 to 10 squares long. You take a penalty to your attack roll equal to the number of squares included in the area attack.

You cannot make a strafe attack in starship scale.

COLLISIONS

A collision occurs whenever your vehicle moves into a space occupied by a creature, structure, another vehicle, or hazard (such as an asteroid), or whenever such things move into your vehicle's fighting space. A collision is treated as an area attack (see Area Attacks, page 155). You can reduce or negate the damage from a collision as a reaction by succeeding at a DC 15 Pilot check (see Avoid Collision, above).

Ramming Vehicles: When the source of the collision is a ramming vehicle, the pilot of the ramming vehicle makes a Pilot check (instead of an attack roll) and compares the result to the Reflex Defense of the target. If the check succeeds, the ramming vehicle, the target, and all passengers aboard vehicles involved in the collision take the amount of damage listed on Table 10-3: Collision Damage. If the check fails, reduce the damage by half.

Mobile Hazards: When the source of the collision is a mobile hazard of Large size or greater (such as an asteroid or unguided vehicle), the colliding hazard makes an attack roll against the target's Reflex Defense. The hazard's attack roll is resolved by rolling 1d20 and adding a flat modifier based on its size: Large, +1; Huge, +2; Gargantuan, +5; Colossal or bigger, +10. If the attack hits, the colliding hazard, the target, and all passengers aboard

> ### UNCONTROLLED VEHICLES
> In the event that the pilot is incapacitated or abandons a vehicle before using the full stop action, the vehicle's emergency systems automatically kick in. On the pilot's initiative count, the vehicle moves in a straight line a number of squares equal to its speed and then comes to a complete stop.
>
> A vehicle without a pilot cannot land itself while flying, so after coming to a complete stop, it will fall as if it had been disabled.

TABLE 10-3: COLLISION DAMAGE

SIZE OF COLLIDING VEHICLE OR HAZARD	DAMAGE[1]
Colossal (station)	20d6 + Str modifier
Colossal (cruiser)	15d6 + Str modifier
Colossal (frigate)	10d6 + Str modifier
Colossal	8d6 + Str modifier
Gargantuan	6d6 + Str modifier
Huge	4d6 + Str modifier
Large	2d6 + Str modifier

[1] *Double the damage if the colliding vehicle is using all-out movement (see page 172).*

CREW QUALITY

Rather than providing statistics for every member of a vehicle's crew, most vehicle descriptions provide a general "crew quality" descriptor.

The following chart lists the five levels of crew quality for GM-controlled vehicle crews, along with the appropriate check modifier. Use the number in the Attack Bonus column for all attack rolls performed by the crew. Use the number in the Check Modifier column for all skill checks related to the operation of the vessel (including Mechanics, Pilot, and Use Computer checks). Crew quality modifies a vehicle's CL, as shown in the CL Modifier column. These modifiers are already included in the vehicle's statistics.

For unique vehicles where the crew's statistics are included, this table is unnecessary. All crewmembers of a general crew quality are considered to only have nonheroic levels.

CREW QUALITY	ATTACK BONUS	CHECK MODIFIER	CL MODIFIER
Untrained	–5	+0	–1
Normal	+0	+5	+0
Skilled	+2	+6	+1
Expert	+5	+8	+2
Ace	+10	+12	+4

vehicles involved in the collision take the amount of damage listed on Table 10–3: Collision Damage. If the attack fails, reduce the damage by half.

MISSILES AND TORPEDOES

Some vehicles carry guided projectile weapons such as proton torpedoes or concussion missiles. Attacks with these weapons are resolved just as with any other weapon.

If you aim before making an attack with a missile or torpedo, it locks on to the target and can track its target independently. Make your attack roll normally, but if you miss, the missile or torpedo can attempt to attack again on your next turn. This next attack is made using the same attack bonus, but with a –5 penalty. (You do not need to spend an action to make this attack.) If the missile or torpedo misses its target a second time, it self-destructs harmlessly.

Attacking a Missile or Torpedo: If a missile or torpedo misses its target initially, it is possible to shoot it down before it attacks again. A missile or torpedo has a Reflex Defense of 30 and 10 hit points, and it is considered to occupy the same square as its target for purposes of determining range penalties.

It is also possible to attack a missile or torpedo prior to its first attack, but you must have readied an action specifically for this purpose (see Ready, page 162).

TRACTOR BEAMS

Instead of damaging a vehicle's hit points, tractor beams prevent another vehicle from escaping. When attacking with a tractor beam, your attack hits if you equal or exceed the target's Reflex Defense. If you hit, make an opposed grapple check (see Grapple, page 153). If you win the opposed grapple check, the target is grabbed.

If a grabbed target is of your vehicle's size or smaller, then it cannot move and it loses its Dexterity bonus to its Reflex Defense. Each round on your turn, you must make another opposed grapple check; if you win the opposed check, you may pull the target up to 10 squares closer to you (or 1 square closer to you in starship scale) or hold it in place in its current square. If you lose the opposed check, the target manages to slip free from the tractor beam.

If the grabbed target is larger than your vehicle, the target retains its Dexterity bonus to its Reflex Defense and can move freely, but you may move your vehicle up to 10 squares closer to it (or 1 square closer to it in starship scale). If the grabbed vehicle ever moves beyond the range of your tractor beam, the tractor beam's hold is broken automatically.

If you pull your target into your square (or pull your vehicle into a larger target's square), your vehicle may use docking clamps to attach itself to the target. Once this is done, it is possible to board the target ship by blowing open or cutting through an airlock or the hull (see Attack an Object, page 151).

VEHICLE DESCRIPTIONS

This section presents several common vehicles that you can include in your *Star Wars* campaign. Every vehicle description comes with a set of combat statistics. Some statistics are exclusive to vehicles or require more elaboration:

Challenge Level (CL): Heroes gain experience points (XP) for destroying, disabling, or otherwise overcoming the vehicle based on the vehicle's CL (see Awarding Experience Points, page 248). However, they don't gain additional XP for incidental crew or passengers killed as a result of the vehicle's destruction. For example, heroes who blow up a shuttle don't also receive XP for its crew; however, if the shuttle was transporting an Imperial Moff that the heroes were hired to eliminate, they should receive XP for the Imperial Moff as well.

Maximum Velocity: The maximum speed the vehicle can achieve after using all-out movement for at least one full round. Maximum velocity is never used in starship scale.

Grapple (Grp): The vehicle's grapple modifier is mainly used to resist attempts to restrain the vehicle physically (usually via tractor beam).

Fighting Space: The fighting space that the vehicle occupies at character scale, starship scale, or both (see Fighting Space, page 159).

Cover: The amount of cover the vehicle grants to its crew and passengers, listed as none, +5 (normal cover), +10 (improved cover), or total.

Crew: The number and quality of the crew (see the Crew Quality sidebar). The crew modifiers are already included in all other statistics in the vehicle description.

Passengers: The number of passengers (including troops) that the vehicle can carry, in addition to its crew.

Cargo Capacity: The amount of cargo the vehicle can carry.

Carried Craft: Other vehicles that are usually carried aboard this vehicle.

Payload: The vehicle's complement of grenades, rockets, missiles, and torpedoes. If the vehicle has no payload, this line is absent.

Hyperdrive: The multiplier used when calculating hyperspace travel times (see Astrogation, page 237). If the starship has a backup hyperdrive, its multiplier is listed in parentheses. Hyperdrive is never used in character scale. If the vehicle has no hyperdrive, this line is absent.

Availability: See Restricted Items, page 118.

WALKERS

Most walkers are used as armored assault vehicles. Their sheer size and strength enable them to carry more armor and weapons than a similarly sized repulsorlift vehicle, and they can step over smaller obstacles.

All-Terrain Armored Transport (AT-AT)

The 15.5-meter-tall All Terrain Armored Transport (AT-AT) is an imposing, four-legged behemoth that shakes the ground as it plods toward enemy fortifications. (The Empire used AT-ATs to overwhelm Rebel forces on Hoth in Episode V.)

AT-AT   CL 14

Colossal ground vehicle (walker)
Init −2; **Senses** Perception +8

Defense Ref 16 (flat-footed 16), Fort 29; +16 armor
hp 300; **DR** 20; **Threshold** 79

Speed 4 squares (max. velocity 60 km/h)
Ranged heavy laser cannons +7 (see below) and
   blaster cannons +7 (see below)
Fighting Space 6×12; **Cover** total
Base Atk +5; **Grp** +42
Atk Options autofire (medium blaster cannons)

Abilities Str 48, Dex 10, Con —, Int 14
Skills Initiative −2, Mechanics +8, Perception +8, Pilot −2
Crew 5 (expert); **Passengers** 40
Cargo 1 ton; **Consumables** 1 week; **Carried Craft** 5 speeder bikes or 2 AT-STs
Availability Military; **Cost** not available for sale

Heavy laser cannons (gunner)
   Atk +7, **Dmg** 6d10×2, 2-square splash

Blaster cannons (gunner)
   Atk +7 (+2 autofire), **Dmg** 3d10×2

All-Terrain Scout Transport (AT-ST)

The 8.5-meter-tall All-Terrain Scout Transport (AT-ST) is a nimble, two-legged mobile weapons platform that rapidly moves across battlefields and through cramped urban environments, providing reconnaissance and quick-response fire support for ground troops.

AT-ST   CL 8

Huge ground vehicle (walker)
Init +8; **Senses** Perception +8

Defense Ref 14 (flat-footed 12), Fort 20; +4 armor
hp 120; **DR** 10; **Threshold** 30

Speed 6 squares (max. velocity 90 km/h)
Ranged twin blaster cannons +6 (see below) and
   twin light blaster cannon +6 (see below) or
Ranged twin blaster cannons +6 (see below) and
   grenade launcher +6 (see below)
Fighting Space 3×3; **Cover** total
Base Atk +5; **Grp** +25
Atk Options autofire (twin light blaster cannon)

Abilities Str 30, Dex 14, Con —, Int 12
Skills Initiative +8, Mechanics +8, Perception +8, Pilot +8
Crew 2 (expert); **Passengers** none
Cargo none; **Consumables** 2 days; **Carried Craft** none
Payload 12 frag grenades
Availability Military; **Cost** not available for sale

Twin blaster cannons (pilot)
   Atk +6, **Dmg** 4d10×2

Twin light blaster cannon (copilot)
   Atk +6 (+1 autofire), **Dmg** 3d10×2

Grenade launcher (copilot)
   Atk +6, **Dmg** 4d6, 2-square burst

Speeders

Ground-based repulsor vehicles, collectively known as landspeeders, are common on planets throughout the galaxy. They are used widely by military forces, civilian authorities, businesses, and private citizens. Most families own at least one landspeeder, particularly on planets with scant urbanization and little public transportation. Landspeeders are propelled by repulsorlifts, although some racing and military models use ion engines for greater top-end speed.

SoroSuub X-34 Landspeeder

One of the most popular models of civilian speeders is the SoroSuub X-series, which can attain a maximum altitude of 1.5 meters. It is a durable two-person craft that features holographic displays, computer-assisted navigation, and counterbalances for a stable ride over rough terrain. (Luke Skywalker used an X-34 landspeeder on Tatooine in Episode IV.)

SoroSuub X-34 Landspeeder — CL 1
Large ground vehicle (speeder)
Init +8; **Senses** Perception +5

Defense Ref 14 (flat-footed 10), Fort 14; +1 armor
hp 40; **DR** 5; **Threshold** 19

Speed 12 squares (max. velocity 330 km/h)
Fighting Space 2×2; **Cover** +5
Base Atk +0; **Grp** +15

Abilities Str 18, Dex 18, Con —, Int 12
Skills Initiative +8, Mechanics +5, Perception +5, Pilot +8

Crew 1 (normal); **Passengers** 1
Cargo 30 kg; **Consumables** 1 day; **Carried Craft** none
Availability Licensed; **Cost** 10,550 (2,500 used)

Speeder Bikes

These small, fast personal transports appeal to teenagers looking for thrills, military forces that require effective scout vehicles, and law enforcers needing swift pursuit craft. Speeder bike races are popular in the Core systems, where they are viewed as more refined than the extremely dangerous Podraces. Still, speeder bikes emphasize speed and maneuverability over safety and protection.

Aratech 74-Z Speeder Bike

The 74-Z is a basic speeder bike designed for military scouting and urban patrol missions. It consists of a powerful repulsorlift engine with two small thrust engines, a long forward control vane, and a small blaster cannon in a rotating forward mount. It is designed for a single pilot but has room for a passenger as well—both straddling the engine block of the vehicle.

Aratech 74-Z Speeder Bike — CL 4
Large ground vehicle (speeder)
Init +14; **Senses** Perception +8

Defense Ref 16 (flat-footed 10), Fort 14; +1 armor
hp 40; **DR** 5; **Threshold** 19

Speed 12 squares (max. velocity 500 km/h)
Ranged laser cannon +7 (4d10, pilot)
Fighting Space 2×2; **Cover** none
Base Atk +5; **Grp** +14
Atk Options autofire (laser cannon)

Abilities Str 18, Dex 24, Con —, Int 14
Skills Initiative +14, Mechanics +8, Perception +8, Pilot +14

Crew 1 (expert); **Passengers** 1
Cargo 3 kg; **Consumables** 1 day; **Carried Craft** none
Availability Restricted; **Cost** 6,750 (1,200 used)

Laser cannon (pilot)
Atk +7 (+2 autofire), **Dmg** 4d10

Armored Assault Tanks (AATs)

These heavily armored vehicles use wheels, treads, powered legs, or repulsorlifts to move about the battlefield. Although not maneuverable, they pack incredible firepower and can safely transport small teams of troops into hostile territory. The Trade Federation uses AAT-1s propelled by heavy repulsorlifts on the front lines of a battlefield to soften up the enemy before deploying waves of battle droids.

AAT-1 — CL 8
Huge ground vehicle (speeder)
Init +7; **Senses** Perception +6

Defense Ref 16 (flat-footed 13), Fort 23; +5 armor
hp 180; **DR** 15; **Threshold** 33
Weakness ion vulnerability

Speed 6 squares (max. velocity 55 km/h)
Ranged heavy laser cannon +4 (see below) and
  light blaster cannons +4 (see below) and
  repeating blaster cannons +4 (see below) or
Ranged heavy laser cannon +4 (see below) and
  light blaster cannons +4 (see below) and
  missile launchers +4 (see below)
Fighting Space 3×3; **Cover** total (crew), none (passengers)
Base Atk +2; **Grp** +25
Atk Options autofire (repeating blaster cannons)

Abilities Str 36, Dex 16, Con —, Int 14
Skills Initiative +7, Mechanics +6, Perception +6, Pilot +7

Crew 4 (skilled); **Passengers** 6 (external)
Cargo 500 kg; **Consumables** 1 week; **Carried Craft** none
Payload 12 missiles
Availability Military; **Cost** not available for sale

Ion Vulnerability—Due to a design flaw, the AAT takes double damage from ion weapons.

Heavy laser cannon (gunner)
Atk +4, **Dmg** 6d10×2, 2-square splash
Light blaster cannons (gunner)
Atk +4, **Dmg** 2d10×2
Repeating blaster cannons (pilot)
Atk +4 (−1 autofire), **Dmg** 3d10×2
Missile launcher (pilot)
Atk +4, **Dmg** 6d6, 2-square splash

AIRSPEEDERS

Airspeeders are swift flying vehicles that can achieve altitudes of a few hundred kilometers; however, they are not suited for space travel.

Modified Incom T-47 Airspeeder

The Incom T-47 airspeeder, heavily modified, is the favored ground attack airspeeder of the Rebel Alliance. They were used to protect Echo Base during the Battle of Hoth and can be adapted to many environments.

Modified Incom-T47 Airspeeder   CL 6
Huge air vehicle (airspeeder)
Init +10; **Senses** Perception +7
Defense Ref 16 (flat-footed 10), Fort 16; +2 armor
hp 60; **DR** 10; **Threshold** 26
Speed fly 16 squares (max. velocity 1,100 km/h), fly 4 squares (starship scale)
Ranged double laser cannon +4 (see below) and
  blaster cannon +4 (see below) or
Ranged double laser cannon +4 (see below) and
  harpoon gun +4 (see below) or
Fighting Space 3×3 or 1 square (starship scale); **Cover** total (crew)
Base Atk +2; **Grp** +18
Atk Options autofire (double laser cannon, blaster cannon), harpoon gun
Abilities Str 22, Dex 22, Con —, Int 14
Skills Initiative +10, Mechanics +6, Perception +6, Pilot +10
Crew 2 (skilled); **Passengers** none
Cargo 50 kg; **Consumables** 1 day; **Carried Craft** none
Availability Military; **Cost** 50,000 used

Harpoon Gun—A gunner use the harpoon gun to make a grapple check against an enemy walker. The gunner must make an attack roll against the walker; if successful, the pilot must make an opposed grapple check. If the grapple check succeeds, the target walker cannot move without first making a Pilot check (DC = harpoon gun's grapple check result). If this Pilot check fails, the walker suffers an automatic collision, taking twice its collision damage.

Double laser cannon (pilot)
Atk +4 (−1 autofire), **Dmg** 5d10
Blaster cannon (gunner)
Atk +4 (−1 autofire), **Dmg** 3d10
Harpoon gun (gunner)
Atk +4, **Dmg** — (grapple +27)

LAAT/i Gunship

The LAAT/i attack gunship, first deployed at the Battle of Geonosis, is an example of a combat space transport designed to carry combat troops directly into the heat of battle. Its weapons are used to clear a landing zone and lay down suppressing fire as the troops exit the vehicle.

LAAT/i Gunship   CL 12
Colossal air vehicle (airspeeder)
Init +0; **Senses** Perception +8
Defense Ref 15 (flat-footed 13), Fort 26; +13 armor
hp 160; **DR** 15; **SR** 15; **Threshold** 76
Speed fly 12 squares (max. velocity 620 km/h), fly 3 squares (starship scale)
Ranged mass driver missile launchers +7 (see below) and
  anti-personnel laser cannons +7 (see below) and
  4 composite-beam pinpoint lasers +7 (see below)
Ranged rocket launcher +7 (see below) and
  anti-personnel laser cannons +7 (see below) and
  4 composite-beam lasers +7 (see below)
Fighting Space 6×6 or 1 square (starship scale); **Cover** total (none for passengers if doors are open)
Base Atk +5; **Grp** +38
Atk Options autofire (anti-personnel laser cannons)
Special Actions penetration 10 (composite-beam lasers)
Abilities Str 42, Dex 14, Con —, Int 14
Skills Initiative +0, Mechanics +8, Perception +8, Pilot +0
Crew 6 (expert); **Passengers** 30
Cargo 2 tons; **Consumables** 2 days; **Carried Craft** none
Payload 24 missiles, 6 rockets
Availability Military; **Cost** 65,000 (40,000 used)

Penetration 10—The gunship's composite-beam lasers ignore the first 10 points of an enemy's damage reduction.

Mass driver missile launchers (pilot)
Atk +7, **Dmg** 6d10×2, 2-square splash

Rocket launcher (pilot)
Atk +7, **Dmg** 5d10×2, 2-square burst

Anti-personnel laser cannons (copilot)
Atk +7 (+2 autofire), **Dmg** 4d10

Composite-beam laser (gunner)
Atk +7, **Dmg** 3d10

STARFIGHTERS

Starfighters, sometimes known as "snub fighters," are the ships of choice for hotshot pilots. Equipped with light yet strong engines and quick, responsive controls, starfighters can zip in and out of tight spots before most heavier craft can react. Their weaponry is light, and their armor and shields are minimal compared to those of larger ships, but a good pilot in a starfighter can do as much damage as a capital ship bristling with gun turrets.

X-wing Fighter

Often hailed as the best starfighter ever made, the T-65B X-wing was developed in secret when the Incom Corporation began to support the Rebel Alliance. With impressive firepower for a ship of its size, sturdy shields, and even a hyperdrive, the X-wing is as agile as an Imperial TIE fighter and far more versatile. It is equipped with a topside astromech bay, letting the pilot plug in an R2 droid to handle targeting, damage control, and hyperspace calculation.

Incom T-65B X-wing Starfighter　　　　　　　　　　**CL 10**
Gargantuan starfighter
Init +7; **Senses** Perception +6

Defense Ref 18 (flat-footed 12), Fort 26; +7 armor
hp 120; **DR** 10; **SR** 15; **Threshold** 46

Speed fly 16 squares (max. velocity 1,050 km/h), fly 4 squares (starship scale)
Ranged laser cannons +5 (see below) or
Ranged proton torpedoes +5 (see below)
Fighting Space 4×4 or 1 square (starship scale); **Cover** total (pilot), +5 (astromech droid)
Base Atk +2; **Grp** +33
Atk Options autofire (laser cannons)

Abilities Str 42, Dex 22, Con —, Int 16
Skills Initiative +7, Mechanics +6 (+13*), Perception +6 (+3*), Pilot +7, Use Computer +6 (+13*)

Crew 1 plus astromech droid (skilled); **Passengers** none
Cargo 110 kg; **Consumables** 1 week; **Carried Craft** none
Payload 6 proton torpedoes
Hyperdrive ×1, 10-jump memory (astromech droid)
Availability Military; **Cost** 150,000 (65,000 used)

* If the ship has an astromech droid, use these skill modifiers instead.

Laser cannons (pilot)
Atk +5 (+0 autofire), **Dmg** 6d10×2

Proton torpedoes (pilot)
Atk +5, **Dmg** 9d10×2, 4-square splash

Y-Wing Fighter

The workhorse of the Rebel Alliance, the Koensayr Y-wing is not as popular as other snub fighters, being neither as fast nor as maneuverable. However, its impressive shields and weaponry more than make up for its performance flaws.

Like the X-wing, the Y-wing provides a topside port to allow an astromech droid to plug in and handle most of the in-flight "dirty work."

Koensayr Y-wing Starfighter　　　　　　　　　　**CL 10**
Gargantuan starfighter
Init +5; **Senses** Perception +6

Defense Ref 16 (flat-footed 12), Fort 26; +7 armor
hp 120; **DR** 10; **SR** 25; **Threshold** 46

Speed fly 16 squares (max. velocity 1,000 km/h), fly 4 squares (starship scale)
Ranged laser cannons +5 (see below) and
 ion cannons +5 (see below) or
Ranged proton torpedoes +5 (see below) and
 ion cannons +5 (see below)
Fighting Space 4×4 or 1 square (starship scale); **Cover** total (crew), +5 (astromech droid)
Base Atk +2; **Grp** +33
Atk Options autofire (laser cannons, ion cannons)

Abilities Str 42, Dex 18, Con —, Int 16
Skills Initiative +5, Mechanics +6 (+13*), Perception +6, Pilot +5, Use Computer +6 (+13*)

Crew 2 plus astromech droid (skilled); **Passengers** none
Cargo 110 kg; **Consumables** 1 week; **Carried Craft** none
Payload 8 proton torpedoes
Hyperdrive ×1, 10-jump memory (astromech droid)
Availability Military; **Cost** 135,000 (60,000 used)

* If the ship has an astromech droid, use these skill modifiers instead.

Laser cannons (pilot)
 Atk +5 (+0 autofire), **Dmg** 4d10×2
Ion cannons (gunner)
 Atk +5 (+0 autofire), **Dmg** 4d10×2 ion
Proton torpedoes (gunner)
 Atk +5, **Dmg** 9d10×2, 4-square splash

TIE Fighter

Cheap and efficient, TIE fighters are not so much feared for their capabilities as their numbers. Mass-produced by Sienar Fleet Systems, TIE fighters cost only a fraction of what a comparable fighter costs. Keeping the price down means that TIE fighters have no shields, hyperdrives, or life support—not even cockpit gravity. They can't even land without special supports. The Imperial Navy believes that this teaches pilots to rely on higher authorities. In reality, it just teaches them to hope that they live long enough to be promoted to a more advanced TIE variant.

TIE Fighter CL 7
Huge starfighter
Init +8; **Senses** Perception +6
Defense Ref 15 (flat-footed 11), Fort 22; +3 armor
hp 60; **DR** 10; **Threshold** 32
Speed fly 16 squares (max. velocity 1,200 km/h), fly 5 squares (starship scale)
Ranged laser cannons +4 (see below)
Fighting Space 3×3 or 1 square (starship scale); **Cover** total
Base Atk +2; **Grp** +24
Atk Options autofire (laser cannons)

Abilities Str 34, Dex 18, Con —, Int 14
Skills Initiative +8, Mechanics +6, Perception +6, Pilot +8
Crew 1 (skilled); **Passengers** none
Cargo 65 kg; **Consumables** 2 days; **Carried Craft** none
Availability Military; **Cost** 60,000 (25,000 used)

Laser cannons (pilot)
Atk +4 (−1 autofire), **Dmg** 4d10×2

TIE Interceptor

The TIE interceptor was designed specifically to counteract the Rebel Alliance X-wing. To increase speed and firepower, the designers at Sienar gave it large engines, more powerful energy converters, and a package of four fire-linked laser cannons. Although put into production before the Battle of Yavin, these fighters weren't in general use until just before the Battle of Endor.

TIE Interceptor — CL 8
Huge starfighter
Init +11; **Senses** Perception +6

Defense Ref 18 (flat-footed 11), Fort 24; +3 armor
hp 90; **DR** 10; **Threshold** 34

Speed fly 16 squares (max. velocity 1,250 km/h), fly 5 squares (starship scale)
Ranged laser cannons +5 (see below)
Fighting Space 3×3 or 1 square (starship scale); **Cover** total
Base Atk +2; **Grp** +26
Atk Options autofire (laser cannons)

Abilities Str 38, Dex 24, Con —, Int 16
Skills Initiative +11, Mechanics +6, Perception +6, Pilot +11
Crew 1 (skilled); **Passengers** none
Cargo 75 kg; **Consumables** 2 days; **Carried Craft** none
Availability Military; **Cost** 120,000 (50,000 used)

Laser cannons (pilot)
Atk +5 (+0 autofire), **Dmg** 6d10×2

Eta-2 Actis Interceptor

Designed to take advantage of Jedi reflexes and piloting skills, the nimble Eta-2 Actis Interceptor is the foremost starfighter used by the Jedi during the Clone Wars. Unlike many other starfighters, the Eta-2 does not boast any shields, relying on the pilot's ability to avoid incoming damage rather than protective shielding.

Eta-2 Actis Interceptor — CL 11
Huge starfighter
Init +18; **Senses** Perception +12

Defense Ref 19 (flat-footed 11), Fort 22; +3 armor
hp 70; **DR** 10; **Threshold** 32

Speed fly 16 squares (max. velocity 1,500 km/h), fly 6 squares (starship scale)
Ranged laser cannons +12 (see below) or
Ranged ion cannons +12 (see below)
Fighting Space 3×3 or 1 square (starship scale); **Cover** total (pilot), +5 (astromech droid)
Base Atk +10; **Grp** +32
Atk Options autofire (laser cannons, ion cannons)

Abilities Str 34, Dex 26, Con —, Int 14
Skills Initiative +18, Mechanics +12 (+13*), Perception +12, Pilot +18, Use Computer +12 (+13*)

Crew 1 plus astromech droid (ace); **Passengers** none
Cargo 60 kg; **Consumables** 2 days (1 week with booster ring); **Carried Craft** none
Hyperdrive ×1 (with booster ring), 10-jump memory (astromech droid)
Availability Military; **Cost** 140,000 used

If the ship has an astromech droid, use these skill modifiers instead.

Laser cannons (pilot)
Atk +12 (+7 autofire), **Dmg** 4d10×2

Ion cannons (pilot)
Atk +12 (+7 autofire), **Dmg** 4d10×2 ion

ARC-170 Starfighter

These rugged and durable attack fighters can handle independent raids as well as assaults on capital ships. Their powerful shields, robust armor, and tail gunner give them good odds even when surrounded by enemy droid fighters.

ARC-170 Starfighter — CL 12
Gargantuan starfighter
Init +6; **Senses** Perception +8

Defense Ref 16 (flat-footed 13), Fort 28; +8 armor
hp 150; **DR** 10; **SR** 25; **Threshold** 48

Speed fly 16 squares (max. velocity 1,050 km/h), fly 4 squares (starship scale)
Ranged heavy laser cannons +7 (see below) and
proton torpedoes +7 (see below) and
laser cannons +7 (see below)

Fighting Space 4×4 or 1 square (starship scale); **Cover** total (crew), +5 (astromech droid)
Base Atk +5; **Grp** +38
Atk Options autofire (medium laser cannons, laser cannons)
Abilities Str 46, Dex 16, Con —, Int 14
Skills Initiative +6, Mechanics +8 (+13*), Perception +8, Pilot +6, Use Computer +8 (+13*)
Crew 3 plus astromech droid (expert); **Passengers** none
Cargo 110 kg; **Consumables** 1 week; **Carried Craft** none
Payload 8 proton torpedoes
Hyperdrive ×1.5, 10-jump memory (astromech droid)
Availability Military; **Cost** 155,000 (70,000 used)
If the ship has an astromech droid, use these skill modifiers instead.

Heavy laser cannons (pilot)
  Atk +7 (+2 autofire), **Dmg** 6d10×2

Proton torpedoes (copilot)
  Atk +7, **Dmg** 9d10×2, 4-square splash

Laser cannons (gunner)
  Atk +7 (+2 autofire), **Dmg** 4d10×2

"Vulture" Droid Starfighter

"Crewed" by a droid brain and controlled by a remote processor, the droid starfighter is a completely mechanized vessel. Armed with blaster cannons and torpedo launchers, droid starfighters are fast and agile. Unlike conventional fighters, however, they can reconfigure themselves into "walk mode," allowing them to patrol on the ground as well as in space. Switching between flight mode and walk mode requires a standard action.

"Vulture" Droid Starfighter — CL 7
Huge starfighter/ground vehicle (walker)
Init +9; **Senses** Perception +8

Defense Ref 14 (flat-footed 11), Fort 22; +3 armor
hp 60; **DR** 10; **Threshold** 32
Immune droid traits (see page 187)

Speed 6 squares, fly 16 squares (max. velocity 1,180 km/h), fly 4 squares (starship scale)
Ranged laser cannons +7 (see below) or
Ranged concussion missiles +7 (see below)
Fighting Space 3×3 or 1 square (starship scale); **Cover** —
Base Atk +5; **Grp** +27
Atk Options autofire (laser cannons)

Abilities Str 34, Dex 16, Con —, Int 14
Skills Initiative +9, Perception +8, Pilot +9, Use Computer +8
Crew 0 (expert); **Passengers** none
Cargo none; **Consumables** 2 days; **Carried Craft** none
Payload 6 concussion missiles
Availability Restricted; **Cost** 19,000

Laser cannons
  Atk +7 (+2 autofire), **Dmg** 4d10×2

Concussion missiles
  Atk +7, **Dmg** 8d10×2, 4-square splash

Droid Tri-Fighter

Featuring a more advanced droid brain than the "Vulture" droid starfighters, the droid tri-fighter has proven itself a capable and versatile addition to the Separatist fleet. Its weapons can be fired at the same or separate targets, giving it the ability to capitalize on a target-rich environment.

Droid Tri-Fighter — CL 9
Huge starfighter
Init +10; **Senses** Perception +8

Defense Ref 16 (flat-footed 12), Fort 24; +4 armor
hp 100; **DR** 10; **Threshold** 34
Immune droid traits (see page 187)

Speed fly 16 squares (max. velocity 1,050 km/h), fly 4 squares (starship scale)
Ranged laser cannon +7 (see below) and
  3 light laser cannons +7 (see below) and
  concussion missiles +7 (see below)
Fighting Space 3×3 or 1 square (starship scale); **Cover** —
Base Atk +5; **Grp** +29
Atk Options autofire (medium laser cannon, light laser cannons)

Abilities Str 38, Dex 18, Con —, Int 14
Skills Initiative +10, Perception +8, Pilot +10, Use Computer +8
Crew 0 (expert); **Passengers** none
Cargo none; **Consumables** 2 days; **Carried Craft** none
Payload 6 concussion missiles
Availability Restricted; **Cost** 40,000

Laser cannon
  Atk +7 (+2 autofire), **Dmg** 4d10×2

Light laser cannons
  Atk +7 (+2 autofire), **Dmg** 3d10×2

Concussion missiles
  Atk +7, **Dmg** 8d10×2, 4-square splash

"You came in that thing? You're braver than I thought."
— Leia Organa

Space Transports

A dizzying variety of commercial transports ply the space lanes of the galaxy, carrying goods and passengers from system to system and world to world for a reasonable price. Most are controlled by independent operators or corporate interests, though governments employ their fair share of transports, sometimes for peaceful purposes . . . and far too often not. Space transports are nearly always armed, shielded, and hyperdrive-capable, allowing merchants to survive pirate attacks—and smugglers to avoid authorities—while traveling from place to place.

Corellian YT-1300 Transport

Perhaps the most adaptable light cargo transport in the galaxy, the YT-1300 design is built on a modular design to suit the needs of a wide variety of clients, many of whom aren't Human, let alone bipedal. The YT-1300 is an excellent all-purpose cargo transport, with powerful engines and a sturdy hull. The Corellian Engineering Corporation was quick to realize that it had a winner on its hands and made almost as many credits selling conversion kits as it did selling the transports themselves.

Corellian YT-1300 Transport   CL 6
Colossal space transport
Init −5; **Senses** Perception +5
Defense Ref 12 (flat-footed 12), Fort 26; +12 armor
hp 120; **DR** 15; **Threshold** 76

Speed fly 12 squares (max. velocity 800 km/h), fly 2 squares (starship scale)
Ranged laser cannon +2 (see below)
Fighting Space 12×12 or 1 square (starship scale); **Cover** total
Base Atk +0; **Grp** +36

Abilities Str 42, Dex 10, Con —, Int 14
Skills Initiative –5, Mechanics +5, Perception +5, Pilot –5, Use Computer +5

Crew 2 (normal); **Passengers** 6
Cargo 100 tons; **Consumables** 2 months; **Carried Craft** none
Hyperdrive ×2 (backup ×12), nav computer
Availability Licensed; **Cost** 100,000 (25,000 used)

Laser cannon (gunner)
   Atk +2, **Dmg** 4d10×2

CAPITAL SHIPS

Capital ships are the backbone of any star fleet, more than compensating for their lack of speed and maneuverability with their weapons, armor, and powerful shields. The largest carry hangars full of starfighters to supplement their own impressive banks of blasters and ion cannons, gravity-well projectors to stop fleeing opponents from entering hyperspace, or thousands of ground troops and their support vehicles. Capital ship commanders take great pride in knowing that they can make a difference just by bringing their guns to bear, let alone firing them.

Corellian Corvette

The Corellian corvette is the logical step up from the YT-1300 transport—a larger configurable space vessel for larger jobs. The corvette can serve as a cargo transport, a passenger liner, a troop ship, or an escort. Corvettes frequently find their way into civilian use, and a significant number fall into the hands of pirates.

Corellian Corvette   CL 16
Colossal (frigate) capital ship
Init +0; **Senses** Perception +6

Defense Ref 16 (flat-footed 12), Fort 38; +12 armor
hp 1,200; **DR** 15; **SR** 100; **Threshold** 138

Speed fly 3 squares (starship scale)
Ranged 3 turbolaser batteries +12* (see below)
Fighting Space 1 square (starship scale); **Cover** total
Base Atk +2; **Grp** +50

Abilities Str 66, Dex 18, Con —, Int 18
Skills Initiative +0, Mechanics +10, Perception +6, Pilot +0, Use Computer +10

Crew 30 to 165 (skilled); **Passengers** 600
Cargo 3,000 tons; **Consumables** 1 year; **Carried Craft** none
Hyperdrive ×2, nav computer (+3)
Availability Licensed; **Cost** 3.5 million (1.5 million used)
* Apply a –20 penalty on attacks against targets smaller than Colossal size.

Turbolaser battery (4 gunners)
   Atk +12 (–8 against targets smaller than Colossal), **Dmg** 5d10×5

Imperial I-class Star Destroyer

An indelible symbol of the Empire's military might, the Star Destroyer is a powerful incentive for troublesome worlds to submit to the will of the Emperor. Fast, tough, and armed to the teeth, an Imperial I-class Star Destroyer can reduce a fleet of lesser ships to so much floating debris.

Imperial I-class Star Destroyer   CL 20
Colossal (cruiser) capital ship
Init –2; **Senses** Perception +6

Defense Ref 18 (flat-footed 16), Fort 56; +16 armor
hp 2,100; **DR** 20; **SR** 150; **Threshold** 256

Speed fly 3 squares (starship scale)
Ranged 5 turbolaser batteries +17* (see below) and
   5 ion cannon batteries +17* (see below) and
   10 point-defense laser batteries +13 (see below) and
   10 tractor beams +7* (see below)
Fighting Space 2×2 (starship scale); **Cover** total
Base Atk +2; **Grp** +68

Abilities Str 102, Dex 14, Con —, Int 20
Skills Initiative –2, Mechanics +6, Perception +6, Pilot –2, Use Computer +6

Crew 37,085 (skilled); **Passengers** 9,700 (troops)
Cargo 36,000 tons; **Consumables** 6 years; **Carried Craft** 72 TIE fighters (any variant), 8 Lambda-class shuttles, 20 AT-ATs, 30 AT-STs, various support vehicles
Hyperdrive ×2 (backup ×8), nav computer
Availability Military; **Cost** not available for sale
* Apply a –20 penalty on attacks against targets smaller than Colossal size.

Turbolaser battery (6 gunners)
   Atk +17 (–3 against targets smaller than Colossal), **Dmg** 5d10×5
Ion cannon battery (6 gunners)
   Atk +17 (–3 against targets smaller than Colossal), **Dmg** 3d10×5 ion
Point-defense laser battery (4 gunners)
   Atk +13, **Dmg** 2d10×2
Tractor beam (2 gunners)
   Atk +7 (–13 against targets smaller than Colossal), **Dmg** — (grapple +68)

Chapter XI
Droids

A droid is a kind of intelligent robot, a mechanical automaton electronically programmed to act, think, and behave in a certain way.

Droids facilitate various tasks that organic beings find tedious, difficult, or hazardous. They are typically fashioned in the likeness of their creators or in a utilitarian design that stresses function. Their usefulness makes them a common sight on nearly every inhabited world in the galaxy. They provide assistance, advice, and sometimes even friendship to trillions of sentient beings on a daily basis.

A Droid's Life

Droids are usually property, bought and sold like any other piece of equipment. Although some droid owners come to think of their droids as friends, the fact remains that droids are programmed to serve whoever is designated as their master. To the vast majority of droids, the concept of droid independence is unthinkable. Without someone to command them, what would they do?

Even so, ownership and control are two very different things. Droids must do what they are commanded to do to the best of their ability, but their programming dictates how they accomplish their orders. Ordered to find a replacement part for an X-wing, a droid might commence a systematic search of the repair bay, then the docking facility, then the neighborhood, then the countryside, and so on—all the while thinking its actions are perfectly logical. Droids often need very specific instructions to do what their masters command, in a manner meeting their master's expectations.

Occasionally, events conspire to lead a droid to independence. These so-called "self-owned" droids are few, but not as rare as many believe. One might hear stories of droids that escape their masters after years of abuse, or of an entire line of droids that manifest violent personalities as the result of a programming glitch. However, independent droids are rarely haywire, rampaging killers. Independent droids often enter into partnerships with organic beings, particularly on worlds where a lone droid without a master draws a lot of unwanted attention. Independent droids sometimes even seek each other out, hoping to find strength and security in numbers. Some independent droids are thrust into the unlikely role of hero, helping to defend the galaxy from the depredations of evil as personified by the likes of the Empire and the Yuuzhan Vong.

Creating a Droid Hero

If you want to play a droid as a hero, you can either play an existing droid from this chapter or create your own unique droid hero. Droid heroes are assumed either to be "self-owned" or to be owned by another player character (with the approval of both the Gamemaster and the player in question). Even if owned by another member of the party, the Gamemaster should ensure that the owner does not abuse his authority by giving unreasonable or unwanted orders to the other player's droid character. A droid player character should be treated the same as any other player character, and in most cases it is best to give suggestions or advice instead of actual orders. (In fact, most droid heroes have a heuristic processor so that they can creatively interpret orders and thus justify acting as they wish.)

When you decide to play a droid hero, you'll have to pick out a few details about what type of droid your character will be. This is the equivalent of picking a species for a non-droid character.

Option 1: Playing a Custom Droid

You can play a droid of your own design. The only choices you have to make are choosing your degree, size, and accessories, and assigning your ability scores. Once you have taken note of these details on your character sheet, continue with character generation normally.

Determining Ability Scores

Droid characters determine their ability scores the same way non-droid characters do (see Chapter 1: Abilities). However, droids do not have Constitution scores because they are not actually living beings; they only need scores for their five remaining abilities. You can determine your ability scores in one of three ways:

Rolling: Roll 4d6 five times, discarding the lowest die each time. Add up the remaining three dice and assign the result to any one of your five abilities.

Planned Generation: All of your ability scores start at 8, and you have 21 points to spend to increase them (see Planned Generation, page 18).

Standard Score Package: The standard score package for droid heroes is 15, 14, 13, 12, and 10. Assign these five scores to your five abilities as you see fit.

Degree

Droids are classified by degree, reflecting the types of tasks they typically perform. Generally, 1st-degree droids are medical and analytical droids, 2nd-degree droids are mechanical and technical droids, 3rd-degree droids are protocol and domestic droids, 4th-degree droids are security and battle droids, and 5th-degree droids are labor and utility droids. A droid's function does not have to match its degree, but this is uncommon.

Pick a degree (1st, 2nd, 3rd, 4th, or 5th) for your droid. This determines your ability score modifiers, as shown in Table 11-1: Droid Degrees. For example, a 3rd-degree protocol droid increases its Wisdom and Charisma scores by 2 and reduces its Strength score by 2.

Table 11-1: Droid Degrees

DEGREE	ABILITY MODIFIERS	TYPICAL ROLES
1st	+2 Int, +2 Wis, -2 Str	medical, scientific
2nd	+2 Int, -2 Cha	astromech, technical
3rd	+2 Wis, +2 Cha, -2 Str	protocol, service
4th	+2 Dex, -2 Int, -2 Cha	combat, security
5th	+4 Str, -4 Int, -4 Cha	labor, utility

Size

You can choose to play a Medium or Small droid. Droids of other sizes exist, but they are controlled by the GM.

A droid's size determines its ability modifiers, its size bonus to Reflex Defense, its size bonus on Stealth checks, adjustments to hit points and damage threshold, its carrying capacity (see Encumbrance, page 140), and its cost factor (see below), as shown in Table 11-2: Droid Sizes.

Medium: Player character droids of Medium size have no special modifiers because of their size. They have a walking locomotion system (see page 188) and a speed of 6 squares.

Small: Player character droids of Small size apply the following ability score modifiers: +2 Dexterity, -2 Strength. They have a tracked locomotion system (see page 188) and a speed of 4 squares. Small droids gain a +1 size bonus to their Reflex Defense and a +5 size bonus on Stealth checks. However, their lifting and carrying limits are three-quarters of those of Medium characters.

Cost Factor: A droid's cost factor is used to calculate the cost of the droid and some droid systems. Particularly large droids can be very expensive, but particularly small droids are not any cheaper due to the expenses associated with miniaturization.

Class and Level

You are 1st level in one heroic class (noble, scoundrel, scout, or soldier) of your choice. You cannot choose the Jedi class.

Systems and Accessories

You have a heuristic processor (see page 190) and two arm appendages (see page 189).

Your may spend up to 1,000 credits on additional locomotion systems (see page 188), appendages (see page 189), and accessories (see page 193) as you see fit. You do not get to keep any left over credits, but you still gain the appropriate starting credits according to your class (see Chapter 3: Heroic Classes).

Droid Traits

All droids characters have certain traits in common as discussed in Droid Traits below.

OPTION 2: PLAYING A STANDARD DROID MODEL

If you wish to forego creating your own custom droid, you can always play one of the stock models found later in the chapter. If you use this option, you do not roll for ability scores; instead, you automatically have the ability scores listed for the selected model of droid. The droid you select must meet the following criteria, and you may modify the stock model as noted here.

Size: You can only be Small or Medium size.

Processor: You cannot have a remote processor, so you must install a basic processor or heuristic processor if the selected model of droid does not normally include one (see Processors, page 190).

Class and Level: The droid you select can have no more than three levels in the nonheroic class or one level in any heroic class. If the droid you select has only one or two levels in the nonheroic class, you may choose to add one level in a heroic class of your choice; this adds 1,500 credits to your droid's final cost.

You begin play with the minimum number of experience points necessary for your character level. For example, a 2nd-level nonheroic/1st-level scoundrel would begin play with 3,000 XP.

Final Cost: The final cost of your droid, including any necessary adjustments for a processor or adding a level in a heroic class, cannot exceed 5,000 credits. You may add accessories or replace systems as you see fit as long as your final cost remains within this limit. You do not get to keep any unspent credits, but you still gain the appropriate starting credits according to your class (see Chapter 3: Heroic Classes).

Traits: All droids have certain traits in common (see Droid Traits, below).

Once you have made all necessary adjustments and noted these details on your character sheet, continue with character generation normally.

DROID TRAITS

Droids share the following basic traits:

Abilities: Droids are nonliving entities, so they do not have Constitution scores. Droids can increase any two of their five remaining ability scores by +1 each at 4th level and every four levels thereafter, just like any other character. These increases represent improved heuristics and algorithms that the droid has developed from experience as well as upgrades to its components undertaken as a part of routine maintenance. Droid ability modifiers are determined by their degree and size (see Degree and Size, above). A droid can never have an ability score less than 1, regardless of modifications.

Behavioral Inhibitors: Droids (except 4th-degree droids) cannot intentionally harm a sentient living being or knowingly allow a sentient living being to be harmed. Furthermore, all droids must follow orders given to them by their rightful owners, as long as those orders don't require the droid to harm a sentient living being. Droids with heuristic processors can sometimes violate these restrictions by creatively interpreting their behavioral inhibitions (see Processors, page 190).

Ion Damage Vulnerability: As electronic constructs, droids are vulnerable to damage from ion weapons (see Ion Weapons, page 159). Generally, ion weapons have the same effect on droids that stun weapons have on living beings.

Maintenance: Droids do not sleep, eat, or breathe. However, they do need to enter shutdown mode and recharge for 1 hour after 100 hours of operation. If a droid fails to do so, it must make an Endurance check each

TABLE 11-2: DROID SIZES

DROID SIZE	ABILITY MODIFIERS	SIZE MODIFIER TO REF DEFENSE	SIZE MODIFIER TO STEALTH	EXTRA HIT POINTS	SIZE BONUS TO DMG THRESHOLD	CARRYING CAPACITY	COST FACTOR
Colossal	+32 Str, −4 Dex	−10	−20	+100	+50	×20	×20
Gargantuan	+24 Str, −4 Dex	−5	−15	+50	+20	×10	×10
Huge	+16 Str, −4 Dex	−2	−10	+20	+10	×5	×5
Large	+8 Str, −2 Dex	−1	−5	+10	+5	×2	×2
Medium	None	+0	+0	—	—	×1	×1
Small	−2 Str, +2 Dex	+1	+5	—	—	×0.75	×2
Tiny	−4 Str, +4 Dex	+2	+10	—	—	×0.5	×5
Diminutive	−6 Str, +6 Dex	+5	+15	—	—	×0.25	×10
Fine	−8 Str, +8 Dex	+10	+20	—	—	×0.01	×20

hour (DC 10, +1 per additional hour after the first) or move −1 persistent step along the condition track (see Conditions, page 148). This persistent condition can only be removed by the droid recharging for 1 hour.

Memory: A droid's trained skills, feats, and talents can be reassigned with the Use Computer skill. A droid hero can use its own Use Computer skill to perform this reprogramming, but it takes a −5 penalty on its skill check. If a droid is ever subjected to a complete memory wipe, it becomes a basic model of its type, losing any levels and abilities gained (see Processors, below).

Nonliving: A droid is immune to poison, disease, radiation, noncorrosive atmospheric hazards, vacuum, mind-affecting effects, stunning effects, and any other effect that works only on living targets. Droids have no connection to the Force and can't gain the Force Sensitivity feat or learn Force powers. Droids do not have a Constitution score, so they don't get bonus hit points for having a high Constitution, and they apply their Strength modifier to their Fortitude Defense.

Unlike living beings, droids don't "die," but they can be disabled or destroyed. If a droid is reduced to 0 hit points, it is disabled and cannot be reactivated until it is repaired so that has at least 1 hit point. If the attack that reduced the droid to 0 hit points also exceeds the droid's damage threshold, the droid is destroyed instead. A destroyed droid cannot be repaired or salvaged.

Repair: Droids can regain lost hit points only through the use of the Mechanics skill (see page 68). A droid can use this skill to repair itself, but it takes a −5 penalty on its skill check.

Shut Down: A droid that is shut down can take no actions and is effectively unconscious. Shutting down a willing droid is a standard action. Shutting down an unwilling droid is more difficult, requiring that you to grab the droid (see Grab, page 152) and then make a Mechanics check (DC = droid's Will Defense) as a standard action while it's grabbed. You cannot shut down an unwilling droid with locked access unless it is disabled or otherwise helpless (see Locked Access, page 195).

Skills: Droids normally cannot use any skill untrained except for Acrobatics, Climb, Jump, and Perception. A droid with a heuristic processor ignores this limitation (see Processors, page 190).

Systems: Droids can have many of their characteristics changed by installing or replacing existing systems (see Modifying Droids, page 197).

Automatic Languages: Binary plus one language chosen by the designer (usually Basic).

Droid Systems

Unlike characters and creatures, droids are essentially collections of different equipment called systems. A droid's systems can be upgraded, replaced, and modified many times throughout a droid's operational lifetime. A droid system falls into one of four categories: locomotion, processor, appendage, or accessory.

Locomotion

All droids begin with a base movement speed determined by locomotion system (see Table 11-3: Droid Locomotion). Droids can have more than one locomotion system. Add 500 × the droid's cost factor for the second locomotion system, 1,000 × the droid's cost factor for the third, 2,000 × the droid's cost factor for the fourth, and 5,000 × the droid's cost factor for the fifth.

Walking Droids: Walking droids are the most versatile droids, having legs and feet that let them travel like bipeds, quadrupeds, and other similar creatures. The most common chassis for walking droids is the "humanoid" form (two arms, two legs, and a head). They suffer the usual penalties when moving through difficult terrain (See Difficult Terrain, page 159).

Wheeled Droids: Wheeled droids use one or more powered wheels to move and are generally designed to traverse smooth surfaces. Wheeled droids can't use the Climb skill, and the penalties of moving through difficult terrain are doubled.

Tracked Droids: Tracked droids are an improvement on the wheeled droid, having ridged treads that give them more traction. Tracked droids ignore the penalties of difficult terrain, but they take a −5 penalty on all Climb checks.

Hovering Droids: Hovering droids use repulsorlift technology to float slowly above the ground (within 3 meters). They ignore the penalties of difficult terrain.

Table 11-3: Droid Locomotion

LOCOMOTION	UP TO SMALL	MEDIUM	LARGE OR BIGGER	COST
Walking	4 squares	6 squares	8 squares	10 × cost factor × (speed) squared
Wheeled	6 squares	8 squares	10 squares	5 × cost factor × (speed) squared
Tracked	4 squares	6 squares	8 squares	20 × cost factor × (speed) squared
Hovering	6 squares	6 squares	6 squares	100 × cost factor × (speed) squared
Flying	9 squares	12 squares	12 squares	200 × cost factor × (speed) squared

(SPEED (BY DROID SIZE))

Flying Droids: Flying droids use engines of some kind to travel more or less wherever they please. They are not hampered by any type of terrain, but tend to be the most expensive.

Stationary Droids: Stationary droids do not have a locomotion system and cannot move from a fixed location.

Restricted Locomotion System
The cost of a droid's locomotion system can be reduced by placing limitations on its use. The two types of restrictions are exclusive and limited. A restricted locomotion system costs only one-tenth the normal cost.

Exclusive Locomotion System: The droid must spend a move action to engage or disengage this locomotion system. While the system is engaged, the droid can only use the move and run actions.

Limited Locomotion System: The droid can only use this locomotion system for a limited time. After using this locomotion system for 1 round, the droid must make an Endurance check (DC 10, +1 per check after the first) or it cannot use that locomotion system again for 1 minute (10 rounds).

Climbing Claws
Claws designed to grip a surface can be added to any droid with a walking locomotion system. Climbing claws grant the droid a climb speed equal to one-half its walking speed. In addition, a droid equipped with climbing claws may reroll a failed Climb check (keeping the better result) and can take 10 on Climb checks even when rushed or threatened. Climbing claws double the cost of a walking locomotion system.

Extra Legs
Walking droids are usually bipedal, but a walking droid can be built with three or more legs (usually four) to grant the droid extra stability and carrying capacity. This doubles the cost of the walking locomotion system, but the droid's carrying capacity is 50% higher than that of a bipedal droid of the same Strength. In addition, the droid gains a +5 stability bonus on checks to resist attempts to knock it prone.

Jump Servos
Repulsorlift-assisted jump servos can be added to any droid with a walking locomotion system. Jump servos grant the droid the ability to treat all jumps as running jumps, even without the normal running start (see the Jump skill, page 68). In addition, the droid may reroll a failed Jump check (keeping the better result) and take 10 on Jump checks even when rushed or threatened. Jump servos double the cost of a walking locomotion system.

Magnetic Feet
Electromagnetic grippers enable a droid to cling to a ship's hull, even when the ship is moving at high speed. Only droids with walking, wheeled, or tracked locomotion can have magnetic feet.

APPENDAGES
The types of appendages a droid has determines how well it is able to touch, hold, lift, carry, push, pull, or place objects. A limb that isn't used for locomotion or balance has one of the following types of appendages: probe, instrument, tool, claw, or hand.

Droids can use their appendages to make unarmed attacks. The damage dealt by an unarmed attack depends on the droid's size and the type of appendage. Table 11-4: Droid Appendages and Damage lists the base unarmed damage; remember to apply the droid's Strength modifier to this

Table 11-4: Droid Appendages and Damage

DROID SIZE	PROBE	INSTRUMENT	TOOL	CLAW	HAND
Fine	–	–	–	–	–
Diminutive	–	–	–	1	–
Tiny	–	–	1	1d2	1
Small	–	1	1d2	1d3	1d2
Medium	1	1d2	1d3	1d4	1d3
Large	1d2	1d3	1d4	1d6	1d4
Huge	1d3	1d4	1d6	1d8	1d6
Gargantuan	1d4	1d6	1d8	2d6	1d8
Colossal	1d6	1d8	2d6	2d8	2d6

base damage. A droid can have any number of appendages, but this does not increase the number of actions or attacks the droid can make in a round.

Probe: Few droids have no actual manipulators. The bare minimum is a probe that can push or pull objects.

Instrument: Instruments are a step up from simple probes. They might be designed to accomplish specific tasks. For example, a droid with a hypodermic syringe as its sole appendage can use the syringe for its intended purpose, but otherwise can only push objects with it. A few instruments are actually designed to clamp, and can thus hold objects, but they are generally delicate. A droid using an instrument of this nature has a carrying capacity (see Encumbrance, page 140) as if its Strength score were one-quarter of its actual value.

Tool: Tool appendages are somewhat sturdier than instruments. A droid must make a DC 15 Dexterity check to lift, carry, or drag objects for which its tools were not designed. The GM might rule that particularly delicate objects have a higher DC. If the check fails, the droid drops the object.

Weapons mounted on a droid are considered tool appendages unless otherwise noted. A tool mount does not include the cost of the tool or weapon mounted on it.

Claw: Claws are an intermediate step between tools and hands. They are useful for grabbing onto objects to be moved, but aren't very good for tasks that require fine manipulation. While a droid could easily carry a blaster in its claw, it would have difficulty firing it, for example. A droid using a claw to perform a task that normally requires a true hand must make a DC 15 Dexterity check to succeed at the task. If the check fails, the droid drops the object it is attempting to manipulate.

Hand: A droid is considered to have a true hand if its gripping appendage includes at least three digits, one of which is opposable. Factory-model 3PO Series protocol droids and Baktoid Combat Automata battle droids come equipped with hands.

Telescopic Appendage

The droid has an appendage that reaches farther from its body than normal. A telescopic appendage has twice the normal reach for the droid's size. For example, a Medium droid with a telescopic appendage has a reach of 2 squares.

Stabilized Mount

For five times the listed cost and weight, a tool appendage can be stabilized so that it can hold a larger weapon. This allows the droid to use that weapon as if was wielded in two hands.

Processors

A droid can't perform any functions without its processor (also known as a droid brain), which contains all the basic information the droid needs to move its appendages, travel from place to place, behave in a certain way, and so on. A droid's Intelligence score reflects the quality of its processor. Low-intelligence droids tend to specialize in single tasks that require no deductive capability. High-intelligence droids are considerably more versatile—and more expensive.

Basic Processor: Basic processors are not designed for creative thought and problem solving, and as such most droids interpret instructions and behavioral inhibitions very literally. Furthermore, basic processors are very limited in that the droid cannot perform any task for which it was not programmed. For example, a droid that is not trained in the Deception skill cannot lie or otherwise convey false or unknown information. A droid with a basic processor cannot use any skill untrained except for Acrobatics, Climb, Jump, and Perception. Similarly, a basic processor does not allow a droid to use any weapon with which it is not proficient, and a droid's behavioral inhibitors may prevent it from harming sentient living beings altogether (see Behavioral Inhibitors, below).

Every droid comes with a basic processor, at the very least.

Heuristic Processor: This type of processor allows a droid to learn by doing, usually without instruction. The droid is able to reason through several potential solutions to tasks and formulate the best approach. Because of this, a droid with a heuristic processor may use skills untrained, just like any other character. Similarly, the droid can wield a weapon even if it is not proficient in its use (but still takes the normal –5 penalty on attack rolls).

In addition, a droid with a heuristic processor can creatively interpret its instructions, allowing it to complete tasks in a manner that it deems appropriate. A heuristic processor allows a droid to work around its behavioral inhibitors as long as it can justify a given action. For example, a noncombat droid with a heuristic processor can attack and even harm sentient living being as long as it believes that doing so will ultimately save more sentient living beings from harm.

Over time, a droid equipped with a heuristic processor develops a unique personality based on experience. Because of this, memory wipes and restraining bolts are commonly used to ensure that a heuristic processor doesn't allow a droid to stray too far from its intended purpose. Still, some progressive masters actually encourage their droids to break their programming, trusting the droid's judgment to make independent decisions without taking advantage of the situation.

Remote Processor: The droid's processor isn't located in the droid; instead, the droid is actually a drone for a remote processor. The processor is equipped with a transmitter that allows a droid equipped with the appropriate remote receiver to operate as far away as 5 km (for the least expensive model) to as much as 5,000 km (for the most expensive model).

The advantage of a remote processor is that it makes the droid much less expensive because it only needs a receiver instead of a local control system. The drawback is that the droid doesn't react as quickly as a droid with an internal processor, so it takes a –2 penalty to its Dexterity.

Remote Receiver: This unit allows a droid to receive instructions from a remote processor. Only droids without internal processors (such as Baktoid Combat Automata battle droids) can be fitted with remote receivers. A remote receiver can only be connected to one remote processor at a time. Changing the connection to a different remote processor requires a DC 20 Mechanics check and a tool kit.

Backup Processor: A droid with a remote receiver can also have a backup processor that allows the droid to function even if it loses contact with its remote processor. The droid will continue executing its last received orders until contact is reestablished.

Synchronized Fire Circuits: A droid with a remote receiver can have synchronized fire circuits that better coordinate its actions with other droids. When successfully using the aid another action to assist another droid connected to the same remote processor, a droid with synchronized fire circuits grants an additional +2 bonus to the other droid's check or roll.

Behavioral Inhibitors

Even without a restraining bolt or periodic memory wipes, most droids operate according to a rigid set of guidelines. A droid's core programming—the part of its memory that can't be wiped—provides it with strict instructions on how to react to common circumstances, most of which revolve around obedience, safety, ethics, and morality. These instructions are the droid's behavioral inhibitors.

The most common restriction coded into a droid's memory is the notion that it can't harm a sentient living being or, through inaction, allow a sentient living being to come to harm. (Fourth-degree droids do not have this restriction.) Droids are under similar strictures not to allow themselves to be harmed unless specifically ordered to do so. Of course, droids are also hardwired to obey the commands of their designated masters. When a master's orders conflict with the droid's behavioral inhibitors, the droid is required to inform its master immediately.

Restraining Bolt: A restraining bolt turns off a droid's motor impulse without actually shutting down the droid. The restraining bolt is activated with a handheld device called a droid caller (see below). Restraining bolts must be secured to specific locations on droids. Attaching or removing a restraining bolt is a full-round action and requires a DC 10 Mechanics check. A droid fitted with a restraining bolt can't upgrade or improve its skills (see Reprogramming, below).

A droid with a heuristic processor can attempt to remove its own restraining bolt as a standard action with a successful DC 20 Charisma check followed by a successful DC 15 Mechanics check. A droid that fails the Charisma check can't attempt to remove the restraining bolt again until 24 hours pass.

Droid Caller: The droid caller is a handheld transmitter weighing 0.2 kg. It transmits a signal to any droid equipped with a restraining bolt. The droid caller overrides a droid's motor function and impels it toward the caller for as long as the device is activated.

BINARY

Nearly all droids are programmed to understand a binary computer language used by most computers and intelligent machines. The simple version of this is a language skill called Binary. With it, droids can communicate with computers and each other. Binary allows a computer or droid to communicate mathematical or technical information in great detail at a very high rate (approximately 100 times as fast as normal speech), but it has great difficulty expressing nontechnical topics such as emotion, art, philosophy, or the Force. For example, as a free action, a droid could use Binary to describe the exact location and physical description of all objects and characters that the droid detects in a 10-square-by-10-square area, but the droid would be unable to express the nuance of a conversation or the emotion conveyed by body language.

Obviously, some droids can understand additional languages as well—most droids in the galaxy are programmed with Basic, even if they can't actually articulate the language. Some living beings learn to interpret the binary language of droids, even if they can't themselves speak an approximation of it. A living being who understands Binary cannot understand the same volume of information as another droid or computer, so the speaking droid must voluntarily slow its speech to normal rates (that is, the same as Basic or any other language) so that the living being can understand it.

A droid with a heuristic processor fitted with a restraining bolt can resist the droid caller with a successful DC 20 Charisma check. If successful, that droid can't be affected by that specific droid caller for 24 hours.

Reprogramming

A basic model droid comes with factory-preset skills and a certain set of trained skills, feats, and sometimes talents. These factory-presets are embedded in the droid's core programming and cannot be altered, but many droids have one or more trained skills left unassigned so that they can easily be programmed for their specific duties. Unassigned skills as well as feats and talents gained through level advancement can be altered through reprogramming.

Reprogramming a droid requires a Use Computer check (DC = droid's Will Defense) and 30 minutes of uninterrupted work. Reprogramming feats and talents is more difficult, so you take a −5 penalty on your Use Computer check. Furthermore, feats and talents can only be reprogrammed if they are neither a requirement for any of the droid's prestige classes nor a prerequisite for any feat or talent the droid retains. As always, a droid must meet all prerequisites for any replacement feats or talents. Reprogramming requires that the droid be shut down for the duration of the procedure (but see "Droid Self-Reprogramming," below).

To reprogram a skill, the programmer must be trained in that skill or purchase a skill package (100 credits). To reprogram a feat or talent, the programmer must either have that feat or talent or purchase a feat or talent package (1,000 credits).

If the droid's owner is unable to do the reprogramming himself, he can hire a professional programmer to do the task for him. The standard cost of hiring a programmer is (droid's Will Defense squared) × 10 credits for a skill, or 10 times this amount for a feat or talent. This cost includes any necessary skill, feat, or talent packages.

Droid Self-Reprogramming: A droid trained in the Use Computer skill may attempt to reprogram itself. However, the droid must have the appropriate skill, feat, or talent package to do so, and it takes a −5 penalty on its Use Computer skill check. A droid attempting to self-reprogram does not have to be shut down, but it is helpless and unable to take any actions until the attempt is completed.

Memory Wipes

Although intelligent droids consider it frightful and ghoulish and heroic droids regard it as a fate worse than death, the memory wipe is a fact of existence for most droids. Its primary purpose is to eradicate personality quirks that distinguish an independent droid.

Wiping a droid's memory requires a successful Use Computer check against the droid's Will Defense. The droid must be shut down to perform the memory wipe.

> "WE SEEM TO BE MADE TO SUFFER. IT'S OUR LOT IN LIFE."
> – C-3PO

A memory wipe erases one class level per minute. A complete memory wipe reduces a droid to a basic model with no personality quirks and no class abilities. For example, a 3PO Series protocol droid that had been a 1st-level nonheroic/4th-level scoundrel becomes a 1st-level nonheroic basic model after a 4-minute memory wipe, losing its scoundrel levels and all the corresponding benefits.

Downloading and Restoring Memory

Unlike organic beings, droids have a form of mechanical immortality: If a droid's programming is saved to a computer system, and a new chassis and droid brain can be bought or found, others can attempt to load its memory into the new droid and reactivate the droid.

A successful Use Computer check is required to transfer a droid's programming into a new chassis. The DC for the Use Computer check depends on the type of new chassis being used:

Same model	DC 20
Different model, same degree	DC 25
Different model, different degree	DC 35

Each time the transfer is attempted, the droid must make a DC 15 Intelligence check. A failed check indicates that the droid's memory suffers corruption: a permanent reduction of 1d6 Intelligence points. The corrupted programming can't be repaired; if the droid's Intelligence modifier decreases because of corruption, the droid's trained skills must be reduced accordingly. The droid also loses access to feats that have an Intelligence prerequisite higher than the droid's new Intelligence score.

A droid successfully transferred into another droid of the same model resumes functioning as it was before the transfer, retaining all ability scores, class levels, skills, feats, and talents.

A droid successfully transferred into a different model adopts the Strength and Dexterity of the new model but keeps its previous Intelligence, Wisdom, and Charisma scores. The droid retains its trained skills, although skill modifiers based on Strength and Dexterity might need adjusting. Finally, the droid loses one class level (including all associated talents and feats) as it has to reprogram and adapt its memory and sensory inputs for the new chassis.

Accessories

Any miscellaneous system that does not fall under one of the above categories can be considered an accessory. Accessories add functions or improve existing systems on a droid, making them more capable and efficient. Table 11-5: Droid Accessories summarizes the various accessories described in this chapter.

Cost and Weight: Sometimes a droid accessory has a flat cost or weight. Often the cost and/or weight is determined by multiplying a base number by the droid's cost factor, which is determined by the droid's size (see Table 11-2: Droid Sizes, page 187).

Availability: Some droid accessories have limited availability or are strictly regulated, as described in Restricted Items (see page 118).

Armor

Droids can be equipped with built-in armor that provides an armor bonus to Reflex Defense. Bipedal droids with two hand appendages can also wear armor designed for humanoid creatures; however, the armor bonus granted by built-in droid armor does not stack with the armor bonus provided by worn armor. Table 11-6: Droid Armor summarizes the different types of built-in droid armor available.

Speed: A droid with built-in light, medium, or heavy armor takes no penalty to its speed.

Armor Check Penalty: A droid with built-in armor takes an armor check penalty on attack rolls as well as skill checks made using the following skills: Acrobatics, Climb, Endurance, Initiative, Jump, Stealth, and Swim. The type of armor worn determines the size of the penalty: light, -2; medium, -5; heavy, -10. A droid with the appropriate Armor Proficiency feat (see page 82) negates these penalties.

Maximum Dexterity Bonus: Built-in droid armor has a maximum Dexterity bonus, just like normal armor (See Armor, page 131).

Availability: Some armor has limited availability.

Rare: This armor is rarely for sale on the open market. The price of the armor on the black market is usually double the listed cost.

Licensed, Restricted, Military, or Illegal: Ownership of the armor is limited or strictly regulated, as described in Restricted Items (see page 131).

Running in Heavy Armor: When running in heavy armor, a droid can only move up to three times its speed (instead of four times).

Communications

All droids are capable of emitting the sounds necessary to speak Binary, a language used by droids and computers to quickly transmit large amounts of information (see Binary sidebar, page 191).

Vocabulator: The droid is equipped with a speaker that enables it to emulate speech, rather than simply spout machine code. This device is standard if the droid has ability to speak any language other than Binary.

Comlink: The droid is equipped with an integrated comlink system. It is otherwise identical to the standard comlink (see page 134).

Diagnostics Package

Some droids are equipped to perform diagnostics, either as an aid to a technician or as a general safety feature. The diagnostic package gives a droid a +2 equipment bonus on Mechanics checks to diagnose problems.

Hardened Systems

Droids of Large or greater size can be designed to have internal armor and redundant systems that enable it to continue functioning despite heavy damage. This is represented by a multiplier that increases the bonus hit points and damage threshold based on the droid's size. For example, a Large droid with hardened systems ×3 would have +30 hit points and a +15 bonus to its damage threshold instead of the usual +10 hit points and +5 bonus to its damage threshold.

Internal Storage

The droid has a certain amount of open space in its chassis, allowing for the addition of new internal components or compartments for carried items. Droids of Tiny size or smaller cannot have internal storage.

For each 50 credits spent, the droid can carry 1 kg of material or equipment in internal storage. A droid's size determines the maximum weight of items stored in internal storage, as noted below:

DROID SIZE	MAXIMUM WEIGHT LIMIT
Small	5 kg
Medium	10 kg
Large	20 kg
Huge	50 kg
Gargantuan	500 kg
Colossal	5,000 kg

Table 11-5: Droid Accessories

EQUIPMENT	COST	WEIGHT	AVAILABILITY
Appendage			
Claw	20 × cost factor	(5 × cost factor) kg	—
Hand	50 × cost factor	(5 × cost factor) kg	—
Instrument	5 × cost factor	(1 × cost factor) kg	—
Probe	2 × cost factor	(0.5 × cost factor) kg	—
Tool	10 × cost factor	(2 × cost factor) kg	—
Climbing claws	appendage cost × 2	—	—
Jump servos	appendage cost × 2	(2 × cost factor) kg	—
Magnetic feet	appendage cost × 2	—	—
Telescopic appendage	appendage cost × 2	(normal weight × 2) kg	—
Armor	See Table 11-6	See Table 11-6	See Table 11-6
Communications			
Comlink, internal	250	0.1 kg	—
Vocabulator	50	0.5 kg	—
Diagnostics package	250	4 kg	—
Droid caller	10	0.2 kg	—
Hardened systems			
Hardened system ×2	1,000 × cost factor	(100 × cost factor) kg	Military
Hardened system ×3	2,500 × cost factor	(250 × cost factor) kg	Military
Hardened system ×4	4,000 × cost factor	(400 × cost factor) kg	Military
Hardened system ×5	6,250 × cost factor	(650 × cost factor) kg	Military
Internal storage			
Compartment space (per kilogram)	50	—	—
Spring-loaded mechanism	150	3 kg	—
Locked access	50	—	Licensed

Spring-Loaded Mechanism: This device allows a Small, Medium, or Large droid to launch an item held in an internal storage compartment up to 4 squares as a standard action. The item can weight no more than 4 kg, and the droid makes a ranged attack against Reflex Defense 10 to launch the projectile into a designated square. Anyone within reach of the target square who has a readied action can try to catch the item, provided the droid's attack succeeds. (If the attack fails, the item lands in a randomly determined square adjacent to the target square.) Catching the item requires a DC 10 Dexterity check and is considered a move action.

Spring-loaded mechanisms are not typically designed (or practical) for droids of Huge or larger size.

Locked Access

A droid with locked access has its shutdown switch secured or located internally, preventing it from being shut off by an opponent. The droid must be disabled or otherwise rendered helpless before it can be shut down.

Table 11-5: Droid Accessories

EQUIPMENT	COST	WEIGHT	AVAILABILITY
Processors			
Heuristic processor	2,000	5 kg	—
Remote processor			
5-km range processor	1,000	10 kg	—
50-km range processor	10,000	100 kg	—
500-km range processor	100,000	1,000 kg	Military
5,000-km range processor	1,000,000	10,000 kg	Military
Remote receiver	−500	1 kg	—
Backup processor	100	—	—
Synchronized fire circuits	150	1 kg	Military
Restraining bolt	5	—	—
Secondary battery	400	4 kg	—
Self-destruct system	maximum damage × 20	(maximum damage × 0.1) kg	Restricted
Sensors			
Improved sensor package	200	2.5 kg	—
Darkvision	150	1.5 kg	—
Shield generator			
SR 5	2,500 × cost factor	(10 × cost factor) kg	Military
SR 10	5,000 × cost factor	(20 × cost factor) kg	Military
SR 15	7,500 × cost factor	(30 × cost factor) kg	Military
SR 20	10,000 × cost factor	(40 × cost factor) kg	Military
Translator unit			
DC 20	200	1 kg	—
DC 15	500	2 kg	—
DC 10	1,000	4 kg	—
DC 5	2,000	8 kg	—

Table 11-6: Droid Armor

ARMOR (CHECK PENALTY)	COST	ARMOR BONUS TO REF DEFENSE	MAX. DEX BONUS	WEIGHT	AVAILABILITY
Light Armor (−2)					
Plasteel shell	400 × cost factor	+2	+5	(2 × cost factor) kg	—
Quadanium shell	900 × cost factor	+3	+4	(3 × cost factor) kg	—
Durasteel shell	1,600 × cost factor	+4	+4	(8 × cost factor) kg	—
Quadanium plating	2,500 × cost factor	+5	+3	(10 × cost factor) kg	Licensed
Durasteel plating	3,600 × cost factor	+6	+3	(12 × cost factor) kg	Licensed
Medium Armor (−5)					
Quadanium battle armor	4,900 × cost factor	+7	+3	(7 × cost factor) kg	Restricted
Duranium plating	6,400 × cost factor	+8	+2	(16 × cost factor) kg	Restricted
Durasteel battle armor	9,600 × cost factor	+8	+3	(8 × cost factor) kg	Restricted
Heavy Armor[1] (−10)					
Mandalorian steel shell	8,100 × cost factor	+9	+3	(9 × cost factor) kg	Military, Rare
Duranium battle armor	10,000 × cost factor	+10	+2	(10 × cost factor) kg	Military
Neutronium plating	12,100 × cost factor	+11	+1	(20 × cost factor) kg	Military

1 *When running in heavy armor, a droid can only move up to three times its speed (instead of four times).*

Secondary Battery
A secondary battery (sometimes called a redundant battery or backup battery) provides the droid with additional power, allowing it to operate for a longer duration. The secondary battery enables the droid to remain operational for 200 hours (instead of the normal 100 hours) before it needs to shut down and recharge.

Self-Destruct System
To prevent capture and analysis, the droid comes equipped with a powerful explosive. The charge destroys the droid from within (no attack required), and a droid destroyed in this fashion cannot be repaired or salvaged. The explosion is treated as an area attack (+5 attack bonus). The damage to all targets with the area is determined by the droid's size (see below), and the burst radius of the explosion is 2 squares per 4d6 of damage (minimum 2 squares). Droids of Tiny size and smaller do not deal collateral damage when they self-destruct.

DROID SIZE	DAMAGE
Small	4d6
Medium	6d6
Large	8d6
Huge	10d6
Gargantuan or larger	20d6

Sensors
Sensors allow the droid to perceive its surroundings. Most droids are equipped with a standard sensor array that gives them the visual and auditory acuity of an average Human. For an additional cost, a droid can be outfitted with an improved sensor package or with darkvision.

Improved Sensor Package: A droid with an improved sensor package gains a +2 equipment bonus on Perception checks. In addition, the droid

> ### Droid Costs
> Some droids have their cost reduced or inflated based on other circumstances. Although the rules in this chapter provide an accurate means of determining the cost of a droid, some models may deviate from this cost. For example, mass production may reduce labor costs, a droid may be priced to match a competitor, prices may increase due to legal restrictions for a particular droid (particularly common for 4th-degree droids), or a manufacturer may have a virtual monopoly on a particular type of droid that allows higher prices.

gains low-light vision, ignoring concealment (but not total concealment) from darkness.

Darkvision: The droid with darkvision ignores concealment (including total concealment) from darkness.

Shield Generator

The droid is fitted with a deflector shield generator—the same type mounted on starships. Whenever the droid would take damage, reduce the damage by the droid's shield rating (SR). If the damage is equal to or greater than the droid's shield rating, the droid's shield rating is reduced by 5. By spending three swift actions on the same or consecutive rounds, the droid may make a DC 20 Endurance check to restore lost shield power. If the check succeeds, the droid's shield rating increases by 5 points (up to its normal shield rating).

Due to the size and energy requirements of shield generators, only droids of Small size or larger can be equipped with a SR 10 generator. Only droids of Medium size or larger can be equipped with a SR 15 generator. Only droids of Large or bigger size can be equipped with a SR 20 generator.

Translator Unit

The droid is equipped with a device that allows it to understand and convey information in a variety of languages, including nonverbal ones. When the droid experiences a form of communication for the first time, it makes an Intelligence check to determine whether it can identify and understand the language. The DC is based on the translator unit's database, with the better units having a lower DC.

Modifying Droids

A droid can be modified to carry additional equipment simply by attaching the new equipment to the droid's chassis and connecting the new component to the droid's processor. Adding equipment increases the droid's weight. Droids suffer from encumbrance penalties the same way organic characters do: They slow down. Adding, removing, or replacing the systems on a droid requires a Mechanics check, the DC set by the type of system.

Locomotion: DC 25 Mechanics check, representing 1 day of work.

Processor: DC 20 Use Computer check and DC 20 Mechanics check, representing 1 day of work.

Appendage: DC 20 Mechanics check, representing 1 hour of work.

Accessory: DC 15 Mechanics check, representing 1 hour of work.

Tool, Weapon, or Instrument Mounted on an Appendage: DC 15 Mechanics check, representing 10 minutes of work. You take a –5 penalty on your Mechanics check when installing a weapon on a 1st-, 2nd-, 3rd-, or 5th-degree droid.

Self-Modification: A droid may install or replace a locomotion system, appendage, or accessory on itself, but it takes a –5 penalty on its Mechanics check. A droid cannot replace or install a processor on itself.

Sample Droids

The following sample droids are presented as basic models, in their factory-preset state. The trained skills and feats possessed by a basic model represent the droid's core programming—characteristics the droid maintains even after being subjected to a memory wipe (see page 192).

First-Degree Droids

First-degree droids are usually medical, analytical, or scientific droids.

2-1B Medical Droid

Programmed by some of the finest medical minds in the galaxy, Industrial Automaton's 2-1B Series was the first commercially successful surgical droid. Each 2-1B is equipped with a computer interface socket and tether; what it doesn't know about a patient's species or medical history, it can download from any medical mainframe.

The 2-1B's servogrip pincer hands are precision-engineered for smooth, steady action. The core programming of 2-1B surgical droids includes the "physician's code." This prevents the droid from refusing medical aid to any being (unless specifically ordered otherwise by an authorized operator), as well as preventing it from deliberately inflicting harm on an organic creature (except as defined by extensive guidelines for saving a life). This includes a stricture against engaging in combat.

2-1B Series droids can be played as droid heroes.

2-1B Medical Droid   CL 0
Medium droid (1st-degree) nonheroic 2
Init +1; **Senses** low-light vision; Perception +5
Languages Basic, Binary, 2 unassigned

Defenses Ref 10 (flat-footed 10), Fort 9, Will 12
hp 5; **Threshold** 9
Immune droid traits

Speed 6 squares (walking)
Melee unarmed +0 (1d3–1)
Fighting Space 1 square; **Reach** 1 square
Base Atk +1; **Grp** +0

Abilities Str 8, Dex 11, Con —, Int 14, Wis 15, Cha 9
Feats Cybernetic Surgery, Skill Focus (Knowledge [life sciences], Treat Injury), Skill Training (Use Computer), Surgical Expertise
Skills Knowledge (life sciences) +13, Perception +5, Treat Injury +13, Use Computer +8
Systems walking locomotion, heuristic processor, 2 hands, improved sensor package, vocabulator
Availability Licensed; **Cost** 4,300 credits

Second-Degree Droids

Second-degree droids are typically astromech droids and some technical droids. Specific models include the R2 unit.

R2 Series Astromech Droid

The R2 astromech is Industrial Automaton's most successful series of diagnostic and repair droids, largely due to the compact design that enables it (unlike its predecessors) to fit precisely into the astromech sockets of starfighters. An R2 unit performs all of the most complex astrogation, flight data, technical diagnosis, and power management tasks, freeing fighter pilots to concentrate on staying alive.

The R2 astromech droid is surprisingly versatile for its size. R2s boast an overwhelming array of tools and sensors, all tucked away behind various access panels, keeping the housing largely free of obstructions. Industrial Automaton's designers even found a way to include "wasted space" in the chassis, allowing internal storage, easy upgrades, and modifications. Even the four standard appendages (two manipulator arms, an electric arc welder, and a circular saw) can be quickly and easily switched out with a number of specialty arms available. The two empty slots are typically filled with a fire extinguisher and a computer interface probe (for an additional cost).

Because these droids are quick-witted, sincere, and often insightful, many owners are reluctant to have their memories wiped, resulting in headstrong, independent astromech droids.

R2 Series droids can be played as droid heroes.

R2 Series Astromech Droid   CL 0
Small droid (2nd-degree) nonheroic 2
Init +3; **Senses** darkvision; Perception +3
Languages Basic, Binary, 2 unassigned

Defenses Ref 13 (flat-footed 11), Fort 8, Will 10
hp 7; **Threshold** 8
Immune droid traits

Speed 6 squares (wheeled), 4 squares (walking), 9 squares (flying)
Melee electroshock probe +0 (1d8 ion)
Fighting Space 1 square; **Reach** 1 square
Base Atk +1; **Grp** –4

Abilities Str 9, Dex 14, Con —, Int 15, Wis 10, Cha 7
Feats Skill Focus (Mechanics, Use Computer), Skill Training (Perception), Toughness, Weapon Proficiency (simple weapons)
Skills Mechanics +13, Perception +3, Pilot +8, Stealth +6, Use Computer +13
Systems wheeled locomotion, walking locomotion, flying locomotion (limited), magnetic feet, heuristic processor, 6 tool appendages, 1 claw appendage, diagnostics package, internal storage (2 kg), improved sensor package, darkvision
Possessions astrogation buffer (storage device, 10 memory units), circular saw, electroshock probe, fire extinguisher, electric arc welder, holorecorder, holoprojector
Availability Licensed; **Cost** 4,500 credits

Third-Degree Droids

Third-degree droids are typically protocol droids and replica droids. Specific models include 3PO series droids and translator droids.

Protocol Droid

Supplied with a SyntheTech AA-1 Verbobrain, the 3PO protocol droid is capable of storing huge amounts of information, enabling it to understand over six million forms of communication and respond in nearly all of them. It also has a tremendous capacity for analyzing previously unknown languages and translating them into whatever language its master desires. The 3PO even includes an olfactory sensor for translating pheromonal communication. The 3PO's additional memory storage is generally used to keep specific communication modes in active memory, avoiding lengthy delays while searching for linguistic information in mid-translation.

Each 3PO comes with a factory-installed restraining bolt mount. They are also programmed for passive behavior—a typical 3PO droid never attacks under any circumstances. If the droid becomes a problem, the 3PO's shutdown switch is conveniently located at the back of its neck.

Built to resemble humanoids, 3POs come in a wide variety of colors.

3PO Series protocol droids can be played as droid heroes.

> "I'M PROGRAMMED FOR ETIQUETTE, NOT DESTRUCTION!"
> – C-3PO

3PO Series Protocol Droid   CL 0
Medium droid (3rd-degree) nonheroic 1
Init –1; **Senses** Perception +1
Languages Basic, Binary, 3 unassigned

Defenses Ref 9 (flat-footed 9), Fort 9, Will 11
hp 2; **Threshold** 9
Immune droid traits

Speed 6 squares (walking)
Melee unarmed –1 (1d3–1)

Fighting Space 1 square; **Reach** 1 square
Base Atk +0; **Grp** −1

Abilities Str 8, Dex 9, Con —, Int 12, Wis 13, Cha 15
Feats Linguist, Skill Focus (Persuasion), Skill Training (Knowledge [bureaucracy], Knowledge [galactic lore])
Skills Knowledge (bureaucracy) +6, Knowledge (galactic lore) +6, Knowledge (social sciences) +6, Persuasion +12
Systems walking locomotion, basic processor, translator unit (DC 5), 2 hand appendages, vocabulator
Possessions audio recorder
Availability Licensed; **Cost** 3,000 credits

Fourth-Degree Droids

Fourth-degree droids are combat droids. Specific models include battle droids, destroyer droids, security droids, war droids, probe droids, and assassin droids.

B1 Series Battle Droid

Frail in appearance but deadly in intent, Baktoid Combat Automata's battle droid is a metal skeleton with a blaster. Built by the Geonosians to the Trade Federation's specifications, battle droids are designed to resemble Geonosians, or perhaps desiccated Neimoidian corpses. Most intelligent beings regard them as startling, but Neimoidians see battle droids as positively ghoulish.

Battle droids are drones controlled by a remote processor, taking their commands from a Central Control Computer that operates several thousand battle droids, destroyer droids, and droid starfighters simultaneously. A battle droid communicates with its fellow drones via comlinks, transmission antennae, and encryption computers, making for a control signal that is nearly impossible to jam (DC 40 Mechanics check).

B1 Series Battle Droids can't be played as droid heroes.

B1 Series Battle Droid CL 1
Medium droid (4th-degree) nonheroic 3
Init +0; **Senses** Perception +6
Languages Basic, Binary

Defenses Ref 9 (flat-footed 9), Fort 11, Will 11
hp 10; **Threshold** 11
Immune droid traits

Speed 6 squares (walking)
Melee unarmed +3 (1d3+1)
Ranged blaster carbine +1 (3d8)
Fighting Space 1 square; **Reach** 1 square
Base Atk +2; **Grp** +3

Abilities Str 13, Dex 9, Con —, Int 9, Wis 10, Cha 10
Feats Toughness, Weapon Proficiency (pistols, rifles, heavy weapons, simple weapons)
Skills Perception +6
Systems walking locomotion, remote processor, 2 hand appendages, internal comlink, vocabulator
Possessions blaster carbine
Availability Military; **Cost** 1,800 credits

B2 Series Super Battle Droid

The B2 Series Super Battle Droid is a marked improvement in the original B1 Series Battle Droid design. Larger and armored, the Super Battle Droid relies on a central control computer for guidance, but it doesn't deactivate when it loses contact with the remote processor thanks to a backup internal processor—a droid brain that takes over when the droid loses communication with the central computer. This second brain allows the droid to store its last set of orders and continue acting on them even after the remote processor has shut down.

Super Battle Droids can be played as droid heroes.

B2 Series Super Battle Droid CL 2
Medium droid (4th-degree) nonheroic 6
Init +3; **Senses** Perception +8
Languages Basic, Binary

Defenses Ref 12 (flat-footed 12), Fort 12, Will 10
hp 21; **Threshold** 12
Immune droid traits

Speed 6 squares (walking)
Melee unarmed +6 (1d3+1)
Ranged wrist blasters +4 (3d8) or
Ranged wrist blasters +2 (4d8) with Rapid Fire
Fighting Space 1 square; **Reach** 1 square
Base Atk +4; **Grp** +6
Atk Options autofire (wrist blasters), Charging Fire, Rapid Fire, aid another (+4)

Abilities Str 14, Dex 11, Con —, Int 10, Wis 11, Cha 7
Feats Armor Proficiency (light), Charging Fire, Rapid Shot, Toughness, Weapon Proficiency (heavy weapons, rifles, simple)
Skills Perception +8
Systems walking locomotion, remote receiver, backup processor, synchronized fire circuits, 2 hand appendages, integrated comlink, vocabulator, plasteel shell (+2 armor)
Possessions wrist blasters (as blaster rifle)
Availability Military; **Cost** 3,300 credits

> "IT'S AGAINST MY PROGRAMMING TO IMPERSONATE A DEITY."
> — C-3PO

Droideka Series Destroyer Droid

Designed and built by the Geonosians of Geonosis and the Collicoids of Colla IV, the Droideka Series destroyer droids reflect the savage ferocity of their makers.

The main propulsion method of destroyer droids is a microrepulsor-assisted wheel mode that allows a destroyer droid to fold itself into a roughly wheel-shaped package and roll along at high speeds. Though lightning-swift in this mode, destroyer droids are considerably more ponderous when unfolded for combat.

Destroyer droids have two heavy repeating blasters that can lay down a devastating barrage. To augment its bronzium armor shell, a destroyer droid also comes equipped with a deflector shield generator. The tremendous energy drain of the blasters and shields necessitates that the destroyer droid be equipped with a minireactor.

Destroyer droids can't be played as droid heroes.

Droideka Series Destroyer Droid   CL 4
Large droid (4th-degree) nonheroic 12
Init +8; **Senses** Perception +13
Languages Basic, Binary

Defenses Ref 16 (flat-footed 14), Fort 13, Will 10
hp 40; **SR** 20; **Threshold** 18
Immune droid traits

Speed 2 squares (walking), 10 squares (wheeled)
Melee unarmed +12 (1d4+3)
Ranged 2 laser cannons +11 (3d8) or
Ranged 2 laser cannons +9 (4d8) with Rapid Shot or
Ranged 2 laser cannons +6 (5d8) with Burst Fire
Fighting Space 2×2; **Reach** 1 square
Base Atk +9; **Grp** +17
Atk Options autofire (laser cannons), Burst Fire, Point-Blank Shot, Rapid Shot

Abilities Str 16, Dex 14, Con —, Int 8, Wis 14, Cha 7
Feats Armor Proficiency (light), Burst Fire, Point-Blank Shot, Rapid Shot, Dual Weapon Mastery I, Dual Weapon Mastery II, Weapon Proficiency (heavy weapons, rifles, simple weapons)
Skills Perception +13, Stealth −3
Systems walking locomotion, wheeled locomotion (exclusive), remote receiver, 2 tool appendages, shield generator (SR 20), integrated comlink, bronzium shell (+5 armor; treat as quadanium plating)
Possessions 2 laser cannons (treat as blaster rifles)
Availability Military; **Cost** 21,000 credits

Dwarf Spider Droid

In the Battle of Geonosis, the Commerce Guild deployed forces of dwarf spider droids. Larger than a standard battle droid and armed with a powerful blaster cannon, the dwarf spider droid gives mobile heavy weapon support to advancing infantry.

The original function of dwarf spider droids was to root out hidden mining operations. The Commerce Guild requires a tribute payment for all commercial operations within its borders; however, small independent operations often dig within Commerce Guild borders and attempt to smuggle the precious ore into a neutral region, avoiding tribute payments. Dwarf spider droids are equipped to descend down rocky crags like those found inside rough-hewn mine shafts, to catch offenders red-handed before they can reach the safety of the Commerce Guild border. Commerce Guild star cruisers also carry compliments of dwarf spider droids for security and tribute enforcement.

Dwarf Spider Droid   CL 3
Large droid (4th-degree) nonheroic 9
Init +3; **Senses** darkvision; Perception +12
Languages Basic, Binary

Defenses Ref 13 (flat-footed 13), Fort 16, Will 11
hp 32; **Threshold** 26
Immune droid traits

Speed 8 squares (walking)
Melee unarmed +8* (1d6+10)
Ranged blaster cannon +5 (6d8)
Fighting Space 2×2; **Reach** 1 square
Base Atk +6; **Grp** +17
Atk Options Far Shot, Point Blank Shot, Power Attack

Abilities Str 22, Dex 9, Con —, Int 10, Wis 12, Cha 8
Special Qualities stability
Feats Armor Proficiency (light), Far Shot, Improved Damage Threshold, Point Blank Shot, Power Attack, Skill Focus (Perception), Weapon Proficiency (heavy weapons, simple weapons)
Skills Climb +6 (may reroll, may take 10 when threatened), Perception +12, Stealth −6
Systems walking locomotion (extra legs), climbing claws, magnetic feet, remote receiver, darkvision, improved sensor package, locked access, 1 tool appendage, quadanium plating (+5 armor)
Possessions blaster cannon
Availability Military; **Cost** 8,500 credits

Stability—A dwarf spider droid gains a +5 stability bonus on checks made to resist being knocked prone.

Includes 4 points of Power Attack

Crab Droid

Introduced late in the Clone Wars, the crab droids used by the Confederacy of Independent Systems were designed to function as advanced scouts and trailblazers in harsh environments. Nicknamed "muckrakers" by the clone trooper legions they faced, crab droids were often used on wet, swampy worlds where they could use their powerful vacuum system to clear a path for battle droids to follow.

Crab droids range in size from 2 meters tall for the scout models to 6 meters tall for the assault models. They have metal armor plating on the outside and multiple jointed legs that grant them great stability and flexibility. Though they are well protected from incoming fire, they do have weak spots atop their central bodies that, while difficult to reach, leave vital equipment and computer systems exposed to anyone brave enough to get that close.

Crab droids can't be played as droid heroes.

Crab Droid Scout — CL 4
Large droid (4th-degree) nonheroic 12
Init +5; **Senses** Perception +13
Languages Basic, Binary

Defenses Ref 18 (flat-footed 18), Fort 17, Will 12
hp 80; **Threshold** 42
Immune droid traits

Speed 6 squares (walking), climb 3 squares
Melee claw +16* (1d6+15) or
Melee claw +20* (1d6+21) with Powerful Charge
Ranged twin blaster +8 (3d10)
Fighting Space 2×2; **Reach** 1 square
Base Atk +9; **Grp** +21
Atk Options Power Attack

Abilities Str 24, Dex 9, Con —, Int 10, Wis 14, Cha 8
Special Qualities stability
Feats Armor Proficiency (light, medium, heavy), Crush, Pin, Power Attack, Powerful Charge, Weapon Proficiency (rifles, simple weapons)
Skills Climb +8 (may reroll, may take 10 when threatened), Perception +13, Stealth −6
Systems walking locomotion (extra legs), climbing claws, heuristic processor, 2 claw appendages, hardened systems ×5, duranium battle armor (+10 armor)
Possessions twin blaster (treat as heavy blaster rifle)
Availability Military; **Cost** 20,000 credits

Stability—A crab droid gains a +5 stability bonus on checks made to resist being knocked prone.

Includes 8 points of Power Attack

IG-100 Series Bodyguard Droid

Manufactured by Holowan Mechanicals, the first IG-100 Series MagnaGuard droids were custom-built to General Grievous's specifications. Quick and deadly, the MagnaGuards are designed to protect their charge to their own destruction. MagnaGuard droids have thick metal plating covering a wiry endoskeleton and have specially designed arms that are adept at wielding melee weapons.

A MagnaGuard droid can't be played as a droid hero.

IG-100 Series MagnaGuard — CL 6
Medium droid (4th-degree) soldier 6
Force 1
Init +9; **Senses** darkvision; Perception +12
Languages Basic, Binary, 2 unassigned

Defenses Ref 17 (flat-footed 16), Fort 17, Will 18
hp 53; **Threshold** 17
Immune droid traits

Speed 6 squares (walking)
Melee electrostaff +8 (2d8+6)
Melee electrostaff +3 (2d8+6) and
  electrostaff +3 (2d8+6)

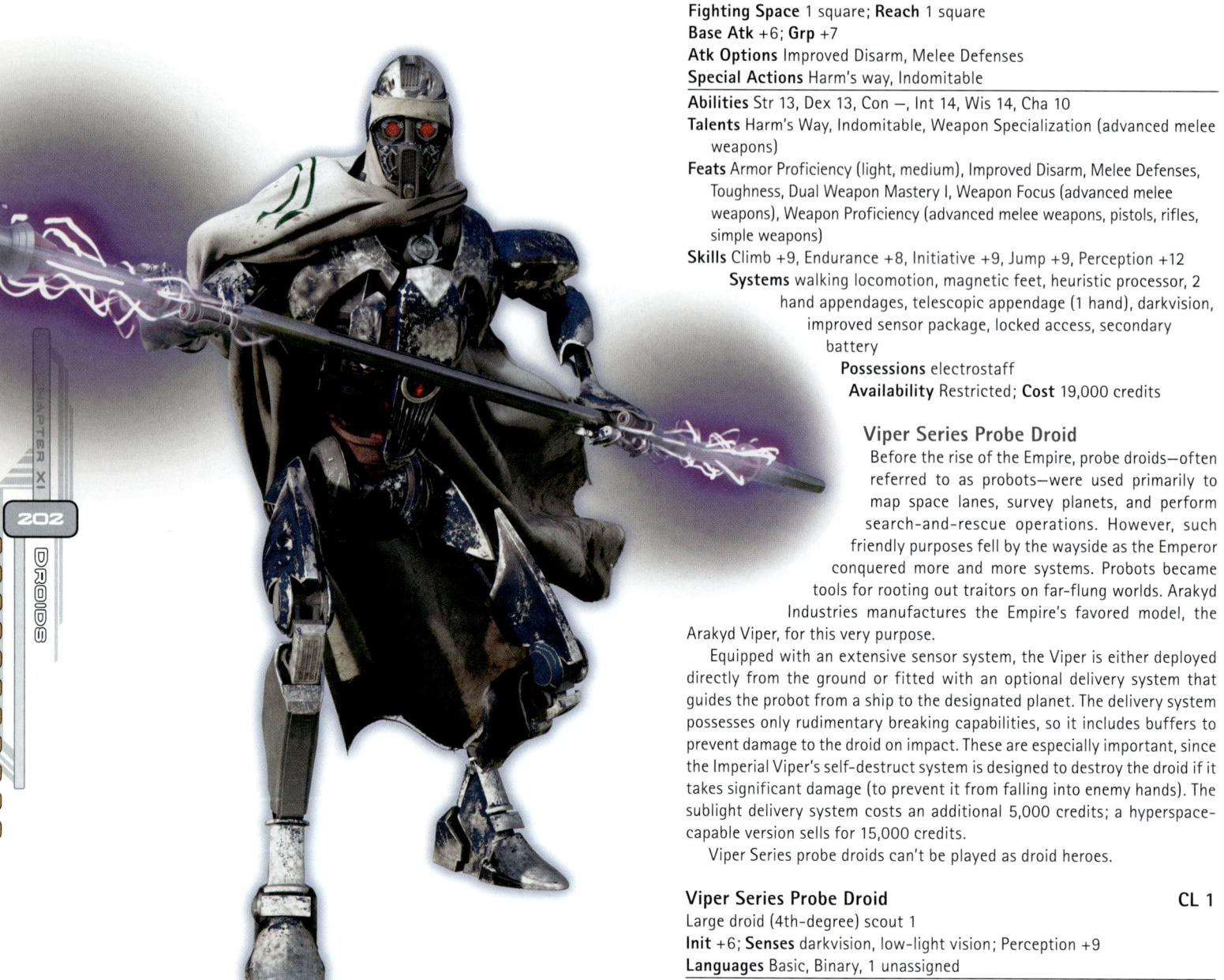

Fighting Space 1 square; **Reach** 1 square
Base Atk +6; **Grp** +7
Atk Options Improved Disarm, Melee Defenses
Special Actions Harm's way, Indomitable

Abilities Str 13, Dex 13, Con —, Int 14, Wis 14, Cha 10
Talents Harm's Way, Indomitable, Weapon Specialization (advanced melee weapons)
Feats Armor Proficiency (light, medium), Improved Disarm, Melee Defenses, Toughness, Dual Weapon Mastery I, Weapon Focus (advanced melee weapons), Weapon Proficiency (advanced melee weapons, pistols, rifles, simple weapons)
Skills Climb +9, Endurance +8, Initiative +9, Jump +9, Perception +12
Systems walking locomotion, magnetic feet, heuristic processor, 2 hand appendages, telescopic appendage (1 hand), darkvision, improved sensor package, locked access, secondary battery
Possessions electrostaff
Availability Restricted; **Cost** 19,000 credits

Viper Series Probe Droid

Before the rise of the Empire, probe droids—often referred to as probots—were used primarily to map space lanes, survey planets, and perform search-and-rescue operations. However, such friendly purposes fell by the wayside as the Emperor conquered more and more systems. Probots became tools for rooting out traitors on far-flung worlds. Arakyd Industries manufactures the Empire's favored model, the Arakyd Viper, for this very purpose.

Equipped with an extensive sensor system, the Viper is either deployed directly from the ground or fitted with an optional delivery system that guides the probot from a ship to the designated planet. The delivery system possesses only rudimentary breaking capabilities, so it includes buffers to prevent damage to the droid on impact. These are especially important, since the Imperial Viper's self-destruct system is designed to destroy the droid if it takes significant damage (to prevent it from falling into enemy hands). The sublight delivery system costs an additional 5,000 credits; a hyperspace-capable version sells for 15,000 credits.

Viper Series probe droids can't be played as droid heroes.

Viper Series Probe Droid   CL 1
Large droid (4th-degree) scout 1
Init +6; **Senses** darkvision, low-light vision; Perception +9
Languages Basic, Binary, 1 unassigned

IG-100 Series MagnaGuard

Defenses Ref 14 (flat-footed 13), Fort 14, Will 13
hp 34; **Threshold** 19
Immune droid traits

Speed 6 squares (hovering)
Melee unarmed +4 (1d6+4)
Ranged blaster +1 (3d6)
Fighting Space 2×2; **Reach** 1 square
Base Atk +0; **Grp** +9
Special Actions self-destruct (+5 area attack, 4d6, 2-square burst)

Abilities Str 18, Dex 12, Con —, Int 12, Wis 15, Cha 11
Talents Acute Senses
Feats Armor Proficiency (light), Weapon Proficiency (blaster pistols, simple weapons, slugthrowers)
Skills Endurance +5, Initiative +6, Perception +9, Stealth +1, Survival +7, Use Computer +6
Systems hovering locomotion, basic processor, 2 hand appendages, 2 claw appendages, 2 tool appendages, improved sensor package, darkvision, self-destruct system (4d6), locked access, integrated comlink, durasteel shell (+4 armor)
Possessions sensor unit, video recording unit, blaster (treat as blaster pistol)
Availability Restricted; **Cost** 18,500 credits

Fifth-Degree Droids

Fifth-degree droids are typically utility droids with low-level functions. Specific models include labor droids and power droids.

ASP Labor Droid

ASP Series labor droids are common throughout the galaxy. They perform a variety of simple tasks, including maintenance, repair, sanitation, delivery, and simple hard labor. Cheap and effective, they are designed as "entry-level" droids for first-time buyers. Many ASP owners modify the droids heavily instead of actually replacing them.

ASPs are built for strength and sturdiness, not intelligence. Since the main virtue of the ASP is versatility, it's programmed with only the most basic functions—leaving the owner to instruct the droid in its specific duties.

ASP Series droids can be played as droid heroes.

ASP Series Labor Droid   CL 0
Medium droid (5th-degree) nonheroic 2
Init +2; **Senses** Perception +1
Languages Basic, Binary

Defenses Ref 15 (flat-footed 14), Fort 13, Will 10
hp 5; **Threshold** 13
Immune droid traits

Speed 6 squares (walking)
Melee claw +4 (1d4+3)
Fighting Space 1 square; **Reach** 1 square
Base Atk +1; **Grp** +4
Abilities Str 17, Dex 12, Con —, Int 6, Wis 11, Cha 5
Feats Armor Proficiency (light), Skill Focus (Endurance), Skill Training (Mechanics), 1 unassigned
Skills Endurance +11, Mechanics +4
Systems walking locomotion, basic processor, 2 claw appendages, durasteel shell (+4 armor)
Availability Licensed; **Cost** 1,000 credits

Place near the "Droideka" stats:

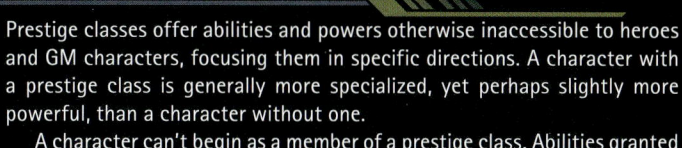

Prestige classes offer abilities and powers otherwise inaccessible to heroes and GM characters, focusing them in specific directions. A character with a prestige class is generally more specialized, yet perhaps slightly more powerful, than a character without one.

A character can't begin as a member of a prestige class. Abilities granted by prestige classes are acquired only by meeting the requirements specific to each example, which almost always demand—in effect—that a character be at least mid-level. Additionally, there may be non-rules-related requirements that must be met in-game, such as group membership fees, special training exercises, or quests.

Prestige classes are purely optional, and always under the purview of the GM. Even though a few examples can be found below, they are idiosyncratic to each campaign, and thus many GMs may choose to not allow them or only use them for GM characters.

Prestige Classes

Table 12-1: Prestige Classes summarizes the prestige classes described in this chapter. Some prestige classes (such as the crime lord, Sith apprentice, and Sith Lord) are more appropriate for GM characters, and the Gamemaster may declare these classes off-limits to heroes. For this reason, a player should consult with her GM before angling her character toward a particular prestige class.

Requirements: All prestige classes have certain requirements that a character must fulfill prior to taking the first level in that class. Among the most common requirements are a minimum character level, a minimum base attack bonus, being trained in certain skills, or having certain feats. These requirements make it easier for certain types of characters to become members of a given prestige class. For example, a scout could potentially take his first level of bounty hunter as an 8th-level character.

Table 12-1: Prestige Classes

PRESTIGE CLASS	BASIC DESCRIPTION
Ace pilot	Extraordinary vehicle pilot
Bounty hunter	Expert at locating and capturing fugitives
Crime lord	Leader of a criminal organization
Elite trooper	Highly trained soldier or bodyguard
Force adept	Member of lesser-known Force tradition
Force disciple	Master of the deepest mysteries of the Force
Gunslinger	Freelance gun-for-hire or troubleshooter
Jedi Knight	Galactic defender who follows the Jedi code
Jedi Master	Galactic guardian and Jedi instructor
Officer	Leader of a military task force or group
Sith apprentice	Handpicked student of a Sith Lord
Sith Lord	Powerful master of the dark side

Ace Pilot

The ace pilot is to vehicle combat what the elite trooper is to personal weapons combat. Her arms and armor are the weapons and shields of a sleek starship soaring through space or an airspeeder shrieking through the atmosphere. A veteran of countless engagements, the ace pilot has proven her skill again and again by virtue of facing the enemy and surviving—and making sure the enemy did not. She has several kills to her credit, and her combat maneuvers are occasionally studied and discussed in training academies for their ingenuity and effectiveness.

For her part, the ace pilot only feels truly alive in the cockpit, where she can pit herself against her peers in a life-and-death contest to see who is the better pilot. For some ace pilots, the contest is enough, and they don't care whether they win or simply get away with their lives. For others, the important thing is the kill. The adrenaline surge they feel when finishing off an enemy brings them back again and again. The best ace pilots learn to stop enemies without destroying them, but those aces are rare, and their exploits are legendary.

Ace pilots define themselves by the vehicles they fly. Some are starfighter aces, while others fly space transports. Ace pilots can also be found at the controls of a Podracer, Coruscant air taxi, or even a large assault vehicle such as an AT-AT.

Examples of Ace Pilot in Star Wars

Han Solo, Wedge Antilles, Sebulba, Wes Jansen, Tycho Celchu, Baron Fel, Corran Horn.

Requirements

To qualify to become an ace pilot, a character must fulfill the following criteria.
Minimum Heroic Level: 7th.
Trained Skills: Pilot.
Feats: Vehicular Combat.

Game Rule Information

Ace pilots have the following game statistics.

Hit Points

At each level, ace pilots gain 1d8 hit points + their Constitution modifier.

Force Points

Ace pilots gain a number of Force Points equal to 6 + one-half their character level, rounded down, every time they gain a new level in this class.

Class Features

The following are features of the ace pilot prestige class.

Table 12-2: The Ace Pilot

LEVEL	BASE ATTACK BONUS	CLASS FEATURES
1st	+0	Defense bonuses, talent
2nd	+1	Vehicle dodge +1
3rd	+2	Talent
4th	+3	Vehicle dodge +2
5th	+3	Talent
6th	+4	Vehicle dodge +3
7th	+5	Talent
8th	+6	Vehicle dodge +4
9th	+6	Talent
10th	+7	Vehicle dodge +5

Defense Bonuses

At 1st level, ace pilots gain a +4 class bonus to their Reflex Defense and a +2 class bonus to their Fortitude Defense.

Talents

At every odd-numbered level (1st, 3rd, 5th, and so on), the ace pilot selects a talent. This talent may be selected from the Expert Pilot or Gunner talent trees (see below) or from the Spacer talent tree (see page 47). The ace pilot must meet the prerequisites (if any) of the chosen talent. No talent can be selected more than once unless expressly indicated.

EXPERT PILOT TALENT TREE

The ace pilot relies on finely honed instincts and years of pilot training to outmaneuver and destroy enemy starships.

Elusive Dogfighter: When engaged in a dogfight, any enemy pilot engaged in the same dogfight takes a –10 penalty on attack rolls when you succeed on the opposed Pilot check (see Attacking in a Dogfight, page 171).

Full Throttle: You can take 10 on Pilot checks made to increase your vehicle's speed (see the Pilot skill description, page 71). In addition, when you use the all-out movement action while piloting a vehicle, your vehicle moves up to five times its normal speed (instead of the normal ×4).

Juke: When you fight defensively as the pilot of a vehicle (see page 171), the dodge bonus to your vehicle's Reflex Defense increases to +5 even if you make an attack.
Prerequisite: Vehicular Evasion.

Keep It Together: Once per encounter, when a vehicle you're piloting takes damage that equals or exceeds its damage threshold, your vehicle avoids moving down the condition track (see Conditions, page 148).

Relentless Pursuit: You may roll twice for any opposed Pilot check made to initiate a dogfight, keeping the better result (see Dogfight, page 171).

Vehicular Evasion: If the vehicle you are piloting is hit by an area attack (see Area Attacks, page 155), it takes half damage if the attack hits. If the area attack misses your vehicle, it takes no damage. You cannot use this talent when your vehicle is stationary or disabled.

GUNNER TALENT TREE

Many starship gunners are skilled both in and out of the cockpit and are deadly with ranged weapons of any kind.

Dogfight Gunner: While your vehicle is engaged in a dogfight, you take no penalty on your attack rolls with vehicle weapons even if you are not the pilot.
Prerequisite: Expert Gunner.

Expert Gunner: You gain a +1 bonus on attack rolls made using vehicle weapons.

Quick Trigger: Whenever an enemy vehicle moves out of your square or an adjacent square, you may make a single attack against that vehicle as an attack of opportunity.
Prerequisite: Expert Gunner.

System Hit: Whenever you deal damage to a vehicle that equals or exceeds its damage threshold, you move that vehicle an additional –1 step on the condition track (see Conditions, page 148).
Prerequisite: Expert Gunner.

Vehicle Dodge

Beginning at 2nd level, you apply a dodge bonus to the Reflex Defense of any vehicle you pilot. The dodge bonus is equal to one-half your class level, rounded down. Any condition that makes you lose your Dexterity bonus to Reflex Defense also makes you lose dodge bonuses. Also, dodge bonuses stack with each other, unlike most other types of bonuses.

BOUNTY HUNTER

The bounty hunter capitalizes on the vendettas of others, tracking down fugitives for their enemies, their masters, or simply for justice. The best bounty hunters are the ones who can stay emotionally detached from either their employers or their quarry—although bounty hunters who hate their prey often make more spectacular kills.

Not all bounty hunters kill. Some employers reserve that pleasure for themselves, or plan to give the quarry a more or less fair trial. Some bounty hunters have reservations about taking lives unnecessarily. Regardless of his methods, a bounty hunter still has to produce the quarry in order to receive payment. Overkill is generally not a good idea.

Male Sullustan Ace Pilot

At one time, organized bounty hunter guilds apportioned contracts and policed their membership. They dwindled in both power and organization during the rise of Emperor Palpatine.

Whether working alone or in groups, bounty hunters revel in the thrill of the hunt. Given the nature of their work, it goes without saying that few bounty hunters die of boredom.

Examples of Bounty Hunters in Star Wars

Aurra Sing, Boba Fett, Bossk, Dengar, 4-LOM, Greedo, IG-88, Zuckuss.

Requirements

To qualify to become a bounty hunter, a character must fulfill the following criteria.

Minimum Heroic Level: 7th.
Trained Skills: Survival.
Talents: At least two talents from the Awareness talent tree (see page 49).

Game Rule Information

Bounty hunters have the following game statistics.

Hit Points

At each level, bounty hunters gain 1d10 hit points + their Constitution modifier.

Force Points

Bounty hunters gain a number of Force Points equal to 6 + one-half their character level, rounded down, every time they gain a new level in this class.

Class Features

The following are features of the bounty hunter prestige class.

Defense Bonuses

At 1st level, you gain a +4 class bonus to your Reflex Defense and a +2 class bonus to your Fortitude Defense.

Talents

At every odd-numbered level (1st, 3rd, 5th, and so on), you select a talent. The talent may be selected from the Bounty Hunter talent tree (presented below), the Misfortune talent tree (see page 46), or the Awareness talent tree (see page 49). You must meet the prerequisites (if any) of the chosen talent. No talent can be selected more than once unless expressly indicated.

BOUNTY HUNTER TALENT TREE

The nature of their work requires bounty hunters to associate with the scum of the universe. You are among the finest bounty hunters in the galaxy, relying on the element of surprise and your hunter's instincts to catch your prey.

Hunter's Mark: If you aim before making a ranged attack (see Aim, page 154), you move the target −1 step along the condition track if the attack hits (see Conditions, page 148).

Hunter's Target: Once per encounter as a free action, you may designate an opponent. For the rest of the encounter, when you succeed on a melee or ranged attack against that opponent, you gain a bonus on damage rolls equal to your class level.

Prerequisite: Hunter's Mark.

Notorious: Your skill as a bounty hunter is known throughout the galaxy, even on fringe worlds. When you are not disguised, you can reroll any Persuasion checks made to intimidate others, keeping the better result (see the Persuasion skill, page 71).

Nowhere to Hide: You may choose to reroll any Gather Information checks made to locate a specific individual (see the Gather Information skill, page 67), but you must keep the result of the reroll even if it is worse.

Relentless: This talent applies only to an opponent you've designated as your hunter's target (see Hunter's Target, above). Any attack or effect originating from the target that would normally move you along the condition track (see page 149) does not, in fact, move you along the condition track.

Prerequisites: Hunter's Mark, Hunter's Target.

Ruthless Negotiator: When haggling over the price of a bounty (see the Persuasion skill, page 71), you can reroll your Persuasion check and keep the better result.

Prerequisite: Notorious.

Male Quarren Bounty Hunter

Table 12-3: The Bounty Hunter

Level	Base Attack Bonus	Class Features
1st	+1	Defense bonuses, talent
2nd	+2	Familiar foe +1
3rd	+3	Talent
4th	+4	Familiar foe +2
5th	+5	Talent
6th	+6	Familiar foe +3
7th	+7	Talent
8th	+8	Familiar foe +4
9th	+9	Talent
10th	+10	Familiar foe +5

Familiar Foe
By observing your enemy in combat, you know how to defeat him more easily. If you spend a full-round action observing an opponent in combat, you gain a bonus on attack rolls against that opponent and a bonus to your Reflex Defense against attacks made by that opponent equal to one-half your class level (rounded down). The effects last until the end of the encounter. You cannot use this ability until after your opponent has acted during the combat.

Crime Lord

Few societies manage to eradicate crime altogether. In the underworld, someone always rises to the top, either through vision, organization, or sheer intimidation. The life of a crime lord isn't for the timid. After conquering an unseen empire, the crime lord wages a daily struggle not only to stay on top but also to stay alive.

Of course, not every crime lord is bent on corrupting society and making a profit. Some use their criminal connections to wage lucrative guerilla wars against tyrants and despots. Indeed, some of the lesser-known heroes of the Rebellion began as smugglers or pirates, and eventually rose through the ranks of their organization to provide a more noble direction for their groups' activities. Although some did so to remove an obstacle to making more money, others recognized that ridding the galaxy of the Empire's evil was a more important long-term goal.

Problematically, crime lords are notoriously bad at cooperating with one another. The head of any given criminal empire has as much to fear from a gang war as he does from internal dissent and ambitious underlings. Even those with altruistic intentions sometimes learn the hard way that their troops are more interested in gaining power and wealth than saving the galaxy from greater evils.

Examples of Crime Lords in Star Wars

Jabba the Hutt, Prince Xizor, Talon Karrde, Ploovo Two-for-One, Davik Kang, G0-T0.

Requirements

To qualify to become a crime lord, a character must fulfill the following criteria.

Minimum Heroic Level: 7th.
Trained Skills: Deception, Persuasion.
Talents: At least one talent from the Fortune, Lineage, or Misfortune talent tree (see pages 44 and 46).

Game Rule Information

Crime lords have the following game statistics.

Table 12-4: The Crime Lord

Level	Base Attack Bonus	Class Features
1st	+0	Defense bonuses, talent
2nd	+1	Command cover, talent
3rd	+2	Talent
4th	+3	Talent
5th	+3	Talent
6th	+4	Talent
7th	+5	Talent
8th	+6	Talent
9th	+6	Talent
10th	+7	Talent

Hit Points
At each level, crime lords gain 1d8 hit points + their Constitution modifier.

Force Points
Crime lords gain a number of Force Points equal to 6 + one-half their character level, rounded down, every time they gain a new level in this class.

Class Features
The following are features of the crime lord prestige class.

Defense Bonuses
At 1st level, you gain a +2 class bonus to your Reflex Defense and a +4 class bonus to your Will Defense.

Talents
At 1st level and each level thereafter, you select a talent. The talent must be selected from the Infamy or Mastermind talent trees (presented below) or the Influence talent tree (see page 43). You must meet the prerequisites (if any) of the chosen talent. No talent can be selected more than once unless expressly indicated.

INFAMY TALENT TREE
You are wanted in multiple systems for criminal acts, and your manner of doing business has earned you an unsavory reputation in the criminal underworld.

Inspire Fear I: Your infamy and reputation are such that any opponent whose level is equal to or less than your character level takes a –1 penalty on attack rolls and opposed skill checks made against you, as well as Use the Force checks made to activate Force powers that target you. This is a mind-affecting fear effect.

Inspire Fear II: As Inspire Fear I (see above), except that the penalty increases to –2.
Prerequisite: Inspire Fear I.

Inspire Fear III: As Inspire Fear I (see above), except that the penalty increases to –5.
Prerequisites: Inspire Fear I, Inspire Fear II.

Notorious: Your reputation as a crime lord is known throughout the galaxy, even on fringe worlds. When you are not disguised, you may reroll any Persuasion checks made to intimidate others, keeping the better result (see the Persuasion skill, page 71).

MALE RODIAN CRIME LORD

Shared Notoriety: When your minions invoke your name, others take note. If you have minions (see the Attract Minion talent, below), they may reroll any Persuasion checks made to intimidate others (see the Persuasion skill, page 71), but the result of the reroll must be accepted even if it is worse.
Prerequisite: Notorious.

MASTERMIND TALENT TREE
You have the ability to attract loyal minions and are skilled at redirecting allies on the battlefield.

Attract Minion: You attract a loyal minion. The minion is a nonheroic character (see page 277) with a class level equal to three-quarters of your character level, rounded down.

You may select this talent multiple times; each time you select this talent, you gain another minion. Normally, you can have only one minion with you at a time. Any other minions you have are assumed to be looking after your various interests. If you lose a minion, you can send for another minion if you have one (although normal travel time still applies).

Each minion that accompanies you on an adventure is entitled to an equal share of the total experience points earned for the adventure. For example, a minion that accompanies a party of five heroes on an adventure receives one-sixth of the XP that the group earns.

Impel Ally I: You can spend a swift action to grant one ally the ability to move its normal speed. The ally must move immediately on your turn, before you do anything else, or else the opportunity is wasted. You can use this talent up to three times on your turn (spending a swift action each time).

Impel Ally II: You can spend two swift actions to grant one ally the ability to take a standard action or move action. The ally must act immediately on your turn, before you do anything else, or else the opportunity is wasted.
Prerequisite: Impel Ally I.

Command Cover
Starting at 2nd level, you can use your allies to shield you from harm. You gain a +1 cover bonus to your Reflex Defense for each ally that is adjacent to you, up to a maximum bonus equal to one-half your class level (maximum +5 at 10th level).

ELITE TROOPER

The elite trooper represents an individual who has received advanced combat training. More than a mere soldier, the elite trooper is highly trained and capable of taking on any number of combat-related missions, such as guarding an important location, assaulting an enemy base, or participating in a stealthy insertion into enemy territory. She's a crack shot and, though trained in the use of armor, can easily operate without it if the situation warrants. When the fighting gets particularly brutal, the elite trooper can dispatch foes hand-to-hand as easily as she does with a blaster.

Elite troopers exist in a variety of roles, but unlike Imperial stormtroopers—the "elite troops" of the Empire—they rely on skill and ingenuity more than sheer force and blind obedience to the Emperor's will. Thus, the best missions for them involve penetrating attacks deep behind enemy lines, or guerilla warfare conducted on enemy-held worlds—situations where versatility and sheer determination are the elite trooper's best armaments and armor.

EXAMPLES OF ELITE TROOPERS IN STAR WARS

General Madine, Major Derlin, Kyle Katarn, Lieutenant Page, Kell Tainer, ARC Trooper Alpha-02.

REQUIREMENTS

To qualify to become an elite trooper, a character must fulfill the following criteria.

Base Attack Bonus: +7.
Feats: Armor Proficiency (light), Armor Proficiency (medium), Martial Arts I, Point Blank Shot.
Talents: At least one talent from the Armor Specialist, Commando, or Weapon Specialist talent trees (see pages 51–53).

GAME RULE INFORMATION

Elite troopers have the following game statistics.

Hit Points

At each level, elite troopers gain 1d12 hit points + their Constitution modifier.

Force Points

Elite troopers gain a number of Force Points equal to 6 + one-half their character level, rounded down, every time they gain a new level in this class.

Class Features

The following are features of the elite trooper prestige class.

Table 12-5: The Elite Trooper

LEVEL	BASE ATTACK BONUS	CLASS FEATURES
1st	+1	Defense bonuses, delay damage, talent
2nd	+2	Damage reduction 1
3rd	+3	Talent
4th	+4	Damage reduction 2
5th	+5	Talent
6th	+6	Damage reduction 3
7th	+7	Talent
8th	+8	Damage reduction 4
9th	+9	Talent
10th	+10	Damage reduction 5

Defense Bonuses

At 1st level, you gain a +2 class bonus to your Reflex Defense and a +4 class bonus to your Fortitude Defense.

Delay Damage

Elite troopers are among the toughest individuals in the galaxy. After being exposed to numerous threats, foes, and combat situations, you've developed the ability to delay effects that would drop lesser creatures.

Once per encounter as a reaction, you can choose to delay the effect of a single attack, ability, or effect used against you. The damage or effect does not take hold until the end of your next turn.

Talents

At every odd-numbered level (1st, 3rd, 5th, and so on), you select a talent. The talent may be selected from the Weapon Master talent tree (presented below), the Commando talent tree (page 52), or the Camouflage talent tree (page 49). You must meet the prerequisites (if any) of the chosen talent. No talent can be selected more than once unless expressly indicated.

WEAPON MASTER TALENT TREE
You are skilled at wielding a variety of weapons and can wield choice weapons with deadly precision and force.

Controlled Burst: Your penalty when making an autofire attack or using the Burst Fire feat is reduced to –2. In addition, if you brace an autofire-only weapon, you have no penalty on your attack roll.

Exotic Weapon Mastery: You are considered proficient with any exotic weapon, even if you don't possess the appropriate Exotic Weapon Proficiency feat.

Greater Devastating Attack: Choose a single exotic weapon or weapon group with which you're proficient. Whenever you make a successful attack against a target using the chosen exotic weapon or a weapon from the chosen group, you treat your target's damage threshold as if it were 10 points lower when determining the result of your attack. This replaces the effects of the Devastating Attack talent (see page 53).

Prerequisites: Greater Weapon Focus, Devastating Attack (see page 53), and Weapon Focus feat (see page 89) with the chosen exotic weapon or weapon group.

Greater Penetrating Attack: Choose a single exotic weapon or weapon group with which you're proficient. Whenever you make a successful attack against a target using the chosen exotic weapon or a weapon from the chosen group, you treat your target's damage reduction as if it were 10 points lower when determining the result of your attack. This replaces the effects of the Penetrating Attack talent (see page 53).

Prerequisites: Greater Weapon Focus, Penetrating Attack (see page 53), and Weapon Focus feat (see page 89) with the chosen exotic weapon or weapon group.

Greater Weapon Focus: Choose one exotic weapon or weapon group with which you're proficient. You gain a +1 bonus on attack rolls with the chosen exotic weapon or a weapon from the chosen group. This bonus stacks with the bonus granted by the Weapon Focus feat (page 89). You must be proficient with the weapon to gain this benefit.

You may select this talent multiple times. Each time you select this talent, it applies to a different weapon group.

Prerequisites: Weapon Focus feat (see page 89) with chosen exotic weapon or weapon group.

Greater Weapon Specialization: Choose one exotic weapon or one of the following weapon groups: advanced melee weapons, heavy weapons, pistols, rifles, simple weapons. You gain a +2 bonus on damage rolls with the chosen exotic weapon or a weapon from the chosen group. This bonus stacks with the bonus granted by the Weapon Specialization talent (page 53). You must be proficient with the weapon to gain this benefit.

You may select this talent multiple times. Each time you select this talent, it applies to a different weapon group.

Prerequisites: Greater Weapon Focus, Weapon Focus feat (see page 89), and Weapon Specialization (see page 53) with the chosen exotic weapon or weapon group.

Multiattack Proficiency (heavy weapons): Whenever you make multiple attacks with any type of heavy weapon as a full attack action (see Full Attack, page 154), you reduce the penalty on your attack rolls by 2.

You can take this talent multiple times; each time you take this talent, you reduce the penalty on your attack rolls by an additional 2.

Multiattack Proficiency (rifles): Whenever you make multiple attacks with any type of rifle as a full attack action (see Full Attack, page 154), you reduce the penalty on your attack rolls by 2.

You can take this talent multiple times; each time you take this talent, you reduce the penalty on your attack rolls by an additional 2.

Damage Reduction

At 2nd level, you gain damage reduction 1 (DR 1), which means that you reduce the damage you take from any attack by 1 (see Damage Reduction, page 158).

At every even-numbered level after 2nd, your damage reduction improves by 1 (DR 2 at 4th level, DR 3 at 6th level, and so on).

Force Adept

The Force adept is strong in the Force but follows a different path than that of the Jedi. To the Force adept, the Force and the aid it provides are more mysterious, more supernatural. A Force adept comes from a different tradition, with different beliefs and codes of conduct than those of the Jedi. There are precious few Force adepts in the galaxy, and even fewer become adventurers. Some call the Force by its familiar name, while others refer to it by some other term entirely.

Some Force adepts become adventurers as part of a quest to learn more about the Force (or whatever they choose to call it). Others do so out of necessity. They are forced from their world, hunted by unscrupulous agents, or are interested in what the galaxy might have to offer them. Force adepts might be called wizards, shamans, witches, or prophets, depending on where they come from and what traditions they follow. Most Force adepts follow

FEMALE HUMAN ELITE TROOPER

the light side (or at least their version of it), but some fully embrace the dark side and use the Force for evil or selfish intent.

Force adepts usually hail from primitive cultures that revere or fear them for their Force powers. Some strive to keep their powers secret, both because they do not fully understand them and because they are afraid of how others might treat them.

Examples of Force Adepts in Star Wars
Asajj Ventress, Inquisitor Tremayne, Maarek Stele, Sly Moore, Teneniel Djo.

Requirements
To qualify to become a Force adept, a character must fulfill the following criteria.
Minimum Heroic Level: 7th.
Trained Skills: Use the Force.
Feats: Force Sensitivity.
Talents: Any three Force talents (see Force Talents, page 100).

Game Rule Information
Force adepts have the following game statistics.

Hit Points
At each level, Force adepts gain 1d8 hit points + their Constitution modifier.

Force Points
Force adepts gain a number of Force Points equal to 6 + one-half their character level, rounded down, every time they gain a new level in this class.

Class Features
The following are features of the Force adept prestige class.

Defense Bonuses
At 1st level, you gain a +4 class bonus to your Will Defense and a +2 class bonus to your Reflex Defense and Fortitude Defense.

Talents
At every odd-numbered level (1st, 3rd, 5th, and so on), you select a talent. The talent may be selected from the Dark Side Devotee, Force Adept, or Force Item talent trees (presented below). You must meet the prerequisites (if any) of the chosen talent. No talent can be selected more than once unless expressly indicated.

DARK SIDE DEVOTEE TALENT TREE
Your powerful negative emotions allow the dark side to flow through you, giving you great power.

Channel Aggression: If you succeed on an attack against a flanked opponent or any target that is denied its Dexterity bonus to Reflex Defense, you may spend a Force Point as a free action to deal additional damage to the target equal to 1d6 per class level (maximum 10d6).

Channel Anger: You let your anger swell into a rage. As a swift action, you may spend a Force Point to gain a +2 rage bonus on melee attack rolls and melee damage rolls for a number of rounds equal to 5 + your Constitution modifier. At the end of this duration, you move -1 step along the condition track (see Conditions, page 148).

While raging, you cannot use skills that require patience and concentration, such as Mechanics, Stealth, or Use the Force.
Prerequisite: Channel Aggression.

Crippling Strike: Whenever you score a critical hit, you may spend a Force Point to also reduce the target's speed by half until he is fully healed (that is, restored to maximum hit points).
Prerequisite: Channel Aggression.

Embrace the Dark Side: Whenever you use a Force power with the [dark side] descriptor, you may reroll your Use the Force check, but you must accept the result of the reroll even if it is worse.

Upon choosing this talent, you can no longer use Force powers with the [light side] descriptor.
Prerequisites: Channel Aggression, Channel Anger.

Table 12-6: The Force Adept

Level	Base Attack Bonus	Class Features
1st	+0	Defense bonuses, talent
2nd	+1	Force technique
3rd	+2	Talent
4th	+3	Force technique
5th	+3	Talent
6th	+4	Force technique
7th	+5	Talent
8th	+6	Force technique
9th	+6	Talent
10th	+7	Force technique

FORCE ADEPT TALENT TREE
Force adepts use the Force to survive on fringe worlds, and they often have signature Force powers that they use particularly well.

Force Power Adept: You are skilled at using a particular Force power. Select one Force power you know. When using that Force power, you have the option of spending a Force Point to make two Use the Force checks, keeping the better result.

This talent may be selected multiple times. Its effects do not stack. Each time you select this talent, you must choose a different Force power.

Force Treatment: You can make a Use the Force check in place of a Treat Injury check (see the Treat Injury skill, page 74). You are considered trained in the Treat Injury skill for purposes of using this talent. If you are entitled to a Treat Injury check reroll, you may reroll your Use the Force check instead (subject to the same circumstances and limitations).

In addition, you can administer first aid, treat disease, treat poison, and treat radiation without the requisite medical kit or medpac.

Fortified Body: The Force shields you against ailments, toxins, and radiation poisoning, making you immune to disease, poison, and radiation.

Prerequisite: Equilibrium (see page 101).

FORCE ITEM TALENT TREE
You can imbue weapons and objects with the power of the Force.

Attune Weapon: You may spend a Force Point to attune a melee weapon. Attuning the weapon takes a full-round action. From that point forward, whenever you wield the attuned weapon, you gain a +1 Force bonus on attack rolls. The weapon is attuned to you alone; others who wield the weapon do not gain the Force bonus.

Empower Weapon: You may spend a Force Point to empower a melee weapon. Empowering the weapon takes a full-round action. From that point forward, the empowered weapon deals an additional die of damage, but only when wielded by you. (For example, an empowered lightsaber deals 3d8 points of damage instead of 2d8 points of damage.) Others who wield the weapon do not gain the bonus damage die.

Force Talisman: You may spend one Force Point to imbue a weapon or some other portable object with the Force, creating a talisman that provides protection to you. Creating the talisman takes a full-round action. While you wear or carry the talisman on your person, you gain a +1 Force bonus to one of your defenses (Reflex, Fortitude, or Will). You may only have one Force talisman active at any given time, and if your Force talisman is destroyed, you may not create another Force talisman for 24 hours.

Greater Force Talisman: As Force Talisman (above), except that the talisman's Force bonus extends to all three of your defenses (Reflex, Fortitude, and Will).

Prerequisite: Force Talisman.

Force Technique
You have learned improved techniques to feel the rhythm the Force. At every even-numbered level (2nd, 4th, 6th, and so on), you gain one Force technique that, once selected, cannot be changed (see Force Techniques, page 101, for more information).

FORCE DISCIPLE
Through meditation and contemplation of the deepest mysteries of the Force, some individuals transcend the dogma in which they were raised as they reach a new and deeper understanding of their connection to the universe around them. The ebb and flow of life—quickening, growing, struggling, dying—becomes a ceaseless chorus of destiny. Some Force disciples tap into this power, become one with it, and speak its wisdom to others. Others might instead enslave destiny, twist its vision, and corrupt others for the sake of power.

Force disciples, like Force adepts, exist in every Force tradition. Even the Jedi and the Sith have had Force disciples among their ranks, but the dogma of these traditions tends to discourage such an eclectic approach to the Force. However, in less well-known dominant traditions—the Baran Do sages, the witches of Dathomir, the Gand findsmen, the Seyugi dervishes—Force disciples hold great power and influence, shaping their traditions for centuries to come. Force adepts who become Force disciples may wield power and influence over entire civilizations.

FEMALE HUMAN FORCE ADEPT

Examples of Force Disciples in Star Wars

Kadann, Lord Cronal ("Blackhole"), Rokur Gepta, the Saarai-kaar, Wialu.

Requirements

To qualify to become a Force disciple, a character must fulfill the following criteria.

Minimum Heroic Level: 12th.
Trained Skills: Use the Force.
Feats: Force Sensitivity.
Talents: Any two talents from the Dark Side Devotee, Force Adept, or Force Item talent tree (see page 214).
Force Powers: *Farseeing*.
Force Techniques: Any one (see Force Techniques, page 101).

Game Rule Information

Force disciples have the following game statistics.

Hit Points

At each level, Force disciples gain 1d8 hit points + their Constitution modifier.

Force Points

Force disciples gain a number of Force Points equal to 7 + one-half their character level, rounded down, every time they gain a new level in this class. (Due to their strong connection to the Force, Force disciples gain more Force Points than most other prestige classes.)

Class Features

The following are features of the Force disciple prestige class.

Defense Bonuses

At 1st level, you gain a +6 class bonus to your Will Defense and a +3 class bonus to your Reflex Defense and Fortitude Defense.

Indomitable

You are immune to mind-affecting effects.

Prophet

Every time you gain a level in this class, you receive two Destiny Points instead of the usual one. In addition, you may sacrifice this extra Destiny Point immediately after gaining a class level. If you choose to do so, you instead receive a prophetic vision from the Force; the content of this vision is determined by the GM. The vision is instantaneous, so no time is required to exercise this option. Upon seeing the vision, you have the option to choose a new destiny (see page 112) so long as the new destiny is related in some way to the vision. The GM is the final arbiter of what new destiny (or destinies) are appropriate.

Talents

At every odd-numbered level (1st, 3rd, and 5th), you select a talent. The talent may be selected from the Force Adept talent tree (see page 214) or any Force talent tree in Chapter 6: The Force. You must meet the prerequisites (if any) of the chosen talent. No talent can be selected more than once unless expressly indicated.

Force Secret

You have glimpsed an eternal truth through your contemplation of the Force. At 2nd level and every level thereafter, you gain one Force secret that, once selected, cannot be changed (see Force Secrets, page 103, for more information).

Table 12-7: The Force Disciple

Level	Base Attack Bonus	Class Features
1st	+0	Defense bonuses, indomitable, prophet, talent
2nd	+1	Force secret
3rd	+2	Force secret, talent
4th	+3	Force secret
5th	+3	Force secret, talent

Male Ithorian Force Disciple

Gunslinger

Since the first primitive slugthrower was developed thousands of years ago, there have been soldiers of fortune focused on pistol fighting. The tradition grew with the technology, creating a special breed of blaster-wielding freelancers who shoot first and ask questions later. Often wandering guns-for-hire, bodyguards in fringe areas, professional duelists, or even assassins, these fighters know everything there is to know about pistols of all descriptions. They can draw faster, shoot faster, and aim more accurately with their weapons of choice than any other category of warrior. Some use their prowess to defend the weak and battle injustice, while others use their skill to gain fast and easy credits. Regardless of motivation, gunslingers seek to use their focused combat techniques to gain greater fame, and wield that fame as a weapon against less well-known foes.

Examples of Gunslingers in Star Wars

Jango Fett, Han Solo, Gallandro, Dash Rendar.

Requirements

To qualify to become a gunslinger, a character must fulfill the following criteria.

Minimum Heroic Level: 7th.

Feats: Point Blank Shot, Precise Shot, Quick Draw, Weapon Proficiency (pistols).

Game Rule Information

Gunslingers have the following game statistics.

Hit Points

At each level, gunslingers gain 1d8 hit points + their Constitution modifier.

Force Points

Gunslingers gain a number of Force Points equal to 6 + one-half their character level, rounded down, every time they gain a new level in this class.

Class Features

The following are features of the gunslinger prestige class.

Defense Bonuses

At 1st level, you gain a +4 class bonus to your Reflex Defense and a +2 class bonus to your Will Defense.

Talents

At every odd-numbered level (1st, 3rd, 5th, and so on), you select a talent. The talent may be selected from the Gunslinger talent tree (presented below), the Fortune talent tree (see page 46), or the Awareness talent tree (see page 49). You must meet the prerequisites (if any) of the chosen talent. No talent can be selected more than once unless expressly indicated.

GUNSLINGER TALENT TREE

You never travel anywhere without a blaster (or two), and you know how to handle yourself in a gunfight.

Debilitating Shot: If you aim before making a ranged attack (see Aim, page 154) and the attack hits, you move the target −1 step along the condition track (see Conditions, page 148) in addition to dealing damage.

Deceptive Shot: Select one target in line of sight within 6 squares. You can spend two swift actions on the same turn to make a Deception check; if the check result equals or exceeds the target's Will Defense, the target is denied its Dexterity bonus to Reflex Defense against your attacks until the beginning of your next turn.

Improved Quick Draw: If you are carrying a pistol (either in your hand or in a holster), you may draw the pistol and make a single attack during a surprise round even if you are surprised. If you are not surprised, you may take any single action of your choice, as normal.

Knockdown Shot: If you aim before making a ranged attack (see Aim, page 154) and the attack hits, you knock the target prone in addition to dealing damage. You can't use this talent to knock down targets two or more size categories bigger than you.

Multiattack Proficiency (pistols): Whenever you make multiple attacks with any type of pistol as a full attack action (see Full Attack, page 154), you reduce the penalty on your attack rolls by 2.

Male Wookiee Gunslinger

Table 12-8: The Gunslinger

LEVEL	BASE ATTACK BONUS	CLASS FEATURES
1st	+1	Defense bonuses, talent
2nd	+2	Trusty sidearm +1
3rd	+3	Talent
4th	+4	Trusty sidearm +2
5th	+5	Talent
6th	+6	Trusty sidearm +3
7th	+7	Talent
8th	+8	Trusty sidearm +4
9th	+9	Talent
10th	+10	Trusty sidearm +5

You can take this talent multiple times; each time you take this talent, you reduce the penalty on your attack rolls by an additional 2.

Ranged Disarm: You can disarm an opponent using a ranged attack. If your ranged disarm attack fails, your opponent doesn't get to make a free attack against you (see Disarm, page 152).

Trigger Work: You take no penalty on your attack roll when using the Rapid Shot feat.

Trusty Sidearm

Starting at 2nd level, you gain a bonus on damage rolls equal to one-half your class level (rounded down) when wielding a pistol. This damage is in addition to the character's usual level bonus to damage. This damage is doubled on a successful critical hit, as normal.

JEDI KNIGHT

Among the Jedi, those of the order who have proven capable, wise, self-sufficient, and stable are given the rank of Knight. A Jedi apprentice must learn to use the Force without instability or strain, build his or her own lightsaber, and show an understanding of the Code of the Jedi (though such understanding may shift from era to era, as the nature of the Jedi differs somewhat in each era). During most eras, a Jedi must pass a series of tests before becoming a Jedi Knight, which may be as simple as fulfilling a single important mission assigned by a Jedi Master, or as complex as a series of trials to test the Jedi's mettle, ethics, and dedication. In a few times of chaos and uncertainty, Jedi apprentices are forced by circumstance to push themselves past the normal boundaries of their training and become knights in function, if not in name, with no formal testing. In these rare cases, the ruling Jedi generally acknowledge the Jedi's status as a knight as soon as circumstances allow.

Jedi Knights are trusted to teach apprentices, carry out missions with little aid or support, and use their best judgment when handling the unexpected. A Jedi Knight is expected to deal with any problem in a manner that reflects well on the Jedi as a whole, and carry out the Jedi goals of defending justice and maintaining peace. Jedi are the guardians of the galaxy, and the Jedi Knight is a skilled individual expected to uphold that trust.

Examples of Jedi Knights in Star Wars

Anakin Skywalker (Episode III), Barriss Offee, Bastila Shan, Kyle Katarn, Luke Skywalker (Episode VI), Nomi Sunrider, Ulic Qel-Droma.

Requirements

To qualify to become a Jedi Knight, a character must fulfill the following criteria.

Base Attack Bonus: +7.
Trained Skills: Use the Force.
Feats: Force Sensitivity, Weapon Proficiency (lightsabers).
Special: Must have built your own lightsaber (see the Building a Lightsaber sidebar, page 40).
Special: Must be a member of the Jedi tradition (see page 104).

Game Rule Information

Jedi Knights have the following game statistics.

Hit Points

At each level, Jedi Knights gain 1d10 hit points + their Constitution modifier.

Force Points

Jedi Knights gain a number of Force Points equal to 6 + one-half their character level, rounded down, every time they gain a new level in this class.

Class Features

The following are features of the Jedi Knight prestige class.

Defense Bonuses

At 1st level, you gain a +2 class bonus to your Reflex, Fortitude, and Will Defense.

Talents

At every odd-numbered level (1st, 3rd, 5th, and so on), you select a talent. The talent may be selected from the Armor Specialist talent tree (see page

51), the Lightsaber Combat talent tree (see page 41), the Duelist talent tree (presented below), or the Lightsaber Forms talent tree (presented below). You must meet the prerequisites (if any) of the chosen talent. No talent can be selected more than once unless expressly indicated.

DUELIST TALENT TREE

Through rigorous training and experience, you become one of the greatest swordfighters in the galaxy.

Force Fortification: As a reaction, you can spend a Force Point to negate a critical hit scored against you and take normal damage instead. You can spend this Force Point even if you've already spent a Force Point earlier in the round.

Greater Weapon Focus (lightsabers): You gain a +1 bonus on melee attack rolls with lightsabers. This bonus stacks with the bonus granted by the Weapon Focus (lightsabers) feat.

Prerequisite: Weapon Focus (lightsabers) feat (see page 89).

Greater Weapon Specialization (lightsabers): You gain a +2 bonus on melee damage rolls with lightsabers. This bonus stacks with the bonus granted by the Weapon Specialization (lightsabers) talent.

Prerequisites: Greater Weapon Focus (lightsabers), Weapon Focus (lightsabers) feat, Weapon Specialization (lightsabers) (see page 53).

Multiattack Proficiency (lightsabers): Whenever you make multiple attacks with any type of lightsaber as a full attack action (see Full Attack, page 154), you reduce the penalty on your attack rolls by 2.

You can take this talent multiple times; each time you take this talent, you reduce the penalty on your attack rolls by an additional 2.

Severing Strike: When you deal damage with a lightsaber that is equal to or greater than both the target's current hit points and the target's damage threshold (that is, when you would deal enough damage to kill your target), you may choose to use this talent. Instead of dealing full damage, you instead deal half damage to your target and move it −1 step on the condition track (see Conditions, page 148). In addition, you sever one of your target's arms at the wrist or elbow joint, or one of its legs at the knee or ankle joint (your choice).

Severing part of an arm prevents the target from wielding weapons or using tools in that hand and imposes a −5 penalty on skill checks and ability checks keyed to Strength and Dexterity. Severing part of a leg knocks the target prone, reduces the target's speed by half, reduces its carrying capacity by half, and imposes a −5 penalty on skill checks and ability checks keyed to Strength and Dexterity.

Because of the severity of such an injury, losing a part of a limb causes a persistent condition that can only be removed by having surgery successfully performed on you (see Treat Injury skill, page 74). A cybernetic replacement limb (see page 137) negates these reductions and penalties.

LIGHTSABER FORMS TALENT TREE

You have refined your knowledge of lightsaber technique, your blade becoming an extension of your self. Anyone using a lightsaber may use one of these forms, but you have the discipline and patience to become a true master of the form.

Ataru: You may add your Dexterity bonus (instead of your Strength bonus) on damage rolls when wielding a lightsaber. When you wield a lightsaber two-handed, you may apply double your Dexterity bonus (instead of double your Strength bonus) to the damage.

Djem So: Once per round when an opponent hits you with a melee attack, you may spend a Force Point as a reaction to make an immediate attack against that opponent.

Jar'Kai: When you use the Lightsaber Defense talent, you gain twice the normal deflection bonus to your Reflex Defense when you are wielding two lightsabers.

Prerequisites: Lightsaber Defense (see page 41), Niman.

Juyo: Once per encounter, you may spend a Force Point as a swift action to designate a single enemy in your line of sight. For the remainder of the encounter, you may reroll your first attack roll each round against that opponent, keeping the better result.

Prerequisites: Weapon Focus (lightsabers) feat (see page 89), Weapon Specialization (lightsabers) (see page 41), base attack bonus +10.

Makashi: When wielding a single lightsaber in one hand, the deflection bonus you gain from the Lightsaber Defense talent (see page 41) increases by 2 (to a maximum of +5).

Prerequisite: Lightsaber Defense.

Niman: When wielding a lightsaber, you gain a +1 bonus to your Reflex Defense and Will Defense.

Shien: Whenever you redirect a deflected blaster bolt (see the Redirect Shot talent, page 41), you gain a +5 bonus on your ranged attack roll.

FEMALE TWI'LEK JEDI KNIGHT

Table 12-9: The Jedi Knight

LEVEL	BASE ATTACK BONUS	CLASS FEATURES
1st	+1	Defense bonuses, talent
2nd	+2	Force technique
3rd	+3	Talent
4th	+4	Force technique
5th	+5	Talent
6th	+6	Force technique
7th	+7	Talent
8th	+8	Force technique
9th	+9	Talent
10th	+10	Force technique

Prerequisites: Deflect (see page 41), Redirect Shot (see page 41).

Shii-Cho: When using the Block or Deflect talents, you only take a −2 penalty on your Use the Force check for every previous block or deflect attempt since your last turn (see page 41).

Prerequisites: Block (see page 41), Deflect (see page 41).

Sokan: You may take 10 on Acrobatics checks to tumble even when distracted or threatened. Additionally, each threatened or occupied square that you tumble through only counts as 1 square of movement.

Prerequisite: Acrobatic Recovery.

Soresu: You may reroll a failed Use the Force check when using the Block or Deflect talents.

Prerequisites: Block (see page 41), Deflect (see page 41).

Tràkata: By harnessing the unique characteristics of a lightsaber, you can catch your opponent off guard by quickly shutting off and reigniting the blade. When wielding a lightsaber, you may spend two swift actions to make a Deception check to feint in combat (see page 66).

Prerequisites: Weapon Focus (lightsabers) feat (see page 89), Weapon Specialization (lightsabers) (see page 41), base attack bonus +12.

Vaapad: When attacking with a lightsaber, you score a critical hit on a natural roll of 19 or 20. However, a natural 19 is not considered an automatic hit; if you roll a natural 19 and still miss the target, you do not score a critical hit.

Prerequisites: Juyo, Weapon Focus (lightsabers) feat (see page 89), Weapon Specialization (lightsabers) (see page 41), base attack bonus +12.

Force Technique
You have learned improved techniques to attune yourself to the Force. At every even-numbered level (2nd, 4th, 6th, and so on), you gain one Force technique that, once selected, cannot be changed (see Force Techniques, page 101, for more information).

Jedi Master
Jedi Masters represent the pinnacle of the Jedi order. They are Jedi who are both strong enough in the Force and patient enough in life to pass on their skills by teaching a new generation of Jedi. The journey from Padawan learner to Jedi Master usually takes decades, and many who start upon the path never reach its final destination.

Becoming a Jedi Master requires patience, inner strength, wisdom, and a deep connection to and understanding of the Force. Further, a Jedi Knight usually doesn't become a Jedi Master until he trains a student to completion. Jedi are allowed only one Padawan at a time, and the training of a single Padawan can take years.

The most respected Jedi Masters are invited by their peers (and, in some cases, their former masters) to join them on the Jedi Council. Those who join the council use their wisdom and influence to instruct others in the ways of the Force and preserve peace in the galaxy. The Jedi Council is also tasked with identifying Force-sensitive children across the galaxy and offering them instruction in the Jedi tradition. These lessons are fairly rudimentary—usually intended to teach a student "the basics" until he or she is old enough to receive formal training as a Padawan.

During the Rise of the Empire era, the Jedi Council would confer the title of Jedi Master upon those deemed qualified to teach others in the ways of the Force. During the Rebellion era and The New Jedi Order era, Jedi require no such approval; however, they must adhere to the tenets of the Jedi Code to become Jedi Masters.

Examples of Jedi Masters in Star Wars
Adi Gallia, Eeth Koth, Luke Skywalker (The New Jedi Order era), Kit Fisto, Luminara Unduli, Mace Windu, Obi-Wan Kenobi (Episode III), Plo Koon, Shaak Ti, Yoda.

Requirements
To qualify to become a Jedi Master, a character must fulfill the following criteria.
Minimum Heroic Level: 12th.
Trained Skills: Use the Force.
Feats: Force Sensitivity, Weapon Proficiency (lightsabers).
Force Techniques: Any one (see Force Techniques, page 101).
Special: Must be a member of the Jedi tradition (see page 104).

Game Rule Information

Jedi Masters have the following game statistics.

Hit Points

At each level, Jedi Masters gain 1d10 hit points + their Constitution modifier.

Force Points

Jedi Masters gain a number of Force Points equal to 7 + one-half their character level, rounded down, every time they gain a new level in this class. (Due to their strong connection to the Force, Jedi Masters gain more Force Points than most other prestige classes.)

Class Features

The following are features of the Jedi Master prestige class.

Defense Bonuses

At 1st level, you gain a +3 class bonus to your Reflex, Fortitude, and Will Defense.

Fearless

You are immune to fear effects.

Serenity

You may enter a brief meditative state as a full-round action. You may remain in this trance as long as you wish, and you are still aware of your surroundings; however, you do lose your Dexterity bonus to your Reflex Defense. Upon emerging from the trance (a swift action), your first attack roll or Use the Force skill check made in the following round is considered to be a natural 20.

Table 12-10: The Jedi Master

LEVEL	BASE ATTACK BONUS	CLASS FEATURES
1st	+1	Defense bonuses, fearless, serenity, talent
2nd	+2	Force secret
3rd	+3	Force secret, talent
4th	+4	Force secret
5th	+5	Force secret, talent

Talents

At every odd-numbered level (1st, 3rd, and 5th), you select a talent. The talent may be selected from the Duelist talent tree (see page 218) or any Force talent tree in Chapter 6: The Force. You must meet the prerequisites (if any) of the chosen talent. No talent can be selected more than once unless expressly indicated.

Force Secret

You have meditated on the deeper mysteries of the light side of the Force. At 2nd level and every level thereafter, you gain one Force secret that, once selected, cannot be changed (see Force Secrets, page 103, for more information).

Officer

Even the best-trained troops need someone to make decisions and provide direction. The officer fills that role but also takes responsibility when the troops fail in their appointed tasks. They frequently also suffer the disrespect of their subordinates, who often see the uniform as a symbol of oppression. Many soldiers can't perceive the honor of the person inside the uniform. Very few officers earn the universal respect of their troops and their superiors, but to those who understand the concepts of leadership and valor, it often just comes naturally.

An officer must be comfortable in command, willing to make tough decisions when his men need guidance, and occasionally ordering individual soldiers to their deaths so that the unit can survive. A good officer learns to do so without hesitation and only agonizes over his decision when lives are no longer at stake. The best officers don't let their distaste for life-or-death decisions paralyze them when their troops are counting on them. Those who can't find the courage to face such dilemmas rarely stay officers for long—though certainly, a few somehow manage to avoid the issue by shifting blame elsewhere.

Examples of Officers in Star Wars

Admiral Ackbar, Captain Needa, General Dodonna, General Grievous, General Rieekan, General Veers.

Male Kel Dor Jedi Master

Requirements

To qualify to become an officer, a character must fulfill the following criteria.

Minimum Heroic Level: 7th.
Trained Skills: Knowledge (tactics).
Talents: At least one talent from the Leadership talent tree (see page 44) or Commando talent tree (see page 52).
Special: Must belong to an organization with a military or paramilitary division. Examples include the Trade Federation, the Galactic Empire, the Rebel Alliance, and the New Republic.

Game Rule Information

Officers have the following game statistics.

Hit Points

At each level, officers gain 1d8 hit points + their Constitution modifier.

Force Points

Officers gain a number of Force Points equal to 6 + one-half their character level, rounded down, every time they gain a new level in this class.

Class Features

The following are features of the officer prestige class.

Defense Bonuses

At 1st level, you gain a +2 class bonus to your Reflex Defense and a +4 class bonus to your Will Defense.

Talents

At every odd-numbered level (1st, 3rd, 5th, and so on), you select a talent. The talent may be selected from the Military Tactics talent tree (presented below), the Leadership talent tree (see page 44), or the Commando talent tree (see page 52). You must meet the prerequisites (if any) of the chosen talent. No talent can be selected more than once unless expressly indicated.

MILITARY TACTICS TALENT TREE

Officers study old battles, looking for historic examples of good military tactics. You are an expert at leading troops into battle and using the battlefield to your advantage.

Assault Tactics: As a move action, you may designate a single creature or object as the target of an assault. If you succeed on a DC 15 Knowledge (tactics) check, you and all allies able to hear and understand you deal +1d6 points of damage to the target with each successful melee or ranged attack, until the start of your next turn. This is a mind-affecting effect.

Table 12-11: The Officer

LEVEL	BASE ATTACK BONUS	CLASS FEATURES
1st	+1	Defense bonuses, talent
2nd	+2	Command cover, share talent
3rd	+3	Talent
4th	+4	Share talent
5th	+5	Talent
6th	+6	Share talent
7th	+7	Talent
8th	+8	Share talent
9th	+9	Talent
10th	+10	Share talent

Deployment Tactics: You can use your tactical knowledge to direct allies in battle. As a move action, you can make a DC 15 Knowledge (tactics) check. If the check succeeds, you and any allies that can see, hear, and understand you gain a +1 competence bonus on attack rolls against flanked opponents or a +1 dodge bonus to Reflex Defense against attacks of opportunity (your choice). The bonus lasts until the start of your next turn. This is a mind-affecting effect.

If you have the Born Leader talent (page 44) or the Battle Analysis talent (page 52), the bonus granted by this talent increases to +2.

Field Tactics: You know how to use existing terrain to best advantage. By using a move action, you can make a DC 15 Knowledge (tactics) check. If the check succeeds, you and all allies within 10 squares of you can use whatever cover is available to gain a +10 cover bonus to Reflex Defense (instead of the normal +5 cover bonus). Allies must be able to hear and understand you to gain this benefit, and the bonus lasts until the start of your next turn. This talent provides no benefit to anyone who doesn't have cover. This is a mind-affecting effect.

Prerequisite: Deployment Tactics.

One for the Team: As a reaction, you can choose to take one-half or all of the damage dealt to an adjacent ally by a single attack. Similarly, as a reaction, an adjacent ally can choose to take one-half or all of the damage dealt to you by a single attack (even if he doesn't have this talent).

Prerequisite: Deployment Tactics.

Outmaneuver: An officer learns to counter the tactics of his enemies. As a standard action, you can make a DC 15 Knowledge (tactics) check. If the check succeeds, enemies in your line of sight lose all competence, insight, and morale bonuses on attack rolls, as well as any dodge bonuses to Reflex Defense, until the start of your next turn.

If one or more enemy officers are within your line of sight, the highest-level officer among them can attempt to oppose your Knowledge (tactics) check as a reaction. If her skill check result is higher than yours, your attempt to outmaneuver your enemies fails.

Prerequisites: Deployment Tactics, Field Tactics.

Shift Defense I: As a swift action, you can take a –2 penalty to one defense (Reflex, Fortitude, or Will) to gain a +1 competence bonus to another defense until the start of your next turn.

Shift Defense II: As a swift action, you can take a –5 penalty to one defense (Reflex, Fortitude, or Will) to gain a +2 competence bonus to another defense until the start of your next turn.

Prerequisite: Shift Defense I.

Shift Defense III: As a swift action, you can gain a +5 competence bonus to one defense (Reflex, Fortitude, or Will) by taking a –5 penalty to your other two defenses.

Prerequisites: Shift Defense I, Shift Defense II.

Tactical Edge: You can use the Assault Tactics, Deployment Tactics, or Field Tactics talent as a swift action instead of a move action, provided you have the talent in question.

Command Cover
Starting at 2nd level, you can use your allies to shield you from harm. You gain a +1 cover bonus to your Reflex Defense for each ally that is adjacent to you, up to a maximum bonus equal to one-half your class level (maximum +5 at 10th level).

Share Talent
At every even-numbered level, choose a talent that you already possess. The talent you select must be under the Influence talent tree (page 43), the Inspiration talent tree (page 43), the Commando talent tree (page 52), or the Military Tactics talent tree (see above). Once per day as a standard action, you can impart the benefits of the chosen talent to one or more allies, effectively granting them the talent (even if they don't meet the prerequisites). An ally must be within 10 squares of you and must be able to see and hear you to gain the talent; once gained, its benefits last until the end of the encounter.

You can share the talent with a number of allies equal to one-half your officer class level (rounded down).

Each time you gain this ability, it applies to a different talent. By 10th level, an officer has five different talents that he can share with up to five allies at a time.

Once you select a shared talent, it cannot be changed.

Sith Apprentice

The Sith apprentice combines combat mastery with the power of the dark side to create a living embodiment of rage and savagery. Physical conditioning and punishing discipline make the Sith apprentice into a formidable opponent, and facility with the powers of the dark side add a wicked barb to an otherwise deadly weapon. The Sith apprentice is dedicated to the conquest and subjugation of any obstacle to the Sith tradition. Throughout history, a single Sith apprentice has usually been more than a match for most Jedi. When Sith apprentices gathered in numbers, as they did four thousand years before the days of Darth Maul and Darth Tyranus, the galaxy trembled.

But those times are gone, and the few Sith apprentices to appear since the rule of Darth Bane have worked in secrecy to preserve the Sith tradition and prepare for their ultimate conquest of the galaxy. In the thousand years since Bane established the rule of "one master and one apprentice," foot soldiers, outlaws, warlords, mercenaries, pirates, fighter pilots, survivalists, duelists, and even the occasional Jedi Knight have turned to the dark side and embraced the way of the Sith, becoming mighty warriors, dying brutal deaths, or both. The way of the Sith apprentice is a constant, unforgiving test of will and ability, honing each into a blade fearsome enough to cut through the heart of the hated Jedi order. Every Sith apprentice dreams of being the one who will destroy this ancient foe of the Sith tradition.

The training of a Sith apprentice is always one of deprivation and hardship. Mercy and forbearance create a weak weapon, and such a weapon is useless. The Sith apprentice is subjected to endless conditioning and drilling. Displays of fear or uncertainty are rewarded with painful and educational punishment. Displays of strength and ruthlessness are rewarded with another day's survival. The Sith apprentice learns to live for the precious few words of encourage-

Male Duros Officer

ment his master gives, and the dream that he will one day stand atop a pile of slain Jedi. For the Sith apprentice, furious battle is its own reward.

Examples of Sith Apprentices in Star Wars

Lumiya, Darth Bandon, Darth Sion, Visas Marr, Carnor Jax, Warb Null.

Requirements

To qualify to become a Sith apprentice, a character must fulfill the following criteria.

Minimum Heroic Level: 7th.
Trained Skills: Use the Force.
Feats: Force Sensitivity, Weapon Proficiency (lightsaber).
Dark Side Score: Your Dark Side Score (see page 94) must be equal to your Wisdom score. If your Dark Side Score ever becomes less than your Wisdom score, you lose access to all class features granted by this class (including talents) until your Dark Side Score again equals your Wisdom score.
Special: Must be a member of the Sith tradition (see page 105).

Game Rule Information

Sith apprentices have the following game statistics.

Hit Points

At each level, Sith apprentices gain 1d10 hit points + their Constitution modifier.

Force Points

Sith apprentices gain a number of Force Points equal to 6 + one-half their character level, rounded down, every time they gain a new level in this class.

Class Features

The following are features of the Sith apprentice prestige class.

Defense Bonuses

At 1st level, you gain a +2 class bonus to your Reflex, Fortitude, and Will Defense.

Talents

At every odd-numbered level (1st, 3rd, 5th, and so on), you select a talent. The talent may be selected from the Armor Specialist talent tree (see page 51), the Duelist talent tree (see page 218), the Lightsaber Combat talent tree (see page 41), or the Sith talent tree (presented below). You must meet the prerequisites (if any) of the chosen talent. No talent can be selected more than once unless expressly indicated.

SITH TALENT TREE

The Sith tradition believes in order through tyranny. In ancient days, Sith warriors battled Jedi Knights for galactic supremacy until, finally, the few surviving Sith were driven into hiding. Since then, the Sith have conspired to annihilate the Jedi and everything they stand for.

Dark Healing: You can spend a Force Point to heal wounds by drawing life energy from another creature within 6 squares of you. Using this ability is a standard action, and you must succeed on a ranged attack roll. If the attack equals or exceeds the target's Fortitude Defense, you deal 1d6 points of damage per class level to the target and you heal an equal amount. If the attack fails, there is no effect.

Dark Scourge: You have dedicated your life to wiping out the Jedi, and your hatred of them knows no bounds. Against Jedi characters, you gain a +1 dark side bonus on attack rolls.

Dark Side Adept: Force powers that are strongly tied to the dark side flow through you more easily. You can reroll any Use the Force check made when activating Force powers with the [dark side] descriptor, but you must keep the result of the reroll, even if it is worse.

Dark Side Master: As Dark Side Adept (see above), except that you can spend a Force Point and keep the better of the two Use the Force checks.
Prerequisite: Dark Side Adept.

Force Deception: You can use your Use the Force check modifier instead of your Deception check modifier when making Deception checks,

"AT LAST WE WILL REVEAL OURSELVES TO THE JEDI. AT LAST WE WILL HAVE REVENGE."
– Darth Maul

Male Human Sith Apprentice

Table 12-12: The Sith Apprentice

LEVEL	BASE ATTACK BONUS	CLASS FEATURES
1st	+1	Defense bonuses, talent
2nd	+2	Force technique
3rd	+3	Talent
4th	+4	Force technique
5th	+5	Talent
6th	+6	Force technique
7th	+7	Talent
8th	+8	Force technique
9th	+9	Talent
10th	+10	Force technique

as you use the Force to cloak your vile treachery. You are considered trained in the Deception skill for purposes of using this talent. If you are entitled to a Deception check reroll, you may reroll your Use the Force check instead (subject to the same circumstances and limitations).

Improved Dark Healing: Your dark healing ability (see above) improves. The range of this ability increases to 12 squares, and even if the attack fails the target takes half damage while you heal an equal amount.

Prerequisite: Dark Healing.

Wicked Strike: When you score a critical hit with a lightsaber, you may spend a Force Point to move the target -2 steps along the condition track (see Conditions, page 148).

Prerequisites: Weapon Focus (lightsabers) feat (see page 89), Weapon Specialization (lightsabers) (see page 41).

Force Technique
You have learned improved techniques to control the Force. At every even-numbered level (2nd, 4th, 6th, and so on), you gain one Force technique that, once selected, cannot be changed (see Force Techniques, page 101, for more information).

Fallen Jedi
A Jedi who turns to the dark side and becomes a Sith apprentice retains all of his Jedi class features, including talents, Force powers, bonus feats, and other abilities. The only exceptions are Force powers with the [light side] descriptor, which the character can no longer use.

Sith Lord
The Sith Lord is the pinnacle of the Sith tradition. Her most sacred tasks include preserving the lore and glory of the Sith and plotting their eventual ascendance to their place as rulers of the galaxy. The Sith Lord must allow nothing to stand in the way of this goal: not all the forces of the Republic military, nor the entirety of the Jedi order. When the time comes, the Sith Lord must be prepared to ruthlessly crush all opposition, leaving no traces behind.

The Sith Lord cultivates individuals with the potential for both great power and great evil, training them from childhood, when possible, to be every bit as ruthless as herself. The training can be better described as physical and mental torture, but it is designed to create someone strong, fast, cunning, and deadly. The Sith Lord passes on her knowledge of the dark side of the Force, instilling in her apprentice both a lust for power and a fear of failure.

Arguably, only the truly ambitious or deeply twisted ever seek to become Sith Lords. Following the path of the Sith dominates one's destiny, requiring a constant devotion to engineering the ascendance of the Sith. A Sith Lord cannot afford the luxury of friends, mercy, or even rest. The dark side sustains her through decades of scheming and planning, of masterminding plots subtle and grandiose. Even then, a Sith Lord may meet her end without ever seeing her contributions to the Sith grand scheme come to fruition. Each must content herself with knowing that her apprentice, or a descendant of her apprentice a hundred generations down the line, will one day honor his sacrifice by destroying the Jedi order and replacing it with the dark empire of the Sith.

In the early days of the Sith, only one of their rank could ever gain the title "Dark Lord of the Sith." Seizing this prestigious position generally required the support of a significant portion of the Sith—and the death of the previous Sith Lord. With the twilight of the Sith and the rise of Darth Bane, the rules of the old Sith were supplanted by new rules. There could only be two Sith at

Table 12-13: The Sith Lord

LEVEL	BASE ATTACK BONUS	CLASS FEATURES
1st	+1	Defense bonuses, fearless, talent, temptation
2nd	+2	Force secret
3rd	+3	Force secret, talent
4th	+4	Force secret
5th	+5	Force secret, talent

any time: One was the master, and the other was the apprentice. While both of these could be Sith Lords, neither could take on an apprentice until the other was dead. Sometimes this resulted in vicious battles between master and student. But more commonly, a Sith Master would pass on all he knew before expiring, leaving his former apprentice to take on an apprentice of his own, and thus continue the tradition of the Sith.

Examples of Sith Lords in Star Wars

Darth Bane, Darth Sidious, Darth Maul, Darth Tyranus, Darth Vader, Darth Malak, Darth Nihilus, Darth Krayt, Exar Kun.

Requirements

To qualify to become a Sith Lord, a character must fulfill the following criteria.

Minimum Heroic Level: 12th.
Trained Skills: Use the Force.
Feats: Force Sensitivity, Weapon Proficiency (lightsaber).
Force Techniques: Any one (see Force Techniques, page 101).
Dark Side Score: Your Dark Side Score (see page 94) must be equal to your Wisdom score. If your Dark Side Score ever becomes less than your Wisdom score, you lose access to all class features granted by this class until your Dark Side Score again equals your Wisdom score.
Special: Must be a member of the Sith tradition (see page 105).

Game Rule Information

Sith Lords have the following game statistics.

Hit Points

At each level, Sith Lords gain 1d10 hit points + their Constitution modifier.

Force Points

Sith Lords gain a number of Force Points equal to 7 + one-half their character level, rounded down, every time they gain a new level in this class. (Due to their strong connection to the dark side of the Force, Sith Lords gain more Force Points than most other prestige classes.)

Class Features

The following are features of the Sith Lord prestige class.

Defense Bonuses

At 1st level, you gain a +3 class bonus to your Reflex, Fortitude, and Will Defense.

Fearless

You are immune to fear effects.

Talents

At every odd-numbered level (1st, 3rd, and 5th), you select a talent. The talent may be selected from the Sith talent tree (see page 223) or any Force talent tree in Chapter 6: The Force. You must meet the prerequisites (if any) of the chosen talent. No talent can be selected more than once unless expressly indicated.

Temptation

You are adept at using Dun Möch, an ancient and vile technique for tempting others to tap into the dark side of the Force. As a standard action, make a Persuasion check and compare it to the Will Defense of a single opponent within line of sight. If the check succeeds, the target is filled with fear or anger, briefly giving in to the dark side. If the target spends a Force Point before your next turn, it must either add 1 point to its Dark Side Score or move −1 step on the condition track (see Conditions, page 148) as it is overcome by doubt and remorse. If the target spends a Destiny Point before your next turn, it instead must add 2 points to its Dark Side Score or move −2 steps on the condition track.

Force Secret

You have learned forbidden secrets of tapping the dark side of the Force. At 2nd level and every level thereafter, you gain one Force secret that, once selected, cannot be changed (see Force Secrets, page 103, for more information).

FEMALE HUMAN SITH LORD

Chapter XIII
Galactic Gazetteer

The *Star Wars* universe is populated with a wide variety of species hailing from thousands of worlds. Each of these worlds has its own unique qualities and cultures. Since fantastic locales are a big part of what makes *Star Wars* exciting and fun, it is important to know a little bit about the established worlds in order to base adventures there.

Life in the Galaxy

Because the galaxy has had some form of interrelated society for more than twenty thousand years (be it Old Republic, Empire, or New Republic), most everyone is used to a mix of species and cultures. There are some beings who are prejudiced against one or another species (and this is especially noticeable during the Empire's control of the galaxy), but most others appreciate the diversity the galactic society has to offer. From planetary spaceports to orbiting space stations, it isn't unusual for Humans and Twi'leks and Mon Calamari to work side by side or otherwise interact. They don't always get along, but that could be said about any individuals in any species. This diversity has led to a spread of ideas, philosophies, sciences, and cultures. Markets throughout the galaxy feature a wide assortment of exotic goods from a variety of worlds. Again, such opportunities for species and cultures to mingle aren't unusual—they're just part of everyday life.

Finally, a galactic society requires open communications to flourish. The Old Republic developed the HoloNet to handle this. A near-instantaneous communications network, it provides a free flow of holograms and other forms of communications among member worlds. Using hundreds of thousands of non-mass transceivers connected through hyperspace simutunnels and routed through massive computer sorters and decoders, the HoloNet allows news and communications to flow from one world to another in almost real time. During the time of the Empire, large portions of the HoloNet system were shut down, and the remaining portions were mostly restricted to government and military use. This reduction of the system cut off rebellious worlds and kept news of the Empire's actions from spreading too quickly. In addition, datacards and other forms of news and information are carried from place to place by starships. This means that even without the HoloNet, in many cases information is only a hyperspace trip away.

Planets of the Galaxy

This section provides a brief gazetteer detailing information on a variety of planets throughout the galaxy. Each entry lists not only pertinent information for the Gamemaster but also Knowledge check DCs for players. This sort of information allows the GM to determine how much a character (and not necessarily the player) knows about a given world.

Bespin
Region: Outer Rim
Climate: Temperate (in the Life Zone)
Gravity: Standard
Moons: 2
Length of Day: 12 standard hours
Length of Year: 5,110 standard days
Sapient Species: 68% Human, 8% Ugnaught, 6% Lutrillian, 18% other species
Government: Guild
Capital: Cloud City
Major Exports: Foodstuffs, technology
Major Imports: Tibanna gas, tourism, cloud cars

Knowledge (Galactic Lore)
DC RESULT
15 The gas giant of Bespin is renowned for its rich stores of Tibanna gas, a key component in blaster ammunition.
20 Cloud City was built by Ugnaughts, the descendents of whom now work the Tibanna gas mines above the planet.
25 The beldon is a huge, floating creature that lives in Bespin's atmosphere and feeds off of airborne plankton floating around the planet.

Knowledge (Social Sciences)
DC RESULT
15 Bespin's primary outpost of civilization is Cloud City, an independent mining colony and haven port for travelers in the Anoat Sector.
20 Though Bespin is a mining colony, they are not a part of the Mining Guild and have rejected any attempts by the Mining Guild to bring the colony into the fold.
25 Bespin maintains neutrality most due to its size, making it a favorite port-of-call for smugglers and others that do not wish to attract governmental attention.

Bothawui
Region: Mid Rim
Climate: Temperate
Gravity: Standard
Moons: 3
Length of Day: 27 standard hours
Length of Year: 351 local days
Sapient Species: 98% Bothan (native), 1% Human, 1% other species
Government: Bothan council
Capital: Drev'starn
Major Exports: Information, technology
Major Imports: Technology

Knowledge (Galactic Lore)
DC RESULT
10 Bothawui is a world covered in mountains and ridges separated by deep, wide valleys inhabited by dangerous wildlife.
15 Bothans eventually discovered that espionage and infiltration were far more convenient methods of waging war, and soon it became the "Bothan way."
20 Settlers from Bothawui established colonies on the planet of Kothlis, making the Bothans one of the few species to maintain permanent colonies on other worlds.
25 As a result of the suspicious and treacherous nature of life on Bothawui, the Bothan SpyNet developed and became the foremost information gathering network in the galaxy.

Knowledge (Social Sciences)
DC RESULT
10 Bothan society is extremely focused on the flow and exchange of information, even impacting the daily lives of ordinary citizens.
15 Bothan politicians rise to power by displaying a mastery over the flow of information and the application of political force.
20 othan politics can be extremely dangerous, and sabotage, assassination, and espionage are as common on Bothawui as debates and normal legislation on other worlds.

Cerea
Region: Mid Rim
Climate: Temperate
Gravity: Standard
Moons: 1
Length of Day: 27 standard hours
Length of Year: 386 standard days

Sapient Species: 98% Cerean (native), 1% Human, 1% other species
Population: 450 million
Government: Council of Elders
Capital: Tecave
Tech Level: Interplanetary (industrial)
Major Exports: Foodstuffs
Major Imports: Technology

Knowledge (Galactic Lore)

DC	RESULT
15	Cerea is a lush temperate world covered in thick forests and jungles.
20	Cerea's isolation from the rest of the galaxy has resulted in the planet remaining largely untouched by industry or civilization, allowing it to maintain a nearly complete natural ecosystem.
25	During the Clone Wars, Cerea struggled to maintain its freedom and neutrality, opting to stay out of the fighting whenever possible.
30	In the waning days of the Old Republic, a generation of Cerean youths rebelled against their elders and sought out the culture and technology of the galaxy at large, leading to a conflict within their society that resulted in bloody uprisings.

Knowledge (Social Sciences)

DC	RESULT
15	Cerea is largely isolationist, preferring to stay out of interstellar conflicts.
20	Despite their isolationist views, many Cereans have risen to positions of prominence, though their decision to leave the home planet has made them outsiders in the eyes of their own people.
25	Cereans have strict laws in place that limit the import of high technology and goods from other worlds, as the planet's rulers seek to prevent technology from corrupting their society.

CORUSCANT

Region: Core
Climate: Temperate (urban)
Gravity: Standard
Moons: 4
Length of Day: 24 standard hours
Length of Year: 368 local days
Sapient Species: 78% Human (native), 22% other species
Government: Republic or Dictatorship (depending on era)
Capital: None
Major Exports: None
Major Imports: Foodstuffs, medicinal goods

Knowledge (Galactic Lore)

DC	RESULT
10	Coruscant is one of the oldest and most populated planets in the galaxy, its surface completely covered by cities.
15	Coruscant long ago became the seat of galactic politics, and it is from this planet that all major interstellar governments have ruled.
20	Coruscant relies on vast weather control stations to regulate everything from temperature to humidity.
25	In the lowest depths of Coruscant, citizens of the planet have degenerated into barbarism or scavenging, making the city depths dangerous to all but the most prepared.

Knowledge (Social Sciences)

DC	RESULT
10	Coruscant is not only the governmental center of the galaxy but also the cultural center of the galaxy, where new trends and fashions debut.
20	Despite the fact that most of the wealthiest members of galactic society live on Coruscant, the world is also home to millions of poor and destitute people, many of whom eke out meager livings as servants and laborers.
30	Coruscant is home to the Black Sun crime syndicate (and other noteworthy criminal organizations) and has a flourishing black market where illegal goods are trafficked on a daily basis.

DORIN

Region: Expansion Region
Climate: Temperate (low oxygen)
Gravity: Standard
Moons: 1
Length of Day: 22 standard hours
Length of Year: 409 standard days
Sapient Species: 100% Kel Dor (native)
Government: Representative Republic
Capital: Dor'shan
Major Exports: None
Major Imports: Technology

Knowledge (Galactic Lore)

DC	RESULT
15	Dorin has a unique atmosphere that is toxic to most sentient species but perfectly breathable to the Kel Dor species.
20	Situated between two black holes, Dorin was not discovered by galactic settlers until several centuries before the Galactic Civil War.

25 Though Kel Dor are generally altruistic and helpful, their justice system is very swift (perhaps frighteningly so to outsiders who make a habit of breaking laws).
30 The Kel Dor once had a proud and influential Force-using tradition known as the Baran Do sages, but since the planet's entry into galactic society, the tradition's influence and prestige have waned as young Kel Dor are drawn to other Force traditions.

Knowledge (Life Sciences)
DC RESULT
15 Dorin's atmosphere is composed mostly of helium and native gases, with very little oxygen. As a result, Kel Dor cannot breathe on other worlds without the assistance of a breath mask.

DURO
Region: Core
Climate: Temperate (polluted)
Gravity: Standard
Moons: 0
Length of Day: 33 standard hours
Length of Year: 420 local days
Sapient Species: 53% Duros (native), 36% Human, 11% other species (on world); 91% Duros, 9% other species (orbital cities)
Government: Corporate
Capital: None
Major Exports: Starships, technology
Major Imports: Foodstuffs, ore, labor

Knowledge (Galactic Lore)
DC RESULT
10 Duro is one of the most reliable and prolific sources of starship manufacturing in the galaxy.
15 Many years ago, the government of Duro opted to consolidate all of the starship manufacturing companies into one government corporation, at which time the entire planet came under corporate rule.
20 The citizens of Duro were moved off of the surface of the world and into floating domed cities that orbited the planet, in order to make way for terrestrial manufacturing plants and resource harvesting systems.

Knowledge (Social Sciences)
DC RESULT
10 Duro's corporate government controls the planet's starship manufacturing facilities as well as almost every other industrial site on the world.
15 Only those that own stock in Duro's corporate government can participate in lawmaking and world politics.
20 The government on Duro permeates every aspect of the lives of its citizen-employees, and those citizens who remain on Duro are almost guaranteed to work for some branch of the starship manufacturing business.

ENDOR, FOREST MOON OF
Region: Outer Rim
Climate: Temperate
Gravity: Standard
Moons: —
Length of Day: 18 standard hours
Length of Year: 402 local days
Sapient Species: 95% Ewok (native), 4% Yuzzum (native), 1% other species
Government: None
Capital: None
Major Exports: None
Major Imports: None

Knowledge (Galactic Lore)
DC RESULT
20 Traditionally ignored by most of the galaxy, the forest moon of Endor is a lush and nearly untouched satellite orbiting the gas giant Endor in the Moddell Sector.
25 The forest moon of Endor is a favorite spot for galactic travelers passing through the Moddell Sector, and numerous visitors (both legitimate travelers as well as smugglers and outlaws) have used the moon as a temporary safe haven.
30 During the height of the Empire, the forest moon of Endor was used as an Imperial base of operations far away from the rest of civilization. The second Death Star was built in orbit of the forest moon.

Knowledge (Social Sciences)
DC RESULT
20 The native sentient species on Endor have no significant cities or technology, living in tribal groups and small villages.
25 The native Ewoks are shamanistic, superstitious, and clever. They built their villages in the boughs of great trees and are known to build complex traps and pitfalls to snare much larger predators.

GAMORR
Region: Outer Rim
Climate: Temperate
Gravity: Standard
Moons: 1
Length of Day: 28 standard hours

Length of Year: 380 local days
Sapient Species: 100% Gamorrean (native)
Government: Feudal clans
Capital: None
Major Exports: Warriors, slaves
Major Imports: Foodstuffs, technology

Knowledge (Galactic Lore)

DC	RESULT
15	Gamorr's past is filled with tales of war and violence, with conflicts so numerous that almost no historians outside of the Gamorreans themselves can truly understand them.
20	Gamorr is a verdant world covered in forests and jungles that boast a diverse array of flora and fauna.
25	When the first Humans arrived on Gamorr, they enslaved large numbers of the native populace and carried them off as slaves.
30	The Hutts are particularly notorious for visiting Gamorr and pressing the natives into service, a problem the Gamorreans have been powerless to prevent.

Knowledge (Social Sciences)

DC	RESULT
15	The concept of warfare is central to Gamorrean society, with their culture and traditions revolving around neverending conflicts.
20	Gamorrean males often travel offworld to work as mercenaries and criminal enforcers.
25	Gamorreans are divided into clans, each of which represents a family or group of families that constantly clashes with other clans.
30	While Gamorrean males are the primary warriors and hunters, Gamorrean females are the matriarchs and rulers of the society.

IRIDONIA

Region: Mid Rim
Climate: Arid (hot)
Gravity: Standard
Moons: 2
Length of Day: 29 standard hours
Length of Year: 413 local days
Sapient Species: 99% Zabrak (native), 1% other species
Government: Dictatorship
Capital: Malidris
Major Exports: None
Major Imports: Foodstuffs, technology

Knowledge (Galactic Lore)

DC	RESULT
10	Iridonia's environment is extremely harsh, so much so that even the native Zabrak have a difficult time surviving exposed on the surface.
15	Iridonia was one of the first worlds of join the Old Republic and is reputed to be one of the first planets to achieve hyperspace travel.
20	The Zabrak of Iridonia developed cities deep inside canyons carved into the planet's surface, clustering together in refuge and developing their society in the cramped caverns.

Knowledge (Social Sciences)

DC	RESULT
10	Iridonia is a strong, independent world whose people resist oppression of any kind.
15	Though the Zabrak are spread out over eight worlds (including their homeworld of Iridonia), all eight governments have a standing agreement to come to one another's defense in times of crisis.
20	Nationalism is a major part of Zabrak politics, and Iridonians believe that despite their homeworld's harsh environment, it is the greatest among all Zabrak worlds.
25	Iridonians place a large emphasis on the will to survive, and as such their government, while civilized, believes that "survival of the fittest" is a philosophy that can be used to determine fitness to rule.

ITHOR

Region: Mid Rim
Climate: Tropical
Gravity: Standard
Moons: 1
Length of Day: 41 standard hours
Length of Year: 422 standard days
Sapient Species: 99% Ithorian (native), 1% other species
Government: Herds
Capital: None
Major Exports: Foodstuffs, medicine, spices
Major Imports: Technology

Knowledge (Galactic Lore)

DC	RESULT
10	Ithor is a tropical world covered in dense rainforests and wild jungles.
15	Ithor's natural ecosystem remains relatively untouched despite having millions of native sentient inhabitants.
20	The Ithorians first explored space in "herd ships," massive repulsorlift-powered cities.

Knowledge (Social Sciences)
DC RESULT
- 10 Ithorians live in self-described herds, which travel in massive floating cities above the planet's surface.
- 15 All Ithorians adore harmony with nature, and they are known to react violently when confronted with someone threatening that way of life.
- 20 Each herd is completely independent from the others, remaining both autonomous and self-sufficient.

KASHYYYK
Region: Mid Rim
Climate: Temperate
Gravity: Standard
Moons: 1
Length of Day: 26 standard hours
Length of Year: 381 local days
Sapient Species: 100% Wookiee (native)
Government: Representative Tribal
Capital: Rwookrrorro
Major Exports: Technology, natural resources
Major Imports: Medicines

Knowledge (Galactic Lore)
DC RESULT
- 10 Despite being covered in a thick forest of trees populated by ferocious predators, Kashyyyk gave rise to the Wookiee species that now travels the space lanes. The Wookiees have warred with their interplanetary neighbors, the Trandoshans, frequently throughout history.
- 15 The Wookiee natives built huge cities within the trees, high above the most dangerous sections of the planet's forest, allowing them to live in relative safety.
- 20 Kashyyyk only joined the galactic community a few millennia before the rise of the Empire, developing space travel as a result of disassembling Trandoshan technology.

Knowledge (Social Sciences)
DC RESULT
- 10 Wookiee society revolves around the importance of family and honor.
- 15 Wookiees are extremely trustworthy, and a Wookiee's word is a bond so strong that only death can break it.
- 20 Wookiee society has little tolerance for anything seen as detrimental or oppressive, and Wookiees are quick to dispose of problems using violence.
- 25 The concept of the life debt (becoming someone's loyal protector for saving a Wookiee's life) is one example of the strength of Wookiee honor.

MON CALAMARI
Region: Outer Rim
Climate: Temperate
Gravity: Standard
Moons: 3
Length of Day: 21 standard hours
Length of Year: 398 local days
Sapient Species: 39% Mon Calamari (native), 60% Quarren (native), 1% other species
Government: Representative Council
Capital: Foamwater City
Major Exports: Warships, weapons
Major Imports: Foodstuffs, medicine, technology

Knowledge (Galactic Lore)
DC RESULT
- 10 Mon Calamari is an aquatic world dotted with small continents and islands spread throughout its vast oceans.
- 15 Mon Calamari has supplied the galaxy with starships of superior quality ever since it first made contact with the Old Republic.
- 20 Unlike other worlds covered by oceans, Mon Calamari has almost no tectonic activity or violent weather, making the planet both placid and attractive to tourists.
- 25 Over time, a rift has developed between the Quarren and the Mon Calamari, which now manifests itself as an animosity that disrupts any attempts at cooperation.

Knowledge (Social Sciences)
DC RESULT
- 10 **Mon Calamari boasts two distinct societies:** one for the Mon Calamari species, and one for the Quarren species.
- 15 Ill will between the Mon Calamari and the Quarren comes as a result of outside interference. The Quarren see the Mon Calamari as meddlers in galactic affairs, while many Mon Calamari see the Quarren as cowards and isolationists.
- 20 The animosity between the two species is the result of conflicts with other species, some of which have nearly erupted into full-blown wars.
- 25 Interacting with either of the two societies is likely to make it difficult to interact with the other, as the prejudices found in both species can extend to outsiders as well.

Naboo

Region: Mid Rim
Climate: Temperate
Gravity: Standard
Moons: 3
Length of Day: 26 standard hours
Length of Year: 312 local days
Sapient Species: 72% Gungan (native), 27% Human, 1% other species
Government: Democratic monarchy (Human), Council (Gungan)
Capitals: Theed (Human), Otoh Gunga (Gungan)
Major Exports: Grains, art, cultural items
Major Imports: Technology, processed foods

Knowledge (Bureaucracy)

DC	RESULT
15	Though the Humans on Naboo support a democratic government, they elect a sovereign monarch to rule over them. There are no age limitations on voting or even leadership.

Knowledge (Galactic Lore)

DC	RESULT
10	Naboo is a peaceful planet that has remained a relatively insignificant, if beautiful, member of galactic society for centuries.
15	Naboo is a world covered in beautiful oceans, sweeping grasslands, and rich forests. Human settlements tend to incorporate waterfalls, cliffs, and other natural terrain features. Gungans live in beautiful submerged cities hidden beneath great lakes.
20	Many years ago, the Humans of Naboo came into conflict with the native Gungans, thus beginning a centuries-long animosity between the two peoples.
25	Naboo, unlike most other habitable worlds, does not have a molten core. Instead, the center of the planet is hollowed out and filled with water.

Knowledge (Social Sciences)

DC	RESULT
10	The Human society on Naboo is peaceful and artistic, focusing on promoting cultural greatness over political power.
25	Gungan society is extremely isolationist and xenophobic, to the point where they typically use violence first and ask questions later.
30	Gungan law is usually considered extremely harsh, with even the smallest offenses warranting exile or even the death penalty.

Nar Shaddaa

Region: Mid Rim
Climate: Temperate (urban)
Gravity: Standard
Moons: —
Length of Day: 87 standard hours
Length of Year: 419 local days
Sapient Species: 20% Human, 1% Evocii, 79% other species
Government: Hutt crime lords
Capital: None
Major Exports: Illegal goods, narcotics, weapons
Major Imports: Foodstuffs, illegal goods, medicine, technology

Knowledge (Galactic Lore)
DC RESULT
- 10 Nar Shaddaa, also known as the Smuggler's Moon, orbits Nal Hutta (the Hutt homeworld). Nar Shaddaa is a haven for criminals of all stripes who gather to conduct illicit business.
- 15 Nar Shaddaa, though technically within Hutt Space and under Hutt rule, has no true organized government and is divided into sectors ruled by individual species, gangs, and crime lords.
- 20 Nar Shaddaa is an urban sprawl with soaring towers and dizzying depths. Many sectors of Nar Shaddaa are in poor repair, boasting unstable architecture and zones where even a wise Jedi fears to tread.

Knowledge (Social Sciences)
DC RESULT
- 10 Nar Shaddaa boasts a strong black market economy. Almost any sort of contraband can be found on Nar Shaddaa for the right price.
- 15 Millions of smugglers, crime lords, and information brokers make their homes on Nar Shaddaa. Their organizations hold sway over different zones of the Smuggler's Moon, and small wars break out between rival gangs on a regular basis.
- 20 Almost every major criminal organization in the galaxy, from the Hutt crime lords to the Black Sun Syndicate, has agents working behind the scenes on Nar Shaddaa.

RODIA
Region: Mid Rim
Climate: Tropical and arid (hot)
Gravity: Standard
Moons: 2
Length of Day: 29 standard hours
Length of Year: 305 local days
Sapient Species: 99% Rodian (native), 1% other species
Government: Rodian Grand Protector
Capital: Equator City
Major Exports: Bounty hunters, foodstuffs, exotic animals, weaponry
Major Imports: Technology, agricultural goods, weapons

Knowledge (Galactic Lore)
DC RESULT
- 10 Rodia's thick, lush jungles provide an ample breeding ground for savage predators, and as the Rodians themselves evolved, they learned to survive among even the deadliest of creatures.
- 15 The Old Republic first made contact with the Rodian people thousands of years ago when scouting vessels arrived on their homeworld, and this first meeting resulted in violent conflict.
- 20 Prior to joining the greater galactic community, the Rodian people had become violent and prone to hunting one another down, killing indiscriminately for the thrill of the hunt.
- 25 Since the jungles of Rodia provide plenty of food in the form of fruits, vegetables, and easily hunted prey, the Rodian people never developed any skill at agriculture.

Knowledge (Social Sciences)
DC RESULT
- 10 Prestige in Rodian society is based on the individual Rodian's ability to hunt and track.
- 15 The Rodian people learned to channel some of their violent tendencies into works of theater, and Rodian dramas are violent but compelling performances that are well regarded throughout the galaxy.
- 20 The highest aspiration of many Rodian natives is to go out into the galaxy and obtain a great quarry, bringing their prey back to Rodia as proof of their excellent hunting skills.

RYLOTH
Region: Outer Rim
Climate: Subarctic, temperate, and arid
Gravity: Standard
Moons: 5
Length of Day: 305 standard days
Length of Year: 1 local day
Sapient Species: 76% Twi'lek (native), 24% other species
Government: Feudal meritocracy
Capital: Kala'uun
Major Exports: Ryll spice, slaves
Major Imports: Foodstuffs, medicine, technology

Knowledge (Galactic Lore)
DC RESULT
- 10 The planet Ryloth has long been a relatively neutral and out-of-the-way planet, avoiding conflict more deftly than most other worlds.
- 15 Ryloth is an incredibly dangerous world that has a unique orbit that causes one side of the planet to perpetually face the world's sun. As such, the sunlit side of the planet remains incredibly hot, while the dark side of the planet is frigidly cold year-round.
- 20 Ryloth produces an extremely rare kind of spice known as ryll, which is harvested and sold by Twi'lek traders.
- 25 The only way life forms can survive on Ryloth is by living in a band of perpetual dusk right at the sunlight's terminator line, where the temperatures are moderate and life can flourish.

Knowledge (Social Sciences)

DC	RESULT
10	Ryloth is usually perceived as lawless world by the galaxy at large, thanks to its lax views on both slavery and the trafficking of spice.
15	Twi'leks native to Ryloth are extremely loyal to their families, also called head-clans, as they are not only family members but also avenues to power.
20	When enough members of a head-clan ascend to positions of leadership within Ryloth society, that head-clan grows in power and stature, rising as one through the ranks of the government.

Sullust

Region: Outer Rim
Climate: Superheated
Gravity: Standard
Moons: 2
Length of Day: 20 standard hours
Length of Year: 263 local days
Sapient Species: 96% Sullustan (native), 2% Human, 1% Bith, 1% other species
Government: Corporation
Capital: Byllurun
Major Exports: Starships, computers, droids, hyperdrive and astrogation technology
Major Imports: Foodstuffs, water

Knowledge (Bureaucracy)

DC	RESULT
10	The SoroSuub Corporation serves as the acting government of Sullust and runs planetary affairs like a business.
15	SoroSuub is not a profit-driven monstrosity like those found in the Corporate Sector, and most of the company's policies and decrees are well accepted by the populace because they are not intrusive or oppressive.

Knowledge (Galactic Lore)

DC	RESULT
10	Sullust is the homeworld of the Sullustan people, as well as the base of operations for the powerful SoroSuub Corporation.
15	Sullust is a volcanic and tectonically unstable planet. The Sullustans have adapted to living in massive, subterranean lava tubes.
20	Sullust became a major trading hub quickly after making contact with the rest of the galaxy, and as galactic commerce became more frequent on the world, so too did the presence of corporations and manufacturing.
25	As the planet's prestige grew, so did the SoroSuub Corporation, which eventually grew so large that it seized control of the planet's government.

Tatooine

Region: Outer Rim
Climate: Arid
Gravity: Standard
Moons: 3
Length of Day: 23 standard hours
Length of Year: 304 local days
Sapient Species: 70% Human, 5% Jawa (native), 5% Tusken Raider (native), 20% other species
Government: Hutt crime lords
Capital: Bestine
Major Exports: Illegal weapons, minerals, narcotics
Major Imports: Foodstuffs, medicine, technology

Knowledge (Galactic Lore)

DC	RESULT
10	Tatooine is a backwater desert world dotted with cities, villages, and moisture farms. Native species include the primitive Tusken Raiders and the Jawas.
15	Controlled by the Hutts, Tatooine is a haven for criminal activity and is often used as a hiding place for lawbreakers on the run.
20	Tatooine hosts numerous dangerous sporting events, including Podracing. One of the most famous Podracing events is the Boonta Eve Classic, which is frequently attended by the planet's Hutt overlords.

Knowledge (Social Sciences)

DC	RESULT
10	Tatooine is controlled by the Hutts, and many criminals seek refuge there.
15	The Jawas of Tatooine have a reputation for being scavenging junk dealers and swindlers, but they are mostly harmless.
20	The Tusken Raiders of Tatooine are referred to locally as Sand People. They live in nomadic tribes and often ride around on large herd animals called banthas. Sand People are extremely violent, attacking anyone who sets foot in their territory. They typically wield gaderffii ("gaffi sticks"), but some tribes use primitive slugthrowers as well.

Trandosha

Region: Mid Rim
Climate: Arid
Gravity: 62% Standard
Moons: 1
Length of Day: 25 standard hours
Length of Year: 371 local days
Sapient Species: 99% Trandoshan (native), 1% other species
Population: 42 million
Government: Tribal
Capital: Hsskhor
Tech Level: Interstellar (advanced)
Major Exports: Slaves, mercenaries
Major Imports: Technology

Knowledge (Galactic Lore)

DC	RESULT
10	Trandosha is located in the same system as Kashyyyk, the Wookiee homeworld. The two species rarely see eye to eye.
15	Trandosha boasts lighter than average gravity, which allows the sluggish Trandoshans to move with ease on their homeworld.
20	Trandosha joined the galactic community many millennia ago but has always been indirectly represented in galactic affairs by a Wookiee representative, which has led to some animosity between the two species.

Knowledge (Social Sciences)

DC	RESULT
10	Trandoshans make poor diplomats and have trouble dealing peacefully with others.
15	Trandoshan slavers have captured or killed more Wookiees than any other species.
20	Trandoshans revere their tribal elders. Breaking Trandoshan traditions or disrespecting one's elders often leads to exile from individual cities or even the entire planet.

Travel in the Galaxy

All the worlds in the galaxy mean nothing to a character if they are unreachable. Fortunately, hyperspace travel has become common, affordable, and (usually) safe.

Astrogation

Moving from a given location to a desired destination through hyperspace requires a successful Use Computer check. Because every object in the galaxy is constantly in motion, the precise path between two locations changes from day to day. If the astrogator uses current data (one day old at most), he can plot a safe course. Doing so takes 1 minute and requires a successful DC 10 Use Computer check.

If an astrogator has no data with which to plot a jump through hyperspace, the base DC for the Use Computer check is 30, and the astrogator must spend 1 hour calculating coordinates and vectors before attempting the check.

As a general rule, data for a particular route through hyperspace is available to anyone with access to the HoloNet—although that data might be outdated if the route in question is not frequently traveled by other ships.

Certain situations or circumstances can also modify the check, as shown in Table 13–1: Astrogation DC Modifiers. The lack of a nav computer (or, failing that, an astromech droid with stored coordinates) makes the task much more difficult. If time is of the essence, the astrogator can perform the check as a full-round action round by taking a –10 penalty on his Use Computer check.

If the Use Computer check is successful, the starship enters hyperspace without incident and arrives at its destination in a number of days equal to 1d6 × the ship's hyperdrive multiplier..

A failed Use Computer check indicates that the astrogator has made a potentially dangerous error in his calculations. Make another Use Computer check using the same modifiers and against the same DC. If this second Use Computer check is successful, the error is caught before entering hyperspace, and the process of plotting a course must begin anew. If this second Use Computer check fails, the starship moves –1 persistent step on the condition track (see Conditions, page 148) and takes damage equal to 5% of its total hit points for every point by which the check fails. (The persistent condition and damage remain until the ship undergoes maintenance.) If the ship is not disabled or destroyed, it arrives at the intended destination in double the expected travel time. If the ship is disabled, it drops out of hyperspace in a random location somewhere between the point of origin and the destination (the exact location is determined by the GM).

Table 13-1: Astrogation DC Modifiers

SITUATION	CHECK MODIFIER
Using nav computer	+5
No nav computer used[1]	–10
No HoloNet access	–5
Attempt to make check in 1 round	–10

[1] *Do not apply the penalty if the ship has current astrogation data stored in an astromech droid or receives accurate transmitted data from another ship.*

Chapter XIV
Gamemastering

The Gamemaster is the guiding force of the game. If the game is fun, it will be to your credit. If it isn't, you'll need to make some adjustments. But don't worry—running a *Star Wars* game is nowhere near as daunting as it might seem at first.

Described below are the different duties of the GM. As with any hobby, focus on what you enjoy the most, but remember that the other duties are also important.

The Role of the Gamemaster

The Gamemaster is storyteller and referee, creator of terrible threats against the galaxy, secret master of the villainous, criminal, and ruthless, and hidden protector of the brave. The GM's responsibilities include several important tasks; each of these is outlined in this section.

Creating Adventures

As the GM, your primary role in the game is creating and presenting adventures in which the other players can play their heroes. To accomplish this, you need to spend some amount of time before the game preparing your stories. This is true whether you create your own adventures or use published ones.

Creating adventures takes time. Many GMs find this creative process the most fun and rewarding part of being a Gamemaster. Creating interesting characters, settings, plots, and challenges to present to your friends can be a great creative outlet. In fact, creating good adventures is so important that it receives its own section in this chapter (see Building an Adventure, page 249).

Teaching the Game

Sometimes, but not always, it's the GM's responsibility to teach newcomers how to play the game. This isn't a burden; it's a wonderful opportunity. Teaching other people how to play provides you with new players and allows you to set them on the path to becoming top-notch roleplayers. It's easier to learn to play with someone who already knows the game. Players who are taught by a good teacher in a fun game are more likely to stick with the hobby over the long haul. Use this opportunity to encourage new players to become the sort of gamers you want to play games with.

Here are a few pointers on teaching the game:

- You need to know the character creation rules so that you can help new players build characters. Have each player tell you what sort of hero he or she wants to play, then show the players how they can create those heroes with the *Star Wars* rules. If they don't know what to play, show them the five heroic classes, briefly describe each, and let them choose the one that most appeals to them.

- Don't worry about teaching all the rules ahead of time. All the players need to know are the basics that apply to understanding their heroes (what hit points are, how to make attack rolls, how to use skills, and so on), and they can pick up most of this information as the game progresses.
- You need to know how to play the game. As long as you know the rules, the game can move along, and the players can simply focus on their characters and how they react to what happens in the game. Have players tell you what they want their characters to do and translate those decisions into game terms for them. Teach them how the rules work when they need to learn them, on a case-by-case basis. For example, if a player wants her Jedi to use the Force, the player tells you what the hero attempts and you tell her what die to roll, which modifiers to add, and what happens as a result. After a few times, the player will know what to do without asking.

Providing the Backdrop

The Gamemaster is the creator of his or her own campaign. Even though you'll be basing your adventures in the *Star Wars* universe, it's still your campaign.

Consistency is the key to creating a backdrop that feels real to the players. When the heroes go back to Mos Eisley for supplies, they should encounter some of the same characters they met before. Soon, they'll learn the cantina owner's name—and she'll remember them as well. Once you've achieved this level of consistency, however, provide an occasional change. If the heroes come back to have their starfighter repaired again, they may discover that the man who ran the starport went back home to Corellia, and his nephew now runs the family business. That sort of change—one that has nothing to do with the heroes directly, but which they'll notice—makes the players feel as though they're adventuring in a living universe as real as themselves. It's not just a flat backdrop that exists only for them to battle stormtroopers or the villain-of-the-week.

Determining the Style of Play

While the GM provides the adventures and the universe, the players and the GM work together to create the game as a whole. However, it's the GM's responsibility to guide the way the game is played. The best way to accomplish this is by learning what the players want and figuring out what you want as well. Many styles of play exist, but a few are detailed below.

Blast 'Em All!

The heroes blow open the blast door, fight the stormtroopers, and rescue the princess. This style of play is very straightforward. It's fun, exciting, and action-oriented. Very little time is spent on developing personas for the heroes, engaging in roleplaying encounters, or mentioning situations other than what's going on in the adventure. If you're running this type of game, let the heroes face obviously evil opponents and meet obviously helpful characters. Don't expect heroes to anguish over what to do with prisoners. Don't bother too much with credits earned or time spent recovering. Do whatever it takes to get the heroes back into the action as quickly as possible. A hero's motivation does not need to be much more than a desire to fight evil (and maybe acquire credits).

Rules and game balance are important in this style of play. Having heroes with combat ability greater than that of their companions can lead to unfair situations; the more powerful heroes can handle more of the challenges, and thus their players have more fun. If you're using this style, be mindful about adjudicating rules. Think long and hard about additions or changes that you want to make.

Immersive Storytelling

The Galactic Senate is threatened by political turmoil. The heroes must convince the senators to resolve their differences, but can only do so after they've come to terms with their own differing outlooks and agendas. This style of gaming is deep, complex, and challenging. The focus isn't on combat, but on talking, developing in-depth personas, and character interaction. Whole gaming sessions may pass without a single blaster being fired.

In this style of game, most characters should be as complex and richly detailed as the heroes—although the focus should be on motivation and personality, not game statistics. Expect digressions about what each player

Gamemaster Accessories

The following items are available to enhance your game:

Miniatures: The rules in this book assume that you are using *Star Wars* miniatures—attractive, pre-painted plastic figures that can be used to represent heroes and adversaries in the game. Combined with the miniatures-scale battle maps, they make it easy to keep track of character position, tactical movement, line of sight, and other combat factors. Miniatures also add an exciting visual element to the game by giving players a stronger idea of what GM characters, creatures, and other heroic characters look like.

Battle Maps: Battle maps provide spacious, ready-to-use encounter locations for epic *Star Wars* battles. Battle maps can be found in the *Star Wars* Miniatures Game and other *Star Wars Roleplaying Game* products.

Galaxy Tiles: A creative alternative to the battle maps, the *Star Wars Galaxy Tiles* accessories provides cardstock corridors, chambers, and map features that the GM can assemble to create Rebel bases, Imperial installations, and other unique adventure locations.

wants his or her hero to do, and why. Buying spare parts might be as important an encounter as fighting battle droids. (And don't expect the heroes to fight the battle droids at all unless their heroes have a good reason to do so.) Heroes will sometimes take actions against their players' better judgment because "that's what a hero would do." Adventures deal mostly with negotiations, political maneuverings, and character interaction. Players may even talk about the "story" they're collectively creating.

Quoting the rules is less important in this style of play. Since combat isn't the focus, game mechanics take a back seat to hero development. Skills take precedence over combat bonuses, and even then, the numbers don't have to be absolutes. Feel free to change things to fit the players' roleplaying needs, perhaps even streamlining the combat system so that it takes less time away from the story.

Something in Between

Most campaigns are going to fall between these two extremes. There's plenty of action, but there's also a plot line and interaction between heroes and nonheroic characters. Players develop their heroes, but they're eager to get into fights as well. The "in between" style provides a nice mixture of roleplaying encounters and combat encounters. Even in combat missions, you can present characters who don't need to be killed. Instead, you can interact with them through diplomacy, negotiation, or a simple conversation.

> "PERHAPS YOU THINK YOU'RE BEING TREATED UNFAIRLY?"
> – DARTH VADER

ADJUDICATING THE RULES

When everyone gathers around the table to play the game, the Gamemaster is in charge. That doesn't mean that you can tell people what to do outside the boundaries of the game, but it does mean that you're the final arbiter of the rules within the game. Good players always recognize that you have the ultimate authority over the game mechanics. Good GMs know not to change or overturn an existing rule without a good, logical justification so the players don't grow dissatisfied.

This means that you need to know the rules. You're not required to memorize the rulebook, but you should have a clear understanding of what's in the book so that when a situation comes up that requires a ruling, you know where to reference the proper rule in the book.

STACKING BONUSES

The term "stacking" means combining for a cumulative effect. It refers to modifiers (bonuses and penalties) that combine instead of replacing one another.

Generally, factors that apply modifiers to a statistic, roll, or check combine if they have different descriptors. For example, a competence bonus will combine with a morale bonus, but two competence bonuses will not combine.

Modifiers with the same descriptor apply only the best bonus. For example, a competence bonus of +2 is used instead of a competence bonus of +1 when both bonuses are applied to the same statistic, roll, or check.

Any bonus without a descriptor (sometimes called an "unnamed bonus") stacks with all other bonuses, including bonuses without a descriptor.

The only descriptor bonuses that stack with others of the same type are circumstance bonuses and dodge bonuses. (Even then, circumstance bonuses stack only if they're not provided by essentially the same circumstance.) Other descriptor bonuses do not stack with others of the same type unless specifically noted otherwise.

All penalties stack regardless of source.

Often a situation arises that isn't explicitly covered by the rules. In such a situation, it's the GM who needs to provide guidance as to how it should be resolved. When you come upon a situation that doesn't seem to be covered by the rules, consider the following:

- Look to any similar situation that is covered in the rules. Try to extrapolate from what you see presented there and apply it to the current circumstance.
- If you have to make something up, stick with it for the rest of the campaign. (This is called a "house rule.") Consistency keeps players satisfied and gives them the feeling that they are adventuring in a stable, predictable universe, not in some random, nonsensical place subject only to the GM's whims.
- When in doubt, remember this handy rule: Favorable circumstances provide a +2 circumstance bonus to any d20 roll; unfavorable circumstances impose a –2 penalty. You'll be surprised how often this "GM's secret rule" solves problems.

KEEPING THE GAME BALANCED

Game balance ensures that most hero choices are relatively equal. A balanced game is one in which one hero doesn't dominate over the rest because of a choice that he or she made (species, class, talent, feat, Force power, weapon, and so on). It also reflects that the heroes aren't too powerful for the threats they face, yet neither are they hopelessly overmatched.

Two things drive game balance: good management and trust.

Good Management
A GM who carefully watches all portions of the game so that nothing gets out of control helps keep the game balanced. Heroes and characters, victories and defeats, awards and afflictions, items found and credits spent—all these things must be monitored. No one hero should ever become significantly more powerful than the others. If this does happen, the others should have an opportunity to catch up in short order. The heroes as a whole should never get so powerful that all challenges become trivial to them. Nor should they be constantly overwhelmed by what they must face. It's no fun to always lose, and always winning gets boring fast. When temporary imbalances do occur, it's easier to fix them by altering the challenges than by changing anything about the heroes and their powers or equipment. No one likes to get something, only to have it taken away again because it was too unbalancing.

Trust
Players should trust the GM. This trust can be gained over time through consistent use of rules, by not taking sides (that is, not favoring one player at another's expense), and by making it clear that you're not vindictive toward the players or their characters. If the players trust the GM—and through you, the game system—they will recognize that anything that enters the game has been carefully considered. If you adjudicate a situation, the players should be able to trust it as a fair call and not question or second-guess you. That way, the players can focus their attention on playing their characters, succeeding in the game, and having fun, trusting their GM to take care of matters of fairness and realism. They also trust that you will do whatever you can to make sure that they can enjoy playing their heroes, potentially succeed in the game, and have fun. If this level of trust can be achieved, you'll have greater freedom to add or change things in your game without worrying about the players protesting or scrutinizing every decision.

Handling Unbalanced Heroes
Sometimes, the unexpected happens. The heroes may defeat a villain, foil an unstoppable escape plan, and steal a custom starfighter you never intended to fall into their hands. Or, even more likely, the combination of some new acquisition with an item or power a hero already has will prove unbalancing in ways you didn't foresee.

Once a mistake has been made, and a hero ends up too powerful, all is not lost. In fact, it's almost never difficult to simply increase the challenges the hero faces to keep him or her from breezing through encounters. However, this solution can be unsatisfying, since the encounters can become too difficult for the other, more balanced heroes. At the same time, it's never fun to lose some aspect of your hero that turns out to be unbalancing. From the player's point of view, it's not his or her fault.

You have two options: Deal with the problem in-game or deal with the problem out-of-game.

Dealing with the Problem In-Game: "In-game" is a term used to describe something that happens in the story created by the play of the game. For example, suppose a hero becomes unbalanced by building a droid servant that fights better than any of the heroes in the group. (This is something that the GM shouldn't have let happen to begin with, but all GMs occasionally make mistakes.) An in-game solution might be to have an enemy scoundrel sabotage the droid, or suspicious guards might confiscate the droid the next time the heroes visit Coruscant. Whatever you do, try not to make it obvious that the situation is actually just a tool to balance the game. Instead, make it seem just a part of the adventure. (If you don't, indignant players will get very angry.)

Dealing with the Problem Out-of-Game: "Out-of-game" means something that happens in the real world, but has an impact on the game itself. An out-of-game solution to the problem described in the previous paragraph would be to take the player aside between sessions and explain that the game has become unbalanced because of her too-powerful droid and that things need to change or the game may fall apart. A reasonable person will see the value in continuing the game, and she'll work with you either in-game (perhaps donating the droid to an appropriate allied organization) or out-of-game (perhaps by erasing the droid from her hero sheet and just pretending it was never there). Be warned, however, that not every gamer is reasonable in this way. Many will not appreciate this level of intrusion on your part and will resent giving up a great ability or item their hero "earned." After an unfortunate exchange of this type, it will seem obvious and contrived if you try to balance things with an in-game solution.

Running a Game Session
After everything is prepared, and everyone sits down at the table, you're on. It's your show. Here are some things you should consider, at the table and before you ever get there, to help make the game run as smoothly as possible.

Knowing the Players
Normally, but not always, the GM is in charge of inviting players to play in his or her game. If this is the case, it's your responsibility to know and understand each of these people well enough that you can be reasonably sure that they'll all get along, work well together, and enjoy the sort of game you run.

A lot of this has to do with playing style. Ultimately, you have to know the kind of game your players want to play. With players new to the game or a newly formed group, this may take a while to define. Recognize that while you're in charge, it's really everybody's game. The players are all there, coming back session after session, because they trust that you'll help them have a fun and rewarding experience.

TABLE RULES

One thing that will help everyone, players and GM alike, to all get along will be establishing a set of rules—rules that have nothing to do with the actual game but that govern what happens with the people around the table.

The following are some "table rules" issues you'll need to deal with eventually. It's best to come up with the answers before you start a regular campaign. You can establish these yourself, or you can work them out with your players.

No-Show Players

Sometimes a regular player can't show up for a game session. The GM and group are faced with the question of what to do with his or her hero. There are several possibilities:

- Someone else runs that hero for the session (in addition to their own hero). This is easiest on you, but sometimes the fill-in player resents the task or the replaced player is unhappy with what happens to the hero in his or her absence.
- You run the hero, doing your best to make the decisions that you think the hero's player would make. This might actually be the best solution, but don't do it if running a hero and running the game at the same time is too much for you and hurts the whole session.

- The hero, like the player, can't be present for this adventure. This only works in certain in-game situations, but if it makes sense for the character to be absent, that's a handy way to take the hero out of the action for a game session. Ideally, the reason for the hero's absence is one that allows him or her to jump back in with a minimum of fuss when the player is available again. (The hero may have some other commitment, for instance.)
- The character fades into the background for this session. This is probably the least desirable solution, because it strains everyone's suspension of disbelief.

Recognize that players come and go. Someone moves away, another gets busy, and yet another grows tired of the game. They'll quit. At the same time, new players will want to join. Make sure to always keep the group at a size that you're comfortable with. The normal-sized group has four or five players (not including the GM). However, some groups are as small as two, and others as large as seven or more. You can also play the game one-on-one, with just one player and one GM, but that's a very different sort of play experience. (It's a good way to handle special campaign ideas, such as a Jedi Master's mentorship of a young Padawan learner.)

If you can, try to find out from the players how long they're interested in playing. Try to get a modest commitment from them to show up on a regular basis during that time.

Integrating New Players
When someone new joins the campaign, his or her hero needs to be integrated into the game. At the same time, the player needs to be integrated into the group. Make sure that a new player knows the house rules and the table rules, as well as the game rules.

Rules Discussions
It's probably best if players don't question your rulings or established rules, propose new house rules, or conduct discussions on other aspects of the game (aside from what's immediately at hand) during the game itself. Such matters are best addressed at the beginning or end of the session.

Jokes and Off-Topic Discussions
There are always funny things to be said, movie quotes, good gossip, and other conversations that crop up during the game, whether they're inspired by what's going on in the session or completely extraneous. Decide for yourself (and as a group) how much is too much. Remember that this is a game and people are there to have fun, yet at the same time keep the focus on the action of the heroes so the whole session doesn't pass in idle talk.

Working with the Players
Two players want the same newfound item. Each thinks his character can use it best or deserves it for what he's done. If the players can't find a way to decide who gets it, you will have to arbitrate or impose a solution. Or, worse, one player is angry with another player for something that happened earlier that day outside the game, so now his hero tries to harass or even kill the other player's hero. The GM shouldn't sit back and let this happen. It's up to you to step in and help resolve conflicts like that. As GM, you're both a master of ceremonies and an umpire during the game. Talk with the arguing players together or separately outside the game session and try to resolve the conflict. Make it clear as nicely as you can that you can't let anyone's arguments ruin the game for the other players, and you won't tolerate real-world hard feelings affecting the way characters within the game react to each other.

Another case is when a player gets really mad when you rule against him. Again, be firm but kind in telling him that you try your best to be fair. You can't have angry outbursts spoiling everyone else's fun. Settle the matter outside the game session. Listen to the player's complaints, but remember that you're the final arbiter. By agreeing to play in your game, that player has also agreed to accept your decisions as GM. (See When Bad Things Happen to Good Heroes, page 246.)

Sometimes one player's actions ruin the fun for everyone. An obnoxious, irresponsible, troublemaking player can make the game really unpleasant. Sometimes he gets others' heroes killed because of his actions. Other times he stops the game with arguments, tantrums, or off-topic conversations. Or he might keep everyone from playing by being late or not showing up at all. Ultimately, you should get rid of this player. Just don't invite him next time. Don't play the game with someone that you wouldn't enjoy spending time with in another social setting.

Decide how many players you want in your game and stick with it. If someone leaves, try to get a new player. If someone new wants to join an already full group, resist the urge to let him or her in unless you're sure you can handle the increased number of players. If there are too many players, consider dividing them into two groups that play at different times. If there are too few, you might want to recruit more or have each player play more than one hero. (It's good to have at least four heroes on a mission team.)

If one player dominates the game and monopolizes your time with her hero's actions, the other players will quickly grow dissatisfied. Make sure everyone gets his or her turn. Also, make sure each player gets to make his or her own decisions. Overeager or overbearing players sometimes try to tell the others what to do. If one player insists on controlling everything, talk to him outside the game session and explain that his actions are making things less fun for everyone.

Metagame Thinking
"I figure that there'll be a lever on the other side of the chasm that extends the bridge," a player says to the others, "because the GM would never create a trap that we couldn't deactivate somehow." That's metagame thinking. Any time the players base hero actions on logic that depends on the fact that they're playing a game, they're "metagaming." This activity should always be discouraged, because it detracts from real roleplaying and spoils the suspension of disbelief.

Surprise your players by foiling this mode of thinking. Maybe there is a lever on the other side of the chasm—but it might be malfunctioning. Keep your players on their toes, and don't let them second-guess you. Tell them to think in terms of the game universe, not of you as the GM. In the game universe, someone put the trench in the Death Star for a purpose. Figure out the hows and whys for what they have done. The heroes will need to do the same.

In short, where possible, encourage the players to employ in-game logic. Confronted with the situation given above, an appropriate response from a clever hero is, "I figure there'll be a lever on the other side of the chasm that extends the bridge, because you'd have to be able to cross from either side." In fact, this is wonderful—it shows smart thinking as well as verisimilitude in the game universe.

Recapping
"Last time, you had just discovered the secret entrance to the Imperial shield generator on the forest moon of Endor. We ended the session with you on a nearby ridge overlooking the entrance. Arani suffered a terrible wound while fighting the biker scouts. Vor'en wanted to go straight to the entrance and shoot it out, but the rest of you talked him into helping you find a suitable place to watch and plan. What do you want to do?"

In the middle of an ongoing campaign, recapping activity from the previous session at the start of a new session often helps establish the mood and reminds everyone what was going on. In most games, heroes continue what they're doing from day to day (or even hour to hour), but most players (in the real world) have several days of real time between game sessions. Some players might forget important details that will affect their decisions if they don't get reminders.

Of course, that means that you, as the GM, need to keep notes of what happens so you don't forget, either. At the very least, jot down a few sentences about what's going on at the end of each game session. Leave your notes where you can find them right away at the beginning of the next session. You'll probably find that, as the GM, you tend to think about the game between sessions more than the other players do, and thus you'll remember more details. You'll quickly get to the point where you won't forget what happened in past sessions, especially if the adventures you're currently working on build off those events.

Setting the Pace
The pace of the game determines how much time you spend on a given activity or action taken by the heroes. Different players enjoy different paces. Some search every room they come across, but some think doing that is not worth the game time. Some roleplay every encounter, while some want to skip on to the "good bits."

Do your best to please the group, but when in doubt, keep things moving. Don't feel that it's necessary to play out rest periods, replenishing supplies, or carrying out daily tasks. Sometimes that level of detail is an opportunity to develop heroes, but most of the time it's unimportant.

You should decide ahead of time, if possible, how long the playing session will last. This not only allows everyone to make plans around the game but also enables you to judge about how much time is left during a session and pace things accordingly. You should always end a session at a good stopping point (see Ending Things, below). Three to four hours is a good length for an evening game. Some people like to play longer sessions, usually on a weekend. Even if you normally play for shorter periods, sometimes it's fun to run a longer "marathon" session.

Referencing Rules

Try to look at the rules as little as possible during a game. Although the rules are there to help you, paging through the book can slow things down. Look something up when necessary (and mark things you'll need to refer to again with a bookmark), but recall a rule from memory when you can. Even if you're not exactly correct in your recollection, the game keeps moving.

Cheating (and Player Perceptions)

Terrible things can happen in the game because the dice just go awry. Everything might be going fine, when suddenly the players have a run of bad luck. A round later, half the heroes are down for the count and the other half almost certainly can't take on the opponents that remain. If everyone dies, the campaign might very well end then and there, and that's bad for everyone. Should you stand by and watch the heroes get slaughtered? Or should you "cheat" and have the opponents run off, or fudge the die rolls so that the heroes still miraculously win in the end? There are really two issues at hand.

Do you cheat? The answer: GMs really can't cheat. You're the umpire, and what you say goes. As such, it's certainly within your right to sway things one way or another to keep people happy or keep things running smoothly. It's no fun losing a beloved hero because he fell down a flight of stairs. A good rule of thumb is that a hero shouldn't die in a minor way by some fluke of the dice unless he or she was doing something really stupid at the time.

However, you might not feel that it's right or even fun unless you obey the same rules the players do. Sometimes the heroes get lucky and kill an opponent you had planned to have around for a long time. By the same token, sometimes things go against the heroes and disaster befalls them. Both the GM and players take the bad with the good. That's a perfectly acceptable way to play, and if there's a default method of running a game, that's it.

Just as important an issue, however, is whether the players realize that you bend the rules. Even if you decide that sometimes it's okay to fudge a little to let the heroes survive so the game can continue, don't let the players in on this decision. It's important to the game that they believe they're always in danger. Consciously or subconsciously, if they believe you'll never let bad things happen to their heroes, they'll change the way they act. With no element of risk, victory will seem less sweet. And if thereafter something bad does happen to a hero, the player may believe you're out to get him. If he feels you saved other heroes when they were in trouble, he might become disaffected with the game.

When Bad Things Happen to Good Heroes

Heroes suffer setbacks, lose prized equipment, and sometimes even die. It's all part of the game, almost as much as success, gaining levels, earning rewards, and attaining greatness. But players don't always take it well when something bad happens to their heroes.

Remind players that bad things happen sometimes. Challenges are what the game's all about. Mention that setbacks are an opportunity to succeed later. Reassure the player of the dead hero that there are lots of opportunities for new hero types she hasn't tried yet. The dead hero's surviving allies will tell tales of their fallen comrade for years to come. The game goes on.

It's rare (but possible) that an entire group of heroes can be wiped out. In such a case, don't let it end the whole game. Encourage the players to try new heroes, perhaps of a class or species they haven't played before. Even that's not really so bad—in fact, it's an opportunity for a dramatic change of pace. This new group of heroes might even be charged with retrieving the bodies of the fallen heroes for honorable burial.

Ending Things

Try not to end a game session in the middle of an encounter. Leaving everything hanging in the midst of combat is a terrible way to end a session. It's difficult to keep track of things such as initiative order, in-game effects, and other round-by-round details between sessions. The only exception to this is ending with a cliffhanger. A cliffhanger ending is one in which things end just as something monumental happens or some surprising turn of events occurs. The purpose is to keep players intrigued and excited until the next session. A cliffhanger ends a session right before an encounter begins, prior to initiative checks, and you pick up the action with initiative checks in the next game session.

If someone was missing from that session, and you had his hero leave for a while, make sure that there's a way to work his hero back in next time. Sometimes, even in a cliffhanger, this can work out well. The hero might come racing into the thick of things to help out his beleaguered friends and help save the day.

Allow some time—a few minutes will do—at the end of the session to have everyone discuss what happened. Listen to their reactions and secretly learn more of what they like and don't like. Reinforce what you thought were good decisions and smart actions on their part (unless such information gives too much away for the adventure). Always end things positively.

You may want to award experience points at the end of each session, or you might wait until the end of each ad-venture. That's up to you. However, the standard approach is to give out experience points at the end of each adventure, so players whose heroes go up a level have time between adventures to choose new skills, feats, and so forth.

Building an Encounter

For purposes of the *Star Wars Roleplaying Game*, an encounter is defined as an obstacle, threat, or situation (whether it be an opponent, several opponents, or a hazard) that prevents the heroes from achieving a specific goal important to the adventure. An obstacle, threat, or situation can be overcome through smart roleplaying, combat, or skill use. Persuading a crazed Force disciple to surrender might require heroes to enter difficult and perhaps life-threatening negotiations, while capturing a crime lord might require heroes to fight their way past a squad of thugs or infiltrate the crime lord's headquarters without setting off the security system.

Challenge Levels

Every opponent or hazard the heroes face has a Challenge Level (CL), which tells GMs how tough it is to overcome. For example, every stormtrooper has a CL, as does every wampa and garbage compactor. The more opponents and hazards the heroes face at once, the more difficult the encounter and the more experience points (XP) the heroes get for overcoming it (see Awarding Experience Points, below).

A challenging encounter is one the heroes should overcome with minor to moderate damage to themselves and some depletion of their resources. A single obstacle, threat, or situation of Challenge Level *n* is challenging for a single character of similar level. For example, a 1st-level hero should find a CL 1 stormtrooper challenging. By extension, four CL 1 stormtroopers should prove challenging to four 1st-level heroes.

A difficult challenge is one that seriously taxes the heroes' resources and may require the heroes to withdraw and recover, while an unfair challenge could easily lead to a total party kill. Difficult and unfair challenges are discussed below (see Measuring Encounter Difficulty).

Complications: An encounter can be made harder by adding complications that make overcoming certain obstacles, threats, and situations more difficult. In general, adding a complication to an encounter increases the CL of every affected obstacle, threat, or situation by 1. For example, if the heroes confront four CL 1 battle droids and two of them have the benefit of improved cover (and the heroes do not), the GM should treat the two battle droids with cover as CL 2 threats and award experience accordingly. However, the two battle droids without cover would still be counted as CL 1 threats.

Beneficial Circumstances: Sometimes an encounter is made easier by circumstances beyond the heroes' control. In such cases, you may reduce the amount of XP the heroes earn for achieving their encounter goals by as much as half. For example, if the heroes run across two bounty hunters who are moderately injured from a previous skirmish, the GM may elect to award only half normal XP for overcoming them. A GM should avoid reducing the XP awards when the beneficial circumstances are the direct or indirect result of good planning or roleplaying on the heroes' parts. For example, if the heroes use treachery or bribery to turn one bounty hunter against the other, they should receive full XP for both bounty hunters even though the encounter was made easier by their actions.

Measuring Encounter Difficulty

Creating balanced and fun encounters is more art than science. However, the following guidelines will help you build encounters that aren't so straightforward that players will be bored and aren't so difficult that the heroes aren't likely to survive:

Multiple Opponents: Encounters with two to six opponents work best. Save the single-opponent encounter for higher-CL "bosses" like the rancor or Darth Vader. Avoid encounters with more than a dozen opponents unless you want the heroes to feel overwhelmed.

Variety: The best encounters combine different sorts of obstacles, threats, and situations. Battling four Rodian soldiers in a corridor is much less interesting than fighting a Rodian noble, two Rodian soldiers, and the noble's trained nexu in a storage bay filled with cargo containers.

Combining Different CLs: When building encounters that involve multiple threats, obstacles, or situations of different Challenge Levels, add together the various CLs and divide this sum by 3 (round down). If the result is within one level of the heroes' average level, it's probably a tough but fair challenge for the heroes. If the result is 2 to 3 levels above the heroes' level, expect a difficult encounter that seriously taxes the heroes' abilities and resources. If the result is 4 or more levels above the heroes' level, expect the heroes to have a real fight on their hands, and also brace for one or more hero deaths. Note that these calculations are based on the assumption that there are four heroes in the party. Four each additional hero, subtract 1 from the result. For each missing hero, add 1 to the result.

Here are some sample encounters to illustrate the formula:

- An encounter with four CL 2 clone troopers and one CL 3 elite clone trooper has a combined CL of 11. Dividing 11 by 3 and rounding down, you get 3. Based on this result, you can expect this encounter to be a challenge for four 2nd-, 3rd-, or 4th-level heroes and a less challenging encounter for higher-level heroes.
- An encounter with two CL 15 elite troopers has a combined CL of 30. Dividing 30 by 3, you get 10. Based on this result, you can expect this encounter to be a challenge for four 9th-, 10th-, or 11th-level heroes; a challenge for five 8th-, 9th-, or 10th-level heroes; or a challenge for six 7th-, 8th-, or 9th-level heroes.
- An encounter with a CL 8 crime lord and five CL 5 assassins has a combined CL of 33. Dividing 33 by 3, you get 11. This encounter is a challenge for four 10th-, 11th-, and 12th-level heroes and a difficult challenge for four 8th- and 9th-level heroes. It's an unfair challenge for heroes of 7th level or less.

Awarding Experience Points

Heroes receive experience points (XP) for overcoming opponents, hazards, and other obstacles that stand in the way of achieving the goals of an adventure. Every opponent and hazard has a Challenge Level (CL) that determines how much XP the heroes get for overcoming it, as shown in Table 14-1: Experience Point Awards. Note that overcoming an obstacle doesn't always mean defeating it. Heroes who trick or bribe a Gamorrean guard into letting them pass should get full XP for the Gamorrean, just as if they'd bested him in combat.

The GM has the right to adjust XP awards depending on how rapidly he or she wants the heroes to gain levels and how easily the heroes achieve their encounter goals. Wherever possible, the GM should split XP awards equally between the heroes so that they're gaining levels at the same rate. Once the heroes accumulate enough XP to gain a level (see Table 3-1: Experience and Level-Dependent Benefits, page 37), it's time to increase the difficulty of the challenges they must overcome.

Beginning at 6th level, heroes receive less XP awards for obstacles with a CL significantly lower than their character level. At some point, low-level threats become fodder, and little experience can be gained from overcoming them. Heroes receive one-tenth XP for anything with a Challenge Level equal to or less than the heroes' average level − 5. For example, a group of 6th-level heroes receive 20 XP for defeating a CL 1 stormtrooper (instead of 200 XP).

Other Rewards

In addition to experience points, the heroes can earn other rewards for their actions. As a general rule, a challenging yet fair encounter should net the heroes resources equal their average level × 2,000 credits, to be divided equally among them. Easy encounters may deliver half as many resources or none at all, and difficult encounters should give 50% more at least. You don't have to hand out resources at the end of every encounter; often it is best to save the heroes' rewards until the end of the adventure, in the form of a lump-sum payment given to them for completing the adventure's goals.

Resources can take several different forms, as detailed below. For purposes of comparison, all resources are measured in credits.

Credits

For many characters, no reward is better than cold, hard cash. This category includes credit vouchers, electronic deposits of credits into a character's account (if the character owns a credit chip), credit coins, or trade goods (often precious metals).

Credits may be found during the course of an adventure—inside a vault in a Hutt crime lord's palace, in the form of trade goods found in a freighter's cargo hold, or perhaps even in the pockets or baggage of a defeated foe. However, heroes are more likely to receive the bulk of their wealth from grateful benefactors for jobs well done.

Table 14-1: Experience Point Awards

Challenge Level	XP Award[1]
0	0
1	200
2	400
3	600
4	800
5	1,000
6	1,200
7	1,400
8	1,600
9	1,800
10	2,000
11	2,200
12	2,400
13	2,600
14	2,800
15	3,000
16	3,200
17	3,400
18	3,600
19	3,800
20	4,000

[1] *Divide the XP award by the number of heroes in the party to determine how many XP each hero receives. Heroes receive one-tenth XP for anything with a Challenge Level equal to or less than their character level − 5.*

Equipment

Heroes invariably acquire new equipment in the course of an adventure, recovering it from the field of battle, seizing it from enemies they defeat, or stealing it from a less-than-secure place (such as the hold of a captured starship or a poorly defended warehouse).

Be judicious when giving out valuable equipment as a reward. If the heroes find valuable equipment too often, they will be tempted to spend several minutes after every battle looting bodies for usable gear and later selling their hawked goods, and this can quickly derail or slow down an adventure.

Always point out notable equipment that you want the heroes to have ("The scout trooper's sniper rifle seems intact, and you can see a targeting scope mounted on it"). Meanwhile, never mention mundane equipment that isn't meant to be useful, or emphasize why the equipment is either unusable or undesirable ("The smuggler's blaster pistol is dirty and rusted, a cheap knock-off of a BlasTech model. You doubt he ever took the time to clean or maintain the weapon"). If your players still spend too much time looting, you should strictly enforce the encumbrance rules (see page 140) and subtract the value of salvaged equipment from the rewards you give them.

Building an Adventure

An adventure—sometimes called a mission—is a collection of related encounters designed to fit together, creating a cogent storyline for the game. Some adventures are only short episodes in the campaign or interludes between longer adventures. Others represent significant missions, while still others form the backbone of the campaign.

When building a campaign, adventure, or encounter, try to think in terms of heroic goals. What must the heroes achieve or accomplish? A heroic goal usually begins with a descriptive verb that best defines the required action: capture, defeat, discover, destroy, escape, find, negotiate, obtain, protect, rescue, and survive are good examples. Once you have a suitable verb, flesh out the details: Rescue the princess from the detention cellblock. Capture the plans for the Emperor's newest superweapon. Negotiate safe passage aboard the smuggler's space transport.

Every encounter should have a specific, attainable goal that heroes can achieve. For example, an encounter might require the heroes to obtain a code cylinder from a Rodian thug. The encounter setup could be as simple as cornering the thug in a cantina or as complex as a landspeeder chase through the dusty streets of Mos Eisley. (Capturing the thug alive could be a secondary or additional goal.) Whether or not the heroes obtain the code cylinder will determine or affect their goals in subsequent encounters.

Just as each encounter has a clearly defined goal, so too does every adventure. For short adventures, the goal might be very simple: Find R2-D2 in the Tatooine desert and bring him back safely. A longer adventure might have an ultimate goal that can be accomplished only after the heroes achieve minor encounter goals and overcome various obstacles. For instance, an adventure's ultimate goal might be to destroy a new Imperial superweapon, but accomplishing this goal might require the heroes to capture an Imperial spy, discover the location of the superweapon's secret construction facility, infiltrate the facility, defeat the Imperial forces in the facility's control room, and activate the superweapon's self-destruct system.

A campaign need not have a clear goal (particularly when it begins), but it should have a theme or context. When Luke and Ben meet Han and Chewbacca in Mos Eisley, they (and their "players," in this model) had no idea that the ultimate end of their "campaign" would be the overthrow of

the Empire and the establishment of the New Republic. However, the GM of this "campaign" probably had a good idea that these heroes would become involved with the Rebellion during the campaign, and the Empire would be their primary opposition. (See Building a Campaign on the next page.)

What Makes an Adventure Exciting?

Creating a memorable adventure requires more than just an interesting plot or a grand finish. Remember that in most cases, the heroes won't be able to see the behind-the-scenes machinations of the villain or the clever plot twists that occur on the bridge of the Imperial starship. While you want your adventures to feel like they could come from a movie, you can't always rely on the same techniques that the moviemakers use. Here are a few tricks to help you keep your adventures memorable and exciting.

Intriguing Interactions

Too often, players (and GMs) see an adventure as little more than a string of firefights separated by "talking." This shortchanges one of the most compelling parts of a roleplaying game: playing a role. In addition to creating interesting characters, the GM must treat these characters as more than just cardboard props to be interacted with and then discarded.

In general, run a GM character just as a player would run a hero—take whatever actions the character would take, assuming the action is possible. That's why it's important to determine a GM character's general outlook and characteristics ahead of time if possible, so you know how to play the character properly.

When a GM character interacts with heroes, the GM determines the characters' initial attitude (hostile, unfriendly, indifferent, friendly, or helpful). A hero might try to influence this attitude with a Persuasion check. However, not all interactions require a check. Calling a Wookiee a "walking carpet" might shift the Wookiee's demeanor from indifferent to hostile. It doesn't take a roll—just the right words and deeds—to turn someone more hostile. In general, a hero cannot repeat attempts to influence someone.

Although a GM character can use the Persuasion skill to influence another GM character, the attitudes of the heroes are never influenced by a skill check—the players always decide those.

Worthy Adversaries

While it's all well and good for the heroes to mow through a few ranks of battle droids or stormtroopers during an adventure, this type of encounter grows tiresome quickly. Be sure to include competent adversaries for the heroes to encounter, whether as common enemies, archvillains, or even occasional foils.

An easy mistake is making an adversary too powerful, believing that the heroes will have it "too easy" unless their opponent is another Darth Vader. Not every opponent has to be a Dark Lord of the Sith. An intelligently played enemy can often seem much more powerful than he appears on paper.

In the same vein, nothing is more disappointing than a climactic battle with a villain who turns out to have a glass jaw. If you know that your villain will face the heroes in combat, make sure he can stand up to them (or has plenty of assistance from underlings).

Exciting Combats

One reason that the lightsaber duels in the *Star Wars* movies are so exciting is that they tend to take place in interesting locations. From a pitched battle on a narrow ledge above a Cloud City airshaft to a death duel interrupted by leaps between platforms and opening and closing energy fields, these elements add twists to traditional combat scenes.

While any combat can be exciting, you should occasionally have the heroes face opponents in a nontraditional setting. Sometimes mounted combat (or aerial mounted combat) can provide a change of pace. Underwater settings can be interesting as well. A short list of other suggestions appears below. For more ideas, look to the *Star Wars* movies, novels, and comics.

Daring Escapes

Sometimes heroes get captured. It happens all the time in the movies. While it would be fairly easy for the bad guys to simply kill the heroes at that point, it's more interesting and fun to "take them alive." Maybe the villains plan to interrogate the heroes, or maybe the heroes are worth more to them alive.

When heroes are knocked unconscious or otherwise force to surrender, the game isn't over. Quite the contrary! Instead, try setting up a situation in which the heroes can perpetrate a daring escape, either alone or with some unexpected assistance. In *The Empire Strikes Back*, Leia and Chewbacca escape Imperial custody with the unexpected help of Lando Calrissian. In *Return of the Jedi*, the heroes escape the clutches of Jabba the Hutt through resourcefulness, teamwork, and sheer luck. Daring escapes are staples of good adventure stories and an opportunity for heroes to turn an unfortunate situation into an advantageous one.

Compound Encounters

You can spice up an otherwise boring scenario by adding new elements after the action has already started. After the players think they know what's going on, make the encounter more complex by adding a new threat, new goal, or new opportunity. The simplest kind of compound encounter adds a new foe halfway through a fight. If a group of assassins attacks the heroes in a cantina, have their bounty hunter leader show up 4 rounds later. Similarly, if the heroes are convinced they focus of a fight in Mos Eisley is to defeat a few stormtroopers, they're not expecting a bantha stampede.

It's important to remember the overall Encounter Level of a compound encounter. Heroes haven't had a chance to recover and heal since the beginning of an encounter, so anything they face is all part of the same encounter, and should be added together to determine the Encounter Level. It is slightly easier to deal with foes that attack a few rounds apart (since not all enemies can attack the heroes off the bat), but in general you don't want to throw more challenges at the heroes just because their arrival time is staggered. A compound encounter is a good way for a typical scenario to become more interesting, not a way to sneak in more foes that the heroes can deal with.

For example, the heroes know an Imperial Inquisitor is hunting them down to capture their Force Sensitive members. They've been attacked by his troops once already, and know how tough those nonheroic characters are. When the heroes are trying to convince a junk dealer to sell them a datapad with critical information, the Inquisitor's troops attack. The junk dealer hides at first, but after three rounds he screams he's leaving, and if the heroes want the datapad they can get it themselves. He throws it onto a conveyer belt, where it's carried toward a smelter. The next round, local guards show up and also start shooting at the heroes. Not only must they beat twice as many foes, but the heroes must reach the datapad before it's melted.

Building a Campaign

The term "campaign" refers to the ongoing game created by the Gamemaster, a linked set of adventures or missions that follow the escapades of a group of heroes. A campaign might have a single ongoing storyline—such as the overthrow of the Empire—or several, shorter plots. The "classic" trilogy (*A New Hope*, *The Empire Strikes Back*, and *Return of the Jedi*) is an example of a campaign with a single ongoing storyline. In this "campaign" we follow the adventures of a central group of heroes—a group that changes slightly over time as individual heroes come and go—who generally work together to accomplish their goals.

Building a good *Star Wars* campaign is more than just stringing together a bunch of adventures, though. The guidelines below should help you create a rich, immersive campaign that is fun for both the players and the GM.

Create a Context

Before any other campaign-building task, you should decide the context in which the players can place (and play) their heroes. While this context doesn't have to be obvious to the players at the beginning of the campaign (and indeed can change as play goes on), it greatly helps the Gamemaster in designing adventures and encounter goals for the game.

Of course, this context will vary dramatically based on the era in which you set your campaign. A plotline appropriate to heroes of the Rebellion era might well be out of place in the days of the Old Republic. A variety of context options exist for the *Star Wars Roleplaying Game*, a few of which are listed below.

- Rebels plotting the overthrow of the Galactic Empire
- Envoys of the Jedi Council searching for evidence of the Sith
- Diplomats working for the Galactic Senate to foster peace and harmony in the galaxy
- Representatives of the New Republic charged with hunting down remnants of the Empire
- Private traders looking to gain wealth and influence
- Members of a mercenary team willing to work for the highest bidder

Incorporate Interesting GM Characters

It's your job to portray everyone in the galaxy who isn't one of the heroes. These people are all your characters, running the gamut from the feisty Jawa who sold the heroes their astromech droid to the foul Sith Lord out to destroy the Rebellion, or the Hutt crime lord holed up in the Tatooine desert.

Most people go about their own lives, oblivious to the actions of the heroes and the events around them. Ordinary people whom they meet in a spaceport won't notice them as being different from anyone else unless the heroes do something to draw attention. In short, the rest of the galaxy doesn't know the heroes are, in fact, heroes. It either treats them no differently from anyone else, gives them no special breaks (or special penalties), or gives them no special attention whatsoever. The heroes have to rely on their own actions. If they are wise and kind, they make friends and garner respect. If they are foolish or unruly, they make enemies and earn the enmity of all.

As you run your campaign, you need to portray all sorts of characters. Use the following tips for creating and controlling interesting characters.

Villains and Opponents

Villains and opponents provide an outlet for play that is unique to being a GM. Running the foes of the heroes is one of your main tasks, and one of the most fun responsibilities. When creating opponents for the heroes, keep the following in mind.

Plausible Villains: Flesh out enemies. Give a fair amount of thought toward why enemies are doing what they do, why they are where they are, and how they interact with all things around them. If you think of them as just bad guys for the heroes to defeat, so will your players.

Intelligent Villains: Make the enemies as smart and resourceful as they really would be—no more, no less. An average Trandoshan might not be the best strategist, but Hutts are very intelligent and usually have schemes and contingency plans.

Fallible Villains: Villains don't know everything, and even smart villains sometimes leap to the wrong conclusions. Avoid the temptation to make your villains omniscient, and let the heroes surprise them once in a while. It'll make your villains seem more realistic and help the players feel like they have the advantage from time to time.

Lackeys: Give your major villains underlings, employees, bodyguards, and other lackeys whenever possible. At the same time, don't deny the heroes the satisfaction of eventually having the opportunity to defeat the major villain.

Allies

Most allies provide assistance to the heroes in the form of information, resources, or safe places to hide from the Empire. These allies may be friends, relatives, school chums, former coworkers, or anyone the heroes have met during their adventures. The Gamemaster should plan such characters in as much detail as necessary for the campaign. At the very least, a name, species, and personality should be included in the GM's notes. Allies will have attitudes of friendly or helpful toward the heroes.

On rare occasions, heroes may have allies who will join them on their missions. This is most useful when the group of heroes is small or doesn't cover the requisite skills for an adventure. Either the GM or one of the players can run this type of GM character. Be careful not to overuse them, because you don't want the players (and their heroes) to become reliant on them.

Build on Campaign Events

Once you've finished setting up the campaign, don't think your work is done. Without a living, reactive environment, even the most exciting context will become stale. Use what's come before and prepare for what's still coming. That's what makes a campaign different from a series of unrelated adventures. Some strategies for maintaining a campaign by building on the past include using recurring characters, having the heroes form relationships beyond the immediate adventure, changing what the heroes know, hitting them where it hurts, preparing the heroes for the future, and foreshadowing coming events.

Recurring Characters: While this includes Tarnree, the bartender who's there each time the heroes visit Mos Eisley, it extends to other characters as well. The mysterious stranger they saw in a back alley of Coruscant reappears on Naboo, revealing his identity and original intentions. The rogue officer responsible for inciting mutiny returns, this time with a pirate crew at his command. The other Jedi the heroes beat out for a prime position as Council Envoy shows up again, after he has turned to the dark side. The scoundrel who helped the heroes free the princess returns just in time for a climactic battle. Overused recurring characters can make things seem artificial, but when you reuse existing characters judiciously, it not only lends realism, but also reminds heroes of their own past, reaffirming their place in the campaign.

Deep Relationships: The heroes make friends with a local bartender and visit him every time they are in town, just to hear another of his jokes. A hero falls in love with a princess, and eventually, they marry. Old Yaris, a retired soldier, looks upon the heroes as the children he never had. The Gungans of Otoh Gunga deliver a present to the heroes every year on the anniversary of the characters' heroic victory over a battle droid army. These relationships flesh out a campaign.

Change What the Heroes Know: The Senator of Corulag is replaced by a usurper. The once-dangerous trade routes are safe now, thanks to increased patrols. A powerful group of corsairs defeats most of the pirates in the area. Change a few details that you have already established. You establish both what the players know now and what they knew before more firmly in their minds. They'll also be intrigued to know why things changed.

Hit Them Where They Hurt: If a hero makes friends with the bartender at the spaceport, then rule that his son was among those kidnapped when the Imperials attacked. If the heroes really enjoy visiting Mos Espa, put Mos Espa in the path of the worst sandstorm in memory. Don't overdo this, or the heroes will never grow attached to anything for fear that it will put that thing in danger. This strategy works as a powerful motivator when used in moderation.

Foreshadowing: If you know that later in the campaign you want to have an order of Dark Jedi rise up from secrecy and begin hunting Jedi, foreshadow that event beforehand. Have the heroes hear rumors about Dark Jedi, or even see evidence of them on an unrelated adventure long before they hunt down and destroy Jedi. It will make the later adventure much more meaningful. Threading information into previous adventures while hinting at future events helps weave a campaign into a whole.

Hazards

A hazard includes any effect that can cause harm but does not have a stat block. Most hazards are self-contained dangers that affect anyone or anything that comes into contact with them. A scorching desert, a toxic or corrosive atmosphere, and a virulent disease are all examples of hazards.

Hazards affect organic creatures, machines, or both. A hazard resolves its effects by making an attack roll against one of the target's defense scores; if the attack succeeds, the target suffers the effects of the hazard, including damage that may require special actions to treat. A hazard may affect all targets within an area or a single target, depending on its nature and its range.

Acid

Corrosive acid deals damage on contact.

Acid (CL 2): When a target comes into contact with acid, make an attack roll (1d20+5) against the target's Fortitude Defense. If the attack succeeds, the character takes 2d6 points of acid damage. If the attack misses, the target takes half damage that round. This attack occurs again each round until the acid is washed off or treated (requiring a DC 15 Treat Injury check and a medical kit).

Atmospheric Hazards

Atmospheric hazards cannot be avoided, although gear can sometimes protect a character from them. Atmospheric hazards are not considered area effects.

Corrosive Atmosphere (CL 4): A corrosive atmosphere has chemicals that can eat away at everything from armor to organic flesh. Each round a character is exposed to a corrosive atmosphere, make an attack roll (1d20+5) against the character's Fortitude Defense. If the attack succeeds, the character takes 2d6 points of acid damage. If the attack misses, the character takes half damage that round.

Toxic Atmosphere (CL 6): A toxic atmosphere is filled with chemicals that harm most living beings. Each round a creature is exposed to a toxic atmosphere, make an attack roll (1d20+5) against the character's Fortitude Defense. If the attack succeeds, the creature takes 1d6 points of damage and moves −1 persistent step on the condition track (see Conditions, page 148). If the attack misses, the creature takes half damage that round and does not move down the condition track.

Vacuum (CL 8): When a creature is exposed to vacuum, make an attack roll (1d20+20) against the character's Fortitude Defense. If the attack succeeds, the creature takes 1d6 points of damage and moves −2 steps down the condition track. If the attack fails, the creature takes no damage but moves −1 step down the condition track. The target cannot move back up the condition track until it is returned to a breathable atmosphere. A creature knocked unconscious by exposure to a vacuum automatically takes a cumulative 1d6 points of damage each round (that is, 1d6 the first round, 2d6 the second, 3d6 the third, and so on). If this damage ever exceeds the creature's damage threshold, it dies.

BLINDNESS

A blinded creature can't see and takes a –2 penalty to Reflex Defense, loses its Dexterity bonus to Reflex Defense (if any), moves at half speed, and takes a –5 penalty on Perception checks. All opponents are considered to have total concealment (page 156) to the blinded creature. All checks and actions that rely on vision (such as reading) fail automatically.

CRUSHING HAZARDS

Some hazards, such as hydraulic walls or doors, can deal continual crushing damage to anyone or anything trapped inside. Crushing hazards require no attack roll as long as the target is completely encompassed by the hazard.

Trash Compactor (CL 10): The powerful hydraulic walls of a trash compactor normally take 10 rounds to close. Any creature inside the trash compactor once it closes completely takes 10d6 points of damage per round (no attack roll required). After 5 rounds, the walls retract, taking 10 rounds to open fully.

DISEASE

Diseases are viruses and other organisms that attack the immune systems of living creatures. Disease hazards always attack the Fortitude Defense of a target, ignoring equipment bonuses to Fortitude Defense, damage reduction, and shield rating. They cause persistent conditions if they move you down the condition track (see Conditions, page 148). The persistent condition cannot be removed until the disease is cured (see Treat Injury skill, page 74) or until the disease fails its attack roll against you twice. Unlike other hazards, some diseases may require special equipment or medicine to treat. Diseases affect only living creatures; droids and vehicles are immune. Airborne diseases are considered atmospheric hazards.

Cardooine Chills (CL 2): The first time a character is exposed to the Cardooine chills, make an attack roll (1d20+2) against the character's Fortitude Defense. If the attack succeeds, the character takes 1d6 points of damage and moves –1 persistent step down the condition track (see Conditions, page 148). This attack occurs again each day the disease remains untreated. Treating the disease requires a successful DC 15 Treat Injury check.

Krytos Virus (CL 5): The Krytos virus is a bioengineered disease produced by the Empire. The first time a creature is exposed to the Krytos virus, make an attack roll (1d20+10) against its Fortitude Defense. Apply a –5 penalty to the attack roll if the target is Human. If the attack succeeds, the creature takes 2d6 points of damage and moves –1 persistent step down the condition track (see Conditions, page 148). This attack occurs again each day the disease remains untreated. Treating the disease requires a successful DC 20 Treat Injury check. Using a bacta tank reduces the Treat Injury DC to 15.

EXTREME TEMPERATURES

The blistering desert of Tatooine or the chill winds of Hoth can quickly overcome even the toughest heroes, and creatures ill-equipped to handle such conditions quickly succumb to heatstroke or hypothermia. Extreme temperatures are not considered area effects.

Extreme Heat or Cold (CL 4): Each hour a creature is exposed to extreme heat or cold, make an attack roll (1d20+5) against the character's Fortitude Defense. If the attack succeeds, the character takes 2d6 points of damage from heatstroke or hypothermia and moves –1 persistent step down the condition track (see Conditions, page 148). If the attack misses, the character takes half damage and does not move down the condition track. Heavy clothing or armor provides a +5 equipment bonus to your Fortitude Defense to resist extreme cold but imposes a –5 penalty to your Fortitude Defense to resist extreme heat.

A creature suffering from heatstroke or hypothermia cannot regain hit points or improve its condition until it spends at least 1 hour in a normal environment.

FALLING OBJECTS

Just as creatures take damage when they fall, so too do they take damage when hit by falling objects. When a creature could be hit by a falling object, make an attack roll (using the attack bonus listed in Table 14-2: Damage from Falling Objects) against the target's Reflex Defense. If the attack succeeds, the target takes the listed damage. If the attack misses, the target takes half damage. This is considered an area attack. Objects of Fine and Diminutive size are too small to deal damage, regardless of the distance fallen. A falling object must land wholly or partly in a creature's fighting space to damage the creature.

The GM may adjust the damage depending on the circumstances. For example, a Colossal object might be extremely light (such as a gas-filled

TABLE 14-2: DAMAGE FROM FALLING OBJECTS

OBJECT SIZE	EXAMPLE(S)	ATTACK BONUS	DAMAGE	STRENGTH CHECK DC
Tiny	Blaster, datapad	–5	1d4	—
Small	Blaster rifle	–2	1d6	—
Medium	Locker, heavy armor	+0	2d6	5
Large	Speeder bike	+2	4d6	10
Huge	Landspeeder	+5	8d6	15
Gargantuan	Starfighter	+10	12d6	20
Colossal	AT-AT	+20	20d6	25

> **FALLING DAMAGE**
>
> When a creature, droid, object, or vehicle falls, make an attack roll (1d20+20) against its Fortitude Defense. If the attack succeeds, the subject takes 1d6 points of damage for every 3 meters fallen (to a maximum of 20d6 damage). If the attack fails, the subject only takes half damage. A falling character or droid also lands prone (see Prone Targets, page 161).
>
> **Acrobatics:** If you are trained in the Acrobatics skill, you can reduce the damage you take from a fall with a successful Acrobatics check (see page 62). If the check succeeds and you take no damage from the fall, you land on your feet.

passenger balloon). Objects that are forced downward (such as a piston in a droid factory or a closing door) deal damage as if they were two size categories larger than they actually are. Additionally, if the target is at least three size categories smaller than the falling object, the target cannot move unless it succeeds on a Strength check to lift the object off itself (see Table 14-2 for the Strength check DC) or a DC 15 Acrobatics check to crawl out from underneath. The GM can modify the DCs for either check based on the circumstances; for example, a character might find herself trapped under an object that has openings or gaps that allow her to wriggle free.

Fire

A creature or character that takes fire damage also catches on fire. For each round that a creature is on fire, make an attack roll (1d20+5) against the target's Fortitude Defense. If the attack succeeds the target takes 1d6 points of fire damage; if the attack fails, the target takes only half damage. A character can put out the flames as a full-round action.

Poison

In *Attack of the Clones*, Zam Wesell attempts to assassinate Senator Padmé Amidala using poisonous centipedelike creatures called kouhuns. Later, Zam herself is slain by a poisoned Kamino saberdart. In *The Phantom Menace*, the Neimoidians pump poisonous gas into the conference room of their Trade Federation battleship in a vain attempt to dispatch Qui-Gon Jinn and Obi-Wan Kenobi.

Poison hazards are toxins that can be ingested, inhaled, or contracted through contact. They always attack the Fortitude Defense of a target, ignoring equipment bonuses to Fortitude Defense, damage reduction, and shield rating. They cause persistent conditions if they move you down the condition track (see Conditions, page 148). The persistent condition cannot be removed until the poison is cured (see Treat Injury skill, page 74) or until the poison fails its attack roll against you once. Contact poisons can be applied to weapons; when a poisoned weapon damages the target, the poison then makes its attack against the target's Fortitude Defense.

A creature that dies from poison damage can be revived (see the revivify ability of the Treat Injury skill, page 74). However, reviving a creature doesn't remove the poison from its system; the poison must be treated separately.

A character wearing a functional breath mask (see page 136) is immune to inhaled poisons, including toxic gases and atmospheres. Poisons affect only living creatures; droids and vehicles are immune.

Dioxis (CL 8): Dioxis is an inhaled gas. Each round a living creature is exposed to dioxis, make an attack roll (1d20+10) against the target's Fortitude Defense. If the attack succeeds, the target takes 4d6 points of damage and moves –1 step along the condition track (see Conditions, page 148). If the attack fails, the target takes only half damage and doesn't move down the condition track. The poison attacks each round until cured with a successful DC 25 Treat Injury check.

Knockout Drops (CL 2): When a creature ingests knockout drops, make an attack roll (1d20+5) against the target's Fortitude Defense. If the attack succeeds, the target takes moves –1 step along the condition track. The poison attacks each round until cured with a successful DC 15 Treat Injury check.

Paralytic Poison (CL 5): When a living creature is injected with a paralytic poison, make an attack roll (1d20+10) against the target's Fortitude Defense. If the attack succeeds, the target moves –1 step along the condition track. A target moved to the end of the condition track by the poison is immobilized, but not unconscious. The poison attacks each round until cured with a successful DC 15 Treat Injury check.

Radiation

Radiation hazards always attack the Fortitude Defense of a target, ignore damage reduction and shield rating, and cause persistent conditions if they move you down the condition track (see Conditions, page 148). The persistent condition cannot be removed until the radiation is cured (see Treat Injury skill, page 74).

Table 14-3: Radiation

RADIATION TYPE	ATTACK BONUS	RADIATION DAMAGE	TREAT INJURY DC
Mild (CL 2)	+1	2d6	15
Moderate (CL 4)	+2	4d6	20
Severe (CL 7)	+5	6d6	25
Extreme (CL 10)	+10	8d6	30

Each round a creature is exposed to a harmful dose of radiation, make an attack roll (1d20 + the radiation's attack bonus) against the target's Fortitude Defense. If the attack fails, the target shrugs off the radiation and suffers none of its effects. If the result hits, the target moves the −1 persistent step along the condition track (see Conditions, page 148) and takes an amount of radiation damage based on the radiation's strength, as shown in Table 14–3: Radiation. The Treat Injury check DC to heal this radiation damage is dependent on the classification of the radiation.

A creature that dies from radiation exposure can be revived (see the revivify ability of the Treat Injury skill, page 74). However, reviving a creature doesn't remove the radiation from its system; the radiation must be treated separately.

Smoke

Characters breathing heavy smoke, ash, or other toxic gases are subject to smoke hazards. Each round a character is exposed to a smoke hazard, make an attack roll (1d20+5) against the target's Fortitude Defense. If the attack succeeds, the target takes 1d6 points of damage and moves −1 step down the condition track (see Conditions, page 148). If the attack fails, the target takes half damage and does not move down the condition track.

Smoke grants concealment to characters within it (see Concealment, page 156). Smoke is an atmospheric hazard.

Traps and Security Systems

Military bases, criminal hideouts, and other facilities often have security systems in place to deter intruders. The Detention Block of the Death Star is an example of a location laden with traps designed to halt unauthorized incursions.

Set Explosive (CL 2 or 5): A set explosive usually takes the form of detonite or an explosive charge (see Explosives, page 130). When a set explosive detonates, make an attack roll (1d20+10) against the Reflex Defense of every creature and object in its blast radius. (Any creature or object to which the explosive is attached is hit automatically.) If the attack succeeds, the creature or object takes full damage. If the attack misses, the creature or object takes half damage. This is considered an area effect. Detonite is a CL 2 hazard; an explosive charge is a CL 5 hazard.

Blaster Turret (CL 2): This robotic blaster turret is usually mounted to a section of floor, wall, or ceiling. It has the range of a pistol, can fire in any direction, and has the following trained skills: Initiative +5, Perception +5. It is equipped with darkvision (page 257) and makes one attack per round against the closest target within its line of sight. Make an attack roll (1d20+5) against the target's Reflex Defense. If the attack succeeds, the target takes 3d6 points of energy damage; on a miss, the target takes no damage.

Blaster Rifle Turret (CL 3): The blaster rifle turret is a slightly larger variant of the blaster turret. It is statistically identical to its smaller cousin except as noted here. It has the range of a rifle and can fire either single shots or switch to autofire mode (see Autofire, page 156). It deals 3d8 points of energy damage with each successful attack.

Gravity

The force that gravity exerts on a person determines how they develop physically as well as their ability to perform certain actions. In addition, gravity affects the amount of damage a character takes from falling.

Gravity conditions may vary considerably from one environment to the next. However, for ease of play, the *Star Wars Roleplaying Game* presents four simplified gravity environments: normal gravity (0.8 to 1.2 g), low gravity (0.1 to 0.8 g), high gravity (more than 1.2 g), and zero gravity (less than 0.1 g). The following sections summarize the game effects for each type of environment.

Normal Gravity

Normal gravity imposes no special modifiers on a character's ability scores, attack rolls, or skill checks. Likewise, normal gravity does not modify a creature's speed, carrying capacity, or the amount of damage it takes from a fall.

Low-Gravity Environments

In a low-gravity environment, it becomes easier to move and lift heavy objects as well as perform Strength-related tasks. In addition, you take less damage from falling.

Speed: Your speed increases by one-quarter (round down to nearest square, minimum 1). This bonus applies to all of your modes of movement.

Carrying Capacity: Your normal carrying capacity is doubled. In addition, you gain a +2 bonus on any Strength check made to lift or move a heavy unsecured object.

Skill Check Bonuses: You gain a +2 circumstance bonus on Strength-based skill checks (including Climb, Jump, and Swim checks).

Weight vs. Mass

While an object in zero gravity loses weight, it does not lose mass or momentum. Thus, while a character could push a 10-ton piece of equipment around in space, albeit slowly, getting it to stop is a bit more difficult. If a character were to come between that piece of equipment and a solid object, that character would be crushed as if he were in full gravity—just more slowly.

For simplicity, assume that a Strength check to lift or move an object in zero gravity gains a +10 circumstance bonus. However, stopping an object already in motion does not receive this same bonus.

Attack Roll Penalty: You take a –2 penalty on attack rolls unless you are native to low-gravity environments or have the Spacehound talent (see page 47).

Damage from Falling: Roll d4s instead of d6s when calculating falling damage (see Falling Damage, page 255).

High-Gravity Environments

In a high-gravity environment, the pull of gravity is significantly greater than normal. Although an object's mass doesn't change, it becomes effectively heavier. It becomes harder to move and carry heavy objects as well as perform Strength-related tasks. In addition, you take more damage from falling. Even the simple task of walking or lifting one's arms feels more laborious.

Speed: Your speed decreases to three-quarters normal (round down to the nearest square, minimum 1 square). This penalty applies to all modes of movement.

Carrying Capacity: Your normal carrying capacity is halved. In addition, you take a –2 penalty on any Strength check made to lift or move a heavy unsecured object.

Skill Check Penalties: You take a –2 penalty on Strength-based skill checks (including Climb, Jump, and Swim checks).

Attack Roll Penalty: You take a –2 penalty on attack rolls unless you are native to high-gravity environments or you have the Spacehound talent (see page 47).

Damage from Falling: Roll d8s instead of d6s when calculating falling damage (see Falling Damage, page 255).

Zero-Gravity Environments

Creatures in a zero-gravity environment can move enormously heavy objects. As movement in zero gravity requires only the ability to grab onto or push away from larger objects, Climb and Jump checks no longer apply.

Most creatures find zero-gravity environments disorienting, taking penalties on their attack rolls and suffering the effects of space sickness. In addition, creatures in zero gravity are easier to bull rush than in other gravity environments.

Space Sickness: When a living creature is exposed to weightlessness, make an attack roll (1d20+0) against its Fortitude Defense. If the attack succeeds, the character moves –1 persistent step down the condition track (see Conditions, page 148). This persistent condition cannot be removed without a DC 20 Treat Injury check, or after eight hours, whichever comes first. This attack recurs after 8 hours but does not recur again after that. Creatures with the Spacehound talent (see page 47) and droids do not suffer the effects of space sickness.

Speed: In a zero-gravity environment, a creature gains a fly speed equal to its base land speed, or it retains its natural fly speed (whichever is greater). However, movement is limited to straight lines only; a creature can change course only by pushing away from larger objects (such as bulkheads).

Carrying Capacity: Your normal carrying capacity increases by 10 times in a zero-gravity environment. In addition, you gain a +10 circumstance bonus on any Strength check made to lift or move a heavy unsecured object.

Attack Roll Penalty: You take a –5 penalty on attack rolls and skill checks while operating in a zero-gravity environment unless you are native to that environment or have the Spacehound talent (see page 47).

Long-Term Exposure: Long-term exposure to zero-gravity conditions can cause serious problems when returning to normal gravity. A creature that spends 120 hours or more in a zero-gravity environment moves –2 persistent steps down the condition track upon returning to normal gravity. These steps down the condition track cannot be removed unless the character spends at least 24 hours in normal gravity.

Visibility

It's a rare mission that doesn't end up in the dark somewhere, and heroes need a way to see. See Table 14–4: Light Sources for the radius that a light source illuminates and how long it lasts. A light source also provides shadowy illumination out to twice this distance; targets within shadowy illumination gain concealment (see page 156), but they are visible. Without a light source, heroes are effectively blinded (see Blindness, page 254).

Darkvision

A creature or droid that has this ability can see in the dark, ignoring concealment and total concealment due to darkness. Darkvision is black and white only, so there must be at least some light to discern colors. It is otherwise like normal sight, and a creature with darkvision can function with no light at all.

Low-Light Vision

A creature or droid that has low-light vision can see without penalty in shadowy illumination, ignoring concealment (but not total concealment) due to darkness. It retains the ability to distinguish color and detail under these conditions.

Table 14-4: Light Sources

ITEM	LIGHT	DURATION
Candle	1 square	12 hours
Torch	3 squares	2 hours
Fusion lantern	6 squares	24 hours
Glow rod	3 squares*	6 hours

Creates a beam 6 squares long and 1 square high.

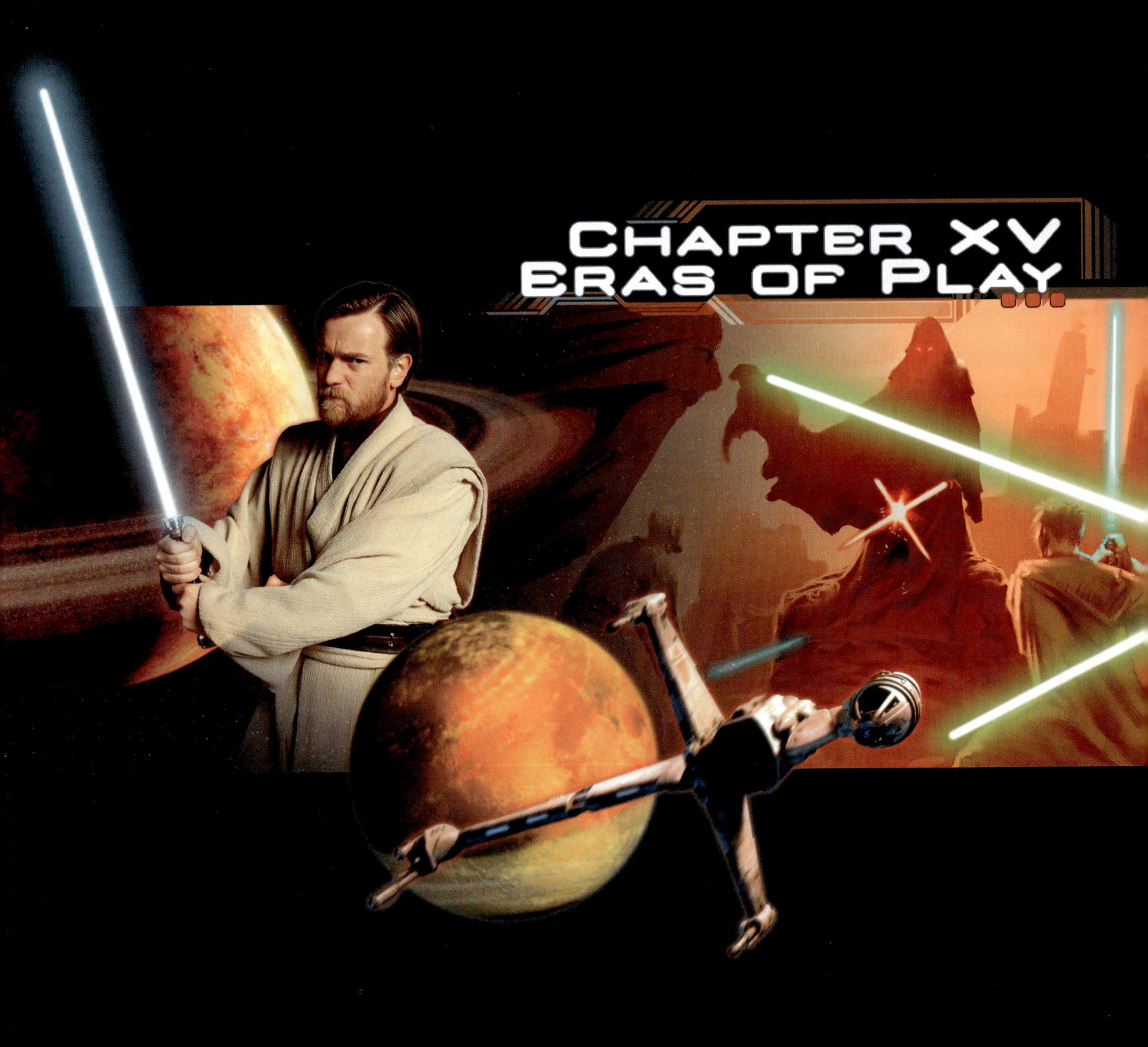

Chapter XV
Eras of Play

As the Gamemaster, you are free to set your *Star Wars* campaign in any time period. However, the core rulebook focuses on three eras in particular: the Rise of the Empire era, the Rebellion era, and The New Jedi Order era. The information presented in this chapter is intended to give you enough of a backdrop to comfortably set adventures in any of these eras.

The Rise of the Empire era represents a time of political unrest: the slow dissolution and ultimate demise of the Old Republic, the rise to power of Chancellor Palpatine, and the Clone Wars. Specifically, it's the years around *Star Wars* Episode I: *The Phantom Menace*, Episode II: *Attack of the Clones*, and Episode III: *Revenge of the Sith*.

The Rebellion era covers the time of the Galactic Civil War, as depicted in Episode IV: *A New Hope*, Episode V: *The Empire Strikes Back*, and Episode VI: *Return of the Jedi*.

Finally, The New Jedi Order era is set twenty-five years after *A New Hope*. The New Republic has been established, and Luke Skywalker's Jedi Knights are growing stronger. This era begins with the costly Yuuzhan Vong War, which reshapes much of the politics of the galaxy. This is the time period detailed in the Del Rey novel series.

Other *Star Wars* eras have achieved popularity in both comic books and video games, and these will be covered at length in future *Star Wars Roleplaying Game* supplements.

The Rise of the Empire Era

22 to 32 Years before *A New Hope*

A campaign set in this era focuses on the slow decline and corruption of the Republic. As *The Phantom Menace* comes to an end, the future for the galaxy looks bright. The charismatic and popular Palpatine has been elected as Supreme Chancellor, the Trade Federation has seemingly been dismantled, and the Jedi Knights are at their peak of power and influence. However, there's a sinister shadow creeping across the galaxy. The vile Sith have returned. Crime is on the rise. Politicians continue to bicker and look after their own petty interests. Nothing is what it seems.

The Phantom Menace unfolds with a galaxy torn asunder by strife, hatred, and greed. Led by a charismatic Separatist named Count Dooku, thousands of worlds have broken away from the Republic. This "confederacy of independent systems" wants to free itself from the yoke of the corrupt Senate, unaware that their galactic insurrection could spell the rise of an even greater evil.

As war foments and erupts between the Republic and the Separatists, plenty of opportunities for adventure present themselves. Heroes working for the Supreme Chancellor, the Jedi Council, or Count Dooku might undertake assignments to stem the tide of decay that grows stronger with every passing year. Remember that no matter what you or your players might think they know about Chancellor Palpatine, most people living in this era consider

Palpatine a good, fair leader and the best hope of the Republic. His true machinations have yet to reveal themselves. Similarly, Count Dooku seems to have the best interests of the galaxy at heart. Under his august leadership, he seeks a galaxy restored to order and prosperity. No one suspects that this former Jedi Master has fallen to the dark side of the Force.

During the era, all species are equal. For every Human senator, there are many more alien species on the Senate. Some species from the later eras haven't been encountered yet (such as Ewoks), and some have made only cursory visits to the galaxy (such as the advance scouts from the Yuuzhan Vong). The order of the Jedi Knights is held together by the Jedi Council, and some ten thousand Knights roam the galaxy as the defenders of the Republic. Many more Force-sensitive beings train in Jedi academies throughout the Republic, each hoping to be selected as a Padawan learner. Those who aren't selected for advanced training use the skills they have acquired to help the Republic in some other way. Some, for example, become farmers in the Agri-Corps or healers in the Medi-Corps.

Corrupt officials, various criminals, evil corporations, assassins, petty warlords, and dark Jedi abound in this time frame. New worlds still await discovery, and new alien species are encountered all the time. Any of these topics can become the seeds for great adventures. Remember also that the Jedi Council wants to learn more about the new Sith menace. From its chamber high atop the Jedi Temple in Coruscant, the capital world of the Republic, the Jedi Council quietly directs key members of the Jedi order to investigate incidents that might somehow be tied to the Sith. Although the Sith started as an empire controlled by corrupt Jedi, eventually Darth Bane altered the nature of the Sith forever. He dictated the rule of the new Sith order: There could be only two Sith at any time, a master and an apprentice. This doesn't limit the number of followers and lackeys the Sith could utilize, just the number of actual Sith.

In *Revenge of the Sith*, Chancellor Palpatine reveals to Anakin Skywalker that he is, in fact, the Sith Lord Darth Sidious. By this time, he has already lost two apprentices (Darth Maul and Darth Tyranus) battling the Jedi. However, he creates an apparent crisis that encourages the senators of the Republic to vote him permanent powers, making him emperor of the galaxy. Darth Sidious strikes down the Jedi with his new clone trooper army and takes Anakin Skywalker as his new Sith apprentice, Darth Vader. His victory nearly complete, Darth Sidious sets Darth Vader on a path to hunt down the remaining Jedi while he sweeps away the last vestiges of the Old Republic. Heroes of this time might be Jedi on the run or fledgling members of what will eventually become the Rebel Alliance.

The Rebellion Era

(0 to 5 Years after *A New Hope*)

The Emperor rules with an iron will. His key supporters include Dark Lord Darth Vader, Moffs and Grand Moffs of varying degrees of power and influence, military commanders, and a variety of secret police, spies, and assassins. The feared agents of the Imperial Security Bureau (the ISB) scour the galaxy for traitors and Rebels. The once-great Jedi Order has been eliminated, and only a handful of Force-sensitive individuals remain in hiding on out-of-the-way planets—other than those darksiders working for the Emperor's New Order.

The Senate has been disbanded. The HoloNet has been restricted. The Core worlds have been effectively cut off from the rest of the galaxy. Alderaan, a world of peace and influence, has been destroyed. The Emperor's Grand Admirals command the vast Imperial military machine, and hundreds of worlds have been tasked with keeping that machine going—no matter what the cost. New weapons of war appear regularly, from modified stormtroopers to walkers, TIE fighters to Star Destroyers. Interdictor cruisers capable of pulling ships out of hyperspace are seeing

DARTH VADER

wider use. No starship, private or otherwise, is safe from Imperial inspection, and boardings occur on a regular basis.

Heroes in this era probably work for the Rebel Alliance. They can be part of a Rebel cell, attached directly to Alliance High Command, or independents drawn to the Alliance's cause. In addition to the Empire, opponents in this period include crime lords, smugglers, bounty hunters, and traitors to the Alliance. It's up to the heroes to help turn the tide of Imperial domination.

The New Jedi Order Era

(25 Years after *A New Hope*)

In this era the New Republic is in place, although a small Imperial remnant maintains control of a portion of the galaxy. The Jedi, on the rise again thanks to the efforts of Luke Skywalker, are at a crossroads. Some members of the order, which numbers about one hundred individuals, want to take a more direct and deliberate role in galactic affairs. Skywalker, meanwhile, is struggling with whether or not he wants to reestablish the Jedi Council. Rash Jedi have led New Republic officials to be wary of the Knights and suspicious of their true motives. Indeed, this leads to varying degrees of mistrust and even fear in the general populace, many of whom still remember the Emperor's anti-Jedi rhetoric from years before.

The first galaxy-wide threat in the New Jedi order era is the Yuuzhan Vong invasion. It begins with Nom Anor, a spy who sows additional seeds of discord throughout the galaxy. His efforts give rise to antitechnology cults dedicated to the destruction of innocent droids. Masking his true identity, he recruits agents from the native populations to carry out acts of sabotage and subversion. Nom Anor, however, is only the beginning of the Yuuzhan Vong threat.

The Yuuzhan Vong are humanoids that follow a religion of pain and nature. They hate machines of all kinds, using instead living technology that they have bioengineered to serve as ships, weapons, and tools. These fierce, holy warriors seek to conquer the galaxy and bring their faith to the infidels who regularly make use of unclean machines. Their invasion begins on far-flung worlds such as Belkadan and Helska, but they quickly widen their hold on key sectors of the Outer Rim and Mid Rim, terraforming worlds to produce the yorik coral and other living materials that serve as their ships and weapons. The Jedi learn, to their horror, that this intractable new enemy cannot be sensed through the Force. The Jedi, former guardians of peace, become the hunted prey of the Yuuzhan Vong. Meanwhile, the extragalactic intruders continue their relentless advance toward the Core, crushing any force that dares stand in their way. A few worlds surrender without a fight, while those that resist are rendered uninhabitable. In time Coruscant itself falls, signaling the death of the New Republic.

Eventually the Yuuzhan Vong discover their history may not be as they thought, when the living planet Zonama Sekot came to Coruscant and fought defensively against the Yuuzhan Vong, "welcoming home it's true inhabitants." The new Galactic Federation of Free Alliances (Galactic Alliance) allows the Yuuzhan Vong to surrender and take Zonama Sekot as their homeworld. While not all Yuuzhan Vong accept this, the primary threat of the Yuuzhan Vong ends as Zonama Sekot flies into hyperspace to seek a new home for the Yuuzhan Vong in the Unknown Regions.

Though the war is over, many threats still exist. Some Yuuzhan Vong and their cults still fight against technological civilization. The Galactic Alliance has to rebuild the galaxy. And the New Jedi Order seeks out threats to peace and justice.

Main Characters

The following section describes the main protagonists from the *Star Wars* feature films.

> "I find your lack of faith disturbing."
> – Darth Vader

Anakin Skywalker (Darth Vader)

Anakin Skywalker's destiny and the fate of the entire galaxy are linked inexorably. After being freed by Qui-Gon Jinn, Anakin studies the ways of the Jedi under Obi-Wan Kenobi, but he allows feelings of anger, fear, and hate to enslave him. The death of his mother and visions of Padmé's death drive him to seek out the wisdom offered by a Sith Lord. In pursuing the power necessary to preserve Padmé's life, Anakin becomes death incarnate.

As Darth Vader, he uses the power of the dark side of the Force to betray and murder his fellow Jedi and enslave the galaxy. Over two decades later, his son Luke—now a Jedi himself—leads Anakin back to the light. He finds redemption in his sacrifice, bringing balance to the Force by ending the tyranny of the Emperor and the Sith.

Darth Vader (Episode IV)   CL 19
Medium Human Jedi 7/Jedi Knight 5/ace pilot 2/Sith apprentice 2/Sith Lord 3
Destiny 3; **Force** 8, Strong in the Force; **Dark Side** 14
Init +17; **Senses** low-light vision; Perception +11
Languages Basic, Binary, Huttese
Defenses Ref 39 (flat-footed 36), Fort 36, Will 33; Block, Deflect
hp 181; **Threshold** 36

Immune fear effects, atmospheric and inhaled poison hazards
Weakness life support

Speed 6 squares
Melee lightsaber +22 (2d8+17) or
Melee lightsaber +20 (3d8+17) with Rapid Strike or
Melee lightsaber +17/+17 (2d8+17) with Double Attack or
Melee lightsaber +15/+15 (3d8+17) with Double Attack and Rapid Strike
Ranged by weapon +20
Base Atk +17; **Grp** +20
Atk Options Double Attack, Rapid Strike, Severing Strike
Special Actions Djem So, Redirect Shot, temptation
Force Powers Known (Use the Force +17): *farseeing, Force disarm, Force grip, Force slam, Force thrust, move object, negate energy, rebuke, surge*
Force Secrets Distant Power, Multitarget Power
Force Techniques Force Point Recovery, Improved Move Light Object, Improved Sense Force

Abilities Str 16, Dex 16, Con 17, Int 14, Wis 14, Cha 15
Special Qualities life support
Talents Armored Defense, Block, Dark Side Adept, Deflect, Djem So, Force Pilot, Improved Armored Defense, Redirect Shot, Severing Strike, Vehicular Evasion, Weapon Specialization (lightsabers)
Feats Armor Proficiency (light), Double Attack (lightsabers), Force Sensitivity, Force Training (3), Rapid Strike, Skill Focus (Use the Force), Strong in the Force, Vehicular Combat, Weapon Focus (lightsabers), Weapon Proficiency (lightsabers, simple weapons)
Skills Initiative +17, Mechanics +16, Pilot +17, Use the Force +17 (may reroll when using *[dark side]* Force powers)
Possessions custom armor (treat as armored flight suit with helmet package; modified, +8 armor bonus), lightsaber (self-built), cybernetic prosthetics (4, both arms and legs), Sith robes, utility belt with medpac

Life Support—Due to injuries sustained on Mustafar, Darth Vader is completely dependent on the life support granted by his armor or by special sealed chambers designed specifically for him. Without this special life support, Vader begins to suffocate (see Hold Breath, page 66).

Obi-Wan Kenobi

A student of Yoda and Qui-Gon Jinn, Obi-Wan Kenobi exemplifies all that is noble and heroic about the Jedi. As a Padawan, he defeats Darth Maul after the Sith Lord strikes down Qui-Gon Jinn. Later, he is promoted to the rank of Jedi Knight and given the responsibility to train Anakin Skywalker, then just a child. Over the next thirteen years, even into the Clone Wars, the two Jedi become more than student and teacher—they became the truest of friends.

As a general in the Clone Wars, Obi-Wan survives his clones' assassination attempt when Palpatine issues Order 66, and in the Jedi Temple he sees horrible evidence of Anakin's fall to the dark side. Despite the crushing pain it causes him, Obi-Wan faces Anakin (now Darth Vader) on Mustafar, ultimately leaving the new Sith apprentice half-dead by a river of lava. Obi-Wan, together with Yoda and Bail Organa, arranges to hide Anakin and Padmé's newborn twins. Almost two decades later, Obi-Wan Kenobi comes out of the Tatooine desert on one last desperate mission, realizing his destiny to once more face his old apprentice.

Obi-Wan Kenobi (Episode III)   CL 14
Medium Human Jedi 7/Jedi Knight 5/Jedi Master 2
Destiny 2; **Force** 7
Init +15; **Senses** Perception +9
Languages Basic, Shyriiwook

Defenses Ref 30 (flat-footed 27), Fort 29, Will 29; Block, Deflect, Soresu
hp 129; **Threshold** 29
Immune fear effects

Speed 6 squares
Melee lightsaber +20 (2d8+13) or
Melee lightsaber +15/+15 (2d8+13) with Double Attack
Ranged by weapon +16
Base Atk +14; **Grp** +17
Atk Options Double Attack, Severing Strike
Special Actions Combat Reflexes, Equilibrium, Redirect Shot, serenity
Force Powers Known (Use the Force +19): *farseeing, Force slam (2), mind trick (2), move object, rebuke, surge, vital transfer*
Force Secrets Quicken Power
Force Techniques Force Point Recovery (2), Improved Move Light Object

Obi-Wan Kenobi

- **Abilities** Str 15, Dex 16, Con 14, Int 13, Wis 14, Cha 15
- **Talents** Block, Deflect, Equilibrium, Greater Weapon Focus (lightsabers), Redirect Shot, Severing Strike, Soresu, Weapon Specialization (lightsabers)
- **Feats** Armor Proficiency (light), Combat Reflexes, Double Attack (lightsabers), Force Sensitivity, Force Training (3), Skill Focus (Use the Force), Weapon Finesse, Weapon Focus (lightsabers), Weapon Proficiency (lightsabers, simple weapons)
- **Skills** Acrobatics +15, Initiative +15, Use the Force +19
- **Possessions** lightsaber (self-built), comlink (encrypted), Jedi robes, utility belt with medpac

Padmé Amidala

Once the youngest elected Queen of the planet Naboo, Padmé Amidala later becomes the senator for her homeworld. Throughout her political career, she remains a tireless champion of democracy and diplomacy, fighting until the end to prevent Supreme Chancellor Palpatine from creating the Grand Army of the Republic and later transforming the government into the Galactic Empire. Her efforts to coordinate dissidents ultimately lead to the formation of the Rebel Alliance.

Padmé falls in love with Anakin Skywalker when he is assigned to protect her at the outset of the Clone Wars. They are married secretly and keep their relationship hidden, even when she becomes pregnant. After Anakin falls to the dark side, she confronts him with tragic consequences. Though she survives her injuries, her destiny is realized when she trades her life for the lives of her newborn twins.

Senator Padmé Amidala (Episode III)   CL 10
Medium Human noble 10
Destiny 2; **Force** 5, Strong in the Force
Init +12; **Senses** Perception +18
Languages Basic, Gran, Gungan, High Galactic, Mon Calamarian, Rodese

Defenses Ref 24 (flat-footed 22), Fort 22, Will 26
hp 59; **Threshold** 22

Speed 6 squares
Melee unarmed +7 (1d4+5)
Ranged sporting blaster pistol +9 (3d4+5) or
Ranged sporting blaster pistol +4/+4 (3d4+5) with Double Attack
Base Atk +7; **Grp** +9
Atk Options Double Attack, Point Blank Shot, Precise Shot
Special Actions Born Leader, Coordinate +1

- **Abilities** Str 10, Dex 15, Con 12, Int 15, Wis 16, Cha 18
- **Talents** Born Leader, Coordinate, Trust, Wanted Alive, Wealth
- **Feats** Double Attack (pistols), Improved Defenses, Linguist, Point Blank Shot, Precise Shot, Skill Focus (Deception, Gather Information, Knowledge [bureaucracy], Perception, Persuasion), Strong in the Force, Weapon Proficiency (pistols, simple weapons)
- **Skills** Deception +19, Gather Information +19, Initiative +12, Knowledge (bureaucracy) +17, Knowledge (galactic lore) +12, Knowledge (social sciences) +12, Perception +18, Persuasion +19
- **Possessions** sporting blaster pistol, comlink, senatorial wardrobe, astromech droid (R2-D2)

Luke Skywalker

A farm boy on the remote desert world of Tatooine, young Luke Skywalker never dreamt that his destiny would shape the fate of the entire galaxy. He studies under Obi-Wan Kenobi, destroys the Death Star over Yavin, and becomes a Jedi Knight with Master Yoda's guidance. He goes on to redeem

SENATOR PADMÉ AMIDALA

his father, Anakin Skywalker (now Darth Vader), helping to end the reign of the Empire.

In the decades that follow, Luke helps to build the fledgling New Republic, founds the Jedi Praxeum on Yavin 4, raises a new order of Jedi, and fights back the menace of the Yuuzhan Vong invasion.

Luke Skywalker (Episode VI)   CL 11
Medium Human scout 1/Jedi 7/ace pilot 2/Jedi Knight 1
Destiny 2; **Force** 5, Strong in the Force; **Dark Side** 3
Init +13; **Senses** Perception +12
Languages Basic, Huttese, Shyriiwook

Defenses Ref 26 (flat-footed 23), Fort 25, Will 25; Block, Deflect, Evasion
hp 99; **Threshold** 25
Speed 6 squares
Melee lightsaber +14 (2d8+11) or
Melee lightsaber +9/+10 (2d8+11) with Double Attack
Ranged blaster pistol +12 (3d6)
Base Atk +9; **Grp** +12
Atk Options Double Attack, Severing Strike
Special Actions Melee Defense Redirect Shot
Force Powers Known (Use the Force +16): *mind trick, move object, surge*
Abilities Str 14, Dex 16, Con 14, Int 14, Wis 14, Cha 15
Talents Block, Deflect, Evasion, Redirect Shot, Severing Strike, Weapon Specialization (lightsabers)
Feats Double Attack (lightsabers), Force Sensitivity, Force Training, Melee Defense, Skill Focus (Use the Force), Strong in the Force, Vehicular Combat, Weapon Finesse, Weapon Focus (lightsabers), Weapon Proficiency (lightsabers, pistols, rifles, simple weapons)
Skills Initiative +13, Mechanics +12, Perception +12, Pilot +13, Ride +13, Survival +12, Use the Force +16
Possessions blaster pistol, lightsaber (self-built), cybernetic prosthesis (1, right hand), flight suit, robes, utility belt with medpac

LUKE SKYWALKER

"AREN'T YOU A LITTLE SHORT FOR A STORMTROOPER?"
— LEIA ORGANA

Leia Organa

As the Senator of Alderaan, Leia Organa secretly serves the Rebel Alliance, determined to bring down the tyranny and injustice that her adopted father (and her late mother) had fought so hard to destroy. Leia is instrumental in every turning point of the Galactic Civil War, and her influence shapes the government of the New Republic, particularly after she becomes the Chief of State in the wake of Mon Mothma's retirement. Over time, Leia becomes increasingly devoted to the Jedi tradition, until finally she begins to live up to the legacy of the Skywalker name.

Leia Organa (Episode VI)   CL 10
Medium Human noble 8/soldier 2
Destiny 2; **Force** 5, Strong in the Force
Init +12; **Senses** Perception +18

Languages Basic, Bothan, High Galactic, Mon Calamarian, Shyriiwook, Ubese
Defenses Ref 23 (flat-footed 21), Fort 23, Will 24
hp 63; **Threshold** 23
Speed 6 squares
Melee unarmed +9 (1d4+6)
Ranged sporting blaster pistol +10 (3d4+5) or
Ranged sporting blaster pistol +5/+5 (3d4+5) with Double Attack
Base Atk +8; **Grp** +10
Atk Options Deadeye, Double Attack, Point Blank Shot, Precise Shot
Special Actions Bolster Ally, Born Leader, Inspire Confidence, Rally
Abilities Str 13, Dex 14, Con 13, Int 15, Wis 14, Cha 16
Talents Bolster Ally, Born Leader, Inspire Confidence, Rally, Weapon Specialization (pistols)
Feats Deadeye, Double Attack, Linguist, Point Blank Shot, Precise Shot, Skill Focus (Deception, Knowledge [tactics], Perception, Persuasion), Strong in the Force, Weapon Focus (pistols), Weapon Proficiency (pistols, rifles, simple weapons)
Skills Deception +18, Gather Information +13, Knowledge (bureaucracy) +12, Knowledge (garactic lore) +12, Knowledge (tactics) +17, Initiative +12, Perception +17, Persuasion +18
Possessions sporting blaster pistol, datapad, utility belt with medpac, Rebel uniform

Han Solo

Once an Imperial officer discharged for saving the life of a Wookiee slave, Han Solo goes on to become one of the best pilots and smugglers in the galaxy. One lost shipment of spice, however, leads to a debt to Jabba the Hutt that Han can't repay, and his shady past comes back to haunt him on Cloud City after the Battle of Hoth. Still, his friends manage to free Han from the clutches of the Hutt gangster, and Han leads the Rebel commando team that destroys the shield generator on Endor.

Years later, Han and Leia are married and have children, all of whom grow to be Jedi studying under their Uncle Luke. When the Yuuzhan Vong invade the galaxy, Han's suffers one loss after another, beginning with the deaths of Chewbacca and, later, his youngest son, Anakin Solo. Even after the end of the war, Han's personal pain continues as he watches the Galactic Alliance and his native Corellia square off... and the fear of losing his only remaining son to the dark side begins to grow.

Han Solo (Episode VI)   CL 12
Medium Human scoundrel 5/soldier 2/ace pilot 3/gunslinger 2
Destiny 2; **Force** 6
Init +18; **Senses** Perception +12
Languages Basic, Huttese, Rodese, Shyriiwook
Defenses Ref 28 (flat-footed 26), Fort 25, Will 24
hp 77; **Threshold** 25
Speed 6 squares
Melee unarmed +10 (1d4+7)
Ranged heavy blaster pistol +14 (3d8+6)
Ranged heavy blaster pistol +12 (4d8+6) with Rapid Shot
Base Atk +9; **Grp** +11
Atk Options Point Blank Shot, Precise Shot, Rapid Shot, Sneak Attack +1d6, Trigger Work
Special Actions Full Throttle, Quick Draw, Stellar Warrior
Abilities Str 13, Dex 15, Con 13, Int 14, Wis 12, Cha 14

HAN SOLO AND LEIA ORGANA

Talents Full Throttle, Keep It Together, Sneak Attack +1d6, Spacehound, Stellar Warrior, Trigger Work, Weapon Specialization (pistols)
Feats Point Blank Shot, Precise Shot, Quick Draw, Rapid Shot, Skill Focus (Initiative, Pilot), Vehicular Combat, Weapon Focus (pistols, heavy weapons), Weapon Proficiency (heavy weapons, pistols, rifles, simple weapons)
Skills Deception +13, Initiative +18, Knowledge (galactic lore) +13, Mechanics +13, Perception +12, Pilot +18
Possessions heavy blaster pistol with targeting scope, tool kit, modified YT-1300 transport *(Millennium Falcon)*

Supporting Characters

The following section presents sample supporting characters from the *Star Wars* feature films.

Chewbacca

The mighty Chewbacca fights in the Clone Wars to defend the Republic, working closely with Jedi Master Yoda. When the Jedi are destroyed by the traitorous clone army, Chewbacca decides he is no longer interested in fighting for the Republic. After a brutal battle, he is captured by the Empire and rescued by a young Imperial officer named Han Solo. Moved by Solo's courage, Chewbacca decides that he owes Solo a life debt. He promptly attaches himself to Han Solo and follows him everywhere, becoming Solo's closest friend and sometimes conscience.

Chewbacca (Episode VI)   CL 10
Medium Wookiee scout 6/scoundrel 4
Destiny 2; **Force** 5
Init +6; **Senses** Perception +10
Languages Basic (understand only), Huttese (understand only), Shyriiwook
___
Defenses Ref 24 (flat-footed 22), Fort 27, Will 21
hp 110; **Threshold** 27; extraordinary recuperation
___
Speed 6 squares
Melee unarmed +11 (1d6+9) or
Melee unarmed +15 (1d6+14) with Powerful Charge
Ranged bowcaster +8 (3d10+5) or
Ranged bowcaster +6 (4d10+5) with Rapid Shot
Base Atk +7; **Grp** +11
Atk Options Careful Shot, Crush, Deadeye, Pin, Point Blank Shot, Powerful Charge, Precise Shot, Rapid Shot
Special Actions rage 2/day
Abilities Str 19, Dex 13, Con 20, Int 12, Wis 10, Cha 10

Talents Acute Senses, Extreme Effort, Jury-Rigger, Spacehound, Stellar Warrior
Feats Careful Shot, Crush, Deadeye, Extra Rage, Martial Arts I, Pin, Point Blank Shot, Powerful Charge, Precise Shot, Rapid Shot, Skill Training (Use Computer), Weapon Proficiency (pistols, rifles, simple weapons)
Skills Climb +5 (may take 10 when distracted), Endurance +10, Mechanics +10 (may reroll when making jury-rigged repair), Perception +10 (treat range as one category less), Persuasion +5 (may reroll attempts to intimidate), Pilot +10, Use Computer +10 (may reroll and keep better result when plotting hyperspace jump)
Possessions bowcaster, bandolier, tool kit

CHEWBACCA

Lando Calrissian

A gambler, smuggler, con artist, opportunist, and all-around scoundrel, Lando Calrissian considers himself more of an entrepreneur than a criminal. Although his capital sometimes comes from questionable sources, Lando almost always puts it into more or less legitimate operations, with the sole purpose of turning it into even more capital. He is nothing if not ambitious—though sometimes his ambition gets the better of him.

Lando Calrissian (Episode VI)　　　　　　　　　　　CL 8
Medium Human scoundrel 8
Destiny 1; **Force** 4; **Dark Side** 1
Init +6; **Senses** Perception +10
Languages Basic, Shyriiwook, Sullustese

Defenses Ref 22 (flat-footed 20), Fort 19, Will 20; Dodge, Mobility
hp 50; **Threshold** 19

Speed 6 squares; Running Attack
Melee unarmed +7 (1d4+5)
Ranged blaster pistol +9 (3d6+4) or
Ranged blaster pistol +4/+4 (3d6+4) with Double Attack
Base Atk +6; **Grp** +8
Atk Options Dastardly Strike, Double Attack, Point Blank Shot
Special Actions Fool's Luck, Fortune's Favor, Gambler

Abilities Str 12, Dex 14, Con 12, Int 14, Wis 13, Cha 16
Talents Dastardly Strike, Fool's Luck, Fortune's Favor, Gambler
Feats Dodge, Double Attack, Mobility, Point Blank Shot, Running Attack, Skill Focus (Deception), Vehicular Combat, Weapon Focus (pistols), Weapon Proficiency (heavy weapons, pistols, simple weapons)
Skills Deception +17, Gather Information +12, Mechanics +11, Perception +10, Persuasion +12, Pilot +11
Possessions blaster pistol, comlink, expensive clothes

R2-D2

At first glance, R2-D2 seems an unassuming astromech droid, typical of his series. But Artoo is unusual in that he has a unique personality quirk: courage. Artoo demonstrates his bravery again and again, taking the typical R2 unit's helpfulness to an unheard-of extreme.

Although he serves faithfully, Artoo does so in the manner he feels is best—which doesn't always coincide with the instructions given to him. In addition to being innovative and resourceful, he is often absolutely right about the best course of action.

R2-D2 (Episode VI)　　　　　　　　　　　CL 6
Small droid (2nd-degree) nonheroic 2/scoundrel 6
Destiny 1; **Force** 4
Init +3; **Senses** darkvision; Perception +6
Languages Basic, Binary, Huttese, Mon Calamarian, Shyriiwook

Defenses Ref 23 (flat-footed 20), Fort 16, Will 18; Dodge, Mobility
hp 34; **Threshold** 16
Immune droid traits

Speed 4 squares (wheeled), 1 square (walking), 6 squares (flying)
Melee electroshock probe +10 (1d8+3 ion)
Ranged by weapon +14
Base Atk +5; **Grp** +3
Special Actions Melee Defense, Point Blank Shot
Special Actions Gimmick

Abilities Str 8, Dex 16, Con —, Int 16, Wis 10, Cha 7
Talents Gimmick, Master Slicer, Trace
Feats Dodge, Improved Defenses, Melee Defense, Mobility, Point Blank Shot, Skill Focus (Mechanics, Use Computer), Skill Training (Perception), Toughness, Weapon Finesse, Weapon Proficiency (simple weapons)
Skills Deception +7, Mechanics +17, Perception +9, Pilot +12, Use Computer +15 (may reroll and keep better result when improving access to a computer)
Systems wheeled locomotion, walking locomotion, flying locomotion (limited), magnetic feet, heuristic processor, 6 tool appendages, 1 claw appendage, diagnostics package, internal storage (2 kg)
Possessions circular saw, electroshock probe, fire extinguisher, electric arc welder, holorecorder, holoprojector

C-3PO

The gleaming golden protocol droid C-3PO is typical of his model: outspoken, fussy, and even a bit high-strung. But since these qualities hardly interfere with his work, his personality quirks are mostly tolerated. Threepio is unusual in that he was not manufactured by Cybot Galactica, like most protocol droids. He was, in fact, assembled from spare parts by young Anakin Skywalker on the remote planet of Tatooine. Still, Threepio meets all the safety and performance standards of the original manufacturer, so he has managed to serve several masters adequately.

C-3PO (Episode VI)　　　　　　　　　　　CL 5
Medium droid (3rd-degree) nonheroic 1/noble 5
Destiny 1; **Force** 4
Init −1; **Senses** Perception +0
Languages Basic, Binary, Bocce, Bothan, High Galactic, Huttese, Mon Calamarian, Shyriiwook

Defenses Ref 16 (flat-footed 16), Fort 15, Will 19
hp 26; **Threshold** 15
Immune droid traits

Speed 6 squares (walking)

Melee unarmed +2 (1d3+1)
Ranged by weapon +2
Base Atk +3; **Grp** +2
Special Actions Coordinate +2

Abilities Str 8, Dex 9, Con —, Int 12, Wis 12, Cha 16
Talents Coordinate (2), Educated
Feats Improved Defenses, Linguist (2), Skill Focus (Persuasion), Skill Training (Deception, Knowledge [bureaucracy], Knowledge [galactic lore], Perception), Toughness
Skills Deception +11, Knowledge (bureaucracy) +9, Knowledge (galactic lore) +9, Knowledge (social sciences) +9, Perception +9, Persuasion +16
Systems walking locomotion, standard processor, translator unit (DC 5), 2 hand appendages, vocabulator
Possessions audio recorder

YODA

The wizened Jedi Master Yoda is a living legend to the Jedi order, the personification of its ideals. He is nearly 900 years old when Senator Palpatine is elected Supreme Chancellor of the Republic. Yoda plays a significant part in the events surrounding the start of the Clone Wars. He forges close friendships with the Wookiees during the war and spends much of his time away from Coruscant. He escapes the destruction and death caused by Order 66, and when the Jedi order is destroyed, Yoda retreats into hiding on Dagobah to await the day he will be needed to help restore balance to the Force. To that end, Yoda trains Luke Skywalker in the ways of the Jedi and helps prepare him to confront Darth Vader and the Emperor. This task complete, Yoda finally succumbs to age and, like so many Jedi before him, becomes one with the Force.

Yoda (Episode III) CL 20
Small Jedi 8/Jedi Knight 7/Jedi Master 5
Destiny 4; **Force** 8, Strong in the Force
Init +18; **Senses** Use the Force +24
Languages Basic, Cerean, Shyriiwook

Defenses Ref 37 (flat-footed 34), Fort 33, Will 38; Block, Deflect
hp 174; **Threshold** 33
Immune fear effects

Speed 4 squares
Melee lightsaber +25 (2d8+16) or
Melee lightsaber +24/+24 (2d8+16) with Double Attack or
Melee lightsaber +29/+29/+29 (2d8+16) with Triple Attack
Ranged by weapon +23
Base Atk +20; **Grp** +14
Atk Options Acrobatic Strike, Double Attack, Triple Attack
Special Actions Redirect Shot, serenity, Skilled Advisor
Force Powers Known (Use the Force +24): *battle strike* (2), *farseeing*, *Force disarm*, *Force slam* (2), *Force thrust*, *mind trick* (2), *move object* (2), *negate energy*, *rebuke* (3), *surge* (2), *vital transfer*
Force Secrets Devastating Power, Distant Power, Multitarget Power, Quicken Power
Force Techniques Improved Sense Force, Force Point Recovery (2)

Abilities Str 8, Dex 16, Con 11, Int 15, Wis 21, Cha 19
Talents Ataru, Block, Deflect, Force Perception, Foresight, Multiattack Proficiency (lightsabers ×2), Redirect Shot, Severing Strike, Skilled Advisor, Visions
Feats Acrobatic Strike, Double Attack, Force Sensitivity, Force Training (3), Running Attack, Skill Focus (Use the Force), Skill Training (Acrobatics), Strong in the Force, Triple Attack, Weapon Finesse, Weapon Focus (lightsabers), Weapon Proficiency (lightsabers, simple weapons)
Skills Acrobatics +18, Initiative +18 (may spend a Force Point to reroll and keep better result), Knowledge (galactic lore) +17, Knowledge (tactics) +17, Use the Force +24 (may substitute for Perception checks)
Possessions lightsaber (self-built), cane, Jedi robes

EMPEROR PALPATINE (DARTH SIDIOUS)

Possessed of the boundless power of the Force and adept in the ways of the dark side, the Emperor is one of the most dangerous and evil Humans in galactic history. The Emperor began his career of evil so subtly that no outward change evidenced the darkness in his heart. Those who encountered him considered him a kindly fellow, perhaps even a bit outclassed by the pace and magnitude of the political arena into which he had been thrust when he became a senator. But even then he was scheming, forging alliances with influential figures in the Senate and the great learning centers.

Ten years after he is elected Supreme Chancellor of the Senate, Palpatine sways Count Dooku to the dark side and uses him to found the Confederacy of Independent Systems. The ensuing conflict between the Republic and the Separatists enables Palpatine to trick the Senate into forming the Empire and voting him in as Emperor. Following the death of Dooku, he secures the service of Anakin Skywalker as his new apprentice, using him as a foil against the Jedi and the Separatists. His master stroke is the secret Order 66, with which he orders the clone troopers, programmed to obey him, to betray and assassinate the Jedi.

With the resources of a million worlds at his disposal and an endless supply of political malcontents to serve as slave labor, the Emperor builds great engines of destruction to ensure his domination of the galaxy. The greatest of these weapons is the planet-destroying Death Star. To oversee its construction and deployment, the Emperor turns to his new apprentice, Darth Vader. Although the Emperor foresees the return of the Jedi Knights in the form of Luke Skywalker, he can't foresee (or won't accept) the impact that young Skywalker will have on Darth Vader—or the ultimate betrayal that would spell the Empire's doom.

Emperor Palpatine (Episode III) — CL 20
Medium Human noble 6/Jedi 1/Sith apprentice 8/Sith Lord 5
Destiny 4; **Force** 8; **Dark Side** 20
Init +16; **Senses** Improved Sense Surroundings; Use the Force +24
Languages Basic, Bothan, Geonosian, Gran, High Galactic, Neimoidian, Rodese, Ryl, Sith, Zabrak

Defenses Ref 35 (flat-footed 33), Fort 34, Will 38; Block, Deflect
hp 132; **Threshold** 34
Immune fear effects

Speed 6 squares
Melee lightsaber +21 (2d8+10/×3) or
Melee lightsaber +20/+20 (2d8+10/×3) with Double Attack or
Melee lightsaber +15/+15/+15 (2d8+10/×3) with Triple Attack
Ranged by weapon +20
Base Atk +18; **Grp** +20
Atk Options Dark Scourge, Double Attack, Melee Defense, Triple Attack, Whirlwind Attack
Special Actions Redirect Shot, temptation

Force Powers Known (Use the Force +24): *dark rage, farseeing, Force disarm, Force lightning* (4), *Force slam, Force thrust, move object* (3), *rebuke* (2), *surge* (3), *vital transfer*
Force Secrets Devastating Power, Distant Power, Multitarget Power, Quicken Power
Force Techniques Force Point Recovery, Improved Move Light Object, Improved Sense Force, Improved Sense Surroundings

Abilities Str 10, Dex 15, Con 12, Int 18, Wis 20, Cha 19
Talents Block, Connections, Dark Scourge, Dark Side Adept, Deflect, Force Perception, Multiattack Proficiency (lightsabers ×2), Redirect Shot, Visions, Wealth
Feats Double Attack, Force Sensitivity, Force Training (3), Linguist, Melee Defense, Skill Focus (Use the Force), Triple Attack, Triple Crit (lightsabers), Weapon Finesse, Weapon Proficiency (lightsabers, pistols, simple weapons), Whirlwind Attack
Skills Deception +19, Gather Information +19, Initiative +16, Knowledge (bureaucracy) +19, Knowledge (galactic lore) +19, Knowledge (social sciences) +19, Knowledge (tactics) +19, Persuasion +19, Use Computer +19, Use the Force +24 (may reroll when using *[dark side]* Force powers, may substitute for Perception checks)
Possessions lightsaber (self-built), Sith robes, comlink (encrypted)

THE EMPEROR

Boba Fett

The most feared bounty hunter of his time, Boba Fett racks up an unheard-of number of successful bounties that earns him a reputation as a force to be reckoned with. His name fills outlaws and criminals with dread. Boba Fett seems bereft of conscience. It means nothing to him to accept help from someone, then minutes later turn that person in for a bounty.

Boba Fett (Episode IV)　　　　　　　　　　　　　　　**CL 15**
Medium scout 3/soldier 5/bounty hunter 5/elite trooper 2
Destiny 3; **Force** 6; **Dark Side** 7
Init +16; **Senses** low-light vision; Perception +16
Languages Basic, Huttese, Mando'a

Defenses Ref 34 (flat-footed 32), Fort 33, Will 27
hp 122; **DR** 1; **Threshold** 33

Speed 6 squares, fly 6 squares (jetpack); Running Attack
Melee unarmed +16 (1d6+9)
Ranged blaster carbine +18 (3d8+7) or
Ranged blaster carbine +15/+15 (3d8+7) with Double Attack or
Ranged grenade launcher +18 (4d6+7, stun, 2-square burst) or
Ranged flamethrower +18 (3d6+7, 6-square cone) or
Ranged missile launcher +18 (6d6+7, 2-square splash) or
Ranged stun grenade +18 (4d6+7, 2-square burst) or
Ranged whipcord +18 (grab)
Base Atk +14; **Grp** +18
Atk Options Double Attack, Hunter's Mark, Keen Shot, Point Blank Shot, Precise Shot
Special Actions familiar foe +2, Hunter's Target, Quick Draw

Abilities Str 15, Dex 18, Con 15, Int 14, Wis 14, Cha 13
Talents Acute Senses, Armored Defense, Hunter's Mark, Hunter's Target, Improved Armored Defense, Juggernaut, Keen Shot, Multiattack Proficiency (rifles), Notorious
Feats Armor Proficiency (light, medium), Double Attack, Exotic Weapon Proficiency (flamethrower), Martial Arts I, Point Blank Shot, Precise Shot, Quick Draw, Running Attack, Weapon Proficiency (heavy weapons, pistols, rifles, simple weapons)
Skills Endurance +14, Initiative +16, Knowledge (tactics) +14, Perception +16, Persuasion +8 (may reroll and keep better result when intimidating), Pilot +16, Stealth +11, Survival +14
Possessions Mandalorian armor (+8 armor, +2 equipment; as battle armor with helmet package; 4 weapon attachments), blaster

Boba Fett

carbine with mounted grenade launcher, 4 stun grenades, flamethrower (5 shots), missile launcher, 4 missiles, whipcord (treat as net), blaster gauntlet (treat as hold-out blaster), jet pack (10 charges), utility belt with medpac

General Grievous

General Grievous learned the art of war as a Kaleesh warlord fighting against the Huk species. That war ended when the Jedi Council decreed the Huks to be the victims of Kaleesh aggression and made the Kaleesh people pay for their actions. Angered by the Jedi order, Grievous is further embittered when he barely survives a shuttle crash. His broken body is rebuilt on Geonosis, an act paid for by the InterGalactic Banking Clan as a gift to their Separatist leader, Count Dooku.

Count Dooku trains Grievous in lightsaber dueling techniques, and Grievous proudly collects the lightsabers from the Jedi he defeats. Grievous has four metal arms and can fight with four lightsabers at once, making him a terrifying opponent in melee combat. He faces Anakin Skywalker and Obi-Wan Kenobi during the Battle of Coruscant but manages to elude them. He is not so fortunate when he fights against Obi-Wan on Utapau, dying at the end of an epic confrontation.

General Grievous CL 14
Medium Kaleesh (cyborg) soldier 8/elite trooper 3/officer 3
Destiny 2; **Force** 6; **Dark Side** 10
Init +16; **Senses** darkvision; Perception +14
Languages Basic, Kaleesh, Muun, Geonosian
Defenses Ref 30 (flat-footed 27), Fort 28, Will 28
hp 101; **DR** 1; **Threshold** 28
Immune atmospheric and inhaled poison hazards
Weakness vulnerable to ion damage and stunning effects

Speed 8 squares, climb 4 squares
Melee lightsaber +21 (2d8+21) or
Melee lightsaber +19 (2d8+15) and
  lightsaber +19 (2d8+15)
Melee lightsaber +14 (2d8+15) and
  lightsaber +14 (2d8+15) and
  lightsaber +14 (2d8+15) with Double Attack
or
Melee lightsaber +11 (2d8+15) and
  lightsaber +11 (2d8+15) and
  lightsaber +11 (2d8+15) with Double Attack and
  lightsaber +11 (2d8+15) with Triple Attack
Ranged heavy blaster pistol +17 (3d8+7)
Base Atk +13; **Grp** +19
Atk Options Double Attack, Dual Weapon Mastery, Melee Defense, Point Blank Shot, Triple Attack
Special Actions Battle Analysis, Deployment Tactics, Outmaneuver, Tough as Nails
Abilities Str 22, Dex 19, Con 11, Int 15, Wis 10, Cha 14
Special Qualities command cover +2, share talent (Outmaneuver)
Talents Armored Defense, Battle Analysis, Deployment Tactics, Greater Weapon Focus (lightsabers), Improved Armored Defense, Outmaneuver, Tough as Nails, Weapon Specialization (lightsabers)
Feats Armor Proficiency (light, medium), Double Attack (lightsabers), Dual Weapon Mastery I, Dual Weapon Mastery II, Martial Arts I, Melee Defense, Point Blank Shot, Triple Attack (lightsabers), Weapon Focus (lightsabers, simple weapons), Weapon Proficiency (lightsabers, pistols, rifles, simple weapons)
Skills Climb +8 (may take 10 when distracted, may reroll and keep better result), Endurance +12, Initiative +16, Jump +13 (may take 10 when distracted, may reroll and keep better result), Knowledge (tactics) +14, Perception +14, Survival +7 (may reroll and keep better result in hot or arid environments)
Systems walking locomotion, climbing claws, jump servos, 6 hand appendages (legs may be used as hands), unique armor (+8 armor), improved sensor package, darkvision
Possessions 4 lightsabers, heavy blaster pistol, cloak

Cyborg Hybrid—As a cyborg hybrid, General Grievous may use any type of droid system except a processor. His cyborg chassis includes a life support system, making him immune to atmospheric and inhaled poison hazards.

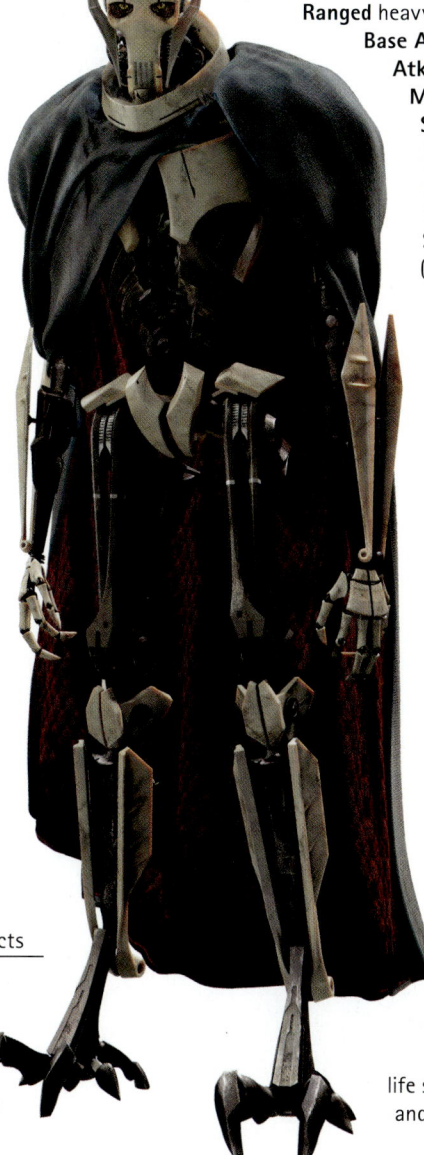

General Grievous

Chapter XVI
Allies and Opponents

The *Star Wars* universe is home to a dizzying array of sapient species. Despite the fact that Humans have been traveling the stars for tens of thousands of years, and many aliens have been doing the same for an equal amount of time, scouts discover new inhabited worlds all the time.

This chapter presents various creatures and characters that GMs can use as potential allies or adversaries for the heroes, from rampaging rancors to clone troopers. Each ally or opponent comes with ready-to-play statistics to make the GM's job a little easier.

Beasts

All animals and other nonsentient life forms have levels in the beast class (a nonheroic class). In the *Star Wars* universe, beasts are usually encountered as threats (such as acklays, rancors, and wampas) or as mounts (such as dewbacks and tauntauns).

Beasts have an Intelligence of 1 or 2. They roll their other five ability scores normally (see Chapter 1: Abilities). Beasts that show above average cunning usually have a good Wisdom score.

Beasts increase only one ability score by one point every fourth level (instead of increasing two scores by one point each). However, they gain feats normally as they advance in level, as shown in Table 3–1: Experience and Level-Dependent Benefits (page 37). A beast that gains an Intelligence of 3 or higher as a result of an ability increase is eligible to multiclass (see Multiclassing, below).

Beasts do not gain talents or starting feats, do not add their beast class level to their defense scores, and do not gain Force Points or Destiny Points.

Examples of Beasts in Star Wars

Acklay, dewback, nexu, rancor, reek, tauntaun, wampa.

Game Rule Information

Beasts have the following game statistics.

Hit Points
At each level, beasts gain 1d8 hit points + their Constitution modifier.

Force Points
Beasts do not gain Force Points.

Table 16-1: The Beast

Level	Base Attack Bonus	Level	Base Attack Bonus
1st	+0	11th	+8
2nd	+1	12th	+9
3rd	+2	13th	+9
4th	+3	14th	+10
5th	+3	15th	+11
6th	+4	16th	+12
7th	+5	17th	+12
8th	+6	18th	+13
9th	+6	19th	+14
10th	+7	20th	+15

Class Skills (trained in 1 + Int modifier, minimum 1): Acrobatics, Climb, Endurance, Initiative, Jump, Perception, Stealth, Survival, Swim.

Class Features

Beasts gain the following class features at 1st level.

Natural Armor
Many beasts have thick hides or scales that grant a natural armor bonus to their Reflex Defense. The amount of natural armor varies from creature to creature. A beast's natural armor bonus is never higher than its beast class level.

Natural Weapons
A beast has one or more natural weapon attacks (see below). It applies its Strength bonus on melee attack rolls made with natural weapons and its Dexterity bonus on ranged attack rolls made with natural weapons. If a beast has two or more natural eeapons, it may make attacks with all of them at no penalty when using the full attack action.

A beast gains a bonus on damage rolls made with its natural weapons equal to one-half its beast class level, rounded down. A beast is proficient with its own natural weapons, but not with any other weapon group.

The most common natural weapon attacks for beasts are summarized here:

Bite: A bite attack deals an amount of piercing damage determined by the beast's size: Fine, 1; Diminutive, 1d2; Tiny, 1d3; Small, 1d4; Medium, 1d6; Large, 1d8; Huge, 2d6; Gargantuan, 3d6; Colossal, 4d6.

Claw: A claw attack deals an amount of slashing damage determined by the beast's size: Fine or Diminutive, 1; Tiny, 1d2; Small, 1d3; Medium, 1d4; Large, 1d6; Huge, 1d8; Gargantuan, 2d6; Colossal, 3d6.

Gore: The creature impales opponents with a horn or antler, dealing an amount of piercing damage determined by the beast's size: Fine, 1; Diminutive, 1d2; Tiny, 1d3; Small, 1d4; Medium, 1d6; Large, 1d8; Huge, 2d6; Gargantuan, 3d6; Colossal, 4d6.

Table 16-2: Beast Size Modifiers

Beast Size	Ability Modifiers[1]	Size Modifier to Ref Defense	Size Modifier to Stealth	Size Bonus to DMG Threshold	Carrying Capacity[2]	Height or Length
Colossal	+32 Str, +32 Con, –4 Dex	–10	–20	+50	×20	19.3 m or more
Gargantuan	+24 Str, +24 Con, –4 Dex	–5	–15	+20	×10	9.7 to 19.2 m
Huge	+16 Str, +16 Con, –4 Dex	–2	–10	+10	×5	4.9 to 9.6 m
Large	+8 Str, +8 Con, –2 Dex	–1	–5	+5	×2	2.5 to 4.8 m
Medium	None	+0	+0	—	×1	1.3 to 2.4 m
Small	–2 Str, +2 Dex	+1	+5	—	×0.75	0.7 to 1.2 m
Tiny	–4 Str, +4 Dex	+2	+10	—	×0.5	0.4 to 0.6 m
Diminutive	–6 Str, +6 Dex	+5	+15	—	×0.25	0.2 to 0.3 m
Fine	–8 Str, +8 Dex	+10	+20	—	×0.01	0.1 m or less

1 *An ability score can never be lower than 1.*
2 *Beasts with four or more legs double their carrying capacity.*

Slam: The creature batters opponents with an appendage, dealing an amount bludgeoning damage determined by the beast's size: Fine or Diminutive, 1; Tiny, 1d2; Small, 1d3; Medium, 1d4; Large, 1d6; Huge, 1d8; Gargantuan, 2d6; Colossal, 3d6.

Sting: A sting deals piercing damage and may also inject a poison (see Poison, page 255). Sting damage is determined by the beast's size: Fine or Diminutive, 1; Tiny, 1d2; Small, 1d3; Medium, 1d4; Large, 1d6; Huge, 1d8; Gargantuan, 2d6; Colossal, 3d6.

Species Traits

Some beasts have adapted to living in extreme environments and gain special bonuses and traits, as summarized below:

Airborne: May reroll Initiative checks but must keep the second result, even if it's worse.

Aquatic: Can't drown in water and doesn't need to make Swim checks; low-light vision (see page 257).

Arctic: May reroll Survival checks made to endure extreme cold, keeping the better result.

Desert: May reroll Survival checks made to endure extreme heat, keeping the better result.

Subterranean: May reroll Perception checks but must keep the second result, even if it's worse; darkvision (see page 257).

Multiclassing

A beast with an Intelligence of 3 or higher can multiclass into any heroic class (see Chapter 3: Heroic Classes). Beasts with an Intelligence of 1 or 2 cannot multiclass.

Size Modifier

A beast applies a size modifier to its Reflex Defense and Stealth checks based on its size. A beast of Large size or bigger also gains a size bonus to its damage threshold. Table 16-2: Beast Size Modifiers summarizes this information.

Beast Descriptions

This section contains sample beasts from the *Star Wars* feature films. Each description includes statistics for a typical member of the species.

Acklay

The most dangerous predator native to Geonosis is the savage acklay, a monstrous arthropod with an armored exoskeleton and slashing foreclaws.

Acklay CL 10
Huge beast 11
Init +9; **Senses** Perception +10
Defenses Ref 15 (flat-footed 15), Fort 19, Will 10
hp 148; **Threshold** 29
Immune mild, moderate, and severe radiation

Speed 8 squares
Melee 2 claws +11* (1d8+18) and
  bite +11* (2d6+18)
Fighting Space 3×3; **Reach** 2 squares
Base Atk +8; **Grp** +26

Abilities Str 27, Dex 9, Con 29, Int 2, Wis 11, Cha 11
Feats Cleave, Power Attack, Skill Training (Initiative, Perception)
Skills Climb +18, Initiative +9, Perception +10
* Includes 5 points of Power Attack

Dewback

Of all the creatures indigenous to Tatooine's vast deserts, the dewback is the most respected. While the plodding bantha makes for shelter at the first hint of a sandstorm, a dewback marches resolutely on without so much as a grunt, even right through the heart of the storm.

Acklay

Dewback CL 2
Large desert beast 3
Init +0; **Senses** Perception +0
Defenses Ref 12 (flat-footed 12), Fort 18, Will 9
hp 43; **Threshold** 28
Speed 6 squares
Melee bite +6 (1d8+5)
Fighting Space 2×2; **Reach** 1 square
Base Atk +2; **Grp** +11
Abilities Str 19, Dex 8, Con 26, Int 1, Wis 8, Cha 3
Feats Improved Damage Threshold, Toughness
Skills Survival +5

NEXU

Native to the jungles of Indona and Cholganna, the nexu is a fierce, stealthy predator with little fear of larger opponents, or even the weapons of sentient beings. Hunted for sport on their native planet, nexu often turn the tables on their would-be hunters and slash them to ribbons before they can fire a shot.

Nexu CL 5
Medium beast 6
Init +12; **Senses** low-light vision; Perception +10
Defenses Ref 16 (flat-footed 12), Fort 13, Will 12
hp 45; **Threshold** 13
Speed 8 squares
Melee 2 claws +8 (1d4+7) and
   bite +8 (1d6+7)
Fighting Space 1 square; **Reach** 1 square
Base Atk +4; **Grp** +8
Atk Options ambush +2d6, Pin
Abilities Str 18, Dex 18, Con 17, Int 2, Wis 14, Cha 12
Feats Pin, Skill Training (Initiative, Perception)
Skills Initiative +12, Perception +10, Stealth +12

Ambush—A nexu deals +2d6 points of damage with its natural weapons against a flat-footed opponent.

RANCOR

While there are certainly larger and more vicious creatures in the galaxy, the rancor holds a special place in the nightmares of countless sentient creatures. Creatures of vast rage and single-minded carnage, rancors are periodically captured by big game hunters and shipped to new worlds as exotic pets.

Rancor CL 11
Huge beast 12
Init +5; **Senses** low-light vision; Perception +9
Defenses Ref 17 (flat-footed 17), Fort 16, Will 8
hp 138; fast healing 5; **Threshold** 36
Speed 8 squares
Melee 2 claws +11* (1d8+20) or
Melee bite +11* (2d6+20)
Fighting Space 3×3; **Reach** 2 squares
Base Atk +9; **Grp** +27
Atk Options Cleave, Crush, Pin, Power Attack
Abilities Str 26, Dex 9, Con 23, Int 2, Wis 7, Cha 15
Special Qualities fast healing 5
Feats Cleave, Crush, Pin, Power Attack, Toughness
Skills Perception +9

Fast Healing 5—A rancor automatically regains 5 hit points every round at the end of its turn, up to its normal maximum, until it is killed.
*Includes 6 points of Power Attack

REEK

Reeks wander the plains of Ylesia in great herds, contentedly munching on grass and lichens. Although immensely strong, they generally reserve their violent behavior for the mating season, when the sound of two bull reeks fighting for dominance rumbles like thunder across the plains.

When a reek attacks, it lowers its head, charges, and attempts to gore with its large horn. Should the initial attack miss, the reek flails its head about blindly, hoping to chase away its prey so that it can attempt another charge.

Reek CL 8
Huge beast 8
Init +3; **Senses** Perception +3
Defenses Ref 15 (flat-footed 15), Fort 20, Will 9
hp 124; **Threshold** 30
Speed 6 squares
Melee gore +10* (2d6+16) or
Melee gore +12* (2d6+20) with Powerful Charge
Fighting Space 3×3; **Reach** 1 square
Base Atk +6; **Grp** +24
Atk Options Power Attack, Powerful Charge
Special Actions rage
Abilities Str 27, Dex 8, Con 30, Int 2, Wis 8, Cha 2
Feats Power Attack, Powerful Charge, Toughness
Skills Endurance +20

Rage—The first time a reek takes damage greater than its Will Defense from a single attack, it flies into a terrible rage. While enraged, the reek temporarily gains a +2 rage bonus on melee attack rolls and melee damage rolls. The reek's fit of rage lasts for a number of rounds equal to 5 + its Constitution modifier. At the end of its rage, the reek moves −1 persistent step along the condition track (see Conditions, page 148). The penalties imposed by this condition persist until the reek takes at least 10 minutes to recuperate, during which time it can't engage in any strenuous activity. A reek can be pulled out of its enraged state by making it friendly (see the Persuasion skill, page 71).

Includes 4 points of Power Attack

Tauntaun

Dirty and smelly, the reptilian tauntaun is perfectly suited to life on the barren ice world of Hoth. The tauntaun's thick fur and layers of fat keep its body temperature high enough for it to operate during the day, but it must seek shelter from the bitter cold at night.

Tauntaun CL 1
Large arctic beast 2
Init +2; **Senses** scent; Perception +0
___
Defenses Ref 13 (flat-footed 12), Fort 13, Will 9
hp 17; **Threshold** 18
___
Speed 8 squares
Melee claw +5 (1d6+5) or
Melee bite +5 (1d8+5)
Fighting Space 2×2; **Reach** 1 square
Base Atk +1; **Grp** +10
___
Abilities Str 18, Dex 12, Con 16, Int 2, Wis 8, Cha 6
Feats Toughness
Skills Survival +5

Scent—Tauntauns ignore concealment and cover when making Perception checks to notice opponents within 10 squares, and they take no penalty from poor visibility when tracking (see the Survival skill, page 73).

Wampa

The wampa is a fearsome predator, both aggressive and subtle. Displaying uncanny cunning, a wampa sometimes ventures into even heavily guarded areas to slaughter and drag a victim away, leaving the survivors confused, terrified, and ripe targets for another attack later.

Wampas are covered in dirty white fur and move with amazing stealth. Only their claws, horns, and gleaming yellow eyes show up against the backdrop of Hoth's endless snowfields. Most of the time, especially in a raging storm, that simply isn't enough to betray the wampa's presence.

Wampa CL 4
Large arctic beast 5
Init +2; **Senses** darkvision; Perception +2
___
Defenses Ref 15 (flat-footed 15), Fort 16, Will 12
hp 52; **Threshold** 21
___
Speed 6 squares
Melee 2 claws +7* (1d6+8) and
  bite +7* (1d8+8)
Fighting Space 2×2; **Reach** 2 squares
Base Atk +3; **Grp** +13
Atk Options rend +2d6
___
Abilities Str 20, Dex 10, Con 22, Int 6, Wis 15, Cha 10
Feats Power Attack, Skill Training (Stealth)
Skills Stealth +7, Survival +9

Rend—If a wampa hits with both of its claw attacks in the same turn, it rends its opponent for an additional 2d6 points of damage.

Includes 1 point of Power Attack.

Nonheroic Characters

Nonheroic characters include everything from professional workers to petty criminals, police officers to common thugs. They lack the inclination or training to be heroes, but they are capable in their own fields. Skilled engineers, educated professors, and master architects are all nonheroic characters, as is the local governor, the self-serving spice merchant, and the baseline Imperial stormtrooper.

Nonheroic characters do not gain talents, do not add their nonheroic class level to their defense scores, and do not gain Force Points or Destiny Points. In addition, they only get to increase one ability score by one point every fourth level (instead of increasing two scores by one point each). However, they gain feats normally as they advance in level, as shown in Table 3-1: Experience and Level-Dependent Benefits (page 37).

Examples of Nonheroic Characters in Star Wars

Battle droids, clone troopers, ordinary civilians, Rebel troopers, stormtroopers.

Game Rule Information

Nonheroic characters have the following game statistics.

Hit Points

At each level, nonheroic characters gain 1d4 hit points + their Constitution modifier.

Force Points
Nonheroic characters do not gain Force Points.

CLASS FEATURES
Nonheroic characters receive no special class features other than some starting feats at 1st level.

Starting Feats
A nonheroic character gains three starting feats at 1st level, chosen from the following list:

Armor Proficiency (light), Armor Proficiency (medium), Skill Focus*, Skill Training*, Weapon Proficiency (advanced melee weapons), Weapon Proficiency (heavy weapons), Weapon Proficiency (pistols), Weapon Proficiency (rifles), Weapon Proficiency (simple weapons).

This feat may be selected more than once. Each time the feat is selected, it applies to a different skill (see the relevant feat description in Chapter 5: Feats).

MULTICLASSING
A nonheroic character can multiclass into a heroic class. The normal multiclassing rules apply (see Multiclass Characters, page 54).

TABLE 3-3: THE NONHEROIC CHARACTER

LEVEL	BASE ATTACK BONUS	LEVEL	BASE ATTACK BONUS
1st	+0	11th	+8
2nd	+1	12th	+9
3rd	+2	13th	+9
4th	+3	14th	+10
5th	+3	15th	+11
6th	+4	16th	+12
7th	+5	17th	+12
8th	+6	18th	+13
9th	+6	19th	+14
10th	+7	20th	+15

Class Skills (trained in 1 + Int modifier, minimum 1): Acrobatics, Climb, Deception, Endurance, Gather Information, Initiative, Jump, Knowledge (all skills, taken individually), Mechanics, Perception, Persuasion, Pilot, Stealth, Survival, Swim, Treat Injury, Use Computer.

CHARACTER ARCHETYPES
The following pregenerated characters are examples of typical allies and opponents that you can throw into an adventure or campaign. They represent some of the more common characters seen across the various *Star Wars* eras. Add personalities and histories to these archetypal characters as you see fit.

CREATING NON-HUMAN CHARACTERS
The statistics provided here use the Human species as the baseline (see Humans, page 23). If you wish to change the character's species, follow these simple rules:

- Remove one of the character's feats. (Human characters gain a bonus feat.)
- Remove one of the Human's trained skills. (Human characters gain a bonus trained skill.)
- Add the relevant species traits for the selected species (see Chapter 2: Species or Other Species, page 284).

THE GALACTIC EMPIRE
The Galactic Empire is a vast and highly organized government ruled over by Emperor Palpatine. The Galactic Empire seized power at the end of the Clone Wars following an unprecedented military build-up and the destruction of the Jedi order.

The Empire is divided into sectors, each of which is governed by a Moff and guarded by military forces. The Empire's authority on any given world can range from a single garrison (found mostly on backwater planets like Tatooine) to an intense presence with a stormtrooper on every street corner (as in the Deep Core and important Core worlds).

Stormtrooper
Stormtroopers are the elite troops of the Empire, trained to fight and die without fear or question. Squads of stormtroopers strike terror into the hearts of civilians throughout the galaxy, enforcing the Emperor's will with ruthless zeal and efficiency.

Stormtroopers are a separate force from the troops of Imperial Forces and do not answer directly to Imperial military officers. They are obedient and devoted to the Emperor. They cannot be bribed, blackmailed, or seduced. Any such attempt automatically fails.

After recognizing the need for troopers with special equipment and training, the Emperor ordered the development of additional types of stormtroopers, including (but not limited to) snowtroopers, sandtroopers, and scout troopers.

Stormtrooper   CL 1
Medium Human nonheroic 4
Dark Side 1
Init +2; **Senses** low-light vision; Perception +9
Languages Basic

Defenses Ref 16 (flat-footed 16), Fort 12, Will 10
hp 10; **Threshold** 12

Speed 6 squares
Melee unarmed +4 (1d4+1)
Ranged blaster rifle +4 (3d8) or
Ranged frag grenade +3 (4d6, 2-square burst)
Base Atk +3; **Grp** +4
Atk Options autofire (blaster rifle)
Special Actions Coordinated Attack

Abilities Str 12, Dex 11, Con 11, Int 10, Wis 10, Cha 10
Feats Armor Proficiency (light), Coordinated Attack, Weapon Focus (blaster rifles), Weapon Proficiency (pistols, rifles, simple weapons)
Skills Endurance +7, Perception +9
Possessions stormtrooper armor (+6 armor, +2 equipment), blaster rifle, frag grenade, utility belt with medpac

Heavy Stormtrooper   CL 2
Medium Human nonheroic 8
Dark Side 1
Init +4; **Senses** low-light vision; Perception +10
Languages Basic

Defenses Ref 16 (flat-footed 16), Fort 12, Will 9
hp 20; **Threshold** 12

Speed 6 squares
Melee unarmed +8 (1d4+2)
Ranged light repeating blaster +2 (3d8) with autofire or
Ranged light repeating blaster +5 (3d8) with braced autofire or
Ranged frag grenade +6 (4d6, 2-square burst)
Base Atk +6; **Grp** +8
Atk Options autofire (light repeating blaster), Burst Fire, Point Blank Shot
Special Actions brace (light repeating blaster)

Abilities Str 15, Dex 11, Con 10, Int 12, Wis 9, Cha 8
Feats Armor Proficiency (light), Burst Fire, Point Blank Shot, Weapon Focus (rifles), Weapon Proficiency (heavy weapons, rifles, simple weapons)
Skills Endurance +9, Mechanics +10, Perception +10
Possessions stormtrooper armor (+6 armor, +2 equipment), light repeating blaster, 3 explosive charges, frag grenade, utility belt with medpac

Scout Trooper   CL 2
Medium Human nonheroic 6
Dark Side 1
Init +4; **Senses** low-light vision; Perception +10
Languages Basic

Defenses Ref 15 (flat-footed 14), Fort 11, Will 10
hp 21; **Threshold** 11

Speed 6 squares
Melee unarmed +4 (1d4)
Ranged blaster pistol +5 (3d6) or
Ranged blaster rifle +5 (3d8) or

Ranged frag grenade (4d6, 2-square burst)
Base Atk +4; **Grp** +4
Atk Options Burst Fire

Abilities Str 10, Dex 13, Con 12, Int 10, Wis 11, Cha 8
Feats Armor Proficiency (light), Point Blank Shot, Skill Training (Stealth), Vehicular Combat, Weapon Proficiency (pistols, rifles, simple weapons)
Skills Perception +10, Pilot +9, Stealth +9
Possessions scout trooper armor (+4 armor; as combat jumpsuit with helmet package), blaster pistol, blaster rifle with standard targeting scope, frag grenade, utility belt with medpac, Aratech 74-Z military speeder bike

Imperial Officer

Admired, respected, and feared, the officers of the Imperial Army and Imperial Navy are drawn from prestigious families with long histories of military service. Few are promoted up from the lower ranks. Most are inducted straight into officer training academies, instructed in doctrine, leadership, and tactics, and then awarded commissions. There, if they distinguish themselves, they finally get a chance to rise through the upper echelons—but rarely do they find occasion to dirty their hands.

Imperial Officer   CL 5
Medium Human nonheroic 4/noble 3/officer 1
Force 2; **Dark Side** 5
Init +3; **Senses** Perception +10
Languages Basic, Bocce, Durese, High Galactic

Defenses Ref 15 (flat-footed 15), Fort 14, Will 18
hp 33; **Threshold** 14

Speed 6 squares
Melee unarmed +6 (1d4+2)
Ranged blaster pistol +5 (3d6+2)
Base Atk +6; **Grp** +6
Special Actions Born Leader, Coordinate, Trust, Vehicular Combat

Abilities Str 10, Dex 8, Con 10, Int 12, Wis 12, Cha 14
Talents Born Leader, Coordinate, Trust
Feats Armor Proficiency (light), Linguist, Skill Focus (Persuasion), Skill Training (Deception, Pilot), Toughness, Vehicular Combat, Weapon Proficiency (pistols, simple weapons)
Skills Deception +11, Knowledge (tactics) +10, Perception +10, Persuasion +16, Pilot +8
Possessions blaster pistol, code cylinder, comlink (encrypted), officer's uniform

Rebel Alliance

The Rebel Alliance fights against the tyranny of the Empire in order to restore justice and freedom to the galaxy. Formed by loyalists such as Mon Mothma and Senator Bail Organa, the Rebel Alliance struggles against the Empire at every turn. It uses guerilla warfare and undercover violence to weaken the Imperial machine and help free the oppressed people of the galaxy. Though the Alliance sometimes engages in direct military action against the Empire, as seen at the Battle of Yavin or the Battle of Endor, most of the efforts of the Alliance take place under the guise of legitimate activity. For this reason, the Alliance has attracted not only freedom fighters but also outlaws, smugglers, and even pirates.

The Rebel Alliance is loosely organized into cells that can operate relatively independently of Alliance command. Each cell operates on Imperial worlds or out of hidden bases, such as the base on Hoth. Any worlds that sympathize with the Alliance find themselves the targets of Imperial wrath. Alliance agents are always on the run from the Empire, and Rebels that are captured are dealt with swiftly and harshly.

Rebel Trooper

The basic Rebel Trooper is stationed on Rebel bases and aboard Alliance starships throughout the galaxy, serving as the first line of defense against the Empire's stormtroopers. They are also used as scouts and saboteurs.

Rebel Trooper   CL 1
Medium Human nonheroic 3
Init +7; **Senses** Perception +6
Languages Basic

Defenses Ref 13 (flat-footed 12), Fort 11, Will 10
hp 10; **Threshold** 11

Speed 6 squares
Melee unarmed +2 (1d4)
Ranged blaster pistol +4 (3d6) or
Ranged frag grenade +3 (4d6, 2-square burst)
Base Atk +2; **Grp** +3
Special Actions Point Blank Shot[H]

Abilities Str 11, Dex 13, Con 12, Int 9, Wis 10, Cha 8
Feats Armor Proficiency (light), Point Blank Shot[H], Weapon Focus (pistols), Weapon Proficiency (pistols, rifles, simple weapons)
Skills Initiative +7, Perception +6[H]
Possessions blast helmet and vest (+2 armor), blaster pistol, comlink (encrypted)

[H] *Human bonus feat or trained skill*

Elite Rebel Trooper CL 2
Medium Human nonheroic 6
Init +9; **Senses** Perception +8
Languages Basic

Defenses Ref 13 (flat-footed 12), Fort 11, Will 10
hp 21; **Threshold** 16

Speed 6 squares
Melee unarmed +5 (1d4+1)
Ranged blaster pistol +6 (3d6) or
Ranged frag grenade +5 (4d6, 2-square burst)
Base Atk +4; **Grp** +5
Special Actions Point Blank Shot[H]

Abilities Str 12, Dex 13, Con 12, Int 9, Wis 10, Cha 8
Feats Armor Proficiency (light), Improved Damage Threshold, Point Blank Shot[H], Weapon Focus (pistols), Weapon Proficiency (pistols, rifles, simple weapons)
Skills Initiative +9, Perception +8[H]
Possessions blast helmet and vest (+2 armor), blaster pistol, 2 frag grenades, comlink (encrypted)

[H] *Human bonus feat or trained skill*

Galactic Republic

Consisting of thousands of civilized worlds, the Galactic Republic is the oldest governing body in history. Senators from its constituent worlds determine policy and enact laws, ensuring that peace and prosperity reign throughout the galaxy.

The greatest threat to the Galactic Republic is the Confederacy of Independent Systems, a coalition of worlds that believes the Republic has become corrupt. The Senate authorizes the deployment of a vast clone army to quell the Separatist threat, leading to the Clone Wars and ending with the destruction of the Separatist leadership and the dissolution of the Republic in favor of a new Empire.

Clone Trooper

To counter the threat of the Trade Federation's droid armies, the Republic deploys an army of cloned warriors. The clones' creators, the Kaminoans, conceive the clones from a single genetic blueprint (that of the bounty hunter Jango Fett), making a few alterations to ensure the troopers' rapid maturation and unwavering obedience. The true loyalty of the clone troopers is revealed at the end of the Clone Wars, when Darth Sidious issues Order 66 and turns the clones against the Jedi order.

Although identical in appearance, clone troopers have different levels of training, which accounts for their varying levels of ability. Clone troopers can't be bribed, blackmailed, or seduced. Any such attempt automatically fails.

Clone Trooper CL 2
Medium Human nonheroic 6
Init +9; **Senses** Perception +4
Languages Basic

Defenses Ref 17 (flat-footed 16), Fort 13, Will 9
hp 21; **Threshold** 13

Speed 6 squares
Melee by weapon +5
Ranged blaster rifle +5 (3d8+3)
Base Atk +4; **Grp** +5
Atk Options Careful Shot
Special Actions Point Blank Shot

Abilities Str 12, Dex 13, Con 12, Int 10, Wis 9, Cha 8
Feats Armor Proficiency (light), Careful Shot, Point Blank Shot, Weapon Proficiency (pistols), Weapon Proficiency (rifles), Weapon Proficiency (simple weapons)
Skills Initiative +9, Perception +4
Possessions clone trooper armor (+6 armor, +2 equipment), blaster rifle, comlink

CLONE TROOPER

Clone Trooper Commander   CL 5
Medium Human nonheroic 6/soldier 2/officer 1
Force 3; **Dark Side** 5
Init +4; **Senses** low-light vision; Perception +11
Languages Basic, High Galactic

Defenses Ref 18 (flat-footed 18), Fort 17, Will 17
hp 30; **Threshold** 17

Speed 6 squares
Melee unarmed +7 (1d4+1)
Ranged heavy blaster rifle +8 (3d10+1) or
Ranged frag grenade +7 (4d6+1, 2-square burst) or
Ranged ion grenade +7 (4d6+1 ion, 2-square burst)
Base Atk +7; **Grp** +7
Atk Options autofire (heavy blaster rifle)
Special Actions Assault Tactics, Battle Analysis, Coordinated Attack, Vehicular Combat

Abilities Str 11, Dex 10, Con 10, Int 13, Wis 10, Cha 12
Talents Assault Tactics, Battle Analysis
Feats Armor Proficiency (light), Coordinated Attack, Point Blank Shot, Skill Training (Perception, Pilot), Vehicular Combat, Weapon Focus (rifles), Weapon Proficiency (pistols, rifles, simple weapons)
Skills Endurance +9, Knowledge (tactics) +10, Perception +11, Persuasion +10, Pilot +9
Possessions clone trooper armor (+6 armor, +2 equipment), heavy blaster rifle, frag grenade, ion grenade, comlink (encrypted, long-range [miniaturized], holo capability), utility belt with medpac

ARC Trooper

The ARC Troopers (Advanced Recon Commandos) are elite clone units that were personally trained by Jango Fett. Whereas most clone troopers are trained to work as a unit, ARC Troopers function well as individuals, making them even more formidable as foes.

ARC Trooper   CL 8
Medium Human nonheroic 6/soldier 3/elite trooper 3
Destiny 1; **Force** 4; **Dark Side** 2
Init +12; **Senses** low-light vision; Perception +13
Languages Basic, Mando'a

Defenses Ref 21 (flat-footed 20), Fort 24, Will 16
hp 57; **DR** 1; **Threshold** 24

Speed 6 squares
Melee unarmed +12 (1d4+5) or
Ranged heavy repeating blaster +10 (5d10+5) with Burst Fire or
Ranged heavy repeating blaster +10 (3d10+5) with autofire or
Ranged missile launcher +12 (6d6+5, 2-square splash) or
Ranged heavy blaster pistol +6 (3d8+3) and heavy blaster pistol +6 (3d8+3) or
Ranged frag grenade +11 (4d6+3, 2-square burst) or
Ranged ion grenade +11 (4d6+3 ion, 2-square burst)
Base Atk +10; **Grp** +12
Atk Options autofire (heavy repeating blaster), brace (heavy repeating blaster), Burst Fire (heavy repeating blaster)
Special Actions Point Blank Shot

Abilities Str 15, Dex 13, Con 10, Int 12, Wis 10, Cha 8
Talents Armored Defense, Controlled Burst, Improved Armored Defense, Weapon Specialization (heavy weapons)
Feats Armor Proficiency (light, medium), Burst Fire, Dual Weapon Mastery I, Martial Arts I, Point Blank Shot, Weapon Focus (heavy weapons), Weapon Proficiency (heavy weapons, pistols, rifles, simple weapons)
Skills Initiative +12, Perception +13, Stealth +10
Possessions ARC trooper armor (+6 armor, +2 equipment), heavy repeating blaster, missile launcher, 4 missiles, 2 heavy blaster pistols, 2 frag grenades, 2 ion grenades, utility belt with medpac

THE FRINGE

Fringers live at the edges of society. Criminals, independents, traders, and mercenaries of all kinds consider themselves fringers. While not all members of the fringe are criminals (certainly, many are hard-working and honest folk), anyone who operates far from the seat of galactic power or outside the bounds of the law can be considered part of the fringe.

Assassin

An assassin usually maintains a cover that enables him to travel freely, yet also explains why he's in a given location at a given time. Many assassins hold jobs as merchants, sales representatives for interstellar corporations, or diplomats. A truly villainous assassin has a "signature" consisting of a unique weapon, a particular approach, or some memento left with his victims.

Assassin   CL 5
Medium Human scoundrel 5
Force 1; **Dark Side** 12
Init +10; **Senses** Perception +8
Languages Basic plus 2 other languages

Defenses Ref 20 (flat-footed 17), Fort 14, Will 17
hp 27; **Threshold** 14

Speed 6 squares
Melee vibroblade +6 (2d6+2) or
Melee vibroblade +4 (3d6+2) with Rapid Strike
Ranged blaster rifle +6 (3d8+2)
Base Atk +3; **Grp** +6

Atk Options Careful Shot[H], Dastardly Strike, Rapid Strike, Sneak Attack +2d6
Special Actions Point Blank Shot, Precise Shot

Abilities Str 10, Dex 16, Con 8, Int 14, Wis 12, Cha 13
Talents Dastardly Strike, Sneak Attack +2d6
Feats Careful Shot[H], Point Blank Shot, Precise Shot, Rapid Strike, Weapon Finesse, Weapon Proficiency (advanced melee weapons, pistols, simple weapons)
Skills Acrobatics +10[H], Deception +8, Gather Information +8, Initiative +10, Perception +8, Persuasion +8, Stealth +10
Possessions blaster rifle with enhanced targeting scope, hold-out blaster, vibroblade, vibrodagger, comlink (encrypted), utility belt with medpac
H *Human bonus feat or trained skill*

Bounty Hunter

Bounty hunters track and recover sentient beings to bring them to "justice"—even if that's little more than a Hutt's personal vendetta. Before the Empire, most bounty hunters were members of a galaxywide guild that worked openly, taking contracts to hunt down criminals for various authorities. During the Emperor's reign, the guild fragmented, leaving a large number of independent operatives. Though they occasionally band together to tackle particularly difficult targets, most of the time they work alone, vying against each other to collect the largest rewards. Bounty hunters differ from assassins in that they usually seek to capture their targets, not kill them.

Bounty Hunter CL 7
Medium Human nonheroic 4/scout 3/bounty hunter 3
Force 2; **Dark Side** 4
Init +13; **Senses** low-light vision; Perception +14
Languages Basic

Defenses Ref 23 (flat-footed 21), Fort 20, Will 18
hp 64; **Threshold** 20

Speed 4 squares
Melee vibrobayonet +10 (2d6+7) or
Melee vibrobayonet +10 (3d6+7) with Mighty Swing
Ranged blaster carbine +11 (3d8+3) or
Ranged blaster carbine +9 (4d8+3) with Rapid Shot or
Ranged stun grenade +9 (4d6+3 stun, 2-square burst)
Base Atk +8; **Grp** +11
Atk Options Hunter's Mark, Mighty Swing, Rapid Shot
Special Actions familiar foe +1, Hunter's Target, Point Blank Shot, Precise Shot[H]

Abilities Str 15, Dex 16, Con 14, Int 8, Wis 14, Cha 10
Talents Acute Senses, Expert Tracker, Hunter's Mark, Hunter's Target
Feats Armor Proficiency (light, medium), Mighty Swing, Point Blank Shot, Precise Shot[H], Rapid Shot, Weapon Proficiency (advanced melee weapons, pistols, rifles, simple weapons)
Skills Initiative +13, Endurance +12[H], Perception +14, Survival +12
Possessions Corellian powersuit (+7 armor) with helmet package, blaster carbine, vibrobayonet, 2 stun grenades, utility belt with medpac, bounty hunter's license, datapad
H *Human bonus feat or trained skill*

Crime Lord

Crime lords come from all strata of society. Some began their careers as streetwise thugs, crawling up from the darkest, filthiest pits of the galaxy to positions of power within the criminal underworld. Others are noble-born, using their money and influence to support their fiendish syndicates.

Crime Lord CL 8
Medium Human scoundrel 4/noble 3/crime lord 1
Force 2; **Dark Side** 9
Init +6; **Senses** Perception +10
Languages Basic, High Galactic, Huttese, plus 5 other languages

Defenses Ref 22 (flat-footed 20), Fort 18, Will 23; Dodge
hp 51; **Threshold** 18

Speed 6 squares; Running Attack
Melee unarmed +4 (1d4+3)
Ranged heavy blaster pistol +7 (3d8+4) or
Ranged heavy blaster pistol +5 (3d8+4) and heavy blaster pistol +5 (3d8+4)
Base Atk +5; **Grp** +7
Atk Options Acrobatic Strike, Dastardly Strike, Dual Weapon Mastery II, Sneak Attack +1d6
Special Actions Point Blank Shot, Presence

Abilities Str 8, Dex 14, Con 10, Int 17, Wis 12, Cha 15
Talents Connections, Dastardly Strike, Minion, Presence, Sneak Attack +1d6
Feats Acrobatic Strike, Dodge, Dual Weapon Mastery I, Dual Weapon Mastery II, Linguist, Point Blank Shot, Running Attack, Skill Focus (Deception), Toughness[H], Weapon Proficiency (pistols, simple weapons)
Skills Acrobatics +11, Deception +16, Gather Information +11, Knowledge (bureaucracy) +12, Knowledge (galactic lore) +12[H], Perception +10, Persuasion +11, Stealth +11
Possessions 2 heavy blaster pistols, datapad, comlink (encrypted), enforcers (including several thugs and a 6th-level minion), 1,000 credits
H *Human bonus feat or trained skill*

Dark Side Marauder

Though the Jedi are the most powerful Force-users in the galaxy, they are by no means the only ones. Dark side marauders are Force-sensitive individuals consumed with rage, hatred, or an insatiable hunger for personal power.

Dark Side Marauder CL 4
Medium Human soldier 4
Force 1; **Dark Side** 14
Init +7; **Senses** Perception +4
Languages Basic

Defenses Ref 19 (flat-footed 19), Fort 19, Will 16
hp 50; **Threshold** 24

Speed 4 squares
Melee vibro-ax +7 (2d10+10) or
Melee vibro-ax +7 (3d10+10) with Mighty Swing
Ranged hold-out blaster +4 (3d4+2)
Base Atk +4; **Grp** +7
Atk Options Mighty Swing
Special Actions Indomitable, Tough as Nails
Force Powers Known (Use the Force +8): *dark rage* (2), *surge*

Abilities Str 16, Dex 10, Con 13, Int 8, Wis 14, Cha 12
Talents Indomitable, Weapon Specialization (advanced melee weapons)
Feats Armor Proficiency (light, medium), Force Sensitivity, Force Training, Improved Damage Threshold[H], Mighty Swing, Weapon Proficiency (advanced melee weapons, pistols, rifles, simple weapons)
Skills Endurance +8[H], Initiative +7, Use the Force +8
Possessions battle armor (+8 armor, +2 equipment), vibro-ax, hold-out blaster, comlink, 100 credits

[H] *Human bonus feat or trained skill*

Thug

Thugs are basic bruisers. They are street toughs aspiring to become swoop champions, grunts working for a local crime lord, security guards, or law enforcers prone to breaking heads and taking bribes.

Thug CL 1
Medium Human nonheroic 2
Dark Side 3
Init +6; **Senses** +5
Languages Basic

Defenses Ref 10 (flat-footed 10), Fort 11, Will 9
hp 9; **Threshold** 11

Speed 6 squares
Melee vibro-ax +2 (2d10+2)
Ranged blaster pistol +1 (3d6)
Base Atk +1; **Grp** +2
Atk Options Cleave[H]

Abilities Str 13, Dex 11, Con 12, Int 8, Wis 9, Cha 10
Feats Cleave[H], Toughness, Weapon Proficiency (advanced melee weapons, pistols, simple weapons)
Skills Initiative +6, Perception +5[H]
Possessions Blaster pistol, vibro-ax

[H] *Human bonus feat or trained skill*

Other Species

All of the character stat blocks in this chapter use Human as the base species. However, you can easily use these stat blocks to represent non-Human characters as well by removing the Human species traits (one bonus trained skill and one bonus feat) and applying the new species' traits. You may use the species described in Chapter 2: Species or any of the species presented below.

Aqualish

Aqualish are walrus-faced humanoids with skin ranging in color from dark green or blue to deep russet or black. Some Aqualish subspecies have four eyes instead of two or fins instead of hands. The Aqualish admire strength and are openly hostile toward the weak. In fact, it is customary and accepted social behavior among Aqualish to be pushy and belligerent upon first meeting others.

Aqualish Species Traits

- **Ability Modifiers:** +2 Constitution, –2 Wisdom, –2 Charisma.
- **Size:** Medium.
- **Speed:** 6 squares.
- **Breathe Underwater:** As amphibious creatures, Aqualish can't drown in water.
- **Expert Swimmer:** An Aqualish may choose to reroll any Swim check, but the result of the reroll must be accepted even if it is worse. In addition, an Aqualish may choose to take 10 on Swim checks even when distracted or threatened.
- **Bonus Feat:** Toughness.
- **Languages:** Aqualish, Basic.

Hutts

Hutts are immense, sluglike, creatures with bulbous heads. Two catlike eyes rise from the surface of a Hutt's face, while a lipless mouth spreads from ear hole to ear hole. Most Hutts are vicious megalomaniacs who consider their kind to be beyond morality as perceived by lesser beings. They have a talent for manipulating others and enjoy exerting power over others.

Hutt Species Traits

- **Ability Modifiers:** +2 Strength, +2 Constitution, +2 Intelligence, –6 Dexterity.

- **Size:** Large. Hutts take a −1 size penalty to their Reflex Defense, a −5 size penalty on Stealth checks, and a +5 size bonus to their damage threshold. Their lifting and carrying limits are double those of Medium characters.
- **Speed:** 2 squares.
- **Force Resistance:** +5 species bonus to Will Defense against any Use the Force check.
- **Supreme Stability:** Hutts can't be tripped or knocked prone.
- **Skills:** A Hutt may reroll a Persuasion check, keeping the better result.
- **Languages:** Basic, Huttese.

Neimoidians

Neimoidians stand between 1.6 and 2 meters tall and are of slight build. Their skin ranges from mottled green to gray, and their vaguely reptilian faces are flat and elongated. They have red eyes, thick lips, and no noses. Neimoidians have two primary motivations: to control their surroundings at all times and to acquire as much wealth and power as they can. The latter goal might seem a logical means of attaining the former, but to a Neimoidian, the pursuit of wealth and power is an end unto itself. Such traits gave rise to the Trade Federation, one of the most powerful and influential economic forces in the Galactic Republic.

Neimoidian Species Traits
- **Ability Modifiers:** +2 Intelligence, +2 Wisdom, −2 Strength.
- **Size:** Medium.
- **Speed:** 6 squares.
- **Conditional Bonus Feat:** Neimoidians with Deception as a trained skill gain Skill Focus (Deception) as a bonus feat.
- **Skills:** A Neimoidian may reroll a Deception check but must keep the second result.
- **Languages:** Basic, Neimoidian, Pak Pak.

Yuuzhan Vong

Conquerors from beyond the galactic rim, the Yuuzhan Vong are organized, bloodthirsty, ritually scarred warriors driven by religious fervor. They are masters of biotechnology; their clothing, weapons, and equipment are genetically engineered life forms. They despise mechanical technology (droids in particular) and destroy any such technology they encounter. They are also disconnected from the Force in a way that Jedi and other Force-sensitive beings find unsettling.

The culture of the Yuuzhan Vong is based on the domination of lesser species. To the Yuuzhan Vong, most other species are unworthy and suitable only as slaves. The worthy are regarded with enough tolerance to grant them a clean death.

Yuuzhan Vong Species Traits
- **Ability Modifiers:** +2 Strength, −2 Wisdom.
- **Size:** Medium.
- **Speed:** 6 squares.
- **Force Immunity:** Yuuzhan Vong can't take the Force Sensitivity feat, can't make Use the Force checks, and never gain Force Points. In addition, they are immune to any Force effect that targets their Will Defense (including Force powers and aspects of the Use the Force skill).
- **Technophobic:** Yuuzhan Vong take a −5 penalty on attack rolls and skill checks made when using mechanical weapons or tools.
- **Weapon Familiarity:** Yuuzhan Vong with the Weapon Proficiency (simple weapons) feat are considered proficient with the amphistaff.
- **Language:** Yuuzhan Vong.

INDEX

Entries in black type are talents.

Acrobatic Recovery 40
Acute Senses 49
Adept Negotiator 39
Adept Spellcaster 107
aid another 151
aim 154
area attacks 155
armor check penalty 132
Armor Mastery 51
Armored Defense 52
Assault Tactics 221
astrogation 237
Ataru 218
attack an object 151
attacks of opportunity 155
attack roll 144
Attract Minion 210
Attune Armor 107
Attune Weapon 214
autofire 156
automatic misses 145
Barter 49
base attack bonus 36
Battle Analysis 52
Battle Meditation 40
Block 41
Bolster Ally 43
Born Leader 44
challenge level (CL) 247
Channel Aggression 213
Channel Anger 213
charge 152
Charm Beast 107
Clear Mind 40
Command Beast 107
concealment 156
conditions 148
Connections 44
Controlled Burst 212
Coordinate 44
coup de grace 154
cover 157
Cover Fire 52
Crippling Strike 213
critical hits 145
damage 145
damage reduction (DR) 158
damage threshold 146
Dark Healing 223
Dark Presence 101
Dark Scourge 223
Dark Side Adept 223
Dark Side Master 223

Dark Side Sense 40
dark side score 93
Dark Side Scourge 40
darkvision 257
Dastardly Strike 46
death 148
Debilitating Shot 216
Deceptive Shot 216
defenses 145
    class bonuses 36
Deflect 41
delay 161
Demand Surrender 43
Demolitionist 52
Deployment Tactics 221
destiny 112
Devastating Attack 53
difficult terrain 159
disarm 152
Disciplined Strike 100
Disruptive 46
Distant Command 44
Djem So 218
Dogfight Gunner 207
Draw Fire 52
Educated 44
Elusive Dogfighter 207
Elusive Target 40
Embrace The Dark Side 214
Empower Weapon 214
encumbrance 140
Equilibrium 101
Evasion 50
Exotic Weapon Mastery 212
experience points (xp) 248
Expert Grappler 52
Expert Gunner 207
Expert Tracker 49
Extreme Effort 50
falling unconscious 147
Fearless Leader 44
Field Tactics 221
fight defensively 152
fighting space 159
flanking 159
Flight 107
Fool's Luck 46
Force Cloak 107
Force Cloak Mastery 107
Force Deception 223
Force Focus 101
Force Fotification 218
Force Haze 40
Force Intuition 40
Force Perception 101
Force Persuasion 40
Force Pilot 101

force points 92
Force Power Adept 214
force powers 95
Force Recovery 101
force secrets 103
force talents 100
Force Talisman 214
Force Treatment 214
Foresight 101
Fortified Body 214
Fortune's Favor 46
Fringe Savant 50
full attack 154
Full Throttle 207
Gambler 46
gambling 47
Gauge Force Potential 101
Gimmick 47
grab 152
grapple 153
Greater Devastating Attack 212
Greater Force Talisman 214
Greater Penetrating Attack 212
Greater Weapon Focus 212
    Lightsabers 218
Greater Weapon Specialization 212
    Lightsabers 218
Gun Club 52
Harm's Way 52
hazards 252
helpless opponents 159
heroic level 36
Hidden Movement 49
hit points 146
Hunter's Mark 208
Hunter's Target 208
Hyperdriven 47
Ignite Fervor 43
Impel Ally I, II 210
Improved Armored Defense 52
Improved Dark Healing 224
Improved Initiative 49
Improved Quick Draw 216
Improved Stealth 49
Improved Weaken Resolve 43
Indomitable 52
initiative 149
Inspire Confidence 44
Inspire Fear I, II, III 210
Inspire Haste 44
Inspire Zeal 44
ion damage 159
Jar'kai 218
Juggernaut 52
Juke 207
Jury-rigger 50

Juyo 218
Keen Shot 49
Keep It Together 207
Knack 46
Knockdown Shot 216
languages 22
Lightsaber Defense 41
Lightsaber Throw 41
line of sight 160
Linked Defense 107
Long Stride 50
low-light vision 257
Lucky Shot 46
Makashi 218
Master Negotiator 40
Master Slicer 47
Melee Smash 52
movement
    diagonal movement 158
    run 155
    speed 146
    squeezing 162
    through occupied squares 161
Multiattack Proficiency
    Heavy Weapons, Rifles 212
    Lightsabers 218
    Pistols 216
multiclass characters 54
natural healing 148
Niman 218
Notorious 208, 210
Nowhere to Hide 208
One for the Team 221
Outmaneuver 221
Penetrating Attack 53
Power of the Dark Side 101
Presence 43
prone targets 161
Quick Trigger 207
Rally 44
Ranged Disarm 217
reach 161
ready 162
recover 154
Redirect Shot 41
Relentless 208
Relentless Pursuit 207
Resilience 40
Resist the Dark Side 41
restricted items 118
retractable stocks 125
Revenge 101
Ruthless Negotiator 208
Second Skin 52
second wind 146
Severing Strike 218
Shared Notoreity 210

shield rating (SR) 161
Shien 218
Shift Defense I, II, III 222
Shii-cho 219
shooting or throwing into a melee 161
Skilled Advisor 40
skills
    opposed check 58
    "taking 10 or 20" 61
    trained vs. untrained 57
Skirmisher 46
Sneak Attack 46
Sokan 219
Soresu 219
Spacehound 47
Spontaneous Skill 44
Sprint 50
Starship Raider 47
Stellar Warrior 47
stacking bonuses 241
stunning 162
Stunning Strike 52
Surefooted 50
surprise 149
Swift Power 101
System Hit 207
Tactical Edge 222
Telekinetic Power 100
Telekinetic Savant 100
Total Concealment 49
Tough as Nails 53
Trace 47
Tràkata 219
Trigger Work 217
Trust 44
unarmed attacks 163
Unbalance Opponent 52
Uncanny Dodge I, Ii 49
Vaapad 219
Vehicular Evasion 207
Visions 101
Walk the Line 46
Weaken Resolve 43
Wealth 44
Weapon Specialization 53
    Lightsabers 41
weapons
    draw or holster 153
    switch weapon mode 154
    weapon batteries 170
    weapon groups 119
    weapon sizes 120
Wicked Strike 224
withdraw 153

CHARACTER RECORD SHEET

NAME _____ **PLAYER** _____

CLASS _____ **SPECIES** _____ **LEVEL** _____

AGE _____ **GENDER** _____ **HEIGHT** _____ **WEIGHT** _____ **DESTINY** _____

STAR WARS ROLEPLAYING GAME

Ability Scores

	SCORE	MODIFIER
STRength		
DEXterity		
CONstitution		
INTelligence		
WISdom		
CHArisma		

Hit Points

TOTAL: ____
CURRENT: ____

FORT DEFENSE ____ + MISC BONUS ____ = DAMAGE THRESHOLD ____

SPEED: ____
INITIATIVE: ____
PERCEPTION: ____
BASE ATTACK: ____
FORCE POINTS: ____
DESTINY POINTS: ____

Condition

NORMAL

-1 TO ALL DEFENSES, TO ATTACKS, SKILL, & ABILITY CHECKS.

-2 TO ALL DEFENSES, TO ATTACKS, SKILL, & ABILITY CHECKS.

-5 TO ALL DEFENSES, TO ATTACKS, SKILL, & ABILITY CHECKS.

-10 TO ALL DEFENSES, TO ATTACKS, SKILL, & ABILITY CHECKS. MOVE AT HALF SPEED.

HELPLESS (UNCONSCIOUS OR DISABLED)

Defenses

	TOTAL		LEVEL OR ARMOR	CLASS BONUS	ABILITY MOD	MISC
Fort	____	= 10 +	____	____	CON ____	____
Ref	____	= 10 +	____	____	DEX ____	____
Will	____	= 10 +	____	____	WIS ____	____

Weapons

WEAPON	ATK	DAMAGE
CRIT	TYPE	NOTES

WEAPON	ATK	DAMAGE
CRIT	TYPE	NOTES

WEAPON	ATK	DAMAGE
CRIT	TYPE	NOTES

WEAPON	ATK	DAMAGE
CRIT	TYPE	NOTES

Special Combat Actions

_____
_____
_____
_____
_____
_____
_____

Dark Side Score

1	2	3	4	5	6	7	8	9	10	11	12
13	14	15	16	17	18	19	20	21	22	23	24

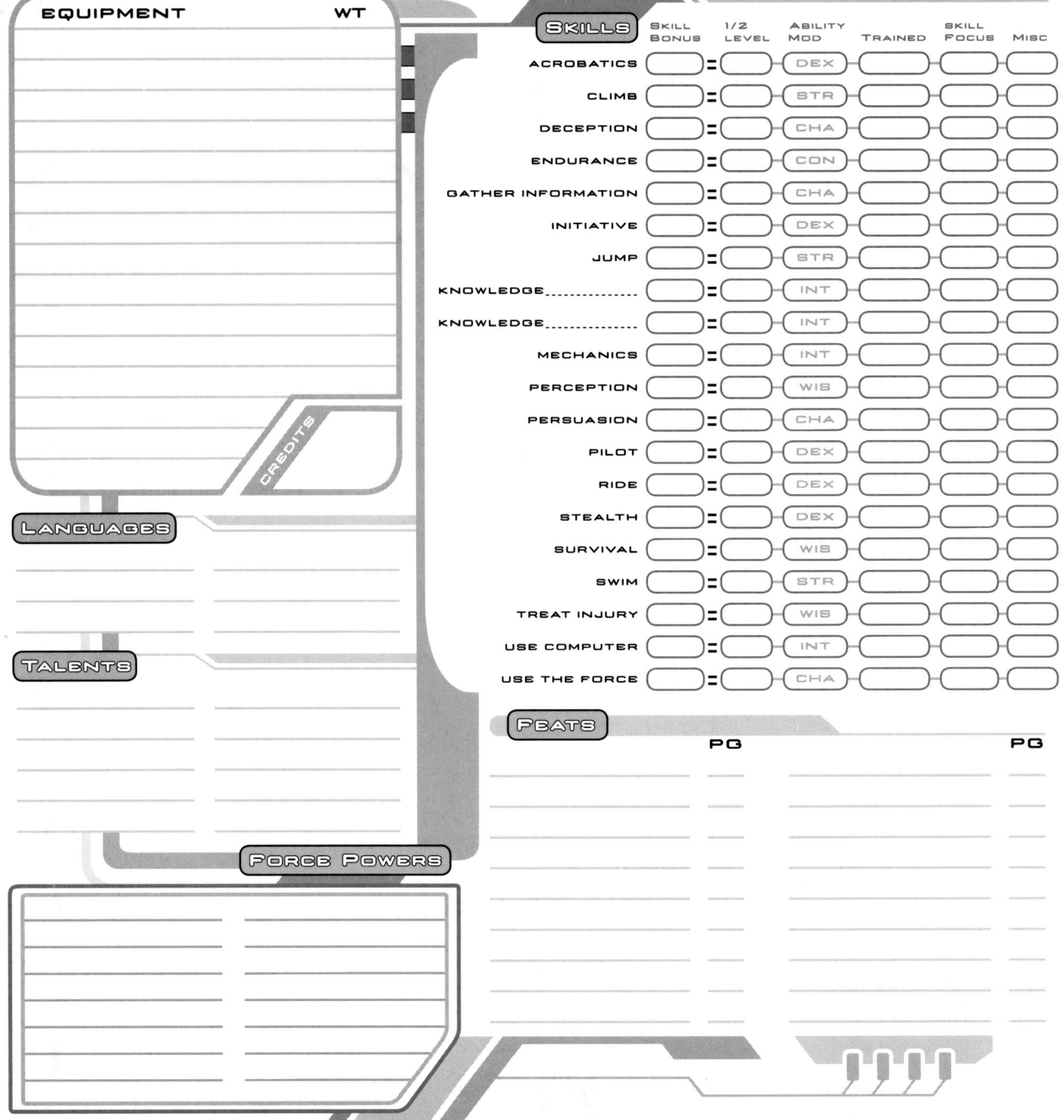